D0330600

My Old True Love

My Old True Love

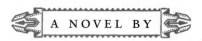 A NOVEL BY

Sheila Kay Adams

ALGONQUIN BOOKS
OF CHAPEL HILL

2004

Published by
Algonquin Books of Chapel Hill
Post Office Box 2225
Chapel Hill, North Carolina 27515-2225

a division of
Workman Publishing
708 Broadway
New York, New York 10003

This is a work of fiction. While, as in all fiction, the literary perceptions
and insights are based on experience, all names, characters, places,
and incidents are either products of the author's imagination or are used
fictitiously.

Library of Congress Cataloging-in-Publication Data
    Adams, Sheila Kay.
      My old true love : a novel / by Sheila Kay Adams.—1st ed.
        p. cm.
      ISBN 1-56512-407-3
      1. North Carolina—History—Civil War, 1861–1865—Fiction.
2. Triangles (Interpersonal relations)—Fiction.   3. Appalachian
Region, Southern—Fiction.   4. Ballads—Fiction.   5. Cousins—
Fiction.   6. Singers—Fiction.   I. Title.
PS3551.D395315M9 2004
813'.54—dc22   2003070809

10 9 8 7 6 5 4 3 2 1
First Edition

This book is in loving memory of my parents Ervin
and Neple Norton Adams, who kept the family stories
and memories in their hearts and passed them on to me.
And it is lovingly dedicated to June Anders
and James C. Taylor—there could be no better in-laws.

Come in, come in, my old true love,
And spend this night with me.
For I have a bed, it's a very fine bed,
And I'll give it up for thee, thee.
I'll give it up for thee.

"Young Hunting," traditional ballad

My Old True Love

SOME PEOPLE IS BORN at the start of a long hard row to hoe. Well, I am older than God's dog and been in this world a long time and it seems to me that right from the git-go, Larkin Stanton had the longest and hardest row I've ever seen.

Granny had an old cow that was skittish back then that would kick anybody but her, so I knowed things was bad when she said to me, "Arty, go do the milking."

My heart laid in my chest as heavy as the milk bucket on my way back. See, my aunt Polly had been trying to have a baby for days and had screamed till her voice had plumb give out. I heard Mommie crying when I started up on the porch and just as I reached for the latch, the door opened and the granny-woman Hattie come out. She had a bright red stain on her forehead and try as I might I couldn't get my eyes to look nowheres else but at that red swipe mark. She never even had to say it. I knowed Aunt Polly was dead. Hattie's eyes was soft as a doe's as she took the bucket of milk and handed me the one she'd carried out of the house and told me to empty it at the far edge of the cornfield. Oh, Lord, I did not want to see what was in that bucket, but just like that red stain, I couldn't look nowheres else, and I gagged the whole time I was burying the afterbirth.

Even though they was a candle burning on the rough-planked table inside the cabin, it seemed dark to me. But there was that bucket of milk, and since they was all talking, I figured it fell to me to strain it. I kept looking at the bed where Aunt Polly was covered up by one of Granny's best quilts. It seemed like the gay colors caught what little light there was and I got sick to my stomach thinking about what lay beneath them. Mommie and Granny stood next to the bed and Mommie was still crying. Crazy-like, the words to an old love song run through my head.

> The doctor he come, to her bed he drew nigh
> Her chambers all parted and moved to the side.

And quick as lightning, another line from another song.

> No doctor's hand, just God's own hand.

Granny's face was so full of sorrow and hurt that I could barely stand to look at her, and I busied my hands to straining the milk. But that didn't stop my ears from hearing every word. In the softest voice ever was, Granny allowed as how Aunt Polly had plumb give up after Luke was killed. Mommie was holding Emily who had cried so long she had the snubs. Hackley had his fists twisted up in her skirt and when she started to say over and over, "My baby sister, my baby sister," he pushed his little face deeper in the folds. Right about then the baby started to cry, and everybody turned back to the bed. I took Emily from Mommie. It was when I set her on my hip that it come to me that I didn't even know what the baby was. But Emily was crying and fussing and Hattie was out the door and gone before I had a chance to ask.

Then Mommie said, "I'll take him," and Granny said, "No you will not." They quarrelled back and forth for a minute, then Granny said, "Thirty-five ain't young, honey. Ye've got eight young'uns and, God willing, soon to be nine. Ye have to think of your own." And what she said next caused a chill down the whole length of my back. "I'll keep him." And then her voice got real soft. "Till he dies, anyway."

Mommie's voice come out in a wail. "We can't let him die. He's all that's left in this world of Polly and Luke."

Granny held up her hands and said, "All right, all right." Then she said one of us needed to go to the spring and bring back water to wash Aunt Polly with before she stiffened, and my eyes flew back to the bed. I felt all done in and Emily was still making this tired little hiccuping sound like she wished she could stop but kept on anyway.

Mommie folded back the quilt from Aunt Polly's face. She tucked a strand of hair still wet with Aunt Polly's living sweat behind one ear.

"She looks young as a girl," she whispered.

Oh, but I thought I would die when she said that.

Then the baby cried again and Mommie got the funniest look on her face. Her chin jutted out, her eyes went to little slits, and she looked mad as hell. "Come over here, Arty," she said to me in a rough voice. She jerked Hackley loose from her dress skirt and knelt by the bed.

"That there is your cousin," she said. "He's ours to raise. He ain't got nobody in this world but us." Hackley made a little sound in the back of his throat and Mommie looked right at him. "He'll need a good strong name, now. You come up with a stout one, all right?"

Hackley looked at Mommie, then back at the baby. He nodded solemnly.

That must've satisfied her because she stood up, got the water bucket, and said, "I'm going to the spring."

And as Granny followed her out on the porch she allowed as how Mommie ought to take the pitch torch, since dark had probably come on down at the spring.

THE BABY MADE ANOTHER little sound and of a sudden I wanted to see that baby more than anything in this world. The quilt they'd wrapped him in had halfway covered his face and I leaned over and flipped it back. His big pretty head was covered in hair as black as a crow's feather. A tiny hand with fingers all spread wide reached out to us. Hackley stared at the hand, then shot a glance at the open door where Mommie and Granny stood backlit by the yellow light of the torch. I could see what he aimed to do and any other time I'd have smacked his hand. But, I didn't do or say nothing. I only watched Hackley's little hand move toward the baby. Quick as a snake the baby's fingers gripped it hard.

"Well, howdy," Hackley whispered. And I swear, that baby turned its head toward him just like he was listening. Hackley smiled. "Howdy, little feller."

IT WAS A GOOD summer for growing in Sodom, just the right amount of sun and rain. We would have plenty for the coming winter. Granny still spent a lot of time up on the side of the mountain where the garden was. With a sheepish look on her face and never quite meeting my eyes, she'd announce before the fog had even burned off that she had to go pull the biggest cucumbers or old bean vines to feed the hogs. She'd say this even though I knew for a fact she would never go in that garden with the dew still on. She'd stay gone until noontime and come in just long enough to fix us something to eat. She'd fuss the whole while about how everything in the garden was going to come in at the same time, which I had to laugh at because that's the way it *always* was. Then she'd head back out up the mountain, climbing hard to where the first row of corn started. She'd always stop there to bring her apron up to wipe the sweat that run off her face like little freshets, look back toward the house, then disappear in between the rows. But I could always tell where she was by the moving of the corn. And I could tell just as well when she'd leave the patch for the cool of the woods beyond, too. We'd had no fresh corn in many months, and my mouth watered at the thought of it and when she come in with the first little ears covered with watery blisters, we fell on them as though starving.

It was toward the end of August before I realized what Granny was doing. It was way up in the day and she was just heading back toward the house. She'd caught up the hem of her apron and had loaded it with potatoes. I had beat out a path on the porch walking the baby. He'd cried so much that day that even when he weren't crying, my ears rung with the sound of it. Granny was beelining it for the steps when he started to cry again. Her head come up and she made a sudden jag toward the springhouse.

She didn't want to sit here in the house and listen to him cry. It was then I knew it was going to be pretty much me for it. From the day he was born, my arms had carried him, but that very day was when my heart claimed him for my own.

IN OCTOBER, MOMMIE BIRTHED a baby girl. We all crowded into the cabin to celebrate and to hang her with a name. Mommie said she'd be known as Martha Elizabeth, after Granny's mother and the queen of England.

We all shouted out, "Welcome to you, Martha Elizabeth Norton!"

Then Granny stood up and took the floor.

"When Polly's baby was born, Nancy told Hackley he could pick out a name for it. And now the little feller's three months old. It's time to hang him with a name, too. Hackley's been wanting to do this for a spell, but we weren't about to waste a perfectly good name on a young'un that might wind up carrying it to the grave, so we waited till we were certain he'd pull through."

I stood up next to her holding the baby. The room was quiet as could be and everybody was looking at us.

Granny went and put her hand on Hackley's shoulder. "All right, Hack. You hang a name on him, son. The time has come."

Hackley come right across that room and stood in front of me. He looked solemnly at the baby.

"I name you . . ." He looked around at everyone in the room, then back at the baby. "I name you Larkin!" he shouted.

The room rang with the shouts: "Welcome to ye, Larkin Stanton!"

OH, BUT THERE ARE no words to tell how Larkin grabbed hold of my heart forever when he was five months old. They was a big snow on the ground and Granny had just come in from milking the goat she'd got from Jim Leake. Me and Larkin was laying on a quilt in front of the fire and his little face was a constant wreath of the sweetest smiles and he was cooing at me for all the world like a little dove. And then he looked up at me with them big round black eyes and said plain as could be, "Amma." Tears come so quick to my eyes I was blinded. Though it pleased me beyond all knowing I tried to tell him, "No, no."

But Granny stopped me.

"Let him call you Amma, child." Granny's eyes were soft. "He's chose you to love best of all, and with good reason. You been all the mama he knows."

LARKIN TOOK HIS FIRST steps, just shy of nine months old, into Hackley's arms. From then on he was never still. He was slow to smile, but when he did his whole face beamed, and you felt blessed just to be in its light. He was quick to learn and I could make him mind with not much more than a smacked hand.

One summer evening me and Granny was on the porch where we'd be more apt to catch a bit of a breeze should one decide to come up the cove. I'd been trying to learn this really hard love song called "The Silk Merchant's Daughter," and Granny had already sung it through a half-dozen times. Larkin was in my lap, and halfway through her singing it yet one more time he started to rock back and forth in perfect rhythm. A low hum began in his throat.

"Granny!"

Granny never liked being interrupted mid-song like that so she was ill when she opened her eyes.

"What?"

"Watch Larkin," I said.

Granny began to sing again and the low humming started up again. She stopped and his humming stopped. Larkin's eyes were fastened on her mouth. She sang and the humming started again.

"Well, I'll be damned! He's trying his best to sing, ain't he?"

"He *is* singing, Granny. Sure as I'm setting here holding him. That's what he's doing." I turned his body until his face was close to mine, but he wanted none of that. He squirmed away back to Granny, humming impatiently in her direction.

Granny laughed with delight. "Looks like we got us another singer, Arty."

> He called for a knife his business to do.
> "Hold on," said the young maid, "for a moment or two
> It's a silk merchant's daughter from London I be
> Pray see what I've come to from the loving of thee."

Larkin's humming got all mixed in with our singing and it all eased its way into the dark there on the porch.

BY THE TIME LARKIN was five he had already learned every song I knew. Granny had to start reaching far back in her memory for them love songs that were so old she swore they'd come straight from the old country. I had to agree with her since they talked an awful lot about Scotland and England. It made me feel funny to think of singing songs that had been tucked away in people's hearts that had come all the way across the ocean.

But Larkin was too little to think about all that. He never cared where they come from. He was just always begging for one more.

"Lordy, honey." Granny said. "You have to give me time to study about it. You know who you ought to git to sing for ye is Hackley. He's learned from that bunch of singing Nortons, too. He's about the only one I can think of right off that can sing all day and not sing the same one twice't."

And so Granny pieced another square in the quilt that would bind them two boys together.

These were the days that I would look back on once I'd married with such a longing in my heart. Them were times that seemed almost magic—you know how it is when you remember your childhood. The sun is always shining or there's a big pretty snow on the ground, and you're young and never sick or tired, and everybody you ever loved is still living and your whole life is a big wide road stretched out in front of you just waiting for you to take that first step toward the living of it.

It was in the fall of my fourteenth year, just as the leaves had started changing on the highest peaks, when I really noticed Zeke Wallin for the first time. I'd knowed him all my life but this day at church I really *saw* him. Me and Granny were making our way through a knot of people that were still milling about in the church-yard after preaching and Larkin had darted away from us with the final *amen*. I watched his dark head move through the crowd until I saw him catch up with Hackley. Then I saw a flash of teeth from beneath one of the old oaks at the edge of the churchyard.

Zeke Wallin had the same spare build, fine bones, and square jaw-line of his older brothers. Never in his life would he tame his curly black hair, and on this day a glossy lock had sneaked out from under his hat. Oh, but his brows set off his best feature: widely spaced eyes of such dark blue they often looked purple, which they did now as he was looking at me. In that minute he was the prettiest man I'd ever seen in my whole life. He told me later my feelings was all over my face, and I blush even now at what he must've seen there.

His smile got even bigger as he swept off his hat and give me a little bow. A rush of heat started in my stomach and streaked outward. A line from a love song raced through my head, the words changing and reshaping themselves into the version I would sing the rest of my life.

Black is the color of my true love's hair. His face is like some rosy
    fair
With the prettiest face and the neatest hands. I love the ground
    whereon he stands.

It felt like my skin had caught fire and it was all I could do to keep
my eyes on the back of Granny's dress as I went stumbling through
the crowd. But as Granny stopped to speak to the preacher, there I
was face-to-face with Zeke.

"Howdy," he said.

"Howdy." All that fire felt like it had settled in my face and I knew
it were beet red.

"I wanted to speak to you before you took off. Tried to last Sunday, but you got gone."

"Last Sunday?"

He flashed me another smile, then his face went all serious. "See,
I wanted to ask if I could walk you home. Same applies to today. If
you'll let me."

He took a sharp breath. "It ought to be against the law of the land
to have eyes that color, Arty Norton."

It was all I could do to keep my eyes level on his, but after he'd said
that I weren't about to look away.

"So can I walk with you?"

I realized that I'd not be the same again, ever. Already I felt as
though my skin laid over my frame differently. I looked up at the towering peak of Lonesome Mountain, imagining the child I'd been a moment ago standing just yonder.

"I reckon you can if you want to."

ON THE COLD NIGHT before I was to marry Zeke, exactly three months from that warm fall day, I laid in bed listening to the sounds that were as familiar to me as the sound of my own heartbeat. I heard the soft snore from Granny's side of the room. The wood from the banked fire hissed. The wind moaned its way around the cabin. Out on the porch, Belle, the redbone pup Hackley had given Larkin, gave a few sharp barks, then was quiet. Larkin, caught in a dream, muttered something I couldn't make out and flung a hand in my direction.

I reached out and touched his shoulder. He rolled against me, and was still. Suddenly, scalding tears come pouring out of my eyes. I put my chin on top of his head.

"I won't never love nobody the way I love you, Larkin."

Outside, the wind stilled as though listening, then rushed up the mountainside. On its breath was the smell of snow.

2

THE ONLY MAN I'D felt love for was Daddy, and that don't really count. But the thought never crossed my mind that I'd *ever* love a man the way I loved Zeke. I am a hardheaded woman and speak my mind whenever I take a notion, and when we first married, I had the notion often. He was so good and tender and loving. I was bad to fuss and quarrel, not at him but just to be quarreling. At first he'd try to offer advice or try to help me somehow. But he soon figured out that the best thing to do was just let me blow and then I'd be fine. Then I fussed because he never listened to nothing I said.

But Lord, how I loved him.

There were times when we'd be setting at the table eating and I'd just have to reach out and lay my hand on him. Many a dinner went cold because of that. And I know he felt the same for me. We was lucky people. I've knowed some that's passion for each other turned to hate after they'd been married awhile or, worse yet, they growed indifferent to one another. I would've gladly took the hate if I'd had to choose. But they was never nothing between me and Zeke but love. Now that ain't to say we never fussed nor quarreled. I was more than a little jealous though he tried so hard to never give me real cause. It was just that I was not blind. I saw the way women's eyes follered him, but if I mentioned it he would sigh great big and say, "You are seeing what ain't there, honey," or even better, "If they are looking why would I look back when I've got the prettiest gal in this part of the world?"

Zeke knew how to handle me all right.

Another reason I loved him so was that it was fine with him that I brought Larkin with me. He were five year old and I couldn't stand the thoughts of leaving him. He stayed with us for almost two years then he wanted to go back to Granny's. It used to make me mad as the devil when somebody would say, "You'll feel different about your own." I could not imagine loving my own any more than Larkin. And it weren't so much that I did. It's just that Abigail was born before we'd been married not quite a year and within four months I was breeding again with John Wesley. Too many babies for Larkin. He even said he wanted to go stay with Granny where it was quiet. And, truth be known, Granny was not young anymore and needed the help. I missed him and cried when he left but I was so busy. And I did get caught up in the loving of my own, but I still say I loved him just as good.

That spring and summer after he went to Granny's, Larkin and Hackley got to be as close as two beans in a hull. Granny said she would find them sitting facing one another, Hackley patiently singing verse after verse, Larkin with eyes shut, his face still as a looking glass, soaking up every word. They roamed the mountains in search of ginseng, singing the old songs. Hackley's voice was clear and strong. But it was Larkin's voice, high and pure, that seemed to have wings.

Several man-shaped roots of ginseng decorated the fireboard of Granny's cabin. During the long nights of that winter, the boys would often give the roots the names of people that lived only in the old songs. Lord Thomas "dressed himself in scarlet red and wore a vest of green," and all the other roots "took him to be some king." Little Margaret sat in her high hall and sadly watched her sweetheart, William, and his new bride come riding up the the road.

They was in and out of my house all the time and I wish you could've seen the two of them—Hackley fair and hair so blond it looked white, with short, stout arms and legs; Larkin so dark, long, and lanky.

A HEAVY FROST BLANKETED Sodom in late May of 1853 during a cold snap we called blackberry winter. The white blooms of the thorny canes covered the ground looking for all the world like snow, out of place against the backdrop of the greening-up hillsides. Granny said we'd have us a fine blackberry harvest since only the hardiest berries would survive. And by July she knew right where to find them.

Larkin ran ahead of us as we paused to rest. The hill was steep, and this was the second time we'd stopped. He reached the top and turned, black eyes sparkling. His short hair, so black it gave his scalp a bluish tint, was damp with sweat.

"I done beat you to the top!"

"Your legs turned eight year old as of today, son!" Granny called out. "Lot younger than ours, for a fact."

"Not much younger than Amma's," he hollered.

"But mine's got a lot more miles on them and I'm hauling two," I hollered back. I was just four months gone but already showing.

Granny reached into the pocket of her apron and took out a plug of tobacco, bit off a chew, then put the plug back in her pocket. She chewed vigorously for a few seconds, spat, and tongued the moist chew firmly between gum and cheek.

"Larkin?" she called, gazing at the mountains in the distance.

His head popped up from the grass at the top of the ridge.

I laughed. "Your head looks like a guinea fowl sticking up that-a-way!"

He jumped up and come careening down the hill.

Granny waited until he stood next to her, then pointed off into the distance.

"You know what that mountain is a-way off yonder?"

Larkin shaded his eyes and stared. "Ain't that Little Bald?"

"It is. And hit's all the way in Tennessee, honey."

We stood there for a long time without talking as the summer breeze come flowing up the side of the mountain and, finding us in its path, teased and petted us before rushing on.

"Well, now," Granny said. "Them berries ain't gonna jump off the vine and into our bucket by theirselves."

"And we need to make haste, Larkin," I said. "Mommie is probably right now making you a stack cake for your birthday."

"Love Aunt Nancy's stack cake, yes I do!" Larkin sang.

The blackberry thicket had been there for as long as even Granny could remember. Some of the canes were thick as Larkin's arm. The berries were big and sweet and it weren't long before our hands and Larkin's mouth were stained purple.

Granny smiled. "Believe you put as many in your belly as in your bucket, honey."

"Reckon he just might have." I patted Larkin's stomach. "See how big it is?"

She reached and thumped his belly. "Lordy! Tight as a tick! They might not be no room left for no stack cake."

He pulled up his shirt and examined his stomach with a worried look. Then his face relaxed.

"Aw, Granny. You're just deviling me. Anyways, Hackley says I can eat more'n anybody he's ever seen."

"Ah! That Hackley is a trick, ain't he? He's sharp enough to stick in the ground and green enough to sprout," she said. "Don't believe they's a serious bone in his body."

"I don't know, Granny," I said. "He's serious about singing them love songs."

"Honey, let me tell you something. You three young'uns are some of the best singers of them old love songs I've heard since my Pappy passed. Now, he was a fine singer, Pappy was. Mommie would try to make him quit singing love songs. Said it was a sin! Pappy was plumb insulted, I can testify to that. Told Mommie she might want to reference the Good Book. Quoted scripture to her right then and there. 'Make a joyful noise . . . come before his presence with singing,' he said. 'And now these three remain: faith, hope, and love. But the greatest of these is love.' Said if the greatest was love and for us to come before his presence with singing, what better way than by singing a love song! Said if God hadn't meant for us to sing them old love songs, why he wouldn't have give us sense enough to learn the words to them. Weren't much Mommie could say about that. Pappy knew the Bible like the back of his hand, better than anybody in this part of the country." She sighed. "He was a fine fiddler, too. When Pappy took to fiddling, why, I couldn't of kept my feet still if my life depended on it. And sing while he played. Now, that's harder'n hell to do. Yessir. Could sing and play the fiddle at the same time."

"Hackley can, too, Granny. Aunt Nancy said she'd never heard of nobody that could play like him when they's only a young'un."

"Pappy could play the fiddle when he weren't no more than a young'un, too. Must be something in the blood."

"What's that mean, Granny?"

"What, honey?"

"That it must be something in the blood?"

Granny looked at Larkin. "Why, it means it must run in the family."

"Oh." Larkin was quiet for a minute. Then, "Granny, have I got something in my blood? Other than the singing thing? Wish't I could learn how to play like Hack. He's trying to learn me but, for some reason, it just don't make no sense to me."

I knew just how he felt. Hackley had picked up the fiddle when he was five and had flew right into playing. He could pick the banjo, too. But, before I could say a word, Granny answered him.

"Why, I never could play nothing neither, son. Pappy tried to learn me too. Made no sense whatsoever. Pappy said my fiddle playing put him in the mind of two cats fighting." She chuckled, then reached out and give his ear a tug. "Why honey, don't fret, you got plenty of good stuff in your blood." She rubbed her hand over his hair. "You got your daddy's features. He was a dark-eyed, dark-haired, handsome man. You know his mama was a Indian. He was a big, stout man— and you're a big, stout boy. And you got your mommie's cleverness. You got a head full a sense, son. So I'd say you got plenty of good stuff, Larkin Stanton. Follow me around the side of the hill. I want to show you something."

I grinned because I knew right off what she meant to show him. It was one of my favorite places in the whole world.

Granny went striding off toward a big chestnut. Larkin bent to pick up his little bucket, and when he straightened up, Granny was nowhere to be seen.

"Go on, son. Go round the tree," I said.

As we rounded the big tree I heard him gasp. "A cave!"

"I used to play all over these mountains when I was a young'un," Granny said. "My own mommie showed me this here cave when I weren't much older than you." Her eyes got awfully bright. "Me and my brother Josie found all manner of stuff in here—little pieces of bowls, little purties. . . . Josie was closest to me. Lord, hit don't seem like he's been gone fer fifteen year."

We stood there quiet. We'd learned that sometimes many minutes would go by as Granny made her way back down the familiar path that was her long life.

She shook herself, sighed, and stepped away from the memory.

"Well, you know it's here now. You and Hackley can make it your own."

She walked back toward the chestnut tree, leaving me and Larkin at the mouth of the cave.

I looked down at him and couldn't help but smile at the shiny boy-wonder look on his face, but then again maybe it weren't so much a boy-wonder thing cause I'd seen the same look on Zeke's face and him a man grown. And then out of nowheres come this icy finger that laid itself cold right at the base of my spine. *Cat walked o'er my grave,* I thought and made the X sign over my heart against it. And in a voice sharper than it needed to be, I called out, "Come on, Larkin!" And then I wanted away from that place *bad.* I took hold of Larkin's hand tight and turned us both down the path toward home.

• • •

That afternoon me, Granny, Mommie, and Lucindy were sitting on the porch peeling apples. Lucindy had fetched them to Granny when she'd brought her young'uns to eat cake with the rest of us. The sun had been awful hot only an hour ago, but had now made its way behind the apple tree at the edge of the yard. A breeze picked up the fine gold hairs at the nape of Mommie's neck, and I just loved the way she brought her hands up all dainty-like to tuck them back into her bun. Mommie had the prettiest hands and when I noticed them I always thought of the line from "Pretty Saro," "My love she is handsome, all proper and neat." Her eyes were the same color as the little flower on blue-eyed grass just like Granny's. But they didn't have the big life in them that Granny's did. I'm sorry to say that but it's the truth. They didn't.

"I swan, that Larkin is growing like a garden weed," she said. "Why, if you didn't know it, you'd not believe for a minute that they was near four years' difference between him and Hack, would you?"

Lucindy looked up. "You surely can't tell my Mary is older— Larkin's bigger than her already. Hell, he's big as Jonah and him turned twelve. You remember the night Jonah was born?" she said to Mommie.

"Don't reckon I'd ever forget it. Wind howling like as to cut you in two! Papa swore the wind blowed a cow off the mountain above the house."

Granny laughed. "It was the truth. We heard a thump against the wall. Long as I live I'll never forget the look on David's face when he come back in. Never hurt the cow."

"Well, I was hurting!" Lucindy said. "By the time Nancy got there I was screaming bloody hell. If I could of got my hands around Andrew's scrawny neck I'd have choked the life out of him right there on the spot."

They all laughed. But I never. Even though I too remembered they was a brief time when I was laboring with Abby and John Wesley that I could've just squeezed Zeke to death. But somehow it weren't that funny sitting here with my lap budding another one.

"Speaking of birthings?" Lucindy asked me as she spit a brown stream off the porch.

"Due the end of November." Mommie didn't give me time to say. "Probably won't be a year between this one and John Wesley."

I shot a look at Mommie and felt myself draw up inside. She had that prim, hateful look to her, mouth all pursed up and her nose wrinkled like she was smelling something bad.

"Abby was a big baby and so was John Wesley. This one probably will be, too." Granny tossed a rotten apple to the big rooster prancing about in the front yard. "We always did have the biggest babies, 'cept for your Marthy, Nancy."

Bless her for the saint she is, I thought. Trying to get Mommie off the topic she so loves nowadays. That would be the "how-many-youngun's-Arty-has-had-in-as-many-years-talk." Which would be three if you're interested.

"Aunt Hattie said Larkin was the biggest one she'd ever caught." Lucindy examined an apple.

"Eight year ago today. Time goes by so fast."

Granny laughed. "That 'catching babies' reminded me of something my uncle Leland said. You probably don't remember him, but I know you remember Aunt Lily."

I remembered Aunt Lily. She called herself big and stout and she was both. She was a little over six feet tall and strong as a bear. Funny, that. Uncle Leland killed a sow bear and as he was skinning it out heard its cub crying off in the woods. He took it home to Aunt Lily and she raised it grown. She'd just had Little Jack and they said the two of them nursed right alongside each other. That bear follered her around just like a big dog.

Granny must've been thinking the same thing because she up and said, "Now, Little Jack, when he was a boy was a pure-D fool over honeycomb. Aunt Lily had to watch him like a hawk when they robbed a bee tree. He'd git in it and have it all over him. They's all gathered up at Pappy's and Little Jack got into Mommie's honey crock. Lordy at the mess he'd made. Uncle Leland never moved from his chair and Aunt Lily was just raising all manner of hell. Pappy was saying how Little Jack must be part bear, way he loved honey, and Uncle Leland rared back and said, 'Why, didn't you'uns know that's how we got Little Jack. Baited a bear-trap with honeycomb in the Pig-Pen Holler and caught him!' " Granny laughed. "Aunt Lily looked at him, popped them hands on her hips and said, 'Shut up, Leland, damned ole son of a bitch!' "

I got so tickled I couldn't stand it. I could just see all that in my mind. They said Uncle Leland was a fine fiddler and a real cut-up. He must've been awfully brave, too. Aunt Lily carried an awful scar above her right eye where an Indian hit her in the head with a rock. She killed the Indian with nothing but her bare hands.

Granny looked toward the barn where the young'uns were just going through the big double doors. "But Larkin is a big young'un. Like his daddy's people, I reckon. 'Course my Pappy was a tall man. Some of his bigness could have come through him. God knows it never come through your papa's side." She looked at Mommie and snorted. "They was everone little people, women, men, all of 'em." She grinned. "Little all over, too!"

Though I laughed with them, I was watching Hackley and Jonah heading for the lower stalls to hunt snakes while the rest of the young'uns went up the ladder into the hayloft. I knew what a fool Mary was over kittens and figured she was hunting for the newest litter. She told me what happened in the barn that day years later. Funny how I don't need these useless old eyes to see in my heart how it must've been.

The big boys wouldn't let Larkin go with them and I doubt that he cared much. Even then he was always hunting for a chance just to be able to look at Mary. She was such a pretty thing, redheaded and freckled like her mama but wispy, delicate, and small-boned. Of course Hackley claimed her for his own. That was no surprise.

But what happened in the barn that day *did* come as a surprise.

Mary said they found some kittens in the loft and she'd picked one up to pet. She said she happened to look at Larkin and he had such a look of longing on his face that she felt sorry for him. Oh, Lord, how that makes me feel even now. It makes my belly hurt to think of him longing for something, anything. And it makes me mad as hell to know she felt sorry for him. I don't know why, but it does.

She said she put the kitten down and eat some strawberries she'd put in her pocket. And then she offered to scratch his head. Oh, that burns me up. Like he was a dog or something. But that's not what she felt, I know that because she told me so. She said his hair felt coarse as a horse's tail and was black as a crow's wing. Larkin must've been purring loud as that kitten before him. He told her she smelled good. Bless his heart. I guess she did.

Larkin told me himself that he'd watched Hackley kiss her. Then Hackley had gone running after Jonah, laughing how he'd done it on a dare, leaving Mary standing there in the light-striped aisle. And then he'd asked if he could kiss her too, and she let him. Poor Larkin. Always second on the list.

He said I called for him right after and I remember it, plain as day. I remember seeing them big boys run out of the barn all red-faced and I hollered out, "Larkin." He come to me. He always did. He was such a good, decent, and loving boy. And I remember what he said to me his face all lit up and bright as a new penny.

"Mary smells like strawberries, Amma."

Fool that I was, I had no way of knowing that he was carrying with him her very breath.

CAROLINA WAS BORN ON the first day of December that year and time for me after that melts and runs smearing all together. Having three under three is *not* the way I'd say to have them. Now, you talk about being tired, but I was slap wore out.

I wouldn't have thought I'd remember much about them times but it's always an amazement what I can reach back and drag up out of this tired old head. I can recall something that happened fifty, sixty years ago better than what happened just last week. Why, I remember words to love songs I learned when I was just four or five year old. Or stuff that ain't got to do with nothing, except maybe my heart, like how the sky colored up so pretty of a summer morning with that pale red and orange right before that big sun ball peeped its hot face up over the mountain. Or in the wintertime taking that first breath of air so cold that it caused my nose hair to brickle, and how the deep lavender light of dawn would be laying about in every crease and crevice there in the cove and the mountains off toward Tennessee would be wearing their misty shrouds. Or how I asked Granny one time if she thought green might be God's favorite color since he'd made so many different shades of it. I remember sweet things, too.

The way Zeke's eyes changed color with his moods, the wonderment on John Wesley's baby face when he found his hand, the sweet milk breath of all my children, the time little Ingabo pulled all the green 'maters and when I fussed at her she shrugged her shoulders and said, "I'll just have to take them and hang them back."

Maybe it has something to do with what's important to us, and what happens when you get old ain't too important. Granny said it was because them early memories was stored in the uncluttered mind of a child. I reckon that's one of the prettiest ways to explain it that I've ever heard.

CAROLINA WAS ALREADY A month old when the first deep snow of the season fell. It had stayed warm right up till then. Then it was as though winter had just been biding her time, saving it up. It snowed just about every day till way up in March. Most folks just hunkered down, waiting for it to be over. But weather never slowed Hackley and Larkin down even a little bit. They was always together and always out going and doing just like boys probably always have and always will. Some mornings just at daylight I'd look out and there they'd be heading down the main trace. I'd know they was heading for Big Laurel Creek. They had traps sunk in the deepest pools and went to check them at least every other day.

Oh, how I envied them two boys their carefree ways. It had only been four years since I'd gone traipsing along with them. It was *me* that learned them how to set their traps deep so only the biggest muskrats would go for the bait, *me* that Larkin come crying to wondering if the trap hurt when it closed on them, *me* that learned them to swim in the deep water of the Seward Hole, *me* that used to go with them to the creek in the still of a winter's snow. And it was *me* that was standing there with a great yearning in that cold little cabin my husband had built with loving hands, *me* that was now held back by the strong yet flimsy chain of flesh that was my own creation.

THEY WAS NO EASY way to get to the creek where it twisted and snaked its way around the foot of the mountain and was bordered on one side by a sheer rock cliff called Jumped-Up. It got named that 'cause it really did look like it had jumped up out of the water right on to the side of that mountain and it kept a stubborn grip for a hundred feet or more before it finally give way to the laurel hell that went the rest of the way to the top.

In the wintertime the clouds seemed living things that would lower their big faces right to the top of the mountain like they aimed to kiss it. As you went down the path to the only ford, they'd boil all about you, coiling around and sending out little ragged bits like arms and fingers, reaching and touching. Little towhees would come spiraling up off the limbs of the jack pines and dive right over what looked like the edge of the world. About halfway down you'd come out of a switchback and step right out of the clouds but they'd be right above your head, the bottom all bruised-looking with fat flakes of snow falling straight down. And as far as you could see, which was awfully far, was the world made soft by snow. "Granny's beat-up egg whites," Larkin would always say. God, I loved him and the things he'd say sometimes. And we'd all three just sing.

Hackley's voice was always certain, wrapping sure and confident around each note, moving along easy, up and down. Oh, but Larkin's was a wonderment, pure and clear, hitting them high notes and holding them, holding them.

Little Marg'ret a-setting in her high hall chair
Combing back her long yeller hair
Saw Sweet William and his new maid bride
Riding up the road so near.

She threw down her ivory comb,
Threw back her long yeller hair,
Said, "I'll go down and bid him farewell
And never more go there."

It was late in the night,
They were fast asleep.
Little Marg'ret appeared all dressed in white
Standing at their bed feet.

"How do ye like your snow-white pillow?
How do ye like your sheets?
How do ye like that pretty fair maid
That lays in your arms asleep?"

"Very well do I like my snow white pillow,
Well do I like my sheet,
Much better do I like that pretty fair maid
That stands at my bed feet."

He called his serving man to go
Saddle the dappled roan
And he went to her father's house that night
And knocked on the door alone.

"Is Little Marg'ret in her room?
Or is she in the hall?"

"Little Marg'ret's in her cold black coffin
With her face turned toward the wall."

"Unfold, unfold those snow-white robes,
Be they ever so fine,
For I want to kiss them cold, corpsey lips,
For I know they'll never kiss mine."

Three times he kissed her cold, cold chin,
Twice't he kissed her cheek.
Once't he kissed her cold, corpsey lips
And fell in her arms asleep.

Larkin never even strained on the high notes that had me screeching at the top of my lungs. It's a good thing he didn't have to study awfully much about the tune because he just lost himself in them stories. When he was little he'd put his own self *right there,* living it, breathing life into it. Listening to him sing never failed to jerk goosebumps up on my arms. Even Hackley, who went along not noticing much, would sometimes stare at him and say something like, "Damn boy."

But they was no beating Hackley when it come to a tune. He went whistling one all the time and once't he could whistle it good he could play it on the fiddle. Oh, how he could make them strings pull at your insides. "Your very guts," Granny said. When he took a hold of a bow, that fiddle might as well get ready because it was going to *weep.* Don't git me wrong, many was the time I watched all the girls go hungry-eyed when he'd commence to singing. But they went plumb foolish when he played. And Hackley loved the girls, any shape and any size. So he played a lot.

But even then, with Mary fixing to turn eleven and him just thirteen, Hackley told Larkin that day he wanted her for his own and aimed to marry her one day.

Larkin said they'd built a lean-to right next to the creek out of pine boughs and had a big fire going. Hackley was stretched out with his feet almost in the flames and Larkin was setting out in the weather.

"I can hear the snow falling all around me," he said. And Hackley had answered with the same thing I often said: "You say the damnedest things."

But if you think about it, you *can* hear snow falling all crackly-like.

They stayed around down there most of that day, playing in the snow, laying by the fire, eating what they'd brung with them. "I purely love this time of the year," Hackley said. And Larkin asked him, "Do you really aim to marry Mary?" Hard to think that even as boys she was always there between them, but oh, yes, she was. And when Larkin asked him if he'd thought whether Mary wanted to marry him, Hackley had shrugged and said, "Why, I reckon she does. I mean, I ain't thought about it much. Just figured when it come time, she would."

And Larkin said even then he wanted his mind off of that, so he'd asked Hackley to sing something he didn't know, and that was the day he learned "The Cruel Mother."

They was a lady who lived in York, all alone and lone-y,
She fell in love with her father's clerk, all down by the green
   wood-side-y.

They hadn't been courting but a year and a day, all alone and lone-y,
Until her heart he did betray, all down by the green wood-side-y.

As she was a walking across the bridge, all alone and lone-y,
She saw her belly were growing big, all down by the green
wood-side-y.

She turned her back against the oak, all alone and lone-y,
First hit bent and then hit broke, all down by the green wood-side-y.

She leaned her back against the thorn, all alone and lone-y,
There's where her two purty babes were born, all down by the
green wood-side-y.

She pulled out her snow-white breast, all alone and lone-y,
And bid them purty babes suck their best, all down by the green
wood-side-y.

She took her hair so long and neat, all alone and lone-y,
To tie them with, both hands and feet, all down by the green
wood-side-y.

She took a penknife keen and sharp, all alone and lone-y,
And pierced these two purty babes to the heart, all down by the
green wood-side-y.

And with a napkin from her head, all alone and lone-y.
She wrapped them up when they were dead, all down by the green
wood side-y.

She wiped her penknife on her shoe, all alone and lone-y,
But the more she wiped the redder hit grew, all down by the green
wood-side-y.

She placed them under a marble stone, all alone and lone-y,
And prayed this murder would never be known, all down by the
green wood-side-y.

I can just see Larkin, eyes shut tight, already making it his own, imagining that poor girl returning to her father's house pretending to be still a maid, thinking of the ghosts of the murdered children coming to call. Them children then telling their own mommie she was doomed for hell.

He'd be learning it to me in a week's time and asking, "Why do you reckon she let them suck if she just aimed to kill them?" I had no answer unless it was that she was a coldhearted and selfish bitch, which is just what I said to him. And he said he'd asked Hackley the same thing and I asked, "Well, what did he say?"

Hackley said just this: "Hell if I know. Just the way them old songs is, sometimes."

4

I HAD MY FOURTH child that we named Sylvaney the year Larkin turned thirteen, and that was also the year I was afraid he would never sing again.

Hugh Wallin's singing school met every summer where he taught the shape-note singing which went like this: a flag shape for fa, circle for sol, diamond for mi, and a square for la. When we all learned the music, we would sing the poetry. The church was always full to busting and we divided ourselves into the three parts, which was tenor, lead, and bass. The singing always started at 9:00 in the morning and more times than not we'd go straight through until suppertime with the number of folks singing ebbing and flowing as some would quit and eat and come back to sing again.

Every time Hackley got called on to lead a hymn the tenors, which was where all the young girls was setting, would go all a-twitter. He knew it, too; however much he acted like he didn't, he did. And this day was no different. He stood and literally flowed into the open center and even I could see what they did. He might have been little but he had that way of moving that women just loved. He held himself all loose and easy and his eyes looked lazy and quick at the same time. Even some of the older women set into fanning themselves. Maggie Hensley was like a worm in a hot skillet, and if I'd acted like that about another man Zeke Wallin would've slapped me blind. I would not have blamed him neither.

All but Mary Chandler. She set there with her hands folded on top of her book and never offered Hackley so much as a glance. And I believe that's why she was all he could see.

" 'Sacred Throne,' folks. Page thirty-five." He waited until pages had ceased rustling and all eyes were on him. Satisfied, he raised his right hand and began to beat out the time.

"Now sing your parts! Everbody sing!"

This was Hackley's favorite hymn and he had no use for the book in his hand. His eyes were never still as he began to sing the lead shapes. And each section in that little church began to sing in harmony so rich it caused my throat to swell up.

"Now sing the poetry!" He threw back his head, closed his eyes, and I forgot everything except the sound. There was a big silence when we finished. Hugh new what he was doing when he called on Larkin to lead the next. Not many people could follow Hackley.

Larkin stood and walked to the square.

"Let's sing 'Windham,' page two hundred and seven." All eyes gazed at him expectantly. "Let's pitch it." He closed his eyes and relaxed. His voice took the first note, then began the climb up the scale.

"Sol, fa, mi, la, sol."

On the high sol Larkin's voice sang out confident and full. Then it cracked. A little frown puckered his forehead and he cleared his throat and started again.

"Sol, fa, mi, la, sol."

Again he couldn't hold it. It was so quiet in there that I could hear folks laughing and talking out where they was eating.

"That's a good pitch, Larkin. Let's sing the shapes," Hugh said.

I could see his hand trembling as he started to beat out the time and sing the shapes to the hymn.

Finally he just quit singing but stayed on beating out the time for everybody else. I quit, too, and watched the sweat run down his face into his eyes. Then the song ended and he ought to have set down, but he didn't. Instead he brought up his book and stared at it dumb-looking as a cow, as though somewhere in there amongst the shapes he had memorized so easy when he was but a child lay the answer. He looked at me and I swear he looked like he was drowning.

Me and Granny both come to our feet but Hackley beat us to him.

"I'll lead the next one," Hack said, and though he laid a sym-pathetic hand on Larkin's arm, he couldn't quite hold back the grin that skittered across his mouth. And I thought, *Don't do this to him, Hackley, you little shit.* But he'd already done it.

Hackley give him a little shove. "It'll be all right," he said.

"Don't pay Hack no mind," I hollered right out. "Sing with the basses. Your voice won't break if you sing low."

It didn't. For Larkin did not sing another note the rest of that long day.

I DONE SOMETHING THAT day that I rarely did. I left Abby and Zeke to fix their own supper and mind the young'uns and I went over the hill to Granny's. I did take Sylvaney but would've left her too if I hadn't knowed my bosoms would give me a fit if she didn't nurse. And it were a good thing I did 'cause I was there a long time. Granny had her hands full of one awfully pitiful man-child.

He was setting on the porch, long legs drawed up, head resting on his knees, and he never even looked up when I howdied the house.

Me and Granny whispered around out back for a few minutes, then we both went out on him. Granny put her knobby old hand on his hair and her touch was so gentle it jerked tears to my eyes.

"Hit happens that-a-way, honey. Yer voice is changing into that of a man. You'll still be able to sing, just deeper and different. You'll see. Same thing happened to Hackley. 'Course hit went quick fer him. Didn't it, Arty?"

And I said, "Why, he squalled and screeched around at them singings for two, three months. Cut up and made such an ungodly racket just to draw attention to himself that Hugh had to make him hush up more than once't. Remember?"

His voice come out all muffled against his knees. "Didn't seem to bother Hack at all." He give a big heaving sigh and then said, "But what if I can't?"

Granny snorted, tugging at his hair a bit. "Can't sing, you mean? Raise your head and look at me," she said in her best no-foolishness voice.

Larkin looked up and my breath caught in my throat. He'd been crying and I thought, *Oh, honey, bless your heart.*

"Son, do you recall me ever lying to you?" Granny said in the softest voice I'd ever heard her use.

He shook his head.

"Then believe me when I tell you that this will pass. Time takes care of most things and hit'll take care of this."

She got down on her knees right in front of him and pulled him straight into her arms. She rocked him like a baby, singing to him the whole time. He let her do it too. And I stood there rocking Sylvaney and my milk let down and wet the front of my dress.

When she was done he pulled back and said, "What song was that, Granny?"

"Pappy called it 'The Blackest Crow.'" She smiled.

I said, "Aunt Vesty said it were 'My Dearest Dear.' Pretty, ain't it? You ought to sing it."

He said, "That's easy for you to say. But I can't." And he drawed his knees up and pushed his face back between them.

Now I'd had enough and I said so.

But Granny said, "You hush, Arty, and go set down over yonder and feed Sylvaney."

And I went because she told me to and felt foolish in the doing of it. Me a mommie four times and I turned right around like a slip of a young'un and set down.

"You will, Larkin. Don't quit trying. It'll come." When she went to get up her knees popped like a gunshot. "I promised you, didn't I?"

I reckon he needed something. So he held tight to her words as summer give way to fall.

EVERY OCTOBER ME AND Zeke had a frolic at our house. He was a fine banjo picker and loved to make music. We'd move all the furniture out into the yard so we could have lots of room for the dancing, which I loved to do. I will have to say that I was light on my feet and turned many a head when I hit the floor. I went by Granny's the night before to make sure they was coming. Truth be known, I wanted to eyeball Larkin. He hadn't come by the house in ages and my mind kept turning to him, worrying about him. And I do not worry well. I am as bad as a man to want to fix things.

WHEN I WENT IN the door Granny was mending a shirt by the light of the fire and Larkin was setting on the floor beside her. She lapped the shirt and leaned forward to spit in the fireplace. "Look what the cats drug in," she said, but I could tell she was glad to see me. Larkin never even looked up, just stared on like they was some big exciting thing other than the fire going on in the fireplace.

Me and Granny talked about this and that and when I just couldn't stand it no more, I asked both of them if they was coming to the frolic. But I was talking mostly to Larkin and he was the one that answered.

"No," he said.

I flew mad and opened my mouth to say something mean, but Granny stood of a sudden and set herself right down on the floor beside him. They was nothing then for me to do but set down on the other side. We set a while and the only sound was the hissing of the fire. Then Granny said in an easy, talky voice, and she did not even look at Larkin, "I was trying to remember the words to a love song yesterday," and then she stopped and never said nothing for a long time. I knowed she wanted Larkin to say the words but I can be right impatient at times and this was one of them. She give me a quick frown when I started talking but I was already in it now.

"Which song? I can't believe you've forgot words to a song."

She was still frowning at me when she started to hum the tune. I recognized it right off but knew better than to say anything else. I didn't even have Sylvaney to nurse this time and figured she'd just run me off.

"Yes, Arty," she said and her voice was not sweet when she spoke my name. "It is bad when ye get to where ye can't remember words you've knowed for seventy years." She began humming, stopped, shook her head.

"Real fine song, 'Pretty Peggy-o.' Recall the tune just fine, but the words don't come." She started up a low humming and started to sing. I was shocked at how phlegmy and coarse her voice was and tried to remember if it had sounded like this back in the summer and realized with a certain sadness that yes, it had been just this way.

Come a-trippin' down the stairs, Pretty Peggy-o
Come a-trippin' down the stairs, Pretty Peggy-o

She stopped. "That ain't right."

"That's the third verse," Larkin spoke like he just couldn't help himself. "First one starts out, 'As we marched down to Fennary-o.'"

I nodded. "That's right."

The fire gave a mighty crack, and a red chunk of wood shot out. Granny slapped it onto the hearthrock with her hand and at the same time give me such a look as would have shut the lying mouth of Satan himself.

"Saddens me to think I've forgot one of Pappy's favorites." She sucked in a big chest full of air and puffed out her cheeks when she breathed out, as she was wont to do. "Sing it for me."

Larkin's eyes went back to watching that miserable fire.

"You know I can't sing no more. Voice won't do a thing I want it to. Breaks and wobbles around. Sounds sometimes like a girl's."

Granny give a big snort. "My voice ain't likely to grace no stages neither, and I ain't gonna git mine back. This singing ain't about purty voices, nohow." She reached out and grabbed his chin, made him look at her. "It's the story what's important, Larkin, not how purty you sing it."

Something moved in his eyes. Whatever it was, it wrenched my heart and I would have said something but I did not and was later glad that I held my tongue, which, as you have probably figured by now, could be sometimes sharp.

"Sing it." She weren't ordering him to do it, she was pleading with him. "For me."

Finally he began to sing in a low, soft voice.

> As we marched down to Fennary-o
> As we marched down to Fennary-o
> Our captain fell in love with a lady like a dove
> And they called her name Pretty Peggy-o.

And though his voice was uncertain, cracked at times, bounced back and forth between that of man and child, we both could hear what it would become. Granny began to cry and it was this that was his undoing.

"Granny?" he said, coming up on his knees.

She laid the rock hard palm of her hand right on his cheek. "My Pappy has been gone from this world for nigh on sixty years now. I told ye a while ago that I can't remember much a'tall, and that was the truth. They's times when I'm hard pressed to recall Pappy's dear old face, try as I might. But just now, while you was singing, his face come to me so sharp and clear it near about took my breath away. It were your singing, child. You sounded just like him."

"I'm sorry, Granny."

Now Granny was staring at the fire, but she turned from it and looked him right in the face and her face just beamed. "Oh, Larkin, honey, it were a good thing. Just fer a minute I had my Pappy back. Ye give me something just now that I never thought I'd hear ever again." Her bright eyes moved around the cabin then came back to him. "When you're young it's hard to believe when somebody dies that they are gone forever, Larkin. You got nothing to lay forever out next to, nothing to measure it against." Granny hitched a bony shoulder. "You don't even know what you'll miss about them. Oh, you have some notion, I reckon. You figure you'll miss seeing them everyday, stuff like that. But, ye've no idea about them little things—Pappy was deaf in one ear and had a way of turning his good ear toward whoever was talking, sort of cocked his head to one side. He was a big man, and when he walked his feet would slap against the floor real heavy-like. Couldn't sneak up on nothing, that's why he had to be such a good shot with a gun. And, law how he'd laugh. Big booming sound. Why, he'd get so tickled sometimes that his eyes would just pour the water. And he was hot-natured and whenever he's out working he'd sweat enough fer two men. He'd cuss them gnats something fierce." And though her eyes were pouring water she laughed plumb out loud. "Called 'em dog-pecker gnats."

I couldn't help it. I laughed too, and so did Larkin.

Then she said, "I never knowed how quiet my world would be without him in it."

Larkin spread his fingers in a gesture of awkward compassion. "Granny, I—" he began.

"Shhh. I'm studying about things, Larkin. Leave it be."

I KNOW THIS MIGHT sound funny, but what I remember most about that winter was how quiet it was. Always before, and I really do mean most of the time—and especially in the cold weather when sound carried best—you could hear Hackley or Larkin, and usually both, singing all over the cove. But Hackley had set in to some serious sparking with Mary, and though I'd bet you a hundred dollars that if Larkin was trying to sing, he was not doing it where anybody could hear him. He drug around like a whupped dog as Christmas come and went and a new year started. Though I felt sorry for him, it got to where I could not hardly stand to be around him. Granny said it didn't seem to be hurting how much he could eat, which I witnessed firsthand when he come by the house to help Zeke slaughter a shoat that got its head hung between the bars of the hogpen and choked itself. He could flat put it away and was getting way tall and his shoulders was broadening up. He was going to be a pretty thing, but God, he was not pretty now. He slinked around looking like death warmed over, all hunched up and pulled in on himself, never looking nowhere but at the ground. I just wanted to wring a chunk out of him and say, *Larkin Stanton, you straighten up,* or something along them lines. But Zeke told me to let him be, that he'd come along, and I could only believe him since I had no experience at being a big boy. And it was not that I did not already have my hands full of young'uns and work, work, work. I was proud to see spring come on and then the summer, even though it brought biting flies, more fleas, and bloodsucking ticks. I could slap flies, pinch fleas, and pull ticks off. At least now I could work outside and get out of that cabin that got smaller and smaller every year.

ME AND GRANNY WAS hoeing corn up in the Jimmy Field one day that was hot as Satan's house cat. The air was so heavy I swear you could've wrung water from it like wringing out a dishrag. I had this banjo tune stuck in my head that Zeke had played the night before and that always drove me crazy. He said it was "George Booker" and I wished I could've gotten my hands on old George. I'd have killed him as dead as a hammer. Of a sudden Granny stopped hoeing and cocked her head. She was one row down from me and I had been having to really bust it to stay out in front of her so as not to backtrash her row. When she leaned on her hoe you can bet I leaned on mine, too. Granny could hoe most folks plumb out of the field, but not me, and it was with some pride that I'd taken the upper row. But I reckon pride does really goeth before a fall as I felt like I was going to fall up at any minute. "What's the matter?" I hollered and she waved a you-need-to-hush hand at me, which I did. I heard nothing but the very first of the frost bugs starting to sing out in the oaks and then it come to me, almost like a whisper. Larkin was singing. And though he was not singing big and loud, he would have had to be singing a little loud since we could hear him from where he was up in the Dave Newground. Well, I knowed then for sure that the high pure voice of the boy was gone. And then he really let loose and the flesh pebbled up on my arms.

> My dearest dear, the time draws near when you and I must part.
> And no one knows the inner grief of my poor aching heart,
> Or what I've suffered for your sake, the one I love so dear.
> I wish't that I could go with you, or you might tarry here.
>
> I wish't your breast was made of glass, and in it I'd behold
> My name in secret I would write, in letters of bright gold.
> My name in secret I would write, believe me when I say
> You are the one that I'll love best unto my dying day.
>
> And when you're on some distant shore, think on your absent
>   friend
> And when the wind blows high and clear, a line to me pray send.
> And when the wind blows high and clear, pray send it, love, to me
> So I might know by your hand-write how times has gone with
>   thee.

And I knew he was *in* that song. Who knows what had gone on in his head to put him in it, but he was there. I know what was in my head, though, standing there in that hot field with Granny grinning like a mule eating saw briers right below me and this black cloud of gnats dancing a jig right in front of my eyes. And I swear I felt like somebody had took their fist and hit me square in the belly and I almost doubled up. Of a sudden I was in that song too and really knew it for the first time. They was coming a time when all of us would live in a world that Granny did not and I could not help it. I started to cry and Granny must have thought I was doing that because he was singing again. And she said, "Lord, it is really just like hearing Pappy again." And I commenced to hoeing because I could not for the life of me say a word to her.

5

THEY WAS NEVER A time when something was not happening with them boys. And I will not call them men, even though Larkin was fifteen and Hackley was almost nineteen. They is some men that will always be boys, and Hackley was one of them. Some of that, bless his heart, was the way his history wrote itself, but my guess is he would have always been that way. Though Larkin was big as a skinned mule, he acted like nothing but the young bull that he was. I swear him and Hackley had two or three fistfights a week back then. Not with each other all the time, though they did have one or two when Larkin either beat hell out of Hackley or he would let Hackley whup him 'cause he felt sorry for him, because it *was not* in Hackley to quit. One time they got into it down at the store and Larkin hit Hackley so hard both his feet come off the ground and he went over the bank right into the branch. Then here he come back and Larkin knocked him over the bank again and again here he come back. He done that four times and every time Larkin would say, "Stay down, Hackley," but Hackley would not. Finally Clee Buckner took ahold of Hackley and held his feet off the ground till he calmed down enough to be set down. And as soon as he was turned loose, don't you know that he went right back at Larkin. I saw the look on Hackley's face then and knowed what had to be, so I hollered out, "You're going to have to put him down, Larkin." And that time when he hit Hackley he went down like you'd throwed a sack of flour on the floor. It is a good thing for them both that they did not get into it often.

They almost come to blows about Larkin's name of all things. I always wondered when that would break out, and it happened right here at the house, too. We was having a frolic and Hackley had put his fiddle down and was out with the men drinking. Now, do not get me wrong. I am not above having a drink myself now and again, but I am not for getting knee-walking drunk. I never did see no sense in that and still don't. But the men had ganged up and Sol Bullman's liquor was flowing like water that night. And Sol's liquor went down sweet and you didn't realize it had you till you was plumb cross-eyed and talking in tongues. As you probably know, they is happy drunks and mean drunks and crazy drunks. Hackley was a crazy drunk and wanted to go to fighting every time. So he'd had him a few drinks and, foolish like, Larkin set in about his name. Why Granny had mentioned it in the first place is beyond me, but she did. Larkin set right in wanting to know just how it was that Hackley had come up with his name. And Hackley said, "It just come to me." Larkin's eyes was black as the night and he said, "Is that right?" Hackley allowed that it was. They went back and forth for a bit and of a sudden they was both mad as hell and right in each other's face. I run in between them and said for them to both hush. Hackley barked out a laugh and said, "Well, I was just four year old, what did you expect?" And Larkin said, "Something better than being named after a coon dog." And me desperate to keep them from fighting, blared out, "Well, he was a damn good coon dog," which set everybody to laughing including

Hackley and Larkin. Later I told Larkin he ought to have been thankful 'cause Mommie had told me Aunt Polly aimed to name him after Grandpap Shelton. And he allowed as how that might have been better and I allowed back as how no, it would not have, since Grandpap's name was Redderdick.

But they stayed into it with them other boys around home. Zeke come in laughing one night telling me how a bunch of them had got to playing poker, which I do not believe in because it is spending money that none of us has. He said Hoy and Roy McIntosh was there and I knowed what he was going to say before he said it. I really think Hackley just did not like the way they looked or held their mouths or something just as foolish because they got into it every time they run up on each other. That was the first time that I heard how Hackley and Larkin had took to fighting back to back. When I thought of how deadly the two of them would be doing that I got the cold chills. Larkin that had them big fists and Hackley that would not quit.

WHEN DECORATION DAY COME it seemed like everybody in the world headed out to Sodom. It was always on the second weekend in August and folks started coming in on that Friday. Everybody was in a right festive mood and we'd all gang up and clean off every grave in every cemetery. It looked so pretty on that Sunday with all the graves mounded and raked smooth. I have thought about that a lot over the years and know now that they had to have been graves we didn't even know about. When I think of all the folks that has died, been buried, and forgot about, it makes me know that our lives are but a flash in the pan and we really are a short time here and a long time gone.

I have to tell you now that this year was different. I felt it right off

as soon as we got to the church. I am not saying it looked any different. The little church was no big fancy thing, just a little box shape
with a steeple on top in which, I'm proud to say, was a bell that we
had bought from up north. On the inside we had benches that didn't
have splinters on them, which is a good thing. I have set on ones that
did and that was not good, because if you study about it they is no
good way to dig a splinter out of that part. At the front we had a pulpit and Zeke's brother Hugh had rocked in a pretty fireplace. Two big
old sugar maples stood guard on either side and they were a sight to
see in the fall of the year. They give shade in the summer, and that was
a good thing since it was hot as blazes this year. The men had knocked
together a bunch of tables and they were already swagging with food
by the time we got there to add our load. I'd cooked late into the night
and got up before daylight to fry chicken and I know heaven could
not smell no better than it did under them trees.

A clot of men had ganged up on the porch of Jim Leake's store.
Others stood about in the yard. I could not believe how quiet they
was, so I just had to wander over there to see what and all was going
on. They weren't even milling about much, and I could still see where
the dirt showed marks from Cassie's broom.

I went over to where Larkin was leaning against one of the posts
and leaned against him. He was as still as that post listening to Wade
Hensley reading the results of the election for governor from the
Asheville News. Nobody spoke until he finished reading every thing
they was to read.

"Damned if Marshall didn't go big for Ellis. Says here a hundred
and fifty-six for him and eighty-two for Pool."

"What about that!" Ruben Gosnell was whittling away and the
head and neck of a little bird that looked like a living thing was

coming right up out of that stick. "What do you reckon they was thinking?"

"Not much, you want my opinion," Shadrack said. I did not care for Shadrack even if he was Zeke's brother. He put on airs and I told him that one time. I also told him that he put his britches on just like everybody else, so they was no love at all lost between us. "How anybody could vote for that lying suck-ass is beyond me. 'Specially after he shit us with all them promises to git that road in down through Paint Rock."

"Bet Shelton Laurel laid it to Ellis's hide, didn't they?" Hugh said. I did like Hugh, and especially his wife Rosa. Me and her had been friends for all our lives and I knowed how good he was to her and their boys. They is something to be said about a man that is good to his wife and does not use his fists on her like some others I know— which would include Shadrack, I just might tell you.

Daddy was setting next to Wade and he leaned over and squinted at the little print in the paper. *Poor old Daddy,* I thought, *His eyes are getting bad.* "Ellis didn't git a single vote in Shelton Laurel. Pool got fifty-one." He looked up. " 'Course, Ellis got four out of thirty votes in our district."

Andrew Chandler give a wave of his hand that said oh-forget-about-that. "Bet that was them Eckerds off on Spillcorn. They been fools since God's dog was a pup. Can't even hold it against them. They can't help it."

As Wade folded up the paper, Daddy said, "Well, every other district in the county except Little Pine went big for Ellis, as did Buncombe County. It'll be four more years of the same old shit."

"What hurt Pool was that business about putting a tax on everything," Zeke said. Me and him had talked a long time about that over the last month and I had told him that them folks down east ought not to have to pay for our roads and such up here but they ought not to make us pay taxes on stuff we had to have to barely survive, neither.

Andrew snorted. "How exactly you reckon they was going to figure out what we had that they could put a tax on? Ain't nobody coming into my house and nosing about, making lists."

"Felt the same way, Andrew." Daddy said. "But they was no way I was gonna vote for them yeller dogs that's in, either. We was between a rock and a hard place."

"Can't trust none of them politicians far as you can rare back and throw 'em out in the yard, anyways." Ervin Ramsey leaned forward and spit off the end of the porch. "Old Pearlie, God rest him, used to say the only folks fit to be in charge of things is them what don't want to be."

"I really miss old Pearlie," Andrew said. "He had a way of putting things that went right to the quick."

Wiley Franklin wiped his face. He was bad to sweat and his handkerchief was already sopping wet. "Well, now," he said, "Pool said something a week or so ago that was right on the money. He said they's a time coming and coming soon when we're going to wind up gitting into it with each other over this slave thing. Said them what owns niggers here in North Carolina can't raise twenty thousand men." He waved his arm at all of us standing there, "Be up to *us* to come up with the rest of 'em."

Greenberry Chandler said, "Far as I'm concerned, they ought to take all the niggers, load 'em on one of them big boats, take 'em about ten mile out into that big blue ocean and dump the lot of 'em."

"Eh law, Greenberry," Sol Bullman said. "That's the most words you strung together at one time since you married that big-mouthed sister of mine!" We all busted out laughing, for he was married to Hattie. She come from a long line of midwives and she had a way about her that said do not mess with me in any shape, form, or fashion. Most of us had been brought into this world by the rough, work-hard hands of her grandmother, mother, or in mine and Larkin's case, Hattie herself. It was a good thing Greenberry was a quiet man.

"But what about Tillman?" Andrew said.

I had not thought of Tillman Chandler in years. He used to claim me for his sweetheart but I did not claim him. He was tall and skinny, and if you was looking at Zeke you would know that I like men of a different sort. I did recall that Tillman had married a woman from Asheville whose daddy died not long after they'd set up housekeeping and that he had come into over two hundred acres and most of it good flat bottom land. It had never even flittered through my head that he would have to have slaves. But then why would it? They was no slaves in Sodom unless you counted the ones what was white and female.

"Damned if I know what to do about it," Ruben said to them. His eyes never moved from the graceful curve of that bird's wing. "But I do know it's a mess, a pure-D mess. Don't believe I understand all I know about this nigger thing anyhow." He raised the bird, give it a good long eyeball, blew on it, and went back to carving. "Never seen a man of color myself."

"Saw two of 'em last week when I was down in Warm Springs." Zeke said. "Black as the ace of spades."

"Well," Ruben said, "I can just about guarantee it'll come to war. They's too much fussing back and forth amongst 'em in Raleigh and up in Washington."

"Goodness, fellers, I reckon not." This was from old man Swan Ray. He started just about everything he said with *goodness* or *here there*. "Here there, it wouldn't be nothing to us one way or t'other. War amongst rich folks, ye ask me."

"Mayhap," Daddy said. "But somehow it always manages to work itself back around to being a poor man's fight."

"If you'uns could hear half of what I hear on my drumming route," Wade said, "you would know it will come to war. That's all I hear, 'specially down south of here."

Wade was from off down toward Hendersonville and had married Vergie Ray, who was Swan's daughter.

I was so caught up in what was being said that I jumped like somebody had poked me in the ribs when Big John Stanton's deep voice come rumbling out right there beside me. The *Big* part of his name was put there for a reason but I swear he could slip up on you and you would never know it till he wanted you to. We was not related to the Stantons but Larkin's daddy was one. Their grandma was full Cherokee and you could surely see it in both of them. She was never heard from again when they was all rounded up and took off.

Big John crossed arms big as fence posts over his chest and said, "Let it come, boys. I for one wouldn't mind a good fight."

"Maybe so, son." Wiley took his hat off and went to smearing that wet handkerchief around on his shiny bald head. "You're young and most of us ain't. But you'd still have to fight one side or the other."

"Hell, Wiley, I'm for joining the side that looked like it were going to win."

Lord have mercy, did that not set everybody to talking at once.

And would you not know that it was just then that Hackley come up to me and Larkin. He was wearing the white shirt Mommie had made him. Last week I'd gone to see if her beans had come in and they had and I was stringing and breaking them up while she sewed the buttons on it. My John Wesley loves green beans and Mommie's big greasys are the best. I must say Hackley looked like icing on a cake. Right then it come to me that my brother was one of the prettiest men I'd ever laid eyes on, even if he was grinning in a not so pretty way.

He said, "Lark, look out yonder and tell me what you see."

"Don't see much, Hack," Larkin said, though he did not do much more than let his eyes skim over the crowd. I could tell that he was way more interested in them men what was still arguing there in front of the store because of what he said next. "Have you heard any of this talk about a war?"

"War?" Hackley said, and I could have told Larkin that my brother had not lost a bit of sleep nor one waking minute with thoughts about no war. And then he said, "I want you to look at the damn prettiest girl in Madison County."

And I piped right in. "You better be thinking about something other than your jewel among women, Mary Chandler." I was trying to be funny, and Larkin picked right up on this, but it was all lost on Hackley because he got real serious. That in itself was a wondrous thing to behold, because there was not much in life that roused Hackley to seriousness.

"She is just that, sister." He had not called me sister in a long time. Then I did know that Hackley Norton was as serious as the night was long about Mary Chandler. And what he said to us next sealed the deal. The crowd sort of parted, and though I could not see from where I was, Hackley could.

"Why, that son of a bitch! Look-a there!"

Like a shot I was up on my tippy-toes trying to see. "What, what?" I said.

Larkin, being a full head and shoulders over me, said, "Willard's trying to talk to Mary."

And Hackley went rushing off, saying real loud-like, "I'll whup his ass!"

Then the crowd parted like Moses had raised his stick and I could see Willard Bullman leaning toward Mary. She had on a cream-colored dress and her waist looked slim as a boy's. I knowed for a fact that I would never see my own that slender again but I would not have traded places with her if it had meant I had to give up my young'uns and Zeke.

Hackley went out through there like a little banty rooster and when Willard saw him coming he looked around right wild. I knowed what he was looking for was standing right beside me. Everybody with any kind of sense knowed that if you messed with Hackley you had Larkin to fight and that was no fun. This is not to say my brother was not a handful all by hisself. He was. But I had my suspicions that it was Larkin they really dreaded and then I knew it for a fact, because when Willard looked and seen Lark standing there on the porch he sort of slouched off into the crowd without so much as a backward look at Mary.

But Larkin was looking at her, they was no doubt, and if you could have seen the look, it would have tipped his hand to you as it most certain did to me. It was such a look that I swear I had to look myself. And I will tell you what I saw. She was not short but not real tall, she was slender and not busty neither. Her dark red hair kept catching the light that was sifting down through the leaves. She had freckles, but they was not so many and she had that real white redhead skin. Her hands were as slender as Mommie's and I could not help it, I looked at mine. I would never have hands like them, as my fingers were too short, and I would never have the slender waist neither. But I would not complain, since Zeke seemed to like the way I was put together just fine. But Mary Chandler was as close to being beautiful as any girl I'd ever seen and I had not even noticed it until that very moment in time. I must have had my head under a bushel or maybe I'd just been raising young'uns and living my own life, thank you very much.

I could not stand to see Larkin all but slobbering on himself. "If you are going to stare so hard, you ought to at least shut your mouth," I said to him. And then I could have just bit my tongue right off at the look of longing and misery that moved through his eyes. Oh, how I wanted to take him in my arms and say, "Do not let this slip of a girl cause this thing," but felt that I ought not because I'd been so hateful and because I did not want to shame him any more than I already had. Red as a beet, he turned back to the men that was now a big crowd and loud to boot. I was never so glad to see anybody in my life as I was to see that Fee had come up and was standing on the other side of Larkin.

"Howdy, Fee," I said. His big round eyes settled on my face then moved on. Poor Fee. Talk about that hard row to hoe, well, he'd had one too. He had been named Pharaoh of Egypt Gosnell. Now why you would name a child that you loved that I do not know, and you cannot call somebody Pharaoh of Egypt anyhow, so we all called him Fee. Everybody thought he was simpleminded, but he were not and I know it. He did not think like the rest of us is all. And even though he was younger than me, Granny said he knew more about which plants could cure you and kill you than anybody in this part of the world. And, Lord, but he had a way with animals that I have never seen the likes of. The big white dog at his side was a testament to that. She were not a hound dog but looked for all the world like a wolf and might well have been just that, for all I know. But she were a pretty thing with eyes that looked smarter than some folks I know.

Larkin and Fee was in a big way of talking, which meant they were standing around shuffling their feet since neither of them was big on talking and I sneaked a look at Fee. He was not the prettiest thing in the world. When he was just little, he was skinny and his head had looked too big for his body. But when he got to be a big boy, it seemed like overnight he started sprouting coarse hair and his arms and legs literally growed ropey strings of muscle. Now as a man grown his body had surely caught up with his head, and I will have to say that standing next to Larkin Stanton did not help his looks none. Lord, but Larkin was a pretty thing. Fee's big lips skinned back over big wide-spaced teeth that was already stained from chewing 'baccer, and I allowed once more to myself that I would *never* dip snuff or chew until I no longer had teeth in my head. After that I don't reckon it would matter none.

They was talking about the dog and I looked down at her. She was looking up at Fee like he was the best thing in the world and I squatted down next to her. "Hey there, you, pretty girl," I said and she set them eyes on me and her ears stood straight up on her head. Her big red tongue come out quick as a snake and licked me right in the mouth. I couldn't do nothing but laugh and that got her even more excited but all it took was one word from Fee to put her right back to setting. "Down," he said. And I allowed that maybe he ought to come to my house and learn my young'uns how to behave as good and we all three laughed at that thought.

YOU KNOW HOW THEY is things in our life that we always remember right up to remembering right where we was, who was with us, how the sun laid on everything, what people said? Well, this proved one of them days. I'd seen Granny reach and take hold of her back down low and rub since I could remember. She was always lifting something too heavy and straining around. But it was the way she done it this day that I knew something was bad wrong. And I knew it with my very heart. When she'd come from the barn two year ago with a funny look on her face and told me she'd seen blood when she'd wiped herself I begged her to go see Hattie. Hattie told us that she had corruption, that it would get worse, but would take its own sweet time. And it had took so much time that I'd forget about it for days at a stretch. And then I'd get reminded like when we'd dug up some lilac bushes from next to her porch and planted them next to mine. "There," she had said to me, "now every time you get a whiff of them lilacs you will think of this day and us planting them together." And I said, "Lord God, Granny, don't talk like that." And she said, "Why, honey, look at how long I've had. Eighty year in case you can't count that high. I am older'n anybody I know, 'cepting for Lige Blackett and I reckon they'll have to knock Lige in the head with a frying pan on Judgment Day." When I laughed she did, too, but then she said, "Don't you tell I said that. Them Blacketts is mean as snakes and dumber than four buckets of hair." We both snickered about that because it was the truth, and then she reached out and pushed my hair back off my face like she used to do when I was a girl. "Just remember, Arty." And I said, "What?" And she got the funniest look on her face and said just this one word: "Everything."

• • •

Now here we all was, and I knew with every bone in me that this would be the last time we was all together. And with the knowing of that, it seemed like everywhere I looked I saw something to store up to take out and study later on.

That was the first time I noticed that Mary's little sister Julie kept sneaking looks at Larkin. She was a real sweet girl and awfully clever, but Julie did not look like Mary is the kindest way I can think to say it. I recall thinking, *You poor thing,* because Larkin did not look at her even once during that long preaching. His eyes went nowhere but to where Mary and Hackley set. So mine did too and I had to hide my smile behind my hand when Hackley tried to put his arm up around her waist and her back went straight as a poker and he finally took it away and his neck got all red. And I thought, *Good for you, Mary. You keep that up and you might get him yet.*

Mommie was bustling about, making sure all the young'uns had plates and spoons. She'd turned fifty a few months back and was more grayheaded now than blond. She was right in amongst my young'uns slinging food like a crazy woman. I had told her to wait till I finished nursing Zeke Jr. but she went right on with her rat killing like I had never said a word so I let her do it. I leaned back against the tree and looked at my brood. Abigail was like looking Mommie right in the face. John Wesley had my brown hair and green eyes and so did Sylvaney. Ingabo had curly red hair and Zeke Jr. was going to be redheaded too. I had got real tired of folks asking where these two got their red hair. Lige Blackett come right out and spoke what I knew everybody was thinking: "Are you sure these two are Zeke's?" And I fired right back at him, "Don't you think I won't smack you just because you are an old man." But they is no doubt about who daddied

Carolina. She looked like she was picked right out of Zeke's hind end, right down to her shiny black hair and purplish blue eyes. She was a Wallin to the bone.

About then Larkin come wandering up and of course Carolina set up a howling for him to pick her up. She was crazy about him and he petted her something awful.

Mommie shaded her eyes and watched as he settled Carolina on his shoulders. "You have plumb growed up," she said. Larkin blushed like a girl. I couldn't help deviling him a little.

"You better watch out, honey. Won't be long before some of these little gals set their eyes on you and go running for their mommies' brooms."

Carolina perked right up on that and hollered, "Larkin has already promised to marry me, Mama. Ain't you, Larkin?"

"That's right, missy. You need to hurry and get grown 'cause I need me a good cook. You can cook now, I know. And course you can keep house and all? Sweep and scrub the floors, milk the cows, wash my clothes, see to the garden, hoe while I'm plowing, all that stuff? You can manage that, can't you?"

I busted out laughing. I could tell by looking at Carolina's face that she had not thought of all that. Larkin had just lost himself a candidate for wife, and I told him so.

Mommie held out her arms. Larkin bent down and Carolina fairly scrambled off and hit the ground running. I do not think she wanted to hear no more about marrying. But Mommie would not let it go. "She is way too young to be thinking about that stuff. And her and Larkin is too close a kin to even let her think on it."

And I thought, *Oh, no. Here is the pursed mouth and wrinkled-up nose look.* But I had got over that bothering me and could not help ruffling her feathers a little.

"Why, in six years Carolina will be old as I was when I married her daddy. By Larkin's age I already had Abigail and we was working on John Wesley. Not even a full year between any of my first three. We was working mighty hard."

I knew I had got Mommie's goat by how red her neck got. I was sorry the minute it left my lips, but even though Larkin shot me a look, I could not wrap my tongue around the words to tell her I was sorry.

"Arty," she said, and I could tell she was mortified. "Set there and talk about getting babies. I swear sometimes . . . ."

She did not say what. But I knew already. She thought I was way too much like Granny and she looked down at the very things in me that she loved in her mama. Mommie was awful bad to preach religion this and religion that. She tried to make everything you did fit in a right place or a wrong place. But that is not the way of it all the time. They is a wide swath of life that is lived right down the middle. I wished you could have seen her face the time she asked me if I had found Jesus and I told her I did not know he had got lost. Oh, but you should *never* say something like that to them folks what have strong beliefs. I thought Mommie's eyes was going to pop right out on stems. I will never do that again.

About then I saw Granny take a drink from her crock and Mommie seed her too and I thought, *Oh, Lord,* and I was right, because Mommie set in on her right off.

"You ought not to drink spirits," she said.

And Granny said back, "The gripe in my belly's worse. Liquor with willer bark tea is about the only thing that helps it."

Mommie looked right shocked at that but fussed at her, "That liquor ain't good for your body or your soul. You ought to drink tea mixed with water. I don't see how you hold all that liquor anyways."

And Granny said the funniest thing I'd ever heard, but I know exactly what she meant now because I am the same way. She said, "Hell, Nancy, I can hold my liquor a lot better than I can hold my water nowdays."

I laughed so hard that I had to lay down. Zeke Jr. fell asleep. I must've dozed a little, too, since the next thing I recall is hearing Mommie and Granny talking real low as they put food away and gathered up the dishes.

"Why do you reckon Arty won't listen to a word I say? I swear sometimes she acts like I ain't got the sense God give a goose and she just baits me."

Of a sudden I was wide awake and listening to every word.

"Nancy, Nancy, Nancy." Granny give that sound that meant she'd puffed out her cheeks. "Arty's just who she is. And it ain't just how she acts toward you. You got your ways too."

That was surely the truth.

Mommie put on her best I-am-just-killed voice and said, "I have always wanted to be close to her. She is my oldest daughter."

And Granny actually laughed at her. "Ye take yourself way too serious, Nancy Ann. Always your way or no way. Well, in case you ain't noticed Arty is as tough as a pine knot and she has her own way."

Mommie sounded so pitiful then that even I felt sorry for her. "Well, I can done see that you're just going to take her side of it."

I was plumb surprised when Granny cut her off. "I have no time for this. You and Arty need to come of it because it ain't going to be no time till it's just you and her for it. And I don't know what in this world Larkin will do when I am gone."

Of a sudden I felt selfish. All I had thought of was me, me, me, and it were Larkin what stood to lose biggest of all and he probably did not even know. I set straight up then and looked around for him. It did not take me long to find him. He was right back over there at the store where them men was still talking, no doubt that war business. And as if they had read my very thoughts I heard somebody holler out the word *War*.

Granny shook her head and her next words come out on a long sigh that sounded like it had whistled right out of her soul. "All this talk about war. The men might fight it, but it is always the women that suffers it."

And Mommie said, "They'll be no war. But even if they is, it won't be nothing to us."

"They will be sides took, and that will mean a fight," Granny said, and right then it hit me and Mommie at the same time because neither one of us had a word to say back to her. Zeke Jr. slept on, but my mind was flying. How old did you have to be before you did not have to go off to fight? Or how young? Would Daddy have to go? Surely he would not, as he were an old man of fifty-one. If not him, then what of my brothers David and Willy? They was both married and had a dozen young'uns between and surely they would not have to go. But Robert and Hackley would. And I almost laughed at the thought of Hackley in a war, but I did not because I felt that yes, he would have to go too. Then I felt cold all over because I thought of Larkin and Zeke. But I am not one to worry with something that I cannot wrap my mind around. *They will not be a war* is all I could think as I picked Zeke Jr. up off that quilt and hauled myself to my feet. *They will not be a war because Arty will not allow it.*

But they was nobody there to sass me back and tell me that Arty might not be the one in charge on that day.

6

GRANNY WANTED THE DOOR open and the light of the hunter's moon had come dashing itself across the floor like bright-colored water and had crawled its way up in the bed with her. If you had told me that corruption would lay waste to a body the way it had Granny's in just three months, I would have called you a dirty liar. But it had, and laying there in that bed she looked as little as one of my least girls. Larkin was setting in the doorway with his feet on the outside step. He had his elbows propped on his knees and his hands was hanging down loose between them. I almost wished that he had gone on hunting with Hackley and them boys that had stopped by here before good and dark. He looked pitiful setting there. The moon's light laid flat on his face, and had it been a summer moon, it would have been pretty to see. But they is something about moonlight in the fall that I did not like then and do not like now. Granny had twisted and turned and fought the covers so that I was just wore out with trying to keep her covered up. From up on the ridge above the house, a panther squalled and a hen in the chicken coop answered it with a nervous chuckle. Granny opened her eyes and looked right at me.

"That would be the little hen Hattie give me two year ago. She's a good layer and right pert for a hen anyways," she said.

Larkin got up and drug him a chair to set next to me. The slats squeaked as he leaned forward to take her skinny little hand in his big one. He brought up the crock of white liquor we'd been keeping next to the bed. He took a sip and tilted it in her direction. "You ready for some more, Granny?"

"Pour me some and help me set up," her voice come all whispery.

I sloshed a fair amount into a tin cup and Larkin helped her up. He looked at me and I saw his hurt plain as day. How anybody could be as little as her and still live was beyond us both. She slurped noisily from the cup. "Lay me back down now, honey. Hit makes me dizzy to set up long."

I took the cup and looked down in it a minute, then I turned it up and drunk what was left. It burned like fire going down and I was thankful for it. My belly got all warm and I felt a little light-headed and was glad for that as well.

He eased her back onto the mattress and I pulled the quilts up and made a big do of tucking them under her chin. She'd stopped eating a week ago and I kept piling on the quilts because I couldn't stand the thoughts of her being cold.

"Mommie will come tomorrow," I said to Larkin.

"It'll be too late tomorry, honey," she whispered, staring out the door.

We never said nothing and in a little bit she said it again and her voice was a little stronger.

"I said it'll be too late tomorry. I don't aim to be here when the day breaks."

And I could tell by her tone that she meant just what she said.

She dozed off, but Larkin kept on holding her hand. Of a sudden she roused up and her eyes flew open.

"Josie? Oh, Josie, look. Them cats has found the nest of baby rabbits back an under the porch. Oh, no! They've hurt one of 'em bad. Try to catch it. We'll nurse it back. Damn cats!" Her hands sort of twisted around on the quilt and then were still.

Larkin leaned back hard in the chair, brought his hands up to his face, and fisted his eyes. I thought he was fixing to cry and I wanted to say to him, *This dying is hard business,* but I did not because his head nodded forward and his chin dipped toward his chest and I knowed he was asleep. I was tired myself but knew I could not sleep so I set there still as a rock and waited—for what, I did not know. A stretch of time went by and up on the mountain the big cat squalled again and I thought, *If any sound could wake the dead it would be that,* and then I felt all funny because I had even thought it. But it did wake Larkin up. We set a long while with neither of us saying a word. Then I was so glad he had not gone with them boys and left me there by myself. When Granny spoke I think it scared us both.

"Larkin, boy? Carry me out into the moonlight. I want to see it all one more time."

I would have hated to have been the one that tried to stop him from taking her out. It was not going to be me, even if I did think it was too cold. He took her up quilts and all, ducked through the door and they was gone out into the bright of that October moon.

If I close my eyes I can still see it and it was a sight to see. He stood in the middle of all that light and it changed them both into something other than what they had been inside the house. Though I had never seen no haints I allowed as how they must look just like them and though I knowed it was Granny and Larkin I could not help myself making an X over my heart.

Granny sort of sighed and said, "Ain't many folks gits to leave this world by the light of a blue moon. Two full hunter's moons . . ." Her eyes glowed with the light. "Sing for me, Larkin."

"What do you want me to sing, Granny?"

"Why, my favorite," she said.

And though his voice was soft, it was the best I would ever hear him sing "Pretty Saro."

When I first come to this country, in 1749,
I saw many fair love'yers but I never saw mine.
I viewed all around me, saw I was quite alone
And me a poor stranger and a long ways from home.

Fare-thee-well to old mother, fare-thee-well to father, too,
I'm a-goin' for to ramble this wide world all through,
And when I get weary, I'll sit down and cry,
And think of my darlin Pretty Saro, my bride.

Well hit's not this long journey I'm a-dreading for to go.
Nor the country I'm a-leavin' nor the debts that I owe
There's only one thing that troubles my mind,
That's leavin' my darlin' Pretty Saro behind.

Well I wish't I was a poet, an' could write some fine hand.
I would write my love a letter that she might understand,
And I'd send hit by the waters where the islands overflow.
And I'll think of my darlin' wherever I go.

Well, I strove through the mountings, I strove through the main,
I strove to forget her but it was all in vain,

From the banks of old Cowhee to the mount of said brow,
Where I once't loved her dearly, and I don't hate her now.

Well, I wish't I was a turtle dove had wings and could fly.
Right now to my love'yer's lodgings tonight I'd draw nigh,
And there in her lily-white arms I would lay there all night.
And I'd watch them little windows fer the dawning of day.

"Sounded so much like my Pappy," Granny said, and I could not help it, I started to cry. "Hush up," she said, and her voice sounded light as the air. "You ain't never been one to cry and carry on any such a-way." I straightened right up at that. Then she said, "Drop the quilts, Larkin. I want to feel the wind on my arms and legs."

"Granny, it's cold out here. Keep the quilts on." I don't know why I was so worried about them quilts but it was all I could think about.

The quiet got awfully big in the long time it took her to gather up to answer. "Let them fall, Arty. Hit don't matter no more. I feel warm as I did when I was a girl."

And the quilts slid off and I pulled them away from his feet and stood there with them balled up in my arms. The wind come up then and lifted her hair, worried at the hem of her nightgown, and she smiled at us. "My mammy used to tell me that they was no such thing as dying. Said we really was just born twice't. Once to this place, then again into the t'other. Said we entered both like newborn babies. And she said just like we waited for a baby to be born in this world, they's folks waiting fer us to be born over yonder." And her breath kept coming out and coming out, but it was only when Larkin called her name that it rose back up and her eyes opened and she stared right at me.

"You see to everything, Arty," she said.

I had such a knot of tears in my throat that I could barely say to her, "Yes, I will."

"Ye'll be all right, son? Tell me."

"I'll be all right, Granny. I swear."

And I said in a strangled voice, "No, oh, no."

Her eyes moved from his face and got all dreamy as they found the moon. Suddenly her eyes got big and wide and she said, "Oh, they are all here now! Pappy!"

And with them words Sarah Elizabeth Gentry Shelton was born again.

IT WAS FULL DAYLIGHT when Mommie stepped up on the porch of the cabin and saw the open door. She come pounding across the porch, calling "Mama? Arty? Oh, God."

I got up from the fireplace where I was laying a fire. "She's gone. She went last night, or I reckon it was really this morning."

"Oh, Lord, have mercy on her soul," Mommie said, then she went to crying like her heart was broke. I let her cry. Sometimes that's the best we can do for somebody, to just let them cry.

I had already sent Larkin to Greenberry's to tell him and Sol to start charring out the coffin and on to tell Hattie to bring her corpse herbs. While we was waiting for him to get back, I told Mommie what had happened out there in the yard.

"She was looking up at the moon, but her eyes weren't seeing no moon. They was looking far off. And then I got the feeling that the yard was full of people. They was swirling all around us just for a thought, petting her and easing her somehow. And then they was just gone. Her too."

We just set there for a while drinking our coffee and then I said, "Well, I ain't sure what to do next, Mommie."

Mommie looked at me and her eyes was as dry as dust and blue as the sky and she said, "That's all right, honey. *I* know what to do. We'll get through it together."

And she sounded so much like Granny I could not help it then, I started to cry.

GRANNY HAD BURIED PAP on the high ridge that looked out on the whole valley of Sodom. Mommie had fussed that it was too hard a climb and Granny had said to her, "Why, Nancy, they'll carry me ever step of the way one of these days. I want to be planted where I can see the whole cove and be able to watch my people light the lamps in the morning and blow 'em out at night. And bury me with my shoes on 'cause if they's any way to come back, I'm coming. And if I can't, then what better place than up there? They ain't no prettier place in the world."

So we climbed. Up past the blackberry patch, dried up and withered from the early frost. Up past the big old chestnut trees with their limbs almost brushing the ground with nuts. On up past the cave and across the gully wash that held the tracks of a big panther. On up to the very spine of the ridge, where, for all of her talk about it being the prettiest place in the world, all I saw waiting for her was a lonesome hole in the ground. Everybody sung as they lowered her, but I could not. They was not a single word that found its way from my hurting heart.

> We'll camp a little while in the wilderness, in the wilderness, in the wilderness.
> We'll camp a little while in the wilderness, and then I'm a-goin' home.

And then I'm a-goin' home, and then I'm a-goin' home.
We're all a-makin ready, oh ready. And then I'm a-goin' home.

And then Hackley stepped right up to that dark hole that was now full of her and put his fiddle under his chin and played "Pretty Saro" and finally I felt the tears that had strangled me all morning start to let down. It was like that fiddle reached right in my throat and untangled the knot and I thought, *Bless you, Hackley.* I was not the only one. They was not a dry eye amongst us by the time he lowered the fiddle to his chest and, still playing, closed his eyes and sung it through.

Nobody said a word as the bow stroked that final note. Not a single word. Then the preacher just said, "Amen," and the crowd give a big sigh all together and everybody started to straggle off back down the mountain. But when Larkin made to leave I said to him, "No, me and you will stay. She would not have left either one of us." And we not only stayed, we helped Fee and them shovel in the dirt. I had kept her covered with them damn quilts and I felt it was my job to help cover her one last time.

I think the eating and mingling that goes on when somebody dies is to keep everybody from thinking about the thing their mind most wants to dwell on. That would be the person you had just put in the cold ground forever and ever because if we tried to think of all them empty days and nights to come, right then we would all go completely foolish. So we eat and talk and eat some more. Back at Granny's house that day it were no different. Except that this time she were not there to see to things and my eyes would not stay away from her chair by the fireplace or her digging stick hanging by the door or all the things that called out to me, *Here I am, but where is she?*

"SHE WANTED YOU TOOK care of, honey," Mommie said to Larkin as she put out food back at the cabin. "She wanted you to have the home place and that clinches it for all of us. It's yours."

He stood there with the blush of a boy still on him, trying to be a man, and, oh, how my heart just broke for him. "You do not have to stay here by yourself, honey," I said. "You come home with me."

What he said next cut me to the quick because it were the truth. "You don't have the room, Amma."

I wanted to argue with him and did, but he were set against it, and I finally had to turn from him and go to helping Mommie lay out the food that kept coming and coming. I thought to myself, for a bunch of people that has no money, it is a wonder we are not all big as fattening hogs for all that we are rich in food.

Hackley come up about that time and I could not help but hear what he was saying. I swear Hackley never said the right things. But you always knew what he was thinking since that was just what he said. He was gnawing on a piece of cornbread while he talked. "I know you hated to see Granny go. But at least you can go hunting with us and stuff now."

I felt the itch in my hand to jerk him up and just blister him like I used to do.

He went right on, though. "I guess that scared you and Arty when she up and died on you. I don't cotton to being around no dead people."

Before I could open my mouth Larkin put him in his place and did a much better, or at least quieter, job of it than I would have.

"It was not a scary thing, Hackley. I would not have missed being there for nothing in this world."

I was about to put in my two-cents worth but did not have to, because Mary come through the door right then and I become invisible to them both. She come across that floor a girl with a mission, and you would have had to drug me away by the hair of the head.

"I'm sorry about your Granny, Larkin." She sounded all out of breath and I peeped a look at her and thought, *Oh, my,* because there she stood looking up at Larkin with that red hair all tousled by the wind up on the mountain and her cheeks all pinked up from the climb and the sun.

Larkin thanked her and Hackley was squirming around her like a big puppy. I thought he was going to go to pissing on the floor at any minute. But for once her attention was not on my brother. It was leveled right at Larkin.

"Sary was a fine person" was all that young'un said as she put one of them slender hands like I would never have on his arm, and I saw heat red as a flame lick its way up the back of his neck. It was a good thing Hackley was blind to everything except what concerned him and only him, or there would have been a killing right then and there. But I don't know which one he would have killed. I looked her hard in the face and will have to say I saw no sign that she had knowledge of what she was doing to either one of them. If she had a notion she could have fooled the devil himself, for her face looked innocent as the day was long. I thought, *Arty, you must tell her,* but I did not do this until years down the road, and by then it would be too late. But we look back with vision that is crystal clear and we have no eyes whatsoever with which we can see the future.

Hackley done what he always did do, which was turn her where only he filled up her sight. He was jigging about that girl grinning like a fool. "What about me, darling Mary? She was my granny, too, you know." Then he leaned in and I swear he nipped at her neck with his teeth.

Nobody saw it but me and Larkin, but Mary knew that we had. I know you've seen how a cat will scrunch itself up, tuck its head down, and its face will look all insulted. Well, let me tell you that Mary literally hissed at Hackley. She *hissed* at him. "Don't you have no respect for me nor nobody else?" She went flouncing off, and there was that spine as stiff as a poker again.

And I have to say I had a world of admiration for that straight little narrow-shouldered back that was going out the door.

Larkin, however, was completely bewildered. "Ain't you going after her?" he said to Hackley.

"She'll get over it pretty quick. Then there's the making-up part." Hackley sort of groaned.

I told him he ought to go on after her since he appeared to be primed and ready if the front of his britches was any proof of the pudding. And he went on with his tongue dragging out on the floor. Granny always said that most men could make pure-D fools of themselves in way less time than you could bring buttermilk in a churn. I would never see nothing to prove her a liar.

THE MOON WAS ALREADY riding the ridgeline of The Pilot when Larkin come to stand next to me on the porch. Everybody else was gone and I was fixing to leave. I picked out the two pines that marked the spot where Granny was spending her first night in the long time gone. I put my arm around him and snugged up close.

"Come home with me, Lark. Don't try to stay here by yourself. You'll just be lonesome."

"I got to stay sometime." He took a long breath in. "Can't get my mind to take in that she's really gone. I catch myself listening for her."

My mind went back to all her things that had called out to me a while ago. "Granny's been a constant for all of us. I always knowed she was right here where I could git to her if I needed her." I thought of all the times I had come up that path yonder with my ass dragging behind me, heavy-hearted with all the troubles of the world heaped on my shoulders and after being here with her for just a little bit I went back down that path with a lighter step.

Larkin must've been thinking my same thoughts for he said, "Granny had a way of helping you to cut through stuff."

And we both laughed and said at the same time "Bullshit," because that is just what she always said whenever we was taking ourselves way too serious.

Up on Graveyard Ridge, the pines went to moving in the wind.

"Bet that wind's cold up there, Amma."

"She is not up there to feel it, Larkin," I said. I had never seen a more empty corpse than hers in all my life.

We were both quiet for a long time and then he said, "Where do you reckon she's at?"

"Now, that I don't know." I give a wave toward that big old sky packed full of stars. "Out yonder somewheres, maybe." And then it come to me and I patted the front of his shirt. "In here for certain." Then I laid my hand against the side of his head. "Up here forever."

"What about heaven?"

"Mommie would be the one to ask about that business. That's where she would say Granny is. As for me, I don't know what I think when it comes down to it. But I will say if they is such a place, then Granny is there with her Mommie and Pappy and her brother Josie, her children, Uncle Pete, Roscoe, your mommie. And she's right now telling all of them about all of us. And they's probably a big frolic going on, music being played, and old love songs being sung, and she's right in the midst of it all."

Then in the most pitiful voice he said, "It feels like a hole has opened up in my life, Amma. Will it ever go away?"

And though I hated to say it, I surely had to, because again I could only tell him the truth. "It won't never go away, honey," I said. "You will just have to figure out how to live your life around it."

7

Winter come roaring in early that November and four inches of snow fell just a week after we'd buried Granny. Though I had begged and begged Larkin, he had stayed on at the house and had not spent a single night with us. He had come by and eat supper several times but that was all. It was during one of them times that I found out that Hackley was bringing his women to the house. Usually as soon as he finished eating Larkin would be for the door, but this one time he set at the table until even Carolina had finally give up and gone to bed. He did not want to tell me but I finally wrung it out of him and it was like twisting a groundhog out of its hole. He said that he didn't want to go home just yet because Hackley was over there with Maggie. My eyebrows must have looked like they had took flight right off my head. I knowed what and all folks said about her, that she was trashy and loose, but I did not think that way. Maggie had hoed on her own long row.

Maggie was the oldest of Wade and Vergie Hensley's nine children. Her daddy was a big, barrel-chested man what laughed a lot. He had this real easy way with people, which was a good thing since that is how he made his living. His old wagon loaded down with all sorts of things you could buy if you had the money went all over, down into South Carolina and even down into Georgia. He could tell some of the funniest tales you have ever heard in your life. I would reckon it was from him that Maggie learned that the only way to make it in this old world was to laugh about things. But now her mommie was a pure-D trick if there ever was one. And it was from her that Maggie got her cleverness, because Vergie Ray Hensley was one of the smartest people I have ever knowed in my life. I remember asking Granny one time if she was crazy and Granny laughed great big and long and then she said, "Crazy like a fox."

THEY WAS NOTHING MUCH remarkable about Vergie there at the start. She was smack in the middle with two older sisters and two younger brothers. They said all she done for the first few years was run after them two little hellions that was her brothers, neither one of which growed up to be worth killing, though that is just what happened to them both. Carl Robert was hung for stealing horses over in Tennessee and Jessie got shot in a card game down in Warm Springs. But then one night Vergie come down with a bad bellyache and by morning she was howling with pain and couldn't even keep down water she was throwing up so bad. Granny said her nor Hattie neither one thought she'd live after that second day and Vergie's mama, who was a big one for churchgoing, hit her knees and prayed all that next night and lo and behold, it seemed a miracle when the next morning Vergie set up and said she was hungry. They was all the big talk in church that Sunday and Vergie got attention from everybody. I mean it ain't every day that common folks gets to see a living, breathing miracle. Even at home she was treated like the queen of

Sheba with her sisters as step-and-fetch-its and them boys was plumb cowed by her. But the days went along, and it weren't long before things was back to normal. Vergie found out the same thing that I have—folks forget pretty quick. She was back to minding them boys in no time at all. But six weeks to the day of her first sick, she woke up with the bellyache. And this time it come with the worst headache in the world. Them sick headaches come like clockwork every six or eight weeks after that, and every time her family thought she would surely die.

By the time she was twelve, Vergie had them headaches once or twice a *week* and Granny said you could hear her screaming as you were going past the house. Said she was pitiful when they was on her bad. She couldn't stand no light to hit her eyes and no loud noises and sometimes she'd beg somebody, anybody to cut her head off. By the time she was fourteen she was the very center of her little world and I am not faulting her people one little bit. No, I am not. It makes me mad as the devil when people get all high and mighty and say *If it was me I would do this or I would do that.* You don't know *what* you would do if you was faced with the same thing.

Vergie figured it out, but I can't even blame her for it either. Who don't want to make things a little easier for themselves, is what I would like to know. She never struck a lick at nothing from then on as far as I can tell.

Granny said by the time she was fifteen Vergie was her mommie's cross to bear and her daddy's darling. Her daddy made her a rocking chair and she'd set out on the porch all day long just rocking back and forth and waving at folks that went past the house. She was a real pretty thing with the fairest skin and thick hair the color of a rubbed buckeye, and she talked so soft that you had to lean in close to hear what she was saying. It was from the porch that she got her first glimpse of Wade Hensley.

She set great store by her teeth and she cleaned them religiously with a birch twig twice a day and was going after them with such a vengeance that she hadn't even seen him come from the road to the house. As I heard it she liked to have fell out of her chair when Wade spoke to her from the yard saying he had something in his bag that would work better than the twig. She first thought he was the biggest man she'd ever seen because he had a big pack on his back. Wade was a big man and was a pretty thing, too, even when he was old, and he always went about dressed up in a suit with a vest and everything. I just loved the way they said he introduced himself to her and I have to say that if some man had done that to me I might not have married Zeke Wallin. They said he swept off his big floppy hat and said, "Wade Hensley, missy—blacksmithy, mule trader, bear trapper, liquor maker, watch repairer, log splitter, hog killer, 'coon hunter, banjor picker, and drummer, at your service." Don't you just love that?

He dug around in his pack for a minute and whipped out a fancy tooth-brushing contraption and handed it to Vergie. He talked and talked that first day about this being the first time he'd ever come up this far and how he usually follered the river between Asheville and Greenville, South Carolina, and how he was born and raised over in Hendersonville and how on that particular day he'd just decided to foller this road to see where it wound up.

Maggie told me that Vergie had asked him if the road had ended up there at her house and then she'd asked him which end of that tooth contraption to put in her mouth and Wade felt sorry for her. And then her daddy might as well have been one of the tribes of Israel for he was just as lost. From then on everybody felt sorry for *him*.

FROM OUT IN THE yard I bet he had thought she was a young'un not more than ten year old. She was little and had the smallest feet I've ever seen on a woman grown. But she had great big pretty bosoms and when he got a look at them I know he did not still think her a child. Right up till the last time I laid eyes on her she could look at you with them eyes all big and round and as empty of care and trouble just like a young'un. But I bet you a nickel to a quarter it was the eye of a woman that looked Wade up and down that day and decided to have him as her own. Granny said she had culled every boy in this part of the country. Just about every one of them had tried to spark her, but she showed no interest in any of them. But once she set her mind to it, Granny said it were a sight to behold how fast she whipped out her needle and sewed Wade up.

At the end of two headache-free months, she married him, and ten months after that she had Maggie.

Everybody said Wade was a fool over Vergie, and I know that for a fact. Why, even when I was a girl and they lived right below us, he'd round that curve and be almost running for the house, he'd be so glad to see her. And she'd be right there waiting for him too. Maggie said her mommie was somebody who dearly loved the part of being married that she called a woman's duty. We used to laugh about that 'cause me and her loved it too. Mommie had told me—and these are her own words—"Lay still, Arty, and, God willing, it will be over quick." Well, let me tell you they was nothing quick about Zeke Wallin's hands, nor could I be still when he took hold of me that first night. And praise be about *that*. Being a woman is hard work and the man that manages to get him a good one ought to have sense enough to use his hands gentle and slow. My friends, you cannot catch flies by pouring a big platter of vinegar but, oh, how many will flock to just a little dab of honey. They is a real passion in most women—even a cold and selfish one like Vergie—and if you can tap into that you can stand most anything life throws at your head. Study on that for a minute or two all you men.

MAGGIE HAD TO GROW up quick. Bless her heart, she was a good little thing and had nothing in her to fight against her mommie's workings. She was well trained by the time she was six year old. She could cook a full meal, milk the cow, churn butter, keep the house clean, and, most important, Lord, she could change diapers with the best of them. Vergie rocked on, and about the only time she left her chair was to give birth and add yet another burden to Maggie's scrawny shoulders. Maggie started hipping young'uns even earlier than me. She had one on each hip when I was hipping Larkin. And where I had the choice with Larkin, Maggie did not.

But Maggie slowly began to put the puzzle pieces that was her little mommie together. She couldn't help but notice how them headaches hit hardest just as Wade's wagon was rounding the curve on its way out of sight. Or when one of the young'uns fell sick and needed tending. Or when it was clothes-washing day that we always called blue Monday. Or at hog-killing time. Or when the heifer calved.

Yes, sir, I can tell you that under the knife of Vergie's complete and total selfishness Maggie's good nature was peeled away and her raw heart got hard as a rock. She had one of the sweetest voices as a child, but as she aged her tongue got sharp as a straight razor. She got used to giving orders and made them young'uns mind like ringing a bell.

When she was thirteen she married a boy from off Shelton Laurel. Now that was a show. When she told Wade and Vergie she aimed to marry you'd have thought she'd come in and allowed as how she was going to chop off all their heads with an ax. The young'uns cried and Wade carried on for days. But Vergie went to bed with the worst headache of her life. Or so she said.

And I said to her, "Do not let your mommie keep you from marrying Dedrick. She'll come of it."

I do think that if Wade had not told her that her mommie was going to have another baby she would have stayed home. But, boy, that fixed the deal for Maggie. She told her daddy that she would not stay there and raise any more of their young'uns. "I aim to mommie my own," she said. But that was to never be. Maggie proved barren and carried no children in her body. But being the woman she was, she carried several of the heart.

Eight months later, Dedrick stepped on a rusty nail and died of the lockjaw. Three days after putting her man in the ground, here come her daddy carrying the rocking chair up the path with Vergie slowly picking her way behind him, the children strung out behind her, with Laurie Bett carrying baby Kelvin bringing up the rear. She moved in front of the chair before Vergie could settle into it. Vergie had decided she needed to be with her at this awful time, but Maggie didn't put up with that for a minute. She put them all back out into the road. Things were not going back to the way they were.

Maggie had been on her own ever since. And she did like the men, but to my knowledge, she had never messed with another woman's husband. So by my way of figuring they was not nothing wrong with that.

BUT THERE SET LARKIN, so what did I think now? Hackley was not married to nobody and neither was Maggie. She was three year older than me, so therefore older than him, but so what to that as well. I looked at Larkin studying about all this. It was not right that they had run him off from his own place. I told him so and told him I would tell Maggie and Hackley that. He turned real red in the face then and said, "No, don't do that. They didn't make me leave. It don't matter to them one way or the other." And I was just struck dumb at that. All sorts of things went to flying about in my head and I finally just out and said plime blank, "Did they do it in front of you?" And you might be thinking, now, what kind of wicked woman is that Arty anyhow? Well, I was and still am a curious woman, and though it might have killed the cat, it did not kill me. And then it all come rushing out from his mouth, and though it made me feel funny I listened hard anyway.

HACKLEY HAD BROUGHT SOME liquor to the house and all three of them had been drinking. Larkin not as much, or at least that is what he said, although you can take that with a grain of salt. He could lay right in there with the best of them. For all of Hackley's bragging and swaggering he could never hold his liquor and wound up passing out. Larkin and Maggie messed around with the fiddle for a while. He had always wanted to play since he was little and he said Maggie was actually getting to where she could play a few tunes. Maggie finally said she had to go outdoors. While she was gone he said he banked the fire and got in the bed. The next thing he knowed it was morning and there was Maggie straddling Hackley on the pallet in front of the fire. He said she was naked as the day she was born, and though he wanted to look away he could not. I knowed how he must've felt. I wanted to tell him to hush but could not. And he said that Maggie knew he was watching too and I said, "How do you know?" And he said, "Because the whole time she was riding him she was looking me right in the eye."

I did not know what to say about that. You can believe I studied about it a lot over the next few days. I thought about talking to Zeke about it, but I already knew he'd just say *Goodness* or *They law* or something like that. Or he might have surprised me and been real interested in that little tale. I was not real sure how I would have liked him being in such a big way to know about that so I just didn't mention it. And I caught myself wondering what Granny would have said. But then I already knew. *Bullshit.*

I SAW MAGGIE AT the store the day that the big cat had been at my chickens. She'd killed two, leaving feathers and blood all over the snow off the end of the porch. She eat one and carried the other off to her kittens I reckon. Zeke said the cat would have to be hunted down and killed, but I said, "She does not have to be killed, she is just hungry and trying to see to her young'uns just like us. We just need to put the chickens up where she can't get to them." His eyes got all darkish blue like they do sometimes when he looked at me. "I love you, Arty," he said. I said to him, "Why, I love you, too." Men are funny creatures, and I will never figure them out if I live to be a hundred, and ain't that a grand thing? They is some things that needs to remain a mystery in this world and the love between a man and a woman is one of them things.

So I had gone to the store to get some nails and there was Maggie buying some cheese. I sidled right up to her and was hoping she was in the mood for talking, but she did not say much while she was running Cassie's big old tomcat off of the cheese wheel and cutting herself a wedge. We just talked about this and that, and I could not get her to talk about the this or that of which I most wanted to hear. I felt like I was going to start hopping from one foot to the other if I didn't ask her. Finally I just blurted out, "Well, have you seen Hackley or Larkin lately?" And she come right back at me with, "Well, damn, Arty, why don't you just come right out and ask me?" And though I felt awfully sheepish I looked her eyeball to eyeball and said, "Well, I reckon I just did."

We walked home together and she talked and talked. Mostly about Hackley, and I could tell that Maggie had done give her heart away. She denied it to me, though. I told her I hoped she had not because my brother was a lover boy with all the women, but he would wind up marrying just the one—and that would be Mary Chandler because she was the only one that was not letting him have what all the other women did. Maggie turned red as blood when I said that, and I could tell it sort of made her mad. But they is one thing about me, and that is that I will call a spade a spade. She denied all about Larkin and that kind of made me mad. She said, "I don't know nothing about Larkin Stanton, Arty." And I told her I believed that he might be a little bit sweet on her, and she said, "I would not hurt that boy for nothing in this world." And though I wanted to believe her, I thought to myself that Maggie just might bear watching where it concerned Larkin. She got right fiesty when I mentioned Mary again. She said, "Well, the virgin Mary might need to set up and take notice of Miss Maggie." And I looked at her standing there with her head up and her shoulders throwed back and her blue eyes just flashing, and I have to say she was a good-looking woman. But she would not take Hackley from Mary. I knew that as good as I knew my own name. I felt sorry for her but I did not have the heart to tell her what I knew.

• • •

It was getting up towards four o'clock that evening when Larkin come by the house bringing me a mess of deer meat that him and Hackley had killed that morning. As I was washing it, he said they had been in the woods all day. I did not tell him that I had talked to Maggie. I just let him talk and to be honest with you, I only about half listened. They is only so much interest I can keep up for a boy talking about hunting deer all day long. But of a sudden he had all my attention because I heard him say this: "So I told him to marry, then." And I said, "What?" He looked at me with his eyes as dark as the sky on a new moon and said, "I told him to go ahead and marry Mary." And though I knew he was hurt and I was trying to pet him a little, my mind went to wondering what if Mary was to find out about all this business about Maggie. Wouldn't that change a tune or two?

But at that time I was not remembering that my brother was no-body's fool.

Big John and Daisy Stanton had their big frolic right at Christmastime. I was having a big time that night and I must admit to drinking of Sol's liquor. I was even flirting a little with some of the men just to get Zeke's attention. Me and him both knew I would never do anything other than some harmless flirting, but he liked to know that other men still noticed me and, oh, they did. So I didn't even know that Larkin was on the place until I saw him standing in front of the door looking mad as hell with little Julie Chandler looking up at him all serious.

That night when we was going home, Zeke told me that Hackley had told most everybody there that Maggie had been walking out with Larkin. I allowed as how nobody had told me that and Zeke laughed and said, "Honey, they would not have dared to tell you." No wonder Larkin looked so mad and I can't believe that he didn't slap the hell out of Hackley for the lying dog that he was. Poor Larkin. Getting all the talking about but getting none of the goody.

I remember he danced a lot with Julie that night. Maggie come but barely spoke to me and kept herself right in the middle of a big crowd of men laughing too loud with her eyes way too bright. And Hackley never laid that fiddle down a single time. He come by and give me a big kiss on the cheek and told me I was the prettiest girl there, and even though I knew he was full of himself and told him as much, it still pleased me. He was on fire with that fiddle and played some of the best music I'd ever heard him play.

If they was any doubt before as to who he loved and aimed to marry they would not be after. My pretty little brother broke a hundred hearts that night.

They'd just finished a Virginia reel when Hackley went to playing "The True Lover's Farewell," and while he was playing, he went across that floor and stood right in front of Mary. Her face was red as a beet and Hackley was looking her right in the eye. And she looked right back at him too. Rosa Wallin come up to me then and said, "That Hackley could charm the birds right out of the trees, Arty," and I said, "It is not him that is doing the charming." And it was not. Mary Chandler was the charmer, if you want to know the truth. He stood there and sung every word right to her.

> A-rovin' on one winter's night
> And a-drinkin' good old wine,
> A-thinkin' about that pretty little girl
> That broke this heart of mine.

Oh, she is like some pink-a rose
That blooms in the month of June.
She's like a musical instrument
Just late-lie put in tune.

Oh, fare you well, my own true love,
So fare you well for a while.
I'm going away but I'm coming back
If I go ten thousand miles.

And it's who will shoe your pretty little feet?
Oh, who will glove your hand?
Oh, who will kiss them red rosy lips
When I'm in some foreign land?

The crow is black, my love,
It will surely turn to white
If ever I forsaken you,
Bright day will turn to night.

Bright day will turn to night, my love,
And the elements will move
If ever I forsaken you,
The seas shall rage and burn.

So fare you well, my old true love,
So fare you well for a while.
If I go I will come again
If I should go ten thousand miles.

Every girl in that room give up hope right then. But even with the
giving up, they was still wishing he was singing to them. Oh, Lord, I

wished I'd not even looked at Larkin's face. He was staring at Mary like he was just going to die, and I thought to myself, *Don't show everybody here where your affections lay.* And Julie was staring just the same way at Larkin. But it was Maggie's look that caused that cold finger to lay itself at the bottom of my spine. They was a longing in her, too, but there was way more pure old mad. They was the eyes of a woman what has been scorned, and I thought, *Oh, Hackley, what a mess you have made for somebody to get to clean up,* because that is just the way my brother was.

THEY WAS NOTHING I could do about any of what was going on, so I did not worry about it. I just kept dancing and dancing. Sometime after everybody had come back in from hollering and shooting in the Christmas day I realized that Maggie and Larkin were both gone, and Julie was setting off by herself looking like a dying calf in a hailstorm. Somebody hollered out that it had started to snow and since I purely love to watch it snow I went back out on the porch. It was plumb hot in the cabin and the cold air on the porch felt good. I was just standing there taking in some of that sweet air when I heard Maggie's voice from out in the yard. "Talk was worse than we thought," she said. I weren't a bit surprised when Larkin answered her, "Does Mary know?" and my heart squeezed at the foolish hope I could hear in his voice. What little bit was there was dashed I am sure by her reply. "She knows but is acting like she don't. She'd have to quit him if she let on like she knew. So, the virgin Mary won't say nothing." I knew right then that Maggie was exactly right. Mary did know but would never say it. And then she said, "You want to walk an old widder woman home?" And there was a world full of promise in them words. I wanted to holler out and remind her what she had said to me about not hurting him, but I did not. About then Julie opened the door and called out, "Are you out here, Larkin? They're starting up the next dance." She didn't see me standing there at the end of the porch 'cause the light didn't reach that far. But I could see her face and I want you to know that she might not have been the looker that her sister was, but she was not bad looking either. They was not a sound from the yard and she stood there just a minute then closed the door.

By the time my eyes had lost the light from the door, they was nobody out there but me.

8

THERE WOULD BE NO broom jumping for Mary Chandler. She let on that it was on account of her religion, but I believe she figured that if she finally had Hackley hemmed up and headed in the right direction she was going to make sure that everything was done right. She did not even want much drinking to go on, but I told her she might as well put that to rest. I had seen it where the man what was getting married had to be held up on either side and poked in the ribs when it was time for him to take the vow. They was nobody what got married that didn't do it in front of folks what had been drinking. That is just the way it was done. She did raise enough hell with her daddy and brothers and with Hackley to where nobody got really drunk until after the church service, which I told her was four steps beyond what I would have thought Hackley would agree to anyway.

I have never in all my life seen such a crowd as come out for their marrying. Hackley had been all around playing the fiddle and it seemed like everybody that he'd ever played with, or for, come that day. The church was full and people stood all around out in the yard. It is a good thing we was having a weather breeder that day and it was fairly warm. To show you how little Hackley knew about things, he went and asked Larkin to be his best man. Mary asked Julie to stand up with her, and you have never seen a happier bridesmaid. I was very proud of Larkin. At least for this one day he managed to bury his feelings way down deep. I was probably the only one that noticed that muscle that kept jumping about knotting up in his jaw.

Maggie was *not* invited.

It come a big snow that next day but that did not slow us down one bit. It actually made for a real good time. We loaded up on sleds and went all around and about singing and cutting up and there was a frolic at somebody's house every night for a solid week.

Maggie had a big dance at her place, and Hackley and Mary were *not* invited. Poor Maggie. I didn't want to make a big deal out of how this was probably the only night those two had had by themselves since they'd married.

Larkin had a big time and got pretty drunk and danced every dance with Maggie. If they was a single solitary soul who had not known about them before all this, they was not one now. Some folks called it a scandal because she was so much older than him. I did not think it so, but I surely did feel sorry for the lot of them. Everything was all mixed up with everybody wanting somebody else and having to make do with what they could get, and that is not a good way to do business of the heart.

NOW YOU MIGHT BE saying, What is wrong with this here woman Arty? Did Hackley and Mary not marry in the beginning of the year 1861? Is this Arty a blithering idiot? How could she not know what was going on down off the mountain in South Carolina and Georgia and all points south? Is she just a simple-minded person who only knowed how to gossip and pick in everybody's business and not mind her own? And to all that I will say this: No, I was not blind then, or deaf, and we all knowed what was happening all around us. But you must understand it had not come for us yet. We were just people living a hard life and getting by. The men would knot up together and talk. But that was all it was then. Just talk, and some little words on a piece of newspaper somebody would bring in from Warm Springs or Marshall. Why, to us Charleston might as well have been up on the moon. Our biggest sin, I reckon, was being innocent, but we would get well over that. South Carolina proved a whole lot closer to us than we ever thought it would.

AND JUST IN CASE you're interested, I did find myself in the family way for the seventh time. And I knew somehow that this one was a girl and I allowed that I would name her Pearl.

SO THAT WINTER PASSED just like every other one we'd ever lived through. I was not sick a single day, and Zeke said I had never been prettier in my life than I was then. That is how I recall that spring. I felt so good and was strong as a mule.

Mommie was pleased as could be with her new daughter-in-law, which I must say might have in itself been reason enough for me to be hard on Mary. These are Mommie's own words: "I am so glad Hackley did not get trapped up with one of them old road whores in spite of all them what was after him." I flew mad at that because though she did not mention any names I knew she was meaning Maggie. But I just felt too good to argue with her so I did not. I did, however, pick just that time to tell her I was breeding again and must admit I went to feeling even better when that big grin dropped off and she went back to looking all pinched up with that smell-something-bad look.

So I was not at all ready for my feelings about Mary to start soft-
ening up when I went over there to help her cook when Hackley had
his barn raising toward the end of March. But soften up they did. Her
little place was as neat as a pin, and you could tell she was really trying to be a good wife and she seemed as happy as a little girl with red
shoes on. It did not hurt one bit that she was courting my affections
either. She asked my advice a dozen times in that one day, and I could
not help it if that went to my head and by the time supper was on the
table me and her was laughing and talking like old pals. While we
was washing up I told her I was expecting, and, oh, how wistful her
face got with the news. She said, "I want to have Hackley's babies
more than anything in this world, Arty." And I laughed and said,
"You ought to be enjoying the time you have with just him, honey.
The babies will start and then they'll just keep coming and coming."
Later in mine and her life we would talk about that conversation and
each and every time her face would carry that same look. I would
reckon she thought about it right up till when she died. They would
be just the one child born to her that was my brother's. And that
would end like so much in life what turns out to be sweet as honey
and bitter as gall at the same time.

But during that spring I decided that whatever had come before
might as well be forgiven and forgotten, and me and her put together
a good friendship that weathered well the rest of our lives. I cannot
help but believe that if things had just been allowed to go their natural course and times had not changed for us in the awful way they
did, I would surely not be telling this tale. But telling it I am, for the
times they did change.

It come a big wet snow right about the time the sarvice trees were blooming, and some of it was still on the ground when Larkin come by the house. He was on his way over to help Hackley do some fencing. He was looking fine as snuff and twice as dusty, which means he was a big pretty man. I couldn't keep the grin off my face when I said, "And how is Miss Maggie getting on?" And he blushed plumb to the roots of his hair and mumbled that she was fine. I had high hopes then that maybe he was moving beyond his old feelings for Mary and I felt a debt of gratitude in my heart for Maggie. As soon as the sun climbed high enough, I told Larkin I had to go let the cows out and he said he'd walk that far with me and then he probably needed to get on over the hill. I linked my arm through his and we strolled along looking at how green everything was. I found the first violets peeping out of the grass along the path to the barn, and we talked about how he used to pick them for me and put them in the water bucket where I'd be sure to see them.

Up in the day I took my littlest young'uns and crossed the ridge myself to see Mary. We set on the porch talking, and I thought, *It does not get much better than this.* There was a little breeze playing about the yard and the sun felt so warm and the young'uns were just drunk with it all. Larkin and Hackley come in and we all set for a while just watching the young'uns. Then Larkin asked if we'd heard they was having a big politicking over at Laurel on Thursday. I allowed that me and Zeke were aiming to go and Mary said her and Hackley was too. I said we ought to go camping and stay all night and they all allowed what a fine idea that was. We flew to making us some plans and by the time I got up to go home, I was looking forward to a big time. I wished Zeke Jr. had not come running to me crying with a skinned elbow. Then I would not have reached over in that water bucket for a handful to wash it off with. But things happen for a reason, even if we do not know what it might be. All I know is that when I brought my hand out, it was covered with violets and I did not even have to think twice't about who might have put them there.

I COULD NOT BELIEVE how many people were on the roads that Thursday and every one of them heading for Shelton Laurel. By the time we got there the big cleared field beside the store was already full of wagons, horses, and mules. And the whole place was just throbbing with hundreds and hundreds of people. And this was a rare thing in the spring of the year. Any other year would have found us at the house working in the fields, so they was a right festive air with everybody wanting to visit. Men was standing around clumped up in little groups, talking and waving their arms around while they did it. Us women left them to it and clumped up ourselves. And a thousand sweating young'uns was wild as bucks running and winding their way through what must've looked like a forest of legs. Carolina's eyes was as bright as new pennies, and when she found Sophie Rice she squealed and grabbed her hand and said "Let's pretend we're two blind girls" and they went staggering off like two drunks. I hollered after them that they'd better keep their eyes wide open if they knowed what was good for them. She was the only one of my bunch that took off but then she always was one that could not be still. Abigail flew right into helping me set up camp while the little ones stood looking about with great big eyes. I said, "John Wesley, quit standing there like you've took root and help your sister." I guess my voice must have got that tone to it that makes Zeke nervous because he said, "Arty, honey, why don't you go get what all we need at the store."

It took me forever to finally get down there because they was so many folks I knew. I could not go any more than a step or two when somebody would holler out, "Arty, Arty, come over here a minute."

When I finally made it, who did I meet coming through the door but Larkin. Him being way taller than me, I was asking him to look out there and tell me who he could see. Of a sudden this big, red-faced man come jostling his way up onto the top step, elbowing everybody out of the way. It was only when he nodded at me and I saw his big round bald head that I knew him to be the great preacher Lester Lydell. Back when he was young and more slender he would take a run-a-go and jump clear over the pulpit, but he was not so young now nor was he slender, so I reckon his jumping days was over. He could still talk a good preaching though. "Brothers and sisters, God spoke to me in a dream. He said to me, 'Preacher, you get out yonder and deliver my message. I didn't call you to set around and say nothing. I called you to preach.' Clear as a bell I heard Him say what I'm saying now. He says we are to leave the Union, separate ourselves from the heathens in the North. God would be on our side if we leave. If we stay in it'd be a sin and disobedience. They'll be punishments heaped upon us if we don't heed his wishes."

Just then a great flood of people come pouring out of the store and he got caught up in them, and the last I saw of him he was waving his Bible in the air still preaching while being carried along by the tide.

Larkin laughed and I did, too. Oh, it was a wonderful day we was having. I turned around still laughing and come smack up against Vergie Hensley. She was as round as could be and had on an orange dress and what went through my mind was, *Oh, how much like a punkin she looks,* but what come out my mouth was, "Why, howdy, Vergie."

Her eyes was all glassy-looking and they sort of slid over my face and then they fastened themselves right onto the front of Larkin's britches and they did not move the whole time we stood there talking. I swear to you that this is no lie, and I thought to my never that I was going to bust wide open I wanted to laugh so bad. I just kept on talking asking her questions about her young'uns, if Maggie was there, when was the last time she'd seen Mommie. I was talking about anything just to see how long she would stand there staring right at Larkin. Finally I said, "Larkin and me have to go, Vergie," and I took him by the arm and pulled him off the porch.

When we got around the corner, I fell against him just dying and all he could do was shake his head. "What do you reckon that was all about?" I said, "I reckon she's heard you like them older women, honey." And he said, "Not that damn old," which set me off to laughing again. We was standing there laughing so hard we was crying when Mommie come around the corner. She come bustling up calling out, "Arty, you, Arty," and she looked and sounded so much like Granny it come near to taking my breath away. I could not help myself, I started to just bawling. "Don't pay me no never mind," I said to Larkin. "I am just some woman who is bigged."

You would have thought I had stuck Mommie with a hot poker the way she sucked in her breath. "Arty Wallin, don't talk about such to him."

I said, "Why not? Is this not a grown man here that has seen me in the family way before?"

I will spare you further details. Suffice to say it was like a thousand other arguments that me and Mommie somehow managed to get into every time we caught a whiff of one another.

• • •

AFTER WE'D EATEN I wandered over to where Mary was talking to Gracie Franklin and Patsy Bowman. And for all of you that thinks Arty's big nose must be stuck in everybody's business, I must tell you that I had not heard the story what was being told.

"Clemmons just up and left," Gracie was saying. I reckoned they must be talking about Red Boyce's son since he was the only Clemmons I knew. "He come in one evening and throwed a big fit. Lindy had been to the barn and already done the milking. Had her buckets setting on the table and he took his arm and swiped bucket, milk, and all right off into the floor. They ain't seen hide nor hair of him since. Lindy's having an awful time of it, they say."

"I reckon she would be having it hard! Her and them two little babies." Patsy was red-faced and mad. "Tell you one thing, if it was me he'd done that-a-way he'd better never come back around me again. He'd better just keep going!"

There was that saying I mentioned before, *If it was me.*

Mary patted Patsy's arm. "I swan. And nobody has seen him since?"

"A man like that ain't worth the powder it would take to kill him." Patsy said.

Hackley popped up where he'd been stretched out on a pallet of quilts laid out on the wagon bed. "Sound like you girls has done got poor old Clemmons tried by jury and hung."

"You better watch it, Hackley Norton, you rogue," Gracie said. "You keep running that mouth and I'll have to come over there and straighten you out."

Butter would not have melted in her mouth and I thought to myself, *You had your chance a long time ago, honey, and you didn't do it then.*

"Ah, Miss Gracie. How you make my head spin with all them pretty words." Hackley swept his old flop hat off and laid it over his heart.

And I said, "I'll loan you my gun if you want it, Mary, just don't aim for his head. Shooting him in the head wouldn't even addle him, let alone kill him."

Mary stood and shook out her skirt as she studied him. "I don't know if I want to waste a perfectly good bullet."

"Oh, God!" Gracie whooped. "I'll bet you folks would give money to hire it done. I'll go to collecting it right now!" She went off looking back over her shoulder at Hackley and went twisting right up to these two men what was propped up on another wagon.

I looked back at Hackley, and them lazy eyes that never missed a trick was watching Gracie. He had his thumbs hooked in the waist of his britches, and for the first time in my life I wanted to see him as a man and not my own brother.

He was not much taller than me but his shoulders was wide for a man his size and for all that he was blond, he had what Granny called a good high color. His eyes were the prettiest shade of blue I have ever seen. Standing there beside that wagon, I believe I come awfully close to seeing what it was that turned the head of most every woman. Some of it was just in how he held himself sort of slouchy-like. But they was a coiled-up something in him, something that was not tame, and when he fixed them eyes on you, it felt like he was just going to spring on you and eat you up.

And then with a little smile he picked up his fiddle and bow and started to play.

I've played cards in England, I've gambled in Spain,
I'm going back to Rhode Island, gonna play my last game.

Jack a diamonds, Jack a diamonds, I know ye from old.
You've robbed my poor pockets of silver and gold.

I'll tune up my fiddle and rosin up my bow
And I'll make myself welcome wherever I go.
Jack a diamonds, Jack a diamonds, I know ye from old,
You've robbed my poor pockets of silver and gold.

I'm gonna drink, I'm gonna gamble, my money's my own,
And them that don't like me can leave me alone.
Jack a diamonds, Jack a diamonds, I know ye from old
You've robbed my poor pockets of silver and gold.

If the ocean was whiskey and I was a duck,
I'd dive to the bottom and I'd never come up.
Jack a diamonds, Jack a diamonds, I know ye from old.
You've robbed my poor pockets of silver and gold.

But the ocean ain't whiskey and I ain't no duck,
So I'll play them "Drunken Hiccups" and trust to my luck.
Jack a diamonds, Jack a diamonds, I know ye from old
You've robbed my poor pockets of silver and gold.

Rye whiskey and pretty women have been my downfall,
They beat me and they bang me but I love them 'fore all.
Jack a diamonds, Jack a diamonds, I know you from old.
You've robbed my poor pockets of silver and gold.

I'll eat when I'm hungry, I'll drink when I'm dry.
If I git to feelin much better gonna sprout wings and fly.
Jack a diamonds, Jack a diamonds, I know you from old.
You've robbed my poor pockets of silver and gold.

As he gave a long stroke of the bow to end the tune, I thought to myself, *Now, Arty, what woman would not trade her soul for all of that?*

Hackley nodded to the crowd that was clapping and hollering, bowed to Gracie, placed his fiddle on the quilt, and said "I know you folks didn't just come to hear me and looks like the speech making is fixing to start."

Larkin took me by the elbow and we made our way through the crowd that had gathered around a little stage of a thing that they'd built up for the speakers. I wanted to get as close to the front as I could because I wanted to see this Zeb Vance person. Zeke talked about him like he was God's gift, and his name had been all over the papers for months. Daddy said he had given twelve speeches in fourteen days begging for us to stay in the Union. He was only six years older than me, which would've made him thirty-one. My eyes was scanning the crowd looking for somebody who looked to fit that bill and I must say I was surprised when Larkin poked me in the ribs and nodded at this tall man standing across from us. He looked like he was carrying the weight of the world and was wore out from it. Looking back, I reckon he was carrying it. Much later he said that he knowed that all his speech making was doing little to change people's minds, and that nothing he could say would stop what he called the rush to secede. But he done it anyway. And if what he said to us was any proof, he done everything he could.

I pulled on Larkin's arm and said, "Who is that standing with him?"

"That's Nick Woodfin, one of the biggest slaveholders in Buncombe County. He's come to give us the other side of things," Larkin said.

Oh, I had read about him in the papers. He had wrote this big long piece about how the South was guaranteed the right to pull out of the Union by the Constitution. Him and Vance had argued back and forth about all this down in Raleigh and finally Woodfin had hollered out, "You know the Constitution of the United States, don't you, Mr. Vance?" And Vance had fired right back, "Yes, Mr. Woodfin, I know of the Constitution. Right now I feel like I helped write the damn thing. Whether we have the right is not the issue," he said. "If we're making our political bed, then I want to be certain we can sleep in it." Now that is my kind of man that can talk about sleeping in the bed you have made.

I looked hard at this Woodfin, because to my knowledge I had never seen nobody what owned slaves. He had on a white linen suit and looked like what I had always thought somebody like him would look, which is to say all proper and sort of citified.

"I like Vance the best," I whispered to Larkin.

"How do you know, Amma? You ain't heard them talk yet." He whispered back.

"I just do," I said. And I did. I could see what Zeke saw in Vance. He looked like he could walk right in the store over home and not draw attention to himself. He had big rough-looking hands and Woodfin's hands looked smooth as a woman's. I made fists of my own and hid them in my skirt because his hands did not look like mine.

Go it, Vance, I thought just as he stepped up on the stage. The crowd quieted right down, and he took a deep breath and sort of bowed to us and then he started to talk. I had never heard the likes of that in all my life and do not much expect to hear it again before I die.

• • •

"MY FRIENDS." HE TURNED to the local big shots. "Honored servants of these good folks." He nodded at Woodfin. "My esteemed colleague. I've not come to inform you that these are serious times. You already know that. Our sister state has left the Union, practicing a right given her by the great men that founded this beloved country in which we live. This country that many of our ancestors went to Kings Mountain and fought for during the Revolutionary War. Some of them didn't come back. They died for a purpose. Has it been so long ago that we've forgotten?" He looked out at us with his dark brows all bunched up above his eyes and give a little shake of his head. "I say no, we have not forgotten. Think of them, my friends. Those mountain men that stood and fought with such tenacity against the English. They could look off in the distance and see the mountains." He give a big sweep of his arm that could have took in the whole world.

"Now we are faced with a grim and somber decision. Will we tear asunder that which we have struggled to form? We might. But must we rush forward with ruinous and indecent haste? Mr. Woodfin will no doubt tell you that we must act now. To hesitate would cause the states that have cast their lot in with that of South Carolina to think badly of us, to think us a rider of the fence. I have heard this argument time and time again." Vance looked at Woodfin for a long time, and I can tell you that I would not have wanted him to fix me with that kind of gaze. When he looked back at us his eyes was shiny bright. "I am convinced that this is a decision that must be made by the people. Good, God-fearing, everyday people like you. This decision *cannot, should not* be made for you by politicians! The leaders in the disunion move are scorning every suggestion of compromise and rushing forward with such speed that it appears that they are absolute fools. Yet don't you be deceived. They are rushing the people into a revolution without giving them time to think. They fear lest the people shall think!"

"Damn them what wants to bust up this country, Zeb!" one man hollered.

And they was a bunch of men that hollered *amen* to that. But they was just as many that stood there with their arms crossed and did not say one single solitary word. It was hearing that big silence that caused the first little ripple of fear to run through me. Zeke had come to stand next to me and I reached out and linked my arm through his. He was as stiff as a board and I knew that he was afraid, too. That was the first of many times that I would know he was afraid, but it did not make me love him any less. It made me love him more.

Vance raised his hands patting the air.

"I understand your anger. But, again, I remind you of the need to proceed through these perilous times with caution. We can't afford to rush in the other direction either. The people must think, and when they are given the time they will begin to think and hear the matter properly discussed." He pointed a long finger at us. "Then and only then will we be able to consider long and soberly before we tear down this noble fabric and invite carnage, civil war, financial ruin, and anarchy. I beg you to think, think, my friends. I implore you to think! Neighbors, we have everything to gain and nothing on earth to lose by delay, but by too hasty action we may take a fatal step that we never can retrace. We may lose a heritage that we can never recover, though we seek it earnestly and with tears." He brought up his hand and pointed a finger straight up at the sky.

I was so caught up in listening to him talk that I did not even see that white-suited Woodfin had climbed on the stage with him until he was close enough to lay his hand on Vance's arm. I even know what he said to him though his voice was low and gruff. He said, "I am so sorry, Zeb." I believe he meant it, too, because you could see it in his eyes. But when he faced us the sorry was gone and his eyes was hot as fire.

"My fine friends and neighbors, I have just received word that South Carolina has fired on Fort Sumter. Lincoln has called for seventy-five thousand volunteers."

And that big crowd that had been so quiet just went to blowing up all around me. Everybody was hollering and cussing, but I was standing there numb as a stump. Vance stood right where he'd been and looked right foolish because he still had his finger pointing and I watched him bring it down to shake the hand Woodfin was offering him. I heard years later that Vance said he raised his hand that day a unionist and brought it down a secessionist. He really did just that. Hell, if you had said them words to me on that day I would have looked at you as dumb as a cow. I would not have knowed what either one of them meant. But, oh, you can believe I know what they both mean now.

Woodfin stepped down off the stage and men literally swarmed around and about him and he was quick swallowed up and gone. I done something then that I look back on today and shake my head about. Of a sudden I had to talk to that Zeb Vance and I had to do it eyeball to eyeball. I pulled my arm loose from Zeke, jerked my skirt up, and rushed that stage, catching him just before he stepped down. I climbed right up there with him too. "Wait, wait," I said. "What does this mean for me?"

Now, I have knowed some what I would call men in my time, but when this one looked down at me, I knowed I was looking at a great man. He had looked tired before, but Lord, now he looked absolutely killed. His voice sounded as sad as any sad I have ever heard.

"This means there will be war."

"But not for us," I said. "The war won't come here."

Oh, how cold his next words left me, even though he was trying to be so kind. "It is here already, madam." And then he said, "I must apologize and excuse myself. There's much I need to do." He was telling the truth about that and he had no way of knowing when he said it how true it would turn out to be. His own troubles was just around the corner—in nineteen days he would be made Confederate captain and would form up his own company and would go marching off to fight. They called themselves the Rough and Ready Guards. He did not know as he stood right there talking to me, Arty Wallin, in Shelton Laurel on that pretty day in April, that he would finish out them long and bloody years far off from his home.

I did not know that I was looking in the face of the man that would be elected governor in a little more than a year. But I would remember him the rest of my life, because in that little minute he opened up a world of worry for me. He handed it to me in a box without a lid and it come swirling up right in my face. Of a sudden I knew in my heart that the war was here as sure as I was a foot high because all around me hollering and cussing was men what was foolish enough to fight in it. Oh, God, and what would Zeke do? He was a good man, a decent man, but a man nonetheless. And good and decent men had a bigger dose of honor than them what was not so good or decent. I thought I would fall up when I knew that yes, he would go. And Larkin? Oh, what would happen to the first child I had not carried in my body but snugged up tight against my heart? I looked at him standing right there, and though he was big as a skinned mule and living on his own and already bedded a woman, he was still a boy. A million memories crowded into my mind and went to racing back and forth. The time he'd had the whooping cough and couldn't breathe and I'd sucked the thick snot out of him with my own mouth. The squeals he'd make when he was learning to crawl. How his little face would get all dreamy when he was listening to them old love songs. And in with all them feelings come the words to an old song I hadn't thought of in years.

"The warfare is a-ragin' and Johnny you must fight.
I want to be with you from morning to night.
I want to be with you, that grieves my heart so.
Won't you let me go with you?" Oh, no, my love, no."

"Oh, Johnny, Oh, Johnny, I think it's you're unkind
When I love you much better than all other mankind.
I'll roach back my hair and men's clothing I'll put on
And I'll act as your servant as you go marching along.

"I'll go to your general and get down upon my knees,
Five hundred bright guineas I'll give for your release."
"When you're standing on the picket some cold winter day
Them red rosy cheeks, love, will all fade away."

As for what happened next, I can only say God bless my brother Hackley, because right then he give an ear-splitting whoop and a holler and said, "Well, would you looky here if it ain't Willis and Columbus." I knowed right then that we was in for some fine music, seeing as how them brothers could play banjo and fiddle like nobody's business.

You might wonder why I did not think of Hackley having to go off to the war, but you should not. If you had known him then, you would have knowed too that the very thought of him in a war with people bossing him around would have made you laugh your head off. My brother was not the sort to give much thought to something that was not right in front of him unless it was in a jug or wearing a dress. Oh, do not get me wrong; Hackley had to come of it. Just not on this night. For him this was just one more excuse for a big frolic.

I went to dancing like a fool the minute they swung up in a tune, and if I had not been in the family way, I would have got as drunk as one too. I could not drink one drop when I was that way because it made me have the heartburn so bad. But they was lots of drinking being done. Hackley was as happy with it as I would ever see him. He always loved that mix of Sol's liquor and playing the fiddle. And when you throwed him in with other musicianers like Lum—which is what they all called Columbus—and Willis, you could figure that one tune would follow another, and you could dance all night if your feet and legs could stand it. Between them boys they probably knowed every fiddle tune they was to know.

There are many other things I recall about that one night. It is funny how our mind works that-a-way. For that night I can remember the exact words people said or the clothes they had on and now I can't remember something that somebody said to me just last week. Hackley's face was red and his eyes was so bright they looked like they could burn you. And I remember him laughing and saying, "Why, iffen I'd have knowed how the whiskey flowed at these speech makins and such I reckon I'd have took to politicking a long time ago. I might just run for sheriff." Bless his heart. He didn't have much time left to him and would never live to vote for a sheriff, let alone run for one.

I had to quit dancing for a bit while I made the young'uns lay down. They all went to sleep pretty quick except for Carolina. I knowed she was up and gone before my back was good and turned. That girl has always told me what she figured I wanted to hear and then done what she wanted to start with. I reckon there has to be one that we pay for our raising with, and that would be Carolina for me. I guess I was Mommie's, although I cannot for the like of me figure out what it was my poor little Mommie was having to pay for. She was always such a good thing.

I can still see how it looked as I was coming back. Things has changed so much from what they used to be. Everybody's wagon was now their bedroom and you could hear all sorts of things. Some things I might not ought to have heard right out in the open that way, but I must say I took my time and meandered along trying to determine who was in what wagon. By the time I got back to that little stage a right smart of time had gone by. They was a great big fire that had been built up against the cool of the spring evening, and you could see folks standing black against the orange light. The musicianers was up on the little stage that Vance had talked from and Hackley looked like some kind of haint. I just had to stand there and look at him for a minute. His hair had flopped down over his forehead and he was bowing that fiddle like he meant to saw it in two. He was lost in that music making.

Larkin was not hard to find. He was so much taller than everybody else that he stood right out. And I could tell he was talking to Mary because her hair was all aglow from the fire. Before I got to them she'd turned away. I went to stand beside him. He slid his arm around me and give me a side-armed hug. His breath smelled pretty strong with liquor. I asked him if he was drunk and he said, "Not near enough." And about that time here come Maggie. Me and her talked for a minute, but I could tell she was after Larkin so I just kept talking and talking and she kept raising her eyebrows and giving me these little nods in Larkin's direction. I kept letting on like I didn't know what she was wanting, and she got to the point where her eyes were just about rolling around in her head. So I took pity on her and said, "Oh, there's Zeke. I need to talk to him," and left her and Larkin standing there together. But I didn't go far enough that I didn't hear every word and see everything that happened.

Larkin had his eyes closed and was patting his leg in time to the music.

"Howdy, Larkin," she said, and I wished you could have heard how her voice sounded. Our Maggie could really be something when she set her head to it.

But Larkin had learned a thing or three and said right back to her in a voice *I* had certainly never heard him use on me, "Howdy, Miss Maggie."

"What are you grinning about?" she said as she walked right up in his face as bold as you please.

"Me to know and you to find out."

I couldn't help it. I eased over a little closer where I could see, and I want you to know I blushed plumb to the roots of my hair when I saw the way she was looking him up and down, letting her eyes stare at certain parts which were much easier to see now than they was when he was talking to his Amma just a minute ago. "I love how I keep getting reminded what a pretty boy you are, Larkin Stanton."

"You don't have to forget it, honey. My door is always open to you and you know that." They was not a thing in his voice that would make you think he was anything other than a man grown, and I finally got it through my thick head that they was things about Larkin that I did not know. And that they was things I did not need to know. I made to leave just as she leaned up close against him and whispered something in his ear. I was still close enough to hear what he said back to her.

"Right here in front of God and everybody?" I knew as sure as the world what they was talking about and, with a face as red as that fire, I swear to you I was trying to get my big nosy self out of their way, when all of a sudden there was Hackley standing right next to them. I wished I had just gone on about my rat killing and not heard or saw nothing because this is one time that I would have been better off not knowing. I was friends with both of them women, and I put myself right smack between the devil and the deep blue sea. I had not noticed nor had Maggie and Larkin that the music had stopped. But it had and when they turned toward the woods, there stood my brother with a great big sloppy grin on his face.

"Why, looky here. Two of my favorite folks passing the time of day," he said. And though his words was light and teasing like, his tone was not. They was an edge to his voice that made me think, *Oh, no, Hackley is drunk and wanting to fight.* I stepped right up close then because I meant to put myself between them if I had to. One look at Maggie's face told me she was not missing a thing and was pleased as could be about what was happening and I silently cursed her for this.

"Why, Hackley Norton, if I did not know you was a happy married man, I might think you was flirting with me."

My brother got right up in her face like me and Larkin was not even there and said, "Being married does not mean I died, nor has it caused me to go blind neither. And you do look mighty good, Maggie."

I could not help it. I said his name and I know my voice had to have sounded my dismay to both of them. "Damn it, Hackley Norton, do not even think of doing such a thing."

Him and Maggie barely glanced at me and both of them might as well have said out loud, "You shut your mouth, Arty." Neither one of them give me or Larkin another thought, and they was no way to tell who was leading who toward the woods. It looked to me like they was racing.

Though you might think I am lying, I am not when I tell you that my very first thought was of Mary. I looked around trying to see where she was. I guess I would have wanted somebody to do the same for me, unless they was planning on telling me about it, which I already knew I would not do. For just a minute I forgot it was not just my secret to keep. But one look at Larkin's face cured me of that. He was mad as fire, they was no doubt about that, but there was another look about him too, and as you have probably figured I am not one for the big words, but the only one that works here is *triumphant*. His eyes was plumb hot looking, and they was such an awful thing to look at that I had to turn my face from his. And he said, "Damn his soul," and he slammed his fist into the palm of his other hand. And quick-like I said, "Don't damn nobody's soul, Larkin." And he said, "I'll tell her now, Amma. You just wait and see if I don't." And I said, "Oh, honey, you cannot be the one that tells her this thing. She would hate you for the bearing of this." So once again I was right in the middle of them all.

When people gets old we have at least one or two moments in our lives that we can look back on and say to ourselves, *If I had done thus and such right here, my whole life would have been different.* It might not even look like it would be no big life-changing thing, but it is. Or if we ain't big thinkers, of which I am sometimes sorry to say I am, then we will say *I wish't I had* or *I wish't I'd never have,* and at the end of that you can put just about anything. *I wish't I had looked the other way* or *I wish't I'd never have seen his face* or *I wish't I had been somewhere else that day.* Or *I wish't somebody would've just picked up a rock and knocked my brains out right then.* Or *I wish't I had turned right around and told Mary right then and let them all go to hell in a handbag.* Well, I wished all them things on that night. But it was a long time later when I wished it the hardest. And that is the worst kind of wishing.

Who should come up to us right then but Mary. I swear, it was like she was put on this earth to try them two boys. The bad thing was that I could not hate her for it, for she did not know. I tell you it even tugged at my heart—and it could be hard as a rock sometimes—to see her standing there holding that pie tin. She held it up to Larkin, and her eyes were great big and held the light from the fire like a looking glass.

"I can't find Hack nowhere," she said, and I thought, *Thank God for small favors,* and give a nervous look back over my shoulders but could not see neither one of them as they had already cleared the trees. "I made him a stack cake because he loves it better than anything in this world." And I thought, *Not better than anything, honey.*

I looked at Larkin then, because I knowed it was do-the-business-or-git-off-the-pot time. He would either tell her or not. I watched it run every which way across his face and there was that muscle bunching in his jaw.

"Larkin," I said. And with that one word Mary must've known something because she turned her little face to me.

"What, Arty?" she said, and her voice was soft as down.

But I was looking at him and did not even shift my eyes. And I knew by the way his shoulders slumped that he would take what I had told him a while ago as the bitter truth. He could not tell her.

I spoke up and was amazed at how light my voice sounded but I guess it ought to have since I was so relieved. "Maybe he went to shit and the hogs eat him."

Mary looked at me and her eyes were just dancing and she said, "Oh, Arty, you just won't do," then she laughed and it was such a pretty sound that I could not help but laugh back. Larkin laughed too, but his voice held a trace of bitterness that I knew went all the way to his soul. Mary must have heard it, because she stopped laughing and looked up at him. But he did not stand for her to look at for long. He turned and went off toward where Lum and Willis was tuning up and drinking up. We watched him turn up the jug and Mary said, "Oh, he is drinking. I thought I smelled it on his breath," and for her that was the end of it.

But my hurt went right on. Even so I stood right there and talked to her until Hackley come waltzing up pretty as you please and took that pie pan from her and wolfed it down. The whole time he did not even look at me. I was staring at him as like to burn a hole plumb through him. When he finished his cake he made this big deal of licking his fingers real slow, staring me right in the eyes, and it was like I could read his mind: *See here, Arty, think where my fingers has been.* And I could not stand it. I had to leave them standing there. I did not say a single word to Mary but she called out to me, "Arty?"

But I acted like I did not hear her and what I carried off with me was the sound of Hackley laughing.

• • •

THE FIRE WAS DOWN to red embers when I got up from beside my sleeping husband later. Zeke could sleep through Gabriel blowing his horn. I never could and I believe it had to do with laying half awake listening for Larkin when I was a girl and then my own coming so quick. Every woman knows that all it takes to wake us quick as lightning even in the dead of night is that one word, *Mommie.* And though not one of my young'uns had called to me out loud—I went round and looked—I still could not sleep. All I had to do was see Larkin's big self setting on that little stage to know that he'd been calling to my heart. I set down with him and right then a shooting star went diving through the sky.

"Make a wish quick, honey," I said.

He said, "What would I wish for, Amma? Anything I can think of that I'd want would mean the ruination of somebody's life and probably mine, too."

"Ah," was all I said, because I knew he was telling the truth.

I put my arm through his and hugged it against my side and we set there for a while and neither one of us said a word. Then I thought of something that we could both wish for. "Let's wish that there won't be no war."

"That would be a waste of a wish, Amma."

He sounded so finished, like they was no doubt in his mind. I said, "Why, I don't reckon this war is wrote in stone, Larkin."

He looked over at me and his face was part dark and part red from the fire. His eyes looked like black holes in his head. "I believe they ain't nothing that will stop this war. Did you not hear what that Zeb Vance said?"

I got all puffed up about that because I knew I did not have an educated mind, but I had a decent head on my shoulders. "I was listening and I heard every word. He was a fine speech-giver."

"He was, Amma. But everything he said was culled when Lincoln called out them troops."

Like a fool I said, "Why, what has that got to do with us, honey? It don't make no matter-mind to us. We'll just go on with our day-to-day."

He glanced at me and said, "No. Things are way different for us now than they was just this morning. It is going to be a pure-D mess."

"But we ain't got no slaves nor nothing. And ain't none of us rich."

He sighed and his voice got this real patient sound to it and I must say I felt my temper flare up because it sounded like he was talking to a child. "This here is not about slaves nor being rich, Amma. It is about *South* Carolina."

Oh, and then it all come washing over me. "And we are *North* Carolina," I whispered.

"Exactly," he said back. Then after a while, "But he did have a fine way of speaking."

From out of the dark beyond the fire I heard Maggie give a little bark of a laugh. And Larkin heard it, too, because his shoulders slumped a little more and he give a great big sigh. I patted him on the arm. "You done right there, Larkin."

"Probably. But doing right don't always make it feel right."

I had to admit that was the truth.

"I will not understand Maggie if I live to be a hundred years old. After that business between all of you back at Christmas, how could she go right back to the trough for more?"

Though he laughed, he sounded awful sad. "Ah, she can't help it. She loves Hack. How can I hold that against her when I love him, too?"

I took to spluttering on that note, and he went to laughing and did not sound so sad. "You can't stay mad at him, neither, and you know it."

I thought about him licking his fingers and didn't know so much about that. My voice sounded more hateful than it ought to have. "Well, what about Mary?"

"Poor little Mary."

"Poor little Mary?" I mocked him. "Don't poor-little-Mary me. It ain't as if she did not know my brother before she married him."

"She knowed him. But I wonder, did she really know him?"

"She knowed what she wanted to know and that is the way of most of us. I have learned twice as much about Zeke Wallin since I married him, but if he had turned out to be a runner of women I would have killed him." You note I did not say *If it was me.* "Are you all right about Maggie?"

"Why, yes," he said. "I liked her all right but I would be lying like a dog if I was to say I loved her. To be honest with you, this has sort of made me sick to my stomach with her. I won't never have nothing else to do with her and that's a fact."

And you know he never did have a thing to do with her in that way. The way it ended up, I wished he had. Again Arty was not in charge. But oh, how she would wish she had been.

9

I HAVE THOUGHT ON that spring night often over the years and it has laid ever sweet in my heart. I know now that it would be one of the last innocent times any of us was to have. In my mind I can just see me and him setting there talking with the dawn coming on all around us. We was right on the edge of a great change and, bless us, we did not know it. We might have thought we did but we did not. The change was not long in the coming either.

IT WAS THE MIDDLE of May when Larkin come by the house way before daylight. Zeke had told me the night before that he aimed to go to Marshall with Daddy to vote and that Larkin and Hackley was going with them even though they could not vote. I allowed that I would just go too, but Zeke had said, "No, Arty, it will not be such a place for women on this day. They will be all manner of rough characters milling about and I do not want to have to worry about you." So I was more than a little miffed that morning but got up and fixed breakfast anyway. I could not bear the thoughts of Zeke leaving home hungry but was not a bit happy about having to do it, so I made a great racket with slamming things around. Larkin could tell I was mad and cut a wide berth around me until I set a plate for him at the table. Neither one of them said much and it was only when Zeke was going off the porch that I run to him and give him my list. He pulled me to him then and I let him. I did not want him going off thinking I was mad.

Mary come by that day and we set out under the trees for a bit. The leaves had feathered out really pretty, and the apple tree over our head was just covered up in blooms. She asked me if Hackley had been with Larkin this morning and I said no, that it was just Larkin that had come by. She said nothing for a long time. Carolina come running up and said she'd seen the first hummingbird and I told her she could expect to see them the very same time next year, too. Granny always said you could set your calendar by the coming of the birds. Carolina ran back to the house and I looked at Mary. She'd pulled up some grass and was working it with her hands and was staring down at it.

"What's the matter?" I asked her, though I had a good mind already what it was.

"Did Larkin say anything to you this morning about him and Hack going hunting last night?"

I sighed to myself. "No he didn't, but that don't mean nothing. They might have and Hackley went on to Mommie and Daddy's."

She looked at me and just busted out crying. "You know better. Why is he doing this? Oh, Arty, I am trying the very best I know how. What am I doing wrong?"

I put my arms around her and she just sobbed and sobbed, and I set there cussing my brother to myself. After she'd got through the biggest of the crying I said, "Mary, you knowed how he was when you married him. Surely you didn't think to change him?"

Her chin come up and her eyes was still bright with tears. "I thought he would want to change."

"Why?" I asked her.

She turned bright red but her eyes stayed right on mine. "Well, you know why."

"Because you held him off till after you were married." I knew that was what she was trying to say, so I just saved her the trouble.

She nodded and then her face sort of crumpled up and she started crying again. "I was afraid I wouldn't be enough for him and now my worst dreams has come true. He don't love me." Now she was just wailing.

"Mary, honey, it ain't that. Hackley loves you or he wouldn't have married you. Some men just runs women. It's just how they are." Meanwhile I am fuming inside.

"But it was me he was running this time last year."

Yes it was, I thought, *but then he caught you and now you are all bagged up and he's got you.*

But I did not say any of this. I just set there and let her cry it out. Then we went in the house and she helped me fix supper. She stayed on while I put the young'uns in the bed and was sitting on the porch watching the moon come up when I went out and set down on the step next to her.

"Are you all right, honey?" I asked her.

"Oh, Arty, I'll be fine. I've decided what I'm going to do." Her face was lit all aglow by that soft moon.

"What?" I said fully expecting her to say she was going to leave him or kill him one.

"I'll tough it out till I can get pregnant. Then he'll straighten out."

I felt so sorry for her. I finally had to tell her how that wouldn't change a thing. I told her that I knew women all up and down the cove that had done the same and all that had happened was when their old man come in drunk and raising hell and shooting things up, they would just be young'uns in the way. You cannot make a decent man out of one that is not.

"Arty, he is your brother. How can you say he is not a decent man?"

See what I got for telling her the truth as I saw it? I swan some folks cannot stand the truth even when it is looking them right in the eye.

I WAS STILL SETTING there long after she'd left for home when Zeke come up the path. The moon was almost setting over across the way but I was not about to go to bed until I heard what all had happened on their trip. And I was surely glad I had stayed up, for he had a big tale to tell.

He said they'd gone over the Sim Mountain heading for Marshall. They'd stood around waiting on Hackley at Mommie's, and I said, "Oh, so he was there, then," and he shot me a look and said he'd got there a little before them and took his own sweet time getting ready to go. They had finally walked on and Hack had caught up with them at the top of the mountain. I made some comment about how I reckon he was probably wore out from all the hunting he'd done the night before, and Zeke said, "Now, Arty, do you want to hear my tale or not?" so I hushed. They'd gone down into Marshall right as the sun was burning off the fog that always come in off the French Broad, and he said it looked like everybody and his brother was there. I could not imagine that there would be more than on court days but he said indeed there was. He said, "They was way more of us than they was them what was for pulling out of the Union," and this was the very first time I'd heard my man put into real words that he counted himself for one side. So I said nothing else while he talked but only listened, and my heart grew heavier and heavier.

Sheriff Walter Woods was already drunk and was out roaming about. I had seen him over at Shelton Laurel that day and he was drinking then, too. He had spent that whole day going about praising them what had already left the Union. He did not have a gun over there but Zeke said he had one in Marshall and it was tucked down in the waist of his britches for everybody to see. Right where the men was voting he hollered out, "Huzzah for Jeff Davis and the Confederacy," and somebody hollered right back at him, "Hurrah for Washington and the Union." I would not have been a bit surprised if he had told me it was Daddy that had hollered it. He had told me that we had just managed to wrassle this country away from the English, and he could not for the life of him figure why some folks now wanted to bust this country up.

But it was not Daddy. It was Hense Shelton. The sheriff come staggering up to him and drawed his gun on Hense asking if he was the one what hollered and Hense said he was and that he reckoned this was still a country where you could say what you believed in. And the sheriff cocked back the hammer and come right on. And that was when Daddy stepped out and said for him to hold up a minute, that they was no need in this. I felt like somebody had dashed cold water on my back, but I did not say a word. Zeke said, "Now, don't worry, it turned out all right." The sheriff recognized who Daddy was and said, "Why, William Norton, you old cur dog," and Daddy managed to get him walking back down the street away from the voting place. All would have maybe been saved had the sheriff not seen Virgil

Capps standing there with a gun tucked down in his own britches. Why do men have to do such things is what I want to know, although I did not ask. Zeke was bad to tote his own gun around and about, even if the only thing I've known him to kill with it was my big pretty black snake that lived down at the barn. Men and guns is not a good mix, is what I think.

According to what Virgil told Zeke, he had forgot he even had it, but that made no matter mind to that drunk sheriff. He jerked loose from Daddy and went over to Virgil, but Zeke said he lost interest in him when he seen who was standing right beside him, 'cause he hollered out "Charles Tweed, you black-hearted Tory" and pointed his gun at him. Zeke said he hit the ground right then because he saw the sheriff meant to shoot Charles, but Charles seed it too and he dove for the ground as well. So the bullet did not hit the one it was intended for. It hit Charles's boy Jack. And I thought, *Oh, no, poor Belvie.* Jack was her baby and she thought the sun rose and set on his fifteen-year-old head. I knowed it was bad, too, because Zeke said by the time that boy went down, he was already breathing a bloody froth. The crowd got quiet then and the sheriff must've decided he had stepped in a big pile because Zeke said he turned and run. And Charles come up off that ground looking completely wild out of his eyes. He pulled his own gun out and took off after the sheriff. Zeke said a door slammed somewhere up the street, and then the sheriff come out on the upstairs porch and hollered, "Come up here, all you damned Black Republicans and take a shot about with me." I reckon Charles did just that and one better. He busted into that house and went right up the steps after him and shot him dead right then and there. And I said to Zeke, "Oh, my God, they'll be trouble for sure now."

By then the pretty light of a silvery spring dawn had found its way into the cove and Zeke's eyes was as gray as a goose when he looked at me. "Arty, they was already more trouble than we knowed what to do with and this will make it even worser." He said that a big fight started there in the streets after that, and he turned the other side of his face to me and I saw a big bruise already blooming on his cheekbone. When I jumped up to see to him he only laughed and said I ought to see the other feller and waved me off. He went back to his tale telling but I paid him no mind. I had my own thoughts to study on and I kept hearing what he'd said before, "This will make it even worser."

He was right. This was only one of many things that happened to us here in this part of the world during that damn war. They was so many bad things that took place here that we come to be called Bloody Madison. And oh, God, it were a bloody place even after the damn war. The sheriff's family brought charges against Charles Tweed's family and they fought it out in the courthouse years later. That always seemed funny to me since the sheriff was dead and so was Charles. He got killed up in Kentucky when he was up there fighting. As a matter of fact he went down right beside Zeke. And God forgive me, but all I can say is if a bullet had to take somebody on that day I am glad it was not Zeke.

In case you're interested the vote that day in Marshall went 28 for leaving out and 144 for staying in. I reckon I do not need to tell you that Daddy and Zeke was two of that 144. I reckon I do need to tell you that if us women had been able to cast a vote they would have had to rewrote that ballot. It would have had to read For, Against, and No War A'tall. Do I need to tell you where Arty would have put her *X*? No, I did not think so.

THE WAR COME RIDING in for us on the hot breath of an early summer and the men went pouring out of Sodom like water through a sieve.

Mary's daddy Andrew and her brother Andy rode off for Asheville the day after we caught wind that North Carolina was leaving the Union. Fools went with big grins and shooting off their guns. They went to join up with the South and Zeke never said a word as we stood on the porch and watched them go.

He did say something when his brother Shadrack went with the same intent a week later. He said, "Well, there goes my brother, Arty," and his voice broke at the end. I would not say nothing. I did not care which way Shadrack Wallin went. For somebody who had not spent much time worrying in the past I was making up for it now. The worry that laid in my breast was much bigger than the baby I was five months gone with.

My own brother Robert left and never even told Mommie he was going. Oh, how that broke her heart.

Mary's other brother Jonah that was Hackley's friend went one evening and nobody never heard from him again. Poor Lucindy. She lost all of her boys in that damn war and was not worth killing from then on. She died when she were fifty-four, an old wore-out woman.

You could hear Big John Stanton's ax thwacking for a solid week. He split more wood than I have ever seen in my life before he rode off. Daisy noted it down in her Bible: *this 6th day of July 1861 is one on which my pur hart has brok. John has gone to the war.*

I KNEW IT WOULD come home to roost with me as well, and I vowed to myself that I would not throw a big fit when it come. I spent a lot of time hiding around from Zeke so he would not know how much I was crying. I swear I was just like a young'un apt to go to crying at the least little thing anyway. But this was like I was standing under a big hammer just waiting for it to fall right on my head. And even though I had tried to ready myself for the blow, when it finally fell on me it almost drove me to my knees.

I was out on the porch trying to catch a breeze when he come up behind me. The young'uns were asleep and it was so peaceful and quiet except for the sound of the night bugs out in the trees. My name come from him on a sigh and all the hair stood up on the back of my neck at the word. "Arty," he said and that was all. But I knew what it meant. The child within me gave a great knock and was still. I laid my hand over my belly and it seemed like we stayed like we was for a long time. Finally I said, "Well, tell me what to fix for you to take with you," and he told me later that night as we was laying next to each other in our bed that he had never loved me more than he did right then.

But I did not cry.

The next day he plowed the upper field and all of us went to planting late corn. I kept looking at him wanting to fill my sight with him standing there stripped to the waist and his lean body glowing with sweat. John Wesley, Carolina, and Abigail was out with me covering the last hills. Sylvaney, Ingabo, and Zeke Jr. was playing out under the big poplar at the edge of the field.

"Sylvaney, honey, go get us a bucket of water," he called out and her little head popped up and she was off toward the house at a run. I watched her go and thought again how much she favored me. That is one thing I will have to admit about me and Zeke. We had the prettiest young'uns. And of the whole bunch Carolina was the only one dark like the Wallins.

I looked back at Zeke and found his eyes on me. They was as purple as the lilacs that bloomed down by the house. I felt the tears starting and got really busy covering up that corn.

When I looked back at him he had turned and the plow point was parting the dirt digging a straight dark furrow that looked like water streaming out behind him.

IT WAS IN THE cool dark of the next morning that I grabbed onto him as like to never let him go. I kissed his face all over and his breath smelled like biscuits and gravy. I put my face into the hollow of his throat, but I did not cry. "Don't worry about John Wesley running off. He done that so you would not see him cry," I said, and the face I offered to him was as dry as dust. "How'll you manage?" And his eyes seemed like they was digging around inside of me trying to see my very heart. "Hush," I said and put my palm flat against his mouth. "Don't say no more. If you're going, go on. Larkin said he'll help me and he will. Now go on." I nodded out toward the road where Hugh set his horse. His fingers dug into my arm and he said, "I love you, Arty." I thought then I was going to break down, but I did not. "I know that," I said. "And I never have knowed love with nobody but you." And I tried one more time to memorize his face by the light of the stars. "Don't be no hero, Zeke," I said. And he said "I ain't no hero, Arty," and then he pulled away from me and a space ain't never been as empty as the one he stepped out of. He got up on his horse and I started to turn back toward the house. I could not stand to look at him anymore, and I balled my hands into fists and went almost running. And then I thought, "Arty, you cannot let him go like this," and I made myself stop and watched him go until I couldn't make out his shape anymore.

Then I cried and them tears I had been so stingy with come in such a flood that I thought I would surely drown.

On the day Pearl was born I was as restless and cagey as an old sow bear. I had gone up on the ridge above the house and was allowing my eyes to feast on the colors of that fall to see if that would calm me down. I loved watching the change come on and my eyes picked out the red maples that were always the first to change. On down the slope was the deep gold of the striped maples and the bright orange of the sugars. Mixed all in was the bloodred of the dogwoods. And way up on the very top of the ridges was the soft yellow of the chestnuts. It was almost as though the mountains knowed somehow of what hardships was waiting for us and was trying to put on a big show now. I leaned down to pick up a chestnut burr and the pain grabbed me low in my back. You can just imagine what I thought when I went to straighten up and could not do it. I knew right then that this baby was going to come and come quick. I hollered for John Wesley and he come running with his eyes big as saucers. It is a good thing he come fast as he did, for if he had not I would have had her right out on the mountain. I just barely got back to the house and she was born. Let me tell you, this is surely the way to have a young'un. Abigail was all that was there to help me and all she really did was catch her when she come out. And as I looked at her little round head covered up with all that black hair, I thought, "Well, they will be no doubt as to who daddied this one, Lige Blackett, thank you very much," because it was just like looking at a little bitty Zeke Wallin.

But Lige Blackett never got to see my precious Pearl. He fell dead as a doorknob two weeks later.

Larkin and Hackley had been all day stripping cane when Julie run to get them. Hackley wanted to have a molasses making which as usual was just him an excuse for a big drinking and a frolic. But I must say since he'd mentioned it my mouth had been pouring water at the thought of a big mess of 'lasses. They was nothing better in the winter time than a chunk of cornbread smothered in butter and warm 'lasses.

They was hot and quarreling like two old women when they stopped by the house on their way down to the Blacketts'. Larkin had been stung by a hornet and Hackley was giving him down the road about it. "You still favoring that sweat bee sting, Larkin?" he said. And Larkin said, "Sweat bee, hell, it was big as a damn crow." I fed them and sent them on their way and was glad to see the back of them.

Pearl started to fret and I picked her up and held her while she nursed. She was a good baby and had kept that big thick mat of hair. I smiled at the little bows Abigail had tied all through it and kissed the top of her head. They is nothing in this world that makes your heart go all peaceful like kissing the downy top of your young'un's head. I was not even sore these two weeks after her birth. I reckon what your body has done six times before it has no trouble remembering on the seventh time around. And I was glad of it.

I fixed a big pot of stewed taters to take to the setting up and by the time I got over there the house was standing full. My young'uns scattered and Mary met me on the porch but her eyes were all on Pearl. She took her and I could see the want on her face like somebody had painted *I want me one, too* on it. I went on in the house to speak to the family, and who should I see but Andrew Chandler big as you please standing right by the cooling board where they had Lige already laid out.

"Why, howdy, Arty," he said. And I howdied him right back. It was no secret that my man and Hugh was fighting for the Union. And they was no secret that the Chandlers had casted their lot with the South. But we was still neighbors, and through Mary we was family. I could be as polite as the next one. I had nothing to say when Shadrack come slinking around like the yeller dog that he was, though. As far as I was concerned, he was not family for all that he was Zeke's brother.

Late up in the night Andrew cornered Hackley and set in on him about when he was going to join up. "Ride back with me tomorrow morning. I'll get you in without a bit of trouble."

"I ain't about to go off and leave Mary till I have to," Hackley said. "They's some of us around here starting to wonder who's going to look about our own."

I could tell by how red Andrew's face was that he was getting mad. "That's what I mean. I can get you in with them that's staying around here."

And I could tell Hackley was getting hot, too. "I ain't leaving Mary till I have to."

"You sure it's not that now everybody's leaving you'd hate to give up being the only rooster in the henhouse?"

It went quiet as a tomb in that house, and Hackley sounded sort of strangled-like when he said "You accusing me of something?"

And I thought, *Andrew Chandler, you better hush right now or you will have my brother to kill.*

Thank God for cooler heads, because Sol Bullman stepped right in between them and said, "Why, Hack, Andrew, what is the matter with younse? Acting like two little boys, I say. And us here trying to bury poor old Lige. It always proves an amazement to me how you never know when the angel of death is going to come swooping out of the sky and cut you down." He looked from one to the other.

And you know me. I piped right in with, "Why, what are you talking about, Sol? Lige was ninety year old."

Andrew popped a shaking finger right under Hackley's nose and said big and loud, "You mark my words, Hackley Norton. Time's coming when you won't be able to set on your fence. You'll have to jump one way or the other. So you ought to decide whether you are with us or against us."

"Why, I reckon I'll ride that fence for now. I'm for me and mine, and if you need reminding, mine just happens to be yours, too!" Hackley said, and his voice was just as big and loud.

Andrew flipped the back of his hand at Hack and went on out the door. And I was even gladder to see the back of him.

Sometimes, especially if the person is old, a setting up can be right jolly, but this one was not. It seemed like them harsh words that had been flung back and forth cast a pall over everybody and it was a quiet night spent round poor old Lige. As we was walking home the next morning a big wind come up and it turned off cold. I told Abigail that it was blowing straight out of the north and she said, "Ain't that where Daddy is?" I could not even answer her.

When I went to bed that night the wind had laid down and I knew they would be a big frost come morning. I laid there listening to my young'uns sleep and my eyes just poured water that I could not let leak when they were awake. I missed Zeke so bad that I finally scooched up next to Pearl and held on to what felt like all I had in this world left of him.

It looked like it had snowed the next morning and I had to break a rim of ice to get water from the spring.

We buried Lige that day and I had never seen a bluer sky in all my life.

WE LET OURSELVES BE lulled along that fall. I must say that there is a certain peace in knowing that nature will move things in the direction they've been going for generation after generation. For me they was comfort in knowing that I went along doing the very same things that Mommie had done and that Granny had done before her and so on. The war was still roaring all around us but there in Sodom it was still out of our sight, and as they say, out of sight, out of mind. You couldn't help but notice it when we all got together for a frolic since they was no men to dance with and us women would dance together with one of us taking the man part. I will have to say it was not near as much fun, but Hackley made sure the music was good even though Lum was gone off to the fight.

When we killed our hog it was up to me and Larkin to do the biggest of the work. Bless his heart, he stayed all night with me and we ground sausage till almost daylight. I told him I'd come help cut cane when it was ready, and he said that would be good and if the frosts held true they would be cutting it in a week.

That was some of the biggest cane I've ever seen. It was just full of juice and I was sticky all over with it on the day we cut. That was a good day. Mary looked after all the young'uns, and me, Larkin, Julie, Hackley, Abigail, John Wesley, and Carolina had a big time. I got to telling tales about Granny and we laughed. Daddy showed up about quitting time and we deviled him about coming right when the work was all done. He helped us carry it to the barn and as we was stacking it, he asked Hackley if he knowed how to witch the boilers like Granny used to. She used to have the biggest 'lassie boilings ever was and to my knowledge never lost a single run to scorching, which is an amazement. Daddy used to tell it was because she cast some sort of spell. Everybody in Sodom would come toting every pot and jug they had. One year the color of every run looked like spun gold and it was just as thick. Now them was some of the best I ever put in my mouth.

They was a big crowd that showed up that year too.

That first morning I'd gotten there before the sun was up and Larkin was just hooking old Dock up to the grinder pole. I patted him on the nose and remembered how I used to ride his back turned around so I could talk to Pap while he plowed. Lord, them was the good old days. I wondered if mules had memories and if old Dock missed Granny as much as I did.

"You'll walk twenty miles today, Dock," I said, "even if it is just round and round in a big circle."

"It'll be good for him," Larkin grinned as he give one last tug on the cinch under his belly. "He don't do nothing all the day long but pick."

Daddy was setting out on the chopping block with all my young'uns gathered around him. He had his pocketknife out and was cutting them off some sopping sticks and they was all standing around big-eyed, waiting. He was laughing and cutting up with them, saying how these was the best sticks in the world. Years later I took that same knife out of his pocket on the day he fell dead at the milk gap, and it was sharp as a razor. I carried it myself until Zeke Jr. got up big enough to give to because Daddy always said a pocketknife was a thing to use.

Up in the day as we were taking off the first run Carolina got stung by a yellow jacket and carried on like you would not believe. Somebody was always getting stung, because once the bees found the fermented leavings they would get drunk as hoot owls and would sting you as quick as look at you. I reckon they would fall into that mean drunk category.

It was such a pretty day and by three o'clock it was hot. Larkin stripped off his shirt and he was sure a pretty creature standing there feeding the grinder. I was nursing Pearl, and Mary went over to get a bucket of juice and stood talking to him.

"Ain't you afraid your back will blister?" she asked him.

And I said, "Why, he ain't blistered in his life."

"If I was to stand here five minutes without a shirt, I'd have water blisters as big as your hand."

Now some women would have said that sort of sly-like, trying to get attention, but Mary said it as easy as she would have said, "I believe it might rain this evening." One look at Larkin's face told me that his mind was painting all kinds of pictures.

Julie hollered out wanting to know what she ought to do with the seed heads and Mary said, "Just a minute, I've got a sack I'm putting them in." As she turned the neck of her dress slipped down and for just a thought her round white shoulder popped into view. She went pulling it back up.

Larkin was watching her so hard he forgot to duck as that pole came back around and it give him a pretty good knock on the head. Good enough for him. If I'd been close enough I'd have give him a knock myself. I could not help noticing that Julie made a point of being at the ready each time that bucket needed emptying the rest of that evening.

By the time the night fell, the smell was almost too much for me. It felt like the inside of my mouth had a thick, sweet coat on it, although

I had not helped sop a single boiler. I had sent Abigail on to the house with Ingabo and Sylvaney, both of which had eat so much sweetening they had took to throwing up. Another run had just come to a boil and the women was skimming off the scum when I had finally had enough and eased off with the excuse of feeding Pearl again. She was not really hungry and fell asleep pretty quick. I was dozing a little myself and was not really paying no attention when I heard Julie say to Larkin, "I just get so tired of being Andrew and Lucindy's other girl. Not the pretty one, the other one."

I studied about her saying that the rest of the night. I would have hated to have had to go through life that way, longing to be something I could never be. I don't reckon I was never anything other than just Arty. I vowed right then and there to make it a point to try real hard to never show a preference with my own young'uns. And as you know, that can be hard, for some young'uns is easier to love than others for one reason or another. But I figure life is tough enough to live through as it is.

LATER ON THAT MONTH Mommie and Daddy had a big frolic at their house. We carried every stick of their furniture out and piled it up in a big pile so there would be more room to dance. We danced and danced and it got hot as fire in the house. I went out to catch my breath and while I was standing there I looked back through the open door. We had danced so hard that we'd kicked up a layer of dust that was level with everybody's knees. It looked like they was all floating on a cloud and I was full struck by it.

As was the custom when Hackley and them got tired of playing, we all set into singing the old songs. Them was such good times when we'd be ganged up and all of us would sing. I can still recall the thrill

I'd get when I would hear somebody sing something I did not know. That night Rosa Wallin sung the prettiest version I would ever hear of "The Little Farmer Boy."

> "Well met, well met, my own true love,
> Well met, well met," cried he,
> "For I've lately returned from the saltwater sea
> And it's all for the love of thee."

That song has got Zeke's favorite verse of any song in it and it goes like this:

> "Oh, take me back, oh, take me back
> Oh, take me back," cried she,
> "For I'm too young and lovely by far
> To rot in the saltwater sea."

Seeing as how she'd traipsed off and left her little babe setting in the floor, I can only say, Whatever did she think? She got no more than what she richly deserved.

I had seen Larkin and Carolina with their two black heads together right before we started singing but had no idea of the surprise they was cooking up for me. My mouth hung open like a gate when she stood up right in front of everybody and allowed that she wanted to sing. When she shut her eyes and started, I could not believe the sweet sound that come from her mouth. My girl sung "My Dearest Dear" just like it was meant to be sung and even throwed in a verse she would have had to learn from Hackley since I had never heard nobody but him sing it.

> Oh my old mother's hard to leave, my father's on my mind,
> But for your sake I'll go with you and leave them all behind.

But for your sake I'll go with you, I'll bid them fare-thee-well
For fear I'll ne'er see you no more while here on earth we dwell.

Folks made such a do about her singing that her and Larkin sung
a back-and-forth and it were one of the sweetest things in this world.
Larkin started it out.

I'll give to you a paper of pins and that's the way our love begins
If you will marry me, me, me, if you will marry me.

I won't accept your paper of pins if that's the way our love
begins
And I'll not marry you, you, you, and I'll not marry you.

I'll give to you a dress of red skipped all 'round with a golden
thread
If you will marry me, me, me, if you will marry me.

I won't accept your dress of red skipped 'round with a golden
thread
And I'll not marry you, you, you, and I'll not marry you.

I'll give to you a dress of green and you'll be dressed fit as a queen
If you will marry me, me, me, if you will marry me.

I won't accept your dress of green for I don't care to dress fit like
a queen
And I'll not marry you, you, you, and I'll not marry you.

I'll give to you a key to my desk and you can have money at your
request
If you will marry me, me, me, if you will marry me.

> If you'll give to me a key to your desk and I can have money at
>   my request
> Then I shall marry you, you, you, then I shall marry you.
>
> Oh, I'll take back the key to my desk and you can't have money
>   at your request
> And I'll not marry you, you, you, no I won't marry you.

They about tore the house down over that one and I could not help it, I started to bawl like a baby. I cried because I was proud of her and because I would have give anything in this world if her daddy had been there to hear it. The saddest part was I did not know if he would *ever* get to hear her and that was almost more than my heart could stand.

When I went outside later I realized it was the night of the hunter's moon. My mind flew back to this time last year. I was not the only one remembering. Larkin was out in that strange light standing with his arms out in front of him and I knew in his heart he was holding Granny as she'd breathed her last.

God bless her sweet soul. I hope they're having a frolic wherever she is.

BEYOND THE MOUNTAINS, THE beast of war was literally roaring. We was starting to hear it too. We read in the paper how Tennessee had barely scraped up enough votes to secede. But right over the line in the eastern part, the vote had been two-to-one to stay in the Union. When the Confederacy moved troops over there, they really stirred up a hornets' nest. I can understand it, because most of them saw that as nothing more or less than that they was being invaded. And that pot that had been just sort of simmering boiled plumb over.

Mommie got a letter from her cousin Davina over in Greeneville that said her husband Ross had fell in with a gang that had meant to burn all the railroads that the Rebels controlled. It didn't work out but the Confederates come through anyways and arrested a bunch of men. They tried them and hung every one of them. Davina wrote and these are her words: "They's mor sojers than you can shak a stik at. We aim to mov frum here Nance. We air cumin home." And it was not long before an absolute flood of people come pouring over the border into Madison County. Among them that crossed over was one John Kirk and one David Fry. John Kirk was the brother of the as yet unheard of George Washington Kirk, and David Fry was the ring-leader of them would-be bridge burners. None of them was famous when they first come but, oh, they would be soon enough. It was not long at all till word was going around that they was recruiting for the Union army.

Finally the letters started to roll into Sodom, and in January Daisy got one from Big John. He had hooked up with some like-minded men from over in Mitchell and Yancey Counties, and they had made their way north to Kentucky. He was with the Union army up in the Cumberland Gap. "I'll not mak it hom in tim to plow," he wrote. "Tell Larkin I said to hep you."

Do you know what a happy woman I was when my Zeke's letter come through? I had not knowed where he was or if he'd been killed or nothing for the longest seven months that had ever rolled over my head. I had tried and tried to go along, but Lord, it had been an ever present pure-D torment not knowing where he was or if he'd made it through, but praise be, make it he had. Him and Hugh was also in the Cumberland Gap and he mentioned nothing about no fighting up there, though he did send me twenty dollars. He only talked about how pretty it was and that if he stood just in the right spot, he believed he could see plumb to North Carolina. He was homesick and I could tell it. I was Zeke-sick and he closed his letter out with this and these are his own words: "May God bless and keep you my dear wife and if we never meet any mur on urth Arty let us so live that we may meet abuv."

I cried the whole time I was writing him back but I did not let on to him. I did say to him that we now had a precious Pearl.

Andrew, Andy, and Shadrack were in and out of Sodom so much you'd have thought they was swinging doors set up down at the forks of the road. They called themselves the Madison Rangers, a Confederate company raised up by Lawrence Allen who was the clerk of court over in Marshall. Now reckon who comes up with the names for these outfits and why did all of them sound so high and fancy?

And you could not have blowed Hackley off his fence with a keg of dynamite.

LORD HAVE MERCY, I thought that winter was just going to go on forever. It was cold and snowy right up through the middle of April. When it finally thawed out enough to plow, us women had to go it alone. There was just not enough of Larkin, Fee, and Hackley to go around, although I will say Hackley tried to be *everywhere* at once, if you know what I mean. I had never plowed in my life and to tell you the truth had thought myself to be above it, but by Ned and God I did come of it. But that was not the worst of it. I had to drag the ground with the spiked harrow to bust up the big clods and then come the scrubbing with the big log. Every night it seemed like something else pained me to the point of distraction. Except for my arms. For that first three weeks or so they *always* felt like they was being jerked out of their sockets. After that though they quit hurting, and I swear I was strong as most men. Though I had never been soft-bodied like a lot of women, now I was lean and did not have one bit of fat on me. I want you to know it was with the most satisfaction and no small amount of pride I carried in my heart as I walked through them fields and seen the first shoots of corn and wheat coming up.

When it first started to rain I was so thankful, but after a week my heart went heavy as a rock. Day after day it poured and my spirits sunk even more as I watched the water run and run and keep running. I swear the fields seemed to just melt right before my eyes. It looked like a river of mud coming down the road out from the house and all my seedlings looked like merry little green boats as they went bobbing by.

They had what they called a bust-out on further north of us. I had never heard of such a thing. They said this woman was in her house cooking supper with two of her young'uns and all at once it come the biggest clap of thunder she'd ever heard but it did not come from the natural place. It come from under her *feet* and everything went perfect black and then everything started to slide. They found the house at the bottom of the mountain and it took them over an hour to dig them out. It was a pure and simple miracle that she lived to tell the story as they said every bone in her was broke. The only thing they could figure was that it had rained so much that the ground held as much as it could and then what it could not just busted out. As if I did not have enough to worry about, I laid awake night after night worrying about us having one of them bust-outs here.

Yes, I was getting to be a pretty decent worrier.

But the rain finally slacked off and quit way up toward the first of May and I could hardly stand to wait for it to dry off enough before I hit them fields with a vengeance. Things was no more than up and tender green when it come a hard freeze on the second day of June that killed most everything I had.

I don't know what I would have done without Larkin and John Wesley. I guess we would have starved to death that winter for sure, though we come damn near to it as it was. But I'm trying to get ahead of myself here.

The time come for Hackley to jump off that fence but he didn't jump. They had to push him off.

LARKIN AND ME WAS in the field behind the house planting what few rows of corn I had left when here come Julie just tearing up stumps. She was hollering the whole time saying, "Larkin, Arty, Larkin, Arty, Larkin, Arty." I thought she was going to fall up before she finally managed to say, "Mary wants you to come. A bunch of soldiers has come and took Hackley and a whole passel of others with them. They was just going past Jim Leake's store when I went by down there." And I said as if it really made some sort of difference—but in my own defense I was sort of addle-brained—"What kind of soldiers?" And she looked at me like I was a fool before she went back down the hill at a dead run, "Gun-toting soldiers is all I know." A look went between me and Larkin and then both of us broke to run too.

I dashed by the house and grabbed Pearl and screamed out for Abigail to mind the others and fix them supper. I swear it is a thousand wonders that my young'uns had not took to calling her Mommie. I was truly blessed to have had such a fine oldest child. She, however, might not have thought she had been thusly blessed with her mommie.

I done the milking for Mary and by that time it was dark in their cabin. Mary had not lit so much as a candle, and I had to feel around on the fireboard till I found one. As it sputtered to light, I saw Larkin squatted down by her stool and he had his arm up around her shoulders and she was sort of leaning into him. It rose up in me that this was not right, but what could I say? Holler out big and loud, "You get away from there, Larkin?" I think not, even though one look at Julie's poor stricken face surely made me want to. But I did mean for them to take note that they was not in this house alone, as much as they might want to act that way so I spoke up and my voice was big and loud. "Mary, tell me again what they said." Larkin looked at me and said, "She's already told us once," and I jutted my chin out at him. He knowed better than to mess with me when my chin was out like that so he told me himself.

"Something about them being with the Buncombe County militia. They was a big-mouthed feller that kept saying something about rounding up anti-Confederates, and though Hack kept saying he weren't against nobody they grabbed him up anyways. Said she saw Sol and Greenberry and your brother David and a bunch more and that she even saw Fee and it looked like they'd hit him in the head with something."

As I said a while ago I had already heard this, but him repeating it had served its purpose. He got up from Mary and was just standing there with his hands hanging down.

And it is a good thing, as right about then I heard feet come pounding across the porch and Mommie come flying through the door with her hair out of its bun and I knowed she'd been caught just as her and Daddy was fixing to go to bed.

"Lord have mercy, Mary." Mommie went to her and grabbed up the very same hand Larkin had just been holding. "Oh, honey. Your poor hands are cold as ice." She rubbed them between hers.

"Damn them all to hell in a handcart!" Daddy said and went to pacing back and forth. "What do they mean coming in here and pulling such a trick as this here? It's that damn bunch from Tennessee what's caused this."

"Don't blame them for this. They can't help it." Mommie said.

"Damned if they can't!" Daddy was just this side of screaming. "That bunch over on Shelton Laurel has brought the whole damn southern army down on us, sure as I'm standing here."

Mommie rose and her back was stiff as a poker. "You hush, William Norton. Raring and raising hell ain't going to do nobody a bit a good. You go to the spring and git me a bucket of water, and I need you to have a cool head when you come back."

Now they had never been no doubt in my mind who was really the boss with Mommie and Daddy, but this was the very first time I had ever in my life seen it so out in the open. Mommie always took care to make sure Daddy thought he was in charge, and she could play him like a fine-tuned fiddle. I waited for a blow that never happened. Daddy's eyes was red as blood and he was blinking and blinking and then he finally just grabbed the bucket and went storming out the door.

Mommie's voice was calm as could be. "He'll be all right when he gets back. He's just hidebound as to what to do. He gets that way sometimes, bless his heart." She handed me another candle. "Light this, Arty. It's dark as pitch in here."

And from then on I did not have to worry who was in charge.

Mommie turned to my baby brother Tete. "I want you to go to the house and gather up some of your things. I hoped to wait but it appears the time for waiting is over."

It is funny how I never even paid any attention to that one of my brothers. I was already married and gone long before he'd even been born, and I was thunderstruck to have just seen how big he had got.

"I'm sending him to Knoxville," Mommie said. "A man that Granny Nance is friends with is taking him to Greeneville. He'll be working with a captain in the Union army. Only way I could figure to keep him safe during this mess." She looked Larkin right in the face. "I can send you too, if you want to go."

Oh, how I wish I had throwed the awfulest fit in the world right then and just made him go. That is one of them moments we all look back down our lives at and know that we could've changed everything that was to come.

"I can't, Aunt Nancy." His eyes were dark and I could read nothing in them by the dim light of the candle. "I've got too many folks depending on me—Daisy, Arty. I can't."

And my heart cried out and said, *Not me, but Mary.* I looked at Mary to see if she was setting there all full of herself and felt sorry in an instant. Her poor little face looked like it had caved in on itself and bore such a look of suffering that I felt scalding tears flood my eyes. We was rowing the same boat now, Mary and me was, and I was ashamed of my feelings of a minute before.

I said nothing and simply went to peeling some shriveled up taters because that is what Mommie told me to do.

I HAD LAID DOWN with Pearl way up in the night just to try to rest as I knew I would not sleep, and it was just getting daylight when we heard footsteps on the porch.

Mary come up out of that chair like she'd been scalded and jerked open the door. "Oh, Hack, Oh, Hack!" she kept saying over and over.

But the way he acted you'd have thought he'd just been out hunting. For once I think he was really trying to put our minds at ease, and especially Mary's. "Hell, honey. I ought to git rounded up and took off more often, if this is how I'll be treated when I get back."

"Are you all right, son?" You could tell Daddy was just worried to death.

"Finer than frog hair." And he grinned at all of us but I noted how pinched he looked around his eyes and then knowed for certain it was all just a big show.

"Come and eat," Mommie said, holding his arm and all but dragging him to the table.

"All right, all right. Let me get untangled from Mary and I'll eat. I am plumb starved, sure enough."

It was while he was eating that he told his tale. He said they'd went along rounding up men until they had joined up with another group coming down from Shelton Laurel. They had been asked a bunch of questions, and then they had made some of them join up with the Confederacy on the spot. When it come his turn, one of the fellers had asked him if he was Andrew Chandler's son-in-law. They had asked him to sign his name on a paper and let him come home.

I could see Daddy had went white as a sheet and he said, "Oh, God, son, what did you sign your name to?"

"And that was all?" Larkin asked.

"Well, pretty much." Hackley would not look at Daddy. "I told them I had been planning to join up as soon as I got my crops in anyhow. They reminded me that the Conscription Act had took effect back last month and that it was the law that I sign up, so I did. Then they let me go."

"Oh, God, help us." Mary's voice was barely a whisper.

"So you'll go now?" Daddy asked.

"Nah. I won't have to go right now. Won't have to leave till the end of this month." He give such a big yawn that his jaw popped. "But for right now I'm going to bed. I am wore out."

Larkin followed him all the way to the bed.

"Hack, what about Fee?"

Hackley set down on the edge of the bed and went to pulling off his boots before he fell sideways on the bed. "They took him on. He didn't go quiet neither. Took three of them to drag him off and that damn dog of his was absolutely trying to eat them up. They aimed to shoot it but didn't. Finally just whistled it up and took it off, too."

"But Fee won't fight! Did you tell them that?"

I could tell by how cloudy his voice was that he was already half asleep. "I was having a hard enough time trying to save my own hide, Larkin. Git on, now. I'm wore slap out."

But Larkin would not hush. "Where did they take Fee? Do you know?"

A soft snore was his only answer. Larkin made a move toward the bed, but I laid my hand on his arm. "Let him be. It don't matter where they took Fee. He won't stay long wherever they got him."

AT DAWN ON THE last day of June, thunder shook the very house as a big storm come tearing its way over from Tennessee. Great black clouds boiled up over the highest peaks and lightning streaked down and hit a big oak tree up on the ridge. It caught fire and the flaming limbs was whipping back and forth in the wind. Fat drops of rain soon followed and the fire cracked and popped like something alive and mad as hell before it sputtered and died in the downpour. The storm moaned and howled and then went screaming on across the ridge. By daylight it was as if it had never been, except for the water that was standing a good three inches deep on top of the ground. This was how it was on the day my brother went for the war.

I WOULD NOT HAVE gone over there for the world if Hackley had not come by the night before and asked me to. I said, "Are you sure, honey? Mary might want you to herself." And he looked at me and said, "She's why I'm asking you to come, Arty." Now how could I refuse him that?

By the time I got over there him and Larkin was standing in the yard and he reached out and loved me. I loved him right back and we wound up standing with our arms around each other for a long time. He had on a fine white shirt that Mary had worked on for the past two weeks and he smelled good and clean. When he finally let go of me and I looked at his face, they was not one bit of foolishness nor devilment in the blue sky of his eyes.

"I'd rather eat shit with a splinter than to have to do this," he said to us. "I don't even know when I'll be able to git back." He give a wave all around the place. "The corn out yonder will need hoeing in two weeks or so."

He hushed then and covered up his eyes with his hand. When he looked back at us his eyes was standing full of tears. "I got to go and ain't no other way around it," and then his eyes went to overflowing and I started crying, too, and of course when I done that my milk let down. You could always tell Arty in a bad situation because she'd be the one standing there with the front of her dress wet as water.

And then he looked at Larkin. "You promise me that you'll look about Mary, and you, Arty, have her help you with the young'uns. She loves your little Pearl and we was hoping she was—"and then he hushed again, but I knowed what he'd meant. She had told me she thought she might be expecting but I knowed now she was not.

I said I could always use help with my litter of hellions and he laughed at that, and I was proud to hear it. I did not know if I could have stood seeing him this way much longer. The tears were gone from his eyes now, but he was still talking as serious as a judge.

"Don't let no harm come to her. Somebody come here and tries to bother her, you kill them, Larkin," he said and did not even blink an eye.

And I said, "Why, Lord, Hackley, surely it won't come to that."

He looked at me. "Arty, them was some of the roughest characters I ever seen riding with them fellers last month. And that bunch that's been hiding out on Shelton Laurel from over in Tennessee ain't no better. You could throw every one of them in a sack, Union, Confederate, don't make no matter mind, and you wouldn't be able to tell which one would fall out first. They'll be robbing, pillaging, plundering, murdering—" He looked back over his shoulder at the cabin. "And raping too. You women'll be left to root hog or die. You'll need to watch yourself, too, sister, and I wouldn't let them biggest girls of yours out much neither. That's where I'm counting on you, Larkin. I think I'll be able to go on down that road and leave if I have your word."

I had never even thought of that. In my heart there bloomed a new respect for Hackley Norton.

"You've got my word that I'll do the best I can," Larkin said.

"And you'll take care of yourself, Hack?" I blurted. "Don't you be taking no bullets."

He laughed at me then and seemed more like his old self.

"Hell, Arty. Don't you worry none about me." He looked up at Larkin with a big grin. "Course I'll miss you covering my back. Remember how we used to do that? Fight back to back? Weren't nobody could whup neither one of us if the other was within hollering distance."

Oh, how fast the years had passed us by. Of a sudden I could just see them as boys and my heart squeezed up in my chest.

But the moment went by and there he stood cocky as a little banty rooster.

"Anyhow," he said, "I figure it won't take me but a little while to get this whole mess straightened out and headed in the right direction."

And Larkin said something I will never forget. "Since I ain't going to be there fighting at your back is all the more reason to watch it closer. If you believe what the papers is saying, then both sides is winning. And me and you knows that can't be right. Somebody's got to lose. And it won't be too much longer afore they ain't no men left around here. All of them's being sent off to Virginy."

"Like I said, it'll get a lot worse through here," my brother said. He looked me right in the eye. "Take care of things, Arty." Then at Larkin, "Mind what I asked you to do."

And then he turned and left us standing there in the path.

We watched him go for a minute and then Larkin hollered out. "Hackley!"

He stopped and turned back to us.

"Sing me something I don't know."

Though in the dark shade, I saw the grin that split his face.

Hackley's voice floated back to us on the breeze, strong at first, but faded as he went on down the road.

A soldier traveling from the north
While the moon shined bright and clearly,
The lady knew the gentleman's horse
Because she loved him dearly.

She took the horse by the bridle reins
And led him to the stable.
"They's hay and oats for your horse, my love
Go feed him, you are able."

She reached and took him by the hand,
She led him to the table.
"They's cake and wine for you, my love
Go eat and drink your welcome."

Hit's she pulled off her blue silk gown
And laid it across't the table,
He pulled off his uniform suit
And he hopped in the bed with the lady.

Larkin seemed to be straining to listen as the words became faint and fainter still, and then disappeared altogether. When all we could hear was birdsong and the loud burring of the katydids we turned back towards the cabin and Larkin said real low, "I already know that one."

I did not answer him for I knowed he was not talking to me.

10

THAT SUMMER WAS HOT as hell and dry as a bone. It was a constant fight to save our gardens, while the corn patches in the upper fields just withered up and died. We toted bucket after bucket of water from the streams until they dried plumb up. They was not enough water to wash clothes and everybody went nasty and dirty smelling. We couldn't even wash the dishes, we just wiped them clean and used them again for the next meal. Oh, how I dreaded them white-hot dog days to come that rendered snakes blind and mean. Sores would get all caked up with a yellow scab and would not heal and then would come that red line streaking toward your heart. Dog days—when skunks, coons, bats, and dogs went mad, and the creeks would be standing pools of sickness.

And this year brought the most dreaded of all to us, and that was the fever.

I SAT AT THE table watching a wasp bumble across the cabin. It bumped against the ceiling, dove down, and bumped the ceiling again. It slapped its body several times against the walls trying to find a way out. But it found none so it turned and started the journey back. When I rubbed my eyes it felt like they was full of grit.

Two days ago I'd had to send Abigail, Carolina, Zeke Jr., and my precious Pearl to stay with Mommie when Sylvaney got the headache. Though it was hotter than the hinges of hell, she was saying she was cold. I kept Ingabo at home too because she was warm to the touch. I sent John Wesley to get Larkin and told him to go on to Mommie's after that. My bosoms felt like they were going to bust wide open, but they was nothing to be done about it. I couldn't even get my mind to wrap around how Mommie was managing with Pearl. Pearl had a few teeth and had been eating some mashed-up food but was still nursing regular. She would be weaned for sure when this was all over. The steady thwack of an ax outside offered me some comfort even though I had not allowed Larkin any nearer to the house than the edge of the yard. He was bedding in the barn and allowed as how he'd slept in worse places. Just knowing he was here had at least knocked the sharp edges off this hellish fear that had been working inside of me like a bunch of worms. Lord, I was tired. I had been up all night bathing first one girl and then the other. Poor little lambs with their skin so hot I could only wonder as to how they was not being baked from the inside out. Every time my mind tried to go down that dark path of what I already knew deep in my bones, my heart would jump up and say, *No, no, it is not.*

I know now that when we really know something we can never not know it. But I was not that way then. I thought that if we believed something hard enough, that we could make it so. When we are young we really believe that all it takes is grit and determination, and it is only with the living of life that we come to wisdom. Well, I say that wisdom is wasted on the old. But maybe not. Mayhap if we knew how tough life was going to be when we was just starting out, it would prove more than we could stand. Maybe nature runs its course just as it does for a reason. That is not to say I do not ball my fists up and shake them in the face of life even now, and me an old woman. I am still a hardheaded person and will not take nothing laying down. I will stick my chin out and take it right there, thank you very much. But I have learned what I have come to believe is the most important thing and do not fight against it no more. And that is that we cannot change the way a single hair grows in another person's head. We all have our own row to hoe and nobody can hoe it for us. It is just a heartbreaking thing when somebody we love has such a hard row. But it was right there in that little cabin that I had to learn the hardest lesson of all, which was that some of us are given short rows.

I did not know that I was fixing to get a big dose of life's seasoning. All I knew to do was fight on, so I did.

That day was so white it hurt my eyes, and I propped my arm on the door facing and put my head in the crook of my elbow. Then such a longing went through me that it made my knees weak, and before I could stop myself I said out loud, "Granny," and you could never know how bad I wanted to see her dear old face right then. I would have traded my soul for just ten minutes.

Right next to my head the wasp give a final slap against the ceiling and dove out into the bright sunlight. I watched it go until I could no longer see its little dark shape against the faded green of the mountain.

That night Sylvaney set straight up in the bed and cried out, "Mommie," and the blood just come gushing out of her nose and her fever went sky high. I done everything I knowed to do trying to stop the blood, but it just kept pouring out to where we all three looked like I had slaughtered a hog right there on the bed. Finally I grabbed the nearest thing which just happened to be the ladle Zeke had carved for me and I snapped the handle off and mashed it as hard as I could against her upper lip. I kept saying over and over, "Granny, don't let this happen, please," and finally the blood stopped.

I have the bowl of that ladle on my dresser and oft times I take it up. And though I cannot see it I rub my hands over it and remember what he said to me when he give it to me. "Here, Arty, it is like you, warm to the touch." So that ladle is like just about everything else in this world that is sweet and bitter at the same time.

Toward morning I stretched out on the bed next to the girls and fell into a deep sleep. I didn't even hear Larkin when he hollered for me from the yard at dawn. But when I opened my eyes, there he was, quietly stacking firewood in a neat pile. I was so wooly-headed that I didn't even say nothing to him and he come to stand at the foot of the bed looking at me and the wasted forms of my girls. I saw in his eyes what I could not carry in my heart, and somehow seeing it there helped me to bear it. He come to my side of the bed and said "Amma," and I said to him, "Git out, git out, Larkin. The girls has got the fever," and he just shook his head. Before I could stop him he reached over me and picked Sylvaney up in his arms and carried her to the table and started washing the dried blood off her face. Though his hands was gentle as could be she started to fight him and he went to singing to her low and soothing-like.

> They'll be no night in that bright land,
> No clouds to blight the sun.
> Like little children we shall play
> Oh, how we'll sing and run.

I could not find my tongue to tell him nay.

It was a few days later when the rosy spots bloomed on their scrawny chests and what little doubt I might have held onto was put to rest. I bathed and sung and cried and could not eat a bite. I was running on nothing but pure will and Larkin's strength. Poor thing. If he made one trip to the spring he made a hundred. He did not say much and I did not have to line out for him a single thing to do. He did whatever he saw needed to be done, even down to taking the blood- and shit-soaked rags out behind the barn to burn.

TWO WEEKS BLURRED BY as we battled against that unrelenting foe. One morning before dawn of the third week, Ingabo bled from her guts so bad that the blood went all the way through the corn-shuck mattress and pooled up under the bed. After I changed her I set down and just held her. She died there in my arms and I laid her on the table. I did not even cry. You might wonder at that, but you should not. You see, I did not have time for the dead. I went right back to bathing Sylvaney. Sometimes you have to set grief down and not carry it right then, but do not fret. It will squat right there and wait for you to pick it back up.

Sylvaney went to sleep down in the evening, and I had to get out of that house or take to screaming like a mad person, so I went out on the porch and set down. I heard Larkin come out behind me but he never said nothing.

And then the strangest thing in this world happened to me. In the blink of an eye they was two Artys setting there with Larkin. One was very stout and clear as a bell and able to think even better than usual. The other one was crazy as hell and wanted to jump up and go to running and clawing at her throat because all the pain known to mankind had balled up and lodged itself there to where she could barely breathe around it. So I said, *You, Arty with the clear head, do this thing, because something must be done with Ingabo, for we cannot leave her long in this heat.* So I opened my mouth and to my amazement I found that this Arty could talk though it come out cracked and brickle.

"Put her in the root cellar."

He waited for me to say something else and when I didn't he asked me, "Do you want me to go git somebody?"

It flashed hot as fire through me that somewhere else people was going about their day-to-day and did not have to bury their little red headed girl down in a cold black hole. And them two Artys was one again.

I started shaking all over and could not stop and my mouth opened and the awfullest sound come out, and I began to keen for that little part of me and Zeke that had left from this world.

I did not even know Larkin had moved but of a sudden he was there. He done nothing more than lay his hand on my shoulder and we stayed that way until a near to full moon showed itself above Picked Shirt Mountain. Then we got up together and went back in the house. We stood for a while by the table and then with the gentlest hands ever was, he gathered my baby up and carried her out the door.

Sylvaney died the next day.

They is no way in this world to make losing a child real to folks what has never lost one. You might think you could imagine it, but friend, you cannot. I have lived a long life and I have forgot more than most folks will ever know, but I have never lost a minute of them awful days. And as you know I can lay right in there with the best of them when it comes to talking and telling tales. But watching them two little girls leave this world and then laying them in the ground done something to me, and I was not the same ever again. From that day on when somebody asked me how many young'uns I had I always said seven living two dead because to have done anything else would have been like they'd never been here a'tall, and I could not stand that. They are your young'uns and they remain so until you are laid in the ground. The wound you tote with you, and though it never closes up, it does get to where it does not feel like you are pouring salt in it. Nature helps you in that way at least.

LARKIN AND DADDY HOLLOWED and charred out a coffin log big enough to hold both girls and we buried them up on the ridge next to Granny. I went half foolish when they started covering them up and Mommie had to hold me up. When I was leaning against her I could feel her flesh trembling, but each time I met her eyes they was as clear and still as a blue pool of water. I stayed until they mounded the dirt over them because I knew I had to. But to tell you the truth I just wanted to jump in the hole with them, and Mommie said to me, "Scream, Arty, scream as loud as you can, if you want to," and I could not. It was a pitiful little crowd that gathered that day. Just me, Larkin, Mommie and Daddy, Mary, Julie, and Maggie. Larkin had to half carry me back to the house.

It says a lot for Mary and Maggie, I think. They might not have said nothing to each other, but by God them two set all their differences aside and come that day for me. Women are not like men in that way.

IT WAS JUST ME and Larkin went back to that empty house. We spent the next two days scrubbing it down. Mommie's brother had died of the fever and she had almost died herself, and she said Granny washed everything with lye soap after. I went at it with a vengeance and by the next day, all the skin on my hands was cracked and bleeding. I did not even so much as pay that no mind. The pain in my hands was good because it made me know that at least on the outside I was still alive.

On the second night, Larkin went to the barn and got a jug of liquor that Sol had give him. I got as drunk as a hooty owl, and I will say that is exactly what I set out to do. Granny told me one time that pitching a big drunk is the best cleaning out we can offer to ourselves, so I took her at her word. I do not remember much about that night nor the next day. I got up on the fourth day weak and shaking but clearheaded and knowing I had to get on with things now. I had buried two of my babies but I still had five in the world of the living.

They come in like little scared rabbits. Even Carolina was quiet and big-eyed. Pearl had growed but she reached for me like I was a long-lost friend and I grabbed a hold of her and held her so tight in my arms that I could feel her little heart beating next to mine. When I finally set her down she come right back up off that floor and walked. Abigail give a little grin, like she didn't know whether she ought to or not, and said she started walking about a week ago. And I was struck by something right then that I have never forgot. All my other young'uns would grow and change and all that, but Sylvaney and Ingabo would always stay my little girls.

Somehow that made it a little easier to bear.

It was just then that a soft little hint of a breeze blowed its way in through the door and the sweet smell of lilacs come sighing into the room. Larkin's head come up and he sniffed the air and the corners of his mouth curled up in a smile. Pearl set into laughing and she went to reaching out her little arms just like somebody was standing there to pick her up. My hair was damp with sweat and of a sudden, it felt like a hand had laid itself on my forehead to push it back. And then it seemed like it went to moving about the room stirring around and about all of them, and then it settled on Larkin. His hair blowed about for a little bit and then it was gone. Abigail scooped up Pearl and all the young'uns went running out. And I stood there for a minute with my mouth hanging open and then I started to cry, and it were not a half-crazy crying neither. It was a good cleansing cry.

Larkin put his hand on me and I turned into him and buried my face in the front of his shirt.

"It felt like she moved through me," I said, and I pushed my face into his shirt again and breathed in.

"The smell is all over you," he said.

I had never had such a feeling of peace in my life as when that happened. Nothing will ever make me believe anything other than that Granny come to let me know that my girls was with her and that they was all right.

And though I have missed them and wondered about them, I have never worried about them since.

11

THE FIRST CONFEDERATE BUNCH come foraging five days later, and damn them for the blackguards they was. We were expecting them too. They was talk all through this part of the world then as to how they would come prancing right onto a body's land demanding part of what little food there was without so much as a fare-thee-well, talking their big talk as to how a law had been passed giving them the right to take 10 percent of everything we had managed to coax up out of the ground. Well, to hell with them and their laws, and I told them that. I asked them if they somehow thought I had took them to raise, but it done no good. They took it anyhow and we come damn near to starving that winter. I still get mad as fire just thinking about how they all treated us back during their big fine war.

They went to Mary's the day after they come to my place and this is how she told it to me. And she left nothing out, bless her.

She didn't have much and she allowed if they got it they was going to have to fight her for it. I can just see her little slender frame standing up to all them big rough men. But stand up to them she did. She said the horses was all spattered with mud, and the men was covered with a silvery coat of fine dust. Ain't it funny what your mind latches onto to remember in times like that? Before she could open her mouth one of them kicked his horse out a little further than the others and he touched the brim of his hat.

"Afternoon, ma'am," he said in a slow drawl that fingered him as being from further south than North Carolina.

Mary was not about to let them know how scared she was, but her knees was knocking under her dress. "Howdy."

Then he give a little smile and Mary said that flew all over her, and before she could catch it that redheaded temper popped out and of a sudden she was no longer scared. She was mad as hell.

"Is they something you think is funny here?"

And he sobered right up and said, "No ma'am. I've not found humor in much these last few days. Is your husband around?"

"My husband is off fighting in this damn war, mister, and he's on the same side as you."

Mary said there was a little flicker of something that went across his face, but that did not stop him from saying, "My men are thirsty and hungry," as if that had anything a'tall to do with her.

She answered them better than I would have. "The spring's out yonder. Ye can help yourself. Don't take the horses down in it. They can drink from the branch out yonder behind the barn."

He looked her right in the face then and said, "And we'll be needing food, too, ma'am."

She looked right back and said, "They ain't no food to spare for you, mister," which was the total truth.

His voice was awful quiet then. "Ma'am, I am authorized by the government to collect ten percent of all food growed on your land."

And Mary put it right back to him. "Well, the government ain't setting here in Sodom trying to figure out how it's going to make it through the coming months without starving to death. And besides that, ten percent of nothing is still nothing."

You know what I have to say about that, don't you? I say, "Go it, Mary." I told her that then, too.

But it done no good, because all he said was, "I'll take all that into consideration while we look about. Men, see what you can find."

The men all got down and set into roaming free about the place and Mary said she was so dismayed that she just stood there like she'd took root. The sound of a pistol shot out back of the house unrooted her, though, and she come off that porch like a screeching hellcat. "Don't you kill my chickens. You stop." Wailing like a ban-shee she launched herself at one of the men what come carrying a chicken and a sack of salt, and they both went down in a flurry.

She had no way of knowing that Larkin had just topped the ridge heading from my place to hers and he was just in time to hear her scream.

He told me later that all he saw was her setting on the ground with this feller looming up over her so he acted before he even had time to think. He went in low and caught the soldier unaware and hit him full force. The next thing he knowed he was flat on his back and the soldier was setting astraddle of his chest with a knife blade at his throat. That was awfully hard for me to believe because they come no tougher than Larkin Stanton, but Mary and Larkin both swore it as the truth. Larkin said this feller's eyes was mild as mud pies as he studied him for a minute.

Then he said, "Catch your breath, son, then you can tell me why you come tearing in here intent on knocking the infernal hell out of me."

Mary had crawled over to them by then and said, "Don't you hurt him. Take everything I got but don't hurt him."

The soldier looked at them and then said in the tiredest voice ever was, "Oh, honey, I'm not going to take everything. I'm just going to take what the government says I can." And then he hollered out for them other soldiers to put their guns away, and Larkin said that was when he noticed that they was about fifteen guns pointed right at his head.

Once the rest of them had gone back to their pillaging and plundering, the soldier got up off Larkin and offered his hand to Mary. "Now I'll get back to what I was doing awhile ago," and he helped her get up. Larkin said he felt pretty damn foolish then.

Mary said while she was knocking the salt and dirt off herself, the soldier stuck his hand out to Larkin and said, "Major Silas McMahan," and him and Larkin shook hands. Men are the funniest creatures. Fighting like dogs one minute then shaking hands and grab-assing the next.

He then turned to Mary and held out his hand, and when she give him hers he bowed over it. I wished I could have seen all that as it would have surely been a sight to see. "Please accept my sincerest apologies," he said.

And Mary said he was the sweetest man ever was. I did not believe it at the time but once I myself got to know Silas, I have to say he was one of the most decent humans I would ever know. He'd been a soldier all his life and had come close to losing his leg down in Mexico. That's why he weren't off fighting up where the big fighting was. He was from down in Central, South Carolina, and his family had been there since God's dog was just a pup and he told me us mountain folks was as foreign to him as anybody he'd ever seen and he had traveled all over. But I'll tell you this much. I don't know what we would have done during that damn war without Silas McMahan.

He took only a little that day from Mary and said he was sorry for having to take that.

Poor little Mary said to me later that she had studied about it and come to where it was all right since it might help them feed Hackley, wherever he was.

Knowing my brother she didn't need to worry about that.

Larkin said that Silas told him before he rode off that no woman was safe living by herself. Well, don't that take all. What do you reckon they was thinking when they started their merry little war and took off all our menfolk, is what I'd like to know.

But the one thing Silas done that day without even meaning to was to give Larkin and Mary the go-ahead to get closer to the line than ever before.

And what happened next put them over it.

IT WAS LONG AFTER when Larkin told me the whole of what happened a few weeks later, the day the Union soldiers rode up to the house.

Larkin was out watering what corn they had managed to save when he heard horses coming up the road. He didn't want to draw notice to the corn so he went slipping out of the field and into the barn, thankful that Hackley had butted it up against some trees because he was able to get the cow out and tied up back in the woods without being seen. He eased back and peeped between the logs. He said what he saw caused his blood to run cold as ice. He said it was all in the way them men got off their horses at the same time and started meandering toward the house that caused him alarm. He said he was desperate for a weapon of some sort when his eyes fell on Hackley's big mowing scythe. What he aimed to do with a scythe against guns is well beyond my way of figuring, but then I reckon at least it made him feel like he was fixing to do *something* other than just stand there with his teeth in his mouth. I shudder to think what might have happened had it not been for one of Daddy's razorback shoats. Larkin said he heard a snuffling sound and from out of the stall nearest him come this pig just sauntering along like it had not a care in the world, and I don't reckon it did. Them hogs was as mean as old billy hell and feared neither man nor beast. It must've thought kingdom come when Larkin slapped it on the hind end with the flat of that blade. He said it went squealing for all its might out of the barn and went hell bent for leather straight at them soldiers. One pulled his gun and shot it right between the eyes. Larkin said they loaded it up and went riding off.

That was how the story went for years. Later I got to hear the rest of it.

AFTER THEM MEN LEFT, Mary went to pieces and Larkin done what he always did. He went to comforting her and they wound up in each other's arms. He said when they kissed he felt like he'd been struck by lightning, and it was like his skin was on fire. He said when he come to his senses he tried to shift away from her, but she'd moved with him and pushed against him even closer. And that she'd whispered his name and he was lost. Had it not been for Granny's little hen flying out from under the house, they is no telling what would've happened, but fly out she did, and it scared the livelong hell out of them. He had tried to say he was sorry then, but she would not let him. "Hush," she had said and then run into the house. He said he'd gone to the barn then and cried like a big baby. And he said to me then, "Amma, I am shamed by it still and I am sorry from the bottom of my heart."

When we are young we might have a bushel of sense but we ain't got a lick of reasoning. We have feelings and yearnings, and to deny them is not natural. I will even go so far as to say we cannot deny them. Even you old people can surely recall what it felt like to wake up in the morning next to the one you love with your skin buzzing and sizzling like fatback in a hot skillet and your heart feeling like it would bust wide open with the wants and longings that is ours when we're in the bloom of youth. Recall how it dropped itself in your gut and went to rippling all through you in the blink of an eye? It washed over me with Zeke and I have never knowed it with any other man, and I was a lucky woman because he felt it for me, too. He give as good as he got. And let me tell you right now, he got a lot. We had many years of strong nature between us and when it began to wane, we still had the memory of it and every once in a while it would flare between us and we would act like young'uns again, if only for a little while. Let me say here how much I thought of that man who was my great love and my best friend. He was my heart's desire until the day he died and remains so even now that he is gone. This is so.

Now to think that strong nature is only between a man and his wife is a foolish, foolish thing. Larkin Stanton had no more reasoning when it come to Mary than any other man-creature on God's green earth. He was seventeen year old and had a healthy dose of man nature and them Stantons was hot-natured men, if you know what I mean. She was a nineteen-year-old vision of pure loveliness with a healthy dose of the woman nature. And then you have to throw in that pot the fact that Larkin had loved her most of his life in one way or another. It seemed like he'd climbed on a bullet when he was born and his whole life was headed in her direction like he'd been shot out of a gun.

The only trouble was that Mary was my brother's wife and to get to where that bullet was heading, it first had to go through him.

I WAS PROUD TO mark the end of summer that year and felt a slight easing in my heart when the first cool rain fell up toward the middle of September. For the first time since burying my girls, I really felt like I might live. I have never cared for the end of summer since and figure I will go to my grave that way.

Me and Mary put our heads together and our gardens as well. Thank God there was a bunch of apples and pears that year. We figured if we was *real* careful with a wing and a prayer and everybody going a little hungry, we might just have enough to make it through the winter.

We talked about where to put the crocks of food to keep them away from the soldiers that was in and out of Sodom in a constant stream, and Larkin come up with the best idea. He got a maddock and shovel and crawled way back under the house and hacked out a root cellar that you could not see until you was right on it. Me and Mary and the young'uns worked every day and night putting stuff up, and it was almost like old times. Carolina worried Larkin to death dancing on the floor over his head. The only way he could get her to quit was by singing to her, as she was as foolish over them old songs as he'd been, and she would quit with the stomping to listen. Them was some good old times.

We built a holding pen back in the woods for our cows. Mary said this would not work because the big cats would get them. I allowed I would rather the panthers kill and eat them than for them to be killed to feed a single solitary soldier. I was sick unto death of all them foolish men that we now had to contend with. What the damn Home

Guards weren't ten-percenting, the damn Yankees was raiding, and what little was left, the deserters was plime-blank stealing. To give you an inkling of how it was with us, I will tell you this. Larkin spent one whole day harnessed like a mule to the sled with me and Mary loading it up with hay. We'd no more than got it off and put in the hayloft than the Home Guard come through and took most of it. All you Yankee lovers don't need to get your drawers in too big a self-righteous wad, neither. Your fine boys in blue come through later that evening and took the damn sled itself.

Larkin had give up all thought of staying at home. He stayed a night or two at Mary's just the two of them, and when that was made known to me I throwed three fits and a quare spell. I told them they would be too much talk and that I would not have it. I was trying my best to protect them and was glad when Julie come to stay. I guess my reasoning was that now at least folks might think he was took up with her and that was the better of the two evils, if they is such a thing.

THEY HAS NEVER BEEN no love lost in me for them high-browed folks up in Asheville. They have always thought themselves above us and I have no use for such. That feeling was only shored up in October when that man that I named Little Shitting Colonel come riding up to Mary's when her and Larkin was getting in the last of the squash. Larkin said they'd already been seen so they was no need to even try to hide the squash, so he picked up the full basket and went to meet them. They was five of them and all of them dressed up in their little Confederate uniforms like that made them God's gift. Now, people, I want to tell you that some men is not kind nor decent and they was looking one right in the face. He was the sort of man what is perfect cut out for this business of war and as far as I'm concerned, every last one of them needs to be consigned to the deepest, hottest hole in hell. And I hope they all wind up in that hole with their backs broke. I will not even say I am sorry for the wishing of such an awful thing.

When Larkin told them they was looking at what food that was left, Little Shitting Colonel blared his eyes and said that was not why they was there. He jerked some papers out of his pocket and sort of waved them at Mary and asked if she was the wife of Hackley Norton.

Well, Lord have mercy, of course poor little Mary's mind went to the worst place and her knees buckled under her. She sort of leaned over against Larkin and he had to hold her up for a minute to keep her from falling. But then that chin come up and she stepped out to meet it head on, bless her little heart. "I am his wife," she said. "Where was he killed?" Little Shitting Colonel said, "Oh, no, madam. Nothing quite so noble as that. He is a traitor, Mrs. Norton. I cannot tell you whether your cowardly husband lives or has been murdered by one of his fiendish friends. All I carry are the papers that identify him as a deserter from the army of the Confederate States of America as of September 23, 1862." Can you believe that somebody would use that word *fiendish*? Well, that is them people from Asheville for you.

"Why, that's been over a month," Larkin said. "How come now is the first we heard of it?"

Little Shitting Colonel made this big show of looking off in the distance and sighing big and loud. I guess he was trying to be a big shot and make sure everybody knowed what a high opinion he had of hisself. "I'm certain the government has much better ways to waste the time of its men without rushing about madly to notify the likes of you folks of the goings and comings of men like this here Hackley Norton." As far as he was concerned, he said, it was good riddance to bad rubbish.

Then he must've took a good look at Larkin, because he asked why it was he had not been conscripted. Larkin answered him with the truth, which was that he'd just turned seventeen back in the summer. You can rest assured that this was not the first time that boy had answered that question. But this was the first time he'd been asked to prove it. Larkin allowed as to how he had no way of doing that except the saying of it and that he did not lie.

Little Shitting Colonel had rared back in the saddle and said he wished he had a ten-cent piece for every time he'd heard that little tale. Then with eyes as flat as a snake's he'd asked for Larkin's name and he got a ugly look on his face and his thin little lips got even thinner. I have always said you should not trust a man that has no lips. And then he said to the rest of them men, "What do you think, gentlemen? Is this hulking giant the child he claims to be? Or is he lying to us so he can remain about to diddle this pretty little trick here?" Larkin said if he'd had a gun that would have been one dead son of a bitch. But he did not, and then Little Shitting Colonel said, "I repeat, can you prove your age?"

Larkin said Julie hollering from the porch was all that kept him from getting into it with them men. All I can say is thank the Lord somebody was thinking on that day.

"I can prove it," she said as she come off the porch and marched her little self right up to them. She was carrying a Bible in her arms and talking a mile a minute. Mary might have been the pretty one, but they was no flies on Julie Chandler. "This here is his granny's Bible," she said in a big loud voice. "The date's wrote down when she married and when all of her young'uns was borned. Larkin's in here too," and she went to giggling like a foolish girl, and it was so unlike her that Larkin said all him and Mary could do was stand there and stare. "Though Lord knows," Julie went on, "Larkin couldn't of been her young'un. Why, she'd a been way too old to of birthed a young'un by the time Larkin come along. See, his mommie died giving birth and his granny wrote his name right next to her daughter's name. It was the durndest thing. When he was born they surely didn't 'spect him to live, though you'd never know it now, would ye? He sure is a big ole thing, ain't he?" She made a beeline for Larkin then and locked her fingers around his upper arm and went to batting her eyes at him and looking up at him like she was going to take a bite out of him. "And, why, you know what they done? His Aunt Nancy, I mean. I don't think his granny was for it, or least ways I don't think she was, course I couldn't swear to it since I weren't there. Anyhow, they let Hackley name him." She giggled some more. "Bless his heart! Hackley's, I mean. He weren't but a young'un hisself and, why, he named Larkin after one of his mommie's brother's coonhounds."

I still get tickled thinking about it. She might still be standing there talking that bunch of foolishness if Little Shitting Colonel hadn't hollered out, "Silence!"

Them other men took to laughing and one of them muttered, "They God."

Julie drawed a great wind as though she was going to start in again.

But the little man had heard enough. "Oh, for heaven's sakes, child, be quiet! I am not interested in all this prattle!" He looked at the Bible she was holding up to him and give a snort and allowed he'd take her word for it. He lost all interest in Larkin and turned back to

Mary. "Mrs. Norton, I am here to officially inform you that your husband is considered by the Confederate States of America to be a criminal and as such may be shot on sight, arrested, and hanged, or placed in prison for the rest of his natural life. Many of these men try to return home. Should he do this, it is your duty to your country to persuade him to turn himself in, or you must take it upon yourself to notify the authorities. We will be patrolling this area and will continue searching for your husband. Do you understand what I'm saying, madam?"

Larkin said Mary's back got stiffer and stiffer the longer he talked to where she was ramrod straight by the time he finished and her eyes was blazing mad. "I am not deaf, mister, and I understand ever word. Give me them papers."

Little Shitting Colonel was right taken aback with our Mary. But he still managed to say he'd told her because he'd assumed she wouldn't be able to read.

"Give me your damned papers. I can probably read better than you can." And she grabbed them papers right out of his hand and then she said, "Now git your Rebel asses off my land!"

They left then but not before Little Shitting Colonel had ordered one of his men to take the squash. That aside, I got the biggest laugh when they all three come by the house that evening and told me that tale.

I had only one question for Julie. "Where in the world did you get Granny's Bible?" And with a grin she said, "It weren't your granny's, it were Mary's."

It done my heart good to know that a proper-mouthed Little Shitting Colonel from the big fine town of Asheville could be outfoxed by a skinny little mountain girl.

Some things is just too rich for words.

12

As the days of that year came to an end, Sodom got buried under a big heavy quilt of the first snow. The Home Guard come through just every little whipstitch taking what it wanted, and looking for what was now a crowd of men what had deserted from the army. They was all kinds of God-awful stories being tossed about. This one I know was the truth because Clarissa told me herself.

She was at home with her little baby that was just setting up good when the Home Guard come riding up wanting to know where her husband Craven was. She knew he was hiding out somewheres but did not know the exact spot. They would not believe her and drug her out fighting like a wildcat the whole way and tied her to a tree. Then they set her baby boy in the doorway where she knowed if he fell over he would fall onto the big flat rock they used as a step and bust his brains out. When she still couldn't tell them where Craven was, they rode off and left her tied to that tree. Who knows what would've happened if Little Bob hadn't come along. He'd been blinded by the fever when just a boy, but he was able to follow the sound of that baby crying and then helped her get untied. Poor old Little Bob. He got bit by a mad dog two years later and went mad hisself and died.

They was all manner of stories every bit as bad as Clarissa's, but the worst one I ever heard was the one Pete McCoy told us one evening when Larkin, Mary, and Julie had come by the house and we'd fixed supper. It was way up in the evening and all my little ones was asleep except for Abigail and Carolina.

When Zeke's old dog went to barking something fierce, Larkin got up and went to the door. Old Shag would defend his people like ringing a bell, and I was sort of surprised when he quit barking right off and went to whining like he did when he knowed you. You could have knocked me over with a feather when Larkin come leading Pete McCoy to the table.

"You're a long way from home," I said. "Surely to goodness you ain't out hunting on such a night." He was an old hunting buddy of Larkin and Hackley's.

"Lord, Arty, I wished I was hunting. I hate to bother younse, but I need help." The top of his head barely reached Larkin's shoulder. "They's been some trouble over on Shelton Laurel," he said in a low-pitched voice.

"We've heard some of it." I said. "Come in and eat."

"I'm obliged. My belly's been trying to eat my backbone all day."

I ain't never seen nobody eat like poor old Pete did that night.

After his second glass of buttermilk he closed his eyes and sort of slumped back in his chair. "Nothing never tasted better," he said.

"What all has happened?" Mary said.

He opened his eyes and studied her. "They's been a slaughter over home."

"What do you mean a slaughter?" I said with a look at Abigail and Carolina. I made up my mind right then that they was old enough to hear it. They might have to face a like thing one of these days, and this might help them ready for it.

Pete rubbed his eyes and then rested his forehead on one hand.

"We been having a hell of a time. Like everbody else I reckon. They's a constant flow outen Tennessee. They're having a worse time of it than us, if you can believe it." He looked at me. "How did you manage when it come hog-killing time?"

"We never had no hog to kill, damn them stealing Yankees to hell." I said.

"Oh." Pete said. "Reckon that took care of that. Well, my crowd was in a bad way 'cause we never had no salt. Not even a good handful. Know now what scraping the bottom of the barrel means. Mommie had not only scraped the bottom of her salting barrel, she'd scraped the sides. But word come to us that they was hoards of salt being kept in Marshall. For the soldiers, see. Plenty of it just setting down there in a warehouse. So John Kirk talked up a salt raid. Big gang of us got together and headed toward Marshall. Wednesday— no, Thursday, two weeks ago, the eighth of January. Reason I remember the day was 'cause I remembered that was the name of a fiddle tune Hack used to play for frolics." His face fell in grim lines. "But this weren't no frolic, not a'tall. We crossed through the Tater Gap about midday. Stayed around down in Walnut Creek till dark laid down, then headed out. We made good time. We aimed to get a raft at Macintosh's Ford and make our way down the river, get the salt, and head back." He barked out a laugh. "Hell, weren't no need of a raft. River was froze solid as a rock. We *walked* down the river on the ice to the warehouse. Why, hit were easy as pie. One old man guarding all that salt. He laid o'er quick, even told us they was a wagon hitched up and ready to go right outside. We took as much as we could pile on that wagon. Some of us was even carrying a sack or two. They was some other stuff we took, too, blankets, bales of cloth, and so on. Then as we's going out of Marshall some of the townpeople come out of their houses and started hollering at us. This feller what was named Peek, Captain Peek, dressed up in his uniform come out and hollered fer us to halt. Then all hell broke loose. Peek drawed his gun and fired, and John Kirk shot back and hit him in the right arm. They was a lot of hollering and screaming. Then this one man slapped Johnny Norton. You know Little Johnny. He rared back and hit that fellow right there in the road. Them folks scattered like a bunch of yeller dogs then.

"I don't know who started the plundering. Mayhap it was on all our minds. Anyways, we started going in the houses and taking stuff. Me and Little Johnny went in this big white house and this little woman commenced to screaming like a hellcat. We paid her no attention 'cept to tell her to shut up. Then Ned Woods come in with five or six of them boys off of No-Fat and he hollered that this was Lawrence Allen's house. I told him I didn't give a good goddamn whose house it was. We went upstairs and they was a little nigger girl setting on the floor right at the top of the steps. Little Johnny had never seen one, I reckon. He knelt down in front of her and she sort of shied back from him. He licked his finger then reached out and rubbed her face and she squealed like a stuck hog. We could hear young'uns crying at the back of the house. We started down the hall and here come that woman and them boys from No-Fat right behind her sort of herding her up the steps." He glanced at us. "Her dress was tore at the front. I reached out and took her by the arm and she commenced to fighting me. I shoved her in behind me and told them boys to leave her alone." He shrugged. "We searched about upstairs and took some stuff, clothes, some more blankets. Then we left."

He looked at me. "Reckon I could have another glass of buttermilk?"

Carolina was already up and crossing the floor before I could even move. She fetched the crock and set it on the table. None of us said a word as he tipped it to his mouth and drained the whole thing.

"They's a little something stronger if you want it," Larkin offered.

"Maybe after a while." He dropped his face into his hands and scrubbed as though trying to get the blood flowing. "We hightailed it out of there, heading hell-bent for the Walnut Gap. We crossed through picking our way by starlight since they weren't no moon to speak of. But, hell, we've hunted all through there so I knowed the placement of every rock and chug-hole. We got back to Shelton Laurel afore daylight, and you could hear hunting horns blowing all up and down the creek.

Pete signed. "I wished you could've seen the look on Mommie's face when I give her that salt and blankets and stuff," he said.

Here Pete was telling us this big tale and I was setting there having to swallow one big mouthful of hot water after another. Just at the mention of a damn sack of salt and I was almost drooling. That's what we had come to, friends. I had to make myself go back to listening.

"It snowed for three days and everybody stayed in. You folks got more than we did, I believe. Anyway day 'fore yesterday it turned off cold as hell, and the snow was really coming down good and hard so it was starting to pile up purty good. I was out hauling Mommie in some wood when I heard the horns blowing. I knowed they was bound to be trouble, and I reckon I ought to have left home right after we got back. But I was trying to help Mommie a little, you know what I mean? Since Daddy died she hadn't had really anybody but me and Edison.

"Word got passed along that it was Lawrence Allen's bunch. His blackguard cousin, that James Keith, had crossed over Sugar Loaf and was coming down the other side. All up and down the creek we hid out in the laurel hells. They was out in the open and started shooting blind. I thought fer a while that we was gonna run them out. Then they hit us with the cavalry, and it was just a matter of time afore we had to break and run. They weren't shooting blind no more, 'cause they shot and killed six of us. He rode out with a few of his men. The rest of them stayed on. At the time, we thought they was fixing to quit and go somewheres else. But that weren't what happened." He give a great heaving sigh. "I'll take some of that whiskey now, if you don't care, Lark."

He took a long long pull from the crock before he set it back down real careful-like. "You might want to take a drink. It ain't been pretty up to now and it's fixing to get worse." He looked at me, and what I saw on his face I hoped to never see again. "You might want these young'uns to go to bed, Arty."

And Carolina spoke up and said, "We ain't young'uns no more, Mommie."

I did not argue with her and let them stay.

Mary went to the sideboard to get cups and he waited till she was back in her place.

"Allen got back the next day. We knowed by then about his sick young'uns, and that his little girl had died. Some of our number had been took already. Morris Franklin, his brother Paul, and Mermon Shelton went to Marshall and give themselves up. They sent all of them on to Asheville. It were like Allen and Keith went crazy after that. They's going up and down the creek ordering people to tell them where we was. Why, they weren't about to tell Allen ner his men where we's hiding out. So Allen started whupping people, hanging 'em up by the neck till they turned blue and was almost dead, then they'd let them down and ask them again where we was. They whupped Mary Shelton acrost the back till it busted open."

"Lord have mercy." Mary whispered as she lifted the cup to her mouth.

Pete swung in Mary's direction. "Mercy?" he said and his voice was bitter as gall. "They was no mercy this day."

"They held Ott Tweed's girl, Hannah, down and—" he looked sideways at my girls. "She's about the same age as you, Abigail. They took turns at her.

"We followed 'em down the creek shooting at 'em, trying to kill as many as we could. But they was too many of them. By the time they caught me, Edison, and Little Johnny there at Paul's place, they had took ten other prisoners." He snorted. "Prisoners! They had old man Joe Woods, who was seventy year old if he was a day, and little David Shelton who was but a boy! They did have six er seven of us what was in Marshall that night. Rest of 'em, though, was innocent as Julie here. They made camp that night on Paul's place, and I told Edison and Little Johnny that I aimed to try to make a run for it. Now, they'd told us that evening afore they put us in Paul's shed that they's gonna take us into Asheville for a trial. But I saw the look in Allen's eyes that evening. They was red and flat as a snake's during dog days. Edison allowed as to how I'd get myself killed or maimed, and I told him I figured that was better than what Allen aimed to do to us."

I thought Pete was going to set into crying then, but he did not.

"I let on like I needed to go to the woods. Finally made such a ruckus that one of the soldiers let me out and took me to where the trees started at the edge of the barn lot. I squatted down like I aimed to take a shit and felt around under me till I found me a good-sized rock. Hit him in the head with it and run. I knew if I could make it up to the laurel thicket, they's no way they could catch me. Hell, they didn't even send nobody after me. I sneaked back about daylight and when they pulled out, me, John Kirk, and Hersh Cantrell counted thirteen prisoners. One of them had got away. I knew hit weren't Edison. I could see his red hair in amongst them that was being led off. We watched till they was gone and then there come Little Johnny sneaking out of that shed, purty as you please. I whistled and he come straight as a shot.

"We set out after Allen, keeping to the ridge. When they got down to the flats at Hickey's Fork, they stopped and Keith commenced to giving orders. We eased on down the mountain till we got to where we could hear him. Six of the fellers they had rounded up was jerked out into the open field and they commenced to beating them till they was all on their knees. Then Keith hollered for some of his crowd to shoot 'em. They was all right still and quiet. Then Keith hollered that if they didn't shoot, then they could join the prisoners. Old man Joe asked for time to pray if they were going to kill them. Then Keith dropped his sword and they fired. Killed five of 'em. And Edison." Pete swiped at his eyes. "Edison was begging fer them to let him go. That soldier raised his gun and shot him."

Pete reached for the crock but it was empty and he put it back down on the table. Larkin reached down beside his chair, brought up a full one, and handed it to Pete.

I knowed Abigail was crying before I even looked at her. Though she was just twelve, her and Edison had set together twice during church and we had all deviled her about it. He was the sweetest thing, and I was certain he would have been asking to walk out with Abby this coming summer. But that would never be now, and my heart just broke with the knowing of it. I reached out and took her hand in mine and was just about done in when I noticed it were as big as my own.

"Then they made the rest of them kneel down and shot them too. They gathered up and rode out then. Us there on the mountain didn't dare come off till the next morning. We loaded the dead on Nance Franklin's sled. Had a time digging the holes. The ground was like flintrock.

"After they was buried, I lit out. Struck out by myself. They won't catch me if I'm on my own."

Larkin got up and went over to the fire. He squatted down and laid on three logs and stirred up the red embers until flames caught the dry wood. Pete hunched forward and laced his fingers together on the table. "One of the reasons I stopped in here was to see if Hack was home." His voice seemed loud in the quiet room.

"No," Mary said. "He deserted from Allen's regiment back in September. We ain't heard nothing since. For all we know," she swallowed hard, "he might be dead."

"I don't reckon. Not unless he died in the last week." Pete said.

"You seen him?" me and Larkin said at the same time.

"Seen him? He was with us up till a week ago. He lit out right afore Allen and Keith showed up. I figured he was heading here." Pete rose from the table and stretched. "I'm going to sleep down in the hayloft, if you don't care. I won't sleep in the house. I'll be gone before you milk in the morning." He stopped at the door. "Thank you. I won't forget this."

"Larkin?" Mary whispered.

"I'll see what I can find out."

When Larkin come back in, all he told us was that Hackley had gone to Marshall with them and Pete hadn't seen him since. Something was just not right so I went to the barn before daylight the next morning to ask Pete myself, but he was already gone, and I never saw him again.

Later on that day, Larkin come by the house. "Hackley," he said, staring at the floor, "he's been laying out over on Shelton Laurel since September."

I did not even ask what the woman's name was. I did not want to know.

MARY WAS WORRIED TO death after that, and she was at my house more than she was at her own. Poor little thing. They was many a morning that she'd show up when I was milking the cows and she would be there when I went to milk that evening. She was still foolish over Pearl, and playing with her seemed to take her mind off her troubles.

My precious Pearl was truly a jewel. She was black-headed and black-eyed but did not have the dark skin like you might think she would. The only real pearl I had ever seen was the one that Wade Hensley had give to Vergie, and I swear to you that my Pearl's skin looked just as smooth and, well, pearly, I guess you would say. She had great big slanty eyes and little features like her daddy's people and was singing up a storm by then, even though it was all in baby talk and you could not understand a word she was saying. And she was not spoiled, though it would have been no fault of all of us. By all rights that young'un should have been rotten. She was a real friendly young'un, too, and never knowed a stranger. And Lord, she loved Mary and would go running to her the minute she saw her.

If I could have got my hands on Hackley I would have slapped him halfway to Sunday. Some men ain't worth killing, but I would have pure-D relished the chance to choke my brother senseless right about then. The least that man could have done was to have wrote to Mary and told her he was still among the land of the living. I was always watching for a line or two from Zeke, and bless him, he never let me to wonder long. I got many letters from him during that damn war and I still have every one of them today.

Mary got five letters from Hackley during that whole time.

Right after the killing over on Shelton Laurel, she asked me if it felt like to me that Hackley had just fell off the face of the earth.

She was a strong woman, Mary was. But even the strongest of us has to lay that heavy yoke down every now and again. I knowed beyond reason that she was having a struggle and comforted her the best I could, and I would have worried more about her if I had not knowed her people. They was a strong bunch of women that she was cut from. And she was young, and youth is a blessing when you are going through a hard patch. The very lack of having something to measure against can be a good thing. She would come every morning saying, "This will be the day I hear something," and when it was not she would say, "Well, mayhap tomorrow." Is that not the way of it? But she was awfully lonesome, too. And she'd had plenty of time laying with a man whose hands was not just able to bring pretty songs from a fiddle. She was missing that, just as I was and every other woman I knowed.

But the rest of us did not have a big strapping man around that looked at us with eyes as black as night and full of love. I think that had started to wear on her as much as anything.

Truth be known, it was right about this time that Mary began to harbor a different sort of affection for Larkin, too. But I, for one, knowed my brother would pop back up. And he did.

LARKIN COME TO ME late up in the evening and I knowed the minute I seen his face that something was wrong. I guess I was primed for bad news as I had got a letter from Zeke that day.

> I want you to rite to me as soon as you git this letter.
> Arty I saw you last nite very plain. O that it could
> hav been so this morning. Arty I think if I liv to git
> back we will liv and injoy ourselves better than ever.
> I will be of more use to you than ever before.

I cried my eyes out while I was writing him back. My heart was just broke. I did not have an inkling how in this world I was ever going to be able to live and stand it.

Larkin said he'd been down in the barn milking when the awfulest-looking man ever was had come up on him. Said he was nasty and had the worst smell about him you could ever wrap your nose around. I give a big sigh and said, "Where did you hide him?" because I knowed right then that my brother had come home to roost. Larkin did not even ask me how I knowed. He just said up in the cave and I said that was as good a place as any. I started gathering up quilts, an old coat of Zeke's, and snatched up what was left from supper to take up there. While I was putting it all in a sack, he said he'd had a time keeping Hack from going to the house to see Mary, but he had finally convinced him that it would put her in harm's way if she knowed where he was. I said, "Larkin, you must tell her." But I knowed he would not. He could not even look me in the eye when he muttered around saying how he would have to study about it, that he had to protect Mary.

Poor Larkin. He knowed when he told her it would take what little part of that girl he had managed to wrassle away for himself.

I cooked a little extra after that, and every evening Larkin would take it up on the mountain to my brother. And now Larkin had yet another burden to tote around on shoulders that was already plumb loaded down. It is a thousand wonders that that child did not go stark raving mad. But you know, maybe he did a little bit. And truth be told, I reckon it all probably drove Hackley mad, too. He was never one to be by himself and always wanted to be putting on a big show and having him a big time. He was lonesome up there and worried the hell out of Larkin wanting this, that, and the other. Poor old both of them, and me too, while I'm about it. I knowed it and could not tell a soul and I worried about Hack. In the bottom of my heart I knowed he would not stay hid for long. Everything Hackley wanted was just a stone's throw down the mountain. He said if the wind was blowing just right he could smell the smoke from his own chimney. But at least he was in out of the weather, and I sent all manner of stuff up there to make it more homey for him.

We had so much on our minds that we never give one thought as to what Mary might be thinking about Larkin disappearing for long periods of time. We was too caught up in trying to hide it from her to imagine where her mind might take her. She never so much as wondered that we was hiding Hackley. She just knowed that Larkin was gone a lot more than he used to be, and her mind went right where any woman's would. She decided all on her own that Larkin had him a sweetheart, and who do you think she imagined it to be? Why, of course she thought it was Maggie.

She told me years later that she would lay there in her bed pretending to be asleep with all sorts of things going through her head.

She said if Julie had not been laying right there beside her, they was no telling what she might of done and sometimes she just had to make herself keep from getting up and crossing that floor and laying down on the floor next to him. And one of the reasons she did not do this was because she thought he would have turned from her.

Now that was something that would never have happened. As bad as I hate to admit it, Larkin would have shucked Hackley's corn so quick it would've make your head spin, if only he'd knowed it could have been his for the shucking.

ONE EVENING IN MARCH me and the young'uns went over to Mary's and she fixed supper for all us. Larkin and Julie was both good hands at riddling and my Carolina was right in there with them. It felt good to be out of the house and I was laughing and carrying on too. It took me awhile to notice that Mary was looking at Larkin more often than not. Her eyes would sort of light on him and then go sliding off somewheres else. Then I caught her studying his hands with her whole heart in her face for all to see, and I thought to myself, *Oh, no.* For a woman that goes to studying a man's hands is thinking where she'd like for him to put them, and that is the gospel truth if it was ever told.

Right before we eat Mary got real snappish with Julie, which is no wonderment when you understand that there was a real easiness that had sprung up between her and Larkin. Mary straightened from the hearth where she'd just swung the great iron pot back over the fire, and I could tell by her tone that she was aggravated.

"Git the plates out, Julie. Larkin, strain the milk. I'm tired to the bone of having to do everything."

They was a look flew between Julie and Larkin that let me know this was no new thing. Julie hitched a little shrug and went to the sideboard for plates.

Larkin said in a real easy voice, "I strained the milk, Mary, and already carried it to the spring house 'cept for the crock over yonder that I left out for buttermilk."

Mary bent over the stewpot then, and I could tell she was already sorry for being so hateful. "Reckon I'm just tired of cold weather. Tired of eating the same thing night and day. I'm so sick of cornbread I could just spit!" She bunched up a handful of apron to lift the Dutch oven and carried it to the table.

Larkin smiled and his black eyes just danced over her. "This here is some of the best cornbread in the country."

She glanced at him, then shot a look at me, and her eyes was plumb naked.

That was a long supper. I set there the whole time watching her watch him and Julie watching them and it was just a mess, I'm telling you. I was wore to a frazzle when we left.

I reckon things would've still been all right if Lucindy hadn't sent for Julie a few weeks later. Andy was home with the bad dysentery and Julie had to go help take care of him. Mary come by the house and told me that Larkin was going to stay on. I made ready to tell her what I thought about that, but before I could get a single word out she said, "Now, don't start, Arty Wallin. I have already had it out with Julie and I ain't in no mood to get into it with you, too." I just looked at her. This was the first time Mary had straightened that little back at me, but I was not about to let that slow me down. "Well, you're going to have to hear me out anyways," I said. And she said right back, "I will tell you what I told Julie, then, and save you the breath." So I just held onto my tongue and heard *her* out.

She said they was out on the porch right before Julie left and they'd sort of got into it when Mary told Julie that Larkin was going to stay. Julie had grabbed her by the arm. "Don't do nothing foolish, sister," she said, "as you will live to regret it." As I say, they was no flies on that girl. Mary looked me right in the eyes then. "I have already done it in my heart a thousand times, Arty," she said. "In your heart is not the same as in the flesh, Mary," I said. She turned beet red but raised that chin at me. "He will stay," she said, and I answered her right back, "Then God help you, for you will need it."

And right then I figured God might not watch them two near close enough, so I appointed myself the guardian of them both and that was a very tiresome job.

NOT LONG AFTER THAT Hackley finally begged Larkin into bringing him his fiddle. I figure Larkin thought that would keep Hackley on that mountain, as he was in a constant state of threatening to come down. It did seem to pacify Hack for a while.

SO THAT IS HOW we passed the rest of the cold weather, and then came the greening up of spring. And the sap began to rise, if you know what I mean, and I was in and out of Mary's house or sending my young'uns by just every little whipstitch. I went at different times so they never knew when I was coming.

Mary come by the house one afternoon with her eyes big and round and a flush on her cheeks, and I thought I had not done my job well enough. But I put that thought to rest when she said, "Arty, let me tell you that I think I heard Hackley's fiddle when I was out in the yard today." My heart was in my mouth. I knowed exactly what had happened but could not say a word to her; I had promised Larkin I would not, and I was one to keep my promises. "Now, it could have been anybody, Mary," I said in as normal a voice as I could muster. She looked at me like I had gone lame in the head. "Why, it were the tune 'Elzig's Farewell,' Arty. Do you not think I would know his hands?" And I said to myself, *I reckon you would, honey.* But what I said to her was "Well, then, you should not be out traipsing around in the woods. You should tell Larkin."

And she hied out of there allowing she would do just that.

I studied and studied about all that until well after dark. I knowed there would be no sleep for me, as I had managed to work myself up into a state. I was resolved now that she should know that it was Hackley she'd heard and be damned the consequences. After Pearl went to sleep, I told Abigail I was going to Mary's and lit out.

And so it was that I caught them.

I was not thinking of anything like that romance business when I went across the porch and pushed on through the door. I reckon in normal times I would have howdied the house, but, like I said, I was not thinking. So I can only imagine what went through their minds when they finally come to know I was standing there in the room with them. I will not embarrass you with the details. But suffice to say I saw way more than a body should see concerning the private actions between a man and woman. You could have cut the air with a dull knife when we was all standing there looking at each other. Finally Larkin said, "Amma, we was just talking about Mary thinking she'd heard Hackley playing the fiddle today." And I said, "Larkin, what you was doing was not talking," and he shut his mouth. Then Mary's chin come up and mine come out and before she could say a word that would cause hard feelings between us, I said, "Get your coat, Mary. We're going up on the mountain and you'll be there all night."

I did not even look at Larkin. He'd had all the say about this I was going to let him have.

NOW WE HAD SOME big troubles, because Mary was not the only one that had heard Hackley playing his damned fiddle, and they was folks there that was not lovers of our people. We hid him in the root cellar under the house that Larkin had dug out months ago. But after the Home Guard set fire to Granny Nance Franklin's house and it burned down on top of her three boys, we moved him out from under there. She was another one that lost every last one of her boys in that damn war, but that did not stop her from leading a Yankee charge against some Rebs one time. She was so wadded up in it that she screamed out, "Raise your fire, boys, you're hitting them in the heels."

We spent the better part of a rainy day cutting our way back into a laurel hell on the backside of Picked Shirt Mountain. That's where Hackley got to live now, and though he commenced to whining and taking on, I told him he could just dry it up. This was the best we could do right now and he might as well hurry and come of it. There would be no more foolishness now that Arty Wallin was in charge. I took the damn fiddle home with me.

But I had the awfulest feeling that seeds had been sowed and I knowed we always got to reap what we sowed, even if the harvest proved bitter.

IT WAS THE FIRST of June when I caught Mary hanging onto the porch railing waiting for the dizziness to leave her. I had suspected it and now I knew. "How long have you been breeding, honey," I said, and she said she was three weeks past her bleeding time. She must've thought she seen something in my face that was not there, because she said then, "It is nobody else's but your brother's child, Arty." I looked at her with my kindest face on. "I would never have thought anything else," I said, "and I would dare anybody to say different." "Have you told him?" I asked. "No, I have not yet, but I will as soon as he gets back to the house," she said, and then she leaned over and throwed up. I helped her back in the house and she stretched out on the bed.

It hit me as I was going home that she had meant Larkin.

WELL, LARKIN ALREADY KNEW. He'd seen me too many times not to recognize the early shine that came from the inside-out of a breeding woman. He told me later that he'd watched with a jealous heart her holding her secret close. She went about fairly skipping through those early weeks. He'd seen her lay her hand on her belly and the look that took hold of her when she did it. He'd been short and hateful with her and then immediately sorry. He couldn't stand the thought that he might have hurt her. But it was him that was hurt when he realized that his words hadn't even reached her at all. She'd never even noticed them, just as she never seemed to notice him any more.

IT WAS WHEN HE'D taken the June apples I'd poked up for Hackley that they got into it.

It had rained for a solid week, and Hack was grumpy and mean as a copperhead. Larkin had stuck around trying to cheer him up, and the talk got around to where it always wound up. Hackley wanted to see Mary as he had not seen her since she'd sneaked up there to tell him she was in the family way. Larkin said he was trying to be patient and had reminded him that he could not bring her up there again and that he could not come off the mountain since the Home Guard was all over the place now. That was when Hackley shot him this little look. "What was that look about?" Larkin said. "What look?" Hackley said, and Larkin said he knowed the answer before he asked. "Have you been off the mountain?" "Once't or twice't," he said and then, "Well, I didn't get caught." Larkin said he flew mad as hell and could barely talk. "Jesus, Hackley. Where did you go? Did anybody see you?" And Hackley could not keep the bragging from his voice: "A week ago I really made the rounds. I stopped in and saw Corrie. Then on to Dovie's. I was back here long before any rooster in Sodom crowed. Had me a time. The way they both carried on over me, you could sure tell they was glad to see me." If that was not enough, he really capped the stack with what he said to Larkin next, and he looked for all the world like a little sulled-up boy when he was saying it. "Didn't have near as much luck last night when I went to Maggie's. Somebody was already there."

"You went to Maggie's?"

"Yeah. I was really wanting to see her. Couldn't believe it when I saw the horse."

Larkin said he hit him the first time before he could catch himself. He said the second time was well planned though, and he knocked Hackley ass over apple cart down the bank.

When I went up later to see about him, Hackley was laughing about it and said when Larkin hit him, he thought the stars had come out and went to dancing all about in his head. I told him if he ever come off that mountain again, I would turn him in to the Home Guard myself. He studied me for a long time and then said "Oh, you would not do that, sister girly" and I said "Do not try me, brother boyo, for I will do as I say." He studied me a little while longer and then said, "I need you to find out where Kirk is, as I aim to join up with him as soon as Larkin turns eighteen." I left there having promised him I would find Kirk if I had to run him to ground myself for he was right. Larkin had to go somewhere and better with the Union than slinking around trying to dodge the Home Guard.

Now there was a character just made for this fine big war they was having. I had seen him once and had heard all about George Washington Kirk from Mommie's cousin Davina. Me and him was about the same age, too. He had a long and lanky frame and had a big mustache that drooped over a broad mouth with red lips. He was a good-looking sort of man and might have been called a handsome man, were it not for his eyes.

Davina said his mommie had been run from the woodpile by a panther when she was three months along with him. When he was born she went over him with a fine-toothed comb looking for any sign that he had been marked. She found nothing until his eyes started to change. I know just what she meant by that. I swear that man's eyes was the same exact tannish color as one of them big cats, and they give me a bad case of the all-overs when they settled on me that day.

But eyes or no eyes, I meant to find him. And find him I did. I set up for him to meet Hackley and Larkin there at my house the day of Larkin's birthday. They was no sense in putting it off no longer and, to be honest with you, I was just about sick of them two boys. They needed to go on.

I was not as certain of this when we were all ganged up there at the house the day they left. Mary looked pitiful standing there with her little belly just beginning to show. The night before, we had carried most of her stuff to my house, and she was going to stay with us until this damn war sorted itself and Hackley come home. That was hard on her, I know but they was really nothing else she could do except to go back to Lucindy's. As I told her when I offered at least she would be with Pearl. That seemed to bring her along as much as anything else. Hackley just loved on me and thanked me. Bless his heart. I reckon it was as Mary said, all their married life had been was one parting after another. And I allowed as how this must be some fine war that you could fight on one side for a while and get tired of that, and go to fighting on the other side. I must admit to harboring very bitter feelings. I had not seen my man in over two years; he had never seen Pearl, and she was a big girl already. Little did I know that it would be two more years before I would see his dear face. And that would prove the longest four years that would ever roll over my head.

Larkin was staring and staring at Mary and I wanted to cap my apron over my head so I would not see it. Or mayhap over his, so nobody else would see it. Finally I could not stand it no more so I went and put my arms around him, and the minute I did that he was my baby again. Some things is meant to always be, and that is one of them. I started to cry and then all my young'uns started to howl and Mary was sobbing, and we just had us a regular call to the altar right there in front of my house. I swear, sometimes I get so tired of being from a family what cannot control their feelings. At times I wish we could be more like them folks what never acts raw and what keeps their feelings all iced up. But that is like wishing to have the moon on your porch, which is not possible, so there we was running about like the crazy bunch that we was.

Finally Hackley had had enough and he hollered out, "For the love of God, hush up," and we did, but the reason we did was because we was all wore out by now. "We've got to go," he said, and he looked right at me. Well, that let me know who he was leaving to see to things, as if they was ever any doubt. I went to Mary then and stood right beside her while Hackley kissed her one last time. So I had to stand there and watch Larkin wanting to kiss her, too, and thinking he might just be bold enough to do it. Well, thank God for Carolina, is all I can say. She picked that minute to throw herself right at Larkin's head. I've never in my life seen such a thing and by the time I got her off him we was all laughing, and she was acting like they was in some play or something throwing her arm up against her head and allowing how she felt faint. What a card that young'un could be.

So what could have been a bad and trying thing turned out to be just a look between them. But, oh, what a look it was. They was more said in that little space of silence than if they'd mouthed a thousand words.

But when he turned that horse he did not look back.

13

I AM A KEEPER OF all manner of tales. I sometimes get tales all mixed up in my head, and they is things that I cannot for the life of me separate out and determine if they are my memories or things that have been told to me. I reckon that is a part of getting to be old. But the one thing that I did and am proud that I did it is I kept letters that folks sent to me during the wartime. And lo and behold, when Larkin come back, he come wagging home with him every letter him and Hackley got as well. So here is some of that what was sent and what I wrote myself. They are yours for the reading, and all I can say is that here is Arty laid out for all the world to view.

October 19, 1863
Dear Larkin,

It is with pleasur I am permitted this good sabbath evening to drop you a few lines to let you know that I got your last two letters on the same day which was yesterday and am pleased to hear that you are dooing well and that the army lif is not treating you vary badly. Tell my brother that I am sending him a howdey too and that he needs to rite his wif. She looks in vain for a letter every day. Tell him it would ease her mind if that means anything to him which it mite but I do not no that for sure. She is getting big now and is glad that the heat has laid oer for the cool of fall. And the colors are coming on now as I no they are there as well. You said you was in east Tennessee up around Kingsport. That seems a long way off. Does it look much like around here? When you rite me back let me know as I am curius as always about such things.

You will never guess who I seed yesterdy. I spent some time with Silas McMahan. You will not believe me when I tell you that he has been walking out with Maggie or mayhap you would believe it too for you no her as good as I do. She allows that she might even be for lovin him which is hard for me to believe.

Listen was you with Mr. Kirk when he was down to Warm Springs? We hearn he was down that way and camped out on the yard at the hotel with 800 or mor men. They said that was a sight to see. It was in the newspaper too how they was a fight with a bunch of Rebels and that Nick Woodfins brother was killed. I find it an amazement that we have took to calling one side Yanks and the other Rebels. This is as good as any I would reckon excep I might say Windbags and Bellows. I have heard from Zeke and he says they are coming down to Tennessee and that he will try to look you up and maybe even come home for a day. Oh to be able to see him again would be like a soothing salve to my sore eyes. And he longs to eyeball the younguns. Ever letter I git expresses that longing and it braks my heart every time.

Vergie has left this part of the world. She has scooted down to Hendersonville where Wades people is all frum. She has took all her young'uns and left everything for Maggie to have. I reckon that makes Miss Maggie a woman of some means and what would be called a good catch. This war has changed the face of us all has it not?

You are a sweet thing indeed to ask me about the younguns. They are all dooing well and growing like you would not believe. Pearl is talking up a storm now and sometimes I catch myself wishing this was not so. She wants to know about everthing and I do not no about some of which she asks me. I have no idee why it is that the sky is blue and so on. She gets mad when I can not answer her. Me and Mary just can not help but laf at her. Mayhap she is just like her Mommie. Carolina is getting to be a great big girl and is pretty as a picture. She says to tell you a big howdee. Mary is five months gone now and with her small frame she looks like she might have swallered a big punkin. I told her what you said and she said to tell you that you was full of squash and beans. You are rite to say she is a funny thing. She is every bit of that.

I would be vary glad to see you too honey. May it not be long before this is so. Keep yur hind end close to the ground Larkin.

Your loving Amma

October 27, 1863
Dear Amma,

I received your kind letter that was wrot me on the 19 October. You are good to writ me to tell me that all is well with you all. Things are just the same hear as they was befor. I hav

just returnd frum a frolik where Hackley played with some mu-
siciners frum up in Kantucky. Them boys nos their way around
a fiddle almost as good as Hackley and for the furst time our
Hack is struglin to keep all atention on hisself. Not realy as all
he has to do is comence to singing and they all step back. They
was no women folk at this frolik and some of us made out as
girls. It was a big time and I do not no that I hav had such a big
time since I left home. You would hav busted a gut laughin no
doubt and might yet when you think of me as a vary big and
vary ugle girl.

They jus come by and tol our regmant to cook 3 days rash-
ings and be redy to march of at a minets warning. I no this mite
cause worry to you and Mary but it is not so with us. It is the
setin around that gits our goat.

Amma I must come to a clos. I will rite you more at a later
day. Kiss the young'uns for me and give Mary a howdee. I tol
her man he shud writ to her but have seed no sines of him dooing it yit.

Love to you Amma

Larkin

It looks the same here in one way but is diferent as well. The
water is no count. I kep my tail always on the ground.

November the 22, 1863
Dear Larkin,

I am sendin this pair of britches that I made for you. I do not
no if they will fit you in the lenth but I made them long and you
can cut them off to wher they will fit beter. Do as you will with
them. Tell Hackley that he has never seed no happyer somebody

than his little wif when she got his leter last week and bles her hart she has gon into a fit of riting him back.

I am riting this in a hury as I want to send it back by Roderick as he is comin your way. I am sendin some cake as well and hope you injoy it.

Thank you for the money. Me and Mary put what you sent and what Hackley sent and bout some chickins. It was more money than ether one of us had ever seed. We fed that pore creature what fetched it to us. To see him pored the worrys over me and her both. He was sick unto death Larkin. Rite and tell me that neither you nor my brother suffers sech a way. Tell Hackley to rite Mary and ease her mind.

I love you my bigest boy. The young'uns are dooing fine as are we all. Zeke said to tell you he was back north and would not see you. He did not git home neither and I was not a bit happy with that. Keep yur hind end low to the ground.

                    Amma

December 28, 1863
Dear Amma,

It is with pleasure that I find the opportunity to rite a few lines to let you know I did get the cake you sent to me and tho it were mushed up it were like nectar from heaven. Thank you for figerin out a way to git it to me. I was one happy big old boy. I sliped off to eat it and wood not even let Hackley have a bit and he cussed a black streak at me but I did not care and told him as much. I am sendin you mor money and want you to use it however is best for you and the younguns. If Mary needs it give sum to her and do not fret that I do not have what I need.

They take good care of us hear and I just got me a fine big coat. Colonel Kirk has picked me to be one of his hawkeyes which is just a sharp shooter but they hav to name everthing hear so hawkeye is what I am. They hav give me a vary fine rifle and I am larning the use of it real quik.

We hav been in a few fights but none that was vary bad. One thing I can say about Colonel Kirk is that he is vary good at fighting and his men all thinks that the sun rises and sets on his head. Another thing I can say is he is one to always think of his men and that is why he is so well thot of I am sure.

Tell Mary that her man is not a easy one to liv with. He will not keep his side of the tent neat and tidy. He needs her hear to look about him. I could stand a peek at her face as well.

It was a blesed shame to hear that Roderick has been kilt. He was a good person and I will never forget how he fetched me that cake. It is soon to be a new year Amma. Let us hop this hear war will not carry over much into the year of '64.

I remain one that loves you
Larkin

January the 18, 1864
Dearest Larkin,

It is with a hevy hart that I put down these words to you. They is no way to say them that will ease the telling so I will just say it. Fee was kilt by soljers yesterdy. I know how you felt him to be your frend and I wisht I cud say hit were a quik death fer him but we know hit were not. As I told you when last I rote to you he was keerin for the horses for Lawrence Allen dam him fer his black hart over in Warm Springs. You know how good he alus was with critters. He had come home fer a few days and when he was goin back he was set on by some Yanke soljers and they kilt him. Know that I lov you and I pray for you ever day and nite.

Your lovin Amma

It was the deepest part of the winter and John Wesley had gone out hunting and bagged a big mess of squirrels. Julie had come by and was going to stay the night with us and while the stew was cooking me, her, and Mary was setting around the table talking. I knowed Mary was in a state of pure-D misery. Her ankles and fingers was all swollen and the baby had dropped over a week ago. I had tried to offer her a little hope that it would not be much longer and knew this to be so. I had been that way myself many times and knowed just how she felt.

I fed my crowd and Mary just picked at her plate and said she was not hungry. Abigail and Julie was washing the dishes when I heard what sounded like somebody sneaking about on the porch. I reached for the cap-and-ball pistol Zeke had given me and turned toward the door just as the latch went to easing up. You can just imagine my surprise when the smoke cleared and there stood my brother looking back at me.

"Damn, sister girly. You come near to blowing my brains out."

Mary was off that bench like she'd been what was shot out of that gun.

And then Larkin come through that door and it was a race between me, Julie, and Carolina to see who could get to him first.

They was followed by a little slight man that at first I did not recognize. And then Julie hollered out "Daddy!" and my mouth hung open like a gate.

It was indeed Andrew Chandler. Now, I could not help myself, so I had to say it. "How come you all decked out in Union duds, Andrew? I thought you was took prisoner over at Strawberry Plains."

"I was but when Hackley got wind of it him and Larkin come and busted me out. I'm riding with Kirk now."

See, that is what I mean about this funny man-fighting-at-a-war thing. It seems not so much to matter which side you tote a gun for, as long as killing somebody is your intent. I said as much to them three.

"It don't matter no more, Amma," Larkin said, and he sounded so tired it broke my heart. "We just want this war over."

And I said *amen* to that and then Mary went to running back and forth setting the table and her cheeks was so flushed that she did not even look like the same girl as what had been setting at my table a little bit ago. I was not the only one watching her, neither. Larkin's black eyes followed her every step she made. *Can it be that the rest of them will finally see what is right before them?*, I thought to myself. I sneaked a peek at Hackley and he was talking to Abigail without a care in this world and had no notion whatsoever of how Larkin was watching his wife. And Julie was watching Larkin. So once again it was left to me to watch everybody watching everybody else until my eyes felt like they was run out on stems.

They was one curious thing that happened that night. Julie was washing up the last of their dishes and Larkin moved to help her. Hackley and Mary had left for their house, and Andrew had hied it for his own bed. I was laying on the bed with Pearl and had been there long enough until they probably thought I was asleep.

"How are you, Julie girl?" Larkin said.

This was said with such a tenderness that it sounded as though he was talking to a lover, so I eased my eyes open to little slits and peeped out at them. I know this was not right and though I am not proud of it, I could not help myself.

He was holding her hands and I watched as he run his hands up her arms to cup her elbows. Now I must ask you, does that not make you think they was things between them that neither had shared with me?

But this is what she said to him and her voice was low and hot as fire. "How can it be, Larkin, that you can look at me so sweet like, with your face as still as a deep hole of water? And then you turn them black eyes on my sister and it's like the same deep hole but with a fast current running right below the surface." When he did not answer her, she turned from him and went back to washing the dishes.

HACKLEY WAS STILL THERE when his son was born two weeks later, on February fourteenth. The day was warm and clear and was the perfect false spring day bearing the promise of what was to come.

Larkin come for me early that morning. It was a quick birth and over in almost no time. Up that evening I went with Larkin to milk and leaned against the side of the stall while he done the work. I was in no hurry to get home and knew Abigail and Julie would see to things just fine. The dim light of the barn was a pleasing change to how close it had been in the cabin. I shut my eyes and breathed in deep, fetching in the familiar odors of fresh milk and sweet hay. I could not help it; I grinned great big as I was right proud of myself. I'd had myself a good day's work and brought my first baby all by myself. Mary had offered herself right over and done everything I told her to do. And the baby had been fit and sound. And if the amount of liquor consumed after a birth said they was a proud papa around, then Hackley was near to busting with his son. As me and Larkin left for the barn, Hackley, Mary, and Hack Jr. had all three been piled up sound asleep in the same bed. Now in the barn, I opened my eyes and as soon as I could see good, I went to studying Larkin. His shoulders and back was even broader, and big ropey muscles rolled around in his arms while he milked. His hair was longer and I liked it better that way. There was no doubt about it, my biggest boy had growed into a handsome man.

"You thinking to draw a picture of me?" he asked.

"Do what?"

"Well, the way you're studying me I figured you was aiming to draw yourself a picture."

"No, you mister smart britches. I don't aim to draw your picture. But you keep up that smart-mouthing your Amma, and I might just turn you across my lap and give you a good whupping like I used to have to do. I was just noticing how you'd filled out since you left. They must be feeding ye pretty good."

"That's the truth. Hack and Andrew both said that's probably the main reason that the Union is winning the war."

"Are they, Larkin?"

"That's what Kirk says." He went back to milking. "Now, there's a strange feller."

"That's what you have said."

The milk hissed as it hit the side of the bucket. "All us boys likes him. He's got a way about him that you can't help but like. But when he's out raiding or we're fighting, they's a mean streak that shows itself."

"That is nothing new as I have noticed that most men has got a mean streak in them."

"You'll get no argument from me about that. I've seen it. But they's a difference in Kirk. Back in the fall we's farther west of here over toward Waynesville. We'd raided a little, set fire to a barn or two, and we happened onto this feller out in the field. Looked like he aimed to plow, though I can't see how he aimed to do any plowing. His coat sleeve was pinned up where he'd lost a arm. Kirk and a bunch of us rode up to him. Kirk drawed his gun and leveled it at this feller, and said, 'Sir, you're wearing the wrong color coat.' That was all he said 'fore he shot him right between the eyes. Killed him right then and there."

"Because of the color of his coat?"

"He's wearing a ragtag Confederate coat more holey than it was righteous."

"And nobody said nothing?"

Larkin shook his head. "That's one of the things ye learn early on, Amma. You don't say nary a word unless you're asked to."

"Sounds like the man ain't got no soul. Or the one he's got is black as pitch."

Larkin rose from the stool, picking up the bucket as he straightened. "Well, I don't reckon I've been called to preach, so I won't concern myself with his soul. I just do what he tells me to do." He gave a shrug and the corners of his mouth lifted in the saddest of little old smiles. "But, you know, I don't reckon Kirk's done no worse than what happened over the ridge in Shelton Laurel. Any way you cut this pie, it's a rotten thing."

"I have no love for neither side, Larkin, so you are preaching to the done saved." Of a sudden the good feelings of a while ago fled from me, and I recalled how I had been like a worm in a hot skillet waiting for him to ask me about Fee, but he had never done it. I knowed now was the time but I stayed propped against the door frame and he stood there with the full bucket in his hand. The wind picked up and set the empty limbs to rattling against the sides of the barn. Off in the distance, a dog went *bark bark bark* and then was quiet. My next words rode out on a big sigh. "For God's sake, Larkin. Ask me about it for you have got to want to know."

And he sighed right back and said, "I'll get that bottle I got hid in the other stall that I been saving for when I felt like I could stand to hear it. Then I'll ask about it."

We settled down in the fine dirt of the barn and leaned back against the logs. He took the cork from the narrow neck of the bottle and passed it right over to me. I took a long and slow drink, and it set me on fire as it went down in my gullet. I shuddered and wiped my mouth with my coat sleeve before handing it back to him.

"Not near as smooth going down as Sol's liquor," I said to him, and it were the truth.

"Ain't found none nowhere like Sol's." He offered me the bottle of amberish-colored liquor again. "Some of them boys from Tennessee give it to me. It surely ain't white liquor. They called it sour mash. Once't you get used to it, it ain't too bad. Hackley loves it."

"How's Hack managing?" I took a smaller drink and could not help but shudder again.

Larkin's shoulders hitched up and down in a so-so shrug. "You know Hack. Right off he found some fellers that played music. Laughs and cuts up a lot. Goes about singing purty much all the time. Everbody really likes him."

"How's it for you, Amma?" he asked, and I knowed he was just stalling me for time, but I answered him anyways.

"It's just as well that I ain't never hungry, seeing as how they ain't nothing much to eat." I wrapped my fingers around the bottle, taking note of how skinny they was. "The children is hungry all the time, though. I swear I believe we'd have starved if it hadn't been for you and Zeke sending us money." I knew right then that this liquor had a big kick to it and was already loosening up my jaw, so I got a big grip on it, as I did not want to worry him. "Most of the time I do just fine. Other times I miss Zeke, but sometimes I dread him coming back." I could not believe I had said that but it were the truth if I'd ever told it. See, I was no longer scared of nothing and had got to be tough as an old pine knot. I did not know if my dear sweetheart would like this whet-leather version of Arty or not. I was not ready to talk to any-body about this so I reached for Larkin's hand, and when I had it in mine I said, "Let me tell you about Fee."

He took another long drink, set the bottle between his feet and then he said, "Tell me, then."

My body sagged over against his and I closed my eyes like I was fixing to sing a love song. But this story would be far different than any song he'd ever learned. This one was hung with Fee's broad coun-tenance and big sloping shoulders and gentle hands. This all went flashing through my mind so clear that tears puddled in my eyes and run down my cheeks.

"Everybody just knew that Fee wouldn't stay in the army and would prob'ly light out for home first chance he got. Well, we was all wrong, Larkin. Allen put him to tending horses down at the training camp at Warm Springs. I reckon you already knowed that, didn't you?"

He squeezed my hand and said, "Just tell me, Amma."

I squeezed back. "All right, honey."

"He had been home for a spell but I'd only seen him once't. He come by the house to see if I needed wood cut. He cut down a poplar tree at the edge of the garden and split it up for me. Took him all day and I fed him dinner and supper. He said he had to be gitting back to Warm Springs and figured to head out the next morning. I offered to let him stay at the house with all of us, but he turned me down. Last I saw of him was when he give a sharp whistle and Old White come from behind the house and down the road they went. He must've changed his mind about going back the next day or he might've just been out in the woods. You know how he'd wander about in the woods of a full moon. It were just two or three nights shy of being full.

"Marian Franklin found him next day. He was coming up from the Seward Hole and Old White barred the path barking and just carrying on. Led him right to where whoever'd killed Fee had kicked some leaves and dirt over him. Jim Leake said he'd heard a commotion out in the road in front of the house that same night and, thinking somebody might be aiming to break in the store, he'd went out just in time to see some men in Union blue ride by. We figure they's the ones what killed him. A bunch of us went down and buried him, Larkin. Lucindy said we ought to move him and bury him next to his mama, but Hoy McIntosh allowed as to how Fee would've wanted to be buried where he was. Said he always loved that part of the country so we just dug a grave and left him be. It is awful purty over there in the Gudger Tract. You can see the creek from where we buried him."

"Was he shot up, Amma? You said in your letter that he suffered."

I could have kicked myself right then and there, and my voice was sharp when I said, "I never should've wrote nothing more than that he'd been killed, Larkin. Some things is better left not said. They's nothing none of us can do about it now, anyways."

"Tell me," was all he said, but it made me mad the same as if he'd made a big speech. I jerked my hand away from him. "Why?" I said. "Ain't you seen enough of what men are doing to one another in this damn war to know? Do you need it lined out for you like a song?"

"That's why I'm asking, Amma. What I've seen . . ." and his voice died off here. I knowed he was recalling things what was too awful for me to know and I did not want to leave him conjuring about this for another minute, so I took up his hand again and locked my palm with his.

"His knee-caps was blowed off. And somebody had cut off one of his ears as clean as a whistle. You know well as me he'd have fought them to the end. They was sixteen bullet holes in him that we could count."

Neither one of us spoke for a long time. Larkin was still as the grave.

"Which ear?"

"What?" I said, though I could not believe he'd asked me that.

"Which ear was gone?"

"The left one."

Larkin nodded and then said nothing more.

"Why'd you want to know that?"

"Because you just told me who done it, Amma." He got up before I could say anything else and offered me his hand. "Let's git on back to the house. They'll maybe be awake by now and all."

When I got up blood and that damn sour mash rushed up to my head, and I was swaying like a young tree in a great wind. I grabbed hold of his arm to steady myself. And then it come over me and I could not stop myself. My fingers was like claws digging into his arm. "How much longer will this last, Larkin?"

"What? The killing?"

"You said a while ago that the Union is winning. So I'm asking, how much longer will it go on?" I shook his arm like a dog worrying a bone. "The war?"

"Hackley says only God knows, and He ain't telling."

I give a mighty snort and almost laughed at how much I sounded like Granny. "Don't you stand too close to him. He's liable to get struck by lightning right in the top of the head."

He laughed out loud and I knowed his thoughts had turned to her too. "Remember when we's little and we'd get scared when it would come one of them big thunderstorms?"

"And Granny would take us out on the porch and tell us not to be afraid. That God was just loading his taters on his wagon and the racket was them hitting the wagon bed." I busted out laughing, and things was of a sudden easy and light with us again. "I ain't a bit afraid of storms. I love them. Makes me feel all wild inside." My words was coming slow and slurry like, and I knowed I was pert near drunk. "Sort of like this sour mash has made me feel." I poked Larkin with my elbow and handed the drained bottle back to him. "A thunderstorm in a bottle."

He laughed at me and said, "Let's go and we'll see to rustling up something to eat." He took the bucket and we stepped out into a fog that had rolled in while we was milking.

We had only taken a step or two. "Look at it, Larkin," I said.

"What, Amma?"

I breathed out into the fog and my breath hung in the air right there in front of my face. "Walk on ahead of me. I want to see something."

He walked on slow out in front of me.

"That's the prettiest thing I believe I've ever seed in nature," I could only whisper because it was just that and I wanted him to see it too. "Stand still honey, and watch what happens when I pass you."

The fog just draped itself on me as I moved, frothing my hair and brows with silver, and the ice crystals in the fog parted as I moved through and left my shape behind me. It looked like I'd walked through a tunnel until it filled itself back in.

When he come to stand beside me, I leaned my shoulder into him and sighed. We stood that a way for a while.

"It held for a long time, didn't it?" he said.

"Maybe that's what living is like," I said. "Maybe Fee just moved on through and left his shape." I knowed my voice was sad but could not help it, as that is how I felt.

He never said nothing else and we went toward the house. I looked behind us and saw our shapes leaving a trail that slowly faded away.

I HAD HOPED TO my never that Hackley would straighten up now that he had a son. And he did for a little while. He behaved for a little over a week and was the perfect picture of what a good husband ought to be, but it did not last. He would just up and be out of pocket for hours at a time, and he wore his secrets like a set of loose clothes. Now you might ask me why he would be any such a way, and the only thing I can say to you is just what I had said a long time ago to Mary. Some men is just runners of women. My brother was just a runner of women, and that is all there is to say about it, really. I will have to say here that I do not understand this, as I have caught many babies in my lifetime and all of the equipment looks pretty much the same to me.

Larkin was staying pretty much with us, and it was from him that

I heard about Hackley going by Maggie's and that she'd run him off. "Well, go it, Maggie," I said. He allowed as how he'd told her them very words. He said that Hackley had let on to Maggie that he did not know about Silas being her feller. I said, "That's a damn lie, because I told him so." We both shook our heads at that. I asked him how our Maggie was getting on and Larkin said she looked really good. When I shot him a look, he grinned. "Oh, no, it were nothing like that," he said. "She let me know right off that she was very happy with Silas." Larkin got real quiet after that, and it was like I could see right into his head and read his mind. I said, "You cannot take it upon yourself to tell Mary, honey," and he got up real quick and said he knowed all about that. As he was leaving he looked at me and said something I have never forgot to this day, nor the look on his face when he said it. "Why don't you tell her, Amma?" And then he was out the door and gone.

In March, Zeke's brother Hugh come home to see his brand-new son. Rosa had not had an easy time and I was glad that he was able to come, though I was jealous too. This would be his second time home since they'd left. He come by the house to tell me Zeke was well and fit over at Strawberry Plains and it tore me all to pieces to think of my sweetheart just across the ridge. Hugh had rode the last few miles dozing in the saddle but I could tell he was wide awake now. He was all for beating a path home. He grinned when I told him this one had come a boy and allowed how Rosa had probably had a fit since she'd wanted a girly-child so bad. I told her she'd just have to use the name she'd picked out for it, which was Cora June, the next time around. This one he'd name Douglas Eugene and call him Doug. We spoke of his other boys. Regular stair-steps they was too, Bose,

Mitch, Tom, and Jess. He made for the door then, and I let him go. But I watched his horse plumb out of sight, because from the back he surely looked like my man Zeke. It would have give me great satisfaction to have seen his dear face right then.

THE NEXT MORNING HUGH had got up just at daylight and headed for the spring. Hugh and Rosa had one of the sweetest springs in this part of the world, and they both took great care to keep it cleaned out. I know exactly what he did that morning because I'd seen him do it myself a hundred times before. He would have splashed some of the icy water on his face and cupped some water to his mouth to drink. That water was so cold it would make your teeth ache plumb to the bone. Then he would have just set back and looked out down the valley and been quiet for a little while. That's what all of them did that come from the war, all of them craved the quiet. The one thing they all said they hated most about the war was the loudness of it. Rosa said he was gone for a long time, and she finally had to send Bose for him. He'd come back all sheepish and she could tell he'd dozed off. And that was why he'd not seen the blackguard that was his brother Shadrack slinking about up on the ridge.

Hugh's brother Shadrack was not even supposed to be home. He'd left Asheville the morning before with orders from Silas McMahan to ride straight downriver to Marshall, and it were only by chance that he'd decided to take the long way around and come through Sodom. And it were only by chance that Tildy had mentioned their cow had found a calf somewhere up on the ridge, and he'd gone to look for it. But he had not found no calf. He'd found Hugh instead. Shadrack rode hard as he could go until he got to the Confederate encampment at Warm Springs, where he told upon Hugh, and they sent out some men to get him. Cassie Leake watched them go by, and when they took the right fork in the road she run to the barn calling for her boy as she went. Jimmy beat them up there, too. Hugh run out the back of the house and headed up the patch of new ground. Poor old thing had grubbed the day before clearing roots as big as his arm out of the rich dirt, and now the field offered nothing to hide or shield him from the Rebels what was coming up the road. They was already so close he could hear their horses. Rosa said he was running hell bent for leather and she saw him raise his eyes toward the trees at the edge of the clearing. She said it was funny how she'd thought earlier that the clearing was so small, and she'd aimed to ask him to clear more of it off before he left. Now she said it seemed as wide as a mile.

They were shooting at him now and he went to zigging back and forth with his eyes fastened on them trees. Rosa said bullets was hitting all about him, jerking up big clods of dirt. Hope rose in her as she realized he was going to make the trees. Just another three or four strides and he'd be there. She strained forward herself willing him on. A flash of blue caught her eye and her heart almost stopped. It was Jess! Right there straight in front of him was their boy Jess.

And she'd screamed out at him and he'd faltered, then turned and run back out into the field they'd shot him down.

THAT NIGHT HACKLEY, LARKIN, and Andrew rode out heading back to Tennessee.

IT WAS LATER THAT month that I got a letter from Larkin that ended like this:

They was a man here what had a necklace of ears that was found stabbed in his guts. He died yesterdy and was

carryin on in the awfulest way about the Pharaoh of
Egypt. Is it not funy what comes to us at the time we are
leeving this old world?

> Your bigest boy,
> Larkin

I tore off that part of the letter and buried it next to Fee's grave.
In my way of figuring, that's right where it needed to be.

14

FINALLY WE GOT US a good spring. That year of '64 they was no rain that would not stop, and I did not have to worry about one of them bust-outs happening to us. We got the corn in and we moved the garden far from the house so the soldiers could not just ride by and take it. If they got it now, they would have to work a little for it. But I will tell you I did not aim for them to get so much as one ear of my corn. I would kill them for it now as my ten-percenting days was long past.

Hack Jr. was one of the prettiest babies I had ever seen. His hair was so blond it looked white and he had Hackley's blue eyes. He was the smilingest little thing too. I reckon he looked plime-blank like his daddy, and Mary was a big fool over him. Pearl was as jealous as she could be, and we had to watch her like a hawk because I was afraid she would hurt him somehow. Mary had took to staying during the day some at her own house. I could understand that. She had her own baby now and wanted to be home, though she always come back with us around suppertime and slept with us.

I had waited till the dew had dried off of the bean patch that day in late June, and as I was picking my mouth was watering. I was not thinking about a thing other than that big mess of beans I was going to be fixing for dinner, when of a sudden all the hair on the back of my neck stood up and I raised my eyes to the end of the row and there stood Larkin. He did not say a word to me, just stood there with his big hands hanging down empty, but I swear to you I knowed it.

And I can never say what and all went through my mind. I reckon every memory I had of my little brother went to crowding up in my head till I centered on how he would stand there with his blond hair shining like gold and make that fiddle just talk. It hit me right then and there that I would never hear a single note come from his hands again. Still, I did not think it was real until I run to that mule and saw that thing what was wrapped up and throwed over its back like a sack of taters. I reached out my hand and touched it, and still it was not real to me. And then I looked down and saw shoes sticking out and the britches had rode up and I could see a pale line of flesh. They was just something so helpless and pitiful about that little stretch of white and I felt the tears coming and could not have stopped them if I had tried. And Larkin's eyes was like black holes that had been bored out in his head and they had the awfulest look out of them you have ever seen. Me and Larkin held onto one another, and we both cried. Then he said, "Amma, I've got to do the hardest thing I've ever done now," and I said, "You will not do it by yourself." I went in to tell the young'uns that their laughing and cutting-up uncle had come home throwed across the back of a strange mule.

As we went across the ridge Larkin told me Hackley was the only man killed on the Union side in the battle that was being called Winding Stairs. He made no further motions to tell me more, and I did not ask, for I was plumb numb inside and it made no real difference. We had a bad thing to do and they was no sense in making it worse.

It was getting up toward late morning when we topped the ridge and stood looking down at the house. I could see where Mary had swept the yard, and there was a curl of smoke rising out of the chimney. Even from up here I could smell that she was baking bread. "Oh, Amma," he said, "I don't know that I can do this." And I said, "You can do it because you have to."

Mary was coming up the path from the spring when she saw us. A big smile bloomed over her face and she dropped the buckets and come running toward us laughing and calling out Larkin's name in the same breath. When she got close enough to see his face, she stopped and lost her laughter and her great big eyes looked from me to him and back to him again. I don't know that I will ever feel as sorry for anybody as I felt for her right then.

"Mary," was all he had to say.

"No," she brought her hand to her mouth. "No," she said again and she started backing up and her forehead got all bunched up.

"Honey," I said.

Her heart broke then. I saw it happen as clear as day, right as she was turning to run back toward the spring. Neither one of us knowed what to do except go to running after her. From the corner of my eye, I spied Julie standing on the porch holding the baby. Larkin's legs was so much longer than mine that I thought for a minute that he was going to catch her. I knowed for a fact that there was no room for nothing else in his heart except for that little figure ahead of him, just now entering the cool, dark path that ended at the deep pool where the spring broke ground. But then he had to slow down. Mary's bare feet grabbed hold of the damp rocks going down there, but his heavy boots were slick. I was right behind him and we both heard the splash.

"Oh, God, Larkin," I hollered out and he broke to run again, boots be damned.

Mary's hair was all fanned out around her small head and she was laying face down in the water.

Larkin hit the shallow water at a run, but it was only when he touched her that she began to fight him.

"Let me be. Leave me alone!" Her fists bounced off his chest as he lifted her up out of that cold water and started toward the bank with her cradled against him like a baby.

"Mary, honey, shhh." His voice was soft and he set a long time holding her close. A bright shaft of sun found its way down through the leaves and he scooted until they were in it. They were both shivering from the icy water.

The smell of honeysuckle came to me and the sweetness of it seemed somehow out of place.

She fought him for a while longer but finally stopped. He began to rock her slowly.

I squatted beside them and went to rubbing her hair. Nobody said nothing for a long time, then finally I said, "Scream, Mary. Scream as loud as you want to."

And finally with a great wail she started to cry. I knowed she would be all right then.

WE ALL PILED UP and stayed at Mary's that night. She said she wanted to stay at her own house, and I knowed I would have felt the same exact way. The young'uns right down to Hack Jr. were quiet and went off to sleep early. Mary had not wanted us to tell nobody until the next morning. I reckon she wanted some time to gather herself. She clutched onto Larkin like a drowning woman and could not stand for him to be out of her sight. We was out on the porch about all night and she wanted to hear it all over and over again until I thought if I heard how my brother had died one more time I would start screaming at the top of my voice and not quit.

"Did he tell you anything to tell me before he died, Larkin?" she asked again.

He said what he'd already told her at least ten times and his voice sounded so tired but so patient with her, that I felt so sorry plumb to the bottom of my soul. "He was dead by the time I got to him, honey."

She looked all done in, and I cast around for something that I might ask him myself. "Not even before you went to fighting?"

He looked up at me and was in such a struggle and a misery that I wished I had kept my big mouth shut. "We'd had a fuss the night before, Amma. I had not talked to him that morning."

"Oh, God. Larkin, honey, I feel the worst in the world for you," I said and went to them both and put my arms around them. We set there till it was daylight.

Poor, poor Mary. This was her first big loss in her life, and God knows I knew as much as anybody about grieving, and now she had a big mess of it to do.

AND SHE DID JUST that and I done a lot myself over that next year. I got only a few letters from Larkin after he left, and he was doing his fair share, too.

Then just like that the war was over. It had started a way off in South Carolina and it ended a way off in Virginy, and as the hot months of the summer of 1865 went by, men what had been gone off fighting in it started to come home. You can only guess at how I searched every face hoping it to be the one I loved.

In late June, Daisy Stanton was out at the chop block shaving enough splinters from a piece of firewood to use for kindling. The evening sun was slanting in at her and had throwed her shadow up against the side of the cabin. Suddenly a great big shadow popped up right beside hers there on the house. Big John had come home.

That blackguard Shadrack Wallin knowed things would probably not go well for him back here in Sodom. The hand he'd had in the death of his brother would not be forgotten, let alone forgiven. And, yeller dog coward that he was, he didn't have the heart to face neither Rosa nor his baby brother Zeke. He timed his homecoming with the new moon and he snuck in here and gathered his belongings and collected his wife and family, and they was gone by daylight, bound for Virginy. On the way he changed the spelling of his name to Wallen, and we never saw hide nor hair of him ever again. Good riddance to bad rubbish is what I have to say about that.

Brother William come up on Mommie at the spring and she hit her knees right there on the bank of the stream, praising the Almighty for delivering her oldest son back to her arms.

Soon after William Jr. showed back up, we heard from Robert, who was living in Mississippi with his new bride after having served out the war with the Confederacy.

Tete come home from Knoxville, where he'd been released from his duties as office clerk to General Hartwell Jackson.

Old Lawrence Allen and his cousin James Keith was afraid for their lives over the Shelton Laurel massacre. And well they should have been, for Pete McCoy had swore he would kill them. Them two made a beeline away from here and headed out for Arkansas.

• • •

THEN THERE WAS THEM what did not return.

Roderick Norton, Larkin's bearer of apple stack cake, was killed by the Home Guard while on a recruiting mission for Kirk.

Andy Chandler got better from the dysentery, went back to fighting, and was killed over at Strawberry Plains.

Little Johnny Norton deserted from Allen's regiment and was killed in a poker game by another deserter over on Shelton Laurel.

Pete McCoy hid out on Shelton Laurel until the war ended. After his mother died in August, he headed for the western country, but made a trip to Charlotte first, where he shot and killed a man that had been with Allen's murdering bunch on Shelton Laurel. Pete died in a dispute over a gold-mining claim in California.

But neither Zeke nor Larkin come, and I was beginning to wonder if they ever would.

ONE WARM NIGHT TOWARD the middle of July, I woke from a dead sleep by a rustling of the mattress as someone sat down on the foot of my bed. Quick as a cat I was up and running for the door when Zeke's voice stopped me right where I was standing. I come back to the bed on slow feet and could hardly believe it was really him and not his haint.

"I'm home," he said.

"I see that," I said, but was not certain until I laid my hand on him and felt him warm beneath it.

We set for a minute with our shoulders touching.

"At night sometimes I dreamed so hard that you was next to me that I would wake in the morning with my hand closed tight like this," I said and held up my clenched fist to him.

He closed his fingers around my little fist and raised it to his mouth where he kissed every one of my knuckles. "I wouldn't let myself dream, Arty," he whispered to me. "Dreaming done me no good. Only made me long for you more."

I palmed back a thick lock of hair from his wide forehead. His eyes was plumb purple in the light of the moon that was coming through the open door. "You won't never have to long for me next to you again, Zeke. You ain't never getting away from me again. I don't ever aim to be no further away from you than I am right now."

He laughed. "It'll make it hard to plow joined at the hip this way."

"There don't need to be no plowing for a while, Zeke. Except for the plowing that needs doing right here."

And he needed nothing else said when I patted the bed.

AND IN AUGUST LARKIN came home.

I WAS STUDYING HIM and he knew I was doing it. This was his third time by the house in as many weeks since he'd come home, and he was awful quiet. He'd been in the upper field with Zeke all morning, and they'd come in for dinner all hot and sweaty but easy with one another, like men can be when they've spent time working together. I followed them out onto the porch talking up a storm while they'd washed and poured water over their heads. Neither had said much, but then Zeke was always spare with his words. But it hurt me that the easy way I had always had with Larkin seemed gone. Even when Carolina had bounded onto the porch like a big puppy and went to poking him in the ribs and batting her eyes at him, flirting with him a little, Larkin had barely smiled. And it was hard not to laugh plumb out loud when Carolina was around. She was always cutting up and going on, slinging that big mane of glossy black hair, with them big blue eyes just dancing with fun. Zeke had finally sent her to the spring for buttermilk just to get her out of the way.

After supper, Zeke had give me a look that was not lost on Carolina and had announced that he had a harness that needed mending, and when Larkin started to rise, he'd placed a hand on his shoulder.

"No need for you to come. Carolina's been wanting to talk to me anyhow." They'd gone out together, leaving me and Larkin at the table.

Larkin leaned back on the bench and looked at me. "You aiming to draw a picture of me?"

I laughed and felt a little better. "No, I ain't, you smart-mouthed whelp, you."

He smiled and it almost blossomed in his eyes, but not quite. "I don't mean to worry you, Amma."

And with that he unlocked the words that had been near about choking me to death, and I let him have it. "Well now why in the world would I be worried? Just because you don't talk to me no more? That you act like you owed me money or something? That when you do come here to the house, you latch onto Zeke like you're in deep water and he's the only one about that knows how to swim? No need for me to be worried about none of that." I had to lay my hand on him then, so I brushed the hair back from his forehead and hunkered down so I could look him eyeball to eyeball. "Or that Julie left Mary's and went to stay with their aunt over at Jewel Hill. Or that Mary won't speak to her mommie since Julie left. Or that Rosa told me that they ain't been no lamps lit of an evening at your place since you come home. Or that you been seen coming from Maggie's real early in the morning." I took my hand away, but stayed close to him in case I needed to put it back. "No need for me to worry about none of that?"

His eyes were flat. He shook his head. "No."

I let out my breath in a big puff and leaned back. "Well, I won't then." And I come up off that bench like it was red hot. His hand shot out and grabbed my arm, but I was so mad I was about to cry and would not look at him.

"It's not as it might seem, Amma."

That flew all over me. "How do you even know how it might seem to me, mister? You ain't bothered to ask."

He sighed. "I'm not a boy anymore, Amma. Can't you see that?"

I jerked my arm loose. "Well, now that you ain't a boy, just don't wind up being a stupid man, Larkin." I went to washing them dishes with a vengeance and out come that chin of mine.

After a while I heard him get up from the table and go out the door.

THOUGH I HAD ROSA looking every morning for weeks after that, she never saw Larkin at Maggie's again.

But we all saw Larkin and Mary walking out together most every evening after supper. And as the tired green of summer gave way to the bright colors of fall, I knowed that Larkin had made his choice not to be a stupid man.

They took to walking up on the mountain, and I would see them go by the house with Hack Jr. riding high up on Larkin's shoulders. I could hear him laughing all the way down at the house. Larkin was a pure-D fool over that young'un, and from the very first he acted like he was his own flesh and blood. But let me say right here that this could not be. That child was the spitting image of my poor dead brother and became more like him the older he got. I swear it was just like looking at him. And you know mayhap that was the very reason why Larkin took such a shine to him. He loved Hackley, too.

They walked up to Hackley's grave a lot. Mary said they was standing next to the grave and Hack Jr. was setting right on it when Larkin asked her to marry him. When she said she would, he had grabbed up both of them and had danced all over the place. I felt like something cold went to crawling right up my spine when she told me that. Somehow, even though I cannot say the why, it did not seem right that he'd asked her there.

15

I OFFERED TO LET them marry in my house, but Mary allowed that she wanted it done in the church. So off we went. Do not think I did not feel happiness in my heart for them, for I did. The only reason I offered them my house was that they was some men what had come from the damn war that carried very hard feelings. I would mention here one Tyler Ray what had been up in Virginy with Mister Lee when he'd surrendered. Tyler's eyes would just fill up with water at the mention of that man's name. Some on the other side was just as bad. As I have said before, and will take this opportunity to say again, men is foolish sometimes when it comes to whether their honor might be slighted in some way. So I say to them, keep your damn honor placed somewhere that it cannot be slighted. But Tyler pulled out his pistol and shot Vernon Lewis in the hand at a poker game back in the fall just for saying that the king of spades sort of reminded him of old Marse Robert. They said the cards went every which way. 'Course in my way of figuring, Vernon Lewis ought to have been shot a long time ago for being a fool, but if we start shooting folks for being fools then we'd be shooting right up till the end of time.

So when I got to the church and it was packed with folks, I got the all-overs, but I did not get them too bad. Larkin had summed it up right as we was leaving the house and, oh, let me say that my biggest boy was as pretty a man as I had ever seed in my life. He had shrugged his big wide shoulders and said to me, "The war is done, Amma. It is time we got on."

And I had said to him something I had never said, but had meant to for a long time. "I am proud of you, son," I said. "This is a decent thing that you are doing for Hackley here on this day."

His voice was all choked up when he answered me. "I am not doing it for Hackley, Amma. This is all for me."

I had nothing to say to that and figured just as he said and so it is.

THE MARRYING THAT DAY went off without a single hitch, and it looked as though old grudges, slights, hurts, and more honor than you could shake a stick at had at least for this day been left outside the door. But do not fret all you people. It was all sorted out and picked right back up when that night ended.

LET ME TELL YOU right now that I had never give much thought to this word *beautiful*. To me people was seldom if ever beautiful. But on this day Mary was beautiful. Her hair was all down and loose and covered her shoulders for all the world like a rich wavy red shawl. There had been no need to pinch her cheeks for color, and them big brown eyes never left Larkin's face one single time while the preacher was talking.

Larkin stood straight and looked right back at her, and his voice was deep as a well when he said the words that bound his heart to hers.

They was those among us that shed tears setting on them hard wooden benches that morning. Mommie capped her hands over her face and just sobbed as the preacher said, "Till death do you part." I was bawling myself and me setting there with my lap budding yet another child. I swear to you, it seemed that every time Zeke Wallin hung his britches up on the peg on the back of the door, Arty found herself in the family way. I reached out and took Zeke's hand in mine and held onto it the whole time. I had made good as I could that threat of not letting him out of my sight. This might explain me being four months gone again. Lord, I felt so sorry for Julie, who did not sob. It would have been better if she had but only one single tear slid down her little face when Larkin said, "I do."

I had seen Maggie at the back of the church when I'd come in and my eyebrows flew straight up. She grinned at me, and I could tell she was having a big time knowing that everybody in there was watching her. Bless her, at least this would lay to rest any ugly thoughts folks might be carrying about her and Larkin. I knowed it was him that had gone and asked her to come, and I also knowed that they had been nothing between them since he'd come home. I know this because she had come by the house the week before and we'd had us a big talk. All them times he'd come to her in the early misty mornings back in the summer, it had been only to sit with her on the porch. She said sometimes they'd talked together, but most times she'd just listened. "He's got a world of horror in his heart, Arty. The things he has seen is bad enough to have killed most men." He'd told her too of how he feared he was ruined now for any woman. She'd let him talk and when he run out of words, she'd let the silence be. They never once touched, though she would have, had he asked. Then he'd stopped coming. She'd let that be as well.

She'd told me then about Silas, too.

She'd lit a fire that night so the windows would be glowing warm and welcoming in the chill of the early fall evening. He was awfully quiet as they ate supper, and Maggie said his eyes followed her everywhere she went and they were the saddest things she'd ever seen. I wanted to stop her right there and I would have a year ago, but she needed to talk to somebody and I was it. She said when he loved her that night his hands was so gentle that it jerked tears from her eyes. The fire had burned down to just red coals when he'd said the words she'd been dreading to hear fall from his lips for as long as she'd known him. "I've got to go home, Maggie."

And there they was now and she could not say nothing. When she didn't answer, he rolled his head to look at her. "I'm taking the train out the end of this week." And all she said was, "Well."

And that was it. He'd left the next morning and she'd kissed him, held him one last time and let him go. She said there'd been a little moment there on the porch when he'd have stayed if she'd asked. She had seen it in his eyes. But she had not asked him.

I asked her then why and she said she'd known, clear as anything, that if he'd left his wife and family for her, that he'd forever have held the best part of himself back from her. And she wouldn't have had him that way. So she'd had to turn from him as he'd climbed on his horse, set her back to him as he'd ridden off down the road. It had been the hardest thing she'd ever done.

I have to say that a big flower of respect bloomed in my heart on that day for Maggie. She was a good and decent person for all that she was hotter than a ginger mill. But then I had knowed that for as long as I had knowed her. I had always allowed that she had just never found the right sweetheart. I told her how sad I was that she had found him only to have to let him go, and she allowed as how it had been her experience that more often than not, life is just that way.

THAT NIGHT WE HAD such a time as it put me in the mind of the way it used to be here around home. When we left the church house we never even broke stride and went right straight to Jim Leake's and had a great big frolic in the front room of his house. I started off trying to act my age but soon got over that. They was a little bit of time right there at the beginning when Lum and Willis took up their banjo and fiddle that it got real quiet. I knowed every single soul in that place was thinking the same as me, that the best of the lot was not here with us. With my eyes burning like fire I hollered out, "Play a good fast frolic tune for my brother, boys." That broke things up and they commenced to playing a tune they'd learned off some boys over in Tennessee what was called "The Cumberland Gap," which is a fine tune with good words which we all took to singing.

Me and my wife and my wife's pap walked all the way to the
    Cumberland Gap.
Cumberland Gap ain't my home and I'm gonna leave old
    Cumberland alone.

I was singing as loud as I could and grinning at Zeke the whole time. A bunch hit the floor dancing for all they was worth, and before I could catch myself and go back to acting my age, I jumped up and was dancing every which way. When that song ended I was winded but thought I had done pretty good for an old married woman and told Zeke as much. All he could do was shake his head at me and allow how I would not do.

Me and him danced the whole livelong night, and my young'uns had themselves a great big time. Pearl played so hard her hair was plastered to her head with sweat, and she was as ill and mean as a copperhead when I finally made her go lay down. I let the biggest ones stay up and was glad I did, because Carolina wound up being the one to sing the song that sent Larkin and Mary down the road to their married bed.

We was all waiting for the musicianers to rest up when Rosa Wallin asked me if I would sing something. Lord, they was no way I could have denied that poor woman a song nor nothing else. She looked like death warmed over ever since Hugh had died, and I felt guilty as sin standing there beside my big pretty man knowing that she'd had to crawl out of her birthing bed to bury hers. I went to running songs through my head trying to figure which one would be the best to sing that would hurt her the least. You have to be careful with these old songs sometimes, for they can reach right in and twist up your heart if you ain't. Carolina give me just a minute and then whispered to me, "Can I sing one, Mommie?" And I told her to go right ahead and I was thankful for the chance to figure which to sing. But I needn't have bothered. That young'un stepped right out and sung exactly what needed to be sung. It were not too much but it were just enough.

> The heart is the fortune of all womankind.
> They're always controlled and they're always confined—
> Controlled by their parents until they are wives
> Then bound to their husbands for the rest of their lives.
>
> I am a poor girl and my fortune is sad,
> I've a long time been courted by the wagoner's lad.

He courted me truly by night and by day
And now he is loaded and driving away.

"Your parents don't like me because I am poor,
They say I'm not worthy to enter your door.
I work for my money, my money's my own,
And folks that don't like me they can leave me alone."

"Go stable your horses and feed them some hay,
Come and sit down beside me for as long as you can stay."
"My horses ain't hungry, they won't eat your hay,
So fare-thee-well, darling, I'll be on my way."

"Your horse is to saddle, your wagon to grease,
Come sit you down by me before you must leave."
"My horse it is saddled, my whip's in my hand,
So fare-thee-well, darling, I can no longer stand."

"I can love little or I can love long,
I can love an old sweetheart till a new one comes 'long.
I can hug and can kiss them and prove to them kind,
I can turn my back on them and also my mind."

I'll go to yon mountain the mountain so high,
Where the wild birds can see me as they pass me by,
Where the wild birds can see me and hear my sad song,
For I am a poor girl and my lover has gone.

When she finished it was like everybody in that room was holding their breath. And then I looked at Zeke, and the tears was just pouring down his face and he did not even try to swipe them and make like he was not crying for all the world to see. He grabbed her up in his arms, and it hit me then that this was the first time he had heard our girl sing.

Nobody needed to tell me what a lucky woman Arty Wallin was, because she already had a pretty good idea of that herself.

Larkin and Mary made their move to leave just then, and we all follered them out the door hollering and carrying on. I have always wondered about that sort of thing. I mean, why them men feels the need to scream out instructions is just beyond me. And some of the women is just as bad. And it was not as if Mary or Larkin either one needed instructing, if you know what I mean. But anyway, out onto the porch we went with everybody hollering the same-old same-old, and then somebody hollered that it was snowing and I crowded right up next to the front. Oh, how I loved the snow, and it were really coming down, too. The ground just barely had a little skift on it, but great big fat flakes was coming down offering us the promise of a big snow if it kept up till morning. Just then two of Edmund Chandler's big boys come toting a big sack between them and I could not believe it when they opened the door and throwed that sack right into the middle of the room. Now I am here to tell you that sack was packed full of possums, and they come out of that sack and went every which way. I have never laughed as much in my life as we spent the rest of the night collecting possums off the beams and out from behind stuff, and everywhere else you can just imagine. Boys is something else, ain't they?

While we was possum gathering, me and Maggie hung together and talked. She pulled a letter out of her sleeve and told me to read it. It was from Silas, and when I read the part that said his wife had died of a fever of some kind I looked up at her. I want you to know they was nothing in her face but sorrow. "In all my wishing I did not wish this, Arty," she said, and I know she was telling me the truth. I looked her right in the eye and said, "Maggie, honey, they will not let me or you neither one be in charge of things even for a minute, so it does not matter what we wish." I went back to reading and found that he aimed to come for her as soon as a decent time had passed. "What will you do, Maggie?" I said. And she said, "Why, I'll go raise our young'uns." And you know, that is just what she done. She turned out quite the lady down there in South Carolina.

Me and Zeke walked out for home just as it was getting daylight, and all our young'uns was stumbling along with us looking like sleepy chickens. Zeke was carrying Pearl, and seeing the two of them together looking just like each other made my heart swell near to busting.

As we come by Mary's little cabin it was closed up tight without so much as a candle lighting the window. It looked so pretty in the snow and my face got all warm when I went to thinking about what was going on just on the other side of them walls. I hoped for Larkin's sake it had been well worth the wait. My gut told me it probably had been.

When we got home I put Pearl in the bed with Abigail and Carolina, and the boys went up in the loft. Soon they was all sound asleep and me and Zeke laid there talking about this, that, and the other. That was the best thing in the world to me. During the damn war, I had learned the hard lesson that is to take nothing for granted in this world.

I got right playful then and asked Zeke what he thought Larkin and Mary were doing right now, and he looked at me like I was a crazy woman. "Why, what do you think they're doing, Arty?" And I could not help it, I just busted out laughing.

But I did not laugh too long, as just about then was when he showed me just what they might be doing. And all I have to say about that is, Lordy, I hope they was.

16

THERE AT THE FIRST, they was no two that was any happier than Larkin and Mary, and that's a fact. I can still see in my mind's eye how he looked when he come by the house and told me that they was pretty certain Mary was in the family way. I mean that man was plumb tickled to death. But when I said, "Well, now, son, you'll be a daddy," he looked at me all funny and said quick as a snake, "I'm already a daddy, Amma." I knowed exactly what he meant by that and knowed too just how he felt. So I held my tongue and did not say what everybody had said to me when I was carrying my own. I knowed he loved Hack Jr. like he would his own and nobody could ever tell him any different. In my way of figuring Larkin was my firstborn. I was always ready to fight anybody that allowed he was not.

As them months come and went, Mary hardly had to lift a hand to do a single thing. Larkin was like a winding blade and would fuss and carry on if she even so much as done work in her garden. She was pretty sick, though. I went by there right after my April was born and she was out on the porch throwing up. I done my best to tell her that some women was sick the whole time they was breeding, and that she was not to worry. I reckon most women cannot be like Arty and pop them out with little or no effort. April was born in about an hour, and I guess that is just as well since I aimed to call her April and if she'd waited one more hour she'd have come in May, so I was in sort of a hurry. And when I saw April's little red head, I was pleased as could be. She was the picture of her sister Ingabo and that was somehow fitting.

That summer was such a good time for all of us, I reckon. Me and Zeke got along really good, even though they was some getting used to each other again. It took me awhile to settle back into him being around all the time. I was used to doing everything for myself and had got right bullheaded. I was not as agreeable about things as I once was. Bless Zeke for having the patience of Job and letting me keep on being the person I had become. That is hard for some men, you understand. They was lots of women what had trouble with their men that first year. I think if Zeke had been like most, we would not have stayed together. Arty had done come around the fence during that damn war, and they was no way on earth she could have gone back to yes-siring all the livelong day and night.

ME AND MARY WAS setting on the porch one evening late in the summer watching the lightning bugs come up all around us. They is nothing on God's green earth to beat that. I feel sorry for folks that has never had the chance to set on the porch and watch that little miracle happen. A warm breeze was blowing and the young'uns was out catching bugs and putting them in a jar. Is that not a wonderful thing to spend your time doing?

Mary had gone all soft-eyed watching me nurse April and allowed that she could hardly wait for her own to be out in the world with us.

I laughed and said she'd better be for enjoying the rest while she could. Then Larkin started to sing down at the barn, and we just set there and listened. Lord, what a voice that man had, and it jerked the chillbumps out on me big as goose eggs. "What's that song?" Mary asked me and I said " 'Pretty Fair Miss,' honey," and I shushed the young'uns just to hear it better.

> Said a pretty fair miss all in her garden and a handsome young
>   soldier come a-riding by,
> Said, "Could I impose on a fair young maiden and ask her for
>   my bride to be?"
>
> Said, "Handsome young soldier standing by the gateway, a man
>   of honor you may be.
> How could you impose on a fair young maiden who never intends
>   your bride to be?"
>
> Said, "I've got a true love-yer that gone to the army and he's
>   been gone for seven years long.
> And if he stays gone seven years longer, no man on earth could
>   marry me."
>
> "Prayhaps your love-yer drownded in the ocean, prayhaps he's
>   on some battlefield slain,
> Prayhaps he's taken another girl and married, his face you'll
>   never see again."
>
> "Well, if he's drownded I hope he's happy, or if he's on some
>   battlefield slain,
> Or if he's taken another girl and married, why, I'd love the girl
>   that would marry him."

His fingers being long and slender, into his pockets they did go.
Said, "Here's the ring that you once gave me before I started for
 the war."

She threw her lily white arms around him and straight before
 him she did fall,
Said, "You're the man that used to court me before you left here
 for the war."

Said, "I been on the deep sea sailing and I been sailing for seven
 years long,
And if I'd stayed gone seven years longer no woman on earth
 could've married me."

That was the prettiest I would ever hear that sung. They was nobody could sing like Larkin Stanton, and that was all there was to it.

We set on for a while after he'd quit, and then Mary looked at me
and said, "Arty, I sometimes feel like I have somehow betrayed your
brother." I took a long time to answer her and what I finally said to
her was this. "Life is not for the dead and gone. It is just for the living. That is the only way it can ever be. As hard as it might sound, we
have to turn loose of the dead and let them go."

SOMEBODY ASKED ME ONE time if now that I was a old
woman, if I had got things sorted out in my mind and was used to the
idea of dying. I said to them what I will say now to you. No, I have
gotten more used to living. That's just how it is.

I CAUGHT MARY'S BABY in September that year, and she
was just like looking her mommie in the face. When I took her to

Larkin, he held out his big hands and I put her in them. He looked down into that little heart-shape of a face and he literally went to swaying. I reached out a hand to steady him and laughed. But then he lifted his face up and I saw his eyes. They was a great stillness in them, and my breath caught in my throat. Before I could say anything to him, he took and shoved that baby back at me, a sob tore itself loose from his throat, and he turned and went running hell bent off the porch. I took the baby back in to Mary and told her some men was profoundly touched when they see what their loins have created. But I was troubled to my very soul. As soon as I could, I lit out after him and found him down at the spring. What he was doing down there was not natural.

The deep water that had pooled for the spring was still as glass. All around us the summer bugs was churring and singing, but he didn't even seem to hear them. He was staring right down into that water like he was waiting for something to rise right up out of it. He give a little shake of his head like he was telling somebody I could not see, *no, no.* Then he slapped the water with the flat of his hand and ripples went to streaking out every which way. "Can't I have this thing?" he said right out loud. "Can I live it? Can I?"

My heart was feeling like it was going to bust out of my body, but I did not say a word. This was for him to figure. I watched as he put his face right down next to the water for all the world like he aimed to kiss his reflection. And then he said to himself, "They is nothing left but to live it."

I slipped off and he did not even know I was there.

OF COURSE ROXYANN OWNED her daddy's heart from the first birth cry. Larkin loved her so much that he would have walked a rotten foot-log over hell to have got to her. And he caught her heart in them big hands of his as well. I ain't never in all my days seen a young'un wean itself as quick as she did, and I believe she done it on purpose so she could go around with her daddy. And in the love he had for her, for a while at least, Larkin Stanton was a man content.

I reckon that was a good thing too, for right before Roxyann's first birthday, Mary was breeding again. Now, they was no sickness with this one and she worked like a man through that winter. I was not a bit surprised when she birthed Luke right on time. He was a great big boy and I could not help it that my mind went back to when his daddy come into this world, which seemed like a lifetime ago. They named him Luke, after Larkin's own daddy.

The older Luke got, the more he looked like his daddy. He was a quiet and serious young'un, and him and Hack Jr. was close from the very start. They was the same difference in age as what was between Larkin and Hackley. I swear for me it was just like I'd been tossed back in time watching them grow. One was sturdy, small, and blond and already taking up his daddy's fiddle and singing the old love songs. And Luke so big and dark, dogging Hack Jr.'s every step. Most of the time I called Luke Larkin and could not help it.

I reckon it was when Rosalie was born that Larkin began to change.

I GUESS SOMETIMES WE just get so caught up in the living through life that we miss the living of it. I know that is what happened them years right after Larkin and Zeke come from the war. We went along, and went along, and in what seemed no time a'tall, Abigail was getting married.

And with each year that rolled over our heads, Larkin got stiller and quieter.

I was like Mary and slow to notice. We was all so busy that we hardly had time enough to think, let alone notice how quiet Larkin had come to be. He was a lot like Zeke in that way, and I guess we'd just got used to him being about and not saying much. And he was in and out, working as hard as the rest of us. So when she come by the house with her face all pinched up with worry, I told her what had taken me a long time to figure with Zeke, that men is just different and don't always feel the need to face bark back and forth like us women do. She seemed to feel a little better by the time she left.

But I kept on studying about it and was plumb taken aback with just how long it had been since Larkin had darkened my own door. I decided right then and there that I had to catch hold of that big young'un and see what and all was churning around and about in that big head of his. A few days later I struck out for their house. But when I got over there I could not for the life of me figure out what was happening right in front of my eyes.

Mary was setting in front of the fire with a lap full of mending and Larkin was setting at the table. I went by him and dropped a big smacking kiss on the top of his head but he barely grunted at me. I never let on and started talking a blue streak with Mary, but I was sneaking looks at him every chance I could. Lord, but his eyes looked like little black chips and there was a still watchfulness in them. His mouth all thinned out and a big muscle was jumping in his jaw. Finally I couldn't stand it no more and I said just his name, "Larkin?" and my voice sounded funny even to me. The look he shot me was gone so fast my head wondered if I had seen it at all. But my heart had caught it all right, and his eyes were still holding on to some of it as well.

"What?"

Mary was watching us and her little face was looking like she was going to take to crying just any minute. I just stared at him and then said the first thing that popped into my mind. "I love you, son."

The dark thing in his eyes was gone in a flash and he smiled. "Why, I love you, too."

I did not know what had just happened, but I knew with the awfulest feeling of despair that this was not the first time whatever it was had squatted in him. And with something that felt an awful lot like fear, I knew it would not be the last.

MARY REACHED FOR THE cup of coffee in front of her, but her hand trembled so that she had to set it back down without even taking a drink. "I don't even know how long he's been this way. But, Lord have mercy, Arty, I see it everywhere now and it does nothing but get worser between us."

She had lost so much weight that her eyes looked to be sunk back in her head. "What are you seeing in him that is troubling you so?"

"With me he's quiet as the grave," Mary said. "But he talks to them boys like they are dogs. *Worse* than dogs. And they are *good* boys, Arty. You know that. They don't sass, they do what they're told." She swiped at her eyes. "For the most part they do, but they're boys and sometimes they get off to playing, you know?"

"I know, honey. Mine's the same way," I said and then, trying to soothe her, I said, "Zeke gets so mad he could spit. Hollers at them sometimes, too."

Mary folded her little hands and put them in her lap. She looked down, studying them, and when she spoke her voice was low. "Hollering ain't all he does."

I reached out and patted her hand. "Mary, hollering ain't all Zeke does. It ain't all I've done, neither."

"Has Zeke ever kicked them?" She raised eyes that seemed to carry all the pain in the world.

I felt myself go cold as ice on the inside and even my heart stilled. "Kick them? You mean kicks with his foot?" Now I knowed she meant with his foot. How else would you kick something, or worse yet someone, but I was just so shocked, you have to understand.

When I said that it was like I had reached out and uncorked a jug and turned it over as one ugly story after another come pouring out. My heart sunk lower and lower as she talked, and I kept thinking to myself, *What in this world has happened?*

Mary talked for a long time and then she just stopped. The room was quiet and a bright square of sun came through the small window that was my pride and joy. The only sound was from the clock on the fireboard and we both jumped when it chimed out the hour.

"Lord, I've got to go," Mary said. "I left Rosalie with Roxyann, and she'll be crying the house down wanting her mommie."

I followed her onto the porch. Mary looked so thin. I put my arms around her and hugged her up, and I was mad as hell and my voice was just shaking. "I have a mind to talk to Larkin Stanton, Mary, whether you want me to or not." At the look on her face I could not stay mad and softened my voice up. "But I won't if you think it'll just make it worse."

Mary swiped her hair back with both hands. "Don't say nothing to him right now."

I looked her hard right in the eyes. "All right. But all you've got to do is ask."

"Thanks so much, Arty."

She was almost to the edge of the yard when I hollered out, "Mary?"

She turned.

"He ain't hit you or the girls, has he?"

Mary shook her head. "Oh no, he's gentle as ever with them. And no, he ain't hit me neither." Her shoulders sagged. "I know it sounds crazy as hell, but sometimes I wish he would. Him hitting me would be better than this awful watching that he's doing."

Mary had never seen Larkin really drunk, so the first time he come up the path singing at the top of his lungs, she really thought things might be fixing to change. She said he laughed, took her on his lap, said sweet things to her and aside from the strong smell of his breath, he seemed more like himself than he had in months. He'd sat at the table wearing a big toothy grin while she'd fixed supper. It was the first relaxed meal they'd all had together in a long while.

She said it just broke her heart when the boys come sneaking in after washing up and that they'd perched on the bench like birds ready to take flight. Luke actually flinched when Larkin dropped his knife. She had looked at Hack Jr. and caught his look of pure old relief when it dawned on him that the awful quiet would not rule this time. Larkin was actually laughing and cutting up and deviling him about this or that young girl. For all that his speech was slurred, at least he was talking to them.

She said she was feeling pretty good, but that had come to an end when they finished supper and Hack Jr. had said, "Daddy?"

Larkin had looked up from his plate with his eyes glassy and his grin on all crooked. "What, son?"

"Willis and a bunch of them are going to let their dogs run. Can me and Luke take Hummer and go with them?"

She said she'd thought to herself, *Oh, no. Don't ruin this, son. Don't.*

But her quick glance at Larkin realized it was already done.

His eyes had gone flat as a snake's and his smile was gone. "You wanting to lay out all night?"

Hack Jr. heard the change but he was already in it now. He swallowed and went on, "We'd be back before daylight, plenty of time to do our work." He glanced quick at Larkin, and even though he saw the stillness on his face, the dark knitting of his brow, he plunged ahead. "We ain't done nothing like that in so long, Daddy. Not since—" and one more look at his daddy had stopped him right there.

Mary said everybody went quiet, and even Roxyann stopped dead still on her way to the sideboard with a stack of plates.

Larkin placed both hands flat on the table. "Since what, Hack?" Of a sudden they was no slurring of words, and that happened so quick it scared the hell out of Mary. "Hack," she said, "you and Luke take the slop bucket out."

"Hush, Mary." His voice had gone soft and his eyes was holding that awful dark thing.

But when Hack Jr. lifted his chin, Mary said she'd felt something almost joyful rise up in her breast. Her son's jaw was set and they was a certain cockiness about him. His lower lip came out in a bit of a pout, and the blue eyes that he offered Larkin was not one bit afraid. I reckon his daddy popped out in him, and that was not lost on Larkin.

Them big hands what was on the table made into big fists and he brought both of them up and slammed them both down on the table so hard that the dishes bounced. "Don't you look at me that way."

But, though it was a shout, it carried no anger. His voice had held such pain it sounded almost like a plea.

Without thought Mary had put her hand out to him.

"Don't, just don't," he'd said as he'd swatted her hand away. Then he'd jumped up and went to staggering for the door. By the time Mary had gathered her wits enough to go after him, the night had swallowed him up.

That was the first night he didn't come home.

17

THAT FALL WAS A misery for them all. When Larkin was home, he was mean drunk. There were the few odd times when he'd come swaggering in, right playful, laughing, singing, grabbing her around the waist. Mary come to dread those times worst of all. He'd run the children off from the house and they would flee ahead of him like a bunch of scared little animals.

And then he'd turn for her.

> FOR THE FIRST TIME in my life I could not reach him, though it was not for lack of trying. I done everything I knowed to do. I tried being easy with him. I rared and threatened and cussed him. I begged and cried. I even dragged Zeke into it and had him try to talk reason with him. Zeke did not want to do it and I had to beg him to. That was hard for me, as I am not a woman what begs. But Larkin would just hump up like a big log and I might as well been spinning moonbeams for all the good it done. I kept on because I could not stop. I could not stop because I loved him and it seemed like he was dying right before my eyes and by God, I would not have it. I would not.

IT WAS COLD AS a witch's ninny pies that day when Hack Jr. come by the house and said Mary was at her wits' end. Larkin had not been home for a solid week. I told him to wait and I would get Zeke to go with him to look. I watched them out of sight and then stepped to the edge of the porch to look up at the sky. It had clouded over a heavy frost that morning and the low clouds that had moved in seemed bigged with snow. I hoped they found Larkin and found him quick.

Thank the Lord, they did just that.

They had gone straight to the cave, just as I'd said for them to do. He was up there all right, and had drunk so much he'd passed out deader than a doorknob. Zeke said he was laying out in the weather on top of Buzzard Rock.

When they come carrying him in I started crying. He was so sick we loaded him on the sled and took him to Granny's old place. They was just no telling what he had, and I could not run the chance of my least ones getting it. He looked rough as a cob and had not washed off nor shaved in way too many a day.

Poor little Mary come by and it took a bunch of fast talking on my part to get her to go back home. She so wanted to help, but I told her for all I knowed he had the fever though I knowed in my heart it was not that old foe. Do not get me wrong, Larkin's body was as sick as any I'd ever seen and it might very well have been something what could be caught. But the worst of his sick could not have been caught by nobody else, for it was the greater sick of his soul. I knowed that I had to first wrassle his flesh from death's jaws and then he could at least have a shot at curing himself of the other. And they was something else I knowed though I cannot really tell you how I knowed it. Mary could not help him through this because she was a part of it.

So though she did not want to go, and I hated to let her go with a lie between us, I finally scared her enough to where she went. Oh, Lord, how sorry for her I did feel as I watched her thin little person all humped up against the cold turn down the path towards home.

Then I balled up my two fists and went to fight what I did not know. But by God, that was one battle I aimed to win. I know for a fact he would have died out there on the mountain, because it come the awfulest snow ever was over the next few days.

Hell, Larkin come damn near to dying anyways.

WHEN HE FINALLY STARTED to come around, the first thing he said was, "Oh, God, it feels like my eyes is full of broke-up glass," and then he tried to set up.

"Lay still, Larkin," I said.

He was so damn weak, and I could tell by how easy-like he swallowed that his throat must be hurting something bad. I put a cold wet cloth on his forehead and he peeped at me through slitted eyes. "Who's that?" he said, and I was surprised at how hoarse he was.

"It's Arty," I said, "and you've been sick as I've ever seen anybody that didn't die. And you still might, so lay still."

"How'd I get here?" he croaked. "God, my throat hurts."

"When it started to snow, Mary sent Hack Jr. to get Zeke. And it's a good thing she did, or you'd be dead, boyo." I leaned over him with the cold rag again. "They's a foot or more on the ground and it's still coming down."

I could see him trying to study about that, but he could not keep his mind on it. I watched him struggle with it, then he dosed back off and for the first time since they'd brought him in, he slept a good sleep.

I was still setting there when he woke up the next time. "Arty?"

"Right here, honey." I pushed the hair back from his forehead and let my hand stay for a bit. "Good. The fever's broke."

"I'm starved to death," he said.

I had to laugh at that. "No, honey. You *cheated* death as sure as the world. I'll get you some broth."

He was so hungry that I had to fuss at him a little. "Not so fast, Larkin. Take it slow."

When I'd spooned the last drop into his mouth I waved a hand in front of my nose. "I'll get some water and we'll clean you up a bit. You've smelled like yesterday's minners for days now."

He turned his head and looked at me. "Days?"

"You've been sick for almost two weeks, Larkin. And you're weak as cat pee."

He stared off up at the top of the cabin while I was heating up some water. When I commenced to washing him, his face got red as a beet. "I hate you're having to do this, Amma."

I grinned at him and just kept on washing. "That's the first time you've called me that in a long time, honey. And don't you be bashful. This ain't the first time I've scrubbed you down, and I ain't gonna see a thing I ain't seen a hundred times before."

He was quiet after that and let me wash him and was back asleep before I got halfway across the room with the dirty water.

IT TOOK TWO MORE weeks before he could get out of bed and put on his clothes, and they just hung on him.

I couldn't help but laugh. "Why, we'll use you in the garden come spring. You can scare the crows away."

Those clear dark eyes looked at me and finally, finally I could see a little sparkle. "You remember how Granny would sew that thread through each kernel of corn before she planted them?"

Now that really got me tickled. "Lord yes, and them crows would kick their own heads off trying to get it out."

Now you have no knowledge of how good that felt to set there and laugh with him.

He set down on the bench I'd pulled over next to the fire, and I set down next to him. We watched the fire for a while and the quiet between us was a good one.

He cleared his throat. "Thank you, Arty."

"You don't need to even say that, honey." I patted his bony knee. "My memory is long, and I ain't forgot for a minute how many times you've helped me."

So much flew between me and him as we set there.

"I was a mess, weren't I?" he said.

"You was." I gathered up his hand but kept my eyes on the fire. "Are you better?"

He knew just what I meant. "I believe."

"Then you need to think about going home, honey. They need you." And then I looked at him. "But only if you're better."

He sighed. "I know it. I'll go in a few days."

"Go only if you can, honey. You was born right here in this room and they was times when I thought you was going to die here. I swear I could feel Granny right here with us. At the first I thought she'd come for you, come to get you, and I kept telling her she could not have you yet. But one night I woke up from a sound sleep and just knowed in my heart that she was here to help me. And then I knew you wouldn't die."

"I hope part of me did die, Amma."

I looked at him, studied his face, and what I saw there made me smile. "They's something cleansing about a good sick, Larkin. Just don't do it again anytime soon."

I squeezed his hand and we set that-a-way, just holding hands, for a long time.

Three days later, Larkin went home.

CHRISTMAS FELL ON SUNDAY that year and they was a big preaching at the church. The young'uns always got up and said some little play parts and such, and some one of us would get up and read from St. Luke about the holy birth. That year of all things they asked me to read it and I spent the better part of two weeks studying on it so I would not get up and make a fool out of myself. I figured I would be nervous as a sore-tailed cat in a room full of rocking chairs. And I was, until I read the first verse, and the beauty of that sweet story seeped right into my bones and I was just fine. *And there were in the same country shepherds abiding in the field keeping watch over their flock by night. And lo the angel of the Lord came upon them and the glory of the Lord shone round about them and they were sore afraid.*

There was a big hush when I finished reading and then there was a little commotion at the back of the church, and you could have knocked me over with a feather when I saw Larkin step out into the aisle and head toward the front of the church. I thought he was coming to say something to me, but he did not even look at me. He went right past me and hit his knees right there in front of the altar. It was when Mary began to shout that I understood what was happening.

I HAVE NEVER SEEN anybody commence to loving up on salvation the way Larkin did.

Larkin took to reading the Bible that very night and he sort of whispered the words to himself. *"In the beginning God created the heaven and the earth."*

It was hard reading sometimes, and there were things he didn't understand. Preacher Daniel had told him to read all of Genesis, and through the cold winter days he would come by the house and me or Zeke one would try to help him. Carolina was a good hand at reading, too, and many was the night the two of them would set and read by the firelight. Now, let me say that they was a time or two when I was tempted to quarrel at him for not being at home, but he seemed so much better that it was almost like he'd been charmed, and I did not want to be the one to break whatever spell he was under.

There were times when he got plumb aggravated with it. *Now these are the generations of the sons of Noah, Shem, Ham, and Japheth and unto them were sons born after the flood.* I agreed with him there. I mean, who was all them folks anyway, and why did they have to list every name plumb back to the beginning of time?

There were times when he pondered the words and even I was plumb struck with some of the tales. *And Abraham stretched forth his hand, and took the knife to slay his son. And the angel of the Lord called unto him out of heaven, and said, Abraham, Abraham: and he said, Here am I.*

By spring, he'd finished Genesis. By summer he'd finished Exodus and Preacher Daniel advised him to skip to Psalms and Proverbs. He even carried his Bible into the field with him, and I saw him many a time propped up on his plow right in the middle of a row with it out reading. Why, sometimes he'd set into crying and I could not help myself, I'd cry too. *Why standest thou afar off, O Lord? Why hidest thou thyself in times of trouble?* We both set there bawling like two calves

in a hailstorm for a good thirty minutes when he found the words
Granny had told us all those years ago when her own Pappy refused
to stop singing the old love songs. *Make a joyful noise unto God, all
ye lands: . . . All the earth shall worship thee, and shall sing unto thee;
they shall sing to thy name.*

In church he took to singing solo, songs he chose from the old
singing books. The one he held most dear was the one called "French
Broad."

High o'er the hills the mountains rise, their summits tow'r toward
the skies,
But far above them I must dwell, or sink beneath the flames of hell.

Oh, God! Forbid that I should fall and lose my everlasting all;
But may I rise on wings of love, and soar to the blest world above.

Although I walk the mountains high, ere long my body low must
lie,
And in some lonesome place must rot, and by the living be forgot.

I allowed as how as long as me and him lived, Granny would not
be forgotten. And he wondered how many would remember as soon
as me and him went to the grave, and it hit me that he was right. That
is not hard to figure if you think about it the least little bit. Recall
that he had no memory of his very own mommie and daddy. I reckon
that was what he meant when he said that time, "Why, Amma, once
we die we might as well have been dead a million years."

But there for a while he seemed to move away from his thoughts
of death and dying and put his mind on the living. He spent hours and
hours with them two boys, and it was not long before you saw them
out working together and hunting all through the cove and yes, you

could hear them singing, too. He was finally starting to get back to himself, even if I thought he was leaning a little heavy on the church-going.

Mary had laughed to me and said, "Do you know what that Larkin said to me yesterday?"

And I was so glad to hear her laughing again and putting on weight that I felt like my face was going to split wide open, I was grinning so hard. "What did he say, honey?"

She looked at me and her cheeks was flushed with high color and her eyes was just shining. "He called me a virtuous woman whose price was far above rubies."

Yes sir, it sounded like our Larkin was back, and that he'd come a long way in figuring out how to deal with Mary just fine.

HE HAD STEPPED OUT of doors there at the house one cold winter's day right after he'd started in on the New Testament. I just happened by the table where he had his Bible out and I saw it was open to Philippians. I saw where he'd maked a passage and leaned down to read it: . . . *Work out your own salvation with fear and trembling.*

Now, that's the part of this church business that I do not like. They talk about God as a stern and vengeful one that will break a switch and just go to wearing you out at the least little thing. And it appears to me that all these people what gets a good dose of the religion gets awful high and mighty and commences to thinking that somehow they is only one way of doing things and that would be their way. They always allow that God has showed them or told them this, that, or the other. I am not too keen on this, as God has never told me nor showed me nothing.

It looked to me like Larkin Stanton was not being talked to much by God, neither, but from the looks of how his Bible was marked up, he was hunting for something awfully hard.

18

I HAVE HEARD FOLKS say that the biggest calm comes right before a storm. As I look back down through all these years that have made up my long life, I will have to say that this is the way it is sometimes. We'll be going right along and have no notion that things are fixing to change for us and then we'll get blindsided, and our life will just go hind end over apple cart. They was no warning a'tall that spring and summer. And I will even go so far as to say they was indeed a time of calm right before Preacher Daniel set things in motion that would change all the rest of our days.

Zeke and Larkin had gone off that spring and fetched back some tobacco seeds and we had all throwed in to grow it together. See, they was the promise of real money in 'baccer, and Lord knows we had need of that. My boys and Luke and Hack Jr. would hit them fields and work like dogs without Zeke or Larkin either one having to stay after them. And Larkin seemed more like himself than he had since he'd come from the war.

I reckon that's why it was so hard on us when it all come to pass.

ROXYANN WAS A BIG girl that summer and I remember she tended to all the young'uns while the rest of us was in the field. In that way she reminded me of myself. Seems like she was born with her hip stuck out to set a young'un on and she was always tending to and nussing young'uns. That was the first summer I really noticed what a fine voice she had. I was coming from the 'baccer field all sticky and hot and heard her singing to one of the young'uns and it was some of the best singing I'd heard in a long time. I made a note in my mind to learn her some of the old love songs and put Carolina on her as well.

See, that is what I mean about it being a peaceful time, which is not to say I don't go to singing when times is tough. Hell, sometimes that's all a body can do is sing, but it is better when the times is good.

Well, that summer went streaking by and they is several things that makes it stand out for me. I was forty years old and in June I found myself breeding again. This would be Arty's last lap-budding, and he come a big old pretty boy that would be the joy of my old age. We named him Joe Larkin. The "Larkin" ought to warn you that I was in a big way of missing my biggest boy. So here is the story of what and all happened that summer right before Larkin was set to have his thirty-second birthday.

MARY HAD ALREADY TOLD me that he was not sleeping and that he had took to wandering around and about the place in the dark. Now I knowed that meant he was fighting with something that he did not want to share with nobody, but I am sorry to have to say here that the didoes he'd cut back before he got so sick had made me not want to trust him much. I was watching him awful close. He started to fall off and his clothes got too big for him. Zeke allowed as how they was not standing around up in them fields, they was all working real hard with that 'baccer, and that this might be a good time for me to just mind my own business. That flew all over me as how I always prided myself on staying out of other people's business. I told him that sometimes I thought men was blind as bats and it was an amazement to me how they managed to find their own hind ends. So after he looked at me and shook his head and went off mumbling down into the front of his shirt, that is the last he mentioned it. I guess he knowed I was not feeling too good, and that he'd had a big part in why that was so. He pretty much left me alone over that summer. And it is probably just as well that he did.

It was not even daylight when Roxyann come running into the yard that Sunday morning. She said her mommie had sent her to fetch me. Rosalie was sick and her daddy was not home. I went with a heavy heart, scared sick thinking that awful squatting thing had somehow found its way back down the path to my biggest boy.

Mary met me at the door and her face was all pinched up. I went off the end of the porch meaning to find Larkin Stanton if I had to hunt all blessed day. That was not to be the case. I found him right off, as he had gone no further than the spring.

I didn't see him at first as the pearly light of that summer dawn had not found its way in under them big trees that stuck out over the water. I had turned to leave when he called out to me. "Amma?"

"Lord have mercy, you done about scared me to death."

"I didn't mean to scare you. You've got that chin stuck out and I know better than to mess with you now." He squatted beside me and smiled.

I looked at the sheen of dew on his clothes and his hair was wet with it. "What are you doing?"

"Just been out here woolgathering." He scooped a handful of water and wet his face. His eyes was red and he looked so tired.

"How long you been out here?"

His mouth give a little quirk. "Awhile."

I looked at him a long time without saying nothing.

Of a sudden he give me a big grin. "You aiming to paint a picture of me?"

Though he was trying awfully hard to be sweet, I did not even try to take the sharp edges off my voice. I was not going to put up with the foolishness I'd let roll over my head before. "Mary sent Roxyann for me before daylight. Rosalie is sick, Larkin, and you'd laid out all night." I know my chin was way out and I let her stay there.

His face got all worried and on the inside I give a big sigh of relief. Maybe me and God did not have so big a fight on our hands as I'd been getting my pigs set for. We headed back toward the house and he never said a word. And I never neither. I left him going in the house and I went on home. This was a preaching Sunday and I had my own herd to get ready.

PREACHER DANIEL WAS ALREADY in the chair behind the altar by the time we got there. All that running about before daylight had caused me to run late, and my bunch was as grumpy and sulled up as a bunch of possums. Hack Jr. and Luke was setting at the back when we went in, but Larkin and Roxyann was up next to the front and had saved us a seat. I asked Roxy where her mommie was and she whispered she'd stayed at home with Rosalee. I hushed then because the preacher stood up and smoothed back his thinning hair and walked to the altar. He laid his worn Bible gently on the stand, and looked out at us and everybody seemed to set up a little straighter and leaned toward him. He managed to keep my mind from wandering, which in my estimation made him a very fine preacher.

"Welcome, brothers and sisters!" His big strong voice boomed out into the room, and he motioned his hand toward the open windows. "It is a glorious day God has provided us with to come together to worship in his holy name. Amen?"

A bunch of people hollered "amen" back at him.

"Then I say let's raise our voices up to Him in song. Just like David told us to do. Let's sing 'Ninety-fifth.'" He held his Bible up and raised it above his head. He laughed delightedly. "And like the song says, 'When I can read my title clear to mansions in the skies, I bid farewell to every fear, and wipe my weeping eyes!'"

The congregation broke into full-voiced singing of the old hymn.

When I can read my title clear to mansions in the skies
I bid farewell to ev'ry fear and wipe my weeping eyes.

Would earth against my soul engage, and fiery darts be hurl'd,
Then I can smile at Satan's rage and face a frowning world.

Let cares like a wild deluge come, let storms of sorrow fall,
So I but safely reach my home, my God, my heav'n, my all.

There I shall bathe my weary soul in seas of heav'nly rest,
And not a wave of trouble roll across my peaceful breast.

Preacher Daniel had a look of pure-D rapture on his face and he rared back and hollered, "So I but safely reach my home, my God, my heaven, my all! Hallaleuer! Glory be to His blessed, blessed name! Amen! And amen!" He took out his handkerchief and wiped his brow and then his mouth. "As I was riding here yesterday I was a worried man. I usually am led by strong conviction. I *know* what I'll be preaching on before I ever get on that old horse tied out yonder!

The Lord puts them thoughts in my heart and the words come pouring out like He wants 'em to."

Preacher Daniel looked down at us and his face wore a wreath of sorrow. "But not a word come into my heart yesterday, ner last night, ner even this morning as I was coming here. But when I heard that song, that old wonderful song, I knowed what God wanted me to talk about here today. Listen to hit again: 'So I but safely reach my home...' No sweeter thought, brothers and sisters, than to know I'm going home one of these days. I'm going home!" He quit talking and looked back and forth at us all. "Do you know whether you're going home one of these glorious days? Can ye say, in the darkest part of the night, to yeself, 'Yessir! One of these days me and old Preacher Dan'l will stroll arm in arm over heaven together'?"

Throughout the room several folks closed their eyes and started rocking back and forth, and a few of them went to shouting.

"Some of ye can say, 'Yes, Preacher! I *will* see ye up yonder!'" He pointed his finger toward the ceiling, then set in to pointing at different people in the crowd. "Sister Ethel! I know, praise the Lord, that me and you will celebrate one of these days around the throne! And you, Brother Carl!" The preacher began to laugh. "Ever single time that door back yonder opens, Brother Carl is pawing the ground to git in. And them little babies, if they went right now, in the blink of an eye, why they'd be rocking in the arms of angels!" He wiped his face and opened his Bible up. "Some of ye knows what hit takes to git into heaven, praise God. You've lived it! Amen! But there's them amongst you that ain't guaranteed your place in Glory. Hit's them that God wants me to talk to today." He lowered his eyes and began to read, "Luke, chapter fifteen, verse seven. 'I say unto you that likewise joy shall be in heaven over one sinner that repenteth more than over ninety-nine just persons, which need no repentance.'" He looked at us and his countenance was sad. "Them's Jesus' words folks. More joy over one sinner that seeks redemption than ninety-nine folks that needs none."

"Bless him, Lord!" screamed out Ethel from right behind me. I swear that scared me so much that my hind end come plumb off that bench.

"That's a big old word, ain't it? Redemption. But that's what hit's all about, friends. Redemption. What did the prodigal son receive from his daddy? Even after he'd took his daddy's gold and squandered it? Even after he'd broke his old daddy's heart? When he come back dragging his tail end behind him, what did his father do? He forgive him. Took him in his old arms and loved him. He give him redemption. And that's what God does fer us. When we beg, and I mean *beg*." He pointed his finger at Carl. "Ain't that right, Brother Carl?"

"That's right, Preacher." Carl answered.

"Amen! And amen!" the preacher shouted. "And when we beg long enough and hard enough, long enough to where"—he laughed and patted his knees—"till they's scabs and calluses on these old kneecaps, then we receive redemption. And we're forgived of all the sins, all the pain of this old life is lifted off us, and we are pure again. Pure as any of these little babes laying in their mommies' arms. All them black spots that sin marks our souls with are gone!"

He smiled. "The Lord's moving in this little church today!" He gazed out at the congregation and paused. "I feel it so strong I want to sing about it. Let's all sing the old song 'Redemption.'"

Come all ye young people of ev'ry relation, come listen a while
    and to you I will tell

How I was first called to seek for salvation, redemption in Jesus,
  who saved me from hell.

I was not yet sixteen when Jesus first call'd me, to think of my
  soul and the state I was in;
I saw myself standing a distance from Jesus, between me and him
  was a mountain of sin.

The devil perceived that I was convinced, he strove to persuade
  me that I was too young,
That I would get weary before my ascension, and wish that I had
  not so early begun.

Sometimes he'd persuade me that Jesus was partial, when he was
  setting poor sinners free
That I was forsaken and quite reprobated, and there was no
  mercy at all for poor me.

The preacher looked out at us and waved his Bible. "It's all right here. The word and the way. You'll find everything you need right here." He tapped the cover with a gentle hand. "There is mercy and salvation for us all. All we need do is confess our sins, beg forgiveness. And then we have it. It's ours." He smiled. "Redemption."

19

I T IS FUNNY HOW words can be treated different by folks. I felt it
was a pretty decent service and I told the preacher as much as I was
leaving that day. And it's funny as I have often said what we recall
from days when our life takes a turn from the way it seemed destined
to go. I mean, for all the world I thought we was all in good shape —
me, Zeke, Mary, Larkin, and all our young'uns. We was doing good
with the 'baccer, and money would soon be rolling in. We stood out
in front of the church house that day and talked with Larkin about
what and all needed doing in the next few days. He never so much as
let on that something had settled down right next to his very soul and
was taking great big bites out of it. And I am sorry to say that I did
not catch it, though I stood right up in his face yapping away about
'baccer and the topping of it. The last I seed of him was his big broad
back going off down the road with his young'uns.

It would be almost two years before I'd see him again.

I HONESTLY DON'T KNOW what I'd have done if it had not
been for Zeke, God bless him. I was big as a cow with Joe Larkin that
fall and though I was not sick one bit in the body, my heart was ab-

solutely broke. Every time Aunt Susan come by the house on her mule carrying the mail I would go rushing out to ask, "Is they anything a'tall for me?" and she would look at me with a world of sadness and say "No, honey, they ain't a thing." You will just have to imagine how it was for me because they is no words to tell you of how I suffered.

When Larkin went walking off with his young'uns that day he'd got about halfway home and then had told Roxy to tell Mary he had to do something and would be on in a bit. Then it was like he'd fell off the face of the earth. All the next day they hunted for him and come up with nothing, and they kept on hunting for a solid week. As you might figure, Mary was perfectly wild. When Zeke made the call to stop looking, she was fit to be tied and I was too. I went up to the cave and they was no sign of him. I stood there in it and looked around at what was there and felt all done in. They was still some of Hackley's things and I don't know, it just made me feel so lonesome and hurt. Zeke finally said, "Arty, you're going to have to let this go." And though I knowed he was speaking the truth, it was hard for me to do. That was one of the few times in my life that all I could do was pray. But as with lots of them times, I did not know if God had Arty on the top of his list and sometimes I felt I might as well be praying to the wind for all the good it done.

I knowed when Mary got a letter from Larkin because Aunt Susan told it to me. I went straight as a shot to Mary and stood around for the better part of a whole day waiting for her to offer to let me read it, but she did not. I went home and cried for an hour to Zeke. Carolina finally said, "Mommie, it is between them." And Zeke said, "Leave your mommie alone, missy." I tried and tried to do that, but finally I had to ask Mary if she could just tell me that he was all right and she looked up at me and I ain't never seen such a look on nobody's face as the one she offered me. "He is in Charleston and is well, Arty." I did not dare ask anything else. At least I knowed he had not gone off somewheres and lost his mind. I done the best I could to comfort myself with just the knowing of that.

JOE LARKIN WAS BORN in March and I knowed in my heart somehow that he would be my last. There is something in a woman that goes to mourning when she births for the last time, and so it was with me. But you know it seemed like I was in a constant state of mourning that next little bit. Mommie died in May and Daddy fell dead at the milk gap that summer. That was an awful time for me as it seemed like everybody I loved was leaving me. They is something that happens to us when our mommie and daddy dies. It is like we have to step up into their shoes and they is no bigger footprints in this world. I grieved and grieved and then grieved some more. And I was watching Mary grieve, too, and she was not like me in that she had no grave to go to and mourn over. A grave does serve some purpose, you know.

LARKIN HAD BEEN GONE over a year when I was out hunting the cows and come up on Mary there on the ridge between the Shop Holler and the Munsen Cove. She was just standing there all wrapped up in Larkin's big blue coat, and I felt sorry for her when I looked in her face. I said howdy to her in my softest voice, and she looked at me with eyes as old as time itself and I was struck with how she looked to have aged ten years in the last two. I asked her what she was doing out. She sort of smiled and said, "Probably for the same reason as you." And we stood for a while looking off back into Tennessee where you could see the snow coming in. And then in a voice as flat as a flitter, she said these words to me that I have never forgot.

"I am so very tired, Arty. I woke up this morning and thought I heard somebody screaming, but it were just the wind hitting the side of the house. I laid there a long time trying to draw comfort from the sounds of my young'uns sleeping, but it did not work its charm on me like it usually does. I find no comfort nowhere."

I went to stand next to her and took her cold little hand in mine. It was like ice and I chapped it between mine till she finally pulled it back. Oh, how I wanted to ask her if she'd heard from him, but I held my tongue. To tell you the truth, I don't think I wanted to hear what she might have to say.

Then it started to snow. "We ought to get in out of the weather," I said.

"They is nowhere I can go that it is not cold, Arty," she said.

That hurt me as bad as anything I'd ever heard, and I'm ashamed to say that I wanted away from her and her cold little hands and her sad little face and her heart that was so badly broke. I went off and left her standing there by herself.

My heart was not just broke, it was shattered, and I could not stand no more.

LATE THAT SPRING MAGGIE come by the house. She was a sight to see and was all decked out in a fine dress and soft leather shoes and had that big mane of glossy hair done up in coils on top of her head. She looked a vision and I told her so. Her and Silas was up there seeing about her house and she asked about Larkin and Mary. Her eyes got bigger and bigger when I told her what had happened. They stayed on for supper and it was a good visit. She wrote to me when she got back home and said they'd gone by Mary's on the way out the next day, and peace had been made between her and Mary. Time does have a way of fixing things up. Though you might not believe that, I will tell you that it does. What she said in her letter is this: "Me and you and Mary has many things between us, Arty, the least of which is your brother and Larkin. We are all women what has eaten us a big mess of life and I suspect they is more of it on our plates to eat before we leave this world. We need to try to help each other as we go along."

And Maggie was exactly right. The three of us went right on eating for a long, long time.

LATE THAT SUMMER AUNT Susan hollered me from the house and she had a grin on her face as big as a mile. There was the letter that had been two years in the coming, but for all that time it were but a short thing.

> Dearest Amma,
> I am coming home.
> > Larkin

And it was like a dam busted inside of me and I cried and cried and cried.

I did not feel honor-bound to tell Mary as she had not done so with me. And it were a good thing, as the days passed and he did not come. My heart would set up a great racing with each sound from the road, but each time they would pass me by. By the end of August it was like the letter had never come at all.

Do not get it wrong here. I harbored no hard feelings toward Mary. I loved her better than my own sister. It is just that when you mixed her sad in with mine, it was a heavier load than I could tote. But I did feel bound to help her in any way I could, and when she sent Luke to get me to help her put up her corn, I went with nary a word.

That day was hot as Satan's housecat and we'd been out in the field most of the day and had left the boys to keep pulling corn. Me and Mary was out behind the house shucking as hard as we could and I could hear Roxy out in front singing where we'd put her to silking and washing it. I even recall that she was singing "Little Margaret." And then right in the middle she just quit. Now, my head come up right off, because we generally do not stop in the middle of a song, and my ears was straining for the next words. Mary was, too, and so it was that both of us was listening hard and had no trouble hearing her give a little scream. Quick as lightning me and her was up running for the house. Mary went in low through the back door and I knowed she was going for the shotgun that was always loaded and setting in the corner. I went around the house at a run and did not even stop to think of myself. My heart leapt into my throat when I come out into the clearing and saw Roxy sort of grappling around with a big man with shoulder-length black hair and I thought to myself, *Lord have mercy, what is a Indian doing here?* That is exactly what it looked like. Out of the corner of my eye I saw Mary come out on the porch and bring the gun up to her shoulder. I thought for all the world that she was going to shoot them both, so I hollered, "No, no, Mary, you'll hit her too." And when he heard my voice the big man turned Roxy loose and I saw his face.

Oh, but it was Larkin standing there.

Then a voice called from inside the cabin. "Mommie, Luke is at his back with the rifle and I'm coming out onto the porch." Hack Jr. come out then and stood beside his mommie. From where I was, I could see that he knowed Larkin but his eyes stayed as cold as ice.

It seemed like we was all froze in time. All except for my eyes and it seemed like they was everywhere at once. It seemed like I could see everything that was happening in a glance, and I thought that at any minute Mary would lay down the gun and everything would be as it should. But that did not happen for too long, and then I knowed something was bad wrong.

"Come over here, Roxy," Mary said, and my heart literally quit beating.

"Mommie, it's Daddy. Can't you see that?"

"I see him. You come on over here anyways."

Roxy looked at me. "Aunt Arty?" she said, and then she took a step away from her daddy and I heard the hammers on that shotgun being pulled back and it sounded loud as hell in that little clearing. I did not even think about it.

I just stepped out into that hot sun and put myself in between Mary and Larkin.

"Luke, you get on up here," I said, and I waited until he was standing there with his daddy.

When he saw his boy Larkin said, "Ah, Luke," and reached and gathered him up close to him. I could see Luke's face over Larkin's shoulder, and his eyes held no welcome for his daddy.

"Get on in the house with all of you young'uns," I said. My voice was rough as a cob and I meant for it to be that way.

"Do not interfere with this, Arty," Mary said to me. I felt my chin come out like a rock cliff.

"You make them young'uns go in that house, Mary, and I mean it. They are innocent lambs in this and should not have to bear it."

This give her pause just as I'd hoped it would, and while she was arguing with them I planted myself closer to Larkin. I never took my eyes off Mary and did not even have time to so much as speak to him before the door shut on them young'uns.

"Get out of my way, Arty."

I felt my guts go to water, but I did not move. "No, I will not."

We all stood there and I could feel the sweat break loose and go to running down between my shoulder blades. I could not stand it no more, and I turned my back on her and faced my biggest boy.

His black eyes was watching me like a hawk and his hair was wet with sweat. His shirt looked wet enough to where I could've wrung the water from it with my hands. "Oh, Larkin," I said right low to him, "what is this about?"

From behind me Mary said, "Tell her, Larkin, as I have not."

He flinched at her words. Finally he said to her, though he was looking me eyeball to eyeball, "You should have told her as I asked you to."

Mary give a big sigh and I heard the shotgun thump down on the porch. When I looked back at her, she was setting on the top step with the gun beside her. "What, Larkin? What should she have told me?"

And Mary laughed, but it was not a happy laugh. "Tell her, Larkin."

Larkin reached out a hand to me but let it drop back to his side before I had time to do anything. "Oh, God. Where will I start?"

"At the beginning, Larkin," Mary said and her voice seemed to echo around in my head.

Of a sudden I couldn't stand there in that sun another minute, and I said, "We're coming to set on the porch, Mary. I feel like I'm going to fall up."

Larkin grabbed hold of my arm and I went and set down beside Mary. He moved a little away from us but kept to the shade of the porch. And then he started to talk.

He said he'd been west to Missouri, south to Florida, and north to Boston since he'd been gone. He'd seen some pretty places and kept company with some pretty rough characters and allowed as that was all right since he was every bit as rough. He had even joined up with a minstrel show and had done a fair bit of singing from the stage. But he said he knowed now that every single step he'd made away from home that he was just making his way back.

I peeped at Mary and she was just staring out toward the barn. I couldn't help it when I said, "I know this is bad, Mary, but surely not bad enough to kill him for. I mean I'd feel the same way I reckon if it was Zeke, but I don't know that I'd take a shotgun after him." I have to tell you here that when I set down, I put my hind end right square on that gun and nothing short of Gabriel blowing his horn could have got me off of it. And maybe not even that.

She give me a look. "Quit wallering the truth around, Larkin," she said. "Tell her like you told it to me in your letter. Or I will one."

We set there and all was quiet. Then he give a great sigh and all the hair stood up on my arms, and I almost capped my hand over his mouth to keep him from saying what he aimed to say.

"Amma," he breathed and then he told me.

"It seems I have carried this thing for all my life, but it has only been with me since the day before I brought Hackley home throwed over that mule. Me and him had a big fuss the night before the Battle of Winding Stairs. It seems like that's all we done there at the last was fuss and fight with each other. I did love him." Mary made a little sound on that and he glanced quick at her, but then his eyes come right back to where they'd been holding mine. "You will probably hate me all the more for the saying of that one thing, Amma. But I did love him.

"I didn't hardly sleep a wink the night before the fight. To tell you the truth, I just sort of dozed around dreaming all manner of foolish things. I was up long before we was called to form up. Right at daylight I went to find Hackley and try to put things right between us. But when I found him he was sound asleep and I did not wake him.

"We formed up in a double V on either side of the road as it topped the mountain. Kirk put the tallest of us in the back and the shortest out in front and us sharpshooters was right in the middle. I could see Hackley right down in front of me. Then the Rebels come around the curve below us and all hell broke loose. It didn't take us long to turn them back and of a sudden a big wind come blowing down the hill and took the smoke off with it, and I saw Hackley getting up. He come up on his knees and sort of turned toward me. He was looking me right in the eyes and he knowed it before he hit the ground. I had shot him and he was dead and gone by the time I got to him."

And there it was. Now you might wonder how I felt hearing him relate the death of my brother to me like that, and I will have to say that I am still in amazement to this day. They was a brief little flare of pain way down in my heart and I immediately thought how this would hurt Mommie and Daddy and then I recalled that they was beyond this. So I let that go. Then I thought on their young'uns and I knowed right off that they had all knowed it for a long time and that's why they had acted the way they had a while ago. The only one that would not forgive him was maybe Hack Jr. and I couldn't swear to that. I searched my own heart again and for just a minute Hackley's face danced in the air right in front of me. But he'd been gone for so very long and though I was sorry, they was no way to change it. We have to go on and life is for the living.

I LOOKED OVER AT Mary and she was staring at Larkin. "What is it?" she said, and then she laughed. "Oh, I know what it is. You're thinking Roxyann looks more like me than I do myself."

I saw on his face that she'd caught him fair and square, but, bless his heart, he tried to deny it. "No, no," he said. "You look just like you always did."

And I thought to myself, *You still can't lie worth a damn.* Then I realized that was what hurt me more than anything else about all this mess. He had not come to *me* with it.

Then Mary said in a real soft voice. "Well, did you find your redemption, Larkin Stanton?"

"Leave him be, Mary," I said and my voice sounded old as Methuselah.

"Oh, I aim to leave him be, Arty. I just want to know since he wrote me so many letters about how he was searching for redemption."

Larkin stepped toward her but I held up my hand at him. "No. You leave her be, too," and I meant that as much as I'd ever meant anything in my life.

"Your forgiveness is all that matters to me, Mary."

She laughed out loud. "I think not, Larkin. The only thing that has mattered to you for a long time is yourself."

I could tell that her laughing had hurt him as bad as her words.

"That's not true, Mary. I've always done for everybody else. Amma, you, and, yes, even Hackley. He always had everything, the best of everything. He always got everything he wanted. Even you. He was not a good man, Mary, and he didn't deserve you."

Mary stared at him. "What are you talking about? His women, his not wanting to fight in the war, what?"

"Well, all of that."

She nodded. "Let's talk about that word redemption some more, Larkin." She leaned toward him. "What do you think would've happened if Hackley had lived?"

"Why, I don't know, nobody knows." He was flustered and I could tell this was not something he wanted to talk about, but I was curious and I wanted to hear what she had to say.

"You know what I think? I think he would've probably got shot by some woman's husband or bigged some young gal and left me for her." She pushed the hair back from her face. "I've not aged well."

What he did then reminded me of Carolina when she was in a big playacting fit and was going about the house all draped in one of my quilts and talking foolishness. I couldn't even feel sorry for him, though I did almost laugh. "You are the darling of my life. Will you say you've forgiven me, honey?"

She waved a tired hand at him. "Oh, get up, Larkin. Go on. Leave."

He got up and his face was red as fire. She looked at his big self there in the yard, sweaty and dusty, and she give him the gentlest of smiles.

That sliced him plumb to the bone.

"You wanted a big show of some kind, didn't you?" she asked him. "Me crying, the young'uns wailing and carrying on, you orating, vowing to love me forever and all. Larkin, you have worn me out. Go on and leave. I'm not taking you back."

My head was going back and forth between them so fast that I was making myself drunk, and I swear they were acting like I was not even setting there.

"But you've got to," he sputtered.

"No, I don't. I went from Daddy's daughter to Hackley's wife to your wife and I'll not have it again where a man can boss me and tell me what to do."

And I could not help it, I thought, *Go it, Mary.*

"But, Mary, I can't live without you. You're my redemption."

This time her laughter carried a measure of sadness with it. "No, honey, I ain't your redemption now no more than I was before. I'm just a real tired woman."

"Hackley would've wanted me to look after you. He told me that before he went off to the war."

"I know, I know. Poor little Mary, she needs tending to, looking after. Well, not no more she don't." She stood up. "It's sort of funny, Larkin. How you provided for me and Hackley."

He looked at her. "Lord have mercy, Mary, I ruined everybody's life."

"No, Larkin, you didn't. You give me the chance to be something I always wanted to be. Strong and able to do things for myself, depending on nobody but me."

He gave a bitter laugh. "Well, so I helped you by going off and making you be strong. I didn't help Hackley, though. I just murdered him."

I could hold my tongue no longer. "Oh, Larkin, didn't you hear what she said awhile ago? About what might've happened to Hackley if he'd lived? Don't you see, honey? He died with dignity, not caught in the bed with some man's wife. You give him a noble death in the war. In a way you give Hackley a good, decent way out."

The smile that lit Mary's face offered us the girl she once was. "Now you all go on while I go in and try to make sense of this for the young'uns." A frown puckered her brow. "I can't promise you'uns nothing where they're concerned. Roxy has always been her daddy's

girl, Rosalie will go with her sister. Luke I don't know about; he's awfully close to Hack Jr." The frown deepened. "Hack Jr. is not a good
age for this. He's all full of piss and vinegar. Larkin, I don't want you
to even try to talk to him right now. He's a lot like his daddy was.
Arty, maybe you can try a bit later." Her eyes met mine and held.

I give her a little smile and said "Time will take care of it. Just like
it takes care of everything else," I said.

Her eyes went to Larkin when he said, "Can I come to see you?"

"I don't think so," she said. "I don't think I want you to."

"But I love you," he said and the truth of it was in his eyes.

"Time will take care of that, too. You go on now, Larkin."

"The young'uns?"

"Roxy will find you, don't worry." I come up off the porch and offered her the gun. Her hand was on the latch when she turned.
"You're not a bad man, Larkin. You really ain't."

And she closed the door softly behind her.

20

I HAVE LAID THE picture out one more time and have run my hands over it. I do not need to see it to know what it looks like. I wish you could see it. Larkin and Hackley are all dressed up in their uniform suits. They was both such handsome men that you can see why they each got a little piece of Mary's heart. Larkin is setting in the chair and Hackley is standing beside him. I reckon the picture-taking man set them up that way because Larkin was so much higher than my brother. I recall his face looks solemn as a judge and his eyes and hair is black as a crow's wing. Hackley's eyes looks almost white, and it is left for my old blind eyes to remember the color of them, which was like the blue-eyed grass. He is standing with his pistol out and his elbow is resting on Larkin's shoulder. His hat is cocked over to the side of his head and his face is just full of devilment. Hackley's got his fiddle in his other hand. I'm glad in a way that I can no longer see it, as it used to hurt me so. See, the picture was took right before they left for Morganton and Winding Stairs. One month later and the deed was done forever.

I think Larkin did find his redemption. Him and Carolina come by here awhile ago and she fixed supper for me. They sung a few songs while they was in the kitchen and it done my heart good. Oh, I did not tell you that he married Carolina, did I? Well, he did, and though I fought it and threatened all manner of hellfire and brimstone would be throwed at their heads, it has worked out in the end.

Just like everything else. Time has took care of it.

If I live a few more hours it will be 1920. If I live three more months eighty-four years will have rolled over my head. I have hoed a long row. It ain't always been easy, but Lord it has been worth it. I have raised eight young'uns counting Larkin. And never, no, not for a minute, have I forgot the two I buried. My rough old hands was the very ones that eased most of my own grandbabies into this world. I have laughed more than most folks and I have cried just as much. I have lived hard at times, not so hard at others, and even let some days plumb get away from me. But who has not done the same? I have give and I have took. I have had a good run.

The smell of lilacs, cold spring water in my mouth on a hot summer day, the colors of fall, the sound of falling snow.

And what of the greatest of all? What of love? Oh, I have knowed love. Love was blue eyes that growed darker when he looked at me.

My hands move over the wooden bowl of a soup ladle with a broken handle and a verse from an old love song goes through my head.

> So fare you well, my old true love,
> So fare you well for a while.
> If I go I'll come again,
> If I go ten thousand miles.

Some things is just too rich for words.

Acknowledgments

THIS STORY IS BASED on family history. Hackley Norton was my grandfather's uncle and he did die in the Battle of Winding Stairs in June 1864. Larkin Stanton did survive the war. His grave stone is located at Walnut, North Carolina. Arty was indeed Hackley's sister and she is buried on a hilltop in Sodom. The other names, characters, and events exist only in my very active imagination or, if real, are used fictitiously and are not in any way intended to represent specific persons.

There are so many people to thank for their great insight, inspiration, and support: First and most important—Jim Taylor, my husband, traveling buddy, and Muse—*there hath been no greater love*—and I could not have written this book without his ear and support. My beloved children, Melanie Rice, Hart Barnhill, and Andrew Barnhill. Lee Smith, my friend and favorite writer, for her unflagging support and encouragement. My agent, Stella Connell, who believed in me enough to take a chance. My editor, Kathy Pories, for her genius, her amazing insight and sensitivity, and for helping me to turn Arty loose to tell this tale. Aidan Quinn for listening and then convincing me I needed to write this story. Renni Browne for her editing suggestions in the early stages of writing this book. The ballad singers of Sodom—Dellie Chandler Norton, Berzillia Wallin, Cas and Vergie Wallin, Evelyn Ramsey, Inez Chandler, and Doug Wallin—they were the keepers of the old songs and their voices are heard throughout this book. My sister, June Gahagan, for reading the book in its infancy and for being the calm at the center of what can sometimes be life's raging storm. My much loved and appreciated aunt Robenia and uncle Wayne Adams for being two of my most valuable resource people. My cousin Jerry Adams for jogging my memory and for supplying me with so much important information. My other cousins, Sharon Ray, Janet Adams Crowe, Sue Vilcinskas, and Keith Ray for listening, encouraging, and just setting on the porch with me while I rambled on and on. My uncle Ward and aunt Almarie Adams. Joe Penland, Bobby McMillon, and Marilyn McMinn McCredie for their lifelong friendship, music, old sayings, sharp wits, and unfailing ability to keep me grounded and laughing. Josh Goforth for his keen ear and musical genius. Laura Boosinger for the years of friendship and help with the selections and singings of the shape-note hymns. Wayne Martin and George Holt for over thirty years of priceless advice and sharing of frailties. David Perry and Linda Hobson for their much valued input. Lydia Hamessley, Sandy Ballard, William Jolliff, Bill and Fritzi Wisdom, Mimi Wright, Susan Graham, and literally countless other friends and fans that have helped me in so many different ways. Sonia Wallace, Vicki Skemp, James Leva, Amy Rabb, Susan Smith, Robbie Gualding, and Carol Elizabeth Jones for their encouraging words at the very beginning. Martha Fowler for handing me the little "gem" I used in the book. Randall Garrison, who showed Jim and me where the battle of Winding Stairs took place. Taylor Barnhill and Dave McGrew for sharing their knowledge of what this part of the world would have looked like in the 1800s. The Mountain Retreat and Learning Centers for providing the most beautiful place in the world where I wrote most of this book.

The following books and writers provided me with invaluable information on the political climate during this period in western North Carolina's history: *The Heart of Confederate Appalachia: Western North Carolina in the Civil War* by John C. Inscoe and Gordon B. McKinney; *Bushwhackers: The Civil War in North Carolina: The Mountains* by William R. Trotter; *Kirk's Raiders: A Notorious Band of Scoundrels and Thieves* by Matthew Bumgarner; *The Papers of Zebulon Baird Vance* edited by Frontis W. Johnston; *Mason Jars in the Flood and Other Stories* by Gary Carden.

I so wish these people were still here to read the book since it was from their recollections that I got the bones on which I hung the meat: Ervin and Neple Adams, Wayne Adams, Myrtle Ray, Fannie Leake, Jean Adams Sizemore, Bob and Emily Norton, Andrew and Mirlie Adams, and Father Andrew Graves. As Mama and Daddy so often said, "Family really is the most important thing in this world . . ."

For all those I have not mentioned I can only say this—you are of my heart, my family, my culture, and I love you—thank you for allowing me to be a part of your lives. And I have to give special thanks and a world of respect to all my Elderhostelers for their great wisdom and humor, and for teaching me the valuable lesson that no matter where we come from, we are all family in our hearts.

First published in the United States of America, 1978
Copyright © 1977 Patrick O'Brian
All rights reserved
Printed in the United States of America
Stein and Day/*Publishers*/Scarborough House,
Briarcliff Manor, N.Y. 10510

Library of Congress Cataloging in Publication Data
O'Brian, Patrick.
  The Mauritius command.

  I. Title.
PZ3.01285Mau 1978   [PR6029.B55]   823'.9'14   77-26234
ISBN 0-8128-2476-8

To Mary Renault

γλαῦκ' εἰς Ἀθήνας

A general view of the Mauritius Campaign

Comoro Islands

Mozambique Channel

Madagascar

Rodriguez

Mauritius
Port Louis
St. Denis
Port South-East
La Réunion

Cape Town to Mauritius 2885 miles

0 100 200 300 400 Miles

Mauritius to Rodriguez 344 miles
Mauritius to La Réunion 130 miles

50°   60°   70°

Mauritius (Ile de France)

0 5 10 Miles

58°E

Flat Island

St. Louis

Sable Pt.

River Noire

Cape Brabant

19°S

To La Reunion 130 m.

To Rodriguez 344 m

Pt. Diable
Ile de la Passe
Port South-East

Prevailing wind (E.S.E. Trades)

La Réunion (Ile Bourbon)

55°E

Cap Bernard   Riviere des Pluies
St. Denis   Ste. Marie
                                      Ste. Suzanne
Pointe
des Galets
St. Paul

21°S

St. Pierre

To Mauritius 130 m

0 5 10 15 Miles

Author's Note

Sometimes the reader of a novel, particularly of a novel set in another age, likes to know whether the events have any existence outside the author's mind, or whether, like the characters, they are quite imaginary.

There is no doubt a great deal to be said for complete freedom within a context of historical accuracy, but in this case the ground-work of the tale, a little-known campaign in the Indian Ocean, is factual; and as far as the geography, the manoeuvres, the ships taken, burnt, sunk or destroyed, the battles, triumphs, and disasters are concerned, the writer has kept close to contemporary accounts, to the log-books and despatches of the officers who fought the actions, and to the Admiralty records. Apart from the necessary fictions at the beginning and the very end, he has not done anything to neaten history except for the omission of a few confusing, unimportant ships whose fleeting presence was neither here nor there; nor has he thought fit to gild the lily by adding in any way to the Royal Navy's pugnacious resourceful-ness in time of adversity.

P.O'B.

Chapter One

Captain Aubrey of the Royal Navy lived in a part of Hampshire well supplied with sea-officers, some of whom had reached flag-rank in Rodney's day while others were still waiting for their first command. The more fortunate had large, comfortable houses overlooking Portsmouth, Spithead, St Helens, the Isle of Wight, and the constant procession of men-of-war; and Captain Aubrey might have been among them, since as a commander and as a young post-captain he had done so well in prize-money that he was known in the service as Lucky Jack Aubrey. But want of a ship, the failure of his agent, his ignorance of business, and the sharp practice of an attorney had reduced him to half-pay and no more; and in fact his cottage lay on the northern slope of the Downs, not far from Chilton Admiral, and the rising hill shut out all the sea, together with most of the sun.

This cottage, though picturesque among its ash trees and even romantic, ideally suited for two in the early days of his marriage, was neither large nor comfortable: it had always been low-ceilinged, pokey and inconvenient, but now that it also contained two babies, a niece, a ruined mother-in-law, some large pieces of furniture from Mapes Court, Mrs Williams's former home, and a couple of servants, it was something like the Black Hole of Calcutta, except that whereas the Hole was hot, dry and airless, Ashgrove Cottage let in draughts from all sides, while the damp rising from the floor joined the leaks in the roof to form pools in many of the rooms. These people Captain Aubrey maintained on nine shillings a day, paid half-yearly and often long after the anxiously-awaited date; and although in his mother-in-law he had a remarkable economist to help him, the effort of doing so had imprinted an expression of abiding worry on a face that nature had meant to look cheerful – an expression that sometimes had a touch of frustration in it as well, for Captain Aubrey, a scientific as well as a natural-born sailor, devoted to hydrography and navigation, was deeply concerned with a plan for finding the longitude at sea by the moons of Jupiter, and although he ground the mirrors and lenses for his telescope himself he would dearly have loved to be able to spend a guinea or two on brass-work from time to time.

1

At some distance below Ashgrove Cottage a deep lane led up through the fungus-smelling woods. The heavy autumnal rains had turned the clayey bottom into a quagmire, and through this quagmire, sitting sideways upon his horse with his feet so withdrawn from the mud that he appeared to be crouching on its back, like an ape, rode Dr Maturin, Captain Aubrey's closest friend, the surgeon in many of the ships he had commanded, a small, indefinably odd and even ill-looking man with pale eyes and a paler face, topped by the full-bottomed wig that marked him as a physician, if a somewhat old-fashioned one. He was, for him, unusually well dressed in a snuff-coloured coat with silver buttons and buckskin breeches; but the effect was spoilt by the long black sash that he wore wound three times round his waist, which gave him an outlandish air in the English countryside. On his saddle-bow lay a net, filled with a variety of mushrooms – bolets of all kinds, blewits, chanterelles, Jew's ears – and now, seeing a fine flush of St Bruno's collops, he sprang from his horse, seized a bush, and scrambled up the bank. As he did so an uncommonly large black and white bird lifted from among the trees, its vast wings labouring in the calm. Maturin's hand darted into the folds of his sash, whipped out a little spy-glass and presented it well before the bird, now harried by a pair of crows, crossed the valley and vanished over the hill that divided Ashgrove Cottage from the sea. With great satisfaction he stared after it for a while and then lowered his glass to the cottage itself. To his surprise he noticed that the little home-made observatory had been moved a considerable distance to the right, a good furlong, indeed, to a point where the ridge dropped fifty feet. And there, standing by its characteristic dome and overtopping it as Captain Gulliver might have overtopped a temple in Lilliput, stood Captain Aubrey, resting an ordinary naval glass upon the dome and peering steadfastly at some object far remote. The light was full on him; his face was sharp and clear in Maturin's telescope, and with a shock the Doctor saw not only that look of anxiety but also the marks of age and unhappiness. Stephen Maturin had thought of Aubrey as powerful resilient cheerful youth itself for so long that this change and the slow, weary motion as the distant figure closed the instrument and stood up, his hand pressed to an old wound in his back, were unusually distressing. Maturin closed his glass, picked the mushrooms and whistled his horse, a little Arab that came like a dog, looking affectionately into his face as he made his awkward

2

journey down the bank with his hatful of collops.

Ten minutes later he stood at the door of the observatory. Captain Aubrey's bottom now protruded from it, entirely filling the gap. 'He must have his telescope as nearly horizontal as it will go, and he bending double over it,' reflected Dr Maturin. 'There is no weight lost in these posteriors, however: would still tip the beam at fifteen stone.' Aloud he said, 'Hola, Jack.'

'Stephen!' cried Jack, shooting out backwards with surprising nimbleness in so large a man and seizing his friend by both hands. His pink face was scarlet with pleasure, and a slight answering flush appeared in Maturin's. 'How very happy I am to see you, old Stephen! How are you? Where have you been? Where have you been all this time?' But recollecting that Dr Maturin, as well as being a medical man, was also an intelligence agent – that his movements were necessarily obscure – that his appearance might well be connected with the recent Spanish declaration of war upon France – he hurried on, 'Looking after your affairs, no doubt. Splendid, splendid. You are staying with us, of course. Have you seen Sophie?'

'I have not. I paused at the kitchen door, asked the young woman was the Captain at home, and hearing domestic sounds within – the massacre of the innocents came to my mind – I merely left my offering and my horse and came along. You have moved the observatory.'

'Yes. It was no great task, however: the whole contraption don't weigh three hundredweight. Killick and I just unshipped the dome – it is copper from the old *Diomed* that the Dockyard let me have – and then we clapped on a couple of purchases and rolled it up in a forenoon.'

'How is Killick?' asked Stephen. Killick had been Jack's servant these many years; the three had been shipmates in several commissions, and Stephen valued him.

'Very well, I believe. I had news of him from Collard of *Ajax*; he sent a shark's backbone walking-stick for the twins. I had to turn him away, you know.'

Stephen nodded and said, 'Did the observatory not answer by the house, so?'

'Yes, it did,' said Jack hesitantly. 'But I tell you what it is, Stephen: from here you can see the Wight and the Solent, the tip of Gosport and Spithead. Quick, come and have a look – she will not have moved yet.'

Stephen lowered his face to the eyepiece, shading it with his

hands; and there, inverted on a pale luminous background, hung a misty three-decker, almost filling the disc. As he shifted the focus she sprang sharp and clear into view. Brilliantly clear: her sails, topgallants down to courses, limp in the flat calm: the cable out of her hawsehole as her boats ahead carried out the warps to bring her to her mooring. While he gazed he heard Jack's explanations – this was his new six-inch speculum – three months' grinding and buffing – finished off with the finest Pomeranian sludge – Miss Herschel's help invaluable – he had taken off a shade too much on the rim and had very nearly given up heart when she put him in the way of recovering it – admirable woman.

'Why, it is not the *Victory*,' cried Stephen as the ship began to move. 'It is the *Caledonia*. I can see the Scotch arms. Jack, I can positively see the Scotch arms! At this distance! You are the speculum-maker of the world, so you are.'

Jack laughed with pleasure. 'Well, do you see, it is the purest day for viewing,' he said modestly. 'Never a shimmer even by the water's edge. How I hope it will hold out until tonight. I will show you such a double star in Andromeda, less than a second of arc apart. Think of that, Stephen. Less than a second apart! With my three-inch glass I could never resolve anything much better than two. Should you not like to see a double less than a second apart?'

'Sure, it must be prodigious. But for my part I should as soon watch the shipping. Such life, such activity, and we Olympian above it all. Do you not spend hours and hours up here?'

'I do, Stephen, I do indeed. But I beg you will not mention it at the house. Sophie don't mind my stargazing, however late – and we shall have to sit up until three this morning before I can show you Jupiter – but staring at the Solent ain't astronomy. She don't say anything, but it makes her low in her spirits to think I am pining for the sea.'

'Do you pine much, Jack?' asked Stephen, but before Captain Aubrey could answer their attention was distracted by a clamour from the cottage, by Mrs Williams's hoarse martial voice, the shrill, defiant replies of the servant she was rebuking. Sometimes the motionless air carried the words up the hill with perfect clarity, and they heard the cry 'a foreign gentleman left them in my kitchen' several times repeated, but generally the passionate voices overlaid one another, and they were further confused by the echo from the hanging wood on the other side of the valley,

4

by the wail of children, and by the repeated slamming of a door.

Jack shrugged his shoulders: yet after a pause he looked benevolently down at his friend, surveying him. 'You have not really told me how you are, Stephen,' he said. 'How do you do in fact?'

'Amazingly well, I thank you, Jack. I took the waters at Caldas de Bohi not long ago, and derived great benefit from them.' Jack nodded: he knew the place, a village in the Pyrenees not far from Dr Maturin's high sheepwalk; for Stephen, though an Irishman, had property in those parts, coming down to him from his Catalan grandmother. 'And as well as growing as supple as a fawn,' continued Dr Maturin, 'I was able to make a number of valuable observations on the cretins of Bohi. Bohi is largely inhabited by idiots, my dear.'

'Bohi is not the only place, not by a long chalk. Look at the Admiralty, and what do you see? A general as First Lord, that is what you see. Would you believe it, Stephen? And the first thing this infernal redcoat does, is to take away one of the captain's eighths – he reduces our prize-money by a third, which is stark, raving lunacy. And then, quite apart from the idiots in Whitehall, this village has half a dozen; they squeak and gibber in the market-place. And in sober earnest, Stephen, I am sometimes cruelly worried by the twins. They do not look over bright to me, and I should take it very kind, was you to survey them privately. But I dare say you would like to look at the garden first?'

'I should like it of all things. And the bees.'

'Why, as to the bees, they seem to have piped down these last few weeks. That is to say, I have not been very close since I tried to take their honey, but I have not noticed them about. It must be more than a month since I was stung. But if you would like to see them, let us take the upper path.'

The hives stood in a trim row on white painted stools, but never a bee was to be seen. Stephen peered into the entrances, saw the telltale cobweb, shook his head and observed, 'It is the fell wax-moth.' He prised a skep from its stool and held it out, inverted, showing the dirty wreck of combs, with the vile grubs spinning their cocoons.

'The wax-moth!' cried Jack. 'Is there something I should have done?'

'No,' said Stephen. 'Not that I know of.'

5

'I would not have had it happen for the world. I am so concerned. Sophie and I valued them extremely, as your present.'

'Never mind,' said Stephen. 'I shall bring you some more, of a bolder stock. Pray let us view the garden.'

In the Indian Ocean Captain Aubrey had dreamed of a cottage, with a little land to it: rows of turnips, carrots, onions, cabbages and beans; now his dream was realized. But it had taken no account of the blackfly, the wireworm, the turnip-beetle, the leather-jacket, the green-fly and the black, the cabbage white. The rows were there, half an acre of them, dug as straight as a ruler in the poor, shallow, spewy, earth, and in them stood some dwarfish plants. 'Of course,' said Jack, 'there is nothing to be seen at this time of the year; but I mean to get three or four loads of dung on to the land this winter, and that will make a marvellous difference. I have already put some to my Brunswick cabbages, beyond Sophie's rose-garden. This way.' As they skirted the meagre potatoes he pointed over the hedge and said, 'That is the cow.'

'I thought it must be a cow: for milk, I make no doubt?'

'Just so. Vast great quantities of milk, butter, cream, veal: that is to say, we look forward to them presently. At the moment she happens to be dry.'

'Yet she does not look gravid. Rather the reverse, indeed: lean, Pharaonic, cadaverous.'

'Well, the fact of the matter, Stephen,' said Jack, staring at the cow, 'the fact of the matter is that she refuses the bull. He is game enough, oh Lord, yes; but she will have nothing to say to him. Then he flies into a hellfire passion, bellowing and tearing up the ground; and we go without milk.'

'From a philosophical point of view, her behaviour is logical enough. Reflect upon the continual, wearisome pregnancies, the price of a momentary and I may say aleatory pleasure. Reflect upon the physical discomfort of a full udder, to say nothing of the necessary parturition, with its attendant perils. I do not mention the uneasiness of seeing one's offspring turned into a blanquette de veau; for this is peculiar to the cow. Were I a female of any kind, I should beg to decline these general cares; and were I, in this particular case, a heifer, I should certainly choose to remain dry. Yet it must be confessed that from a domestical point of view celibacy in a cow takes on a different aspect entirely: here the general good calls out for teeming loins.'

6

'Yes,' said Jack. 'It does. Now here is Sophie's garden. It will be full of roses, come next June. Do you think they look a trifle spindly, Stephen? Do you think I should cut them back very hard, this winter?'

'Nothing do I know about gardening,' said Maturin. 'Nothing at all. But perhaps they may be a little, shall I say, rachitic?'

'I don't know how it is,' said Jack, 'I don't seem to have much luck with ornamental plants: that was supposed to be a lavender hedge, do you see? The roots came from Mapes. However, come and look at my cabbages. I am quite proud of them.' They passed through a wicket-gate and came to a plot at the back of the cottage: a sea of greenery, with a noble steaming dunghill beyond it. 'There,' cried Jack, 'have you ever seen the like?'

'I have not,' said Stephen.

'You may think them rather close, but I reasoned this way: for slinging hammocks we allow fourteen inches a man; now a man will eat a cabbage, and the part cannot be greater than the whole; so I set them by that reckoning, and it has answered amazingly.' He laughed with satisfaction. 'Do you remember the old Roman that could not bear to cut 'em?'

'Diocletian, I believe.'

'Just so. How I understand him. And yet, you know, whenever I do bring myself to spoil a rank, precious little encouragement do I get. Always this silly cry of caterpillars. Lord, if they had ate a tenth part of what we have ate in the way of weevils and bargemen in our biscuit, month in month out, on blockade, they would thank Heaven fasting for an honest green caterpillar.'

They stood awhile, contemplating the cabbage-patch, and in the stillness Stephen could actually hear the innumerable jaws at work. His eyes wandered from the mass of green to the dunghill: on the top of it he noticed the bolets, chanterelles, blewits and collops that he had picked a little while before. The crash of a slamming door above interrupted their meditations; this was followed by the sound of heavy steps within, and the back-door opened, to display a square, red-faced woman, the spit of Mrs Williams but for a cast in her left eye and, when she spoke, a shrill Welsh voice. She had her box on her shoulder.

'Why, Bessie,' cried Jack. 'Where are you going? What are you about?'

Passion so choked the woman that for a moment her lips moved with never a sound; then all at once the words came darting out, accompanied by so venomous a look that Stephen

7

crossed himself. 'A character, a character, that's all I want. Near with the sugar, nearer with the tea. A character I want, is all.' With this she vanished round the corner of the cottage.

Jack looked after her, and observed in a low voice, 'That makes the fourth this year. It is the damnedest thing, Stephen: I managed a ship's company of three hundred odd as easy as kiss your hand, but I cannot get the least notion of discipline into this establishment.' He paused, brooding, and added, 'You know very well I was no friend to the cat at sea; but rot me, I can see it has its uses.' Another reflective pause in which his face took on the stern, implacable expression of one who orders a dozen lashes to be laid on; then this look was replaced by one of concern and he cried, 'Oh Stephen, what a wretched host I am. You must be clemmed. Come in, come in, and we'll have a glass of grog. This way: you will not mind walking through the scullery – no ceremony, eh? Sophie must be somewhere in front.'

As he spoke a minute window opened above their heads and Sophie's head emerged. Her distracted look instantly changed to open delight, the sweetest smile. 'Oh, Stephen,' she cried, 'how very happy I am to see you. Come in. I shall be down directly.' Stephen plucked off his hat, bowed and kissed his hand, though indeed he could perfectly well have reached hers from where he stood.

'Step in,' said Jack, 'and mind your head on the beam.'

The only thing in the scullery apart from a vast copper and its smell of boiling baby-clothes was a young woman on a chair with her apron over her head, rocking mutely to and fro. Three paces carried them through it however, into a narrow passage and so to the parlour, a pleasant little room with a bow window, made more spacious by a number of sea-going devices such as lockers under the windows and compact brassbound ship's furniture, yet somewhat marred by incongruous great objects never designed for a cottage, such as a high-backed caned seat for five or six people and a long-case clock whose hood would not fit under the ceiling and which therefore stood bareheaded in a corner, shedding desolation. Jack had scarcely time to ask Dr Maturin whether the bow did not remind him of the stern-window of the brig in which they had first sailed together when there was the sound of steps on the stairs and Sophie ran in. She kissed Stephen with sisterly affection and holding him by both hands scrutinized him for his health, his happiness and his general welfare with a tenderness that went straight to his heart, talking all the time

8

with extreme rapidity – 'she was amazed, delighted – where had he been? – had he been quite well? – he could not imagine how pleased she was – had he been here long? – why had not Jack called her? – she had missed a quarter of an hour of him – she was sure the twins would remember him – they would be so excited – and little Cecilia too of course – he was hungry, was he not? – he would take a piece of seed-cake – how *was* he?'

'I am very well, I thank you. And you too, my dear, you are blooming, blooming.' She was indeed. She had caught up most of the wisps of hair he had seen streaming from the window, but one had escaped and its disorder enchanted him; yet for all the complacency with which he gazed upon her he could not conceal from his private mind that the tendency to plumpness he had once warned her of was quite gone, that were the present flush of pleasure not on her face she might look worn and even haggard, and that her hands, once so elegant, were now coarse and reddened.

Mrs Williams walked in. Stephen rose to bow, to ask after her health and that of her other daughters, and to answer her questions. He was about to sit down again after a tolerably detailed account of Mrs Williams' providential recovery when she cried, 'Not on the settle, Doctor Maturin, if you please. It is bad for the cane. You will be more comfortable in Captain Aubrey's chair.'

A thump and a dismal howling above-stairs called Sophie from the room, and presently Jack went after her. Mrs Williams, feeling that she had been a little abrupt in the matter of his sitting, gave Stephen a history of the settle since its manufacture in Dutch William's time: she had brought it with her from dear Mapes, where no doubt he remembered it in the summer drawing-room; she liked Captain A's cottage to have something of the air of a gentleman's house, and in any case she could not bear leaving so valuable, so historical a piece to her tenant, a worthy sort of man no doubt, but something in the commercial line, and people in that walk of life would not scruple to sit on it. The clock also came from Mapes, the most accurate clock in the county.

'A handsome clock it is too,' said Stephen. 'A regulator, I believe. Could it not be set a-going?'

'Oh, no, sir,' said Mrs Williams with a pitying look. 'Was it to be set a-going, the works would instantly start to wear.' From this she carried on to wear in general and the prohibitive cost of repairs, with an aside about Captain A's being handy in the house.

9

Captain Aubrey's voice, though well calculated to carry from one end of a ship to another in a gale, was less suited to the confidential domestic whisper, and at intervals in Mrs Williams's stream of words his deep rumble could be heard, not perhaps quite as good-humoured as once it was, expostulating about a fair-sized piece of ham that could be dressed, a sea-pie that could be knocked up in a moment. Stephen turned his attention to Mrs Williams, and shading his eyes with his hand he studied her carefully. It appeared to him that her misfortune had had remarkably little effect on her: her restless, aggressive urge to dominate seemed if anything to have increased; she looked well, and as happy as it was in her nature to be. Her frequent references to her former grandeur might have been references to a myth in which she did not herself believe, a dream from which she had wakened to her present reality. Perhaps she had been born to play the part of a contriving manager with two hundred a year, so that at last she was fulfilling her real purpose. Was it a remarkable display of courage, or was it stark insensibility? For some time now she had been on the subject of servants, producing the usual threadbare observations with great conviction and volubility. In her young days they had been perfect; now they were difficult to find, impossible to keep, idle, false, dishonest, and often downright evil. 'Only this morning, only this very morning,' she said, 'I caught the cook fingering a heap of toadstools. Can you imagine such wickedness, Dr Maturin? To finger toadstools and then to touch my grandchildren's food with her nasty hands! There's a Welshwoman for you!'

'Did you attend to her explanation, ma'am?'

'Of course not. Lies, all lies, you know, in the kitchen. I flung them out of the door and gave her a piece of my mind. Character, forsooth! Don't she wish she may get it.'

After a short pause Stephen said, 'I saw an osprey this morning in that noble hanger over the way.'

'Did you, sir, indeed? Well, I declare. In that little wood we see from the window? It is quite well, for Hampshire. But when you know the neighbourhood as well as I know it, you will find that it is nothing in comparison of the woods at Mapes. They stretched into the next county, sir, and they were full of ospreys. Mr Williams used to shoot any number of 'em. I dare say this osprey of yours was a stray from Mapes.'

For some time Stephen had been aware of a snuffling behind the door. Now it opened and a little girl with yellow hair and a

10

heavy cold came bursting in. She stared at him with an arch look, then buried her head in her grandmother's lap; to Stephen's relief all Mrs Williams's entreaties that she should stand up, that she should shake the gentleman's hand and give him a kiss, were in vain, and there she reclined, while her grandmother gently stroked her hair.

Mrs Williams had never, to Stephen's knowledge, shown the least kindness to her daughters; her face, voice and manner were unfitted for the expression of kindness; yet here it was, glowing in her whole squat person as she explained that this was little Cecilia, the child of her middle daughter, who was following her husband's regiment and who therefore could not look after her, poor thing.

'I should have known her anywhere,' said Stephen. 'A fine child.'

Sophie returned and the child at once began to shout, 'Aunt, Aunt, Cook tried to poison me with toadstools.' She kept up this unvaried cry for some time, and over it Stephen said to Sophie, 'I am strangely remiss: you must forgive me. I am come to beg you all to dine with me, and I have not yet delivered my invitation.'

'You are very good,' said Mrs Williams at once, 'but I am afraid that would be quite impossible, because –' she looked about for some reason why it should be quite impossible, but was obliged to take refuge in hushing the child. Stephen went on, 'I am staying at the Crown in Petersfield, and have bespoke a variety of dishes.'

Sophie asked how he could be so monstrous; he was staying at the cottage, and dining there too. Again the door opened, and both women eagerly turned to Jack. 'How they do talk,' reflected Stephen: this was the first time he had ever seen the slightest possible evidence of a relationship between Sophie and her improbable mother.

'Uncle Aubrey,' cried Cecilia, 'Cook tried to poison me and the twins with toadstools.'

'What stuff,' said Jack. 'Stephen, you dine and sleep with us. The galley is all ahoo today, but there will be a capital sea-pie.'

'Jack,' said Stephen, 'I have bespoke dinner at the Crown. These dishes will be on the table at the appointed hour, and if we are not there, they will go to waste entirely.'

This remark, he noticed, had a striking effect upon the women. Although they still protested that he should not go, the con-

viction and the volume of their arguments declined. Stephen said nothing: at times he looked out of the window, at others he watched Sophie and her mother, and their kinship became more apparent. Where did it lie? Certainly not in tone of voice, nor in any particular feature or physical movement. Conceivably it arose from a certain not childish but rather un-adult expression common to both, an expression that a French colleague of his, a physiognomist and a follower of Lavater, had called 'the English look', attributing it to frigidity, a well-known characteristic of Englishwomen, and thus to an ignorance of the warming, ripening delights of physical love. 'If Dupuytren was right, and if this is indeed the case,' he reflected, 'then Jack, with his ardent temperament, must be strangely put about.' The flood of talk continued. 'How well he bears it,' thought Stephen, remembering Jack's short way with cackle on the quarterdeck. 'I honour his forebearance.' Compromises made their appearance: some should go, some should stay. Eventually, after a very long typical family discussion that often began again where it had started, it was agreed that Jack should go, that Stephen should return the next morning for breakfast, and that Mrs Williams, for some reason, should content herself with a little bread and cheese.

'Nonsense, ma'am,' cried Jack, goaded beyond civility at last, 'there is a perfectly good piece of ham in the larder, and the makings of a monstrous fine great sea-pie.'

'But at least, Stephen, you will have time to see the twins before you leave,' said Sophie quickly. 'For the moment they are quite presentable. Pray show them, my dear. I will be with you in a moment.'

Jack led him up the stairs into a little sloping room, upon whose floor sat two bald babies, dressed in fresh frocks. They had pale, globular faces, and in the middle of each face a surprisingly long and pointed nose called the turnip to an impartial observer's mind. They looked at Stephen steadily: they had not yet reached the age of any social contract whatsoever and there was not the least doubt that they found him uninteresting, dull, even repellent; their eyes wandered elsewhere, dismissing him, both pairs at exactly the same moment. They might have been infinitely old, or members of another genus.

'Very fine children,' said Stephen. 'I should have known them anywhere.'

'I cannot tell one from t'other,' said Jack. 'You would not

credit the din they can kick up if things are not quite to their liking. The one on the right is probably Charlotte.' He stared at them; they stared at him, unwinking. 'What do you think of them, Stephen?' he asked, tapping his forehead significantly.

Stephen resumed his professional role. He had delivered some scores of babies at the Rotunda in his student days, but since then his practice had lain among adults, particularly among seafaring adults, and few men of his professional standing could have been worse qualified for this task; however, he picked them up, listened to their hearts and lungs, opened their mouths and peered within, bent their limbs, and made motions before their eyes.

'How old are they?' he asked.

'Why, they must be quite old by now,' said Jack. 'They seem to have been here for ever. Sophie will know exactly.'

Sophie came in, and to his pleasure Stephen saw both the little creatures lose their eternal, ancient look; they smiled, wriggled and jerked themselves convulsively with joy, mere human larvae.

'You need not be afraid for them,' he said, as he and Jack walked over the fields towards their dinner. 'They will do very well; they may even turn out a pair of phoenixes, in time. But I do beg you will not countenance that thoughtless way people have of flinging them up into the air. It is liable to do great harm, to confuse their intellects; and a girl, when grown into a woman, has greater need of her intellect than a man. It is a grievous error to fling them to the ceiling.'

'God's my life!' cried Jack, pausing in his stride. 'You don't tell me so? I thought they liked being tossed up – they laugh and crow and so on, almost human. But I shall never do it again, although they are only girls, poor little swabs.'

'It is curious, the way you dwell upon their sex. They are your own children, for all love, your very flesh; and yet I could almost suppose, and not only from your referring to them as *swabs*, a disobliging term, that you were disappointed in them, merely for being girls. It is, to be sure, a misfortune for *them* – the orthodox Jew daily thanks his Maker for not having been born a woman, and we might well echo his gratitude – but I cannot for the life of me see how it affects *you*, your aim being, as I take it, posterity, a vicarious immortality: and for that a girl is if anything a better assurance than a boy.'

'Perhaps it is a foolish prejudice,' said Jack, 'but to tell you the

13

truth, Stephen, I had longed for a boy. And to have not one girl but two – well, I would not have Sophie know it for the world, but it is a disappointment, reason how I may. My heart was set on a boy: I had it all worked out in my mind. I should have taken him to sea at seven or eight, with a good schoolmaster aboard to give him a thorough grounding in mathematics and even perhaps a parson for the frills, Latin and morality and so on. He should have spoken French and Spanish as well as you do, Stephen; and I could have taught him a deal of seamanship. Even if I could get no ship for years and years, I knew just what admirals and captains to place him with; he would not have lacked for friends in the service; and if he had not been knocked on the head first, I should have seen him made post by twenty-one or -two. Maybe I should even have seen him hoist his flag at last. I could help a boy along, at sea; and the sea is the only thing I know. What use can I possibly be to a parcel of girls? I cannot even give them portions.'

'By the law of averages the next is very likely to be a boy,' said Stephen, 'and then you will carry out your benevolent scheme.'

'There is no likelihood of another. None at all,' said Jack. 'You have not been married, Stephen – but I cannot explain – should never have mentioned it. This is the stile to the turnpike: you can see the Crown from here.'

They said nothing as they walked along the road. Stephen reflected upon Sophie's confinement: he had not been present, but he understood from his colleagues that it had been unusually difficult and prolonged – a bad presentation – yet there had been no essential lesion. He also reflected upon Jack's life at Ashgrove Cottage; and standing before the fire in the Crown, a fine great, posting-inn on the main Portsmouth road, he said, 'Were we to speak generally, we might say that upon the whole sailors, after many years of their unnatural, cloistered life, tend to regard the land as Fiddler's Green, a perpetual holiday; and that their expectations cannot be attempted to be fulfilled. What the ordinary landsman accepts as the common lot, the daily round of domestic ills, children, responsibilities, the ordinary seaman is apt to look upon as a disappointment of his hopes, an altogether exceptional trial, and an invasion of his liberty.'

'I catch your drift, old Stephen,' said Jack with a smile, 'and there is a great deal in what you say. But not every ordinary seaman has Mrs Williams to live with him. I am not complaining,

14

mark you. She is not a bad sort of a woman at all; she does her best according to her own lights, and she is truly devoted to the children. The trouble is that I had somehow got the wrong notion of marriage. I had thought there was more friendship and confidence and unreserve in it than the case allows. I am not criticizing Sophie in the least degree, you understand – '

'Certainly not.'

' – but in the nature of things . . . The fault is entirely on my side, I am sure. When you are in command, you get so sick of the loneliness, of playing the great man and so on, that you long to break out of it; but in the nature of things it don't seem possible.' He relapsed into silence.

After a while Stephen said, 'So if you were ordered to sea, brother, I collect you would not rage and curse, as being snatched away from domestic felicity – the felicity, I mean, of a parent guiding his daughters' first interesting steps?'

'I should kiss the messenger,' said Jack.

'This I had supposed for some time now,' murmured Stephen.

'For one thing, I should be on full pay,' continued Jack, 'and for another, there would be a chance of prize-money, and I might be able to give them portions.' At the word prize-money the old piratical look gleamed in his bright blue eye and he straightened to his full height. 'And indeed I have some hopes of a ship. I pepper the Admiralty with letters, of course, and some days ago I wrote to Bromley: there is a frigate fitting out in the Dockyard, the old *Diane*, doubled and braced with Snodgrass's diagonals. I even pester Old Jarvie from time to time, though he don't love me. Oh, I have half a dozen irons in the fire . . . I suppose you have not been up to anything, Stephen? Not another *Surprise*, with an envoy for the East Indies?'

'How come you to ask such a simple question, Jack? Hush: do not gape, but look privily towards the stair. There is a most strikingly handsome woman.'

Jack glanced round, and there in fact was a most strikingly handsome woman, young, spry, a lady very much alive, wearing a green riding-habit; she was aware of being looked at, and she moved with even more grace than nature had provided.

He turned heavily back to the fire. 'I have no use for your women,' he said. 'Handsome or otherwise.'

'I never expected you to utter so weak a remark,' said Stephen. 'To lump all women together in one undiscriminated heap is as unphilosophical as to say . . .'

'Gentlemen,' said the host of the Crown, 'your dinner is on the table, if you please to walk in.'

It was a good dinner, but even the soused hog's face did not restore Captain Aubrey's philosophy, nor give his expression the old degree of cheerfulness that Stephen had known outlast privation, defeat, imprisonment and even the loss of his ship.

After the first remove, which had been entirely taken up with memories of earlier commissions and former shipmates, they spoke of Mrs Williams's affairs. That lady, having lost her man of business by death, had been unfortunate in her choice of a new one, a gentleman with a scheme of investment that must infallibly yield seventeen and a half per cent. Her capital had been engulfed and with it her estate, though up until the present she still retained the house whose rent paid the interest on the mortgage. 'I cannot blame her,' said Jack. 'I dare say I should have done the same myself: even ten per cent would have been wonderfully tempting. But I wish she had not lost Sophie's dowry too. She did not choose to transfer it until the Michaelmas dividends were due, and in decency we could hardly press her, so it all went, being in her name. I mind the money, of course, but even more than that I mind its making Sophie unhappy. She feels she is a burden, which is the greatest nonsense. But what can I say? I might as well talk to the cathead.'

'Allow me to pour you another glass of this port,' said Stephen. 'It is an innocent wine, neither sophisticated nor muddy, which is rare in these parts. Tell me, who is the Miss Herschel of whom you spoke with such warm approbation?'

'Ah, now, that is another case altogether: there is a woman who bears out all you say about heaps,' cried Jack. 'There is a woman you can talk to as one rational being to another. Ask her the measure of an arc whose cosine is nought, and instantly she replies pi upon two: it is all there, in her head. She is sister to the great Mr Herschel.'

'The astronomer?'

'Just so. He honoured me with some most judicious remarks on refraction when I addressed the Royal Society, and that is how I came to know her. She had already read my paper on the Jovian moons, was more than civil about it, and suggested a quicker way of working my heliocentric longitudes. I go to see her every time she comes down to Newman's observatory, which is pretty often, and we sit there either sweeping for

comets all night or talking about instruments. She and her brother must have made some hundreds in their time. She understands telescopes from clew to earring, and it was she who showed me how to figure a speculum, and where to get my superfine Pomeranian sludge. And it is not mere theory: I have seen her walking round and round a post in Newman's stable-yard for a good three hours without a break, putting the last touches to a six-inch mirror – it will never do to take your hand from the surface at that stage, you know – taking snuff from a saucer every hundred paces. An admirable woman; you would love her, Stephen. And she sings, too – hits the note plumb in the middle, as pure as the Carlotta.'

'If she is Mr Herschel's sister, I presume she is a lady of a certain age?'

'Oh, yes, she must be sixty or so: she could never have come by such a knowledge of double stars in less. Sixty at least. Yet it is all one. Whenever I come home from a night with Miss Herschel there are wry looks, a tolerably frigid welcome.'

'Since it has physical effects, the sorrow and woe that is in marriage no doubt belongs to the province of the physician,' said Stephen. 'But I am as little acquainted with it as I am with gardening, or domestic economy.'

He was brought nearer acquainted the next morning, when he walked up to breakfast at the cottage. He was far too early, and the first sight that met his eye was the twins flinging their pap about and shrieking as they did so, while their grandmother, protected by a coarse canvas bib and apron, endeavoured to feed them with a spoon and little Cecilia wallowed in the bowl itself; he recoiled into the arms of the servant-girl carrying a basket of malodorous cloths, and worse might have happened if Sophie, suddenly appearing from above, had not whipped him away into the garden.

After a little general conversation from which it appeared that Jack had enjoyed his dinner, had come home singing, and was now grinding the coffee himself, she said, 'Oh, Stephen, how I wish you could help him to a ship. He is so unhappy here. He spends hours and hours up on the hill, looking at the sea through his telescope, and it breaks my heart. Even if it were only for a short cruise – the winter is coming on, and the damp is so bad for his wound – any sort of ship at all, even if it were only a transport, like dear Mr Pullings.'

'How I wish I could, my dear; but what is the voice of a ship's

17

surgeon in the councils of the great?' said Stephen, with a veiled though piercing glance to see whether any of her husband's knowledge of his double character had been sacrificed to marital confidence. Her next words and her totally unconscious air reassured him: she said, 'We saw in the paper that you were called in when the Duke of Clarence was ill, and I thought that perhaps a word from you . . .'

He said, 'Honey, the duke knows Jack very well, by reputation – we spoke of his action with the *Cacafuego* – but he also knows that recommending Jack for a command would be the worst service he could do him. His Highness is in bad odour with the Admiralty.'

'But surely they could not refuse the King's own son?'

'They are terrible men at the Admiralty, my dear.'

Before she could reply the church clock of Chilton Admiral told the hour, and on the third stroke Jack's hail of 'Coffee's up' followed by his manly form and some remarks about the wind having backed two points in the night – heavy rain for sure – broke up their conference.

Breakfast was spread in the parlour, and they walked into a fine smell of coffee, toast and wood-smoke: the ham stood on the table, flanked by Jack's own radishes, each the size of a moderate pippin, and a solitary egg. 'There is the great advantage of living in the country,' he said. 'You get your vegetables really fresh. And that is our own egg, Stephen! Do help yourself. Sophie's crab-apple jelly is by your side. Damn that chimney; it will not draw when the air is anything south of west. Stephen, let me pass you an egg.'

Mrs Williams brought Cecilia in, so starched that she held her arms from her sides, like an imperfectly-articulated doll. She came and stood by Stephen's chair, and while the others were busily wondering why there was no news from the rectory, where the birth of a child had been hourly expected these many days past, she told him loud and clear that they never had coffee except on birthdays and when there had been a victory, and that her uncle Aubrey usually drank small beer, whereas her aunt and grandmama drank milk: if he liked, she would butter his toast for him. She had buttered a good deal of his coat too before Mrs Williams, with a delighted shriek, plucked her away, remarking that there never was such a forward child for her years; Cecilia, her mother, could never have buttered a piece of toast so prettily at that age.

Jack's attention was elsewhere; his ear was cocked; his cup was poised; several times he looked at his watch. 'The post!' exclaimed Mrs Williams at the thundering double knock on the door, and Jack made a visible effort to sit still in his chair until the servant appeared, saying, 'A letter and a book, sir, if you please, and a shilling to pay.'

Jack felt in his pocket, frowned, and called across the table, 'Have you a shilling in change, Stephen? Here's nothing small.'

Stephen too plunged his hand into his breeches and came up with a mixed bag of currency, English, French and Spanish. 'The gentleman has three gold pieces,' said Cecilia, 'and a large quantity of silver.' But Stephen was deaf: he picked out twelve pence and handed them over, saying 'Never mind me, I beg.'

'Well, if you will all forgive me . . .' said Jack, breaking the seal. Mrs Williams craned her neck to make out all she could from her indifferent point of vantage, but before she could move to a better, her curiosity was satisfied. 'Oh,' said Jack, throwing the letter down, 'it is only that fellow Bromley. I always knew he was a rake; now I know he is a scrub into the bargain. However, here is the *Naval Chronicle*. That is always worth reading. My dear, Stephen's cup is empty.' He turned first to the appointments and promotions. 'Goate is made post at last: I am heartily glad of it.' Considerations upon the merits and demerits of Captain Goate and other acquaintances, also made post. Then, after a calculating pause, Jack said, 'You know, Stephen, our losses last year were not as heavy as I made out last night. Listen: *Jupiter*, 50, wrecked in Vigo Bay; *Leda*, 38, wrecked off Milford Haven; *Crescent*, 36, wrecked off Jutland; *Flora*, 32, wrecked off Holland; *Meleager*, 36, wrecked on Barebush Cay; *Astraea*, 32, wrecked off Anagado. Only five frigates, you see. And as for the post-ships, only *Banterer*, 22, wrecked in the St Lawrence; *Laurel*, 22, taken by the *Canonnière*, 50 – you remember the *Canonnière*, Stephen? I pointed her out to you once, when we were looking into Brest. An ancient old ship, built somewhere about 1710, but an amazing fine sailer; she can still give most of our heavy frigates topgallants on a bowline. Stephen, what's amiss?'

Stephen was gazing through the acrid smoke at Cecilia, who, bored with the conversation, had opened the clock's door with her greasy hands to get at the pendulum, a heavy jar of quicksilver.

'Oh, let the poor little treasure be,' said Mrs Williams, looking at her granddaughter with the fondest admiration.

19

'Madam,' said Stephen, his heart in pain for the exquisite mechanism, 'she will do herself a mischief. That quicksilver is most delicately poised; furthermore it is poison.'

'Cecilia,' said Jack, 'cut along now. Run away and play.'

Contention, tears, Mrs Williams's nimble protective tongue, and Sophie led her niece from the room. Mrs Williams was not at all pleased, but in the silence the sound of the passing-bell came clear from the church; it instantly diverted her mind, and she cried, 'That must be for poor Mrs Thwaites. She was due last week, and they sent for the man-midwife last night. There, Captain Aubrey.' These last words were delivered with an inimical jerk of her head, a retaliation, as it were, for his list of male wreckage and death, an assertion of women's sacrifice.

Sophie returned with the news that a horseman was approaching the cottage. 'It is news of poor Mrs Thwaites, no doubt,' said Mrs Williams, looking hard at Jack again. But she was mistaken. It was a boy from the Crown, with a letter for Jack: he was to wait for an answer.

' "Lady Clonfert presents her compliments to Captain and Mrs Aubrey, and would be most grateful for a passage to the Cape. She promises to take up no room and to give no trouble whatsoever; and flatters herself that Mrs Aubrey will, as a fellow-sailor's wife, understand and support this sadly informal and hurried application. She also proposes, if perfectly convenient to Mrs Aubrey, to do herself the honour of waiting upon her in the forenoon," ' read Captain Aubrey aloud, with a very high degree of astonishment, adding, 'Certainly she may have a lift to the Cape, whenever I happen to be going there, ha, ha.'

'Jack,' said Stephen, 'a word with you, if you please.'

They walked out into the garden, pursued by Mrs Williams's angry voice – 'A most improper application – no compliments to me – and disgracefully ill-wrote; she has spelt promises with one m – I have no patience with these attempts at thrusting oneself into a strange house.'

At the end of the wan row of carrots Stephen said, 'I must beg your pardon for having evaded your question last night. I have in fact *been up to something*, as you put it. But first I must speak very briefly of the position in the Indian Ocean. Some months ago four new French frigates slipped out of the Channel ports, ostensibly for Martinique – that was the general rumour on shore, and that was the destination stated in the orders delivered to their respective captains: but no doubt these captains also carried

20

sealed orders, to be opened somewhere south of Finisterre. At all events the frigates never reached the Antilles. Nothing was heard of them until they reached Mauritius, where they upset the balance of power in those waters entirely. The news of their presence reached England a very short while ago. They have already taken two Indiamen, and clearly they threaten to take many more. Government is extremely concerned.'

'I am sure of it,' cried Jack. Mauritius and La Réunion lay right in the path of the eastern trade, and although the Company's ships were usually well enough armed to deal with the privateers and pirates that swarmed in those seas, while the Royal Navy, by stretching its resources to the utmost, could just contain the French men-of-war, the sudden arrival of four frigates would be catastrophic: furthermore, the Frenchmen had excellent deep-water harbours in Port-Louis and Port South-East and St Paul's, sheltered from the frequent hurricanes and full of marine stores, whereas the Navy's nearest base was the Cape, more than two thousand miles to the south.

Stephen was silent for a moment. 'Do you know the *Boadicea*?' he asked abruptly.

'*Boadicea*, thirty-eight? Yes, of course. A weatherly ship, though slow: fitting foreign for the Leeward Islands station. Charles Loveless has her.'

'Well, listen now: this vessel, this frigate, is to be diverted to the Cape. And Captain Loveless, as you say, was to take her there to form part of a squadron made up of what the Admiral could spare: a force intended not only to counteract the French frigates but to take their bases away from them. In short, to capture La Réunion and Mauritius, to install a governor, and to possess them as colonies, valuable not only in themselves but as posts along this most interesting route.'

'A capital notion,' said Jack. 'It has always seemed absurd to me, that islands should not be English – unnatural.' He spoke a little at haphazard, because he had noted – oh, with what keen attention – Stephen's 'Captain Loveless *was* to take her'. Might this possibly be an acting command?

Stephen frowned. 'I was to accompany this force, together with the proposed governor,' he went on. 'And I was in a position to offer a certain amount of advice; that is to say, I was consulted on various points. It did not appear to me that Captain Loveless was fitted for the political side of the task, either mentally or physically; but he has great interest at the Admiralty. However,

21

his malady increased upon him, and in spite of my colleague's efforts and of my own he is now on shore with an obstinate tenesmus that will keep him there. In London I caused it to be suggested that Captain Aubrey would be admirably suited for the vacant command – ' Jack gripped his elbow with a force that made him catch his breath, but he continued ' – that it was probable he would accept it in spite of his domestic situation and of the very short notice, and that I should be seeing him myself directly. Alternative names were advanced; some very frivolous objections to do with seniority and the flying of some kind of flag, some trumpery mark of distinction, were raised, for it seemed desirable that the person, or the ship, in question should be so ornamented . . .' With a prodigious effort Jack swallowed the words 'A broad pendant, a commodore's broad pendant, for God's sake!' and Stephen continued, 'and most unhappily several people had to be consulted.' He bent to pick a stalk of grass and put it into his mouth; for some time he shook his head, and the farther end of the grass magnified its motion, showing anger, disapprobation, or a most decided negative. Jack's heart, raised by the mere mention of a broad pendant, the sailor's sweetest dream short of the admiral's flag itself, sank into the dark, everyday world of half-pay. 'Most unhappily, I say,' went on Stephen, 'for although I carried my point, it is evident that at least one of those consulted has been talking. The rumour has already spread about the town. Lady Clonfert's appearance is clear proof of that: her husband is on the Cape station, captain of the *Otter*. Oh, oh, it is always the same thing – gabble, gabble, gabble, blab, blab, blab, like a parcel of geese on a common, or a pack of old women . . .' his voice soared shrill in indignation, and Jack was aware that he was giving instances of loose talk, of intelligence conveyed to the enemy by spreading gossip; but Jack's glowing mind was filled with a picture of the *Boadicea*, her simpering figurehead with its vast bosom spreading over the frigate's fine seaworthy bows – a trifle slow, perhaps, and he had seen her miss stays; but a careful stowing of her hold to bring her by the stern might make a world of difference, and cross-cat-harpins; Charles Loveless had no notion of cross-cat-harpins, still less of Bentinck shrouds. He found Stephen's eye fixed angrily upon him, bent his head with an expression of the gravest attention, and heard the words, 'As though the French were deaf, dumb, blind, incompetent! That is why I am most unwillingly obliged to give you this short summary. In any other event I

should infinitely have preferred the news to reach you through the proper channels, without the least explanation – your provisional orders are at the port-admiral's office this minute – for not only does this require speaking openly of what should not be mentioned at all, but I am extremely averse to appearing in the role of fairy godmother, a purely fortuitous fairy godmother in this case. It can inflict an apparent, though fallacious, burden of obligation, and cause great damage to a relationship.'

'Not to ours, brother,' said Jack, 'not to ours. And I will not thank you, since you don't like it; but Lord, Stephen, I am a different man.' He was indeed. Taller, younger, pinker, his eyes blazing with life. His stoop had gone, and a great boyish grin kept ruining his attempted gravity.

'You will not mention this to Sophie, nor to any other person,' said Stephen, with a cold, penetrating glare.

'Must I not even start looking to my sea-chest?'

'What a fellow you are, Jack!' cried Stephen, in great disgust. 'Of course you must not, not until the port-admiral's messenger is come. Cannot you see the obvious cause and effect? I should have thought it plain even to the meanest intelligence.'

'A ship!' cried Jack, springing heavily into the air. There were tears in his eyes, and Stephen saw that he might wish to shake hands at any minute. He disliked all effusion, privately thinking the English far too much given to weeping and the flow of soul; he pursed his lips with a sour expression, and put his hands behind his back. He said, 'Plain to the meanest intelligence: I appear – you have a ship. What must Sophie conclude? Where is my character?'

'How long do you think the port-admiral's messenger will be, Stephen?' asked Jack, with nothing but a loving smile at these harsh words.

'Let us hope he outpaces Lady Clonfert by a few minutes at least, if only to prove that casual gossip does not necessarily have to run faster than official orders every single time. How we shall ever win this war I cannot tell. In Whitehall they know perfectly well that success in the Mauritius enterprise is of capital importance, and yet some fool must be prating. I cannot express my abhorrence of their levity. We reinforce the Cape, and tell them so: they instantly reinforce the Ile de France, that is to say, Mauritius. And so it runs, all, all of a piece throughout: Mr Congreve invents a military rocket with vast potentialities – we instantly inform the world, like a hen that has laid an egg, thus

23

throwing away all the effect of surprise. The worthy Mr Snodgrass finds out a way of rendering old ships serviceable in a short time and at little expense: without a moment's pause we publish his method in all the papers, together with drawings, lest some particular should escape our enemy's comprehension.'

Jack looked as solemn as he could, and shook his head; but very soon he turned a beaming face to Stephen and asked, 'Do you imagine this will be one of your stand-off-and-on capers? Ordered to sea at a moment's notice, recalled, turned on shore for a month, all your hands drafted elsewhere, and then sent to the Baltic at last in your hot-weather clothes?'

'I do not. Quite apart from the absolute importance of the operation, there are many members of the Board and of the ministry that have their money in East India stock: ruin the Company and you ruin them. No, no: there is likely to be a wonderful degree of celerity in this case, I believe.'

Jack laughed aloud with pleasure, and then observed that they must be getting back to the house – the boy from the Crown was waiting for an answer. 'I shall have to give that wretched woman a lift,' he added. 'You cannot refuse a brother-officer's wife, the wife of a man you know; but Lord, how I wish I could get out of it. Come, let us walk in.'

'I cannot advise it,' said Stephen. 'Sophie would detect you instantly. You are as transparent as a bride. Stay here till I desire Sophie to make your joint reply to Lady Clonfert: you cannot be seen until you have your orders.'

'I shall go to the observatory,' said Jack.

It was here that Stephen found him some minutes later, with his telescope trained on the Portsmouth road. 'Sophie has answered,' said Stephen, 'and every woman in the house is now scrubbing the parlour and changing the lace window-curtains; they turned me out with very little ceremony, I can tell you.'

The promised rain began to fall, drumming briskly on the copper dome: there was just room for them both, and there they crouched in silence for a while. Beneath the bubbling current of his pure joy, Jack longed to ask whether Stephen had in some way arranged Captain Loveless's tenesmus; but although he had known Stephen intimately these many, many years, there was something about him that forbade questioning.

Presently, his mind sobering, he reflected on the Indian Ocean, on the fine blue-water sailing with the south-east trade-wind, the perilous inshore navigation among the coral reefs surrounding La

24

Réunion and Mauritius; on the typical Admiralty decision to send one frigate to counterbalance four; on the immense difficulty of maintaining even a blockade, above all in the hurricane months, let alone that of landing upon those islands, with their few harbours (and those fortified), their broad reefs, the perpetual heavy surf on their inhospitable shores; on the question of water, and on the nature of the force likely to oppose him. To oppose him, that is to say, if ever he reached the station. Furtively stretching out to touch a piece of wood, he said, 'This hypothetical squadron, Stephen, have you any idea of its strength, and what it might have to deal with?'

'I wish I had, my dear,' said Stephen. 'The *Néréide* and the *Sirius* were mentioned, to be sure, together with the *Otter* and the possibility of another sloop; but beyond that everything is nebulous. Vessels that Admiral Bertie had at the time of his latest despatches, dated more than three months ago, may very well be off Java by the time the squadron is actually formed. Nor can I speak to what Decaen may have had in Mauritius before this reinforcement, apart from the *Canonnière* and possibly the *Sémillante* – they range so wide. On the other hand I can tell you the names of their new frigates. They are the *Vénus, Manche, Bellone* and *Caroline*.'

'*Vénus, Manche, Bellone, Caroline*,' said Jack, frowning. 'I have never heard of a single one of 'em.'

'No. As I said, they are new, quite new: they carry forty guns apiece. Twenty-four pounders, at least in the case of the *Bellone* and the *Manche*: perhaps in the others too.

'Oh, indeed?' said Jack, his eye still to his telescope. The rosy glow in his mind had strange lurid edges to it now. Those were in fact the French navy's most recent, very heavy frigates, the envy of the British dockyards. Buonaparte had all the forests of Europe at his command, splendid Dalmatian oak, tall northern spars, best Riga hemp; and although the man himself was the merest soldier, his ship-builders turned out the finest vessels afloat; and he had some very capable officers to command them. Forty guns apiece. The *Néréide* had thirty-six, but only twelve-pounders: *Boadicea* and *Sirius*, with their eighteen-pounders, might be a match for the Frenchmen, particularly if the French crews were as new as their ships; but even so, that was a hundred and sixty guns to a hundred and ten to say nothing of the broad-side weight of metal. Everything would depend on how those guns were handled. The other forces at the Cape hardly entered

into the line of count. The flagship, the ancient *Raisonable*, 64, could no more be considered a fighting unit than the antique French *Canonnière*: he could not offhand recall the smaller vessels on the station, apart from the *Otter*, a pretty eighteen-gun ship-sloop: but in any case, if it came to a general action, the frigates alone must bear the brunt. The *Néréide* he knew of, the crack frigate of the West Indies station, and in Corbett she had a fighting captain; Pym he knew by reputation; but Clonfert of the *Otter* was the only captain he had ever sailed with . . . Across the round of his objective-glass travelled a purposeful Marine, mounted on a horse. 'O blessed form,' murmured Jack, following him behind a haystack with his telescope, 'he will be here in twenty minutes. I shall give him a guinea.' All at once the Indian Ocean, the Mauritius command, took on a new, infinitely more concrete reality: the characters of Admiral Bertie, Captain Pym, Captain Corbett and even Lord Clonfert assumed a great practical importance: so did the immediate problems of a new command. Although his intimacy with Stephen Maturin did not allow him to ask questions that might be judged impertinent, it was of such a rare kind that he could ask for money without the least hesitation. 'Have you any money, Stephen?' he said, the Marine having vanished in the trees. 'How I hope you have. I shall have to borrow the Marine's guinea from you, and a great deal more besides, if his message is what I dearly trust. My half-pay is not due until the month after next, and we are living on credit.'

'Money, is it?' said Stephen, who had been thinking about lemurs. There were lemurs in Madagascar: might there not be lemurs on Réunion? Lemurs concealed among the forests and the mountains of the interior? 'Money? Oh, yes, I have money galore.' He felt in his pockets. 'The question is, where is it?' He felt again, patted his bosom, and brought out a couple of greasy two-pound notes on a country bank. 'That is not it,' he muttered, going through his pockets again. 'Yet I was sure – was it in my other coat? – did I perhaps leave it in London? – you are growing old, Maturin – ah, you dog, there you are!' he cried triumphantly, returning to the first pocket and drawing forth a neat roll, tied with tape. 'There. I had confused it with my lancet-case. It was Mrs Broad of the Grapes that did it up, finding it in a Bank of England wrapper that I had – that I had neglected. A most ingenious way of carrying money, calculated to deceive the pick-pocket. I hope it will suffice.'

'How much is it?' asked Jack.

'Sixty or seventy pound, I dare say.'

'But, Stephen, the top note is a fifty, and so is the next. I do not believe you ever counted them.'

'Well, never mind, never mind,' said Stephen testily. 'I meant a hundred and sixty. Indeed, I said as much, only you did not attend.'

They both straightened, cocking their ears. Through the beating of the rain came Sophie's voice calling 'Jack! Jack!' and rising to a squeak as she darted into the observatory, breathless and wet. 'There is a Marine from the port-admiral,' she said between her gasps, 'and he will not give his message except into your own hands. Oh, Jack, might it be a ship?'

A ship it was. Captain Aubrey was required and directed to repair aboard HMS *Boadicea* and to take upon himself the command of the said vessel, for which the enclosed order was to be his warrant: he was to touch at Plymouth, there to receive on board R. T. Farquhar, Esquire, at the Commissioner's office, and any further orders that might be transmitted to him at that place. These stately, somewhat inimical documents (as usual, Captain Aubrey was to fail not, at his peril), were accompanied by a friendly note from the Admiral, asking Jack to dine with him the next day, before going aboard.

Now that direct action was legitimate, it burst forth with such force that Ashgrove Cottage was turned upside-down in a moment. At first Mrs Williams clung tenaciously to her scheme for changing the parlour curtains, clamouring that it must be done – what would Lady Clonfert think? – and protesting that she should not be overborne; but her strength was as nothing compared with that of a newly-appointed frigate-captain burning to join his ship before the evening gun, and in a few minutes she joined her daughter and the distracted maid in brushing uniforms, madly darning stockings and ironing neck-cloths, while Jack trundled his sea-chest in the attic and roared down to know where was his neat's-foot oil, and who had been at his pistols? adjuring them 'to bear a hand', 'to look alive', 'to lose not a minute below there', 'to light along the sextant-case'.

Lady Clonfert's arrival, so much in the forefront of Mrs Williams's mind not an hour before, passed almost unnoticed in the turmoil, a turmoil increased by the howling of neglected children, which reached its paroxysm as her coachman thundered on the door. A full two minutes of strenuous battering passed by

27

before the door was opened and she was able to walk into the naked parlour, whose old curtains lay on one end of the settle and the new on the other.

Poor lady, she had but a sad time of it. She had dressed with particular care in garments designed not to offend Mrs Aubrey by being too fashionable or becoming yet at the same time to beguile Captain Aubrey, and she had prepared an artless speech about sailors' wives, Clonfert's respect and affection for his old shipmate, and her perfect familiarity with life aboard a man-of-war, together with some slight hints as to her acquaintance with General Mulgrave, the First Lord, and with Mrs Bertie, the wife of the Admiral at the Cape. This she delivered to Stephen, wedged into a dim corner by the clock under a drip, with some charming asides to Sophie; and she was obliged to repeat it when Jack appeared, trailing cobwebs from the attic and bearing his chest. It is difficult to sound artless twice in quick succession, but she did her best, for she was sincerely devoted to the prospect of escaping an English winter, and the idea of seeing her husband again filled her with a pleasurable excitement. Her confusion caused her bosom to rise and fall, a blush to overspread her pretty face, and from his corner Stephen observed that she was doing quite well against heavy odds – that Jack, at least, was not unmoved by her distress. Yet he also noticed, with regret, a certain stiffening in Sophie's attitude, a constraint in her civil smile, and something near acerbity in her reply to Lady Clonfert's suggestion that she too might darn the Captain's stockings and make herself useful during the voyage. Mrs Williams's stony reserve, her repeated sniff, her ostentatious busyness, he took for granted; but although he had long known that jealousy formed part of Sophie's character – perhaps the only part that he could have wished otherwise – he was grieved to see it thus displayed. Jack had caught the signals as quickly as his friend— Stephen saw his anxious glance – and his cordiality towards Lady Clonfert, never very great, sensibly diminished; although he did repeat what he had said at the beginning – that he should be happy to carry her ladyship to the Cape. What had preceded that glance, to make it so anxious? Dr Maturin lapsed into a meditation upon the marriage state: monogamy, an aberration? How widely spread in time and place? How strictly observed? From this train of thought he was aroused by Jack's strong voice stating that her ladyship was certainly aware of the tediousness of tiding down the Channel, that he strongly recommended her

28

posting to Plymouth, that he begged stores and baggage might be kept to a minimum, and that once again he must urge the most exact punctuality however short the notice: 'for his part he should gladly lose a tide to be of use, but on the King's service he must not lose a minute.'

Now everybody was standing up: soon Jack had led Lady Clonfert, under an umbrella, to her carriage, had firmly closed the door upon her, and was back in the house, his face radiating universal goodwill, as though she were utterly dismissed.

Mrs Williams was abusing Lady Clonfert's tippet, complexion and morals with a volubility that Stephen could not but admire, yet Jack's statement that a couple of hours would see his dunnage corded up, that Stephen would oblige him infinitely by riding straight to Gosport in order to bring back John Parley in Newman's dogcart to pack the telescope, and that he was determined to go aboard before the evening gun and to get the *Boadicea* to sea on the ebb, struck her dumb. It had no such effect on her daughter, however, who instantly produced a number of reasons why Jack could certainly not join tonight: the state of his linen would bring discredit on the service; it would be shockingly rude to dear, kind Admiral Wells not to dine with him, most impolitic if not direct insubordination; and Jack had always been such a friend to discipline. Besides, it was raining. It was clear to Stephen that she was not only horrified at losing Jack so soon but that she was also sorry for her recent – shrewishness was far too strong a word – for she now ran straight on into praise of their visitor. Lady Clonfert was a most elegant, well-bred woman, with remarkably fine eyes; her wish to join her husband was in every way meritorious and understandable; her presence aboard would certainly please the gunroom, indeed the whole ship's company.

Sophie then returned to arguments against Jack's leaving quite so soon: tomorrow morning would be far, far better in every way; they could not possibly have his clothes ready before then. In spite of her nimble wit, logical arguments soon began to run short, and Stephen, feeling that at any moment she might resort to others, even to tears, or appeal to him for support, slipped quietly out of the room. He communed with his horse in its out-house for a while, and when he came back he found Jack at the door, staring up at the scudding clouds, with Sophie, looking exceptionally beautiful in her anxiety and emotion, beside him. 'The glass is rising,' said Jack thoughtfully, 'but the wind is still

due south . . . and when you consider where she lays, right up the harbour, there is not a hope of getting her out on this tide. No, my dear; perhaps you are right. Perhaps I should not go aboard until tomorrow. But tomorrow, sweetheart,' he said, looking fondly down, 'tomorrow at the crack of dawn you lose your husband to his natural element.'

Chapter Two

Upon that damp element, always unstable, often treacherous, but for the moment both warm and kind, Captain Aubrey dictated an official letter to his happy clerk:

Boadicea, at sea

Sir,

I have the honour to acquaint you, that at dawn on the seventeenth instant, the Dry Salvages bearing SSE two leagues, His Majesty's ship under my command had the good fortune to fall in with a French national ship of war with a prize in company. On the *Boadicea*'s approach she bore up, abandoning her prize, a snow, whose topmasts were struck down on deck. Every exertion was made in this ship to come up with the enemy, who endeavoured to lead us among the shoals of the Dry Salvages; but missing stays in consequence of the loss of her mizen topmast, she struck upon a reef. Shortly afterwards, the wind having fallen to a flat calm, and the rocks sheltering her from the *Boadicea*'s guns, she was boarded and carried by the boats, when she proved to be the *Hébé*, formerly His Majesty's twenty-eight-gun frigate *Hyaena* but now mounting twenty-two twenty-four-pounders, carronades, and two long nines, with a complement of 214 men, commanded by Mons. Bretonnière, lieutenant de vaisseau, her captain having been killed in the action with the prize. She was thirty-eight days out of Bordeaux, on a cruise, and had taken the English vessels named in the margin.

My first lieutenant, Mr Lemuel Akers, an old and deserving officer, commanded the *Boadicea*'s boats and led the attack in the most gallant manner; while Lieutenant Seymour and Mr Johnson, master's mate, displayed great activity. Indeed I am happy to say, that the conduct of the *Boadicea*'s people gave me great satisfaction, and I have no greater loss to deplore than two men slightly wounded.

The snow was secured without delay: she is the *Intrepid Fox* of Bristol, A. Snape master, from the Guinea coast, laden with elephants' teeth, gold-dust, grains of Paradise, hides, and skins. In view of the value of her cargo, I have thought proper to send

31

her into Gibraltar, escorted by the *Hyaena* under the command of Lieutenant Akers.

I have the honour to be, etc.

Captain Aubrey watched his clerk's flying pen with great benevolence. The letter was true in essence, but like most official letters it contained a certain number of lies. Jack did not think Lemuel Akers a deserving officer, and the lieutenant's gallantry had in fact been confined to roaring at the *Hébé* from the stern-sheets of the launch, to which his wooden leg confined him, while the conduct of several of the *Boadicea*'s people had filled their new captain with impatience, and the snow had not been secured without delay.

'Do not forget the wounded at the bottom of the page, Mr Hill,' he said. 'James Arklow, ordinary, and William Bates, Marine. Now be so good as to let Mr Akers know that I shall have a couple of private letters for him to take to Gibraltar.'

Left alone in the great cabin he glanced out of the stern-window at the calm, crowded, sunlit sea, with his prizes lying upon it and boats plying to and fro, the *Hébé*'s or rather the *Hyaena*'s rigging full of men putting the last touches to her repairs, the shrouds of her new mizen rattled down already: he had a first-rate bosun in John Fellowes. Then he reached out for a sheet of paper and began: 'Sweetheart – A hasty line to bring you my dear love and to tell you all is well. We had an amazing prosperous voyage down as far as 35°30′, with a fine double-reefed topsail quartering breeze – *Boadicea*'s best point of sailing in her present trim – all the way from the moment we sank Rame Head right across the Bay and almost to Madeira. We put into Plymouth at the height of flood on Monday night – black, with squalls of sleet and blowing hard – and since we had made our number to Stoke Point, Mr Farquhar was ready waiting, bag and baggage, at the Commissioner's office. I sent to Lady Clonfert's inn, desiring her to be at the quay by twenty minutes past the hour; but through some mistake she did not appear, and I was obliged to proceed to sea without her.

'However, to cut things short, this pretty wind carried us across the Bay, where the *Boadicea* proved she was a dry, wholesome ship, and at one time I thought we should raise the Island in just over a week. But then it backed into the south-east and I was obliged to stretch away for Tenerife, cursing my luck: and at four bells in the morning watch I happened to be on deck

32

to make sure the master, an ignorant old man, did not run us on the Dry Salvages as he had nearly run us on Penlee Point, when there, right under our lee at the dawn of day, was a Frenchman, lying to with her prize. She had scarcely a chance, for the prize, a well-armed Guineaman, had mauled her briskly before she was taken; her rigging was all ahoo, she was bending a new foretopsail, and many of her people were in the Guineaman, setting her to rights: and of course she was not half our size. And since we had the weather-gage we could afford to yaw and let fly with our bow guns: not that it did her much harm, apart from flustering her people. However, she did her best, peppering us with her stern-chaser and trying to lead us into the four-fathom water of the Dog-Leg Passage. But I sounded that channel when I was a midshipman in the *Circe*, and since we draw twenty-three foot, I did not choose to follow her, although there was no swell worth speaking of. Had she got through, we might have lost her, *Boadicea* being a trifle sluggish (though you will not repeat that anywhere, my dear); but we knocked away her mizen topmast – she missed stays in the turn of the passage – ran on to the reef, and there being no wind could not beat across. So we lowered the boats and took her without much trouble, though I am sorry to say her commanding officer was wounded – Stephen is patching him up at this moment, poor fellow.

'There was no glory in it, sweetheart, not the least hint of danger; but the charming thing is, that she can just be called a frigate. She was our old *Hyaena*, a jackass twenty-eight as ancient as the Ark, that the French took when I was a boy: she was overgunned, of course, and they reduced her to what they rate a corvette, with twenty-four-pounder carronades and a couple of long nines – I scarcely recognized her at first, she was so changed. But she is still a frigate for us, and of course she will be bought into the service (she is a fine sailer too, particularly on the wind, and we hauled her clear with no damage at all, bar a fathom or two of her copper being scraped off). And then there is head-money, and above all this Guineaman. She is no prize to us, being English, but she is salvage, and she does represent a certain amount of cash, which, the kitchen copper being in the state it is, will not be unwelcome. Unfortunately the Admiral shares. Although mine were Admiralty orders, the cunning old dog added some nonsense of his own, to make sure of one of my eighths if I took anything; and this he did in the most barefaced way, after dinner, laughing cheerfully, ha, ha. All

admirals are tarred with the same brush, I fear, and I dare say we shall find the same thing at the Cape.' He had scarcely written the last word before Stephen's grave warnings about close counsel came to his mind: he carefully changed it to 'our destination', and then returned to the Guineaman. 'Ordinarily she would have been crammed with blacks for the West Indies, which would have added much to her value; but perhaps it was just as well that there were none. Stephen grows so outrageous the minute slavery is mentioned, that I dare say I should have been obliged to set them ashore to prevent his being hanged for mutiny. Only the last time I dined in the gunroom, Akers, the first lieutenant, got on to the subject, and Stephen handled him so severely, I was obliged to intervene. Mr Farquhar is of the same opinion with Stephen, and I am sure they are right – it is a very ugly thing to see, indeed – yet sometimes I cannot help feeling that a couple of biddable, able-bodied young blacks that attended to their duty and could give no month's warning might come in uncommon handy at Ashgrove Cottage. And now I am on the cottage, I have written to Ommaney to send you all he will advance on the *Hyaena* directly, with which I beg you will instantly buy yourself a pelisse and tippet against its infernal draughts, and . . .' There followed a list of domestic improvements to be made: the copper, of course; the parlour chimney to be rebuilt; Goadby to be set to work on the roof; a newly-calved Jersey cow to be bought with Mr Hick's advice. 'My dear, time is flying,' he went on. 'They are hoisting in *Hyaena*'s boats, and the snow has won her anchor. We may touch at St Helena, but otherwise I must take my leave until we reach our port. God bless and keep you, sweetheart, and the children.' He sighed, smiled, and was about to seal when Stephen walked in, looking mean and pinched. 'Stephen,' he said, 'I have just written to Sophie. Have you any message?'

'Love, of course. And compliments to Mrs Williams.'

'Lord,' cried Jack, writing fast, 'thank you for reminding me. I have explained about Lady Clonfert,' he observed, as he closed the letter up.

'Then I trust you kept your explanation short,' said Stephen. 'Circumstantial details destroy a tale entirely. The longer, the less credible.'

'I merely stated that she did not appear at the rendezvous, and passed on.'

'Nothing about three o'clock in the morning, the hocus-pocus

at the inn, signals disregarded, the boat being made to row as though we were escaping from the Day of Judgment, and the lady ditched?' asked Stephen, with the unpleasant creaking noise that was his nearest approach to a laugh.

'What a rattle you are, to be sure,' said Jack. 'Come now, Stephen, how is your patient?'

'Why, he has lost a great deal of blood, it cannot be denied; but then on the other hand I have rarely seen a man with so much blood to lose. He should do very well, with the blessing. He has the late captain's cook with him, a famous artist, and desires he may be kept aboard, if agreeable to the gallant victor.'

'Capital, capital. A famous artist in the galley will set the crown on a very pretty morning's work. Was it not a very pretty morning's work, Stephen?'

'Well,' said Stephen, 'I wish you joy of your capture with all my heart; but if by "pretty" we are to understand an elegant economy of means, I cannot congratulate you. All this banging of great guns for so pitiful a result as the mizen topmast of a little small slip of a thing, and it embarrassed among the rocks, the creature – Armageddon come before its time. And the infamous backing and filling before the Guineaman is even approached, in spite of her captain's ardent pleas; and all this interminable while no one is allowed to set foot upon these rocks, on the grounds that not a minute is to be lost. Not a minute, forsooth: and forty-seven are wantonly thrown away – forty-seven minutes of invaluable observation that will never be made up.'

'What I know, Stephen, and what you don't know,' began Jack, but a messenger interrupted him: with the Captain's leave, Mr Akers was ready to go aboard. On deck Jack found the southwest breeze setting in steadily, just as if it had been ordered, a perfect breeze to waft the *Hyaena* and her charge to Gibraltar. He gave his letters to the first lieutenant, again recommended the utmost vigilance, and urged him towards the side. Mr Akers displayed a tendency to linger, to express his extreme gratitude for his command (and indeed the recovered *Hyaena* meant his promotion) and to assure Captain Aubrey that if a single prisoner showed his nose above the hatchway it should instantly be blown off with his own grapeshot, but presently he was gone; and leaning over the rail Jack watched the *Boadicea*'s boats carrying him and his companions away. Some went to the man-of-war, to work the ship and guard the prisoners; some to the *Intrepid*

Fox, to strengthen her sickly and diminished crew: a surprising number of men in both cases.

Few captains, far from a press-gang, a receiving-ship or any other source of hands, could have smiled at the sight of so many of them pulling awkwardly away to other vessels, never, in all probability, to be seen again, but Jack beamed like the rising sun. Captain Loveless had had excellent connections, and the *Boadicea* a plethoric crew: a good average crew, upon the whole, with no more than a fair share of landsmen and with a gratifying proportion of hands who deserved their rating of able seaman; yet with a number of hard cases too, not worth the food they ate nor the space they occupied, while the last draft had been made up entirely of quota-men from Bedfordshire, odd misfits, petty criminals and vagrants, not one of whom had ever used the sea. The *Hébé*'s English prisoners, right sailormen taken out of British ships for the most part, together with a couple of prime hands pressed from the *Intrepid Fox*, far more than compensated for their loss; and now, with real satisfaction, Jack watched eight sodomites, three notorious thieves, four men whose wits were quite astray, and a parcel of inveterate skulkers and sea-lawyers go off for good. He was also happy to be rid of a great lout of a midshipman who made the youngsters' lives a burden to them: but above all he was delighted to be seeing the last of his first lieutenant. Mr Akers was a harsh, greying, saturnine man with one leg; the pain from his wound often made him savagely ill-tempered; and he did not see eye to eye with Jack on a number of matters, including flogging. Yet far more important, honourable wound or not, Akers was no seaman: when Jack had first stepped aboard the frigate he found her lying with two round turns and an elbow in her cables, a very disgusting sight; they had lost an hour and twenty minutes clearing their hawse, with *Boadicea*'s signal to proceed to sea flying all the time, reinforced by guns at frequent intervals: and this impression of busy, angry inefficiency had grown stronger day by day.

So there it was: he had made two charming captures; at the same time he had freed himself of men whose presence would have gone far towards preventing the frigate's becoming a fully efficient instrument for distressing the enemy, let alone a happy ship, and he had done so in a way that would confer the utmost benefit on Mr Akers. That was where the prettiness lay. He was now in command of a crew whose collective seamanship was already tolerably good in spite of the remaining fifty or sixty raw

hands, and whose gunnery, though of the lowest standard, as it so often was under officers whose one idea of action was a yard-arm-to-yardarm engagement where no shot could miss, was certainly capable of improvement. 'Vast capabilities, ma'am, vast capabilities,' he murmured; and then his smile changed to an inward chuckle as he recollected that for once his low cunning had over-reached Stephen Maturin: for what Jack knew, and what Stephen did not, was that those forty-seven minutes had made all the difference between salvage and no salvage, between the *Boadicea*'s right to an eighth of the Guineaman's value and a mere letter of thanks from her owners. The *Intrepid Fox* had been taken at forty-six minutes past ten on Tuesday, and if he had accepted the surrender of the French prize-master one moment before twenty-four hours had passed, by sea-law the Guineaman would not have been salvage at all. And as for Stephen's passing three quarters of an hour on the Dry Salvages, searching for problematical bugs, Jack had set him down on remote oceanic rocks before now, and had been obliged to have him removed by armed force, long, long after the appointed time: but, however, he would make it up to him – there were coral reefs in plenty on the far side of the Cape.

'Frigate signalling, sir, if you please,' said the signal midshipman. '*Permission to part company.*'

'Say *carry on*,' replied Jack. 'And add *happy return.*'

The *Hyaena* dropped her topsails neatly, sheeted them home and gathered way, followed by the Guineaman a cable's length to leeward; and having watched them for a while, true on their course for Gibraltar, Jack gave the orders that would carry the *Boadicea* slanting away towards the tropic line, close-hauled on the freshening breeze, and walked into his great cabin. The bulk-heads, knocked down when the frigate cleared for action, were already back in place, and the two massive eighteen-pounders were housed again, fore and aft; but the starboard gun was still warm, and the smell of powder and slow-match hung about the air, the most exhilarating scent by land or sea. The beautiful room was all his own, with its noble space and its gleaming curve of stern-windows, in spite of his distinguished passenger; for although Mr Farquhar was to be a governor, his status was still highly theoretical, since it depended on the defeat of a powerful French squadron and on the conquest of the islands he was to govern; and for the moment he had to be content with what would otherwise have been the captain's dining-cabin. Jack

threw one last loving glance at his captures, dwindling north-wards over the sparkling light-blue sea, and called out, 'Pass the word for Mr Seymour, Mr Trollope and Mr Johnson.'

Seymour, the second lieutenant, and Trollope, the third, fol-lowed by Johnson, a master's mate, hurried in, looking pleased but somewhat apprehensive: they knew very well that the *Boadicea*, though successful, had not distinguished herself, particularly in the operation of hauling the *Hyaena* off her innocuous ledge of rock and towing her clear of the channel and they were by no means sure what their new captain would have to say. Seymour and Johnson might almost have been brothers, short, pink, chubby men with round heads and fresh open faces upon which their expression of respectful sobriety seemed less natural than cheerfulness: they were the kind of men Jack had seen a hundred times in his career, and he was happy to have them aboard. He had seen other Trollopes too; Trollope was a big man, black-haired, with a dark, unhumorous, determined face and a strong jaw; he might be a right hard-horse lieutenant under the wrong kind of commander, or a devil of a captain himself, if ever he reached post rank. But for the moment he was young; he was not yet set. They were all young, though Johnson might be nearing thirty – old for his station.

Jack knew very well what was in their minds; as a lieutenant he had often been summoned to bear the blame for others' shortcomings. But what he did not know was that the deferential expression on the faces of these capable, enterprising, seasoned young men was the outcome not merely of respect for his rank but of something resembling awe of his reputation in the service: in his fourteen-gun brig the *Sophie* he had taken the thirty-two-gun Spanish *Cacafuego*; he was one of the few frigate-captains who had ever attacked a French ship of the line, a seventy-four; as acting-captain of the *Lively* he had compelled the *Clara* and the *Fama*, Spaniards of equal force, to strike to him in the memorable frigate-action off Cadiz; and in cutting-out operations and in generally harassing the enemy he had few equals among those of his standing in the Navy list. Jack neither knew it nor suspected it, partly because he still felt very much their con-temporary, and partly because he sincerely regarded his more outstanding actions as the effect of luck: he had happened to be on the spot, and in his place any other sea-officer would have done the same. This was not false modesty: he had known officers by the score, good officers, excellent seamen, their courage beyond

question, who had served throughout the wars without any chance of distinguishing themselves; men on convoy-duty, in transports, or even in the ships of the line perpetually blockading Brest and Toulon, who very often encountered danger, but from the violence of the sea rather than that of the enemy, and who therefore remained obscure, often unpromoted and always poor: had they been in the right place at the right time, they would have done as well or better: it was a question of luck.

'Well, gentlemen,' he said, 'this is quite a pleasant beginning to a voyage. But we have lost Mr Akers. Mr Seymour, you will be so good as to take his place.'

'Thank you, sir,' said Seymour.

'And Mr Johnson, you have passed for lieutenant, I believe?'

'Oh, yes, sir. On the first Wednesday in August, 1802,' said Johnson, blushing and then turning remarkably pale. He had passed, but as it happened for so many other midshipmen with no influence, the longed-for commission had never come. All these years he had been a master's mate, a senior midshipman, no more, the likelihood of promotion fading with every birthday; it had almost vanished now, and he seemed fated to end his career as a master at the best, a mere warrant-officer until he was thrown on the beach, with never a command of his own. And in the *Boadicea* there were midshipmen with claims far higher than his own: Captain Loveless had shipped the godson of one admiral, the nephew of another, and the heir of the member for Old Sarum; whereas Johnson's father was only a retired lieutenant.

'Then,' said Jack, 'I shall give you an order as acting-lieutenant, and let us hope the Admiral at the Cape will confirm it.'

Johnson, flushing scarlet now, brought out his acknowledgments, and Jack hurried on, 'For I will not disguise from you, gentlemen, that the Cape is our destination. And what you may not know, is that there are four French forty-gun frigates waiting for us round the other side of it. Now today's little brush was very well in its way. It pleased the raw hands – entered 'em, as you might say – and it clapped a stopper over the *Hébé*'s capers; she had been playing Old Harry with our trade these past few weeks. So I believe we may drink a glass of wine to it. Probyn!' he called, Probyn being his steward. 'Rouse out a bottle of Madeira and then jump forward and see that the French captain's cook is comfortably stowed: use him civil. Here's to the *Hyaena*, ex-*Hébé*, then; and a safe landfall to her.' They drank gravely, certain that this was by no means all the

39

Captain had to say. 'Very well in its way,' he continued, 'but I scarcely suppose that any one of you would have called it pretty.'

'Not quite in your Minorca style, sir,' said Trollope.

Jack looked hard at the lieutenant. Had they ever been ship-mates? He could not recall his face.

'I was a midshipman in *Amelia*, sir, when you brought the *Cacafuego* into Mahón. Lord, how we cheered the *Sophie*!'

'Was you, though?' said Jack, somewhat embarrassed. 'Well, I am glad it was not the *Cacafuego* we came upon today, let alone one of those Frenchmen round the Cape; because although the Boadiceas seem a willing, decent set upon the whole – no sign of shyness that I could see – their gunnery is pitiful beyond all description. And as for pulling, never, never have I seen so many creatures in human shape incapable of handling an oar: in the red cutter there was not one single man apart from old Adams and a Marine that knew how to pull. But it is the gunnery that is my chief concern: pitiful, pitiful . . . Broadside after broadside at five hundred yards and even less; and where did they go? Not aboard the Frenchman, gentlemen. The only shot that told was the one fired from the bow-chaser, and that was pointed by Jack of the breadroom, who had no business to be on deck at all. Now do but imagine that we had run into a well worked-up French frigate, hulling us with her twenty-four-pounders at the best part of a mile: for their practice is devilish accurate, as I dare say you know.' In the solemn pause that followed he refilled their glasses and went on, 'But thank God this happened early: it could not have fallen better. The raw hands are over their sea-sickness; they are all pleased with themselves, poor honest lubbers; and every foremast Jack is richer by a year's pay, all won in a sunny morning. They must be made to understand that by teaching them their duty we are putting them in the way of getting more. They will attend now, with a good heart; no need for rattans and the rope's end. By the time we reach the Cape, gentlemen, I trust that every man and boy on the ship's books will at least be able to pull an oar, hand and reef a sail, load, point and fire a musket and a gun: and if they can learn no more than that, and to be obedient to command, why, we shall be in a fair way to meet any French frigate on the far side of it.'

With the lieutenants gone, Jack considered for a while. He had no doubt that they were entirely with him; they were the sort of

40

men he knew and liked; but there was still a great deal to be done. With their help he might make the *Boadicea* into a most lethal floating battery of tremendous power; but still she had to be brought to the scene of action, brought as rapidly as the elements would allow. He sent for the master and the bosun, and to them he stated that he was not satisfied with the frigate's sailing, either in the article of speed or in that of lying close to the wind.

There followed a highly technical conference in which he encountered steady resistance from Buchan, the master, an elderly man set in his ways, who would not admit that any restowing of the hold, any attempt to bring her by the head, would have the least favourable effect. Slow she had always been and slow she always would be: he had always stowed the hold in exactly the same way, ever since he had been in her. The bosun, on the other hand, a young man for his important office, a seaman through and through, brought up in North Sea colliers, was as eager as his captain to get the best out of the *Boadicea*, even if it meant trying something new. He spoke feelingly on the good effect of cat-harpins, well-sniftered in; he entirely agreed with the plan for raking the foremast; Jack's heart warmed to him.

At least a part of Mr Buchan's sullenness arose from hunger. The gunroom dined at one o'clock, an hour now long past; and although today dinner would have been indifferent in any case, its absence rendered the master positively morose. The bosun had dined at noon together with the carpenter and the gunner, and Buchan, smelling both food and grog upon him, hated his cheerful face; even more his steady flow of talk.

Jack too was somewhat given to worshipping his belly, and when he had dismissed them he walked into the coach: here he found Stephen and Mr Farquhar, eating cake. 'Do I interrupt you?' he asked: not at all, they said, clearing a space for him among the books, documents, maps, proclamations and broadsheets that they were trying to reassemble after the abrupt disappearance and reappearance of their quarters. 'I hope I see you well, sir?' he said to Mr Farquhar, who had suffered more than most in the Bay of Biscay and who had spent much of the time since rising from his cot in conference with Dr Maturin, the two of them deep in papers, talking foreign to the intense vexation of their servants, two ship's boys told off to look after them, who liked to indulge their natural curiosity – a curiosity much stimulated by their shipmates before the mast, eager to

41

know what was afoot. Farquhar had lost a stone, and his lean, intelligent, hook-nosed face still had a greenish tinge, but he replied that he had never felt better in his life, that the tremendous din of battle, the more than Jovian thunder of the guns, had completed the work – with a civil bow to Stephen – of Dr Maturin's preternatural physic, so that he felt like a boy again; he had a boy's appetite, a restless eagerness to be at table. 'But,' he went on, 'you must first allow me to congratulate you most heartily upon your splendid victory. Such instant decision, such a determined onslaught, and such a happy issue!'

'You are too kind, sir, too kind by half. But as for the happy issue that you are so obliging as to mention, it has one aspect that cannot but rejoice us all. We have the French captain's cook aboard, and I am come' – turning towards Stephen – 'to ask whether you think he might be persuaded . . . ?'

'I have already attended to him,' said Stephen. 'A sucking pig, one of a large surviving farrow, was one of the few casualties aboard the *Hébé*, and I understand that it is to provide a first example of his powers. I have also seen to it that Monsieur Bretonnière's wine and comforts have been transferred: to these I thought fit to add his late captain's stores; foie gras in jars, truffles in goose-grease, pieces of goose in goose-grease, a large variety of dried sausages, Bayonne hams, potted anchovies; and among the rest of the wine, twenty-one dozens of Margaux of '88, with the long cork, together with an almost equal quantity of Château Lafite. Sure, I cannot tell how we shall ever get through them all; yet it would be the world's shame to let such noble wine go back, and in these conditions another year must see it the mere ghost of itself.'

The claret never saw another year, however, nor did that splendid vintage go to waste: with steady application and with some help from Bretonnière and other guests from the gunroom Jack and Stephen drank almost every drop as the days went by. And there were days enough in all conscience, since the kind winds of their departure deserted them well north of the line, and sometimes they would lie on the oily, heaving sea, drifting slowly towards America on the equatorial current, with the *Boadicea*'s figurehead simpering all round the compass and the frigate nearly rolling her masts by the board. Ten days on end when she wallowed with flaccid sails on the stagnant water, clean in herself but so surrounded by the filth of three hundred men – by Admiral Brown as the old hands called it – and by her

42

own empty beef-casks, peelings and general rubbish that Jack was obliged to take the jolly-boat a quarter of a mile away for his morning's swim, while at the same time he caused the crew to tow their ship, thus rendering the view more agreeable and training them in the art of managing an oar, so beating two birds with one bush, as he put it, or even three, since after they had pulled her for an hour or two it was the *Boadicea*'s custom to lower a sail into the pure, tepid water, buoying its outer corners and thereby making a shallow pool in which those who could not swim – the great majority – might splash about and enjoy themselves, perhaps learning how to stay afloat in the process.

But they crossed the line itself in style, with studdingsails aloft and alow, and with more than the usual merriment, for when they reduced sail to let Neptune come aboard, accompanied by an outrageously lewd Amphitrite and Badger-Bag, he found no less than a hundred and twenty-three souls who had to be made free of the equator by being lathered with rancid grease – tar was forbidden, being in short supply – and shaved with a piece of barrel-hoop before being ducked.

Southward still, with Canopus and Achernar high overhead, and Jack showed his attentive midshipmen the new constellations, Musca, Pavo, Chamaeleon and many more, all glowing in the warm, pellucid air.

Strange, unpredictable weather, for even when the *Boadicea* found the trades in 4° south they proved apathetic and fitful. It was clear that this was not to be a rapid passage, but although Jack often whistled for a breeze, a stronger breeze, he was not deeply worried by the length of their voyage: his ship was well-found, several storms of rain had filled her water, and her men were remarkably healthy; and as the weeks turned into months it came to him that this was a happy period, a time set apart, lying between the anxieties of home on the one hand and those that would surely be waiting for him in the Indian Ocean, where his real work would begin. And then although he longed for the 'real thing' to start, he knew that no power on earth could bring him to it any earlier: he and Fellowes had done all they could to increase the frigate's rate of sailing, and they had accomplished much; but they could not command the wind. So with a tranquil conscience and that fatalism which sailors must acquire if they are not to perish of frustration, he rejoiced in this opportunity for making the *Boadicea* into something like his notion of a

crack frigate, a fighting-machine manned entirely by able seamen, men-of-war's men, every one of them an expert gun-layer and a devil with the boarding-axe and cutlass.

Insensibly the lubberly part of the *Boadicea*'s crew began to resemble sailormen as the unchanging naval routine came to be their only real way of life, a life in which it was natural and inevitable that all hands should be piped just before eight bells in the middle watch and that the sleepers should start from their hammocks to the muster and then to the scrubbing of the decks in the first light of dawn; that all hands should be piped to dinner at eight bells in the forenoon watch, that this dinner should consist of cheese and duff on Monday, two pounds of salt beef on Tuesday, dried peas and duff on Wednesday, one pound of salt pork on Thursday, dried peas and cheese on Friday, two more pounds of salt beef on Saturday, a pound of salt pork and some such treat as figgy-dowdy on Sunday, always accompanied by a daily pound of biscuit; that at one bell dinner should be followed by a pint of grog, that after supper (with another pint of grog) all hands should repair to their action-stations at the beat of the drum, and that eventually hammocks should be piped down so that the watch below might have four hours of sleep before being roused again at midnight for another spell on deck. This and the perpetual living movement of the deck underfoot, and the sight of nothing but the Atlantic Ocean clear round the horizon, nothing but endless sea and sky, cut them off from the land so completely that it seemed another world, with no immediacy at all, and they adopted the values of the sea.

They also came to resemble sailormen in appearance, since one hour and forty minutes after the *Boadicea* had passed under the tropic of Cancer the carpenter's mate banged two brass nails into the deck, exactly twelve yards apart: twelve yards of duck, needles and thread were served out to each man, together with sennet, and they were desired to make themselves hot-weather frocks, trousers and broad-brimmed hats. This they did, helped by their handier colleagues, to such effect that at next Sunday's divisions the landsmen dressed in a mixture of rag-fair clothes and purser's slops, old leather breeches, greasy waistcoats and battered hats, had vanished, and their captain paced along lines of men as clean and white in their way as the Marines, drawn up on the quarterdeck, were clean and red in theirs.

There were still some fools belonging to the afterguard who were only good for heaving on a given rope; there were a dozen

or so in either watch whose heads could not stand the swingeing ration of grog and who were continually punished for drunkenness; and there were some remaining hard cases; but on the whole he was pleased with them: a very decent set of men. He was pleased with his officers too, apart from Buchan and the purser, a very tall yellow-faced man with knock-knees and huge splay feet, upon whose books Jack kept a very sharp eye indeed: all three lieutenants seconded him with admirable zeal, and the older midshipmen were of real value.

Not the least part of that wonderfully lucky stroke off the Dry Salvages was the *Boadicea*'s acquisition of a large quantity of ammunition. Regulations confined Jack to a hundred round-shot for each of his long eighteen-pounders, and he had to hoard them with jealous care, for there was no certainty of any more at the Cape – a wretched situation in which he knew that if he did not train his gun-crews by firing live they would not know how to do it when the moment came, and that if he did then at the same critical juncture they might have nothing left to fire – but from that blessed day onwards the *Boadicea*'s daily exercise with the great guns had not been the usual dumb-show. Certainly the crews rattled their eighteen-pounders in and out, going through all the motions of firing them, from casting loose to housing; but since the *Hébé*'s twenty-four-pound balls fitted the *Boadicea*'s carronades and her nine-pound the two chase-guns, every evening heard their savage roar: every man was accustomed to the deadly leap of the recoiling gun, to the flash and the din and to seizing his tackle, rammer or wad with automatic speed in the dense swirling powder-smoke. And on high days, as when they saluted the Tropic of Capricorn with a double broadside, it was a pleasure to see their spirit: they demolished a raft of empty beef-barrels at something over five hundred yards and ran their guns up again, cheering madly, to blast the scattered remains in a trifle less than two minutes. It was nothing like the mortal rate of fire that Jack so valued; it was not even the three broadsides in five minutes that was coming to be thought normal by those captains who cared for gunnery, far less the three in two minutes that Jack had achieved in other commissions; but it was accurate, and a good deal faster than some ships he knew.

This 'time out', this happy interval with a straightforward and agreeable task in hand, sailing through warm seas with winds that, though often languid, were rarely downright contrary, sailing southwards in a comfortable ship with an excellent cook,

ample stores and good company, had its less delightful sides, however.

His telescope was a disappointment. It was not that he could not see Jupiter: the planet gleamed in his eyepiece like a banded golden pea. But because of the ship's motion he could not keep it there long enough or steadily enough to fix the local time of its moons' eclipses and thus find his longitude. Neither the theory (which was by no means new) nor the telescope was at fault: it was the cleverly weighted cradle slung from the maintopgallant-mast stay that he had designed to compensate for the pitch and roll that did not answer, in spite of all his alterations; and night after night he swung there cursing and swearing, surrounded by midshipmen armed with clean swabs, whose duty it was to enhance the compensation by thrusting him gently at the word of command.

The young gentlemen: he led them a hard life, insisting upon a very high degree of promptitude and activity; but apart from these sessions with the telescope, which they loathed entirely, and from their navigation classes, they thoroughly approved of their captain and of the splendid breakfasts and dinners to which he often invited them, although on due occasion he beat them with frightful strength on the bare breech in his cabin, usually for such crimes as stealing the gunroom's food or repeatedly walking about with their hands in their pockets. For his part he found them an engaging set of young fellows, though given to lying long in their hammocks, to consulting their ease, and to greed; and in one of them, Mr Richardson, generally known as Spotted Dick, because of his pimples, he detected a mathematician of uncommon promise. Jack taught them navigation himself, the *Boadicea*'s schoolmaster being incapable of maintaining discipline, and it soon became apparent to him that he should have to keep his wits as sharp as his razor not to be outstripped by his pupil in the finer points of spherical trigonometry, to say nothing of the stars.

Then there was Mr Farquhar. Jack esteemed him as an intelligent, capable, gentlemanlike man with remarkable powers of conversation, excellent company for the space of a dinner, although he drank no wine, or even for a week; but Mr Farquhar had been bred to the law, and perhaps because of this a little too much of his conversation took the form of questioning, so that Jack sometimes felt that he was being examined at his own table. Furthermore, Mr Farquhar often used Latin expressions that

46

made Jack uneasy, and referred to authors Jack had never read: Stephen had always done the same (indeed, it would have been difficult to refer to any author with whom Jack was acquainted apart from those who wrote on fox-hunting, naval tactics, or astronomy), but with Stephen it was entirely different. Jack loved him, and had not the least objection to granting him all the erudition in the world, while remaining inwardly convinced that in all practical matters other than physic and surgery Stephen should never be allowed out alone. Mr Farquhar, however, seemed to assume that a deep knowledge of the law and of public business embraced the whole field of useful human endeavour.

Yet Mr Farquhar's vastly superior knowledge of politics and even his far more galling superiority at chess would have been as nothing if he had had some ear for music: he had none. It was their love of music that had brought Jack and Stephen together in the first place: the one played the fiddle and the other the cello, neither brilliantly, yet both well enough to take deep pleasure in their evening concerts after retreat; they had played throughout every voyage they had made together, never interrupted by anything but the requirements of the service, the utmost extremity of foul weather, or by the enemy. But now Mr Farquhar was sharing the great cabin, and he was as indifferent to Haydn as he was to Mozart; as he observed, he would not give a farthing candle for either of them, or for Handel. The rustling of his book as they played, the way he tapped his snuffbox and blew his nose, took away from their pleasure; and in any case, Jack, brought up in the tradition of naval hospitality, felt bound to do all he could to make his guest comfortable, even to the extent of giving up his fiddle in favour of whist, which he did not care for, and of calling in the senior Marine lieutenant as the fourth, a man he did not much care for either.

Their guest was not always with them, however, for during the frequent calms Jack often took the jolly-boat and rowed away to swim, to inspect the frigate's trim from a distance, and to talk with Stephen in private. 'You cannot possibly dislike him,' he said, skimming over the swell towards a patch of drifting weed where Stephen thought it possible they might find a southern variety of sea-horse or a pelagic crab related to those he had discovered under the line, 'but I shall not be altogether sorry to set him down on shore.'

'I can and do dislike him intensely when he pins my king and a rook with his lurking knight,' said Stephen. 'At most other

times I find him a valuable companion, an eager, searching, perspicacious intelligence. To be sure, he has no ear at all, but he is not without a tincture of poetry: he has an interesting theory on the mystic role of kings, founded upon his study of tenures in petty serjeanty.'

Jack's concern with petty serjeanty was so slight that he carried straight on, 'I dare say I have been in command too long. When I was a lieutenant, messing with the rest, I used to put up with people far, far more trying than Farquhar. There was a surgeon in the *Agamemnon* that used to play 'Greensleeves' on his flute every evening, and every evening he broke down at exactly the same place. Harry Turnbull, our premier – he was killed at the Nile – used to turn pale as he came nearer and nearer to it. That was in the West Indies, and tempers were uncommon short; but no one said anything except Clonfert. It don't sound much, 'Greensleeves', but it was a pretty good example of that give and take there has to be, when you are all crammed up together for a long commission: for if you start falling out, why, there's an end to all comfort, as you know very well, Stephen. I wish I may not have lost the way of it, what with age and the luxury of being post – the luxury of solitude.'

'So you are acquainted with Lord Clonfert, I find? What kind of a man is he, tell?'

'Ours was a very slight acquaintance,' said Jack evasively. 'He only came into the ship just before we were ordered home, and then he exchanged into the *Mars*.'

'An able, dashing man, I believe?'

'Oh,' said Jack, gazing beyond Stephen's head at the *Boadicea*, a lovely sight on the lonely sea, 'the *Agamemnon*'s wardroom was crowded, she wearing a flag; so I hardly knew him. But he has made quite a reputation for himself since those days.'

Stephen sniffed. He was perfectly aware of Jack's dislike for saying anything unpleasant about a former shipmate, and although he honoured the principle in theory, in practice he found it somewhat irritating.

Jack's acquaintance with Lord Clonfert had in fact been brief, but it had left its mark. They had been ordered away with the boats to take, burn or destroy a privateer lying far up a broad, shallow creek, out of range of the *Agamemnon*'s guns, an estuary lined with mangroves, whose unbuoyed channels through the mudbanks presented many interesting problems of navigation, particularly as the boats had to advance against the fire of the

privateer and of some guns planted on the shore.

Clonfert's boats took the north channel, Jack's the southern; and by the time for the final dash across the open water where the privateer was moored Clonfert's were grouped behind a spit of land somewhat nearer to the ship than Jack's. Jack emerged from the narrow channel, waved his hat, gave a cheer, urged his men 'to stretch out now, like good 'uns' and steered straight for the enemy's starboard mainchains through the heavy smoke, convinced that Clonfert's party would board on the other side. He heard the answering cheer, but it was the cheer of spectators rather than of participants: Clonfert's boats did not intend to stir. Jack realized this in the last fifty yards, but he was committed and it was too late to do anything but race on. The privateersmen fought hard: they killed several Agamemnons, among them a midshipman to whom Jack was much attached, and wounded many more. For some minutes it was doubtful who should drive whom over the side – a cruel, bitter little action, vicious hand-to-hand murder in the fading light – and then the French captain, flinging his empty pistols at Jack's head, leapt the rail and swam for it, followed by most of his remaining men. It was not the safety of the shore that he was seeking, however, but the second battery of guns that he had mounted there; and these he turned straight on to the ship, to sweep her deck with grape at point-blank range. Although Jack had received a shrewd rap on the head, his wits were about him still, and before the first discharge he had cut the cables and let fall the foretopsail to the nascent land-breeze, so that there was already way upon her when the fire began. With the luck that never deserted him in those days he steered her through the one channel in which she would not ground, and the light air took her out; though not before the grapeshot had wounded another man, cut away the crossjack halliards, and scored him across the ribs with a wound like a blow from a red-hot poker, knocking him flat into a pool of blood. They picked up the other boats and returned to the *Agamemnon*, Clonfert taking over.

Jack was scarcely conscious of going up the side. He grieved extremely for the boy who had been killed; his mind was dulled by pain and by the fever that followed so quickly in that climate; and Clonfert's eager explanation – 'he was right up against a mudbank – he was pinned down by the shore-battery – it would have been suicide to move – he was in the very act of landing to take it from behind when Aubrey made his gallant dash' –

seemed to him uninteresting and unimportant. Later, when he was fit for duty again, it did seem to him a little strange that the official letter should have omitted his name and have given Clonfert quite so much credit: though indeed Clonfert was senior to him at that time; and then again half a dozen privateersmen, unable to swim, had taken refuge below, where they had had to be overcome after Clonfert's taking over. But by that time Clonfert had exchanged into the *Mars*; and Jack, homeward-bound in the *Agamemnon*, soon forgot the incident, retaining only an inward conviction that Clonfert was either singularly muddle-headed and unenterprising or that he was somewhat shy. None of the other officers in the wardroom offered an opinion – their silence was significant – and in the turmoil of the succeeding years Jack would scarcely have remembered Clonfert but for the noise he made sometimes in the newspapers, as when he was cast in damages for criminal conversation with Mrs Jennings, or on the occasion of his court-martial for striking another officer on the quarterdeck of HMS *Ramillies*, and sometimes more creditably in the Gazette. His court-martial had led to his being dismissed the service, and although after some time he had been reinstated by order-in-council he necessarily lost seniority: on the other hand, duing the interval he took service with the Turks, and the experience proved uncommonly useful when, as a king's officer once more, he attached himself to Sir Sydney Smith. He was with that somewhat flamboyant gentleman at Acre when Smith forced Buonaparte to retire, and in other creditable actions, mostly on shore; and Smith praised him highly in his public letters: indeed Clonfert and the Admiral agreed well together – they were both seen walking about London wearing Oriental robes – and it was due to him that Clonfert was made a commander, his present rank. Jack was well aware that Gazettes might suppress truth and suggest falsehood, but he knew that they could not possibly invent victories such as the destruction of a Turkish squadron or the spiking of the guns of Abydos; and on these occasions it occurred to him that he might have been mistaken about Clonfert's want of courage. The reflection did not linger, however: quite apart from the fact that Clonfert was not a man whom Jack had taken to, he was a follower of Smith; and Smith, though dashing, was a vain, showy man who had given Nelson much uneasiness in the Mediterranean. Jack's admiration and respect for Nelson was such that his opponents could find no friend in Captain Aubrey. His mind ran on to

admirals, their rivalries, the ill effect of these rivalries, the problems of high and necessarily remote command.

'Why, brother, what a study you are in,' said Stephen. 'We shall certainly row clean through my weed, if you go on at this unconsidered pace. Pray, what is in your mind? Dread of the French, no doubt?'

'Certainly,' said Jack, shipping his oars, 'they make my heart die within me. But what concerns me most, as we get nearer to the Cape, is the possibility of a pendant, and what comes with it.'

'I do not understand you – a little to the left, if you please; I believe I see a cephalopod among the wrack. He is gone, the thief. Row gently, joy, and I shall trail my little net. I do not understand you: the ship has a perfectly good pendant at this moment; surely you must have noticed it.' He nodded towards the *Boadicea*, from whose masthead dropped the long streamer that showed she was in commission.

'What I mean is the broad pendant.' Stephen looked stupid. 'The *broad* pendant, Stephen, that shows you are a commodore: and what comes with it is high command. For the first time you are as who should say a flag, an admiral; and you have an admiral's responsibilities of command.'

'What of it, my dear? To my certain knowledge you have always exercised command efficiently: I doubt I could have done much better myself. You say belay, and he belayeth. What more can you desire, for all love?' Stephen spoke with only a small part of his attention: all the rest was concentrated upon the cephalopod, though indeed he did murmur something about commodores – he remembered them perfectly – the chief Indiaman of the fleet that had succoured them so providentially after their affray with Monsieur de Linois had been called the commodore.

'Why, don't you see,' cried Jack, his mind fixed upon this question of command, 'it has always been the command of a single ship. You are bred up to it – it comes natural. But high command is something you come to suddenly, with no experience. There are captains under you; and handling the captains of a squadron, each one of them God the Father on his own quarterdeck, is a very different matter from handling a ship's company under your own eye. You can rarely choose them and you can rarely get rid of them; and if you do not handle them right, then the squadron is inefficient, and there's the devil to pay with tar.

A good understanding is more important than I can tell you. Nelson could do it as easy as kiss my hand . . . the band of brothers, you know . . .' His voice trailed away, and as he watched Stephen grubbing among the weed he thought of cases where admirals or commodores had lacked the Nelson touch: a melancholy list – bitter ill-feeling, indecisive actions, golden opportunities thrown away for lack of support, strict obedience to the letter of the Fighting Instructions, courts-martial, and above all the enemy roaming about the sea unchecked. 'Corbett's reputation is sound enough, so is Pym's,' he said almost to himself, and then louder, 'But now I come to think of it, Stephen, you should know all about Clonfert. He is a countryman of yours, an eminent chap, I dare say, in Ireland.'

'Sure, it is an Irish title,' said Stephen, 'but Clonfert is as much an Englishman as you are yourself. The family name is Scroggs. They have some acres of bog and what they call a castle near Jenkinsville in the bleak north – I know it well; anthea foetidissima grows there – and a demesne south of the Curragh of Kildare, forfeited Desmond land; but I doubt he has ever set foot on it. A Scotch agent looks after what rents he can rack out of the tenants.'

'But he is a peer, is he not? A man of some real consequence?'

'Bless your innocence, Jack: an Irish peer is not necessarily a man of any consequence at all. I do not wish to make any uncivil reflection on your country – many of my best friends are Englishmen – but you must know that this last hundred years and more it has been the practice of the English ministry to reward their less presentable followers with Irish titles; and your second-rate jobbing backstairs politician, given a coronet of sorts and transplanted into a country where he is a stranger, is a pitiful spectacle, so he is; a flash Brummagem imitation of the real thing. I should be sorry if the Irish peers, for the most part of them, were Irishmen. Apart from certain naval lords, that the ministry dare not have in the English House, they are a shabby crew, upon the whole, out of place in Ireland and ill at ease in England. I do not speak of your Fitzgeralds or Butlers, you understand, still less of the few native families that have survived, but of what is commonly called an Irish peer. Clonfert's grandfather, now, was a mere – Jack, what are you about?'

'I am taking off my shirt.'

'To swim so soon after dinner, and such a dinner? I cannot advise it. You are very corpulent; full of gross, viscous humours

52

after these weeks and months of Poirier's cooking. And now we are come to the point, my dear, it is my clear duty to warn you against gule, against ungoverned appetite . . . a brutish vice, inductive mainly to the sin of Eve . . . bulimy, bulimy . . . dinners have killed more men than ever Avicenna healed . . .' he prosed away while Jack took off his trousers. 'So you are determined on your bathe?' he said, looking at his naked companion. 'Will you let me see your back, now?' He ran his fingers over the dull-blue scar and asked, 'Do you feel it, these days?'

'Just a trifle, this morning,' said Jack. 'But otherwise, from the time we cleared the Channel until yesterday, never a twinge. A swim,' he said, slipping over the side and plunging deep into the pure blue water with his long yellow hair streaming out behind him, 'is the very thing for it,' he continued, rising to the surface and blowing hard. 'God, it is so refreshing, even though it is as warm as milk. Come on, Stephen, bathe while you may. For tomorrow we reach the cold current setting north, the green water and the westerlies, I trust; you will have your mollymawks and your pintadoes and maybe your albatrosses, but there will be no more swimming till the Cape.'

Chapter Three

Ever since the *Boadicea* had made her landfall all hands had been
in a state of feverish activity, putting the last touches to her
beauty: now it was almost over, and she stood into False Bay
with a fair breeze rounding her studdingsails and wafting the
reek of fresh paint along with her. The only stage still to obscure
her spotless black and white Nelson checker was that occupied
by the carpenters' mates, applying carmine with anxious care to
the lips, cheeks and bosom of the opulent though insipid British
queen.

Jack, already fine in his best uniform, stood by the starboard
rail of the quarterdeck with Mr Farquhar beside him. A little
farther forward the gunner blew on his slow-match by the brass
nine-pounder: all the other guns were housed, ranged with the
perfection of the Guards on parade, their breeching pipeclayed.
Seymour was a conscientious first lieutenant, and the deck was a
pleasure to behold – the gleaming pallor of the wood, the ebony
of the seams new-paid with pitch, the falls precisely flemished, a
series of exact helices that no man dared disturb, the few pieces
of brass the captain would permit blazing in the sun, no speck of
dust to be seen from stem to stern, the hen-coops, the surviving
swine struck down into the hold together with the goat, which,
in the general silence, could be heard bleating angrily for its long-
overdue tobacco. The general silence, for all hands were on deck
in their Sunday frocks, and they gazed earnestly, mutely at the
shore, upon which people could now be seen walking about –
walking about on dry land, among trees! – most of them per-
ceptibly black: the only sounds to be heard, apart from the goat,
were the bark of the master conning the ship from the forecastle, the ritual answers of the timoneer, the chant of the
leadsman in the chains: 'By the mark, fifteen: by the mark,
fifteen: and a half, fifteen: by the deep, sixteen: and a half,
fifteen', and the conversational voice of the Captain as he pointed
out various objects to his guest.

'That flat rock is what we call Noah's Ark, and far over there is
Seal Island – the Doctor will like that. And beyond the Ark
where you see the white water is the Roman Rock: we shall pass
between the two. Indeed, we shall open Simon's Bay at any

minute now. Mr Richardson, pray see if the Doctor has finished – whether he can come on deck – he would be sorry to miss all this. 'Yes, there we are,' he went on, with his telescope to his eye as the inner harbour came into full view. '*Raisonable*, do you see? The two-decker. Then *Sirius: Néréide* laying inside her, a very pretty berth: then a brig I cannot make out at all. Mr Seymour, what do you make of the brig with her topmasts on deck?' At this point Stephen appeared, blinking in the strong light, wiping his bloody hands on a woollen nightcap and looking squalid. 'Ah, there you are, Doctor,' cried Jack. 'Have you finished sawing up poor young Francis? How is he coming along? Prime, I dare say?' Francis, until today the most popular topman in the ship, endeavouring to gild the *Boadicea*'s maintopgallant truck, had lost his hold, making a most spectacular fall from that giddy eminence, missing the deck (and certain death) by the grace of the frigate's roll, but grazing her number twelve portlid with such force as to play havoc with his thoracic cage and above all to smear the bleeding paintwork, the grass-combing bugger.

'He may do,' said Stephen. 'These young fellows are made of steel and a particularly resilient leather. So that is Africa.' He looked greedily at the shore, the known haunt of the aardvark, the pangolin, the camelopard; of birds without number, roaming at large amidst a flora of extraordinary wealth, headed by the ostrich. 'And that,' pointing towards a remote headland, 'is the all-dreaded Cape of Storms itself, I make no doubt?'

'Not exactly,' said Jack. 'The Cape is far astern: I am sorry you did not see it. We came round precious close while you was busy. But before that you did see the Table Mountain, did you not? I sent a messenger.'

'Yes, yes. I felt most obliged to you, in spite of the unchristian hour. It might also be compared with Ben Bulben.'

'Curious, ain't it? And now here on the larboard bow – no, the larboard – you have Simon's Bay, a sweet anchorage. And there's *Raisonable*, wearing the flag.'

'Would that be a line-of-battle ship?' asked Farquhar. 'A most imposing vessel.'

'I doubt any sixty-four would ever lie in the line nowadays,' said Jack. 'In any case, the *Raisonable* was built fifty years ago, and if she fired a full broadside she might fall to pieces; but I am glad she looks imposing. Then comes *Sirius*, a much more powerful ship in fact, although she has but one tier of guns; thirty-six eighteen-pounders, much the same broadside weight of

metal as ours. Then another frigate, do you see? *Néréide*, thirty-six; but only twelve-pounders. Then that odd little brig-of-war.'

'Pray, sir, why are they not at sea?' asked Farquhar. 'As I understand it, those and a smaller vessel called the *Otter* are almost all we have to guard the Indian trade. I ask out of mere curiosity.'

'Oh,' said Jack, 'this is the tail-end of the hurricane season up there. They could hardly be blockading the Mauritius in the hurricane season. They are probably in to refit and to take in stores – nothing for them up there, two thousand miles to the north . . . Mr Johnson, I believe you may begin to reduce sail.'

His eyes were fixed to his glass: the *Boadicea* had made her number and he was watching for the master-attendant's boat to put off. There it was, just leaving the pier. Although the frigate was now under fore and main topsails alone, still she glided in, heaved on by the moderate south-east swell and the making tide, and the shore came fast towards him. The moment he had the Admiralty House square on he would begin his salute; and while he waited for that moment to come he had the strangest feeling that at the first gun England and his whole voyage south would vanish into the past.

'Carry on, Mr Webber,' he said, and as he spoke the nine-pounder bawled out its respects with a tongue of fire in a cloud of smoke.

'Fire one,' said the gunner; and the echoes came hurrying back from the mountains. 'Fire two. Fire three . . .' By the seventeeth gun the great bay was alive with crossing reverberations, and before they had died away a puff of smoke appeared on the *Raisonable*'s side, followed a second later by the deep report. Nine guns she fired, the reply due to a captain, and after the ninth the *Boadicea*'s signal-midshipman, young Weatherall, piped, 'Flag signalling, sir.' Then his voice broke to a harsh bass as he went on, '*Captain repair aboard flag.*'

'Acknowledge,' said Jack. 'Lower away the gig. Where's my coxswain? Pass the word for my coxswain.'

'I am sorry, sir,' said Johnson, blushing. 'Moon is drunk.'

'Damn him,' said Jack. 'Crompton, jump into the gig. Mr Hill, are these all my papers? Every last one?' Clasping the packet of sealed, canvas-covered documents to his bosom he ran down the side, caught the heaving gig on the height of its rise, and said, 'Shove off.'

It was many, many years since he had last been here, a mid-

shipman, an oldster, in the *Resolution*, yet how exactly he remembered it all; there were a few more civilian houses in the village at the bottom of the bay, but everything else was just the same – the steady beat of the surf, the mountains, the men-of-war's boats crossing to and fro, the hospital, the barracks, the arsenal: he might himself have been a lanky boy, returning to the *Resolution* after catching Roman-fish off the rocks. He was filled with a pleasurable excitement, with countless memories, yet at the same time with an apprehension that he could not define.

'Boat ahoy?' asked the *Raisonable*.

'*Boadicea*,' replied the acting coxswain in a voice of brass; and then more quietly he said, 'Rowed of all.' The gig kissed against the tall flank of the flagship, the sideboys ran down with their scarlet man-ropes, the bosun started his call, and Jack was piped aboard. As he took off his cocked hat he realized with a shock that the tall bowed white-haired figure who answered his salute was the Admiral Bertie he had last seen in Port of Spain as the lithe, lively, wenching captain of the *Renown*; and some part of his busy mind said to him, beneath all the rest, 'Perhaps you are not so very young yourself, either, Jack Aubrey.'

'Here you are at last, Aubrey,' said the Admiral, shaking his hand. 'I am very happy to see you. You know Captain Eliot?'

'Yes, sir; we were shipmates in the *Leander* in ninety-eight. How do you do, sir?'

Before Eliot could reply with anything more than an extension of the friendly smile that he had worn ever since Jack's face appeared, the Admiral went on, 'I dare say those papers are for me? Come along; let's have a look at them in the cabin.' Splendour; opulence; carpets; a portrait of Mrs Bertie, looking plump and comfortable. 'Well,' he said, wrestling with the outer covers, 'so you had a tedious passage of it: but did you have any luck on your way down? They used to call you Lucky Jack Aubrey in the Mediterranean, I remember. God damn these seals.'

'We saw barely a sail, sir; but we did have a little brush off the Dry Salvages, and retook the old *Hyaena*.'

'Did you? Did you, indeed? Well, I am heartily glad of it . . .' The papers were free now, and as he glanced through them he said, 'Yes. I have been expecting these. We must take them along to the Governor at once. But you have a politico aboard, I see? A Mr Farquhar? He must come too: I shall send my barge, by way of compliment; you cannot be too careful with these

57

political gents. You had better order some cool clothes, too; it is a twenty-mile ride to Cape Town. The Governor will not object to nankeen trousers and a round jacket.' He gave his orders and called for a bottle of wine. 'This is the right Diamant of the year one, Aubrey,' he said, sitting down again. 'Too good for you young fellows; but you did retake the old *Hyaena* . . . I was a midshipman in her. Yes.' His washed-out blue eyes looked back over forty-five years, and he observed, 'That was in the days before carronades.' Returning to the present he drank his wine, saying, 'I trust your luck will hold, Aubrey: you need it, on this station. Well, and so we shall have to fag over that damned mountain, a wearying ride in this infernal dust – dust everywhere, rain or shine; a whole nation of swabbers would never come to an end of it. I wish we did not have to go. If it were not for the political side, I should get you to sea the minute you had your water aboard. The situation is far worse than ever it was before you left England – far worse than when these orders were written. The French have snapped up two more Indiamen, this side of the Ten Degree channel, the *Europe* and the *Streatham*: homeward-bound Indiamen, worth a mint of money.'

'Lord, sir, that is very bad,' cried Jack.

'Yes, it is,' said the Admiral, 'and it is going to get even worse unless we bring it up with a round turn, and smartly at that. That is what we must do: it is feasible, and it must be done. Oh, yes, it is feasible, with a certain amount of initiative . . . and maybe I should add good fortune too, though luck don't bear talking about.' He touched wood, considered for a while, and then said, 'Listen, Aubrey, before your Mr Farquhar comes aboard – before we start getting entangled in political considerations – I shall lay the position before you as clearly as I can. There are four French frigates based on Mauritius and Réunion in addition to the force they had there last year: they can use Port-Louis or Port South-East in Mauritius and Saint-Paul in Réunion, and separately or in pairs they can range out as far as the Nicobars and beyond – the whole Indian Ocean. You can't catch them out there; we can't convoy all the Eastern trade – we do not possess the ships; and you can't blockade them for ever. So you must either destroy them in detail in their home waters or eventually you must take their bases away from them. Now with this in mind, we have seized and garrisoned Rodriguez with part of the Fifty-Sixth and some Bombay sepoys, for your water in the first place, and in the second as a base of the reinforcements that

are supposed to come from India in time. There are only about four hundred men on the island at present, but we hope for more next year – it is a question of transports. You know Rodriguez?'

'Yes, sir. I have not touched there, however.' Rodriguez: a remote and tolerably barren speck of land alone in the ocean, three hundred and fifty miles eastward of Mauritius: he had viewed it from the masthead of his dear *Surprise*.

'So at least you have your water. As for ships, you have *Boadicea*, of course: *Sirius*, with a good steady captain in Pym, as regular as a clock; *Néréide* – she is only a twelve-pounder, and getting on in years, but Corbett keeps her in very good order though he is rather undermanned; *Otter*, a fast, useful eighteen-gun sloop, in very good order too. Lord Clonfert has her: she should be in any moment now. And I can let you have *Raisonable* except in the hurricane months, for she cannot bear a hard blow. She is not all she was when I was a boy, but we careened her a few weeks ago, and she is quite fast. At least she is a match for the *Cannonière*, who is older still; and she makes a show. I might conceivably be able to add the *Magicienne* from Sumatra, in time, and the *Victor*, another sloop. But even without them, I conceive that, *Raisonable* cancelling out *Cannonière*, three well worked-up frigates and a powerful sloop would not be reckoned out of the way for dealing with four Frenchmen.'

'Certainly not, sir,' said Jack. The Admiral was speaking as though Jack's pendant were a certainty.

'No one will pretend it is an easy task, however. The Frenchmen are *Vénus*, *Manche*, *Caroline* – it was she who took the last two Indiamen – and *Bellone*, all new forty-gun frigates. As for the rest, they have the *Cannonière*, as I have said, still mounting her fifty guns, our brig the *Grappler*, several avisos and a few smaller things. And I warn you, Aubrey, if you hoist your pendant, I cannot let you have a captain under you. If you shift into the *Raisonable* for the time being, Eliot can replace you in *Boadicea*; but I cannot let you have a captain under you.' Jack bowed. He had scarcely relied upon it: on the remoter stations there were few post-captains to spare; and then again if a commodore did have a captain under him, that commodore was entitled to a third of the Admiral's share of prize-money.

'May I ask whether we have any intelligence of their land-forces, sir?' he said.

'Yes, but I wish it were more exact. On Mauritius General Decaen has the best part of two regiments of the line, and his militia

may amount to ten thousand or so. Our information from Réunion is more scanty, but it seems that General Desbrusleys has much the same. Oh, it is a tough nut to crack, I grant you; but cracked it must be, and at the earliest possible moment. You have to strike hard and fast with your forces concentrated while theirs are dispersed: in a word, you have to go in and win. Government will be in a rare old taking when the news of the *Europe* and the *Streatham* reaches England, and this is the kind of situation where you must produce results at once. I do not mention the country's interests, of course; but I do say that from a purely personal point of view there is probably a knighthood or even a baronetcy if you succeed; and if you don't, why it is the beach and half-pay for the rest of your life.'

A midshipman darted in. 'The captain's duty, sir,' said he, 'and should you wish a compliment to the gentleman in the barge?'

'Certainly,' said the Admiral. 'As to a flag.' In the pause that followed he gazed abstractedly at his wife's portrait. 'Should you not like a baronetcy, Aubrey? I am sure I would. Mrs Bertie fairly longs to wipe her sister's eye.'

The unofficial part of Simon's Town, though little more than a hamlet, had drinking-booths, wine-shops and places of entertainment enough for a town of moderate size; and into one of those, at dusk, walked Stephen Maturin, bearing a bunch of orchids. He was tired, thirsty, and covered from head to foot with African dust; but he was happy, having spent this first half-day ashore walking up a mountain clothed with a vegetation largely unknown to him and inhabited by remarkable birds, some of which he recognized from their published descriptions: he had also seen three quarters of a female spotted hyaena, and he had found the remaining piece, including its wistful face, removed to some distance, in the act of being devoured by his old friend the bearded vulture – a pleasant combination of the present and the past, of two far-distant worlds.

He called for wine and water, mingled them in proportion to his thirst, placed his orchids in the water-jug, and drank until at last he began to sweat again. Apart from the landlord and three pretty Malay girls at the bar, there were only two other people in the twilit room, a very large officer in a uniform he could not make out, a vast gloomy man with a great deal of dark whisker, not unlike a melancholy bear, and his smaller, inconspicuous companion, who sat at his ease in shirtsleeves, with his breeches

unbuttoned at the knee. The sad officer spoke a fluent though curious English devoid of articles: the smaller man's harsh and grating accent was clearly that of Ulster. They were discussing the Real Presence, but he had not made out the thread of their discourse before they both burst out 'No Pope, no Pope, no Pope,' the sad officer in the deepest bass that Stephen had ever heard. At the bar the Malay girls politely echoed 'No Pope' and as though it were a signal they brought candles and set them about the room. The light fell on Stephen's orchids and upon the contents of his handkerchief, fourteen curious beetles, collected for his friend Sir Joseph Blain, formerly the chief of naval intelligence; he was considering one, a bupestrid, when he became aware of a darkness by his side, the melancholy bear, gently swaying. 'Golovnin, fleet lieutenant, captain of Imperial Majesty's sloop *Diana*,' said he, clicking his heels.

Stephen rose, bowed, and said, 'Maturin, surgeon of Britannic Majesty's ship *Boadicea*. Please to take chair.'

'You have soul,' observed Golovnin, nodding at the orchids. 'I too have soul. Where did you find them, flowers?'

'In mountain,' said Stephen.

Golovnin sighed; and taking a small cucumber from his pocket he began to eat it. He made no reply to Stephen's proffer of wine, but after a while he said, 'What is their name, flowers?'

'Disa grandiflora,' said Stephen, and a long silence fell. It was broken by the Ulsterman, who, tired of drinking alone, brought his bottle over and set it on Stephen's table without the least ceremony. 'I am McAdam, of the *Otter*,' he remarked, sitting down. 'I saw you at the hospital this morning.' Now, by the light of the candle, Stephen recognized him, not from that morning but from many years ago: William McAdam, a mad-doctor with a considerable reputation in Belfast, who had left Ireland after the failure of his private asylum. Stephen had heard him lecture, and had read his book on hysteria with great applause. 'He will not last long,' observed McAdam, referring to Golovnin, now weeping on to the orchids.

'Nor will you, colleague,' thought Stephen, looking at McAdam's pallid face and bloodshot eye.

'Will you take a wee drink?'

'Thank you, sir,' said Stephen, 'I believe I shall stay with my negus. What is it that you have in your bottle, pray?'

'Och, it's a brandy they distill hereabouts. Raw, rot-gut stuff; I drink it experimentally, not from indulgence. He' – pointing an

61

unsteady finger at Golovnin – 'drinks it from nostalgia, as the nearest to his native vodka; I encourage him.'

'You alluded to an experiment?' said Stephen.

'Yes. Strobenius and others allege that a man dead drunk on grain-spirits falls backwards: on brandy he falls forwards. And if that is true, it tells us something about the motor centres, if you understand the expression. This gentleman here is my corpus vile. Yet it is wonderful how he holds out. This is our third bottle, and he has drunk glass for glass with me.'

'I honour your devotion to science, sir.'

'I do not give a fart in hell for science,' said McAdam. 'Art is all. Medicine is an art or it is nothing. Medicine of the mind, I mean; for what is your physical medicine, apart from purges and mercury and bark, what your murderous chirurgical tricks? They may, with luck, suppress symptoms: no more. On the other hand, where is the true *fons et origo* of nine tenths of your vicious constitutions of body? The mind, that's where it is,' he said, tapping his forehead. 'And what heals the mind? Art: nothing else. Art is all. That is my realm.'

It occurred to Stephen that McAdam was perhaps a somewhat seedy practitioner of this or any other árt; a man furthermore whose inward torments were clearly printed on his face. But as they talked of the interaction of mind and body, of interesting cases they had seen – false pregnancies – inexplicable remissions – their experience afloat – the inverse relationship of constipation and courage – the proved efficacity of placebos – his opinion of McAdam rose: indeed, a mutual esteem came into being, and McAdam's arrogant, didactic tone grew even civil. He was telling Stephen about his patients aboard the *Otter* – most of the Otters were, *sensu stricto*, mentally deranged, and there was one case that McAdam would describe and name, were it not for professional secrecy, a fascinating and particularly subtle chain of symptoms – when without any warning Golovnin fell off his chair, grasping the orchids. He lay motionless, still in the attitude of sitting; but he fell sideways, a wholly inconclusive result. At the sound of the crash the landlord paced to the door and whistled. Two enormous sailors walked in, and murmuring, 'Come, Vasily Mikhailovitch; come, little father,' they carried their captain out into the darkness.

'He has not hurt my flowers, however,' said Stephen, smoothing their petals. 'They are, in their essentials, quite intact. You have no doubt remarked the curious spiral convolution of the

ovary, so typical of the whole order. Though perhaps your realm does not extend to botany, at all?'

'It does not,' said McAdam. 'Though twisted ovaries are well within it; and twisted testicles too – I speak in figure, you understand: I am jocose. No. The proper study of mankind is man. And I may observe, Dr Maturin, that this eager prying into the sexual organs of vegetables on your part seems to me . . .'

What it seemed to Dr McAdam did not appear, for his tide too had now reached the full. He rose; his eyes closed, and he pitched straight into Stephen's arms, falling, as Stephen noted, forwards.

The landlord brought one of the wheelbarrows that he kept under the porch, and with the help of a black, Stephen wheeled McAdam towards the pier, passing several bodies of cheerful liberty-men as he went. He hailed each party in turn, asking for any Otters; but no man chose to leave the sheltering darkness and sacrifice a moment of his shore-leave, and Stephen heard nothing but facetious replies – '*Otter*'s bound for the Rio Grande' – '*Otter*'s paid off at the Nore' – '*Otter* was broke up for firewood last Wednesday week' – until he met a group of Néréides. A familiar voice cried, 'It's the Doctor,' and there was the powerful form of Bonden at his side, Jack Aubrey's coxswain from his earliest command.

'Bonden, sir. Do you remember me?'

'Of course I remember you, Bonden,' said Stephen, shaking his hand. 'And am delighted to see you again. How do you do?'

'Pretty spry, thank you, sir; and I hope I see you the same? Now just you shove off, Darkie' – to the black – 'I'll take care of this here barrow.'

'The question is, Bonden,' said Stephen, giving the black two stuivers and a penny, 'the question is, how shall I find the means of conveying my charge to his ship, always supposing that his ship is here at all, which seems to be a matter of some doubt? He is the surgeon of the *Otter*, Bonden, a learned man, though somewhat original; and at the moment disguised in drink.'

'*Otter*, sir? She come in on the turn of the tide, not ten minutes ago. Never you fret, I'll square our boat-keeper directly and take him out.' He hurried away: a little later the *Néréide*'s jolly-boat appeared at the step, and Bonden carried the body into it. In spite of the dimness Stephen noticed that Bonden moved stiffly; and this stiffness became more apparent as he pulled out across the harbour towards the distant sloop.

'You are stiff, Barret Bonden,' said Stephen. 'In another man I should say he had certainly been flogged; but that can scarcely be the case with you. I trust it is not a wound, or a rheumatism from the falling damps?'

Bonden laughed, but without much mirth, and said, 'Oh, it was four dozen at the gangway, all right, sir, and two more for luck: brass on the lock of the number seven gun not bright enough.'

'I am amazed, Bonden: amazed,' said Stephen, and indeed he was. Bonden had never been flogged to his knowledge; and even in a flogging ship fifty lashes was a savage punishment for anything but a most serious crime. 'And grieved. Let us row over to the *Boadicea*, and I shall give you some salve.'

'It's all right now, sir, thanking you kindly. I was aboard you this afternoon, but it was not for no salve: you will find the letter we wrote, a-laying there in your cabin.'

'What is it about, tell?'

'Well, sir,' said Bonden, resting on his oars: but by this time they were close to the larboard side of the *Otter*, and in reply to her hail Bonden called, 'Your doctor coming aboard: request a line.' The *Otter* was perfectly used to this: a whip with a bowline appeared over the side; Bonden slipped it under McAdam's arms; and the surgeon vanished upwards.

'Well, sir,' said Bonden again, pulling slowly towards the *Boadicea*, 'this is the way of it. When me and Killick, on the Leeward Islands station, heard the Captain was afloat again, we went to join him, in course: and there was plenty more in other ships did likewise – old Sophies, old Surprises, even an old Polychrest: Bolton, that slab-sided cove the Captain pulled out of the sea. Oh, was he to new-commission a ship, he'd have no trouble finding a ship's company: not like some – ' He swallowed the coarse expression with a cough and went on, 'Howsoever, we put in our request, and Captain Dundas, a very affable gent and a friend of the Captain's as you know full well, sir, discharged us into *Néréide*, Captain Corbett, for the Cape: which he was so kind as to say he was sorry to lose us, and give Killick a pot of guava-jelly for the Captain. But *Néréide*'s short-handed: because why? because the men run whenever they can. There was Joe Lucas, of our mess, as swam three mile, with bladders, off St Kitts, sharks and all: was brought back, flogged, and swum it again, with his back like a raw steak. And today, with only twelve liberty-men out of the whole crew, two of 'em are off for the mountain, in spite of all them wild beasts, I know for a certain

64

fact, leaving thirty-eight months' pay and their prize-money. So, do you see, we are afraid, Killick and me and the rest, that Captain Corbett will not discharge us into the *Boadicea*; and so we wrote this letter to you, sir. Because not liking to put ourselves in the Captain's way, being that he's to hoist his pendant any minute as they say, and therefore too busy, we hoped you might put in a good word, just casual, at the right moment.'

'Of course I shall. But you could very well have addressed Captain Aubrey himself; he has the kindest recollection of you – often speaks of his real coxswain, and much regrets your absence.'

'Does he, though?' said Bonden, with a chuckle of satisfaction. 'But even so, we'd take it very kind in you to say a word: it would come more proper, like, from you. And we are main anxious to be out of *Néréide*.'

'She is not altogether a happy ship, I collect?'

'No, sir, she ain't.' He rested on his oars again, and looking a little sideways at Stephen he added, 'She's a shot-rolling ship: that's what she is.'

Stephen knew nothing about the sailing of ships, theoretical or practical; but he did know that when a crew started trundling cannon-balls about the deck under the cover of darkness, then something was very much amiss; for the next stage was mutiny. He also knew that in any normal ship it would be unthinkable for an unusually steady, sober man like Bonden to be flogged.

'I'm not complaining, mark you,' said Bonden. 'Nor I'm not setting up in judgment: there are some right bastards in the *Néréide*, before the mast and elsewheres; and when things reach a certain pitch, in such a ship the cat falls on the just and the unjust alike. I can take fifty lashes as well as the next man, I hope; though I may say as how it was the first time the cat and me came acquainted – oh, I was beat like a drum when I was a little chap in the *Thunderer*, but that was only the master-at-arms' admonition, as we say. His cane, sir. No. What I mean is, that in the first place me and Killick and the rest want to get back to our own captain: and in the second, we want to get out before things turn nasty. And at the gait they are going now – well, I shouldn't give much for Captain Corbett's life, nor some of his officers, come an action, or even maybe a dirty night with no moon; and we want no part in it.'

'Ugly, Bonden, very ugly,' said Stephen, and no more until they were alongside the *Boadicea*, when he said, 'Good night,

now; and thank you for rowing me home.'

He turned in with Leguat's Voyage, with its fascinating account of the solitaire, and Sparmann; and late in the middle watch he heard Jack come aboard. But it was not until quite late in the morning that they met, Stephen having been called to the sick-bay to deal with an alcoholic coma that had suddenly started to gush blood at the ears; and when they did meet it was clear to him that both his crapulous night and his crapulous morning (the sick-bay had smelt like a distillery) were to be prolonged. Captain Aubrey had the yellow, puffy look of one who has drunk far too much – so much indeed that his twenty-mile ride back had not worked it off. 'Twenty miles, *more* than twenty miles, on a damned screw that flung me down three times, and spoilt my best nankeen trousers,' he said. His steward had broken the coffee-pot: his French cook had gone ashore with Bretonnière to join the other prisoners of war, and never more would there be brioche for breakfast. But infinitely more than even the missing coffee was the fact that the Admiral had promised Jack his orders and had not produced them. An interminable, inconclusive conference with the Governor, Mr Farquhar and two general officers of a stupidity remarkable even for the army: then an equally long supper with the soldiers, determined to make their guest drunk. And all this while no orders. By the time Jack set off on his glandered mare the Admiral had long since gone to bed; the flag-lieutenant knew nothing about any orders, written or even contemplated. So here he was, as he told Stephen in the cabin, not knowing *where* he was: there had been no word about his pendant at any time. Here he was, left hanging up in the air: perhaps the expedition would not take place at all: and if it did, after months of delay, perhaps he was not intended to command at all – there had been a furtive, evasive look in the eye of the Admiral's secretary, an ill-looking, untrustworthy swab, for all he was a parson. There had been no mention of higher command in his original sailing orders, and although the Admiral had certainly spoken as though the matter were settled, the appointment no doubt lay at his discretion: the Admiral might have changed his mind: he might have been influenced by the opinion of the council. And then earlier there had been that ominous '*if* you hoist your pendant'.

'Let us take a turn on deck,' he said. 'My head seems to be made of hot sand. And Stephen, might I beg you, implore you, not to smoke those vile things in the cabin? It is your pot-house

66

all over again, like that soldiers' mess last night.'

They reached the quarterdeck in time to see an odd figure come up the side, a young man dressed in a gaudy coat and a little gaudy hat. He had come up the starboard side, the officers' side, and as he advanced towards Mr Seymour he saluted. The first lieutenant hesitated: not so Jack. 'Turn that fellow off the ship,' he roared. Then, in a lower voice, holding his hand to his aching forehead, 'What the devil does he mean by it, prancing about the deck of a King's ship improperly dressed, like a jack-pudding?' The young man got into a boat, and was rowed away by a crew of merry-andrews, all in much the same kind of rig.

Jack's steward cautiously sidled near, muttering something about 'the gunroom's pot', and Stephen said, 'I believe he means that coffee's up.'

It was: and as they drank it benignity returned, helped by fresh cream, bacon, eggs, pig's fry, the last of the true French short bastards, toasted, and Sophie's orange marmalade.

'I am sorry I was so cursed snappish just now, about your cigar,' said Jack, pushing back his chair at last and undoing his waistcoat. 'Pray smoke, Stephen. You know I like the smell.'

'Ay,' said Stephen. He broke a cigar in three, crumbled one piece, moistened it with a few drops of coffee, rolled it in paper, and lit it with a voluptuous indraught. 'Listen, now, will you?' he said. 'Bonden, Killick and some others are aboard the *Néréide*, and wish to return to you. All tastes are to be found in nature, we are told; and it is to be presumed that they like the brutal, arbitrary, tyrannical exercise of power.'

'Oh,' cried Jack, 'how very, very pleased I am! It will be like old times. I have rarely regretted anything so much as having to part with them. But will Corbett ever let them go? He's devilish short-handed; and it's only a courtesy, you know, except to a flag. Why, a man like Bonden is worth his weight in gold.'

'Corbett does not seem to be aware of his value, however: he gave him fifty lashes.'

'Flogged Bonden?' cried Jack, going very red. 'Flogged my cox'n? By God, I . . .'

A nervous young gentleman brought the news that the Commander-in-chief's flag-lieutenant had been seen putting off from the shore and the captain of the *Otter* from his sloop, and that Mr Seymour thought Captain Aubrey might like to know.

'Thank you, Mr Lee,' said Jack, and he went on deck: Lord and Lady Clonfert had been far, far from his mind, but they

came back with a rush as he saw the *Otter*'s gig, pulled by the same merry-andrews of just before breakfast, approaching the *Boadicea*. It was at about the same distance as the *Raisonable*'s barge, but the flag-lieutenant paused by the flagship to exchange a bellowed and apparently very amusing conversation with a friend on her poop, and before it was over the gig was alongside.

Clonfert was piped aboard, a slight, strikingly handsome, youthful-looking man in full uniform with a star on the bosom of his coat and a singular expression of expectation and uneasiness on his face. He flushed as Jack shook his hand, saying, 'I am happy to see you again, Clonfert; but I heartily wish I had better news for you. Come into my cabin.' Once there he went on, 'I am very much concerned to tell you, that because of an unfortunate misunderstanding about the time, I was obliged to leave Plymouth without Lady Clonfert.'

'Oh,' said Clonfert, with a look of bitter contrariety on his mobile face. 'I was afraid that might be so. I sent early to enquire, but it seems that the message I sent by one of my officers could not be received.'

'An officer?' cried Jack. 'I had no notion – an officer, in that rig?'

'I am sorry it did not meet with your approval, sir,' said Clonfert stiffly. 'But it is my custom to dress my gig's crew in my own colours – it is usual enough in the service, I believe – and the gentlemen under my command fall in with my humour. I confess it is irregular, however.'

'Well, it can lead to misunderstanding. Still, it is cleared up now, and I have delivered my damned unwelcome news – I regret it extremely, but I am sure that Lady Clonfert will have taken the next Indiaman. She will have travelled in much greater comfort, and she should be here within the next week or so, for we made but a slow passage of it. You will dine with me? We have a sucking-pig, and I recall you was fond of sucking-pig in the *Agamemnon*.'

Clonfert flushed again at the name of the ship: he darted an intensely suspicious glance at Jack, and then with an artificial air he said he must beg to be excused – with infinite reluctance he must plead a previous engagement – but that in taking his leave he must be allowed to express his sense of Captain Aubrey's great politeness in having intended to bring Lady Clonfert to the Cape; he was pénétré, pénétré.

He brought it off well enough to make Jack, whose conscience

68

was far from easy on that score, feel something of a scrub; and if he had not tripped on his way out of the cabin the performance would have been well-nigh perfect. The flag-lieutenant was already on deck, talking and laughing with Seymour, when Jack saw his visitor to the side; and Jack's searching eye saw that the jolly young man was the bearer not of the unimportant inconclusive temporizing verbal order that he had so dreaded – that he had so reasonably dreaded, from the tone of last night's conference – but of an important folder bound up with tape, red official tape.

In the cabin once more he received the folder; but first he had to listen to the flag-lieutenant's message. 'The Admiral desires me to say, sir, that he was taken unwell just after the meeting; that he was unable to give you your orders as he had intended; but that he dictated them from his bed at the earliest possible moment. In fact, sir, he dictated them to me, the secretary not being in the way.'

'So you know what is in them, I dare say?'

'Yes, sir; and may I be the first to wish you joy of your pendant, sir?'

'Thank you, Mr Forster,' said Jack, with the full sun lighting up his heart and bowels, his whole being. 'Thank you very much indeed. I trust the Admiral's indisposition causes him no pain or distress? I could wish him restored to the most amazing health and happiness immediately.' The flag-lieutenant thought that perhaps the Admiral had eaten something; for his part he had recommended a dose of rhubarb; and Jack listened to him with an appearance of steady solicitous attention. Jack looked decently solemn, but his mind was swimming in happiness, a happiness made all the more wholly concrete, real and tangible when the flag-lieutenant's recollections of an occasion upon which he too had eaten something came to an end and Jack could cut the tape and see that his orders were addressed to Commodore Aubrey. Yet underlying this pure felicity there was another level of consciousness, a hard, sober determination to come straight into direct contact with the 'real thing', to see exactly what it amounted to, to gauge the limits of his possible initiative, to weigh up the forces in presence, and to start dealing with the situation at once.

The orders were clear, concise, and urgent: the Admiral had obviously had his way. Commodore Aubrey was directed and required to repair aboard the *Raisonable*; to hoist his pendant;

69

to take the ships and vessels named in the margin under his command; to proceed to sea with the utmost dispatch; to seek out and destroy the French cruisers operating south of 10° S and west of 70° E, and, with the cooperation of the officer commanding the land forces on Rodriguez (which were to be reinforced at the appropriate juncture), to undertake the reduction of the French possessions of the Ile Bourbon, otherwise Ile de la Réunion, otherwise Ile Buonaparte, and of the Mauritius, otherwise Ile de France, together with that of the French ships and vessels in the seas thereto adjacent: he was to attend to the general directions in the attached schedules A and B; and in all political matters or those having a bearing on contact with the civil population he was to seek the advice of William Farquhar, Esquire, H.M. Governor-Designate, and in the absence of Mr Farquhar then that of Dr Stephen Maturin.

The schedules, together with various appreciations, charts, hydrographical notes, and estimates of the French strength, mostly derived from the American merchantmen that passed to and fro, were in separate packets; and among them was a paper bearing the superscription Lieutenant Johnson, R.N., *Boadicea*. 'What is this?' asked Jack.

'The Admiral has confirmed your acting-order for Mr Johnson,' said the flag-lieutenant. 'It is his commission.' Jack nodded, a fresh jet of pleasure overcoming the underlying gravity for a moment, and the flag-lieutenant went on, 'I am also to say, sir, that the Admiral desires you will use your own discretion entirely as far as *Raisonable* is concerned, and shift your pendant just as you see fit: he knows her condition only too well. He asks for this list of followers and servants to be sent to him in Cape Town, and he hopes you will see proper to maintain the following appointments. He much regrets that time and his present indisposition do not allow him to communicate the confidential remarks upon your captains personally, in the usual manner, and begs you will forgive this hasty scribble.' He passed a half sheet of paper, folded and sealed, and said, 'I believe that is all, sir, apart from Mr Shepherd's message: he says that since you will need a commodore's secretary he begs to recommend his cousin, Mr Peter. Mr Peter has been several months on this station and is thoroughly *au courant*. He is in Simon's Town at the moment – rode over with me – if you choose to see him.'

'I should be happy to see Mr Peter,' said Jack, strongly aware of the importance of these civilities, of the importance of good

relations throughout the squadron.

Decency required Jack to refresh the flag-lieutenant; decency required the flag-lieutenant to see his share of the bottle out within ten minutes, in order to leave the new commodore free for the innumerable tasks awaiting him; but although the young man did his best, no period of Jack's life had ever passed so slowly.

When Mr Forster had gone at last, Jack summoned Johnson and said, 'I wish you joy of your commission, Mr Johnson. Here it is. The Admiral has confirmed your acting-order, and I am very sure you deserve it.' He handed over the precious document, even more precious perhaps to Johnson than his pendant was to Jack – certainly less loaded with responsibility – and both to cut short the flood of thanks and to gain a few minutes he said, ·'Pray be so good as to send the bosun as soon as possible,' while to the bosun he said, 'Mr Fellowes, I do not suppose we have a broad pendant in the colour-chest? If not, I should be obliged if you would have one run up directly.'

'Aye aye, sir,' said the bosun, trying to suppress a grin, 'broad pendant it is.' Out of piety, a dread of offending fate by presumption, Jack had never ordered one to be made: he had felt the temptation very strongly – he had longed to cherish it in private – but he had waited until it should be certain. On the other hand the Boadiceas had turned the matter over in their heads well north of the line, ferreting about and fitting odd scraps together; they had become convinced of the need for such an object, and it had been lying by these last four thousand miles.

The bosun hurried off forward: Jack broke the Admiral's seal and read: 'Captain Pym of the *Sirius* is a thoroughly reliable, conscientious officer, but wanting in initiative; Captain Corbett of the *Néréide*, though he keeps excellent discipline and is of outstanding value as a fighting commander, has a tendency to irascibility that is to be regretted; he is on bad terms with Captain Lord Clonfert of the *Otter*, and the two should not be sent together on detached service if it can be avoided. Lord Clonfert has distinguished himself recently in several minor actions of a most dashing nature; and he, like Captain Corbett, has a considerable acquaintance with the waters off Réunion and the Mauritius.' The confidential remarks told Jack perhaps rather more about the Admiral than the captains; but he had scarcely formulated this reflection before Fellowes came hurrying back, bearing the beautiful pendant in his arms. Jack looked at it with an affectation of detachment that could scarcely have deceived

his daughters, far less the bosun. 'Thank you, Mr Fellowes,' he said. 'Pray put it on the locker, and then ask the Doctor, with my compliments, whether he can spare a moment.'

He was drawing on the breeches of his best full-dress uniform when Stephen walked in. 'I thought you might like to see something new,' he said, adding, not without pride, '*Ex Africa surgit semper aliquid novo, ——novi*, eh?'

'To what do you refer?' asked Stephen, gazing about the cabin.

'Cannot you see anything that strikes you dumb with awe, the mark of a living commodore, very nearly the most exalted being on the face of the earth?'

'The ornamental cloth? Oh, that: I had understood you to say something new. That cloth I saw daily in the bosun's cabin when his bowels were disturbed, long ago: I took it for a sign of his office, or perhaps the banner of some bosuns' guild.' Then, feeling obscurely that he had not quite fulfilled his friend's expectations, he added, 'But it is an amazingly handsome flag, upon my honour; and so neatly sewn. I dare say you will hang it up, presently; and sure it will do us all great credit, the pretty thing.'

If there had been little secrecy aboard the frigate, there was even less in the squadron. No one had failed to remark the flag-lieutenant's arrival, nor his prolonged stay in the *Boadicea*, nor the subsequent desertion of the flagship by a troop of the Admiral's servants and followers, nor yet Captain Aubrey's passage across the harbour: when the swallow-tailed pendant broke out at the *Raisonable*'s masthead, therefore, not a ship or vessel present let a second go by before starting the thirteen-gun salute due to the man it symbolized. The salutes merged with one another and with their echoes, filling the bay with a sullen roar, a cloud of smoke that drifted over Jack as he stood there on the poop, not directly looking at his pendant, but feeling its presence with oh such intensity: the moment his thunderous reply was done, he turned to the signal lieutenant and said, '*All captains*, Mr Swiney.'

He received them in the Admiral's great cabin: the *Raisonable* was not the *Hibernia* nor yet the *Victory*, but still this was a noble room, full of dappled reflected light, and as they filed in their blue and white and gold made it look nobler still. Pym of the *Sirius* came first, a big man, as tall as Jack and fatter; his congratulations were as frank and unreserved as his fine friendly open face, and Jack's heart warmed to him. Corbett followed, a small

72

dark round-headed man whose set expression of determined, angry authority was now softened into a look of the deference and the pleasure proper to this occasion. He had fought several most creditable actions in the West Indies, and in spite of Bonden Jack looked at him with respect: with hopeful anticipation, too. Corbett's good wishes were almost as cordial as Pym's, although there might have been the slightest hint of resentment, of merit and local knowledge passed over: but in any event they were far more hearty than Clonfert's formal 'Allow me to offer my felicitations, sir.'

'Now, gentlemen,' said Commodore Aubrey, when this stage was over, 'I am happy to tell you that the squadron is to proceed to sea with the utmost dispatch. I should therefore be obliged for a statement of each ship's readiness, her condition: not a detailed statement, you understand – that can come later – but a general notion. Lord Clonfert?'

'The sloop I have the honour to command is always ready to put to sea,' said Clonfert. That was mere rodomontade: no ship was always ready to put to sea unless she never used up any water, stores, powder or shot; and the *Otter* had just come in from a cruise. They all knew it, Clonfert as well as any once the words were out of his mouth. Without allowing the awkward pause to last more than a moment, however, Jack went straight on, receiving a more rational account from Pym and Corbett, from which it appeared that the *Sirius*, though well-found in general, badly needed careening, and that she was having great trouble with her water-tanks, new-fangled iron affairs that had been wished on her in Plymouth and that leaked amazingly. 'If there is one thing that I detest more than anything,' said Captain Pym, staring round the table, 'it is innovations.' The *Sirius* had rummaged her hold to come at the tanks, so even with the best will in the world, and working double-tides, she could scarcely be ready for sea before Sunday. The *Néréide*, though apparently fit to sail the moment she had filled her water, was really in a much sadder way: she was old, as the Commodore knew, and according to Captain Corbett's carpenter her navel-futtocks could be removed with a shovel; while she was certainly iron-sick fore and aft, if not amidships too; but far worse than that, she was shockingly undermanned. Captain Corbett was sixty-three hands short of his complement: a shocking figure.

Jack agreed that it was a very shocking figure, to be sure. 'But let us hope that the next homeward-bound Indiaman to put in will

solve the difficulty with sixty-three prime hands and a few super-numaries.'

'You are forgetting, sir, that ever since their disagreement with Government about the running of the colony the Company's ships no longer touch at the Cape.'

'Very true,' said Jack, with a covert glance at Clonfert. He covered his lapse by saying that he should visit their ships in the course of the afternoon, when he would hope to see their detailed statements of condition, and suggested that they should now discuss some claret that he had taken from a Frenchman on his way down. The last of the Lafite appeared, together with something in the farinaceous line from the *Boadicea*'s galley.

'Capital wine,' said Pym.

'As sound as a nut,' said Corbett. 'So you found a Frenchman, sir?'

'Yes,' said Jack, and he told them about the *Hébé*: it was not much of an action, but the mere talk of banging guns, the *Hyaena* restored to the list, the prize neatly salvaged, caused the formal atmosphere to relax. Reminiscence flowed with the claret: comparable actions and old shipmates were called to mind: laughter broke out. Jack had never served with either Pym or Corbett, but they had many acquaintances in common throughout the service: when they had spoken of half a dozen, Jack said, 'You knew Heneage Dundas in the West Indies, of course, Captain Corbett?' thinking that this might jog his mind.

'Oh, yes, sir,' said Corbett: but no more.

'That will not wash, however,' said Jack within: and aloud, 'Lord Clonfert, the bottle stands by you.'

All this time Clonfert had been sitting silent. A shaft of light, falling on his star, sent a constellation of little prismatic dots flashing high: now, as he leant forwards to the bottle, they all swept down. He filled his glass, passed the bottle on, and moved perhaps by some notion of repairing his unpleasant relationship with Corbett and possibly at the same time of winning an ally in this meeting where he could not but feel at a disadvantage, he said, 'Captain Corbett, a glass of wine with you.'

'I never drink a glass of wine with any man, my lord,' replied Corbett.

'Captain Corbett,' said Jack quickly, 'I was astonished to learn about the Russian brig lying inside the *Néréide*, and even more astonished when the Admiral told me that her captain had served under you.'

74

'Yes, sir, he was in the *Seahorse* when I had her, serving as a volunteer to learn our ways: and he picked them up pretty well, I must confess. His people are scarcely what we should rate ordinary, but I dare say he will knock some seamanship into them in time. They have a fine sense of discipline in those parts: a thousand lashes are not uncommon, I believe.'

The talk ran on about the unfortunate *Diana* – her sailing from the Baltic on a voyage of discovery at a time of peace between England and Russia – her arrival, all unsuspecting, in Simon's Town to learn that war had been declared – her curious status – her curious build – her people's curious ways ashore.

Eight bells struck: they all stood up. Jack detained Corbett for a moment and said, 'Before I forget it, Captain Corbett, my coxswain and some other men are aboard the *Néréide*. Here, I have jotted down their names. You will oblige me by having 'em sent over.'

'Certainly, sir,' said Corbett. 'Of course . . . But I beg you will not think I intend the least disrespect if I venture to repeat that I am cruelly short-handed.'

'So I understand,' said Jack. 'But I do not mean to rob you: far from it. You shall have an equal number from the *Boadicea*, and I believe I may even be able to let you have a few more. We pressed some good men among the *Hébé*'s prisoners.'

'I should be most uncommon grateful, sir,' said Corbett, brightening at once. 'And I shall send your men back the moment I reach the ship.'

It was with his own coxswain at his side, therefore, that the Commodore put off for his tour of the squadron. 'This is like old times, Bonden,' he said, as they approached the *Sirius*. 'Yes, sir; only better,' murmured Bonden: and then, in answer to the frigate's hail, he roared 'Pendant,' in a voice to wake the dead.

It did not startle the *Sirius*, however: from the moment of Captain Pym's return all hands had turned to – dinner cut short, grog gulped down – in order to give her an entirely artificial and fallacious appearance, designed to make her appear what she was not. They had done so with a will, being proud of their ship, and although there had been no time for any lavish repainting, the *Sirius* that the Commodore beheld was as unlike her worka-day self as the concentrated effort of two hundred and eighty-seven men and several women (some regular, others less so) could make her. Seeing that she was virtually disembowelled because of her tanks, they had not been able to turn her into a larger version of a

royal yacht, as they could have wished; but apart from the pyramids of nameless objects on deck, decently shrouded with awnings and tarpaulins, she was very presentable, and Jack was pleased with what he saw. He did not believe it, of course; nor was he expected to believe it: the whole thing, from the white-washed coal in the galley to the blackened balls in the shot-garlands, was a ritual disguise. Yet it had a relationship to the facts, and he gained the impression of a fine steady ship in moderately good order with competent officers and a decent crew largely composed of men-of-war's men – she had been in commission these three years and more. Captain Pym had set up a splendid array of bottles and cakes in his cabin, and as Jack lowered a Bath bun whose specific gravity somewhat exceeded that of platinum he reflected that its consistency was in all likelihood a fair symbol of the ship – steady, regular, rather old-fashioned, reliable; though perhaps not apt to set the Indian Ocean in a blaze.

Next the *Néréide*. She had had no real need to turn to in order to achieve the full effect that the *Sirius* had aimed at, yet from the mute, weary sullenness of her crew and the anxious, jaded, harassed look of her officers, every man jack aboard had been hard at it, gilding the lily for this occasion. Jack liked a taut ship, and of course a clean ship, but the total perfection of the *Néréide*'s vast expanse of brass alone oppressed him: he went through with his inspection, that being due to those who had toiled so hard and to so little purpose, but he made his tour of the silent, rigid frigate with no pleasure at all. His real business lay below, however, among the navel-futtocks; and there in the depths with the captain, his nervous first lieutenant and his nervous carpenter, he found that Corbett had not exaggerated greatly. Her timbers were indeed in a bad way: yet, he reflected as he prodded about with a spike, the Simon's Town surveyor might be right in saying that they would last another two or three seasons, whereas unless Jack was out in his reckoning the rot on the upper deck would spread more rapidly than that. As a young fellow, a midshipman in those very waters, he had been disrated for misconduct, for venery, and turned before the mast: infinitely against his will he had been a foremast jack for six months. That ship's standard of spit and polish had been nothing remotely like the *Néréide*'s, but she had had a tartar of a captain and a driving first lieutenant, and he knew to his cost just what it took in labour to produce even half this result. And those months,

so wretched at first and indeed most of the time, had also given him something that few officers possessed: an intimate understanding of life at sea from the men's point of view, a comprehension from within. He knew their language, spoken and silent; and his interpretation of the looks he had seen before coming below, the constraint, the veiled sideways glances, the scarcely perceptible nods and signs, the total lack of anything resembling cheerfulness, depressed him extremely.

Corbett was a brisk man with figures, however: he produced his detailed statement of the *Néréide*'s condition, neatly ruled in black and red, at the same time as his Madeira and sweet biscuits. 'You are very well found in powder and shot, I see,' Jack remarked, glancing over the columns.

'Yes, sir,' said Corbett. 'I don't believe in flinging it into the ocean: besides, your genuine recoil does so plough up the deck.'

'It does; and the *Néréide*'s deck is a most remarkable sight, I must confess. But do you not find it answers, to have your men handy with the guns – accurate at a distance?'

'Why, sir, as far as my experience goes, it don't make much odds. I have always engaged yardarm to yardarm, when they could not miss if they tried. But I don't have to tell *you* anything about close engagement, sir, not after your action with the *Cacafuego*, ha, ha.'

'Still, there is something to be said for the other school of thought – something to be said for knocking away the enemy's sticks from a mile off and then lying athwart his hawse,' observed Jack mildly.

'I am sure you are right, sir,' said Corbett, without the least conviction.

If the *Néréide* had been as like a royal yacht as a man-of-war could very well be, the *Otter*, at first glance, was the yacht itself. Jack had never, in all his life, seen such a display of gold leaf; and rarely had he seen all shrouds and stays wormed with vermilion yarn and the strops of the blocks covered with red leather. At second glance it seemed perhaps a little much, touching on the showy, just as the perfection of tailoring on Clonfert's quarterdeck – even the midshipmen had laced cocked hats, breeches, and Hessian boots with gold tassels – had a hint of costume rather than of uniform about it: and as he stood there Jack noticed to his surprise that Clonfert's officers appeared rather a vulgar set. They could not help their undistinguished faces, of course, but their stance, now too rigid, like tailor's dummies, now

too lounging and easy by far, was something else again; so was their under-bred open staring, their direct listening to what their captain had to say to him. On the other hand, no great perspicacity was required to see that the atmosphere aboard the *Otter* was as unlike that in the *Néréide* as possible: the lower-deck Otters were a cheerful, smiling crew, and it was clear that they liked their captain; while the standing officers, the bosun, the gunner and the carpenter (those essential pillars), seemed steady, valuable, experienced men. The *Otter*'s decks, rigging and gingerbread-work had surprised him; her cabin surprised him even more. Its not inconsiderable size was much increased by looking-glasses in gilt frames; these reflected a remarkable number of cushions piled up on a Turkish sofa, and the Arabian Nights were even more strongly called to mind by scimitars hanging on the bulk-head against a Persian carpet, a gilt mosque-lamp swinging from the beam, and a hubblebubble. Among all this the two twelve-pounders looked homely, brutish, drab, and ill-at-ease.

The ritual offerings appeared, brought in by a black boy in a turban, and Jack and Clonfert were left alone: a certain awkward-ness became manifest at once. With advancing years Jack had learnt the value of silence in a situation where he did not know what to say. Clonfert, though slightly older in spite of his youth-ful appearance, had not, and he talked – these baubles were from his Syrian campaign with Sir Sydney – the lamp a present from Dgezzar Pasha – the scimitar on the right from the Maronite Patriarch – he had grown so used to Eastern ways that he could not do without his sofa. Would not the Commodore sit down? The Commodore had no notion of lowering himself to within inches of the deck – what could he do with his legs? – and replied that he should as soon keep an eye on the *Boadicea*'s boats as they pulled briskly between the arsenal and the frigate, filling her magazines and shot-lockers with what he hoped would prove a most persuasive argument. Then the Commodore would surely taste a little of this Constantia and toy with an Aleppo fig: Clon-fert conceived that they made an interesting combination. Or perhaps a trifle of this botargo?

'I am infinitely obliged to you, Clonfert,' said Jack, 'and I am sure your wine is prodigious good; but the fact of the matter is, that *Sirius* gave me a great deal of capital port and *Néréide* a great deal of capital Madeira; so what I should really prize beyond anything at this moment is a cup of coffee, if that is possible.'

It was not possible. Clonfert was mortified, chagrined, desolated, but he drank no coffee; nor did his officers. He really was mortified, chagrined and desolated, too. He had already been obliged to apologize for not having his statement of condition ready, and this fresh blow, this *social* blow, cast him down extremely. Jack wanted no more unpleasantness in the squadron than already existed; and even on the grounds of common humanity he did not wish to leave Clonfert under what he evidently considered a great moral disadvantage; so pacing over to a fine narwhal tusk leaning in a corner he said, in an obliging manner, 'This is an uncommonly fine tusk.'

'A handsome object, is it not? But with submission, sir, I believe horn is the proper term. It comes from a unicorn. Sir Sydney gave it to me. He shot the beast himself, having singled it out from a troop of antelopes; it led him a tremendous chase, though he was mounted on Hassan Bey's own stallion – five and twenty miles through the trackless desert. The Turks and Arabs were perfectly amazed. He told me they said they had never seen anything like his horsemanship, nor the way he shot the unicorn at full gallop. They were astounded.'

'I am sure they were,' said Jack. He turned it in his hands, and said, with a smile, 'So I can boast of having held a true unicorn's horn.'

'You may take your oath on it, sir. I cut it out of the creature's head myself.'

'How the poor fellow does expose himself,' thought Jack, on his way back to the *Raisonable*: he had had a narwhal tusk in his cabin for months, bringing it back from the north for Stephen Maturin, and he was perfectly acquainted with the solid heft of its ivory, so very far removed from horn. Yet Clonfert had probably thought that the first part was true. Admiral Smith was a remarkably vain and boastful man, quite capable of that foolish tale: yet at the same time Admiral Smith was a most capable and enterprising officer. Apart from other brilliant actions, he had defeated Buonaparte at Acre: not many men had such grounds for boasting. Perhaps Clonfert was of that same strange build? Jack hoped so with all his heart – Clonfert might show away with all the unicorns in the world as far as Jack was concerned, and lions too, so long as he also produced something like the same results.

His meagre belongings had already come across from the *Boadicea*; they had already been arranged by his own steward as

he liked them to be arranged, and with a contented sigh Jack sat easy in an old Windsor chair with arms, flinging his heavy full-dress coat on to a locker. Killick did not like seeing clothes thrown about: Killick would have to lump it.

But Killick, who had dashed boiling water on to freshly-ground coffee the moment the *Raisonable*'s barge shoved off from the *Otter*, was a new man. Once cross-grained, shrewish, complaining, a master of dumb and sometimes vocal insolence, he was now almost complaisant. He brought in the coffee, watched Jack drink it hissing hot with something like approval, hung up the coat, uttering no unfavourable comment, no rhetorical 'Where's the money going to come from to buy new epaulettes when all the bullion's wore off, in consequence of being flung down regardless?' but carried on with the conversation that Jack's departure had interrupted. 'You did say, sir, as how they had no teeth?'

'Not a sign of them, Killick. Not a sign, before I sailed.'

'Well, I'm right glad on it' – producing a handkerchief with two massive pieces of coral in its folds – 'because this will help to cut 'em, as they say.'

'Thank you, Killick. Thank you kindly. Splendid pieces, upon my word: they shall go home in the first ship.'

'Ah, sir,' said Killick, sighing through the stern-window, 'do you remember that wicked little old copper in the back-kitchen, and how we roused out its flue, turning as black as chimney-sweeps?'

'That wicked little old copper will be a thing of the past, when next we see the cottage,' said Jack. 'The *Hébé* looked after that. And there will be a decent draught in the parlour, too, if Goadby knows his business.'

'And them cabbages, sir,' went on Killick, in an ecstasy of nostalgia. 'When last I see 'em, they had but four leaves apiece.'

'Jack, Jack,' cried Stephen, running in. 'I have been sadly remiss. You are promoted, I find. You are a great man – you are virtually an admiral! Give you joy, my dear, with all my heart. The young man in black clothes tells me you are the greatest man on the station, after the Commander-in-chief.'

'Why, I am commodore, as most people have the candour to admit,' said Jack. 'But I did mention it before, if you recollect. I spoke of my pendant.'

'So you did, joy; but perhaps I did not fully apprehend its true significance. I had a cloudy notion that the word commodore and

indeed that curious little flag were connected with a ship rather than with a man – I am almost sure that we called the most important ship in the East India fleet, the ship commanded by the excellent Mr Muffit, the commodore. Pray explain this new and splendid rank of yours.'

'Stephen, if I tell you, will you attend?'

'Yes, sir.'

'I have told you a great deal about the Navy before this, and you have not attended. Only yesterday I heard you give Farquhar a very whimsical account of the difference between the halfdeck and the quarterdeck, and to this day I do not believe you know the odds between . . .' At this point he was interrupted by the black-coated Mr Peter with a sheaf of papers, by a messenger from the general at Cape Town, and by Seymour, with whom he worked out a careful list of those men who could be discharged into the *Néréide*, either in the light of their own crimes or in that of the frigate's more urgent needs, and lastly by the Commander-in-chief's secretary, who wished to know whether his cousin Peter suited, to say that Admiral Bertie, now much recovered, sent his compliments: without wishing to hurry the Commodore in any way, the Admiral would be overjoyed to hear that he had put to sea.

'Well, now, Stephen,' said Jack at last, 'this commodore lark: in the first place I am not promoted at all – it is not a rank but a post, and J. Aubrey does not shift from his place on the captains' list by so much as the hundredth part of an inch. I hold this post just for the time being, and when the time being is over, if you follow me, I go back to being a captain again. But while it lasts I am as who should say an acting temporary unpaid rear-admiral; and I command the squadron.'

'That must warm your heart,' said Stephen. 'I have often known you chafe, in a subordinate position.'

'It does: the word is like a trumpet. Yet at the same time . . . I should not say this to anyone but you, Stephen, but it is only when you have an enterprise of this kind on your hands, an enterprise where you have to depend on others, that you understand what command amounts to.'

'By others you mean the other commanders, I take it? Sure, they are an essential factor that must be thoroughly understood. Pray open your mind upon them, without reserve.' Jack and Stephen had sailed together in many ships, but they had never discussed the officers: Stephen Maturin, as surgeon, had messed

with them, and although he was the captain's friend he belonged to the gunroom: the subject was never, never raised. Now the case was altered: now Stephen was Jack's political colleague and adviser; nor was he bound in any way to the other commanding officers. 'Let us begin with the Admiral; and Jack, since we are to work openly together, we must speak openly: I know your scruples and I honour them, yet believe me, brother, this is no time for scruples. Tell, do you look for full, unreserved support from Mr Bertie?'

'He is a jolly old boy,' said Jack, 'and he has been as kind and obliging to me as I could wish: he confirmed my acting-order for Johnson at once – a most handsome compliment. As long as all goes well, I make no doubt he will back us to the hilt; apart from anything else, it is entirely in his interest. But his reputation in the service – well, in Jamaica they called him Sir Giles Overreach, from the fellow in the play, you know; and he certainly over-reached poor James. A good officer, mark you, though he don't see much farther through a brick wall than another man.' He considered for a while before saying, 'But if I made a mistake, I should not be surprised to be superseded: nor if I stood between him and a plum. Though as things stand, I cannot see how that could come about.'

'You have no very high opinion of his head, nor of his heart.'

'I should not go as far as that. We have different ideas of what is good order in a ship, of course . . . no, I shall tell you one thing that makes me uneasy about his sense of what is right. This Russian brig. She is an embarrassment to everybody. The Admiral wishes her away, but he will not take the responsibility of letting her go. He will not accept the responsibility of making her people prisoners, either – among other things they would have to be fed, with everything charged against him if Government disapproved. So what he has done is to make the captain give his word not to escape and has left him lying there, ready for sea: he is trying to starve Golovnin out by allowing no rations for his men. Golovnin has no money and the merchants will not accept bills drawn on Petersburg. The idea is that he will break his word and disappear some dirty night when the wind is in the north-west. His word means nothing to a foreigner, said the Admiral, laughing; he wondered Golovnin had not gone off six months ago – he longed to be rid of him. He took it so much as a matter of course – did not hesitate to tell it – thought it such a clever way of covering himself – that it made my heart sink.'

Stephen said, 'I have noticed that some old men lose their sense of honour, and will cheerfully avow the strangest acts. What else affects your spirits, now? Corbett, I dare say? In that case the beadle within has quite eaten up the man.'

'Yes: he is a slave-driver. I do not say a word against his courage, mark you; he has proved that again and again. But by my book his ship is in very bad order indeed. She is old too, and only a twelve-pounder. Yet with the odds as they are, I cannot possibly do without her.'

'What do you say to the captain of the *Sirius*?'

'Pym?' Jack's face brightened. 'Oh, how I wish I had three more Pyms in three more *Siriuses*! He may be no phoenix, but he is the kind of man I like – three Pyms, and there would be your band of brothers for you. I should have to do myself no violence, keeping on terms with three Pyms. Or three Eliots for that matter: though he will not be with us long, more's the pity. He means to invalid as soon as ever he can. As it is, I shall have to humour Corbett to some degree, and Clonfert; for without there is a good understanding in a squadron, it might as well stay in port. How I shall manage it with Clonfert I can hardly tell: I must not get athwart his hawse if I can avoid it, but with that damned business of his wife I am half way there already. He resented it extremely – refused my invitation, which is almost unheard-of in the service, previous engagement or not: and there was no previous engagement. This is an odd case, Stephen. When we talked about him some time ago, I did not like to say I had my doubts about his conduct – an ugly thing to say about any man. But I had, and I was not the only one. Yet maybe I was not quite as wise as I supposed, for although he still looks like a flash cove in a flash ship, he did distinguish himself up the Mediterranean with Admiral Smith.'

'That, I presume, was where he came by his star? It is an order I have never seen.'

'Yes, the Turks handed out quite a number, but they were thought rather absurd, and not many officers asked permission to wear them: only Smith and Clonfert, I believe. And he has also carried out some creditable raids and cutting-out expeditions in these waters. He knows them well, and he has a native pilot; the *Otter* draws little water, even less than the *Néréide*, so he can stand in among the reefs; and according to Admiral Bertie he might almost be setting up as a rival to Cochrane in the matter of distressing the enemy.'

'Yes: I have heard of his enterprise, and of his ship's ability to go close to the shore. I shall no doubt have to be with him from time to time, to be landed and taken off. But just now you spoke of the odds. How do you see them at present?'

'Simply in terms of ships and guns, and only from the point of view of fighting at sea, they are rather against us. Then if you allow for the fact that we shall be more than two thousand miles from our base while they are in their home waters, with supplies at hand, why, you might say that they are in the nature of three to five. In the Channel or the Mediterranean I should put it nearer evens, since we are at sea all the time in those parts, and they are not: but their heavy frigates have been out the best part of a year now, plenty of time to work up their crews, given competent officers; and upon the whole the French officers are a competent set of men. But all this is very much up in the air – there are so many unknowns in the equation. For one thing, I know nothing of their captains, and everything depends on them. Once I catch sight of them at sea I shall be able to reckon the odds more accurately.'

'Once you have had a brush with them, you mean?'

'No. Once I have seen them, even hull down on the horizon.'

'Could you indeed judge of their abilities at so remote a view?'

'Of course,' said Jack a little impatiently. 'What a fellow you are, Stephen. Any sailor can tell a great deal from the way another sailor sets his jib, or goes about, or flashes out his stuns'ls, just as you could tell a great deal about a doctor from the way he whipped off a leg.'

'Always this whipping off of a leg. It is my belief that for you people the whole noble art of medicine is summed up in the whipping off of a leg. I met a man yesterday – and he was so polite as to call on me today, quite sober – who would soon put you into a better way of thinking. He is the *Otter*'s surgeon. I should probably have to cultivate his acquaintance in any event, for our own purposes, since the *Otter* is, as you would say, an inshore prig; but I do not regret it now that I have met him. He is, or was, a man of shining parts. But to return to our odds: you would set them at five to three in favour of the French?'

'Something of that kind. If you add up guns and crews and tonnage it is a great deal worse; but of course I cannot really speak to the probability until I see them. Yet although I have sent a hundred Boadiceas to lend a hand aboard the *Sirius*, and

84

although I know Pym is doing his utmost to get her ready for sea, our own ship has to take in six months' stores, and I should love to careen her too, the last chance of a clean bottom for God knows how long – I cannot see how we can sail before Saturday's tide. I shall keep the people hard at it, and harry the arsenal until they wish me damned, but apart from that there is nothing I can do: there is nothing that the Archangel Gabriel could do. So what do you say to some music, Stephen? We might work out some variations on "Begone Dull Care".'

Chapter Four

The squadron, standing north-east with the urgent trade-wind on the beam, made a noble sight; their perfect line covered half a mile of sea – and such a sea: the Indian Ocean at its finest, a sapphire not too deep, a blue that turned their worn sails a dazzling white. *Sirius*, *Néréide*, *Raisonable*, *Boadicea*, *Otter*, and away to leeward the East India Company's fast-sailing armed schooner *Wasp*, while beyond the *Wasp*, so exactly placed that it outlined her triangular courses, floated the only bank of cloud in the sky, the flat-bottomed clouds hanging over the mountains of La Réunion, themselves beneath the horizon.

The Cape and its uneasy storms lay two thousand miles astern, south and westward, eighteen days' sweet sailing; and by now the crews had long since recovered from the the extreme exertion of getting their ships ready for sea three tides before it seemed humanly possible. But once at sea new exertions awaited them: for one thing, the perfection of this line, with each ship keeping station on the pendant at exactly a cable's length, could be achieved only by incessant care and watchfulness. The *Sirius*, with her foul bottom, kept setting and taking in her topgallants; the *Néréide* had perpetually to struggle against her tendency to sag to leeward; and Jack, standing on the poop of the *Raisonable*, saw that his dear but somewhat sluggish *Boadicea* was having an anxious time of it – Eliot was fiddling with his royals – while only the pendant-ship, fast in spite of her antiquity, and the *Otter* were at ease. And for another, all the ships except the *Boadicea* were disturbed, upset and harrassed by the Commodore's passion for gunnery.

He had begun as soon as they sank Cape Agulhas, and although they were by no means reconciled to the exercise they were used to his ways; they were quite sure what the Commodore would be at at this point in the forenoon watch when they saw the *Raisonable* signal to the *Wasp* and then bid the squadron wear together. Up and down the line the bosuns' calls shrilled high and clear, the hands stood poised upon their toes (for the competition between the ships was very keen, the horror of public disgrace very great), and the moment the *Raisonable* deviated from her line the others began their turn: round they

came, as trim as could be, forming the line with their larboard tacks aboard, the wind one point free, a reversed line, with the *Otter* leading. They had no great press of sail and this was a simple manoeuvre; even so, it was well executed; there was not much amiss with their seamanship, reflected Jack, looking over the taffrail at the *Néréide*'s masts, all in one line, eclipsing those of the *Sirius*, her next astern. Meanwhile the schooner had cast off the targets, and she was making sail with remarkable diligence, being eager to run out of range as soon as possible.

It was an understandable eagerness, for as usual the *Otter* opened a fine brisk fire a little before her guns could really be said to bear, and her wilder shot whipped up the sea between the schooner and the target. Her second broadside was nearer the mark, and might have hit it if the Otters had waited for the top of the roll: her third resembled the first, except that one ball did skip over the target: and she did not manage a fourth. Jack, watch in hand, was calling the figures to the mathematical midshipman he had brought with him when the *Boadicea* spoke out, pitching her shot a trifle high but sweeping the hypothetical deck; her second broadside struck the enemy square amidships, and with rapturous cries her third and fourth demolished the floating wreckage. 'One minute fifty-five seconds,' wrote Spotted Dick upon his slate, following it with two points of admiration. 'As they bear, Mr Whittington,' called Jack. The *Raisonable* was understood to play no competitive role in all this: because of her age she could not blaze away with the single, timber-shattering roar of a younger ship, but every third gun of her lower deck, half charged, and several of her lighter pieces produced a slow rolling fire that would have done a certain amount of damage. Far more damage than the full but almost comically inept broadsides of the *Néréide*: two broadsides only, and those fired so high that no more than a single shot went home – a shot almost certainly fired by one of the quarter-gunners that Jack had most reluctantly sent into her. Then came *Sirius*, with two deliberate broadsides and then her five aftermost guns as the battered target went astern: slow but quite accurate at this moderate range.

Jack had neither the time nor the powder for any more. As soon as the guns were housed he signalled *Tack in succession* and called the schooner under his lee. From the moment they weighed from Simon's Town he had watched the sailing of the ships under his command with a very close attention, but never had he kept his glass so fixedly upon any one of them as now he

kept it upon the *Wasp* as she came racing up close-hauled, throwing white water right down her lee-rail. She was a beautiful craft, beautifully handled, and she sailed closer to the wind than he would have thought possible; yet his anxious, worn expression did not lighten when she rounded to and lay there under the *Raisonable*'s quarter, her captain looking up at her lofty poop with an inquiring face.

Jack nodded absently to the schooner, told the signal-lieutenant to summon the captain of the *Sirius*, stepped aft with a speaking-trumpet and hailed the *Boadicea*, desiring her acting-captain to come aboard. The Commodore received them rather formally in the fore-cabin, where Mr Peter handed Eliot written orders to proceed to the Mauritius in company with the *Sirius*, there to lie off Port-Louis, the capital and the chief port, in the north-west of the island, and to rendezvous with the rest of the squadron on that station: in the intervening time they were to watch the motions of the enemy and to gain all the information they could. To these orders Jack added a clear direction not to engage in any action unless the odds were heavily in their favour, together with some advice about arriving off Sable Point after dark and sending in boats to look into the harbour at crack of dawn, so that they could pull out against the sea-breeze. Then, in his care for the *Boadicea*, he was going on to beg Eliot not to carry too great a press of sail, not to set his royals – a spar carried away in these latitudes was a terrible loss – she must be humoured, not drove – when he realized that he sounded more like a mother-hen than was quite right. He stifled his recommendation about the *Boadicea*'s starboard cathead, saw them over the side, watched their ships steer north, and went below again, going right aft to the great cabin, where Stephen sat at a table, encoding letters on paper of surprising thinness.

'The great advantage of these ark-like vessels,' observed Stephen, 'is that one can at least speak in privacy. The Admiral, with his luxury of dining-room, bedroom, antechamber, fore-cabin, and then this magnificence with the balcony behind, could riot at his ease: the Commodore can freely speak his mind. A mind that is, I fear, oppressed by melancholy thoughts?'

'Yes: commodious, ain't it?' said Jack, stepping out on to the stern-gallery, from which he could see the *Wasp*, rising and falling ten feet on the long smooth swell and shivering her foretopsail from time to time to keep her pace down to that of the two-decker. Coming back he said, 'Stephen, I do so hate this

vile scheme of yours.'

'I know you do, my dear,' said Stephen. 'You have frequently mentioned it. And each time I have replied, that in the first place the contacts and the information I seek are of essential importance; and in the second, that the risk is negligible. I walk two hundred paces along a strand clearly defined by palm-trees; I call at the second house I see – a house of which I have an accurate drawing – I make a contact of inestimable value, receive my information, deliver these documents, whose extreme tenuity, you see' – holding them out – 'renders them edible, as tradition doth require – I walk back to the boat and so to your swift-sailing machine, to join you, with the blessing, for breakfast. I promise not to linger, Jack, though La Réunion is another Ophir, to the philosophic mind.'

Jack paced up and down: all that Stephen said was perfectly reasonable. Yet not so many years ago Jack had fetched him out of Port Mahon more dead than alive, Port Mahon in Minorca, where he had been caught on a secret mission, interrogated with all the barbarity of the Inquisition, and very nearly destroyed.

'Minorca was entirely different,' said Stephen. 'In that case I had been undermined at home. Here the possibility does not exist.'

'It is not only that,' said Jack, coming to a halt in front of a chart of the coast of La Réunion. 'Just look at these God-damned reefs. Think of the surf. I have told you again and again, Stephen, these inshore waters are hellish dangerous – reefs everywhere, half of 'em uncharted, the most tremendous surf. I know what I am talking about. I was here as a boy. There is scarcely a beach where you can land in safety, even when the swell is more moderate by half. To get into your Petite Anse you must run through a gap in the reef not a cable's length across even at high tide, by moonlight. And what if this Company's chap don't find it? He is no pilot for these waters: admits it candidly.'

'The alternative is to go in the *Otter*. Clonfert does know these shores; and he has a native pilot. And since I shall have to spend some time in the *Otter* sooner or later, I am eager to know her captain. Much will depend upon our understanding.'

'Certainly he knows this coast,' said Jack, 'but then the coast knows him. He has been in and out a score of times on this east side alone. The *Otter* is very recognizable, and if any fishing-boat or aviso or watchman on the cliffs sees her standing in, then

89

every soldier and militiaman on the island will be running about, shooting the first thing that stirs. No: if it has to be, then the schooner is the right choice. Her captain is a steady young fellow and a good seaman; nothing flash or gimcrack about him or his *Wasp*. Besides, there is the time.'

'Sure, I should prefer the schooner. She leaves us at Rodriguez for Bombay, as I understand it, and that will preserve my character a little longer.'

'Well,' said Jack in the most unwilling voice. 'But I tell you, Stephen, I shall give him absolute orders to return immediately if he cannot make out his leading marks at once, or at the least sign of movement ashore. And Stephen, I must tell you this, too: if the scheme goes wrong, I cannot land a party to bring you off.'

'It would be madness to attempt any such thing,' said Stephen placidly; and after a slight pause, 'Honest Jack, would it be uncivil to remind you, that time waits for no man? This also applies, they tell me, to the tide.'

'Then at least,' cried Jack, 'I can send Bonden with you, and have a carronade mounted in the boat.'

'That would be kind; and might I suggest that black men for the boat's crew would be a diabolically cunning stroke, by way of amusing the enemy? For we must assume that he sees in the dark, the creature.'

'I shall attend to it this minute,' said Jack, and he left Stephen to his encoding.

A little before four bells in the afternoon watch Dr Maturin was lowered like a parcel on to the heaving deck of the *Wasp*, where Bonden seized him, cast off the five fathoms of stout line that had held him motionless (no one had the least opinion of his powers of self-preservation, at sea) and led him aft, whispering, 'Don't forget to pull off your hat, sir.'

It was a round hat of French manufacture, and Stephen took it off to the schooner's quarterdeck and to her captain with something of an air; then turning about with the intention of waving it to Jack he found that he was gazing over a broad lane of sea at the *Raisonable*'s stolid figurehead. The schooner had already crossed the two-decker's bows, and she was now flying goose-winged towards the clouds that hung over La Réunion.

'If you will step this way, sir,' said the captain of the *Wasp*, 'I believe we shall find our dinner ready.'

At the same moment Killick mounted to the poop of the *Raisonable*, where Jack was staring after the schooner, and stated, with something of his old acerbity, that 'the gentlemen were treading on one another's toes in the halfdeck this ten minutes past: and his honour still in his trousers.' Abruptly Jack realized that he had forgotten his invitation to the wardroom, that he was improperly dressed – north of Capricorn once more he had reverted to the free and easy ducks – and that he was in danger of committing unpunctuality. He darted below, huddled on his uniform, and shot into the great cabin just as five bells struck. Here he received his guests, the sailors in their best blue coats, the soldiers in their scarlet, and all of them red-faced in the heat, for they had had their finery on for the last half hour at least: presently he led them to the dining-table, where the skylight admitted the rays of the ardent sun, and they grew redder still. At the beginning of a cruise, and often right through it, these feasts, theoretically the gathering of equals for social intercourse but in fact the almost obligatory attendance of men belonging to different steps of a rigid and never-forgotten hierarchy, tended to be ponderous affairs. Jack was perfectly aware of it, and he exerted himself to give some semblance of spontaneity to his entertainment. He tried very hard, and at one point, feeling for the sufferings of the Marine captain whose stock was bringing him nearer and nearer to a cerebral congestion, he even thought of bidding them take off their heavy coats: but that would never do – a disproportioned thought indeed – for although he naturally liked his guests to enjoy themselves, he must not conciliate their goodwill by the least improper concession; they must enjoy themselves within the limits of naval convention, and these limits certainly did not extend to turning the cabin into a bawdy-house. He confined himself to ordering the awning, removed for Stephen's aerial voyage, to be rigged again, and water to be dashed upon the deck.

Although his heart was not in it, he laboured on: yet artificial conviviality is rarely infectious, and still they sat, hot, prim, polite. Convention required that no man but Jack Aubrey should initiate any conversation, and since they had not yet taken the measure of their new Commodore they obeyed it religiously. Presently he began to run short of topics, and he was reduced to urging them to eat and drink. For his own part he could only go through the motions of eating – his stomach was quite closed – but as a grateful coolness began to come down from the shaded

91

skylight, wafted by the unvarying south-east trade, the bottle went about more briskly. Even before the port came to the table each man had a shining, glazed appearance, a tendency to stare and hold himself very straight, and each man behaved with even greater care as the decanter went its rounds – tolerably dismal rounds, as Jack could not but inwardly confess.

Dinner in the *Wasp*'s low triangular cabin was a very different matter. Since this coming night's activity called for a mind as clear as it could be Stephen had begged for thin cold coffee: Mr Fortescue drank no wine at any time, so the bottle he had provided for his guest stood untouched between the lime-juice and the tall brass pot while the two of them devoured a great mound of curry so Vesuvian that it paled the tropic sun. Each had early discovered the other's passionate concern with birds; and now, after a modest though fully-detailed account of petrels he had known, Mr Fortescue observed that there was nothing like a sailor's life for bringing a man acquainted with the world.

'Sir, sir,' cried Stephen, waving a Bombay duck, 'how can you speak so? Every ship I have sailed upon might have been called the Tantalus. They have carried me to remote countries, within reach of the paradise-bird, the ostrich, the sacred ibis; they have set me down in a variety of smelly and essentially identical havens; and then, almost without exception, they have hurried me away. The wealth of the Indies is within my grasp, and I am hurried away to another stinking port a thousand miles away, where exactly the same thing occurs. In candour I must not deny that the intervening ocean may reveal wonders that more than compensate the tedium of one's confinement, the Judaic ritual of life aboard – I have beheld the albatross! – but these are fleeting glimpses: we know nothing of the birds' economy, the interesting period of their loves, their solicitude for their young, their domestic tasks and cares. Yet all this is just at hand, attained by enormous expense of spirit and of the public treasure: and it is thrown away. No: I can conceive of no more deeply frustrating life for a naturalist than that of a sailor, whose lot it is to traverse the world without ever seeing it. But perhaps, sir, you have been more fortunate?'

Mr Fortescue, though freely admitting the justice of Dr Maturin's observations in general, had indeed been more fortunate, particularly in respect of the great albatross, *Diomedea exulans*, to which the Doctor had so feelingly referred: he had

been cast away on Tristan da Cunha, where he had lived with and upon albatrosses, thousands and thousands of albatrosses, to say nothing of the penguins, terns, skuas, prions, the indigenous gallinule and a hitherto nondescript finch. He had sat with albatrosses right through their incubation; he had weighed, measured, and eaten their eggs; he had attended to their nuptial ceremonies; and, having been cast away with a piece of pencil and the Complete Practical Navigator, whose blank pages served for notes and measurements, he had, to the best of his poor abilities, drawn them.

'And were you indeed able to make illustrated notes?' cried Stephen, his eyes gleaming. 'How I wish, oh how I wish, that you might be persuaded to communicate them, at some not too distant time!'

As it happened, said Mr Fortescue, reaching for the book, they were just at hand, entirely at Dr Maturin's service; and he rather thought that there might be some specimens – eggs, skins, and bones – in the locker upon which he sat.

They were still with their albatrosses at nightfall, when the chaotic mountains of La Réunion stood black against the after-glow, and when Jack, with the taste of brass in his mouth and an aching head, began his pacing of the poop, glancing westward at each turn, although there could not be the slightest chance of seeing the *Wasp* much before dawn. It was a pacing that continued as the stars swept widdershins round the southern sky and watch succeeded watch: nervous and uneasy at first, it settled into a mechanical to and fro of his body, leaving his mind to run clear. By this stage he was fairly peaceful, and between watching the stars he ran over his calculations, always coming up with the same comforting result: La Réunion lay at the apex of a triangle whose base was the squadron's course during the afternoon and then the night, its southern arm the *Wasp*'s path taking Stephen in, an arm some fifty miles long. He had kept the squadron under topsails alone, and having checked the rate of sailing each time the log was heaved he was confident that they would have run off eighty miles at about four bells in the morning watch, reaching the point at which the northern arm of the triangle, that of the schooner bringing Stephen back, should meet the base, making a neat isosceles of the whole. In these seas, with their perfectly steady wind, such calculations could be made with remarkable accuracy; and here the only important variable was the time Stephen spent ashore, which

Jack provisionally set at three hours.

The middle watch wore on: once a flying squid struck against the great stern-lantern: otherwise the quiet night-routine of the ship moved along its invariable course. The wind sang an even note in the rigging, the water slipped along the side, the phosphorescent wake stretched out, a straight line broken by the bow-wave of the *Otter*, two cables' lengths astern; and at each stroke of the bell the sentinels called out from their stations, 'All's well', 'All's well', right round the ship and up and down the squadron.

'I hope to God they are right,' said Jack. He stepped down to the quarterdeck and looked at the log-board again. He was strongly tempted to go up into the top or even to the masthead; but that would singularize the whole thing too much – draw too much attention to it – and he returned to his lonely poop, only desiring the officer of the watch to send a good man aloft with a night-glass and bid him keep a sharp look-out.

He was still on the poop when the eastern stars began to pale: the morning watch had been called long since and men were moving about the dim deck, sprinkling sand. Jack's certainties had vanished an hour ago: his neat isosceles triangle had fled down the wind, routed by a thousand fresh unknown quantities. He stood still now, leaning on the rail and searching the horizon from the west to south-west. The blazing rim of the sun thrust up; light shot into the eastern sky; and the lookout hailed 'Sail ho.'

'Where away?' cried Jack.

'On the starboard beam, sir. *Wasp*. A-lying to.'

And there indeed she was, hull-down, well to the east, her triangular sails just nicking the rising sun. Jack called down to the quarterdeck, 'Make sail to close her,' and resumed his pacing. The steady grind of holystones, the slap of swabs: full day-time life returned to the *Raisonable* as she set her topgallants and ran fast along the line that should cut the schooner's path. When his powerful glass had shown him Stephen walking about far over there, Jack went below, said, 'Breakfast in the after-cabin, Killick,' and stretched himself out on his cot for a while. Presently he heard the officer of the watch call for a bosun's chair, agitated cries of 'Handsomely, handsomely, there. Boom him off the backstay,' and a little later Stephen's familiar step.

'Good morning, Stephen,' he said. 'You look as pleased as Punch – the trip was to your liking, I hope and trust?'

'The most delightful trip, I thank you, Jack; and a very good morning to you too. Most delightful . . . look!' He held out his two hands, opened them cautiously and disclosed an enormous egg.

'Well, it is a prodigious fine egg, to be sure,' said Jack: then, raising his voice, 'Killick, light along the breakfast, will you? Bear a hand, there.'

'Other things have I brought with me,' said Stephen, drawing a green-baize parcel from his pocket and a large cloth bag. 'But nothing in comparison with the truly regal gift of that most deserving young man Fortescue. For what you see there, Jack, is nothing less than the concrete evidence of the albatross's gigantic love. Whereas this' – pointing to the gently heaving parcel – 'is no more than a poll-parrot of the common green, or West African, species, too loquacious for its own good.' He undid the baize, snipped the band confining the parrot's wings, and set the bird upon its feet. The parrot instantly cried, 'A bas Buonaparte. Salaud, salaud, salaud,' in a metallic, indignant voice, climbed on to the back of his chair, and began to preen its ruffled feathers. 'The cloth bag, on the other hand, contains some of the finest coffee I have ever tasted; it grows to great advantage upon the island.'

Breakfast appeared, and when they were alone again Jack said, 'So you did not spend all your time ashore bird's nesting, I collect. Would it be proper to tell me anything about the rest of your journey?'

'Oh, that,' said Stephen, setting his egg sideways upon a butter-dish to see it at a better angle. 'Yes, yes: it was a straightforward piece of routine, perfectly simple, as I told you. Fruitful, however. I shall not tell you about my interlocutor – far better to know nothing in these cases – apart from saying that I take him to be a wholly reliable source, exceptionable only in his prolonged retention of this indiscreet fowl, a fault of which he was himself most sensible. Nor shall I trouble you with the political aspect: but I have a clear notion of the military side. I believe it to be a true statement of the position, and am not without hope that it will give you pleasure. In the first place, our accession of strength is as yet unknown: in the second, the two most recently captured Indiamen, the *Europe* and the *Streatham*, are in St Paul's road, on the other side of the island, together with their captor, the frigate *Caroline*, whose inward parts are alleged to require some attention that will keep her there for perhaps a fortnight. In fact

her captain, a most amiable young man called Feretier, is attached to the wife of the Governor, General Desbrusleys, a passionate gentleman who is at odds with Captain Saint-Michiel, the commandant of St Paul's, and with most of the other officers on La Réunion. At present he is at Saint-Denis: his forces amount to something over three thousand men, including the militia; but they are stationed at various points, twenty and even thirty miles apart over difficult mountain country; and although St Paul's is strongly defended by batteries and fortifications mounting, let us see, nine and eight is seventeen – I write seven and I retain one: five and five is ten, and with the one that I retained, eleven – mounting a hundred and seventeen guns, you may consider it practicable, in spite of the difficulty of landing on these shores, to which you have so frequently adverted. This rude sketch shows the approximate location of the batteries. This the disposition of the troops. You will forgive me for labouring the obvious when I say, that if you do decide to act, then celerity is everything. "Lose not a minute", as you would put it.'

'Lord, Stephen, how happy you make me,' said Jack, taking the paper and comparing it with his chart of St Paul's roadstead and the shore. 'Yes, yes: I see. A crossing fire, of course. Forty-two-pounders, I dare say; and well served, no doubt. There is no possibility of cutting the Indiamen or the frigate out, none at all, without we take the batteries. And that we cannot do with our Marines and seamen: but three or four hundred soldiers from Rodriguez would just tip the scale, I do believe. We could not hold the place, of course, but we might take the ships – there is a fair chance that we take the ships.' He stared at the paper and at his chart. 'Yes: a tough nut, to be sure; but if only I can persuade the soldiers on Rodriguez to move at once, and if only we can get our men ashore, I believe we can crack it. St Paul's is on the leeward side, where the surf is not so wicked unless the wind lies in the west . . . but I quite take your point about losing no time, Stephen . . .' He ran out of the cabin, and a few moments later Stephen, turning the egg over in his hands, heard the *Raisonable* begin to speak as she bore up for Rodriguez, spreading sail after sail: the masts complained, the taut rigging sang with a greater urgency, the sound of the water racing along her side mounted to a diffused roar; the complex orchestra of cordage, wood under stress, moving sea and wind, reverberating in the various hollows of her hull, produced a composite, all-pervading sound, exalting to the sea-borne ear – a sound that never slackened day

or night while the squadron made good its five hundred miles with the strong, steady south-east wind just abaft the beam.

Rodriguez: the low dome of the island lay clear on the starboard bow at dawn on Thursday, a greenish dome, its skyline stuck with palm-trees, in a green lagoon; all round the immense surrounding reef the white of breakers, and beyond it the intense blue of the open sea, uninterrupted for five thousand miles to windward. A man-of-war bird passed a few feet overhead, its long forked tail opening and closing as it glided through the swirling currents about the forestaysail and the jibs, but neither Jack nor Stephen moved their steady gaze from the land. On a flat tongue of land with a large house upon it and some huts, neat rows of tents could already be seen: no great number of them, but enough to shelter the three or four hundred soldiers that might make the descent on La Réunion a possibility, if only their commanding officer·could be induced to stir. Jack had seen combined operations by the score, few of them a pleasant memory; and the likelihood of miserable jealousies between army and navy, the divided command, to say nothing of divided councils, were clear in his mind. He was superior to Lieutenant-Colonel Keating in rank, but that gave him a mere precedence, no right to issue orders: it would have to be a true, willing cooperation or nothing. He must rely upon his powers of exposition: and as though an unremitting glare might carry conviction, he kept his glass trained on the house, moving it only occasionally to glance at the gap in the surf that showed the narrow passage into the lagoon.

Stephen's mind was largely taken up with the same considerations; yet part of it was also aware, vividly aware, that the island gliding towards him was the home of an enormous land tortoise, not perhaps quite so vast as *Testudo aubreii*, discovered and named by himself on a comparable island in this same ocean, but even so one of the wonders of the world; and, more important still, that until recently it had been the home, the only home, of the solitaire, a bird in some ways resembling the dodo, equally extinct alas, but still less known to science, even in fragmentary remains. He turned over a number of approaches to this subject, none wholly satisfactory, given Jack's gross insensibility to all science without an immediate application: for Captain Aubrey, as for the rest of brute creation, there were only two kinds of birds, the edible and the inedible. Even after prolonged medita-

97

tion, during which the squadron reduced sail for the first time in fifty-two hours, he could produce no more than a timid 'Were we compelled to stay a short while . . .' that passed unnoticed, for as he spoke Jack raised his speaking-trumpet and hailed the *Néréide*, saying, 'Lead in, if you please, Captain Corbett. And preserve us from evil.'

'Amen,' said a forecastleman automatically, glancing at the Commodore with horror as soon as the word was out of his mouth.

'. . . perhaps I might be allowed a party,' continued Stephen, 'a very small party, consisting only of ambulant cases . . .' He would have added 'to look for bones', if the Commodore's eager determined expression had not convinced him that he might as well have pleaded with the ship's figurehead.

The barge splashed down into the calm waters of the lagoon, its crew stretched out as they were bid, and this same eager determined expression advanced with long strides up the coral beach to meet Colonel Keating. They exchanged salutes, shook hands, and the soldier said, 'You will not remember me, sir, but I was at a dinner given in your honour at Calcutta after your magnificent defence of the China fleet.'

'Certainly I remember you, sir,' said Jack, who had indeed some recollection of this tall, lean figure – a long-nosed, capable face that raised his hopes, 'and am very happy to see you again.'

The Colonel looked pleased, and as he led Jack through a double hedge of his men, Englishmen of the 56th Foot on the one side, turbaned sepoys of the 2nd regiment of Bombay Infantry on the other, he observed, 'How delighted we were to see you coming in. We have been so cruelly bored on this dismal rock, these last few months – reduced to tortoise-races – nothing to look forward to except the arrival of the main body next year – nothing to shoot except guinea-fowl.' Jack instantly seized upon the opening and said, 'If we are of the same mind, Colonel, I believe I can do away with your boredom. I can offer you something better than guinea-fowl to shoot at.'

'Can you, by God?' cried the soldier, with a look as keen as Jack's. 'I rather hoped something might be afoot, when I saw you come ashore so quick.'

In the tent, drinking tepid sherbet, Jack stated the case: he felt almost certain that the Colonel, though mute, was with him, but even so his heart thumped strangely as he spoke the words

98

that must bring the answer, positive, negative, or temporizing: 'And so, sir, I should value your appreciation of the position.'

'Sure, I am of your mind entirely,' said Keating straight away. 'There are only two things that make me hesitate – hesitate as the officer commanding the troops on Rodriguez, I mean, not as Harry Keating. The first is that I have barely four hundred men here, a mere advance-party to build the fort and prepare the lines. It was never imagined that I should move until the arrival of the main body with the next monsoon, and I might be broke for stirring, for leaving my command. Yet as against that, I know the Company loves you like a son, so I might equally well be broke for not falling in with your plan of campaign. As far as that goes, then, I should choose to follow my own inclination, which is the same as yours, sir. The second is this question of landing through the surf – the choice of our disembarcation. As you pointed out so candidly, there lies the crux. For with no more than your Marines and what seamen you can spare – say six hundred men with my few companies – it must necessarily be nip and tuck. My men, and particularly the sepoys, are not clever in boats: if we do not land cleanly and carry their works out of hand, a neat *coup de main*, there will be the Devil to pay, once their columns start coming in from Saint-Denis and the other places. If I could be satisfied on that point, I should cry done directly.'

'I cannot pretend to be well acquainted with the western side of the island myself,' said Jack, 'but I have two captains here with a vast deal of local knowledge. Let us hear what they have to say.'

Colonel Keating's conscience longed to be satisfied, and it would have taken far less to do so than Corbett's vehement assertion that landing on the west side, north of St Paul's, so long as the wind stayed in the south-east, which it did three hundred days in the year, was as easy as kiss my hand, particularly when this was reinforced by Clonfert's still more positive statement that even with a westerly wind he would undertake to set a thousand men ashore in a sheltered cove accessible through gaps in the reef known to his black pilot. But the Colonel was less pleased when the two captains disagreed violently upon the best place for the landing, Clonfert maintaining that the St Gilles inlet was the obvious choice, Corbett that no one but a blockhead would attempt anything but the Pointe des Galets, adding, in reply to Clonfert's objection that it was seven miles from St Paul's, that he conceived the opinion of a post-captain with a *real*

knowledge of these waters, acquired over many years of service on the station during this war and the last, was likely to carry more weight than that of a very young commander. The Colonel retired into a grave, formal absence while the captains wrangled, the veiled personalities growing more naked until the Commodore called both to order, not without asperity. And somewhat later Keating's delight in the company of the sailors was damped again when Lord Clonfert abruptly excused himself before the end of dinner and left the tent as pale as he had been red at the beginning of the meal – a redness attributable to the Commodore's words, delivered in what was meant to be the privacy of the nascent fort: 'Lord Clonfert, I am exceedingly concerned that this display of ill-feeling should have taken place, above all that it should have taken place in the presence of Colonel Keating. You forget the respect due to senior officers, sir. This must not occur again.'

'Lord, Stephen,' cried Jack as he came into the stern-gallery of the *Raisonable*, where Dr Maturin sat gazing wistfully at the land, 'what a capital fellow that Keating is! You might almost think he was a sailor. "When do you wish my men to be aboard?" says he. "Would six o'clock suit?" says I. "Perfectly, sir," says he; turns about, says to Major O'Neil, "Strike camp," and the tents vanish – the thing is done, with no more words bar a request that his Hindus should be given no salt beef and his Mahometans no salt pork. That is the kind of soldier I love! In three hours we shall be at sea! *Néréide* is preparing to receive them at this minute. Are not you delighted, Stephen?'

'Oh, excessively delighted; delighted beyond measure. But Jack, am I to understand that no shore-leave is to be allowed – that we are to be hurried from this place as we were hurried from the parturient whale off Cape Agulhas? I begged Mr Lloyd for a boat, a small boat, but he declared that it was as much as his skin was worth to suffer me to go without an order from you, adding, with an inhuman leer, that he thought the Commodore would have anchors atrip before the ebb. Yet surely it would be of immeasurable benefit to all hands, to be indulged in running about and frolicking, if no farther than the strand?'

'Bless you, Stephen,' said Jack, 'you shall have your boat, for what bugs you may gather in two hours and a half; for two hours and a half it is, mark you well, not a minute more; and I shall send Bonden with you.'

Stephen was making his laborious way down the stern-ladder, his searching foot was already poised over the boat itself, when the *Otter*'s yawl pulled alongside and a midshipman said, 'Dr Maturin, sir?'

Stephen writhed his neck round, directing a grim look at the young man: all his professional life ashore had been haunted by these vile messengers; innumerable concerts, theatres, operas, dinners, promised treats had been wrecked or interrupted by fools, mooncalves, who, to gain some private end, had broken a leg, had fits, or fallen into a catalepsy. 'Go and see my mate, Mr Carol,' he said.

'Dr McAdam's particular compliments to Dr Maturin,' went on the midshipman, 'and would be most grateful for his present advice.'

'Hell and death,' said Stephen. He crept up the ladder, flung some medical objects into a bag, and crept down again, holding the bag in his teeth.

A worried, perfectly sober McAdam received him aboard the *Otter*. 'You wished to see this case in its crisis, Doctor: pray step below,' he said in public; and in private, 'This is the crisis, God damn me, and a tear-my-guts-out crisis too. I am relieved to have you to consult with, colleague – am in three minds at the least.' He led him into the captain's cabin, and there, on the sofa, lay Lord Clonfert, doubled up with pain. He made a real attempt at mastering it to greet Stephen and to thank him for coming – 'Most benevolent – vastly obliged – désolé to receive him in these conditions' – but the strong gripes cut him very short.

Stephen examined him carefully, asked questions, examined him again, and the doctors withdrew. The attentive ears that hung about in the neighbourhood could make precious little of their Latin, but it was understood that Dr Maturin would have nothing to do with Dr McAdam's iliac passion, still less his Lucatellus' balsam; that he slightly inclined to a clonic spasm; that he believed Dr McAdam might do well to exhibit *helleborus niger* in the heroic dose of twenty minims, together with forty drops of thebaic tincture and sixty of antimonial wine, accompanied, naturally, with a little Armenian bole, as a temporary expedient; he had known it answer in tormina of much the same kind (though less intense) that afflicted a purser, a wealthy purser who dreaded detection when the ship paid off; but this was a particularly difficult, interesting case, and one that called for a more prolonged consultation. Dr Maturin would send for the

other lenitives he had mentioned, and when the enemata had had their effect, Dr McAdam might choose to walk on the island to discuss the matter at greater length: Dr Maturin always thought more clearly, when walking. The ears dispersed during the coming and going of the messenger; they made nothing of the administration of the drugs other than the fact that the groans in the cabin stopped; but they did catch some words about 'delighted to attend the opening of the body, in the event of a contrary result' that earned Dr Maturin some brooding glances as the two medical men went over the side, for the Otters loved their captain.

Up and down they strolled among the hurrying soldiers, then through the tortoise-park, where the disconsolate French superintendent stood thigh-deep among some hundreds of his charges, and so towards the interior, until at last the rollers crashing on the reef were no more than a continuous, half-heard thunder. Stephen had seen a flight of parrots that he could not identify, some francolins, a kind of banyan tree which, rooting from its branches, made dark arcades that sheltered countless fruit-bats the size of a moderate dove: and some promising caves; yet his professional mind had also followed McAdam's long and detailed account of his patient's habit of body, his diet, and his mind. He agreed with his colleague in rejecting physical causes. 'This is where the trouble lies,' repeated McAdam, striking the dome of his head, bald, naked and disagreeably blotched with ochre against the pallid, sweating scalp.

'You were not so sure of your diagnosis a little while ago, my friend, with your iliac passion and your strangulation,' said Stephen inwardly; and outwardly, 'You have known him a great while, I collect?'

'Sure, I knew him as a boy – I treated his father – and I have sailed with him these many years.'

'And *peccatum illud horrible inter Christianos non nominandum*, can you speak to that? I have known it produce strange sufferings, though mostly of a cutaneous nature; and none as extreme as this.'

'Buggery? No. I should certainly know it. There is repeated venereal commerce with the other sex, and always has been. Though indeed,' he said, standing while Stephen grubbed up a plant and wrapped it in his handkerchief, 'it is the wise man that can always separate male and female. Certainly men affect him far more than women; he has more women than he can do with – they pursue him in bands – they cause him much concern – but it

is the men he really minds: I have seen it again and again. This crisis, now: I know it was brought on by your Captain Aubrey's checking him. Corbett is bad enough, but Aubrey . . . I had heard of him often and often, long before he ever came out to the Cape – every mention of him or of Cochrane in the Gazette, every piece of service gossip, analysed, diminished, magnified, praised, decried, compared with his own doings – cannot leave them alone, any more than a man can leave a wound in peace . . . Och, be damned to his whimsies – why does he have to be Alexander? Do you want a drink?' asked McAdam, in a different voice, pulling out a case-bottle.

'I do not,' said Stephen. Until now the decent conventions of medical conversation had restrained McAdam's language and even his harsh, barbarous dialect; but spirits worked very quickly upon his sodden frame, and Stephen found the liberated McAdam tedious. In any event, the sun was no more than a hand's-breadth above the horizon. He turned, walked quickly through the almost deserted camp, down the now empty beach with McAdam blundering after him, and into the boat.

'I beg you will take notice, Commodore,' he said, darting on to the poop, 'that I am come aboard seven minutes before my time, and desire it may be made up, whenever the requirements of the service next permit.'

For the time being the service required Stephen, his shipmates, and three hundred and sixty-eight soldiers to bowl along the twentieth parallel, and to cover the hundred leagues between Rodriguez and the rest of the squadron as briskly as ever the *Néréide*, with her heavy load, could be induced to pass through the sea. It would have been far more convenient to stow the troops in the spacious *Raisonable*, but here everything depended upon speed, and Jack dreaded the loss of time in transferring them to the *Néréide*, perhaps with the sea running high: for he had fixed upon Corbett's landing-place, and the *Néréide*, replete with local knowledge and drawing little water, was to set them ashore at the Pointe des Galets; she therefore ran westward horribly crowded and trailing a smell of Oriental cooking.

Cracking on as though yards, booms, gaffs and even topmasts were to be had for the asking in the nearest port, they ran off the distance in two days, and on the evening of the second they found the *Boadicea* and *Sirius* north-east of Mauritius, exact to the rendezvous and, as far as could be told, undetected from the land. This Jack learnt from the soaking Captain Pym, whom he

summoned aboard the *Raisonable* in the most pitiless way through an ugly cross-sea, with a close-reef topsail wind sending warm green water over the waist of the two-decker. Pym had some solid intelligence, gained from two separate fishing-boats taken far off shore: the *Canonnière*, condemned by the surveyors as a man-of-war, had had all her guns but fourteen taken out and was refitting to carry a commercial cargo back to France in a month or so; on the other hand, only one of the powerful new frigates, the *Bellone*, was in Port-Louis, the *Manche* and the *Vénus* having sailed north-eastwards some time before, with six months provisions aboard.

The heavy sea, the increasing wind, the sudden tropical darkness made it impossible to gather a council of war; and having seen the half-drowned Pym regain his ship, Jack called the *Boadicea* under his lee and in a voice that carried loud and clear over the general roar he desired Captain Eliot to proceed to St Paul's with the utmost dispatch, *the utmost dispatch*, to lie there in the offing, and to 'bottle 'em up until we join you – never mind about carrying away a spar or two.' The *Boadicea*, with her fire-power, would hold them if there was any attempt at getting away.

By the next day the squadron had left Saint-Louis far astern; they were clear of the disturbed winds and currents to the leeward of Mauritius, and in the moderate sea the Marines and a hundred seamen went aboard the *Néréide* to join the rest of the landing-party. The captains gathered with the Colonel and his staff in the great cabin of the *Raisonable*, and the Commodore ran over the plan of attack once more. Stephen was there, and Jack presented him, as casually as possible, as the political adviser to the governor-designate: this earned him a broad stare from Corbett and a curiously agreeable smile from Clonfert, but it aroused no emotion in the others, taken up as they were with the coming event. Lord Clonfert was looking pale and drawn, but much stronger than Stephen had expected: before the conference he had taken Dr Maturin aside and had thanked him for his care with an obliging warmth that was evidently intended to convey more than common civility. For most of the meeting he sat silent: only towards the end, moved by some impulse that Stephen could not make out, did he put forward the suggestion that he should lead the detachment of seamen – he had some knowledge of the country, and he spoke French. It made sense: Jack agreed, looked round the table, asked whether anyone had any further

104

point to make, caught Stephen's eye, and said 'Dr Maturin?'

'Yes, sir,' said Stephen. 'I have only this to say: in the event of the capture of St Paul's, it is of the first political consequence that the inhabitants should be well treated. Any looting, rape, or disorderly conduct would have the most prejudicial effect upon the political ends in view.'

They all looked grave, murmuring a general agreement, and shortly afterwards Jack stood up. He wished them all a very good night's sleep, he said, 'for it will be a busy day tomorrow, gentlemen; and if this blessed wind holds, it will start precious early. For my part I shall cut quarters and turn in the minute hammocks are piped down.'

He turned in, but it was not to sleep. For the first time in his sea-going life he lay awake, listening to the wind, watching the tell-tale compass over his cot, and going on deck every hour or so to look at the sky. The blessed wind never faltered, still less did it veer into the dreaded west; indeed it strengthened so much that early in the middle watch he reduced sail.

At the change of the watch he was on deck again. He could feel the loom of the land somewhere on the larboard bow, and as his eyes grew used to the darkness he could in fact see the mountains of La Réunion clear against the starlit sky. He looked at his watch by the binnacle lamp; paced up and down the quarterdeck; called out 'Sharp the bowlines, there,' and heard the answering 'One, two, three, belay oh!' 'Bowlines hauled, sir,' said the officer of the watch, and the hands returned to their cleaning of the decks. 'I wonder what Corbett will do about it,' he thought, 'with seven hundred people aboard and not an inch to shove a swab.' He looked at his watch again, stepped into the master's day-cabin to check it with the chronometer, checked his reckoning once more, and said, 'Signal *Néréide carry on.*' The coloured lanterns soared up, *Néréide* acknowledged and a few moments later he saw the dim form of the frigate shake out her reefs, set her topgallantsails, haul her wind two points, and stretch away for the land, away from the squadron, trailing her string of boats.

According to the plan she was to go in alone to avoid suspicion: the landing-parties were to take the batteries commanding the roadstead, and the squadron was then to sail in and deal with the men-of-war and the town. So far the timing was perfect. Corbett would have just light enough to see: Jack disliked the man, but he believed in his knowledge of the coast. But the

waiting was going to be hard and long, since the troops had seven miles to march: he resumed his pacing. Seven miles to march, and all he could do in the meantime was to stand in quietly for St Paul's under topsails alone. He watched the sand in the half-hour glass: the top emptied, the glass was turned, the bell rang clear; again the sand began its busy journey, tumbling grain by grain, millions of grains. If all had done well they should be on their way by now. The glass turned and turned again, and slowly the sky lightened in the east. Another turn, another bell: 'You may pipe the hands to breakfast, Mr Grant, and then clear the ship for action,' he said, and with a fair show of unconcern he walked into his cabin, into the smell of toast and coffee. How had Killick guessed?

Stephen was already up, sitting there clean, shaved and respectably dressed under the swinging lamp. He said, 'There is the strange look about you, brother?'

'A strange feeling, too,' said Jack. 'Do you know, Stephen, that in about one hour's time the dust will begin to fly, and what I shall do is just lie there in the road and give orders while the other men do the work? It has never happened to me before, and I don't relish it, I find. Though to be sure, Sophie would approve.'

'She would also beg you to drink your coffee while it is hot: and she would be in the right of it. There are few things more discouraging to the mind that likes to believe it is master in its own house, than the unquestionable effect of a full belly. Allow me to pour you a cup.'

The banging of the carpenters' mallets came closer as the bulkheads went down and the cabins vanished to give a clean sweep fore and aft: not that the poor old *Raisonable* could do much, clean sweep or not; but even so the familiar sound, the coffee and the toast brought his heart back to something like a natural state. The carpenter himself appeared at the door, begged pardon, hesitated. 'Carry on, Mr Gill,' said Jack pleasantly. 'Don't mind us.'

'It is irregular, sir, I know,' said the carpenter, not carrying on at all but advancing towards the table, 'and I beg you will forgive the liberty. But I fair dread the notion of a battle, sir. Man and boy I've been in the *Raisonable* these six and twenty year; I know her timbers, and I know her butt-heads; and with respect, sir, I make so bold as to say, the firing-off of they old guns will start 'em.'

106

'Mr Gill,' said Jack, 'I promise you I will use her reasonable. Reasonable, eh, you smoke it?' A ghost of his old merriment showed for a moment; a ghost of a smile appeared on the carpenter's face; but not much conviction.

On deck again, and now the world was full of growing light. The squadron was already right into the broad shallow bay: on the larboard quarter the cape stretched out far westwards into the sea; at the bottom of the bay stood the town of St Paul's, now no more than five miles away; behind rose the savage mountains of La Réunion, barring the eastern horizon; and in the offing lay the *Boadicea*. The wind was steady in the southeast out here, but the different patterns of the sea inshore showed odd local breezes blowing. Jack took his glass, searching for the *Néréide*: he swung it along the cape, the Pointe des Galets – a moderate surf on the outer reef, far less on the beach itself – and all at once he saw her, almost becalmed in the lee of the headland, working slowly out from behind an island against the send of the sea. At the same moment the signal-lieutenant caught sight of her, made out her hoist, and reported, '*Néréide*, sir: *troops on shore.*'

'Very good, Mr – ' The young man's name escaped him. His glass ran along the coast, along the causeway that traversed a long stretch of flat watery ground, farther and farther along, and there they were: three bodies of them: first an exact column of red; then the seamen in a smaller, irregular, but compact blueish mass; and then the sepoys. Already they were much nearer to St Paul's than he had dared to hope: but could they ever take the batteries by surprise? Viewed from the sea, the red coats were horribly conspicuous.

'*Boadicea* signalling, sir,' said the lieutenant again. '*Enemy in sight, bearing due east.*'

That meant that the *Caroline* had not slipped out. 'Thank you, Mr Graham,' said Jack – the name came to him this time – 'Reply *Stand in*: and to the squadron *Make more sail.*' As he spoke a flaw in the wind shivered the *Raisonable*'s jib: he and every other man on board glanced up at the clouds gathering over the island: the dark masses had a look that none of them much cared for. Was the wind going to come foul at last? But in a moment the gust had passed, and the squadron, *Sirius*, *Raisonable* and *Otter*, ran fast and true straight for St Paul's and the powerful batteries guarding the port. And as they ran, so every eye aboard, furtively or openly, watched that distant progress on the

land, for a long, long half hour.

The trim columns far over there were losing shape: they were advancing at the double now, closer and closer to the first battery guarding St Paul's, the Lambousière, closer and closer until they were hidden from Jack by a screen of trees. In a barely tolerable suspense he waited for the sound of the heavy French guns sending grape into the close-packed companies; but what he heard was a remote crackle of musketry, a faint wind-borne cheering. The red coats were swarming all over the battery, and already the sailors were beyond it, racing for the next, La Centière. Still in their dead silence the three ships stood on, *Boadicea* converging upon them from the west, *Néréide* tearing up from the north. In five minutes they would be within the extreme range of the third battery, La Neuve, right by the town, with its forty guns: now the harbour was wide open; there lay the *Caroline*, and there lay the Indiamen; and Jack could see boats plying between the frigate and the shore. She was landing troops. Beyond her the two Indiamen, a brig-of-war, several smaller vessels – total confusion there. Confusion too just outside the town, where the musketry-fire was spreading fast, two distinct lines of fire, as though the French soldiers had formed at last, and were standing firm. Musketry, and then Jack saw the *Caroline* begin to turn; there had been some order amidst all that turmoil, for she had evidently laid out a spring: in his glass he could see the hands at her capstan, slewing her; and as her guns bore so she fired at the English troops, a steady, rapid independent fire. The brig was firing too. Yet scarcely had her first guns spoken but there was an answer from the Lambousière battery: the seamen had turned the guns on the shipping in the port, and they had sent up the union flag. Immediately afterwards the musket-fire round the Centière reached a paroxysm; the British colours ran up on the battery, and its guns joined in. The smoke drifted wide, a cloud with flashes in its heart.

Jack glanced up and down his line. The *Boadicea* had reached her station ahead: the *Néréide* was still half a mile astern. He must stand on past the guns of the third battery, tack and stand closer in. Although his guns would easily fetch the town by now he dared not fire into the mêlée at this range; even a broadside at the *Caroline* meant the risk of hitting his own people, directly behind. The inaction, the passive waiting, was extraordinarily painful, above all as the English soldiers seemed to be falling back. Slowly, slowly on, and silently; they were coming

abreast of La Neuve. The waiting would not last much longer: round-shot would be all about their ears at any moment now. The battery glided by, full on the beam, and he could see the mouths of the guns. But not one spoke, and not a man was there to serve them: the gunners had either run, or they had joined the defenders. The confusion in the town now had a pattern, the French line had broken, and they were retreating up the hill. Yet for all that the round-shot came flying from the harbour. The *Caroline*, still firing fast from her starboard broadside, now gave the squadron her whole tier of larboard guns. She concentrated her fire on the pendant-ship, and at her first discharge she hulled the *Raisonable* three times and struck her maintop. Wreckage, a studdingsail-boom, and some blocks came hurtling down into the splinter-netting over the quarterdeck. The next sent a dozen hammocks flying amidships; yet still the squadron could not reply.

'You have noted the time, Mr Peter?' asked Jack, knotting a stray signal-halliard.

'Immediately, sir,' cried Peter. The secretary was a yellowish white, made all the more evident by his black clothes: his morning's beard showed strongly against his skin. 'Seventeen minutes after eight,' he said.

How the *Caroline* pasted them! She was completely shrouded in her own smoke, but still the twenty-four-pound shot came crashing home. 'Admirable practice,' observed Jack to the secretary. Still another steady broadside, and the ship's bulwark of hammocks had great ragged gaps in it; three men were down. The glass turned; the bell struck one. 'Mr Woods,' said Jack to the master, as he stood conning the ship, 'as soon as the church and the tower are in line, we shall go about. Mr Graham, to the squadron: *Tack in succession at the gun*. And then *Close engagement*.' The minutes dropped by, then at last the signal-gun. The squadron went about as smoothly as a machine, *Boadicea*, *Sirius*, *Raisonable*, *Otter*, *Néréide*; smoothly, but slower, close-hauled on the failing inshore breeze, into the reach of the French guns again. Nearer still, and now the Indiamen let fly, together with the brig and every armed vessel in the port. But now in the town the situation was clear enough. Union flags were flying from all the batteries but one, and at this close range the squadron's guns could at last tell friend from foe. In succession their forward guns began to speak: *Boadicea* fired some deliberate sighting shots, *Sirius* her half-broadside, and the *Raisonable* a moderate

109

rolling fire; *Otter* and *Néréide* nothing but their bow-guns yet. Eliot had a fine notion of close engagement, observed Jack to himself. The *Boadicea* had stopped firing and she was standing straight in to cross the bows of the *Caroline* as she lay there within twenty-five yards off the shore. At this rate she would surely ground in the next few minutes.

'*Boadicea* signalling: *Permission to anchor*, sir,' said a voice in his ear.

'*Affirmative*,' said Jack, and he turned to the waiting carpenter.

'Five foot of water in the well, sir,' reported Mr Gill, 'and we sprung a butt-end, with them old guns.'

'Mr Woods, haul your wind,' said Jack, never moving his eye from the *Boadicea*. 'Ship the pumps.' He saw her small bower splash down, followed by her stream-anchor: there she lay, her sails clewed up, right athwart the *Caroline*, within pistol-shot of the shore. And now her crew's long training showed itself: in a furious eruption of fire and smoke she played with both broadsides on the frigate, the Indiamen, and the remaining battery. The *Sirius*, the *Otter*, and from some distance the *Néréide* supported her: the *Raisonable*, lying to, said nothing apart from a few symbolic shots from her stern-chaser. But Jack's spirit was entirely aboard the *Boadicea*, in the true heart of the battle, approving her every stroke; and when, in less than half a glass, the *Caroline*'s colours came down, followed by those of all the other ships and of the last battery, his heart leapt as though she had struck to him. They came down, and a universal cheer went up from the entire squadron, echoed by a roaring from the land.

'My barge, Mr Warburton,' said Jack to the first lieutenant. 'And my compliments to Dr Maturin: we are going ashore.'

The town had suffered very little, and the square in which they met Colonel Keating, with a group of officers and civilians, might have been living in deep peace – windows open, stalls of bright fruit and vegetables displayed, the fountain playing – but for the dead silence, all the heavier for the recent warlike thunder, and the total absence of inhabitants. 'Give you joy, Colonel,' said Jack in an unnaturally loud voice as they shook hands. 'You have done wonders, sir: I believe the place is ours.'

'For the moment we may say so, sir,' said Keating with a beaming smile, 'but they are rallying on the hills above, and Desbrusleys' column from Saint-Denis is likely to be here by nightfall. We must go to work at the double.' He laughed very

cheerfully, and catching sight of Stephen he said, 'There you are, Doctor: a glorious good morning to you, sir. You politicoes will be pleased with us – we have behaved like lambs, sir, like Sunday-going lambs – not a maiden has been put to the blush, so far, and my men are all well in hand.'

'Might I beg for an officer and a few soldiers, Colonel?' said Stephen. 'I must find the mayor and the chief of police.'

'Certainly you may, sir. Captain Wilson will be delighted to accompany you. But please to remember, that we are likely to be bundled out in less than twelve hours' time; a couple of regiments, with their artillery playing on us from the heights, would make the place untenable.' He laughed again, and from some odd contagion the whole group laughed too: cautious faces peered at the mirth from behind window-curtains; a number of small black boys crept closer under the market stalls. 'Oh, Commodore,' he went on, 'where are my wits? Here are the captains of the Indiamen.'

'I am happy to see you, gentlemen,' said Jack, 'and beg you will go aboard your ships at once. We knocked them about a little, I fear, but I trust they will be ready for sea before . . .' His words were cut off by an earth-shaking explosion, the upward flight of dark lumps of masonry, their corresponding downward crash, as the Lambousière battery disintegrated.

'That will be your friend Lord Clonfert,' remarked the Colonel, chuckling. 'A very active officer. Now, Commodore, shall we attend to the public property?'

They attended to it, and to a great deal besides. Theirs was an enormously busy day, for not only had the more dangerous fortifications to be destroyed, a large number of English prisoners to be released, still more French prisoners to be secured, the wounded seamen from the *Caroline* – half her crew, headed by their captain – to be carried to the hospital, and committees of anxious citizens, clergy and merchants to be reassured, but the wind had fulfilled its earlier threat. It now lay somewhat to the west of south, and the surf was increasing every hour. The *Caroline*, the Indiamen, the *Grappler* brig, and several other vessels having cut their cables at the last moment, had to be heaved off; the *Raisonable* was obliged to be laid in a mud berth at the ebb for the angry Mr Gill to come at her sprung butt-end; while every officer, every bosun and carpenter that could possibly be spared from a thousand other urgent tasks was furiously busy in the French naval yard, an undreamed-of Tom Tiddler's

ground strewn with cordage, sailcloth, and spars of every dimension. Stephen had an equally strenuous time with the mayor, the vicar-general, and the chief of police; while at the same time he made a large number of private contacts. His was a less physically active day than most, but at sunset, when the senior officers gathered at Keating's headquarters, a carefully-chosen cabaret by the port, and sat there refreshing themselves with white wine and an admirable local fish, he was as tired as any of them. The weariness was apparent in their drawn faces, the frequent yawn, the relaxed posture, but not in their expressions, nor their spirits: they were still a band of grigs. Colonel Keating was as merry as ever when he passed Jack his little spy-glass and pointed out the French soldiers gathering on the heights above the town. 'They tell me the main column is to be led by General Desbrusleys himself,' he said, speaking loud to be heard above the surf. 'Yet I wonder a man of such spirit has not placed his artillery before this; there are some capital places up there, you know, for a plunging cross-fire. But no doubt he means to come by another route.'

A frantic Company's supercargo darted by, in search of hands to reload his precious silk. He plunged through the gathering maidens lining the port and vanished with a low, frustrated howl. The maidens resumed their vigil, clasping one another and giggling: none had yet been caused to blush, even by this late hour; but hope was not altogether dead, though the last boats were putting off.

'Make the good woman understand we mean to pay, would you, Stephen? She does not seem to understand French very well,' said Jack privately; and aloud, 'I do not wish to hurry you, gentlemen, but I believe it would be as well to go aboard. Weather permitting, we shall come ashore tomorrow and finish our task. The hands will be rested, and' – nodding at Stephen – 'in daylight they will be out of temptation.'

The weather did not permit. The wind settled into the west, blowing right on the land, and although the squadron, together with its captures and recaptures, rode easily far beyond the breakers, with a fine holding-ground and two cables veered out on end, and although the swell did not prevent a numerous gathering for breakfast in the *Raisonable*, it seemed evident that the thunderous surf, a quarter of a mile deep along the shore as far as eye could reach, must prevent any communication with the town. It was an uncommonly cheerful breakfast, with yesterday's

action on shore fought over point by point, with kind words from the soldiers about the Navy's versatility, discipline and enterprise, and it was a breakfast that made surprising inroads on Jack's mutton hams from the Cape and his soft tack from St Paul's; yet there was not an officer aboard who did not know that they had left a great deal undone in the town, partly from want of time and partly from want of an authoritative list of government as opposed to private property: Stephen had obtained the list a little before dark, but until that time he had strongly insisted that nothing but the most obvious military stores and equipment should be touched. Then again, all the sailors and most of the soldiers knew that if the wind kept in the west the squadron would be in a most uncomfortable position. Desbrusleys would bring his artillery from Saint-Denis under the cover of darkness and lob mortar-shells on to them from behind the nearest hill while they lay like sitting ducks, unable to beat out to sea: for the moment, however, the French seemed disinclined to move. Their forces could be seen on the mountain-ridge above St Paul's; but there they stayed, and their immobility contributed not a little to the gaiety of the meal.

It was not until well after dinner that a column was reported to be advancing over the causeway from Saint-Denis. A remarkably large column, too, with artillery. 'He will never get his guns across the marsh without fascines, however,' observed Colonel Keating, 'because we destroyed the bridge; and it will take him the best part of the day to cut them. The most tedious, wearing task I know, getting guns across a marsh.'

'The surf is growing less,' said Captain Corbett. 'In my opinion we shall be able to land tomorrow – look at the westward sky. Soon come, soon go: that's my experience.'

'Earlier than that, I trust,' said Jack. 'I should never rest easy again, was we not to blow up at least the first three buildings in Dr Maturin's list.'

'And from the political point of view,' said Stephen, 'I should rejoice to see the archives go up in flames: such an invaluable confusion.'

'If I may speak, sir,' said Lord Clonfert, 'I believe it could be attempted now, or at least before the evening. I brought away a couple of surf-boats, and there are more alongside the *Sirius*, if I am not mistaken. My men are used to handling them, and I will undertake to put a party of Marines and seamen ashore.'

'Perhaps in two or three hours,' said Jack, staring at the sea.

How much was this Clonfert's desire to outdo Corbett? Even after yesterday's joint action their relationship was obviously still as bad as ever: even worse, maybe. Yet there was the importance of the objective; and these surf-boats, well managed, could do surprising things. But was Clonfert merely showing away? What kind of capers would he cut on shore? On the other hand, he had certainly done well yesterday . . . Jack felt that Clonfert's mental processes were foreign to him: there was something about the man that he could not make out, either at this point or after some hours of reflection, when he came to his pragmatic decision, gave the order, and stood on the *Raisonable*'s poop, watching the surf-boats pull away. They were on the edge of the whiteness, waiting for the huge roller: it came, sweeping them along at a breakneck pace. They vanished in the hollow of the sea, rose again black against the white water, and again they shot forward: again and again, and the last wave pitched them high on the beach.

Now they were busy. A tower to the left of the town gave a great jerk, its parapet flying bodily into the air: smoke and dust surrounded it, the whole building settled into a low shapeless heap, and the vast boom reached the ship. A long pause, and then smoke appeared behind the administrative buildings. 'Those are my tax-gatherer's records,' said Stephen, beside him. 'If that does not render us beloved, the Bourbonnais are hard to please. General Desbrusleys seems sadly bogged down,' he added, shifting his glass to the far-distant stationary column in the marsh.

They watched: they watched. At one time Jack remarked that the surf was certainly diminishing; and at another he said, 'You know, Stephen, I am growing almost used to being a spectator: yesterday I thought I should hang myself from mere misery . . . I suppose it is what you pay for command. Look at the smoke, over beyond the arsenal. What now, Mr Grant?'

'I beg pardon, sir, but Mr Dale of the *Streatham* Indiaman is in a great taking. He says they are burning his silk – begs you to see him.'

'Let him up, Mr Grant.'

'Sir, sir,' cried Mr Dale. 'They are burning our silk! Pray sir, signal them to stop. Our silk – our chief cargo – half a million pounds' worth of silk – the French stored it in that warehouse. Oh, pray, sir, signal them to . . . oh Lord, Lord' – clasping his hands – 'it is too late.' The smoke gave way to flame, to a great

114

sheet of flame; and all the signals in the world would not put it out.

'Pray, Clonfert,' said Jack, when the captain came to report, 'why did you burn the store behind the arsenal?'

'Behind the arsenal, sir? I was assured it was government property. A most respectable man, a priest, assured me it was government property. Have I done wrong?'

'I am sure you acted with the best intentions, but it seems that the Indiamen's silk was there, to the tune of half a million.' Clonfert's face fell, he looked utterly wretched, and suddenly quite old. 'Never mind it,' said Jack. 'I dare say they exaggerate; and anyhow we have saved them three millions, as they themselves acknowledge. You have done nobly, nobly – how I envied you on shore! It was no doubt a necessary stroke, for if we are drove off, pretty foolish we should look, leaving all that in enemy hands. But come, you are soaking wet: should not you like to shift your clothes? I have plenty in my sleeping-cabin.'

It was no use. Clonfert retired, sad, cast down, his glory quite put out. Nor did he revive the next day, when, the sea almost calm again, the south-east wind re-established, and all the squadron's forces ready in the boats to oppose Desbrusleys, one of Stephen's new acquaintances put off from the shore with the news that the Saint-Denis column was retreating, and that Captain Saint-Michiel, the commandant of St Pauls, was willing to treat for a suspension of arms.

The news was visibly true: the column could be seen withdrawing. All hands returned to their ships, and presently the commandant's emissaries appeared. General Desbrusleys, it seemed, had blown out his brains; but whether this was the outcome of the unhappy gentleman's military or marital reverses, or of the two combined, did not appear. At all events, for the moment the French army command was in a state of hopeless confusion, and Saint-Michiel made no difficulty about signing an agreement that gave the British squadron a long, peaceful week in St Paul's. Peaceful, but active: they were able to destroy or take away a hundred and twenty-one guns and an immense quantity of powder and shot, to blow up the remaining fortifications, to reduce the naval yard to a mere desolation with not so much as a paint-pot in it, and to do wonders for that fine frigate the *Caroline*; while the Commodore and the Colonel had time to write their despatches, a most arduous and delicate undertaking. When Jack's were finished at last, stripped of all humanity and copied

115

fair in Mr Peter's hand, together with the very moderate casualty-list, an exact account of the captured ships and vessels, a somewhat less exact account of the government stores and provisions taken, and many other documents, he came to his difficult decision.

He sent for Corbett and Clonfert, receiving them in some state with his secretary beside him. To the first he said, 'Captain Corbett, since we already have a *Caroline* in the service, I have provisionally renamed her the *Bourbonnaise*; but there is nothing provisional in my offering you the command of her, and at the same time desiring you to proceed forthwith to the Cape with my despatches. I have no doubt the Admiral will send you straight home with them, so I will burden you, if I may, with my own personal letters. I have manned her with something near her complement, barring Marines of course, from the merchant-seamen released at St Paul's, so I must ask you to be very moderate in the article of followers. Here is your order, and this is my private packet.'

Corbett's habitually angry face was ill-suited for the expression of pleasure, but even so it cracked and expanded with delight. The man who carried these despatches – the news of the neatest, completest little victory in his experience – would be much caressed at the Admiralty: would be certain of the next plum going.

'I shall be moderation incarnate, sir,' he said. 'And may I say, sir, that nothing could increase my sense of this command more than the obliging manner in which it has been given?'

To the second he said, 'Lord Clonfert, it gives me great pleasure to appoint you to the *Néréide*, vice Captain Corbett. Tomkinson, your first lieutenant, may have the *Otter*.' Clonfert too flushed bright at the news, the entirely unexpected news, of this decisive step in his career, the vital change from a sloop to a post-ship; he too made his acknowledgments, and more gracefully by far than Corbett; and for a while the full shining glory of the first day on La Réunion returned, indeed a greater glory. Yet it seemed to have some slight bitter aftertaste, for as he was taking his leave he said, with a smile not wholly of unmixed happiness, 'I never thought, sir, when we were lieutenants together, that it would be you that made me post.'

'He is an odd fish, Clonfert,' said Jack to Stephen, between two peaceful duets. 'You might almost think I had done him an injury, giving him his step.'

'You did so advisedly, not from any sudden whim? It is the real expression of your sense of his deserts, and not an alms? He should in fact be made a post-captain?'

'Why,' said Jack, 'it is rather a case of *faute de mieux*, as you would say. I should not like to have to rely upon him at all times; but one of them had to go, and he is a better captain than Corbett. His men will follow him anywhere. Perhaps he may lay out for popularity more than I think right, but whether or no, your foremast Jack dearly loves a lord; and I must take advantage of that just as I should take advantage of a tide or a shift in the wind; I shall let him take most of his Otters into the *Néréide*, and scatter the Néréides about the squadron. That was a damned unhealthy ship.' He shook his head, looking grave, and played a series of deep notes: they changed however, promising a happy development; but before he reached it his dry bow refused its duty, and he reached out for the rosin.

'When you have done with my rosin, Jack – *my* rosin, I say – would you be prepared to reveal our immediate destination?'

'It will please you, I believe. We must take Keating back to Rodriguez first, and you shall have a romp with your tortoises and your vampires; then, while the rest of the squadron is blockading Mauritius, down to the Cape to leave Eliot and the poor old *Raisonable*; then back in the *Boadicea*, which is taking the Indiamen south. Back to these waters, to see what can be done about the remaining frigates, unless you and Farquhar have further designs on La Réunion. I will not say I am sanguine, Stephen, because that might not be very clever; but I remember when you asked me how I should set the odds some weeks ago, I said three to five against us. Now I should say they are evens, or slightly in our favour.'

Chapter Five

The Admiral was pleased with the Commodore, as well he might be, for not only had Jack captured one of the four powerful French frigates that so disturbed Mr Bertie's peace of mind, and retaken two Indiamen together with a useful eighteen-gun sloop, not only had he destroyed one of the strongest French bases in the Indian Ocean, doing so with such briskness that the Admiral's dispositions would be admired even in Whitehall, which always called for quick results, but he had also enriched Mr Bertie to the extent of several thousand pounds. Just how many thousand it was impossible to say until a tribe of officials six thousand miles away should have set a value on a prodigious number of objects such as the three hundred and twenty pikes, forty rammers and forty sponges taken at St Paul's; but in any case Admiral Bertie would eventually receive one twelfth of the total sum that they arrived at: without having stirred hand or foot, without having given any advice more valuable than a general exhortation to 'go in and win', he had acquired a considerable addition to his fortune; and ever since his first charming conference with Captain Corbett, the forerunner of the squadron, he had spent the chief of his time in drawing up detailed plans for new stabling and a pine-house at Langton Castle, where he lived, while in default of the coronet for which she longed, Mrs Bertie should have a suit of lace.

Yet although the Admiral was perhaps a little devious beneath his bonhomie he had a grateful heart – a fairly grateful heart; at least he was no gripe-farthing; and the moment the *Raisonable* was signalled he began to lay on a feast, sending two boats away to the westward for lobsters, his favourite dish.

As he led the Commodore towards this glowing spread, which was attended by almost all the eminent men and all the beautiful women of Cape Town, so long as they were white, he said, 'How happy I am to see you back so soon, Aubrey, and how very well things have turned out! I sent Corbett straight home with your splendid news, as soon as I had dashed off my covering letter: you will have a Gazette to yourself, I am sure. What a pretty ship she is, too, your *Bourbonnaise* – fine narrow entry, and as stiff as a steeple. I wish our yards could turn 'em out like that: yet

after all, if you young fellows take 'em ready made, it saves our shipwrights' time, eh? Ha, ha. I confirmed her new name, by the by, and shall confirm all your appointments: I am glad Clonfert is made post, though that was a sad unlucky stroke with the Company's silk: I dare say you keel-hauled him for it at the time. Still, 'tis of no use crying over spilt milk, as I always tell Mrs Bertie; and all's well that ends well. Clonfert is made post, and you have taken four thumping prizes and half a dozen little ones. You did not see anything else on your way down, I suppose, just for the *bonne bouche*, as they say, ha, ha?'

'Well, sir, we sighted that Russian sloop *Diana* beating about off Rodriguez; but I thought I should best fall in with your views by disregarding her.'

The Admiral did not seem to hear. After a momentary absence he went on, 'Well, and so you knocked their batteries about their ears. I am glad of it, and Farquhar is cock-a-hoop, as far as a dry stick of a man like that can be cock-a-hoop – drinks no wine, and the water has rotted all the joy out of him – I did not ask him to this dinner: in any case, he declines all invitations. He is longing to see you, however, and your Dr Maturin; for the next bite, once Rodriguez is reinforced, is Bourbon for good and all. Or La Réunion, or Ile Buonaparte, as they call it. Damned fools: this chopping and changing is typical of your foreigner, don't you find, Aubrey? That should be with the next monsoon, so long as transports can be provided for three or four thousand men. What kind of man is this Dr Maturin, may I ask? Is he to be trusted? He looks something of the foreigner to me.'

'Oh, I believe he is quite trustworthy, sir,' said Jack, with an inward grin. 'Lord Keith has a great opinion of him: offered him to be physician of the fleet. And the Duke of Clarence called him in, when the whole faculty was at a stand. He thinks the world of Dr Maturin.'

'Oh, indeed?' cried the Admiral, deeply impressed. 'I shall have to take care of him, I find. Not that these clever politicoes can really be trusted, you know. You must take a long spoon to sup with the Devil, I always say. However, let us get to our lobsters. You can trust my lobsters, Aubrey, ha, ha. I sent a couple of boats to the westward for 'em, the moment you made your number.'

The lobsters were trustworthy, so were the oysters, so was the rest of the enormous meal, which carried on, remove after remove, until the cloth was drawn at last and the port appeared, when

Admiral Bertie called out, 'Fill up, gentlemen. Bumpers all round. Here's to Lucky Jack Aubrey with three times three; and may he thump 'em again and again.'

A week later the Governor of the Cape also honoured the Commodore with a feast. It consisted largely of game – blauw-bok, springbok, steinbok, klipspringer, hartebeest, wildebeest, the black and the blue – no lobster at all, and it took even longer to eat; but this was as far as the Governor's originality could take him; once more the meal ended with cabinet pudding, and once more the guests drank their port wishing that Jack might thump them again and again.

At the time of this second toast Stephen was eating bread and cold meat with Mr Farquhar and Mr Prote, his secretary, in an upper room of the government printing-house, a secluded place from which the workmen had withdrawn. They were all of them more or less black, for in the light of Stephen's most recent intelligence they had been recasting a proclamation to the people of La Réunion, as well as a number of handbills and broadsheets that painted, in glowing colours and fluent French, the advantages of British rule, promising respect for religion, laws, customs and property, pointing out the inevitably disastrous consequences of resistance, and the rewards (perhaps a little imprecise and rhetorical) of cooperation. There were similar documents, though in a less forward state of preparation, addressed to the inhabitants of Mauritius; and all these were to be printed as secretly as possible, with the help of two confidential journeymen. Yet since neither of these knew a word of French, Farquhar and Prote had been perpetually in and out of the house, and both had grown fascinated by the technical processes of printing. In their eagerness to show Stephen their proficiency they corrected three long texts in the galley, reading by means of a little looking-glass that they tended to snatch from one another, plucking out letters, inserting others, prating about upper case, lower case, formes, coigns and composing-sticks, setting-rules and justification, and gradually smearing themselves, and him, with an unreasonable quantity of printer's ink.

They were no longer talking about the act of printing, however, nor even about their insidious printed warfare: that, together with Stephen's detailed report of the promising state of public feeling on La Réunion and his account of the agents he had acquired, was far behind them; and now, as they ate their blotted meat, they discussed the poetry of the law, or rather poetry in the

120

law, a subject to which they had been led by considerations on the inheritance of landed property in Mr Farquhar's future kingdom.

'The French system, their new French code, is very well on paper,' observed Farquhar, 'very well for a parcel of logical automata; but it quite overlooks the illogical, I might say almost supra-logical and poetic side of human nature. *Our* law, in its wisdom, has preserved much of this, and it is particularly remarkable in the customary tenure of land, and in petty serjeanty. Allow me to give you an example: in the manors of East and West Enbourne, in Berkshire, a widow shall have her free-bench – her *sedes libera*, or in barbarous law-Latin her *francus bancus* – in all her late husband's copyhold lands *dum sola et casta fuerit*; but if she be detected in amorous conversation with a person of the opposite sex – if she grant the last favours– she loses all, unless she appears in the next manor-court, riding backwards on a black ram, and reciting the following words:

'Here I am
Riding on a black ram
Like a whore as I am;
And for my crinkum-crankum
Have lost my binkum-bankum;
And for my tail's game
Am brought to this wordly shame.
Therefore good Mr Steward let me have my lands again.

'My uncle owns one of these manors, and I have attended the court. I cannot adequately describe the merriment, the amiable confusion of the personable young widow, the flood of rustic wit, and – which is my real point – the universal, contented acceptance of her reinstatement, which I attribute largely to the power of poetry.'

'There may be a significant statistical relationship between the number of black ram-lambs suffered to reach maturity,' said Prote, 'and that of personable young widows.'

'And 'tis no isolated case,' continued Farquhar. 'For in the manor of Kilmersdon in Somerset, for example, we find what is essentially the same purgation, though in an abbreviated form, since no more than this distich is required:

'For mine arse's fault I take this pain.
Therefore, my lord, give me my land again.

'Now is it not gratifying, gentlemen, to find our black rams – unprofitable creatures but for this interesting ceremony – so far apart as Berkshire and Somerset, with no record of a white ram's ever having been admitted? For your black ram, gentlemen, is, I am persuaded, intimately connected with the worship of the Druids . . .'

Mr Farquhar was a man with a good understanding and a great deal of information, but at the first mention of Druids, oak-groves or mistletoe a wild gleam came into his eye, a gleam so wild on this occasion that Stephen looked at his watch, rose to his feet, said that he must regretfully leave them, and gathered up his book.

'Should you not like to wash before you go?' asked Farquhar. 'You are somewhat mottled.'

'Thank you,' said Stephen. 'But the being upon whom I am about to wait, though eminent for precedence, does not stand on ceremony.'

'What can he have meant by eminent for precedence?' asked Mr Prote. 'Anyone who is anyone, apart from us, is at the Governor's.'

'He may well mean a black magus, or a potentate among the Hottentots. Now the Druids, I say . . .'

In fact the being's precedence was merely alphabetical: for in the gaiety of his heart Dr Maturin had referred to the aardvark. It stood before him now, a pale creature with a bulky hog-backed body close on five feet long, a broad tail, an immense elongated head ending in a disk-like snout, short stout legs and disproportionately long translucent ass's ears; it was partially covered with sparse yellowish hair that showed the unwholesome nightwalker's skin below; it blinked repeatedly. The aardvark was acutely conscious of its position and from time to time it licked its small tubular lips, for not only had it been measured and weighed, while a tuft of bristles that could ill be spared had been clipped from its flank, but now it was being looked at through a diminishing-glass and drawn. It was a meek, apologetic animal, incapable of biting and too shy to scratch; and it grew lower and lower in its spirits: its ears drooped until they obscured its weak, melancholy, long-lashed eyes.

'There, honey, it is done,' said Stephen, showing the aardvark its likeness: and calling upwards through the ceiling he said, 'Mr van der Poel, I am infinitely obliged to you, sir. Do not stir, I beg. I shall lock the door and leave the key under the mat: I am

going back to the ship, and tomorrow you shall see the egg.'

Some hours later he beheld Simon's Town again, its inner anchorage scattered with Jack's prizes: it reminded him of Port Mahon long ago, when the *Sophie*'s captured feluccas, trabacaloes and xebecs lined the quay. 'That was very well,' he said, 'and Minorca a delightful island; but even Minorca could never boast the aardvark.' The street was filled with liberty-men, a cheerful crew, for not only had Jack ordered a modest advance of prize-money – two dollars a nob paid down on the capstan-head – but Dr Maturin's words on loot had not been obeyed quite as strictly as he could have wished, and pieces of the finest Oriental silk, slightly charred, covered the lithe forms, the infinitely seductive bosoms of the sailors' companions. He was hailed on all sides; kind hands led his hired nag away; and a Boadicean midshipman, smelling strongly of patchouli, rowed him out to the *Raisonable*. At ease in his spacious cabin he opened his book and looked at the picture again. 'It is perhaps the most gratifying beast I have ever figured,' he said, 'and it displays a touching affection for the good Mr van der Poel; I believe I shall attempt to colour it.' He turned back through the pages. Most were covered with the small close-written text of his diary, but there were several drawings – the Rodriguez tortoise, the seals of False Bay – some washed with water-colour. 'Perhaps not,' he said, considering them. 'My talents scarcely seem to lie that way.' He converted the Dutch weight of the aardvark into avoirdupois, sharpened his pen to a finer point, reflected for a while, gazing out of the scuttle, and began to write in his personal cipher.

'I cannot trace the chain of thought or rather of associations that leads me to reflect upon Clonfert and Jack Aubrey. Conceivably the aardvark plays a part, so ill at ease: but the links are obscure. Clonfert's tormina exercise my mind; for by whatever private scale of pain one may measure them, they must come tolerably high. It seems ludicrously facile to regard them as the direct transposition of his state of mind; yet McAdam is no fool except to himself; and in some not dissimilar cases that Dupuytren and I dissected we were able to eliminate any direct physical cause. The vermiform appendix, so often the villain in these apparent strangulations, as pink as a healthy worm, the whole tract from the oesophagus downwards, devoid of lesion. Clonfert is more of an Irishman, with the exacerbated suscepti-bilities of a subject race, that I had supposed; more indeed than I gave Jack to understand. I find that as a boy he did not attend

a great English public school, as did most of his kind I have known; nor did he go early to sea and thereby wash away the barrier: the first years of his nominal service were book-time, as they call the amiable cheat by which a complaisant captain places an absent child upon his muster-roll. Far from it: he was brought up almost entirely by the servants at Jenkinsville (a desolate region). Squireen foster-parents too for a while, his own being so mad or so disreputable: and he seems to have sucked in the worst of both sides. On the one hand he derived his notion of himself as a lord from people who have had to cringe these many generations to hold on to the odd patch of land that is their only living; and on the other, though half belonging to them, he has been bred up to despise their religion, their language, their poverty, their manners and traditions. A conquering race, in the place of that conquest, is rarely amiable; the conquerors pay less obviously than the conquered, but perhaps in time they pay even more heavily, in the loss of the humane qualities. Hard, arrogant, profit-seeking adventurers flock to the spoil, and the natives, though outwardly civil, contemplate them with a resentment mingled with contempt, while at the same time respecting the fact of conquest – acknowledging their greater strength. And to be divided between the two must lead to a strange confusion of sentiment. In Clonfert's case the result of this and of other factors seems to me an uneasy awareness of his own distinction (he often mentions it), a profound uncertainty of its real value, and a conviction that to validate its claims he should be twice as tall as other men. In spite of his high heels, both literal and figurative, he is not twice as tall as other men: Jack, in particular, tops him by a head and more. He has surrounded himself with a strikingly inferior set of officers, which I do not remember to have seen done in the Navy, where the aristocratic captains are almost always accompanied by aristocratic officers and midshipmen, just as a Scotch commander will gather Scotchmen around him: no doubt they provide him with the approval he longs for; but how much can a man of his understanding value their approval? And if Lady Clonfert and Mrs Jennings are a fair example of his women, to what degree can their favours really gratify him?

'Upon this foundation, and upon what McAdam tells me, I could build up a moderately convincing Clonfert whose entire life is an unsatisfactory pretence: a puppet vainly striving to be another puppet, equally unreal – the antithesis of Jack, who has

never played a part in his life, who has no need for any role. It would not satisfy me, however, for although it may have some truth in it and although it may go far towards pointing at the origin of the tormina and some other symptoms I have noted (McAdam did not appreciate the significance of the asymmetric *sudor insignis*), it does not take into account the fact that he is *not* a puppet. Nor, which is far more important, does it take into account the affection of his men: Jack asserts that sailors love a lord and no doubt that is profoundly true (apart from anything else, the fancied difference diminishes the servitude); but they do not go on loving a lord if he is worthless. They did not go on loving Prince William. No: a continued affection over a long period must be based upon the recognition of real qualities in the man, for a ship at sea, particularly a small ship on a foreign station, is an enclosed village; and whoever heard of the long-matured judgment of a village being wrong? The communal mind, even where the community is largely made up of unthinking and illiterate men, is very nearly as infallible as a Council. And the qualities valued by a community of men are commonly good nature, generosity and courage. Courage: here I am on the most shifting ground in the world. For what is it? Men put different values on their lives at different times: different men value approval at different rates – for some it is the prime mover. Two men go through the same motions for widely different reasons; their conduct bears the same name. Yet if Clonfert has not performed these actions I am very sure that his men would not esteem him as they do. Farquhar's illogicality may well render their affection for Lord Clonfert greater than it would be for Mr Scroggs, but that is merely an addition; the esteem is already there, and so are the actions upon which it is founded. I saw him storm a battery at St Paul's; and in the result his outward gestures, his élan, and indeed his success were indistinguishable from Jack Aubrey's.

'Jack Aubrey. The lieutenant of long ago is still visible in the grave commodore, but there are times when he has to be looked for. One constant is that indubitable happy courage, the courage of the fabled lion – how I wish I may see a lion – which makes him go into action as some men might go to their marriage-bed. *Every man would be a coward if he durst:* it is true of most, I do believe, certainly of me, probably of Clonfert; but not of Jack Aubrey. Marriage has changed him, except in this: he had hoped for too much, poor sanguine creature (though indeed he is sick

125

for news from home). And the weight of this new responsibility; he feels it extremely: responsibility and the years – his youth is going or indeed is gone. The change is evident, but it is difficult to name many particular alterations, apart from the comparative want of gaiety, of that appetence for mirth, of those infinitesimal jests that caused him at least such enormous merriment. I might mention his attitude towards those under his command, apart from those he has known for years: it is attentive, conscientious, and informed; but it is far less personal; his mind rather than his heart is concerned, and the people are primarily instruments of war. And his attitude towards the ship itself: well do I remember his boundless delight in his first command, although the *Sophie* was a sad shabby little tub of a thing – the way he could not see enough of her meagre charms, bounding about the masts, the rigging, and the inner parts with an indefatigable zeal, like a great boy. Now he is the captain of a lordly two-decker, with these vast rooms and balconies, and he is little more than polite to her; she might be one set of furnished lodgings rather than another. Though here I may be mistaken: some aspects of the sailor's life I do not understand. Then again there is the diminution not only of his animal spirits but also of his appetites: I am no friend to adultery, which surely promises more than it can perform except in the article of destruction; but I could wish that Jack had at least some temptation to withstand. His more fiery emotions, except where war is concerned, have cooled: Clonfert, younger in this as in many other ways, has retained his capacity for the extremes of feeling, certainly the extremity of pain, perhaps that of delight. The loss is a natural process no doubt, and one that prevents a man from burning away altogether before his time; but I should be sorry if, in Jack Aubrey's case, it were to proceed so far as a general cool indifference; for then the man I have known and valued so long would be no more than the walking corpse of himself.'

The sound of the bosun's call, the clash of the Marines presenting arms, told him that Jack Aubrey's body, quick or dead, was at this moment walking about within a few yards of him. Stephen dusted sand upon his book, closed it, and waited for the door to open.

The officer who appeared did indeed resemble Commodore rather than Lieutenant Aubrey, even after he had flung his coat and with it the marks of rank on to a nearby locker. He was bloated with food and wine; his eyes were red and there were

liverish circles under them; and he was obviously far too hot. But as well as the jaded look of a man who has been obliged to eat and drink far too much and then to sit in an open carriage for twenty miles in a torrid dust-storm, wearing clothes calculated for the English Channel, his face also had an expression of discouragement.

'Oh for some more soldiers like Keating,' he said wearily. 'I cannot get them to move. We had a council after dinner, and I represented to them, that with the regiments under their command we could take La Réunion out of hand: the *Raisonable* would serve as a troop-carrier. St Paul's is wide open, with not one stone of the batteries standing on another. They agreed, and groaned, and lamented – they could not move without an order from the Horse-Guards; it had always been understood that the necessary forces were to come from the Madras establishment, perhaps with the next monsoon if transports could be found; if not, with the monsoon after that. By the next monsoon, said I, La Réunion would be bristling with guns, whereas now the French had very few, and those few served by men with no appetite for a battle of any kind: by the next monsoon their spirits would have revived, and they would have been reinforced from the Mauritius. Very true, said the soldiers, wagging their heads; but they feared that the plan worked out by the staff must stand: should I like to go shooting warthogs with them on Saturday? And to crown all, the brig was not a packet but a merchantman from the Azores – no letters of any kind. We might as well be at the back of the moon.'

'It is very trying, indeed,' said Stephen. 'What say you to some barley-water, with lime-juice in it? And then a swim? We could take a boat to the island where the seals live.'

To a cooler, fresher Jack he offered what comfort he could provide. He left the stolid torpor of the soldiers to one side – neither had really believed in the possibility of stirring them, after the dismal end of the unauthorized expedition to Buenos Aires from this very station not many years before – and concentrated on the changed perception of time during periods of activity; these busy weeks had assumed an importance unjustified by their sidereal, or as he might say their absolute measure; with regard to exterior events they still remained mere weeks; it had been unreasonable to expect anything on their return to the Cape; but now a ship might come in any day at all, loaded with mail.

'I hope you are right, Stephen,' said Jack, balancing on the gunwale and rubbing the long blue wound on his back. 'Sophie has been very much in my mind these last few days, and even the children. I dreamt of her last night, a huddled, uneasy dream; and I long to hear from her.' After a considering pause he said, 'I did bring back some more pleasant news, however: the Admiral is fairly confident of being able to add *Iphigenia* and *Magicienne* to the squadron within the next few weeks; he had word from Sumatra. But of course they will be coming from the east – not the least possibility of anything from home. The old *Leopard*, too, though nobody wants *her*: iron-sick throughout, a real graveyard ship.'

'The packet will come in from one day to the next, and it will bring a budget of tax-demands, bills, and an account of the usual domestic catastrophes: news of mumps, chicken-pox, a leaking tap; my prophetic soul sees it beneath the horizon.'

The days dropped by while the *Boadicea*, her holds emptied and herself heaved down with purchases to bollards on the shore, had her foul bottom cleaned; Jack set up his telescope with a new counterbalance that worked perfectly on land; Stephen saw his lion, a pride of lions; and then, although it had mistaken the horizon, his prophetic soul was shown to have been right: news did come in. But it was not domestic news, nor from the west: the flying *Wasp* had turned about in mid-ocean and had come racing back to the Cape to report that the French had taken three more Indiamen, HM sloop *Victor*, and the powerful Portuguese frigate *Minerva*.

The *Vénus* and the *Manche*, already at sea when the squadron looked into Port-Louis, had captured the *Windham*, the *United Kingdom*, and the *Charlton*, all Indiamen of the highest value. The *Bellone*, slipping out past the blockade by night, had taken the eighteen-gun *Victor*, and then she and her prize had set about the *Minerva*, which mounted fifty-two guns, but which mounted them in vain against the fury of the French attack. The Portuguese, now *La Minerve*, was at present in Port-Louis, manned by seamen from the *Cannonière* and some deserters: the Indiamen, the *Vénus* and the *Manche* were probably there too, but of that the *Wasp* was not quite sure.

Before the turn of the tide Jack was at sea, the wart-hogs, the soldiers, and even his telescope left behind: he had shifted his pendant into the *Boadicea*, for the hurricane months were not far away, and the *Raisonable* could not face them. He was back

128

in his own *Boadicea*, driving her through variable and sometimes contrary winds until they reached the steady south-east trade, when she lay over with her lee-rail under white water, her deck sloping like the roof of Ashgrove Cottage, and began to tear off her two hundred and fifty and even three hundred nautical miles between one noon observation and the next; for there was some remote hope of catching the Frenchmen and their prizes, cutting them off before they reached Mauritius.

On the second Sunday after their departure, with church rigged, Jack was reading the Articles of War in a loud, official, comminatory voice by way of sermon and all hands were trying to keep upright (for not a sail might be attempted to be touched). He had just reached article XXIX, which dealt with sodomy by hanging the sodomite and which always made Spotted Dick and other midshipmen swell purple from suppressed giggling at every monthly repetition, when two ships heaved in sight. They were a great way off, and without interrupting her devotions, such as they might be with every mind fixed earnestly upon the mast-head, the *Boadicea* edged away to gain the weather-gage. But by the time Jack had reached *All crimes not capital* (there were precious few), and well before he cleared the ship for action, the windward stranger broke out the private signal. In answer to the *Boadicea*'s she made her number: the *Magicienne*; and her companion was the *Windham*.

The *Magicienne*, said Captain Curtis, coming aboard the Commodore, had retaken the Indiaman off the east coast of Mauritius. The *Windham* had been separated from her captor, the *Vénus*, during a tremendous sudden blow in seventeen degrees south; the *Magicienne* had snapped her up after something of a chase, beating to windward all day, and had then stood on all night in the hope of finding the French frigate. Curtis had found her at sunset, looking like a scarecrow with only her lower masts standing and a few scraps of canvas aboard, far away right under the land, creeping in with her tattered forecourse alone. But unhappily the land to which she was creeping was the entrance to Grand-Port; and when the land-breeze set it, blowing straight in her teeth, the *Magicienne* had the mortification of seeing the *Vénus* towed right under the guns of the Ile de la Passe, at the entrance to the haven.

'By the next morning, sir, when I could stand in,' said Curtis apologetically, 'she was half way up to the far end, and with my ammunition so low – only eleven rounds to a gun – and the

Indiaman in such a state, I did not think it right to follow her.'

'Certainly not,' said Jack, thinking of that long inlet, guarded by the strongly fortified Ile de la Passe, by batteries on either side and at the bottom and even more by a tricky, winding fairway fringed with reefs: the Navy called it Port South-East, as opposed to Port-Louis in the north-west, and he knew it well. 'Certainly not. It would have meant throwing the *Magicienne* away; and I need her. Oh, yes, indeed, I need her, now they have that thumping great *Minerva*. You will dine with me, Curtis? Then we must bear away for Port-Louis.' They passed the Indiaman a tow, and lugging their heavy burden through the sea they stood on, the wind just abaft the beam.

Stephen Maturin had been deeply mistaken in supposing that Jack, older and more consequential, now looked upon ships as lodgings, more or less comfortable: the *Raisonable* had never been truly his; he was not wedded to her. The *Boadicea* was essentially different; he entered into her; he was one of her people. He knew them all, and with a few exceptions he liked them all: he was delighted to be back, and although Captain Eliot had been a perfectly unexceptionable officer, they were delighted to have him. They had in fact led Eliot a sad life of it, opposing an elastic but effective resistance to the slightest hint of change: 'The Commodore had always liked it this way; the Commodore had always liked it that; it was Captain Aubrey that had personally ordered the brass bow-chasers to be painted brown.' Jack particularly valued Mr Fellowes, his bosun, who had clung even more firmly than most to Captain Aubrey's sail-plan and his huge, ugly snatch-blocks that allowed hawsers to be instantly set up to the mastheads, there to withstand the strain of an extraordinary spread of canvas; and now that the *Boadicea*'s hold had been thoroughly restowed, her hull careened, and her standing-rigging rerove with the spoils of St Paul's, she answered their joint hopes entirely. In spite of her heavy burden she was now making nine knots at every heave of the log.

'She is making a steady nine knots,' said Jack, coming below after quarters.

'How happy you make me, Jack,' said Stephen. 'And you might make me even happier, should you so wish, by giving me a hand with this. The unreasonable attitude, or lurch, of the ship caused me to overset the chest.'

'God help us,' cried Jack, gazing at the mass of gold coins

lying in a deep curve along the leeward side of the cabin. 'What is this?'

'It is technically known as money,' said Stephen. 'And was you to help me pick it up, instead of leering upon it with a stunned concupiscence more worthy of Danae than a king's officer, we might conceivably save some few pieces before they all slip through the cracks in the floor. Come, come, bear a hand, there.'

They picked and shovelled busily, on all fours, and when the thick squat iron-bound box was full again, Stephen said, 'They are to go into these small little bags, if you please, by fifties: each to be tied with string. Will I tell you what it is, Jack?' he said, as the heavy bags piled up.

'If you please.'

'It is the vile corrupting British gold that Buonaparte and his newspapers do so perpetually call out against. Sometimes it exists, as you perceive. And, I may tell you, every louis, every napoleon, every ducat or doubloon is sound: the French sometimes buy services or intelligence with false coin or paper. That is the kind of thing that gives espionage a bad name.'

'If we pay real money, it is to be presumed we get better intelligence?' said Jack.

'Why, truly, it is much of a muchness: your paid agent and his information are rarely of much consequence. The real jewel, unpurchasable, beyond all price, is the man who hates tyranny as bitterly as I do: in this case the royalist or the true republican who will risk his life to bring down that Buonaparte. There are several of them on La Réunion, and I have every reason to believe there are more on the Mauritius. As for your common venal agents,' said Stephen, shrugging, 'most of these bags are for them; it may do some good; indeed it probably will, men rarely being all of a piece. Tell me, when shall you be able to set me down? And how do you reckon the odds at present?'

'As to the first,' said Jack, 'I cannot say until I have looked into Port-Louis. The odds? I believe they are still about evens for the moment. If they have gained the *Minerva*, we have gained the *Magicienne*. You will tell me that the *Minerva* is the heaviest of the two, and that the *Magicienne* only carries twelve-pounders; but Lucius Curtis is a rare plucked 'un, a damned good seaman. So let us say evens for the moment. For the moment, I say, because the hurricane-season is coming, and if they lie snug in port and we outside, why, there is no telling how we shall

stand in a few weeks' time.'

During the night they brought the wind aft as they went north about Mauritius, and when Stephen woke he found the *Boadicea* on an even keel; she was pitching gently, and the urgent music that had filled her between-decks these last days was no longer to be heard. He washed his face perfunctorily, passed his hand over his beard, said 'It will do for today,' and hurried into the day-cabin, eager for coffee and his first little paper cigar of the day. Killick was there, gaping out of the stern-window, with the coffee-pot in his hand.

'Good morning, Killick,' said Stephen. 'Where's himself?'

'Good morning, sir,' said Killick. 'Which he's still on deck.'

'Killick,' said Stephen, 'what's amiss? Have you seen the ghost in the bread-room? Are you sick? Show me your tongue.'

When Killick had withdrawn his tongue, a flannelly object of inordinate length, he said, paler still, 'Is there a ghost in the bread-room, sir? Oh, oh, and I was there in the middle watch. Oh, sir, I might a seen it.'

'There is always a ghost in the bread-room. Light along that pot, will you now?'

'I dures'nt, sir, begging your pardon. There's worse news than the ghost, even. Them wicked old rats got at the coffee, sir, and I doubt there's another pot in the barky.'

'Preserved Killick, pass me that pot, or you will join the ghost in the bread-room, and howl for evermore.'

With extreme unwillingness Killick put the pot on the very edge of the table, muttering, 'Oh, I'll cop it: oh, I'll cop it.'

Jack walked in, poured himself a cup as he bade Stephen good morning, and said, 'I am afraid they are all in.'

'All in what?'

'All the Frenchmen are in harbour, with their two Indiamen and the *Victor*. Have not you been on deck? We are lying off Port-Louis. The coffee has a damned odd taste.'

'This I attribute to the excrement of rats. Rats have eaten our entire stock; and I take the present brew to be a mixture of the scrapings at the bottom of the sack.'

'I thought it had a familiar tang,' said Jack. 'Killick, you may tell Mr Seymour, with my compliments, that you are to have a boat. And if you don't find at least a stone of beans among the squadron, you need not come back. It is no use trying *Néréide*; she don't drink any.'

When the pot had been jealously divided down to its ultimate

132

dregs, dregs that might have been called dubious, had there been the least doubt of their nature, they went on deck. The *Boadicea* was lying in a splendid bay, with the rest of the squadron ahead and astern of her: *Sirius, Néréide, Otter,* the brig *Grappler* which they had retaken at St Paul's, and a couple of fore-and-aft-rigged avisoes, from the same source: to leeward the *Windham* Indiaman, with parties from each ship repairing the damage caused by the blow and the violence of the enemy, watched by the philosophical French prize-crew. At the bottom of the deep curve lay Port-Louis, the capital of Mauritius, with green hills rising behind and cloud-capped mountains beyond them.

'Shall you adventure to the maintop?' asked Jack. 'I could show you better from up there.'

'Certainly,' said Stephen. 'To the ultimate crosstrees, if you choose: I too am as nimble as an ape.'

Jack was moved to ask whether there were earthbound apes, as compact as lead, afflicted with vertigo, possessed of two left hands and no sense of balance; but he had seen the startling effect of a challenge upon his friend, and apart from grunting as he thrust Stephen up through the lubber's hole, he remained silent until they were comfortably installed among the studding-sails, with their glasses trained upon the town.

'You have the white building with the tricolour flying over it?' said Jack. 'That is General Decaen's headquarters. Now come down to the shore and a little to the right, and there is the *Bellone*: she is swaying up a new foretopmast. Another foot – he holds up his hand – he bangs home the fid: neatly done, most seamanlike. Inside her lies the *Victor*. Do you see the French colours over ours? The dogs; though indeed she was theirs before she was ours. Inside again, the French colours over the Portuguese: that is the *Minerva*. A very heavy frigate, Stephen; and no sign of her having been roughly handled that I can see. Then comes the *Vénus*, with the broad pendant, alongside the sheer-hulk. They are giving her a new mizen. Now she *has* been handled rough – bowsprit done in the gammoning, head-rails all ahoo, not a dead-eye left this side, hardly; and very low in the water; pumps hard at it: I wonder they managed to bring her in. Yet it was early in the year for that kind of blow: she must have been in the heart of it, the Indiaman on the edge, and the *Magicienne* quite outside, for Curtis never even struck his top-gallant masts.'

'Your hurricano has a rotatory motion, I believe?'

133

'Exactly so. And you can be taken aback just when you think you have rode it out. Then over to the right again you have the *Manche* and a corvette: the *Créole*, I believe. A very tidy squadron, once they have put the *Vénus* to rights. What a match it would be, was they to come out and fight their ships as well as that gallant fellow at St Paul's fought his. What was his name?'

'Feretier. Do you suppose they mean to come out?'

'Never in life,' said Jack. 'Not unless I can amuse them – not unless I can make their commodore believe we are no longer in the offing, or only one or two of us. No: it looks like Brest or Toulon all over again: steady blockade until we are down to salt horse and Old Weevil's wedding-cake. We used to call it polishing Cape Sicié in the Mediterranean. But at least it means that I can send you down to La Réunion with the *Grappler*, if you really have to go: she can convoy the *Windham* that far, in case of the odd privateer, and be back the next day. It is barely thirty leagues, and with this steady wind ... Forgive me, Stephen, it is time for my captains. There is Clonfert's gig putting off already, with his damn-fool boat's crew. Why does he have to make such a raree-show of himself?'

'Other captains dress their boat's crew in odd garments.'

'Still, there is such a thing as measure. I do not look forward to this meeting, Stephen. I shall have to call for an explanation – they will have to tell me how the *Bellone* got out. However, it will not be long. Shall you wait for me here?'

The conference was longer than Jack had expected, but Stephen, cradled in his top as it swung fore and aft on the long even swell, scarcely noticed the passage of time. He was warm through and through, so warm that he took off his neck-cloth; and while his eye dwelt on the motions of the seabirds (noddies, for the most part), the routine work on the deck below, the repairs carrying on aboard the *Windham*, and the boats moving to and fro, his mind was far away on La Réunion, following a large number of schemes designed to overcome the French reluctance to becoming British by means less forthright, and less murderous, than a yardarm-to-yardarm engagement with both broadsides roaring loud. He was therefore almost surprised to see the Commodore's large red face heave up over the edge of his capacious nest; while at the same time he was concerned to see its heavy, anxious expression, the comparative dullness of that bright blue eye.

'This is a damned awkward harbour for a close blockade,'

observed the Commodore. 'Easy enough to slip out of, with the wind almost always in the south-east, but difficult to enter, without you are lucky with the sea-breeze and the tide – that is why they use St Paul's so often – and difficult to bottle up tight in the dark of the moon. Still, come down into the cabin, if you would like a wet: Killick has discovered a few pale ancient beans that will just provide our elevenses.'

In the cabin he said, 'I do not blame them for letting the *Bellone* slip between them and the cape; and the *Cannonière* was gone before ever they reached their stations. But I do blame them for falling out over it. There they sat like a couple of cross dogs, answering short and glaring at one another. It was Pym's responsibility as the senior captain, of course; but whose fault it was in fact I could not make out. All I am sure of is that they are on wretched terms. Clonfert seems to have a genius that way, but I am surprised at Pym, such an easy, good-natured fellow. However, I have invited all captains to dine, and let us hope that will smoothe things over. It is a miserable business, these rivalries in a squadron. I thought I had got rid of them with Corbett.'

Although this dinner, whose main dishes were a four-hundred-pound turtle and a saddle of mutton from the Cape, was eaten in a humid ninety degrees, it did restore a semblance of civility, if not more. Pym was no man to keep up a resentment, and Clonfert could command the social graces; they drank wine together, and Jack saw with relief that his entertainment was going fairly well. Curtis of the *Magicienne* was a lively, conversable man, and he had much to tell them about the French squadron and its depredations in the Company's far eastern settlements: Hamelin, their commodore, was a savage, Jacobin fellow, it seemed, though a good seaman, while Duperré of the *Bellone* had a fine, swift-sailing ship, and he fought her with great determination; and the French crews were in a surprisingly high state of efficiency. Curtis's account carried the dinner over its first formal stage, and soon there was plenty of animated talk; although indeed Clonfert addressed almost all his conversation to his neighbour, Dr Maturin, and the two young commanders, Tomkinson of the *Otter* and Dent of the *Grappler*, did not feel it proper to open their mouths except to admit calipash and calipee, fat-tailed sheep and Cape Madeira.

'You and Clonfert got along very well together,' observed Jack, when his bloated guests had gone. 'What did you find to talk about? Is he a reading man?'

'He reads novels. But most of the time we spoke of his exploration of these coasts. He has charted many of the inlets, rowing in with his black pilot; and he has a surprising fund of information.'

'Yes. I know. He outdoes Corbett in that, I believe. He has real abilities, if only . . . What now?'

'All ready, sir,' said Bonden.

'Show me the pockets.'

'Number seven canvas, sir, double-sewn,' said Bonden, spreading his jacket and displaying an array of pouches. 'With flaps.'

'Very good. Now stow these away, and button 'em up tight.'

As he received the little heavy bags Bonden's visage took on a glassy, know-nothing look: he said no word; he extinguished the gleam of intelligence in his eye. 'There we are,' said Jack. 'And here is a chit for Captain Dent. He will ask you if you can make out the leading-marks for the cove where *Wasp* put the Doctor ashore, and if you can *not* – mark me, Bonden, if you are not dead certain of both marks and soundings – you are to say so, whether they think you a jack-pudden or no. And Bonden, you will take great care of the Doctor. Hammer his pistol-flints, d'ye hear me, and do not let him get his feet wet.'

'Aye, aye, sir,' said Bonden.

A few minutes later the boat pulled away; Bonden, though unnaturally stout in his close-buttoned jacket, sprang up the side of the *Grappler* and hauled Stephen aboard; and the brig headed south-west, followed by the Indiaman.

Jack watched them until they were hull-down, and then he turned his gaze to the shore, with its fortifications sharp and clear against the bright green of sugar-cane. He could almost feel the answering gaze of the French commanders training their telescopes on the squadron, particularly that of Hamelin, his equivalent on the other side; and as he gave the orders that would set the long blockade in motion he turned over the possibilities of amusing them and of bringing them out to fight.

He had tried several before the *Grappler* came back, bearing Stephen, loaded with intelligence, a chest of the best coffee in the world, and a new machine for roasting it: he had tried open provocation and lame-duck ruses, but Hamelin would not bite, the cunning dog; the French lay there at their ease, and the squadron was obliged to be content with its steady routine of beating to and fro with only the prospect of Christmas to encourage them.

By no means all the news that Stephen brought was good: the

frigate *Astrée* was expected from France; the disaffection of the commandant of St Paul's had much diminished since General Desbrusleys' death; and an important body of regulars with fervently Buonapartist officers had arrived. La Réunion would be much harder to take with the promised three thousand troops from India than it would have been with half that number from the Cape some weeks earlier. In the opinion of the French officers it could not be successfully attacked, even with good weather for landing, by less than five thousand men. On the other hand, he had learnt a great deal about Mauritius, the more important island of the two by far, with its splendid ports: among other things, a considerable part of the French garrison was made up of Irish troops, prisoners of war or volunteers who still believed in Buonaparte. And Stephen had many contacts to make, some that might be of the greatest value. 'So,' said he, 'as soon as you can let me have the *Néréide*, with Clonfert's local knowledge and his black pilot, I should like to begin the work of preparation. Apart from other considerations, our broadsheets need time to have their effect; and some well-chosen rumour, some indiscretion in the proper place, might conceivably bring your French frigates out.'

Jack freely admitted the importance of the task in hand. 'Yet do not think me weak, Stephen, when I say how I regret the days when we were of no account – when we cruised by ourselves, pretty busy at times, but often free for our hand of piquet in the evening and our music. You shall have *Néréide* tomorrow, if you choose, since *Vénus* has chosen this moment to heave down, and the *Manche* shows signs of doing much the same, so I can spare a ship; but at least let us have this evening to ourselves. While you were away I transposed the Corelli for violin and 'cello.'

The music tied them back to what seemed a very distant past, one in which no commodore's secretary with his heap of papers had to be kept away for a few hours' peace; a past where no susceptible captains had to have their feelings managed, and where what little administration the first lieutenant left to his captain could be settled out of hand, among people he knew intimately well. But the morning brought Mr Peter back with a score of documents; the *Magicienne* was very much afraid that she would have to ask for a court-martial upon her yeoman of the sheets for an almost unbelievable series of offences, starting with drunkenness and ending with a marlin-spike struck into the ship's corporal's belly; and the *Sirius* was running short of

wood and water. Stephen crossed to the *Néréide* after no more than the briefest farewell.

He found Clonfert in high spirits, delighted to be away on his own, delighted to be away from the Commodore's rigid discipline: for although there were many things in which Jack and Lord St Vincent did not see eye to eye, including politics and free speech, they were at one in their notions on keeping station and on prompt, exact obedience to signals. They walked the quarterdeck in the forenoon, and as they strolled up and down the windward side, with the high wooded shore of Mauritius gliding by and shimmering in the heat, Stephen took in the atmosphere of the ship. There were few original Néréides left, since Clonfert had brought all his officers together with most of the *Otter*'s crew, and there was the same feeling in the frigate as there had been in the sloop. In many ways it was much like that in any man-of-war: that is to say, the hands' activities, the employment of their strictly-regulated time, the almost fanatical regard to neatness, were much the same as he had observed in other ships. Yet in none of Jack Aubrey's commands had he ever heard the captain's orders followed by suggestions that things might be better otherwise; and this as it were consultation appeared to be customary right down the hierarchy, from the officer of the watch to Jemmy Ducks, who looked after the poultry. With his limited experience, Stephen could not say that it was wrong: everybody seemed brisk and cheerful and when a manoeuvre was decided upon it was carried out promptly: but he had supposed this loquacity and tergiversation to be confined to the navy of the French, that lively, articulate nation.

The exception seemed to be the warrant-officers, the master, the bosun, the gunner and the carpenter, grave men who adhered to the Royal Navy's tradition as Stephen had seen it, particularly the magnificent granite-faced Mr Satterly, the elderly master, who appeared to regard his captain with a veiled affectionate indulgence and to run the ship with scarcely a word. The commissioned officers and the young gentlemen were far less mute; they obviously desired Clonfert's favour and attention, and they competed for it partly by activity and partly by a curious mixture of freedom and something not far from servility. The words 'my lord' were always in their mouths, and they pulled off their hats with a marked deference whenever they addressed him; yet they addressed him far more often than was usual in any ship that Stephen had known, crossing to his side of the quarterdeck

unasked and volunteering remarks of no great consequence, unconnected with their duty.

Perhaps high spirits did not suit Clonfert quite so well as low. When he led Stephen to his cabin he showed its furnishings with a somewhat tiresome exultation, though insisting that this arrangement was merely temporary: 'not quite the thing for a post-captain – passable in a sloop, but a trifle shabby in a frigate.' The cabin, like most of those in rated ships, was a strikingly beautiful room: in Corbett's time it had been bare scrubbed wood, gleaming brass, shining windows, and little more; now that Spartan interior, rather too large for Clonfert's possessions, looked as though a brothel had moved into a monastery, and as though it had not yet settled down. The size of the room was increased by two large pier-glasses that Clonfert had brought with him from the *Otter*, one to port, the other to starboard: he strode to and fro between them telling Stephen the history of the hanging lamp in some detail; and Stephen, sitting cross-legged upon the sofa, noticed that at each turn Clonfert automatically glanced at his reflection with a look of inquiry, doubt, and complacence.

During dinner the Captain ran on about his Turkish and Syrian experiences with Sir Sydney Smith, and at some point Stephen became aware that for Clonfert he had ceased to be a table-companion and had turned into an audience. It was quite unlike their friendly discourse of some days before, and presently Stephen grew sadly bored: lies or half-lies, he reflected, had a certain value in that they gave a picture of what the man would wish to seem; but a very few were enough for that. And then they had a striving, aggressive quality, as though the listener had to be bludgeoned into admiration; they were the antithesis of conversation. 'They can also be embarrassing,' he thought, looking down at his plate, for Clonfert was now astride that unfortunate unicorn: it was a handsome plate, with the Scroggs crest engraved broad and fair upon the rim; but it was a Sheffield plate, and the copper was showing through. 'Embarrassing and hard work; since in common humanity one must keep the man in countenance. What a state of nervous excitement he is in, to be sure.'

Yet although Stephen kept Clonfert decently in countenance, mutely acquiescing in the unicorn and a variety of unlikely feats, he did not put such violence upon himself as to encourage a very long continuation; eventually Clonfert grew conscious that he had somehow missed the tone, that his audience was not

impressed, was not with him, and an anxious look came into his eye. He laid himself out to be more agreeable, speaking once again of his gratitude for Stephen's care of him during his seizure. 'It is a wretched unmanly kind of disease,' he said. 'I have begged McAdam to use the knife, if it would do any good, but he seems to think it nervous, something like a fit of the mother. I do not suppose the Commodore ever suffers from anything of that kind?'

'If he did, I should certainly not speak of his disorder, nor the disorder of any other patient under my hands,' said Stephen. 'But,' he added more kindly, 'you are not to suppose that there is anything in the least discreditable in your malady. The degree of pain exceeds anything I have seen in any tormina, whatever their origin.' Clonfert looked pleased, and Stephen went on, 'It is a grave matter, indeed; and you are fortunate in having such an adviser as Dr McAdam in daily reach. I believe, with your leave, that I shall wait upon him presently.'

'Honest McAdam, yes,' said Clonfert, with a return to his former manner. 'Yes. He may be no Solomon, and we must overlook certain frailties and an unfortunate manner; but I believe he is sincerely devoted to me. He was somewhat indisposed this morning, or he would have paid his respects when you came aboard; but I believe he is up and about by now.'

McAdam was in his sick-bay, looking frail. Fortunately for the Néréides his mate, Mr Fenton, was a sound practical ship's surgeon, for McAdam had little interest in physical medicine. He showed Stephen his few cases, and they lingered a while over a seaman whose inoperable gummata were pressing on his brain in such a manner that his speech followed an inverted logic of its own. 'The sequence is not without its value,' said McAdam, 'though it is scarcely in my line. For that matter there is little scope for my studies in a ship of war. Come away below, and we will take a drop.' Far below, in the smell of bilge-water and grog, he went on, 'Mighty little scope. The lower deck is kept far too busy for much to develop apart from the common perversions. Not that I would have you understand that I agree for a moment with the wicked old Bedlam chains and straw and cold water and whipping; but there may be some fancies that in the egg cannot stand a wee starting with a rope's end, nor close company. At any rate I have not had a decent melancholia from the lower deck this commission. Manias, yes; but they are two a penny. No: it is aft that you must look for your fine flower of derangement,

not forgetting the pursers and clerks and schoolmasters, all mewed up more or less alone; but above all your captains – that is where the really interesting cases lie. How did you find our patient?'

'In a high flow of spirits. The helebore answers, I believe?'

For some time they discussed valerian, polypody of the oak, and stinking gladwin, their effects, and Stephen recommended the moderate use of coffee and tobacco; then McAdam branched off to ask, 'And did he speak of Captain Aubrey, at all?'

'Barely. In the circumstances it was an omission that I found remarkable.'

'Aye, and significant too, colleague, most significant. He has been on about Captain Aubrey these last days, and I took particular notice of the *sudor insignis* that you pointed out. It coincides within an hour or so. He was obliged to shift his coat after every bout: he has a chestful, and the right side of each one is pale from scrubbing away the salt, the right side alone.'

'It would be interesting to analyse that salt. Belladonna would suppress the sweat, of course. No more grog, I thank you. But it appears to me that for our patient truth is what he can persuade others to believe: yet at the same time he is a man of some parts, and I suspect that were you to attack him through his reason, were you to persuade him to abandon this self-defeating practice, with its anxiety, its probability of detection, and to seek only a more legitimate approval, then we should have no need for belladonna or any other anhidrotic.'

'You are coming into my way of thinking, I find: but you are not come far enough. The trouble lies much deeper, and it is through unreason that the whole nexus must be attacked. Your belladonna and your logic are pills from the same box: they only suppress the symptom.'

'How do you propose to attain this end?'

'Listen now, will you,' cried McAdam, slopping out a full tumbler and drawing his chair so near that his breath wafted in Stephen's face, 'and I will tell you.'

In his diary that night Stephen wrote, 'if he could carry out a reconstruction of the Irish political and social history for the last few ages which has formed our patient, and then a similar rebuilding of his mind from its foundation in early childhood to the present day, McAdam's scheme would be admirable. Yet even for the second part, what tools does he dispose of? A pickaxe is all. A pickaxe to repair a chronometer, and a pickaxe

in drunken hands at that. For my part I have a higher opinion of Clonfert's understanding if not of his judgment than has my poor sodden colleague.'

This higher opinion was confirmed the next evening, when the *Néréide* made her way through a wicked series of reefs off Cape Brabant and the gig put Stephen and the captain ashore in a little creek; and the next, when the black pilot not only took them into a still lagoon but also guided them through the forest to a village where Stephen had a conversation with a second potential ally; and again some days later during a stroll behind Port South-East with a packet of subversive papers.

As he told Jack on rejoining the *Boadicea*, 'Clonfert may not be his own best friend in some ways, but he is capable of a steadiness and a resolution that surprised me; and I must observe, that he perpetually took notes of the depth of the water and of the bearings in what I am persuaded you would call a seamanlike manner.'

'So much the better,' cried Jack. 'I am delighted to hear it, upon my word and honour. I have been doing something in that line myself, with young Richardson: he promises to be a capital hydrographer. We have laid down most of the nearby coast, with double angles and any number of soundings. And I have discovered a watering-place on Flat Island, a few leagues to the northwards; so we shall not have to be perpetually fagging out to Rodriguez.'

'No Rodriguez,' said Stephen in a low voice.

'Oh, you shall see Rodriguez again,' said Jack. 'We still have to put in there for stores, turn and turn about; but not quite so often.'

Turn and turn about they went, while the French remained obstinately at peace in their deep harbour, fitting themselves out anew to the last dump-bolt; and turn by turn, when he was not away in the *Néréide* down the coast, Stephen moved into each departing ship. His limestone caves on Rodriguez fulfilled all their golden promise; Colonel Keating was kindness itself, providing fatigue-parties and draining a small marsh; and by the third turn Stephen was able to report that from the bones found in the mud alone he could almost promise Jack the sight of a complete skeleton of the solitaire within the next two months, while at the same time he might partially clothe it with feathers and pieces of skin found in the caves.

For the rest of the time it was plain blockade, inshore at night,

off the capes by day, but never far, lest a Frenchman should slip out on the land-breeze, go north about in the darkness and bear away for the rich waters of the Indian Ocean, leaving the squadron a great way to leeward. Up and down, up and down, and all the time their thin canvas grew thinner in the tropical sun and the sudden prodigious downpours, their running rigging, incessantly passing through the countless blocks as they trimmed sail, gradually wasted away in those wisps called shakings, and the weed accumulated on their bottoms, while through the gaps in their copper the teredos thrust their augers through the oak.

Christmas, and an immense feast on the upper deck of the *Boadicea*, with a barrel of providently salted penguins from off the Cape serving as geese or turkeys, according to the taste and fancy of the mess, and plum-duff blazing faint blue under the awnings spread against the fiercer blaze of the Mauritian sun. New Year, with a great deal of ship-visiting; Twelfth Night, and the midshipmen's berth regaled the gun-room with a two-hundred-pound turtle – an unfortunate experiment, for it was the wrong kind of turtle: the shell turned into glue, and all who had eaten of the creature pissed emerald green; and now Jack began to consult his barometer every watch.

It was a handsome, heavily-protected brass instrument hanging in gimbals by the table on which they breakfasted, and he was unscrewing its bottom when Stephen observed, 'I shall soon have to think of another trip to La Réunion. This Mauritius brew is sad stuff, in comparison.'

'Very true,' said Jack. 'But drink it while you may. Carpe diem, Stephen: you may not get another cup. I unscrewed this shield, because I thought the tube must have broke. But here is the quicksilver, do you see, lower than I have ever seen it in my life. You had better stow your bones in the safest place you can think of. We are in for an uncommon hearty blow.'

Stephen swept the vertebrae he had been sorting into his napkin and followed Jack on deck. The sky was pure and innocent, the swell rather less than usual: on the starboard bow the familiar landscape lay broad and green under the eastern sun. '*Magicienne* is at it already,' said Jack, glancing at the busy hands over the water, setting up double preventer-stays. '*Néréide* has been caught napping. Mr Johnson: *squadron make sail; course due west; prepare for heavy weather*.' He turned his glass to Port-Louis: yes, there was no fear of the French slipping out. They too could read a barometer, and they too were making all fast.

'Might this portend a hurricano?' asked Stephen privately in his ear.

'Yes,' said Jack, 'and we must have all the sea-room we can win. How I wish Madagascar were farther off.'

They won forty miles of sea-room; the boats on the booms could scarcely be seen for frappings; the guns were double-breached, bowsed up against the side until they made it groan; topgallantmasts were down on deck; storm-canvas bent; spare gaskets, rolling-tackles, spritsail-yard fore and aft – all that a great deal of activity and experienced seamanship could accomplish was done: and all under the same pure sun.

The swell increased long before a darkness gathered in the north. 'Mr Seymour,' said Jack, 'tarpaulins and battens for the hatchways. When it comes, it will blow across the sea.'

It came, a curved white line racing across the sea with inconceivable rapidity, a mile in front of the darkness. Just before it reached them the *Boadicea*'s close-reefed topsails sagged, losing all their roundness; then a tearing wall of air and water ripped them from their bolt-tops with an enormous shrieking howl. The ship was on her beam-ends, the darkness was upon them and the known world dissolved in a vast omnipresent noise. Air and water were intermingled; there was no surface to the sea; the sky vanished; and the distinction between up and down disappeared. Disappeared momentarily for those on deck, more durably for Dr Maturin, who, having pitched down two ladders, found himself lying on the ship's side. Presently, she righted and he slid down; but on her taking a most furious lee-lurch on wearing round, he shot across the deck, through all his remaining stock of Venice treacle, to land on hands and knees upon the other side, clinging to a suspended locker in the darkness, puzzled.

In time gravity reasserted itself; he climbed down, still mazed from the prodigious din and by his tumbles, and groped his way forward to the sick-bay. Here Carol, nominally his assistant but in fact the virtual surgeon of the frigate, and the loblolly-boy had preserved their lantern, by whose light they were disentangling their only patient, a poxed member of the afterguard, whose hammock, twirling in the violent motion, had enveloped him like a cocoon.

Here they remained, hooting lugubriously to one another for a while. Rank had little significance in this pandemonium, and the loblolly-boy, an ancient man once sailmaker's crew and

still good at sewing, told them in his shrill, carrying voice that in Jamaica as a boy he had known seven ships of the line founder with all hands in a blow not half as hugeous as this here. Presently Stephen shouted, 'Come aft, Mr Carol, and let us take all the lanterns we can find. The casualties will soon be coming down.'

They crept aft through the darkness – deadlights shipped long since, and the air that came blasting down was charged with shattered water, not light – and to them were brought the injured men: one from the wheel, his ribs cracked by the flying spokes; a small, light reefer dashed by the wind against the hances, and now limp, insensible; Mr Peter, who had made the same plunge as Stephen, though less luckily; more ribs, some broken limbs. Then, as lightning struck the ship, three men quite dazed and one with a shocking burn, dead before they brought him below.

Bandaging, splinting, operating in a space that heaved through forty-five degrees in all directions and on chests that shifted and slid beneath them, they worked on and on. At one point a messenger from the quarterdeck came with the Commodore's compliments and was all well, together with something about 'eight hours'; and then, much, much later, when the ship had been on a comparatively even keel for some time, with no new cases coming below and the last of the fractured clavicles reduced, there was the Commodore himself, streaming wet, in his shirt and breeches. He looked round, spoke to those casualties in any condition to hear him, and then in a hoarse voice he said to Stephen, 'If you have a moment at any time, Doctor, you will find a curious sight on deck.'

Stephen finished his bandage with a neat double turn and made his way up through the small hole in the canvas-covered hatch. He stood blinking in the extraordinary orange-tawny light, bracing himself against the flying air, as solid as a wall. 'The lifeline, sir,' cried a seaman, putting it into his hand. 'Clap on to the lifeline for all love.'

'Thank you, friend,' said Stephen, gazing about him, and as he spoke he realized that the enormous universal roar had diminished: it was now slightly less than that of continuous battle at close quarters. The *Boadicea* was lying to under a scrap of mizen staysail, riding the tremendous seas nobly, shouldering them aside with her bluff bows: her fore and main topmasts had gone by the board; wild ropes by the score stretched horizontally

aft from the wrecked tops, sometimes cracking as loud as a gun; her remaining shrouds were packed with scraps of seaweed and pieces of terrestrial vegetation – a palm-frond was clearly recognizable. But this was not the curious sight. From the drowned forecastle aft, and particularly on the quarterdeck, wherever there was the slightest lee, there were birds. Seabirds for the most part, but right by him a little creature like a thrush. It did not move as he approached it, nor even when he touched its back. The others were the same, and he looked into the lustrous eye of a bosun-bird within a few inches. In this unearthly lurid glow it was hard to make out their true colours or their kind, but he did distinguish a white-headed noddy, scarcely to be seen within five thousand miles of the Mauritius. As he was struggling towards it a sort of growl in the orange clouds immediately above overcame the general roar, and in a second it was followed by a thunder so intolerably vast that it filled all the air about him; and with the thunder a blaze of lightning struck the ship again. He was flung down, and picking himself up with a confused recollection of a triple stroke, of a forward gun having gone off, blasting out its portlid, he crawled below to wait for the wounded.

There were no wounded. Instead there appeared a piece of jellied veal, brought by Killick with the message that 'the thunderbolt had made hay of the best bower anchor, but otherwise all was well; that unless they were taken aback in the next hour or so, the Commodore thought they might be through the worst of it; and that he hoped Dr Maturin might see better weather in the morning.'

Having slept like a corpse through the middle watch, and having attended his urgent cases at first light, Dr Maturin did indeed see better weather when he came on deck. The sky was the most perfect blue, the sun delightfully warm, the gentle southeast wind refreshing: there was an enormous swell, but no white water, and apart from the desolation of the deck, the steady gush of the pumps, and the worn look of all hands, yesterday might have been a nightmare out of time. Yet there were other proofs: Mr Trollope, the second lieutenant, limped up to him and pointed out two ships of the squadron, far, far to leeward: the *Magicienne*, with her mizen gone, and the *Sirius*, with no topmasts standing.

'Where is the Commodore?' asked Stephen.

'He turned in half a glass ago. I begged him to get some sleep. But before he went below he told me to take care to show you

the best bower, a most amazing philosophical sight.'

Stephen considered the fused, distorted metal, and said, 'We seem to be heading south?'

'South-west as near as ever we can, with our compasses run mad because of the lightning; south-west for the Cape to refit. And don't we wish we may get there, ha, ha!'

Chapter Six

There were no banquets at the Cape for Jack Aubrey; there were few kind words from the Admiral, either, although the Commodore had brought in all his squadron safe after one of the worst blows this last decade; and there were less, if less were possible, when an American barque arrived with the news that the *Bellone*, *Minerve*, and *Victor* were out – she had spoken them off the Cargados Garayos, standing north-east under a press of sail to cruise for Indiamen in the Bay of Bengal.

Not that Jack had any leisure for feasting in Cape Town or for comfortable chat with Admiral Bertie: it was an anxious, hurried time for him, with five ships to be refitted by a small yard with scarcely a spare frigate-topmast in it – supplies were expected from India – and no fit timber much nearer than Mossel Bay. A small, ill-furnished yard, and one governed by men of a rapacity that Jack had never seen equalled in all his long experience: the squadron was known to have done well for itself at St Paul's, and the yard was going to have a proper share come hell or high water, regardless of the fact that all this wealth depended on leisurely decisions to be taken far away at some future date – that the squadron had very little cash in hand, and could only take it up by bills at a usurious rate of interest. An anxious time, with the Frenchmen out; and one rendered more anxious still, as far as Jack was concerned, by a host of factors. By the steady obstruction of those in control of spars, cordage, paint, blocks, copper, iron-work, and the countless other objects the squadron cried out for. By the Admiral's apparent indifference to very gross corruption: Aubrey must be aware that dock-yard people were not plaster saints, observed Mr Bertie, nor yet choir-boys; these things should be settled as they were usually settled in the Navy; and for his part he did not give a straw how the Commodore set about it, so long as the squadron was ready for sea by Tuesday sennight at the latest. By the discovery that his own Mr Fellowes, seduced by the bosun of the *Sirius* and a desire to be rich now rather than at some later period when he might be dead, had not only looked upon the thunderstruck best bower as a perquisite, but had done the same by the kedge, fifty fathom of two-inch rope, and an unreasonable quantity of other stores – a

court-martial quantity. By contention among his captains as to who should be served first from the meagre supplies whose existence the dock-yard could not conceal. And above all by the loss of one vessel carrying mail and by the arrival of another so thoroughly soaked by rain-storms under the line that all letters apart from those wrapped in waxed sailcloth had mouldered and partly coalesced; Sophie had never learnt to use waxed sailcloth, nor to number her letters, nor to send copies in another bottom.

Immediately after the arrival of this blotting-paper packet, Jack snatched an interval between visits to the master-attendant and the rope-walk and tried to disentangle the sequence with the help of such dates as 'Friday' or 'after church'. But this interval was also seized upon by Mr Peter, whose great sheaf of documents reminded Jack of his duty as a commodore: all that he had told the Commander-in-chief by word of mouth had to be cast into official, written form, carefully read over and considered. Very carefully, for although Jack was the least suspicious creature afloat, Stephen was not, and he had pointed out that it might be wise to regard Mr Peter as a functionary with loyalties on land rather than as a confidential ally. And then there was his duty as captain of the *Boadicea*: although his first lieutenant saw to the daily running of the ship, Mr Seymour was now exceedingly busy with the refitting, and in any case there were several things that necessarily fell to the captain. It was he who persuaded Mr Collins, now at eighteen the senior master's mate, that he was not absolutely required to marry the young lady who alleged that, as a direct consequence of Mr Collins' attentions, all her girdles were now too tight; still less to marry her at once. 'A fortnight is not enough, in these affairs,' he said. 'It may be only an indigestion, a pound or two of beefsteak pudding. Wait until we come in from the next cruise. And until then, Mr Collins, I desire you will not leave the ship. Though indeed,' he added, 'was you to marry every girl you play love-tokens with, when ashore, the place would very soon come to look like Abraham's bosom.'

It was he who patiently listened to an indignant, rambling account of sharp practice far away, delivered by Matthew Bolton, forecastleman, starboard watch, in his own name and in that of three mute companions unnaturally shaved and scraped. Bolton had refused Mr Seymour's help, on the grounds that as the Commodore had pulled him out of the sea when they were shipmates in the *Polychrest*, it obviously fell to him to do the

same throughout the length of Bolton's natural life.

This was a logic that seemed convincing to Bolton, the first lieutenant and the Commodore; and when Jack had extracted the facts from the circumstantial details, a description of the grass-combing bugger that had tried this guardo-move, and an account of Mrs Bolton's state of health, he reached for a pen, and, watched very closely indeed by the four seamen, wrote a letter, which he then read out to them in a harsh, all-hands-to-punishment voice that gave the utmost satisfaction:

> *'Boadicea,*
> Simon's Town
>
> Sir,
> Conformably to the wishes of the men named in the margin, late of the *Néréide*, and now on board of his Majesty's ship under my command, I acquaint you that unless the prize-money due to them for Buenos Ayres and Monte Video, and received by you under their power of attorney, is forthwith paid, I shall state the case to the Lords Commissioners of the Admiralty, with a request that their solicitor may be directed to sue for the same.
>
> I am, etc.

There,' he said, 'that will clap a stopper over his antics. Now, Bolton, if the Doctor is aboard, I should like to see him when he is at leisure.'

As it happened the Doctor was not on board. He was half way between Cape Town, where he had left Mr Farquhar, and False Bay, sitting in a sparse grove of proteas in a dust-storm, clasping a loose portfolio of plants to be dried for his herbal, and dividing what attention he had left between a small flock of crested mouse-birds and a troop of baboons. Presently he came down to the harbour, where he washed away some of the dust at his usual tavern and received from the landlord (an obliging African of Huguenot descent) the foetus of a porcupine: and here, as he had expected, he found McAdam, sitting in front of a bottle that would have preserved the foetus almost indefinitely. Little of it had been drunk, however, and McAdam entertained him with a reasonable account of their patient's extraordinary activity and flow of spirits. Lord Clonfert, it appeared, was up well before dawn every day (a rare occurrence), inspiring all hands with a sense of extreme urgency; he had bleared Pym's eye over a couple of topgallant yards by means of a thumping bribe;

and he was now negotiating with a known receiver of stolen goods for a gig. 'Sure it will break his heart if he is not the first that is ready for sea,' said McAdam. 'He has set his soul on out-doing the Commodore.'

'May we not in part attribute his activity to the roborative, stimulating use of coffee, and to the general soothing effect of mild tobacco, which has set his humours in equilibrio? Tobacco, divine, rare, superexcellent tobacco, which goes far beyond all their panaceas, potable gold, and philosopher's stones, a sovereign remedy to all diseases. A good vomit, I confess, a virtuous herb, if it be well qualified and opportunely taken, and medicinally used, but as it is commonly abused by most men, which take it as tinkers do ale, 'tis a plague, a mischief, a violent purger of goods, lands, health; hellish, devilish and damned tobacco, the ruin and overthrow of body and soul. Here, however, it *is* medicinally taken; and I congratulate myself upon the fact, that in your hands there is no question of tinkers' abuse.'

The flying dust, the incessant wind, had made McAdam more gross than usual; he had never cordially liked Stephen's prescription of coffee and tobacco; and from his wavering, red-rimmed eye it seemed that he was meditating a coarse remark. Indeed, he began 'A fig for . . .' but having belched at this point he reconsidered his words, fixed his gaze on the bottle, and continued, 'No, no: you do not have to be a conjuror to see it is all emulation. If the one is your dashing frigate-captain, t'other will be your dashing frigate-captain to the power of ten, whether or no. He will outdo the Commodore though he burst.'

It would not be difficult to outdo the Commodore in his present state, the creature, reflected Stephen as he walked into the cabin: not, at least, in the article of speed. Captain Aubrey was completely surrounded by papers, including those of the courts-martial that were to be held over the next few days – the usual offences of desertion and violence or disobedience or both when drunk: but time-consuming – and upon them all he had laid out the mildewed sheets of his private correspondence.

'There you are, Stephen,' he cried. 'How happy I am to see you. What have you there?'

'An unborn porcupine.'

'Well, there's glory for you. But Stephen, you are a rare one for making out a secret hand, I am sure. Would you help me try to find out the sequence of these letters, and perhaps even the sense?'

Together they pored over the sheets, using a magnifying-glass, intuition, crocus of antimony, and a little diluted copperas; but to small effect.

'I do make out that the Old Nonpareils we planted had three apples apiece, and that the strawberries failed,' said Jack, 'and she obviously heard from Ommaney, because here is the parlour chimney drawing fit to turn a mill, and a Jersey cow – the children have hair, and teeth, any number of teeth, poor little souls. Hair: with all my heart, though she does say it is straight. Straight or frizzled, 'tis all one: they will look far better with some hair – Lord, Stephen, it must have been their hair I blew away, thinking it was shakings that had got into the cover.' He crept about for some time and came up with a little wisp. 'Very like shakings, however,' he said, folding it into his pocket-book and returning to the letters. 'Neighbours most attentive: here is another brace of pheasants from Mr Beach last Thursday. But in this one she says she is well, surprisingly well, underlined twice: says it again in what I take to be the last. I am heartily glad of it, of course, yet why *surprisingly*? Has she been ill? And what is this about her mother? Could the second word be palsy? If Mrs Williams has been sick, with Sophie looking after her, that might explain the surprisingly.'

They pored again, and Stephen almost certainly deciphered a hare, a present from Captain Polixfen, eaten jugged on Saturday or Sunday or both; and something about the rain. All the rest was mere conjecture.

'I think Old Jarvie was altogether wrong in saying that a sea-officer had no business to marry,' said Jack, carefully gathering the sheets. 'Yet I can see what he meant. I should not be un-married for the world, you know; no, not for a flag; but you cannot conceive how my mind has been going back to Ashgrove Cottage these days, when I should be thinking about getting the squadron to sea.' He jerked his head over his shoulder and stared out of the scuttle for a while before adding, 'These God-damned courts-martial: and what to do about the land-sharks in the yard. To say nothing of the bosun and his infernal capers.'

During supper he picked at his mutton, setting out the difficulty of dealing with Mr Fellowes: disposing of His Majesty's property was an immemorial practice among His Majesty's servants – if the objects were damaged it was almost legitimate by length of custom – and in the Navy it went by the name of cappabar. Pursers, carpenters, and bosuns stole most, having more to steal,

and better opportunities; but there were limits, and Fellowes had not confined himself to damaged goods, nor to those of slight value. He had carried cappabar too high by far – the thing was flagrant – and Jack could bring him before a court-martial and have him broke tomorrow. It was Jack's duty to have him broke. On the other hand, it was also his duty to keep his ship in the highest possible fighting-trim: for that he needed a first-rate bosun: and first-rate bosuns did not grow on trees, at the Cape. First-rate bosuns were not twelve a penny. He grew a little heated on the subject, cursing Fellowes for a half-witted zany, a mad lunatic, a fling-it-down-the-gutter sodomite; but his heart was not in it; his epithets lacked real warmth and inventiveness; and his mind was clearly still far away in Hampshire.

'Come,' said Stephen, 'if ever the Madras establishment fulfils its undertakings, and we move on La Réunion, which I begin to doubt, Mr Farquhar will be with us, and that will be an end to our music. Let us play my old lament for the Tir na nOg; I too am mighty low, and it will serve as a counter-irritant. Like will be cured by like.'

Jack said that he would be very happy to lament with Stephen until the moon went down, but with messengers expected from Cape Town and from every official in the yard, he did not expect they should reach any very high flow of soul before they were interrupted. In the event they had not even tuned their strings when Spotted Dick appeared, to state, with Mr Johnson's duty, that *Iphigenia* was off the point, had made her number, and was standing in.

With a brisk south-east wind and the making tide she had dropped anchor before moonrise, and the news that Captain Lambert brought drove all thoughts of England and of music from Jack Aubrey's head. The *Iphigenia*, that fine thirty-six-gun eighteen-pounder frigate, escorting a small fleet of transports, had reinforced Colonel Keating at Rodriguez to the extent of two regiments of European troops, two of Indian, and some auxiliaries: the numbers were fifteen hundred short of what had been hoped for, but the soldiers had done their best: they had kept very nearly to their time, and the definitive attack on La Réunion was now a possibility, though a hazardous one, above all if the French had moved fresh forces into the island. They would certainly have had time to remount their batteries.

The first thing to do was to find out what ships Governor Decaen had in Mauritius, and, if it could be done, to shut them

up in their harbours. 'Captain Lambert,' he said, 'what is the state of the *Iphigenia*?'

He did not know Lambert at all, a recently-promoted young man, but he liked the look of him – a small round jolly sailor with a capable air – and he fairly loved him when he took a paper from his pocket and said, 'These are my officers' reports, sir, made as we were standing in. Purser: provisions for nine weeks in full, of all species, except rum: of that, only thirty-nine days. Master: one hundred and thirteen tons of water; beef very good, pork sometimes shrinks in the boiling; the rest of the provisions very good. I should add, sir, that we watered, wooded, and tortoised at Rodriguez. Gunner: eighteen rounds of powder filled; plenty of wads; forty rounds. Carpenter: hull in good state; knees of the head supported by two cheeks; masts and yards in good state; pretty well stored. Surgeon: in the sick list, three men, objects for invaliding; portable soup, fifty-seven pounds; other necessaries to the 19th of next month only. And as for my people, sir, we are only sixteen short of complement.'

'Then I take it you can sail at once, Captain Lambert?'

'The moment we have won our anchors, sir, unless you wish me to slip. Though I should be happy to take in a little powder and shot, and some greenstuff: my surgeon is not quite happy about his lime-juice.'

'Very good, very good, Captain Lambert,' said Jack, chuckling. 'You shall certainly have your powder and shot. Never trouble with that damned yard at this time of night: I have more than we can safely stow, from St Paul's, and my gunner will have to disgorge the surplus. And you may have six of our bullocks that are waiting on the beach. As for your greenstuff, my purser has an excellent unofficial man on shore, will rouse you out any quantity in half an hour. Mr Peter, be so good as to prepare a letter to the Admiral, to go at once: Mr Richardson is our best jockey, I believe – tell him to never mind the lions and tigers on the road; they are all gammon, for the most part. Then, an order for Captain Lambert – proceed to sea on the ebb, rendezvous off Port-Louis, copies of private signals, alternative rendezvous at Rodriguez after the – let me consider – the seventeenth. And let all captains come aboard. Killick, pass the word for the gunner, and bring a bottle of the Constantia with the yellow seal. The yellow seal, d'ye hear me?'

Between the signing of the papers and the interview with the reluctant gunner they drank their bottle, the best bottle in the

ship, and the captains began to arrive: their coxswains could be heard answering the sentry's hail in quick succession: '*Néréide*', '*Sirius*', '*Otter*', '*Magicienne*'.

'Now, gentlemen,' said the Commodore, when they were all assembled, 'when can your ships proceed to sea?'

If it were not for Pym's vile newfangled iron tanks, the *Sirius* could be ready in a couple of days: if it had not been for the yard's incomprehensible delay over the long-promised iron horse, the *Otter* might say the same. '*Néréide* will be ready for sea in thirty-six hours,' said Clonfert, smiling with intent at Captain Pym: but the smile changed to a look of surprised vexation when Curtis said, 'The *Magicienne* can sail this minute, sir, if I may have leave to water at Flat Island. We are no more than thirty ton shy.'

'I am delighted to hear it, Captain Curtis,' said Jack. 'Delighted. *Magicienne* and *Iphigenia* will proceed to Port-Louis with the utmost dispatch. Mr Peter will give you your orders; and with this wind you might be well advised to warp out into the fairway to catch the first minute of the ebb.'

They received their orders; they warped out into the fairway; and dawn saw the two frigates beating out of the bay, to vanish, close-hauled, round the Cape of Good Hope by the time the cabin's breakfast of eggs and mutton-ham came aft in a cloud of fragrance. Shortly afterwards Captain Eliot arrived with a formal order from the Admiral directing the Commodore to convene his court-martial, and a letter in which he congratulated Jack on this splendid accession of force at Rodriguez, from which the country might confidently expect wonders in a very short time indeed, particularly as for the next few weeks the squadron would have the use of the *Leopard*. The horrible old *Leopard*.

Jack changed into his full-dress uniform; the ominous union flag broke out at the *Boadicea*'s peak; the captains gathered; and with Mr Peter acting as deputy judge-advocate they set about the unpleasant business of trying poor Captain Woolcombe for the loss of the *Laurel* of twenty-two guns, captured by the *Canonnière* – the Frenchman's last fight – off Port-Louis before Jack came to the Cape: for until this time a sufficient number of senior officers had never been in Simon's Town long enough for the court to be formed, and poor Woolcombe had been under nominal arrest ever since he had been exchanged. Everyone knew that in the circumstances, with the *Canonnière* in sight of her home port, carrying an enormous land-based crew and mounting

155

more than twice the number of far heavier guns, no blame could be attached to the *Laurel*'s captain; everyone knew that there must be an honourable acquittal – everybody except Woolcombe, for whom the issue was far too important for any certainty whatsoever and who sat throughout the long proceedings with a face of such anxiety that it made the members of the court very thoughtful indeed. Each one of them might find himself in the same position, faced perhaps with ill-disposed judges, differing from him in politics or service loyalties or bearing him some long-nourished grudge: a court of amateur lawyers, from whose decision there was no appeal. Illogically, perhaps, since they themselves had framed the verdict, every member of the court shared in Woolcombe's glowing relief when the judge-advocate read it out, and when Jack handed back the captain's sword with an elegant if somewhat studied formal speech. They were happy with Captain Woolcombe, and the sentences for some of the desertions and embezzlements that followed were quite remarkably light. Yet for all that the sentences took a great while to reach: the stately process went on and on. In his own ship a captain could deal with any delinquent foremast hand so long as the offence did not carry the death-sentence, but he could not touch any officer holding a commission or a warrant; they had to come before the court; and at times it seemed to Jack, on the boil with impatience to get to sea, to make the most of the situation before the French knew of the forces on Rodriguez, before they had fully reorganized themselves on La Réunion, that no warrant officer in the squadron had found any better use for his time than getting drunk, over-staying his leave, disobeying, insulting, and even beating his superiors, and making away with the stores entrusted to his care. Indeed, a steady diet of courts-martial gave a most unpleasant impression of the Royal Navy: crime, oppression, complaints of illegal conduct, sometimes justified, sometimes fabricated or malicious (one master charged his captain with keeping false musters, on the grounds that he had a friend's son on the ship's books when in fact the young gentleman was at school in England, a perfectly normal practice, but one which would have wrecked the captain's career if the court had not performed some singular acrobatics to save him), brawling in the wardroom, ungentlemanly behaviour, officers against captain, captain against officers, evidence of long-standing ill-will; and all the bloody violence of the lower deck.

Between these grim sessions the presiding judge turned sailor again, and he drove on the refitting of his ships, fighting a most determined battle against obstruction and delay. But having all the time in the world, the dock-yard won hands down; they had gauged his needs and his impatience quite exactly, and he had not only to bleed borrowed gold at every vein, but even to thank his extortioners before the last sack of thirty-penny nails and ten-inch spikes came aboard. These actions took place at dawn and dusk, for at dinner-time the president of the court necessarily entertained the other members.

'Pray, Commodore, do you not find passing sentence of death cut your appetite?' asked Stephen, as he watched Jack carve a saddle of mutton.

'I cannot say I do,' said the Commodore, passing Captain Woolcombe a slice that dripped guiltless blood. 'I don't like it, to be sure; and if the court can possibly find a lesser offence, I think I should always give my vote for it. But when you have a straightforward case of cowardice or neglect of duty, why, then it seems to me plain enough: the man must be hanged, and the Lord have mercy on his soul, for the service will have none. I am sorry for it, but it don't affect my appetite. Captain Eliot, may I help you to a little of the undercut?'

'It seems to me perfectly barbarous,' observed Stephen.

'But surely, sir,' said Captain Pym, 'surely a medical man will cut off a gangrened limb to save the rest of the body?'

'A medical man does not cut off the limb in any spirit of corporate revenge, nor *in terrorem*; he does not make a solemn show of the amputation, nor is the peccant limb attended by all the marks of ignominy. No, sir: your analogy may be specious, but it is not sound. Furthermore, sir, you are to consider, that in making it you liken the surgeon to a common hangman, an infamous character held in universal contempt and detestation. And the infamy attaching to the executioner arises from what he does: the language of all nations condemns the man and *a fortiori* his act: which helps to make my point more forcibly.'

Captain Pym protested that he had not intended the least reflection upon surgeons – a capital body of men, essential in a ship, and on shore too, no doubt: he would not meddle with analogies any more; but still perhaps he might adventure to say that it was a hard service, and it needed a hard discipline.

'There was a man,' remarked Captain Eliot, 'who was sentenced to death for stealing a horse from a common. He said to

the judge, that he thought it hard to be hanged for stealing a horse from a common; and the judge answered, "You are not to be hanged for stealing a horse from a common, but that others may not steal horses from commons." '

'And do you find,' asked Stephen, 'that in fact horses are not daily stolen from commons? You do not. Nor do I believe that you will make captains braver or wiser by hanging or shooting them for cowardice or erroneous judgment. It should join the ordeal of the ploughshare, floating or pricking to prove witchcraft, and judicial combat, among the relics of a Gothic past.'

'Dr Maturin is quite right,' cried Lord Clonfert. 'A capital execution seems to me a revolting spectacle. Surely a man could be . . .'

His words were drowned in the general flow of talk that Stephen's word 'shooting' had set going; for Admiral Byng had been shot to death on his own quarterdeck. Almost everybody was speaking, except for Captain Woolcombe, who ate in wolfish silence, his first meal without anxiety; and the names of Byng and Keppel flew about.

'Gentlemen, gentlemen,' cried Jack, who saw the far more recent Gambier and Hervey and the unfortunate engagement in the Basque roads looming ahead, 'let us for Heaven's sake keep to our own humble level, and not meddle with admirals or any other god-like beings, or we shall presently run foul of politics, and that is the end of all comfortable talk.'

The noise diminished, but Clonfert's excited voice could be heard carrying on, '. . . the possibility of judicial error, and the value of human life – once it is gone, it cannot be brought back. There is nothing, nothing, so precious.'

He addressed himself to his neighbours and to those sitting opposite him; but none of the captains seemed eager to be the recipient, and there was the danger of an embarrassing silence, particularly as Stephen, convinced that two hundred years of talk would not shift his kind, bloody-minded companions an inch, had taken to rolling bread pills.

'As for the value of human life,' said Jack, 'I wonder whether you may not over-estimate it in theory; for in practice there is not one of us here, I believe, who would hesitate for a moment over pistoling a boarder, nor think twice about it afterwards. And for that matter, our ships are expressly made to blow as many people into kingdom come as possible.'

'It is a hard service, and it requires a hard discipline,' repeated

Pym, peering through his claret at the enormous joint.

'Yes, it is a hard service,' said Jack, 'and we often call our uniform buttons the curse of God; but a man – an officer – enters it voluntarily, and if he don't like the terms he can leave it whenever he chooses. He takes it on himself – he knows that if he does certain things, or leaves them undone, he is to be cashiered or even hanged. If he has not the fortitude to accept that, then he is better out of the service. And as for the value of human life, why, it often seems to me that there are far too many people in the world as it is; and one man, even a post-captain, nay' – smiling – 'even a commodore or a jack-in-the-green, is not to be balanced against the good of the service.'

'I entirely disagree with you, sir,' said Clonfert.

'Well, my lord, I hope it is the only point upon which we shall ever differ,' said Jack.

'The Tory view of a human life . . .' began Clonfert.

'Lord Clonfert,' called Jack in a strong voice, 'the bottle stands by you.' And immediately afterwards, aiming at bawdy, in which all could share, and quickly attaining it, he spoke of the striking increase – the potential increase – in the population of the colony since the squadron's arrival: 'a single member of my midshipmen's berth has already contrived to get two girls with child: one brown, the other isabella-coloured.' The others turned with equal relief to similar accounts, to reminiscences of burning wenches in Sumatra, at Port-au-Prince, in the Levantine ports; to rhymes, to conundrums; and the afternoon ended in general merriment.

The *Néréide*, her topgallantmasts and her new gig on board at last, left Simon's Town for Mauritius that evening: and as they stood watching her out of the bay, Stephen said to Jack, 'I am sorry I started that hare; it gave you some uneasiness, I am afraid. Had I recollected, I should not have asked it in public, for it was a private question – I asked for information sake. And now I do not know whether the public answer was that of the Commodore or of the plain, unpendanted Jack Aubrey.'

'It was something of both,' said Jack. 'I do in fact dislike hanging more than I said, though more for myself than for the hanged man: the first time I saw a man run up to the yardarm with a night cap over his eyes and his hands tied behind his back, when I was a little chap in the *Ramillies*, I was as sick as a dog. But as for the man himself, if he has deserved hanging, deserved it by our code, I find it don't signify so very much what happens

159

to him. It seems to me that men are of different value, and that if some are knocked on the head, the world is not much the poorer.'

'Sure, it is a point of view.'

'Perhaps it sounds a little hard; and perhaps I came it a little over-strong and righteous, when I was speaking, speaking as a commodore, to Clonfert.'

'You certainly gave him an impression of unbending severity and perfect rectitude.'

'Yes, I was pompous: yet I did not speak far beyond my own mind. Though I must confess he vexed me with his tragic airs and his human life – he has a singular genius for hitting the wrong note; people will accept that kind of thing from a learned man, but not from him; yet he will be prating. I hope he did not resent my checking him: I had to, you know, once he got on to Whigs and Tories. But I did it pretty civil, if you remember. I have a regard for him – few men could have got the *Néréide* out so quickly. Look, she is going about to weather the point. Prettily done – stays as brisk as a cutter, stays in her own length – he has a very good officer in his master: and he would be one himself too, with a little more ballast – a very good officer, was he a little less flighty.'

'It is curious to reflect,' wrote Stephen in his diary that night, 'that Jack Aubrey, with so very much more to lose, should value life so very much more lightly than Clonfert, whose immaterial possessions are so pitifully small, and who is partly aware of it. This afternoon's exchange confirms all that I have observed in my acquaintance with both. It is to be hoped, if only from a medical point of view, that some resounding action will soon give Clonfert a real basis – a sounder basis than his adventitious consequence. Nothing, as Milton observes, profits a man like proper self-esteem: I believe I have mangled the poor man; but here is Mr Farquhar, the all-knowing, who will set me right. If only there were another thousand men on Rodriguez, I might write Governor Farquhar with some confidence even now.'

Mr Farquhar came aboard, but with no ceremony and with so small a train – one secretary, one servant – that it was clear he had been listening to the military men in Cape Town, who had little opinion of the sepoy in his own country and none at all of his fighting qualities elsewhere. Their considered opinion was that the French officers were right when they said that five regiments of

European troops, supported by artillery, would be needed for a successful attack; that the hazards of landing on such a shore were so great that even five regiments were scarcely adequate, particularly as communication between the sea and the land might be cut off from one day to the next, and with it the troops' supplies; and that perhaps it would be better, all things considered, to wait for further reinforcements at the next monsoon.

'I wish I could share your sanguine outlook,' he said to Stephen, when at last he was in a fit condition to say anything at all (the *Boadicea* had had heavy weather until she reached the twenty-fifth parallel), 'but perhaps it is based upon more information than I possess?'

'No: my reports were tolerably complete,' said Stephen. 'But I am not sure that you or the soldiers attach the same weight to our present superiority in ships. If, as it appears likely, two of their frigates are away from the scene of action, our local advantage is five to two; a very great advantage, and in this I do not count the *Leopard*, which is, I am told, only a smaller *Raisonable*, the kind of vessel that is facetiously termed a coffin-ship by the sailors, of questionable use even as a transport. It was long before I came to appreciate the prodigious force represented by a man-of-war of the larger kind: we can all envisage the dreadful power of a battery, of a fortress belching fire; but a ship seems so peaceful an object, and to the untutored eye so very like the Holyhead packet writ large, that perhaps one does not easily see it as a vast battery in itself, and what is more a moveable battery that can turn its resistless fire in various directions, and then, its work of destruction completed, glide smoothly off to begin again elsewhere. The three frigates, my dear sir, the three frigates by which we presumably outnumber our adversaries, represent an enormous train of artillery, a train that is not painfully dragged by innumerable horses, but is borne by the wind. I have seen them in action upon this very coast, and I have been amazed. There are also the enemy's lines of supply to be considered: superiority at sea means that they may readily be severed.'

'I take your point,' said Farquhar. 'But the decisive battle must be fought on land; and the few regiments we possess must be put down on that land.'

'Yes,' said Stephen. 'What you say is very true. And I admit that these considerations would make me more doubtful of the issue than in fact I am, were I not supported by what you would

perhaps term an illogical source of hope.'

'It would be benevolent in you to share your comfort.'

'As you may know, in the service our Commodore is known as Lucky Jack Aubrey. I am not prepared to enter into the concept of luck, as it is vulgarly called: philosophically it is indefensible; in daily experience we see it to exist. All I will say is, that Captain Aubrey seems to possess it in an eminent degree; and it is that which cheers my sometimes pensive nights.'

'How I hope you are right,' cried Farquhar. 'How sincerely I hope you are right.' After a pause he added, 'For countless reasons: among them the fact that I do not touch emolument or allowance until I enter into my functions.' He paused again, passed his hand over his eyes, and swallowed painfully.

'Let us take a turn on deck,' said Stephen. 'The greenish pallor is invading your face again, no doubt induced by melancholy thoughts as much as by the motion of the ship. The brisk trade-wind will blow them away.'

The brisk trade-wind instantly plucked off Mr Farquhar's hat and wig. They flew forward, to be caught – a miracle of dexterity – by the bosun, who rose from the new best bower, seized the one in his right hand, the other in his left, and sent them aft by a midshipman. For his own part Mr Fellowes had preferred to keep the full length of the gangway between himself and the quarterdeck ever since a memorable day in Simon's Town, when the Commodore had had a private word with him, if private is quite the term for an explosion of honest rage that resounded from the after-cabin to the cutwater, filling the ship's company with mirth, glee, and apprehension, evenly mingled.

Covered once more, Mr Farquhar hooked himself into the rigging at Stephen's side; and as he gazed about him the corpse-like appearance faded from his face: the *Boadicea* was leaning over so that her lee chains were under the tearing white water and her weather side showed a broad streak of new copper; ahead of her the *Sirius*, under the same cloud of sail, kept as precisely to her station as though the two ships were joined by an iron bar; and together they were racing away to the north-east in the track of the *Néréide* to join the *Magicienne* and the *Iphigenia* off Port-Louis. They had already passed the *Leopard*, which had had two days' start (and which, since her captain was related to the Admiral, was strongly suspected of being present only to share in any prize money that might be going), and they were cracking on as though they meant to run off the two thousand miles and

more in under a fortnight – a real possibility, they having picked up the powerful trade so soon. 'Celerity is everything, in these operations,' he said, 'and here we have celerity given form. How we fly! It is exhilarating! It is like a race for a thousand pound! It is like wrestling with a handsome woman!'

Stephen frowned; he disliked Mr Farquhar's warmer similes. 'Sure celerity is all,' he said. 'Yet a great deal also depends upon our finding the other ships at the rendezvous. The sea is so uncommonly vast, the elements so capricious, the instruments for finding the latitude so imperfect, or so imperfectly used, that I have known a vessel cruise ten days and more without finding her consorts.'

'Let us put our trust in the Commodore's mathematical powers,' said Mr Farquhar. 'Or his luck: or both. I believe, Dr Maturin, that if you would so far indulge me, I could relish a little, a very little, of your portable soup again, with just a sippet of toast; and I promise that if ever I come to govern my island, my first care, after the new constitution, shall be to repay you in turtle.'

Their trust was not misplaced. The day after they had seen the mountains of La Réunion piercing the white trade-clouds far to the leeward the two frigates went north about Mauritius, and there, true to the appointed coordinates, they found the rest of the squadron. Lambert, the senior captain, came aboard at once: the position in Port-Louis was just what they had expected, with the *Vénus*, the *Manche*, and the *Entreprenant* corvette lying snug in port and the *Bellone* and *Minerve* still far away; but on the other hand Clonfert, sent to cruise off the south-east of the island, had discovered a new French frigate, the 38-gun *Astrée*, moored under the batteries of the Rivière Noire in an impregnable position, obviously aware of the blockade of Port-Louis and unwilling to emerge. He had also cut out a four-hundred-ton merchantman from Jacotet, spiking the guns of the little batteries and taking some officers prisoner. It was true that the ship had proved to be a neutral, an American, one of the many Americans who used these seas, almost the only neutrals and almost the only source of casual information available to either side: but even so, said Lambert, it was a most dashing affair.

'This is a damned unfortunate object for dashing at and a damned odd moment to choose for dashing,' said Jack afterwards. 'If the *Néréide* had been knocked about in this cutting-out

lark (for it was no more), we should have been put to our shifts to cover the landing, above all now that they have the *Astrée*. I wonder at Lambert, sending him off alone: though indeed it is plain that he knows these waters, and that he don't want conduct. Jacotet is a hellish awkward anchorage to get into. However, I think we must take Clonfert with us to Rodriguez as soon as we have watered, to keep his ardent spirits out of the way of temptation until there is a proper scope for 'em. He may dash till he goes blue in the face, once the real battle is engaged.'

They watered at Flat Island, and then the *Boadicea* and the *Néréide* stretched away to the east for Rodriguez, leaving Pym in command with orders to fade imperceptibly away by night with the *Iphigenia* and *Magicienne*, leaving the *Leopard* and two avisoes off Port-Louis to bring instant warning if the *Bellone* and *Minerve* should return from the Bay of Bengal. 'For there's the rub,' said Jack. 'If those two heavy frigates, together with *Vénus*, *Manche* and *Astrée* were to fall on our rear at the wrong moment, with the troops half on shore and half off, we should be like Jackson, hard up in a clinch, and no knife to cut the seizing.'

Ordinarily Rodriguez presented the appearance of a desert island; perhaps somewhat larger than the ideal desert island, being a good ten miles long, and perhaps somewhat greyer and more sterile inland than might have been wished, though pleasant enough after a long voyage with no sight of land; but now the bay was crowded with shipping, and on the shore exactly squared streets of tents stretched away in all directions, while in these streets hundreds and even thousands of men moved about, their red coats visible from a great way off.

Jack was first ashore, taking Stephen and Farquhar with him: to his intense relief he found that Keating was still in command – no glum, over-cautious general had superseded him. The two commanders instantly and with great goodwill plunged into the details of moving soldiers, ammunition, stores, provisions, arms, and even some howitzers in due order to the scene of action, and Stephen slipped silently away. 'The solitaire could never have borne this,' he reflected as he made his way through the crowded camp. 'And even the tortoise-park is sadly diminished.'

He had not gone a hundred yards before a voice behind him called out, 'Doctor! Doctor!'

'Not again?' he muttered angrily, walking faster among the screw-pines and drawing his head down between his shoulders.

But he was pursued, run down; and in his overtaker he instantly recognized the tall, lank, and still very boyish form of Thomas Pullings, a shipmate from his first day at sea. 'Thomas Pullings,' he cried, with a look of real pleasure replacing the first malignant glare. 'Lieutenant Pullings, upon my word and honour. How do you do, sir?'

They shook hands, and having inquired tenderly after the Doctor's health and the Commodore's, Pullings said, 'I remember you was the first that ever called me Lieutenant P, sir, back in dear old Pompey. Well, now, if you chose to tip it the most uncommon civil, you could say Captain.'

'You do not tell me so? And are you indeed a captain already?'

'Not by land, sir; I am not Captain P by land. But at sea I am the captain of the *Groper* transport. You can see her from here, if you stand from behind the tree. Hey, you, the lobster there,' he called to an intervening soldier, 'your dad worn't no glazier. We can't see through you. There, sir: the brig just beyond the snow. She's only a transport, but did you ever see such lovely lines?'

Stephen had seen just such lines in a Dutch herring-buss, but he did not mention the fact, saying no more than 'Elegant, elegant'.

When her captain had gloated over the squat, thick object for a while he said, 'She's my first command, sir. A wonderful brig on a bowline; and she draws so amazing little water, she can run up the smallest creek. Will you honour us with a visit?'

'I should be very happy, Captain,' said Stephen. 'And since you are in command, might I beg the favour of a shovel, a crowbar, and a stout man of fair average understanding?'

The Commodore and the Colonel worked on their plan of campaign; the staff-officers worked on their lists; the soldiers polished their buttons, formed in squares, formed in fours, and marched off by the right into the boats, filling the transports and the frigates until the harassed sailors could scarcely holystone the decks, let alone come at the rigging; and Dr Maturin, with two Gropers of fair average understanding dug out the remains of the solitaire from the caves into which she had retired from hurricanes, only to be overwhelmed by the ensuing deluge of now rock-like mud.

The last soldier left the beach, a crimson major in charge of the operation; and as he set his weary foot on the *Boadicea*'s quarterdeck he looked at his watch and cried, 'One minute fifty-

three seconds a man, sir: that beats Wellington by a full two seconds!' A single gun to windward from the Commodore, the signal *Make sail*, and the fourteen transports began to file through the narrow opening in the reef to join the men-of-war.

By the evening they had sunk the island. They were sailing towards the setting sun with a fine topgallantsail breeze on the larboard quarter; and nothing but open sea lay between them and the beaches of La Réunion. The enterprise was now in train. Jack was far too busy with Colonel Keating and his maps for anything but the living present, but Stephen felt the long hours of gliding towards the inevitable future more than he had expected. He had been intimately concerned in matters of greater moment, but none in which the issue would be so clear-cut – total success, or total failure with a shocking loss of life – in a matter of hours.

He was not altogether happy about the plan to attack, which assumed that they would be expected at St Paul's, a restored, strengthened St Paul's, and which required a feint and then a landing at two points, the one east and the other south-west of Saint-Denis, the capital, the second being designed to cut off communication between Saint-Denis and St Paul's; nor was Jack, who feared the surf. But since Colonel Keating, a man in whom they had great confidence, and one who had fought over some of the terrain, strongly urged its strategic importance, and since he was supported by the other colonels, the Commodore had yielded, neither Stephen nor Farquhar saying anything, except when they stressed the importance of respect for civilian and ecclesiastical property.

The hours dropped by. At every heave of the log La Réunion was seven or eight miles nearer. Mr Farquhar was busy with his proclamation, and Stephen paced the quarterdeck, silently hating Buonaparte and all the evil he had brought into the world. 'Good only for destruction – has destroyed all that was valuable in the republic, all that was valuable in the monarchy – is destroying France with daemonic energy – this tawdry, theatrical empire – a deeply vulgar man – nothing French about him – insane ambition – the whole world one squalid tyranny. His infamous treatment of the Pope! Of this Pope and the last. And when I think of what he has done to Switzerland and to Venice, and to God knows how many other states, and what he might have done to Ireland – the Hibernian Republic, divided into departments – one half secret police, the other informers – conscription – the country bled white – ' A subaltern of the 86th caught his pale wicked glare

full in the eye and backed away, quite shocked.

In the afternoon of the day after the council three ships were sighted from the masthead: *Sirius*, *Iphigenia* and *Magicienne*, exact to the rendezvous, having seen no sign of the *Bellone* or *Minerve*, nor any hint of movement in Port-Louis. That evening they began to take chosen troops aboard over an easy, gentle sea: and Jack summoned the captains to explain the course of action. While the main force made a demonstration before Sainte-Marie, the *Sirius* was to land Colonel Fraser's brigade and the howitzers at Grande-Chaloupe, a beach on the leeward side of the island between Saint-Denis and St Paul's. At the same time part of the brigades under Colonel Keating were to be landed at the Rivière des Pluies, thus placing Saint-Denis between two fires; and here the other troops should also be landed as the transports came in; for the frigates were now to press on alone under all the sail they could bear.

They pressed on, still over this long easy swell, in a gentle breeze with studding-sails aloft and alow: a magnificent sight in their perfect line stretching over a mile of sea, the only white in that incomparable blue. They pressed on, never touching a sail except to make it draw better, from sunset until the morning watch; and all the time the Commodore took his sights on the great lambent stars hanging there in the velvet sky, checking his position again and again with the real help of Richardson and the nominal help of Mr Buchan the master, calling for the log at every glass, and perpetually sending below for the readings of the chronometers and the barometer. At two bells in the morning watch he gave orders to reduce sail; and coloured lanterns, with a leeward gun, bade the squadron do the same.

Dawn found him still on deck, looking yellow and unshaved and more withdrawn than Stephen cared to see. La Réunion lay clear on the larboard bow, and the soldiers, coming sleepily on deck, were delighted to see it: they clustered on the forecastle, looking at the land with telescopes; and more than one cried out that he could find no surf upon the reefs, nothing but a little line of white. 'They may not be so pleased in twelve hours' time,' said Jack in a low voice, answering Stephen's inquiring look. 'The glass has been sinking all through the night: still, we may be in before it comes on to blow.' As he spoke he took off his coat and shirt, and then, having given his orders to Trollope, the officer of the watch, his breeches: from the rail he pitched head-first into the sea, rose snorting, swam along the line of boats that

each frigate towed behind her, made his way back along them, and so went dripping below: the Boadiceas were perfectly used to this, but it shocked the redcoats, as savouring of levity. Once below and free of good mornings right and left, he went straight to sleep, with barely a pause between laying his long wet hair on the pillow and unconsciousness; and fast asleep he remained, in spite of the rumbling boots of a regiment of soldiers and the din inseparable from working the ship, until the faint tinkle of a tea-spoon told some layer of his mind that coffee was ready. He sprang up, looked at the barometer, shook his head, dipped his face into a kid of tepid water, shaved, ate a hearty breakfast, and appeared on deck, fresh, pink, and ten years younger.

The squadron was coasting along just outside the reef, a reef upon which the sea broke mildly: three lines of rollers that a well-handled boat could manage easily enough.

'Upon my word, Commodore, the weather seems to serve our turn,' said Colonel Keating; and then in a louder voice and waving his hat to a young woman who was gathering clams on the reef, 'Bonjour, Mademoiselle.' The young woman, who had already been greeted by the three leading frigates, turned her back, and the Colonel went on, 'How do you think it will stay?'

'It may hold up,' said Jack. 'But then again it may come on to blow. We must move smartly: you will not object to a very early dinner, at the same time as the men?'

'Never in life, sir. Should be very happy – indeed I am sharp-set even now.'

Sharp-set he might be, reflected Jack, but he was also nervous. Keating set about his very early dinner with a decent appearance of phlegm, yet precious little went down his gullet. He had never had such an important command; nor had Jack; and in this waiting period they both felt the responsibility to a degree that neither of them would have thought possible. It affected them differently, however; for whereas Keating ate very little and talked a good deal, Jack devoured the best part of a duck and followed it with figgy-dowdy, gazing thoughtfully out of the stern-window as the not very distant landscape slipped by: far off, the harsh, precipitous mountains; nearer to, cultivated land, the occasional house: forest, plantations, a hamlet, and some carts creeping against the green. Their dinner did not last long: it was first interrupted by the report of two sail bearing east a half south – they later proved to be the leading transports, *Kite* and *Groper* – and then cut short entirely by the appearance of the

168

little town of Sainte-Marie before Jack had quite finished his first attack upon the figgy-dowdy.

Here the reef trended in towards the coast, and the squadron turned with it, heaving to at the Commodore's signal. Already the town was in a state of turmoil: people were running about in all directions, pointing, screeching audibly, putting up their shutters, loading carts. They had plenty to screech about, for there, right off their anchorage, where the fresh water of the stream made gaps in the coral, and well within gunshot, lay five ships, broadside on, with their ports open and a frightful array of cannon pointing straight at Sainte-Marie. Even worse, large numbers of boats with soldiers in them were rowing about, evidently determined to land, to take, burn, rase, and sack the town. The sergeant's guard from the little post was lined up on the beach, but they did not seem to know what to do, and every man who could command a horse had long since galloped off to Saint-Denis to give the alarm and to implore instant succour from the military there.

'This is going very well,' said Colonel Keating some time later, as he watched the vanguard of the succour through his telescope. 'Once their field-pieces are across the stream, they will have a devil of a time getting them back again. Their horses are quite done up already. See the company of infantry at the double! They will be pooped, sir, pooped entirely.'

'Aye,' said Jack. 'It is very well.' But his mind was more on the sea than on the land, and it appeared to him that the surf was growing: the rollers, perhaps from some blow far to the east, were coming in with more conviction. He looked at his watch, and although it wanted forty minutes of the stated time he said, 'Make *Sirius*'s signal to carry on.'

The *Sirius* paid off heavily, filled, and bore away for Grande-Chaloupe, carrying close on a thousand men and the howitzers. As she moved off, her place was taken by the *Kite*, the *Groper*, and two other transports, increasing the alarm on shore.

The plan had been unable to allot any precise interval between the two landings, since obviously that must depend on the time the *Sirius* should take to pass Saint-Denis and reach the agreed point between that town and St Paul's; but they had hoped for something in the nature of two hours. With the failing breeze, however, it now looked as though at least three would be required: and all the while the surf was growing. The waiting was hard, and it would have been harder still if the newly-arrived

French field-pieces, drawn up on a hill behind the post, had not seen fit to open fire. They threw no more than four-pound balls, but they threw them with striking accuracy, and after the first sighting shots one passed so close to Colonel Keating's head that he cried out indignantly, 'Did you see that, sir? It was perfectly deliberate. Infernal scrubs! They must know I am the commanding officer.'

'Do you not shoot at commanding officers in the army, Colonel?'

'Of course not, sir. Never, except in a mêlée. If I were on land, I should send a galloper directly. There they go again. What unprincipled conduct: Jacobins.'

'Well, I believe we can put a stop to it. Pass the word for the gunner. Mr Webber, you may fire at the field-pieces by divisions: but you must point all the guns yourself, and you must not damage any civilian or ecclesiastical property. Pitch them well up beyond the town.'

With the great guns going off one after another in a leisurely, deliberate fire, and the heady smell of powder swirling about the deck, tension slackened. The soldiers cheered as Mr Webber sent his eighteen-pound balls skimming among the Frenchmen on their knoll, and they roared again when he hit a limber full on, so that one wheel sprang high into the air, turning like a penny tossed for heads or tails. But such an unequal contest could not last long, and presently the French guns were silenced: and all the time the swell increased, sending white water high on the reef and surging through the gap to break in great measured rollers on the strand.

Yet after the lull the breeze had strengthened too, with every sign of blowing hard before the night, and at length Jack said, '*Sirius* should be at Grande-Chaloupe by now. I think we may move on.'

Their move took them briskly past another shallow gap in the reef, where more fresh water broke the coral, and to another anchorage (though still indifferent) off the mouth of the Rivière des Pluies.

'This is it,' said Colonel Keating, map in hand. 'If we can go ashore here, the landing will be unopposed. It will be at least an hour before they can get round: probably more.'

'My God,' thought Jack, looking at the broad belt of surf, the steep-to beach of rounded boulders. He stepped to the taffrail and hailed, '*Néréide*, ahoy. Come under my stern.' The *Néréide*

shot up, backed her foretopsail, and lay pitching on the swell: there was Lord Clonfert on her quarterdeck; and Stephen noticed that he was wearing full-dress uniform – no unusual thing in a fleet-action, but rare for a skirmish.

'Lord Clonfert,' called Jack, 'do you know the deep-water channel?'

'Yes, sir.'

'Is a landing practicable?'

'Perfectly practicable at present, sir. I will undertake to put a party ashore this minute.'

'Carry on, Lord Clonfert,' said Jack.

The *Néréide* had a little captured schooner among her boats, a local craft; and into this and some of her boats she poured an eager party of soldiers and seamen. The squadron watched the schooner run down to the edge of the surf, followed by the boats. Here she took to her sweeps, backing water and waiting for the master-wave: it came, and she shot in through the breaking water, on and on, and they thought she was through until at the very last she struck, ten yards from the shore, slewed round, and was thrown on to the beach, broadside on. As the wave receded all the men leapt ashore, but the backdraught took her into the very curl of the next, which lifted her high and flung her down so hard that it broke her back at once and shattered her timbers. Most of the other craft fared the same: the boats beaten to pieces, the men safe. Only four bodies were to be seen, dark in the white water, drifting westwards along the shore.

'It is essential to carry on,' cried Colonel Keating in a harsh voice. 'We must take Saint Denis between two fires, whatever the cost.'

Jack said to Mr Johnson, 'Make *Groper*'s signal.'

While the transport was coming up he stared at the beach and the floating wreckage: as he had thought, it was only the last stretch that was mortal at this stage. Anything of a breakwater would allow boats to land; and the *Groper* was the only vessel with a draught shallow enough to go in so far. When she was under the *Boadicea*'s lee he called, 'Mr Pullings, you must shelter the boats: take your brig in, drop your stern-anchor at the last moment, and run her ashore as near as you can heading south-west.'

'Aye, aye, sir,' said Pullings.

The *Groper* bore up in a volley of orders, made her way slowly towards the land while her people were busy below, rousing a

171

cable out of a stern-port, and then much faster: into the surf, on and on through it. In his glass Jack saw the anchor drop, and a moment later the *Groper* ran hard aground right by the shore. Her foretopmast went by the board with the shock, but the hands at the capstan took no notice: they were furiously heaving the cable in, forcing her stern round so that she lay just south-west, braced against the seas and creating a zone of quiet water right in by the shore.

'Well done, Tom Pullings, well done indeed: but how long will your anchor hold?' muttered Jack, and aloud, 'First division away.'

The boats ran in, landed and hauled up, half-swamped in most cases but rarely overset: the beach was filling with redcoats, forming neatly in line as they came ashore. Some, with Colonel McLeod, had taken up position a few hundred yards inland. Then the *Groper*'s cable parted. A tall comber took her stern, wrenched it round, and flung her on that unforgiving beach: and since her bows were already stove, she went to pieces at once, leaving the surf the full sweep of the shore. The wave that broke her was the first of a growing series; and presently the belt of surf grew wider and wider, thundering louder still.

'Can another ship be sent in, Commodore?' asked Keating.

'No, sir,' said Jack.

On the road that led from Sainte-Marie to Saint-Denis, and that here curved inland from the coast to avoid a swamp, three separate bodies of French troops could be seen, moving slowly from east to west, towards Saint-Denis. Colonel McLeod's party on shore had already thrown up dry-stone breastworks between the beach and the road, and had formed behind them in good order. To the left of their line the seamen and the Marines had done much the same; but being on wetter ground they had made a broad turf wall, upon which stood Lord Clonfert, conspicuous with his star and his gold-laced hat.

The first body came abreast of the landing-party at a distance of two hundred yards: they halted, loaded, levelled their pieces, and fired. Clonfert waved his sword at them, reached behind him for a Marine's musket, and returned the fire. It was almost the only shot in reply to the French discharge: clearly the landing-party had spoilt nearly all its powder.

As the squadron watched, too far for accurate fire on this heaving sea but near enough for telescopes to show every detail, two cavalrymen came galloping down the road from Saint-

Denis, spoke to an officer and rode on. The troops shouldered their muskets, reformed, and set off towards Saint-Denis at the double. The second and third bodies, also given orders by the horsemen, came fast along the road: each halted long enough for a volley or two, and each was saluted by Clonfert from the top of his wall. He was eating a biscuit, and each time he put it down on his handkerchief to shoot. Once he hit an officer's horse, but most of the time his musket missed fire.

Still more horsemen came riding fast from Saint-Denis, one of them probably a field-officer, urging the troops to hurry. The inference was as clear as the day: Colonel Fraser had landed in force from the *Sirius*, and these men were being called back to protect the capital.

'*Magicienne* and the *Kite* and *Solebay* transports must go and support him at once,' said Jack. 'The rest of the squadron will stay here, in case the sea goes down by the morning.' Colonel Keating agreed: he seemed glad of the authoritative statement, and Stephen had the impression that he had lost his sense of being in control of the situation – that this impossibility of communicating with the visible shore was something outside his experience.

Throughout this time Stephen and Farquhar had stood by the hances, out of the way, two figures as unregarded as they had been at the time of the military councils, where they sat virtually mute, dim among the splendid uniforms; but now, after a hurried consultation with Farquhar, Stephen said to Jack, 'We are agreed that if Colonel Fraser has a firm footing on the other side of the island, I should be put ashore there.'

'Very well,' said Jack. 'Mr Fellowes, a bosun's chair, there. Pass the word for my coxswain. Bonden, you go aboard *Magicienne* with the Doctor.'

What remained of this anxious day off the Rivière des Pluies was taken up with watching the surf. A little before sunset half an hour's downpour of a violence rare even for those latitudes deadened the white water of the breakers so that the channel was a little clearer, and a subaltern of the 56th, born in the West Indies and accustomed to surf from his childhood, volunteered to swim ashore with Colonel Keating's orders to Colonel McLeod. He launched himself into the rollers with the confidence of a seal, vanished, and reappeared on the crest of a wave that set him neatly on his feet at high-water-mark: shortly afterwards McLeod, covering the subaltern's nakedness with a plaid, marched off at

the head of his men to seize the little post at Sainte-Marie, deserted by its occupants, to hoist the British colours, and to regale upon the stores left by the sergeant's guard.

Yet darkness fell with its usual suddenness in the tropics, and it was impossible to send boats in through the reviving turmoil. The ships stood off and on all night, and in the morning the combers were still roaring up the beach. There might, Jack agreed, be a slight improvement, but it was nothing like enough; and his strongly-held opinion was that they should proceed at once to Grande-Chaloupe to reinforce the troops landed from the *Sirius* and *Magicienne*, leaving the *Iphigenia* and some transports to land at the Rivière des Pluies later in the day if the sea went down. Happily Colonel Keating shared this opinion to the full, and the *Boadicea* made sail, passed Saint-Denis, where the soldiers swore they could distinguish gunfire on the far side of the town, rounded Cape Bernard, and stretched south-south-west under a cloud of canvas for the beach of Grande-Chaloupe, obvious from miles away by the congregation of shipping and the now unmistakeable gunfire in the hills above.

They stood in, and here, on the leeward side of the island, what a different state of things was seen! Calm beaches, lapping billows, boats plying to and fro: and up in the hills companies of redcoats regularly formed; companies of turbans; guns at work, and still more guns being dragged up by ant-like lines of seamen.

The Colonel and his staff raced ashore, all weariness forgotten; troops, guns, heavy equipment began to pour from the frigate. Jack's duty bound him to the ship, however, and he stood watching through his telescope. 'This is a damned poor way of being present at a battle,' he said to Mr Farquhar. 'How I envy Keating.'

Colonel Keating, provided with a captured horse on the beach itself, spurred his mount up the paths to Colonel Fraser's forward post, where they both surveyed the scene. 'You have a charmingly regular attack here,' said Keating with great satisfaction, directing his spy-glass right and left. 'And a most judicious defence: the French have made a very proper disposition of their forces.'

'Yes, sir. It is as regular as one could wish, except for the blue-jackets. They will rush forward and take outworks before they are due to fall: though I must confess, they have done wonders in getting the howitzers up. But on the whole it *is* pretty regular: over on the right, sir, beyond the signal-post, Campbell and his

sepoys have made the prettiest set of approaches. They are only waiting for the word to charge: that will carry us two hundred yards nearer their demi-lune.'

'Then why don't you give it, Mother of God? They have clearly outflanked the enemy already. Where is your galloper?'

'He is just behind you, sir. But if you will forgive me, there is a parley in train. The political gentleman from the ship came up with a clergyman and a party of tars and said he must speak to the French commanding officer. So knowing he was the governor's adviser, we beat a chamade and sent him across with a flag of truce. It seemed to me proper; and yet now I half regret it . . . Can he be quite right in the head, sir? He desired me to keep this bone for him, saying he would not trust it to the French for the world.'

'Oh, these politicoes, you know, Fraser . . .' said Colonel Keating. 'It will come to nothing, however. They are very strongly entrenched on the hill; and even if McLeod comes up from the east, it will take us a good week of regular approaches to press them to their main works.'

They were studying the main works with great attention through their telescopes when an aide-de-camp said, 'I beg your pardon, sir, but Dr Maturin is approaching with a French officer and a couple of civilians.'

Colonel Keating walked forward to meet them. Stephen said, 'Colonel Keating, this is Colonel Saint-Susanne, who commands the French forces on the island. These gentlemen represent the civil administration.' The two soldiers saluted one another: the civilians bowed. Stephen went on, 'From a desire to avert the effusion of human blood, they wish to know the terms upon which you will grant a capitulation covering the whole island: and I have taken it upon myself to assure them that the terms will be honourable.'

'Certainly, sir,' said Colonel Keating, with an icy glare at Stephen. 'Gentlemen, pray step this way.'

Jack and Farquhar, prosaically eating an early elevenses and wondering vaguely, repetitively, why there was no longer any firing in the hills, were interrupted first by cheering on the shore and then by an ensign bearing a scribbled note. 'Forgive me, sir,' said Jack; and he read, 'My dear Commodore – Your friend has disappointed us – he has *done us out* of our battle, as neat a battle as you could wish to see. We had driven in their piquets – outflanked their right wing – and then quite out of order a

capitulation is proposed, *to avert the effusion of human blood* forsooth – they accept the usual terms – honours of war, side-arms and baggage, personal effects and so on – so if you are satisfied, please to come ashore to sign together with your obliged humble servant, H. Keating, Lieut.-Col.'

The Commodore laughed aloud, beat his massive thigh, held out his hand and said, 'Governor, I give you joy. They have surrendered, and your kingdom awaits you. Or this island of it, at the least.'

Chapter Seven

His Excellency the Governor of La Réunion sat at the head of his council table: he now wore a uniform as splendid as that of the gold and scarlet colonels on his left hand, more splendid by far than the weather-worn blue of the sea-officers on his right; and now there was no question of his sitting mute. Yet there was no trace of hauteur to be seen on his eager, intelligent face as he tried to guide the meeting towards a unanimous approval of the Commodore's revolutionary scheme, his plan of an instant attack upon Mauritius, with simultaneous landings from Flat Island off Port-Louis and in the neighbourhood of Port South-East at the other end of the island. Colonel Keating had been with him from the first; but a distinct inclination to enjoy the fruits of victory for a while, 'to allow the men a little rest', and, more creditably, a desire to prepare the campaign with due deliberation, so that mortars for example did not arrive without their shells, had yet to be overcome; for if so ambitious and risky an operation as this were to fail, the attempt could be justified only by a unanimous vote.

'I shall echo the Commodore's words, gentlemen,' said Mr Farquhar, 'and cry "Lose not a moment". This is the moment at which we have a superiority of five to three in frigates, when we possess a fleet of transports, troops in the first flush of victory, and exact intelligence of the enemy's strength and dispositions on the Mauritius, supplied by their own records here.'

'Hear him, hear him,' said Colonel Keating.

'With command of the sea we may concentrate our forces wherever we choose. Furthermore, my colleague' – bowing to Stephen at the far end of the table – 'assures me that at this juncture, this very favourable juncture, our efforts at sapping the enemy's morale are more than likely to be crowned with success; and we are all aware of Dr Maturin's powers in that direction.' It was not the most fortunate stroke: some of the colonels who had toiled and sweated extremely in the hope of glory turned a sombre gaze upon Dr Maturin. Feeling this, Mr Farquhar hurried on, 'And perhaps even more important, this is the moment at which our hands are free. The *Leopard* has taken our despatches to the Cape: she will not return. No orders from any

authority unacquainted with the exact state of local conditions can take the guidance of operations from the hands of those who *are* acquainted with them – no new set of staff-officers can, for the moment, arrive with a plan of campaign matured in Bombay, Fort William, or Whitehall. This is a state of affairs that cannot last.'

'Hear him, hear him,' said Colonel Keating, Colonel McLeod and Colonel Fraser; and the fatter, more cautious staff-officers exchanged uneasy glances.

'Far be it from me to decry patient laborious staff-work,' said the Governor. 'We have seen its gratifying results on this island: but, gentlemen, time and tide wait for no man; and I must remind you that Fortune is bald behind.'

Walking away from the Residence through streets placarded with the Governor's proclamation, Jack said to Stephen, 'What is this that Farquhar tells us about Fortune? Is she supposed to have the mange?'

'I conceive he was referring to the old tag – his meaning was, that she must be seized by the forelock, since once she is passed there is no clapping on to her hair, at all. In the figure she ships none abaft the ears, if you follow me.'

'Oh, I see. Rather well put: though I doubt those heavy-sided lobsters will smoke the simile.' He paused, considering, and said, 'It don't sound very eligible, bald behind; but, however, it is all figurative, all figurative . . .' He gazed with benign approval at a strikingly elegant woman accompanied by an even more willowy black slave-girl, stepped into the gutter to let them pass, they looking haughty, unconscious, a thousand miles away, and continued, 'Still, I am glad they have come to see reason. But Lord, Stephen, what an infernal waste of time these councils are! If it had dragged on another day the squadron would have been dispersed – *Sirius* is gone already – and I should have had to follow my own scheme. My first duty is to the sea, and I must get at Hamelin before the *Bellone* and *Minerve* are back. But as it is, I can combine the two. Pullings!' he exclaimed.

On the other side of the street Pullings cast off the girl at his side and crossed, blushing a reddish mahogany yet beaming too. 'Did you find anything you liked, Pullings?' asked Jack. 'I mean, in the professional line?'

'Oh, yes, sir – I was only looking after her for a minute, for Mr – for another officer, sir – but I don't suppose you will let me have her, sir – far too pretty, except for a trifle of worm in her

futtocks, her ground futtocks.' Pullings had been sent to St Paul's in the *Sirius* when the frigate tore down immediately after the capitulation to snap up all the shipping in the road; he had been told to make his own choice of a replacement for the *Groper*, and he had done himself as proud as Pontius Pilate. They watched the young woman attach herself to the arm of Mr Joyce of the *Kite* transport, and as they walked along, Pullings, more coherent now that he was relieved of a sense of guilt – for very strangely his officers looked upon Jack Aubrey as a moral figure, in spite of all proofs to the contrary – expatiated on the merits of his prize, a privateer schooner, copper-fastened, wonderfully well-found.

At the gates of the government stable-yard they parted, and while Bonden led forth a powerful black horse, once the pride of the French garrison, Stephen said, 'This is not the moment to ask how you mean to combine the two schemes; yet I admit that I am curious to know. Bonden, I advise you, in your own best interest, not to stand behind that creature's heels.'

'If you will ride over to St Paul's with me,' said Jack, 'I will tell you.'

'Alas, I have an audience of the Bishop in half an hour, and then an appointment at the printing-shop.'

'Maybe it is just as well. Things will be clearer in the morning. Bonden, cast off afore.'

Things were indeed clearer in the morning: the Commodore had seen all the officers concerned; he had all the facts distinctly arranged; and he received Stephen in a room filled with charts and maps.

'Here, do you see,' he said, pointing to an island three or four miles off Port South-East, 'is the Ile de la Passe. It lies on the reef at the very edge of the only deep-water channel into the port: a devilish channel, narrow, with a double dog-leg and any number of banks and rocks in its bed. The island is pretty strongly held – it mounts about twenty heavy guns – but the town is not. They expect us in the north, where we have been blockading all this while, and most of their forces are around Port-Louis: so if we knock out the Ile de la Passe – and a couple of frigates should be able to manage it –'

'In spite of the intricate navigation? These are very alarming shoals, brother. I see two and three fathoms marked for a couple of miles inside the reef; and here is a vast area with the words *Canoe-passage at high-tide*; while your channel is a mere serpent;

a lean serpent at the best. But I am not to be teaching you your business.'

'It can be done. Clonfert and his black pilot know these waters perfectly. Look, here is the Jacotet anchorage just at hand, where he cut out the American. Yes, they should manage it well enough; though of course it must be done by boats and in the night; ships could not stand in against that fire, without being sadly mauled. Then once the island is seized, the French cannot easily retake it: their batteries cannot reach across the inner bay and since they have no ship of force in Port South-East, nor even gun-boats, they have no means of getting their artillery any nearer. Nor can they starve it out, so long as we victual it from the sea. So if we hold the Ile de la Passe we deny the French their best harbour after Port-Louis; we have a base for our landing; and we open up all the country out of range of the batteries for your handing-out of broadsheets and culling simples. For their little garrisons in the town and along the coast will scarcely stir outside the reach of their own guns.'

'This is a very beautiful plan,' said Stephen.

'Ain't it?' said Jack. 'Keating has already sent some Bombay gunners and European troops into the *Néréide*, to garrison the place when we have taken it: for obviously the *Néréide* possesses more local knowledge than all the rest of the squadron put together.'

'You do not feel that Clonfert's oversetting of the little ship off the Rivière des Pluies throws a certain shade on his qualifications?'

'No, I do not. It could have happened to anyone in those circumstances, with the soldiers ready to call us shy. I should have tried it myself. But I am not going to give him his head at the Ile de la Passe; I do not want him to be coming it the Cochrane: Pym shall command. Pym may not be very wise, but he is a good, sound man, as regular as a clock; so *Néréide*, *Iphigenia* and perhaps *Staunch* –'

'What is this *Staunch*?'

'She is a brig: came in last night from Bombay. A useful little brig, and in excellent order. Narborough has her, a most officer-like cove: you remember Narborough, Stephen?' Stephen shook his head. 'Of course you do,' cried Jack. 'Lord Narborough, a big black man with a Newfoundland dog, third of the *Surprise*.'

'You mean Garron,' said Stephen.

'Garron, of course: you are quite right. Garron he was then,

but his father died last year, and now he is called Narborough. So *Néréide*, *Iphigenia*, and perhaps *Staunch* if she can get her water in quick enough, are to run up to Port-Louis, where Pym is watching Hamelin's motions. *Iphigenia* will stay, and *Sirius* and *Néréide* will come south for the Ile de la Passe.'

'The *Néréide* is not to come back here, so?'

'To wait for the dark of the moon, you mean? No; we cannot afford the time.'

'Then in that case I had better go aboard her now. There is a great deal to be done in the Mauritius, and the sooner I get there the better. For I tell you, my dear, that though they are less lethal, my broadsheets are as effective as your – as your round-shot.'

'Stephen,' said Jack, 'I am convinced of it.'

'I had almost said, as effective as your broad*sides*, but I was afraid the miserable play upon words might offend an embryonic baronet; for Farquhar tells me that if this second campaign should succeed as well as the first the happy commander will certainly be so honoured. Should you not like to be a baronet, Jack?'

'Why, as to that,' said Jack, 'I don't know that I should much care for it. The Jack Aubrey of King James's time paid a thumping fine not to be a baronet, you know. Not that I mean the least fling against men who have won a great fleet action – it is right and proper that *they* should be peers – but when you look at the mass of titles, tradesmen, dirty politicians, moneylenders . . . why, I had as soon be plain Jack Aubrey – Captain Jack Aubrey, for I am as proud as Nebuchadnezzar of my service rank, and if ever I hoist my flag, I shall paint *here lives Admiral Aubrey* on the front of Ashgrove Cottage in huge letters. Do not think I am one of your wild democratical Jacobins, Stephen – do not run away with that notion – but different people look at these things in different lights.' He paused, and said with a grin, 'I'll tell you of one chap who would give his eye-teeth to be a baronet, and that is Admiral Bertie. He puts it down to Mrs Bertie, but the whole service knows how he plotted and planned for the Bath. Lord,' he said, laughing heartily, 'to think of crawling about St James's for a ribbon when you are an ancient man, past sixty. Though to be sure, perhaps I might think differently if I had a son: but I doubt it.'

In the afternoon of the next day, Dr Maturin, preceded by two bales of hand-bills, proclamations and broadsheets, some

181

printed in Cape Town and others so recently struck off in Saint-Denis that they were still damp from the press, came alongside the *Néréide*, six hours late. But the Néréides were not used to his ways; they were in a fuming hurry to be off in pursuit of the *Iphigenia*, which had sailed at crack of dawn; and they let him drop between the boat and the ship's side. In his fall he struck his head and back on the boat's gunwale, cracking two ribs and sinking stunned down through the warm clear water: the frigate was already under way, and although she heaved to at once not a man aboard did anything more valuable than run about shouting for some minutes, and by the time she had dropped her stern-boat Stephen would have been dead if one of the bale-carrying black men had not dived in and fetched him out.

He had had a shrewd knock, and although the weather was so kind, the sun so warm, an inflammation of the lungs kept him pinned to his cot for days. Or rather to the captain's cot, for Lord Clonfert moved from his own sleeping-cabin and slung a hammock in the coach.

Stephen therefore missed their rapid voyage north, the meeting of the ships off Port-Louis, and their return southwards through heavy seas to carry out the Commodore's plan of attack on the Ile de la Passe; he missed all but the sounds of their first abortive attempt at gathering the boats for the assault in a pitch-black night with the wind blowing a close-reef topsail gale, when even the *Néréide*'s pilot could not find the channel and when the weather forced them back to Port-Louis; but on the other hand, in these circumstances of particular intimacy he did grow more closely acquainted with Clonfert and McAdam.

The captain spent many hours at Stephen's bedside: their conversation was desultory and for the most part of no great consequence; but Clonfert was capable of an almost female delicacy – he could be quiet without constraint, and he always knew when Stephen would like a cooling drink or the skylight opened – and they talked about novels, the more recent romantic poetry, and Jack Aubrey, or rather Jack Aubrey's actions, in a most companionable way; and at times Stephen saw, among the various persons that made up his host, a gentle, vulnerable creature, one that excited his affection. 'His intuition, however,' reflected Stephen, 'though so nice in a tête-à-tête, does not serve him when three or more are gathered in a room, nor when he is anxious. Jack has never seen him in his quasi-domestic

character. His women have, no doubt; and it may be this that accounts for his notorious success among them.'

These reflections were prompted by the visit of his old shipmate Narborough, before whom Clonfert pranced away, monopolizing the talk with anecdotes of Sir Sydney Smith, and to whom he behaved with such an aggressive affectation of superiority that the commander of the *Staunch* soon returned aboard her, thoroughly displeased. Yet that same evening, as the *Néréide* and *Staunch* approached the Ile de la Passe once more, coming south about while the *Sirius* took the northern route, to avoid suspicion, Clonfert was as quiet and agreeable and well-bred as ever he had been: particularly conciliating, indeed, as though he were aware of his lapse. And when, at his request, Stephen had once again related Jack's taking of the *Cacafuego*, shot by shot, Clonfert said with a sigh, 'Well, I honour him for it, upon my word. I should die happy, with such a victory behind me.'

With McAdam Stephen's relationship was by no means so pleasant. Like most medical men Stephen was an indifferent patient; and like most medical men McAdam had an authoritative attitude towards those under his care. As soon as the patient had recovered his wits they fell out over the advisability of a cingulum, a black draught, and phlebotomy, all of which Stephen rejected in a weak, hoarse, but passionate voice as 'utterly exploded, fit for Paracelsus, or a quicksalver at the fair of Ballinasloe,' together with a fling about McAdam's fondness for a strait-waistcoat. Yet this, even when it was coupled with Stephen's recovery without any treatment but bark administered by himself, would not have caused real animosity if McAdam had not also taken to resenting Clonfert's attention to Stephen, Stephen's ascendancy over Clonfert, and their pleasure in one another's company.

He came into the cabin, only half-drunk, the evening before the *Néréide* and the *Staunch*, though delayed by head-winds, hoped to rendezvous with the *Sirius* off the Ile de la Passe for the assault, took Stephen's pulse, said, 'There is still a wee smidgeon of fever that bleeding would certainly have cured before this; but I shall allow you to take the air on deck again tomorrow, if the action leaves you any deck to take it upon,' drew his case-bottle from his pocket, poured himself a liberal dram in Stephen's physic-glass, and bending, picked up a paper that had slipped beneath the cot, a single printed sheet. 'What language is this?' he asked, holding it to the light.

'It is Irish,' said Stephen calmly: he was extremely vexed with himself for letting it be seen, for although there was no kind of remaining secrecy about his activities, his ingrained sense of caution was deeply wounded: he was determined not to let this appear, however.

''Tis not the Irish character,' said McAdam.

'Irish type is rarely to be found in the French colonies, I believe.'

'I suppose it is meant for those papisher blackguards on the Mauritius,' said McAdam, referring to the Irishmen who were known to have enlisted in the French service. Stephen made no reply, and McAdam went on, 'What does it say?'

'Do you not understand Irish?'

'Of course not. What would a civilized man want with Irish?'

'Perhaps that depends upon your idea of a civilized man.'

'I'll just give you my idea of a civilized man: it is one thot makes croppies lie down, thot drinks to King Billy, and thot cries — the Pope.' With this McAdam began to sing *Croppies lie down*, and the grating, triumphant noise wounded Stephen's still fevered and over-acute hearing. Stephen was fairly sure that McAdam did not know he was a Catholic, but even so his irritation, increased by the heat, the din, the smell, and his present inability to smoke, rose to such a pitch that against all his principles he said, 'It is the pity of the world, Dr McAdam, to see a man of your parts obnubilate his mind with the juice of the grape.'

McAdam instantly collected his faculties and replied, 'It is the pity of the world, Dr Maturin, to see a man of your parts obnubilate his mind with the juice of the poppy.'

In his journal that night Stephen wrote '. . . and his blotched face clearing on a sudden, he checked me with my laudanum. I am amazed at his perspicacity. Yet do I indeed obnubilate my mind? Surely not: looking back in this very book, I detect no diminution of activity, mental or physical. The pamphlet on Buonaparte's real conduct towards this Pope and the last is as good as anything I have ever written: I wish it may be as well translated. I rarely take a thousand drops, a trifle compared with your true opium-eater's dose or with my own in Diana's day: I can refrain whenever I choose: and I take it only when my disgust is so great that it threatens to impede my work. One day, when he is sober, I shall ask McAdam whether disgust for oneself, for one's fellows, and for the whole process of living was common among his patients in Belfast – whether it incapacitated

them. My own seems to grow; and it is perhaps significant that I can feel no gratitude towards the man who took me from the water: I make the gestures that humanity requires but I feel no real kindness for him: surely this is inhuman? Humanity drained away by disgust? It grows; and although my loathing for Buonaparte and his evil system is an efficient stimulant, hatred alone is a poor sterile kind of a basis. And, laudanum or not, the disgust seems to persist even through my sleep, since frequently it is there, ready to envelop me when I wake.'

The next morning was not one of those occasions, frequent though they were. Having listened in vain at intervals throughout the night for sounds that might herald an action or even a meeting with the other ships, Stephen awoke from a long comfortable dozing state, a wholly relaxed well-being, aware that his fever was gone and that he was being looked at through the crack of the partly open door. 'Hola,' he cried, and a nervous midshipman, opening wider, said, 'The Captain's compliments to Dr Maturin, and should he be awake and well enough, there is a mermaid on the starboard bow.'

She was abaft the beam before Stephen reached the rail, a vast greyish creature with a round snout and thick lips, upright in the sea, staring at the ship with her minute beady eyes. If she was indeed a maid, then she must have had a friend who was none, for in her left flipper she held a huge grey baby. She was going fast astern, staring steadily, but he had time to see her opulent bosom, her absence of neck, hair, and external ears, and to estimate her weight at forty stone, before she dived, showing her broad tail above the wave.

He made the fullest acknowledgments for such a treat – had always longed to see one – had searched the Rodriguez lagoons and those of an island near Sumatra but had always been disappointed until this happy moment – and now he found the realization of his wishes even more gratifying than he had hoped.

'I am glad you was pleased,' said Lord Clonfert, 'and I hope it may be some lay-off against my wretched news. *Sirius* has queered our pitch: see where she lays.'

Stephen took his bearings. Four or five miles away on his right hand rose the south-east coast of Mauritius, with the Pointe du Diable running out into the sea: also on his right hand, but within a hundred yards, the long reef stretched out fore and aft, sometimes dry, sometimes buried under the white rollers, with the occasional island standing on it or rising from the paler

185

shallow water inside; and at the far end, where Clonfert was pointing, there lay the *Sirius*, close to a fortified island from whose walls, clear in the telescope, flew the union jack.

In spite of his pleasure at Stephen's delight, it was clear that Clonfert was profoundly disappointed and put out. 'They must have gained twenty leagues on us, while we were beating up off the cape,' he said. 'But if Pym had had any bowels he would have waited for tonight: after all, I did lend him my pilot.' However, as an attentive host he checked any bitter reflections that might have occurred to him, and asked Stephen whether he would like his breakfast.

'You are very good, my lord,' said Stephen, 'but I believe I shall stay here in the hope of seeing another siren. They are usually found in the shallow water by a reef, I am told; and I should not miss one for a dozen breakfasts.'

'Clarges will bring it to you here, if you are quite sure you are strong enough,' said Clonfert. 'But I must send for McAdam to survey you first.'

McAdam looked singularly unappetizing in the morning light, ill-conditioned and surly: apprehensive too, for he had some confused recollection of harsh words having passed the night before. But, having beheld the mermaid, Stephen was in charity with all men, and he called out, 'You missed the mermaid, my dear colleague; but perhaps, if we sit quietly here, we may see another.'

'I did not,' said McAdam. 'I saw the brute out of the quarter-gallery scuttle; and it was only a manatee.'

Stephen mused for a while, and then he said, 'A dugong, surely. The dentition of the dugong is quite distinct from that of the manatee: the manatee, as I recall, has no incisors. Furthermore, the whole breadth of Africa separates their respective realms.'

'Manatee or dugong, 'tis all one,' said McAdam. 'As far as my studies are concerned, the brute is of consequence only in that it is the perfect illustration of the strength, the irresistible strength, of suggestion. Have you been listening to their gab, down there in the waist?'

'Not I,' said Stephen. There had been much talk among the men working just out of sight forward of the quarterdeck rail, cross, contentious talk; but the *Néréide* was always a surprisingly chatty ship, and apart from putting this outburst down to vexation at their late arrival, he had not attended to it. 'They seem displeased, however,' he added.

186

'Of course they are displeased: everyone knows the ill-luck a mermaid brings. But that is not the point. Listen now, will you? That is John Matthews, a truthful, sober, well-judging man; and the other is old Lemon, was bred a lawyer's clerk, and understands evidence.'

Stephen listened, sorted out the voices, caught the thread of the argument: the dispute between Matthews and Lemon, the spokesmen of two rival factions, turned upon the question of whether the mermaid had held a comb in her hand or a glass.

'They saw the flash of that wet flipper,' said McAdam, 'and have translated it, with total Gospel-oath conviction, into one or other of these objects. Matthews offers to fight Lemon and any two of his followers over a chest in support of his belief.'

'Men have gone to the stake for less,' said Stephen: and walking forward to the rail he called down, 'You are both of you out entirely: it was a hairbrush.'

Dead silence in the waist. The seamen looked at one another doubtfully, and moved quietly away among the boats on the booms with many a backward glance, thoroughly disturbed by this new element.

'*Sirius* signalling, sir, if you please,' said a midshipman to the officer of the watch, who had been picking his teeth with a pertinacity so great that it had rendered him deaf to the dispute. '*Captain to come aboard.*'

'I am anxious to see whether the *Sirius* has any prisoners,' said Stephen, when the Captain appeared, 'and if I may, I will accompany you.'

Pym welcomed them with less than his usual cheerfulness: it had been a bloody little action, one in which he had lost a young cousin, and although the frigate's decks were now as trim as though she were lying at St Helen's, there was a row of hammocks awaiting burial at sea, while her boats still lay about her in disorder, all more or less battered and one with a dismounted carronade lying in a red pool. The anxiety of the night had told on Pym and now that the stimulus of the victory was dying he looked very tired. Furthermore, the *Iphigenia* had sent an aviso with word that the three frigates in Port-Louis were ready for sea, and the *Sirius* was extremely busy, preparing her return. Her captain found time to be affable to Stephen, but his preoccupation made his words to Clonfert seem particularly curt and official. When Clonfert, having offered his congratulations, began to say that the *Néréide* felt she might have been allowed to

187

take part, Pym cut him short: 'I really cannot go into all that now. First come first served is the rule in these matters. Here are the French commandant's signals; he did not have time to destroy them. As for your orders, they are very simple: you will garrison the island with a suitable force – the French had about a hundred men and two officers – and hold it until you receive further instructions; and in the meantime you will carry out such operations ashore as seem appropriate after consultation with Dr Maturin, whose advice is to be followed in all political matters. Doctor, if you choose to see the French commandant, my dining-cabin is at your disposition.'

When Stephen returned after questioning poor Captain Duvallier, he gained the impression that Clonfert had been rebuked for his tardiness or for some professional fault to do with the *Néréide*'s sailing; and this impression was strengthened as they pulled back in the barge, together with the black Mauritian pilot; for Clonfert was silent, his handsome face ugly with resentment.

Yet Clonfert's moods were as changeable as a weather-glass, and very shortly after·the *Sirius* and *Staunch* had vanished over the western horizon, with Pym flying back to blockade the French frigates in Port-Louis, he blossomed out in a fine flow of spirits. They had cleared up the bloody mess in the fort, blasting holes in the coral rock for the dead soldiers; they had installed the Bombay gunners and fifty grenadiers of the 69th, reordering the heavy guns so that one battery commanded the narrow channel and the other all the inner anchorage that was within their range; they had taken the *Néréide* through the narrow channel into a snug berth behind the fort; and now he was a free man,·his own master, with the whole of the nearby coast upon which to distinguish himself. No doubt he was directed to advise with Dr Maturin; but Dr Maturin, having required him to harangue the men on the absolute necessity for good relations with all civilians, black or white, male or female, was quite happy to fall in with his military views, such as an assault upon the battery on the Pointe du Diable and indeed upon any other batteries that might catch his fancy. Dr Maturin's attitude towards these forays was so far remote from the killjoy dis-approval Clonfert had at one time feared that he even accompanied the flotilla which crossed the wide lagoon by night to carry the Pointe du Diable in great style at dawn, without the loss of a man. He watched the destruction of the guns, the carry-

ing-off of a beautiful brass mortar, and the prodigious jet of fire as the powder-magazine blew up, with evident complacency, and then walked off into the country to make a variety of contacts and to spread his subversive literature.

Day after day the raids on military installations continued, in spite of the opposition of the French regulars and of the far more numerous militia; for the French had no cavalry, and boats guided by a pilot who knew every creek and passage could reach their goal far sooner than the infantry. Moreover, as Stephen's printed sheets attained a wider circulation, it became apparent that the militia was growing less and less inclined to fight: in fact, after about a week in which the Néréides had traversed the country in all directions, doing no harm to private property, paying for whatever they needed, treating the private Mauritians civilly, and routing all the meagre troops that the southern commander could bring against them, the attitude of the militia came more to resemble a neutrality, and a benevolent neutrality at that. Day after day the soldiers, Marines, and seamen went ashore: the frigate grew steadily more infested with monkeys and parrots, bought in the villages or captured in the woods; and Stephen, though busy with his own warfare, had an interview with an ancient gentlewoman whose grandfather had not only seen, run down and devoured a dodo, perhaps the last dodo to tread the earth, but had stuffed a bolster with its feathers.

Although there was no loot, this was a pleasant interval for all hands, with plenty of excitement and charming weather to say nothing of fresh fruit, fresh vegetables, fresh meat and soft tack: yet Clonfert exultant was a less agreeable companion than Clonfert oppressed. Stephen found his boisterous energy wearisome, his appetite for destruction distasteful, and his continual dashing about the country, often in full dress with his diamond-hilted sword and his foolish star, as tedious as the dinners he gave to celebrate the sometimes important, sometimes trivial conquests of his little force. They were conquests in which Stephen could detect no coherent plan: to him they seemed no more than a series of raids determined by the whim of the day; though on the other hand their want of logical sequence puzzled the French commander extremely.

These feasts were attended by Clonfert's officers, and once again Stephen noted the curiously vulgar tone of the Néréide's gunroom and midshipmen's berth, the open flattery of the Captain, and the Captain's appetite for this flattery, however gross.

Not a dinner passed without Webber, the second lieutenant, comparing Clonfert with Cochrane, to Clonfert's advantage: the word 'dashing' was in daily use: and once the purser, with a sideways look at Stephen, offered a comparison with Commodore Aubrey – a comparison that Clonfert, with an affectation of modesty, declined to allow. Stephen also observed that when McAdam was invited, which was not always the case, he was encouraged to drink and then openly derided: it grieved him to see a grey-haired man so used by young fellows who, whatever their seamanship and courage might be – and there was little doubt of either – could make no claim to any intellectual powers nor yet to common good-breeding. And he found it still more painful to see that Clonfert never checked their merriment: the Captain seemed more concerned with gaining the approval – even the worship – of his young men than with protecting an old, diminished friend.

It was in the mornings that Stephen found Clonfert's boisterousness more than usually tiresome: and he particularly regretted his company one forenoon, when, in an interval between political activities, he was negotiating with his old lady for the bolster. Clonfert spoke quite good French and he meant to help, but he hit a false note from the beginning. His noisy facetiousness offended and confused her; she began to show signs of incomprehension and alarm and to repeat that 'one never slept so well as upon dodo – sleep was the greatest blessing that God sent to the old – the gentlemen were young, and could do very well on booby-down.' Stephen had almost abandoned hope when Clonfert was called away; but once he was out of the room she reconsidered his argument, and he was paying down the price when the door burst open, a voice shouted 'Run, run for the boats. The enemy is in sight,' and the village was filled with pounding feet. He laid down the last broad piece, caught the bolster to his bosom, and joined the rout.

Far out at sea, to windward, five ships were standing in towards the Ile de la Passe. Steadying himself in the gig, with his spy-glass to his eye, Clonfert read them off. '*Victor*, the corvette, leading. Then their big frigate, the *Minerve*. I can't make out the next. Then, by God, the *Bellone*. I could almost swear the last is the *Windham* Indiaman again. Stretch out, stretch out, there; pull strong.'

The gig's crew pulled strong, so strong they left the two other boats that had been launched far behind – three more in a farther

190

creek had not yet even gathered their men. But it was a long, long pull, the whole length of the two spreading anchorages between the shore and the island, four miles and more against the wind.

'I shall lure them in,' said Clonfert to Stephen. And then, having glanced impatiently back towards the distant boats, he added, 'Besides, if they go round to Port-Louis, *Sirius* and *Iphigenia* will be no match for them, with Hamelin bringing his three frigates out.' Stephen made no reply.

The exhausted crew ran the gig alongside the *Néréide*. Clonfert told the coxswain to stay there and ran aboard; a few moments later the frigate displayed a French ensign and pendant and Clonfert dropped down into the boat, crying, 'The fort, and stretch out for all you are worth.'

Now the fort too showed French colours, and after a short pause the French signal ran up the flagstaff on the island: '*Enemy cruising north of Port-Louis*'. The leading frigate replied with the French private signal; the island answered it correctly; and each ship made her number. Clonfert had been right: *Victor, Minerve, Bellone*; and the two others were Indiamen, outward-bound Indiamen taken in the Mozambique channel, the *Ceylon* and the unlucky *Windham* again.

On nearing the reef the French squadron reduced sail; it was clear that they were coming in, but they were coming slowly now, and there would be time to make ready for them. Stephen chose a high, remote corner of the fort from which he could survey the whole scene and sat there on his bolster. Above him the white trade-clouds passed steadily over the pure sky; in the warm sunlight the breeze cooled his cheek; and overhead a bosun-bird wheeled in perfect curves: but within the ramparts below he saw far more confusion than he had expected. Aboard the *Néréide*, which had warped in closer to the island and which was now anchored with a spring on her cable, everything seemed to be in order, although so many of her hands were away in the boats; she was clearing for action, her guns were run out already, and her old standing officers had the process well in hand. But in the fort people were running hither and thither; there was a great deal of shouting; and the Indian gunners, whose officer was somewhere in the boats or perhaps on shore, were arguing passionately among themselves. Soldiers and sailors were at cross purposes: and even among the seamen there was none of that quiet, efficient cheerfulness that marked the actions Stephen had seen

191

with Jack Aubrey – no impression of a machine moving smoothly into place. No food was served out, either: a small point, but one that Jack had always insisted upon. And the remaining boats, with at least a hundred and fifty soldiers and seamen in them, were still a great way off: as far as he could make out, the launch had run aground on the horn of a bank, and since the tide was on the ebb the others were having great difficulty hauling it off.

In the fort and on the lagoon time seemed to stagnate, in spite of the strenuous activity: out at sea it flowed steadily, perhaps faster than its natural pace, and Stephen felt a large, ill-defined apprehension fill the back of his mind, like that which accompanies a nightmare. Now men could be distinguished aboard the ships: now their faces were becoming visible, and orders came clear upon the wind. The French ships had formed a line to enter the channel, the *Victor* first, then the *Minerve*, then the *Ceylon*. The corvette steadied, hauled up her courses, and led in under topsails alone, the lead going in the chains on either side. The noise in the fort had given place to dead silence, with the smell of slow-match wafting on the breeze, drifting from the spare tubs and those beside each gun. The corvette entered the narrows, glided nearer and nearer, her bell flashing in the sun; came abreast of the fort, where the turbanned gunners crouched behind the parapet, and passed it, still in this dead silence. Her master's order to the helmsman brought her round in a tight curve behind the fort, into the deep water, and within twenty yards of the *Néréide*. The *Néréide*'s French ensign came down, the English colours ran up with a cheer, and her side vanished in a great cloud of smoke as her broadside roared out in a single vast prolonged explosion. Another and another, with incessant cheering: the corvette dropped her anchor under the *Néréide*'s starboard quarter, still under her full traversing fire, and an officer ran aft along her shattered deck, calling out that she had struck.

At this point the powerful *Minerve* was already in the channel, well within the channel, with the *Ceylon* close behind her: now they were right under the heavy guns of the fort; they could not turn nor bear away nor move any faster. This was the deadly moment, and every man was poised for the order. At the flagstaff the tricolour raced down to make place for the union flag; but the cheering fool who hauled it down flung it wide on to a tub of burning match near the upper magazine. Flame leapt across and with a crash far louder than a broadside and more blinding than

the sun a hundred charges exploded all together. At the same second the Bombay artillerymen, still without an officer to stop them overloading, let off their ill-pointed guns, bursting or dismounting six of them and killing a man in the *Néréide*'s gig as it was going to take possession of the *Victor*.

Stephen picked himself up in the clearing smoke, realized that shrieks were piercing through his deafness, and hurried to the dead and wounded men scattered all about the flagstaff and the dismounted guns. McAdam's assistant was there and his loblolly boy, and with the help of a few clear-headed seamen they carried them to the shelter of a rampart. By the time they had done what little they could, dressing horrible burns with their torn-up shirts and handkerchiefs, the scene had changed. The *Victor*, having hoisted her colours again, had cut her cable, and she was following the *Minerve* and the *Ceylon* in towards Port South-East. The *Bellone* and *Windham*, just far enough out to sea, far enough from the narrows, to be able to turn, had hauled their wind. The French ships in the lagoon were standing straight for the narrow pass where the *Néréide*'s other boats were advancing in a confused heap, and it seemed that they must take them in the next few minutes. The *Minerve* showed no obvious damage at all.

Clonfert hailed the fort from the *Néréide*, calling for all the soldiers to come aboard: he was going to attack the *Minerve*, and he needed every man to work his guns. It was not an impossible contest in spite of the *Néréide*'s lighter metal; the *Minerve* was not yet cleared for action, she was approaching the second dog-leg off the Horseshoe bank, where she could not turn, whereas the *Néréide* would still have room in the nearer anchorage to luff up and rake her; and neither the *Victor* nor the *Ceylon* could give her much support. But while the soldiers were in the act of going aboard, the *Bellone* changed her mind. She let fall her topgallantsails and headed for the channel and the island. The moment she was engaged in the narrows there was no doubt of what she meant to do: she must come on. And she did come on, with great determination. As she came, handled no doubt by a man who knew the passage perfectly, for she threw an extraordinary bow-wave for such a dangerous piece of navigation, Stephen looked round to see what Clonfert was at, and to his astonishment he saw that the launch and the cutters were passing, had passed, the French men-of-war without being touched – had passed them in the narrows within a biscuit-toss. It was inexplicable. But in any case there they were, with their

men pouring into the *Néréide*, and cheering as they came. The *Néréide* had not yet slipped her cables.

The *Bellone* stood on. She had already cleared her starboard broadside and as she approached the island she fired her forward guns: the smoke, sweeping before her, veiled the fort, and through this veil she fired her full array as she swept by, sending eighteen-pound ball and countless lethal fragments of stone flying among the small remaining garrison. Swinging round into the *Néréide*'s anchorage she sent in another broadside against the other face of the battery: and to all this the demoralized Bombay gunners, deprived of support from small-arms men, unofficered, unused to ships, returned no more than a ragged, ineffectual fire. The *Bellone* went straight for the *Néréide*, as though to run her aboard; but just before they touched the *Bellone* put her helm hard down and shot by. For a moment the two frigates were yardarm to yardarm, almost touching: both broadsides crashed out together, and when the smoke cleared the *Bellone* was well beyond the *Néréide*, running on, still under her topgallantsails, for the second sharp turn in the channel, apparently undamaged. The *Néréide* had lost her driver-boom and a couple of upper yards, but her turn and a sudden gust had laid the *Bellone* over so that her fire was too high to hurt the *Néréide*'s hull or to kill many of her crew: it had cut the spring to her cable, however, and she slewed round so far and so fast that she could not fire into the Frenchman's stern.

Now the silence fell again. The four French ships – for the *Windham*, shying at the entrance and the fort, had stood out along the coast – moved smoothly down to anchor in twenty fathom water off the Olive bank, half way to Port South-East, and Clonfert returned to the island with a strong party of soldiers. He was in excellent spirits, hurrying about with the army officers to put the fort into such order that it could withstand an attack by the French squadron. Catching sight of Stephen he called out, 'How did you like that, Dr Maturin? We have them in the bag!'

A little later, when the armourers had set up the dismounted guns and spare carronades had replaced those that had burst, he said, 'If it had not been for that infernal luck with the flag, we should have sunk the *Minerve*. But it was just as well – the *Bellone* would have hauled her wind, and as it is we have both of them hard up in a clinch. I am sending Webber in the launch to tell Pym that if he can spare me just one frigate – *Iphigenia*, or *Magicienne*

194

if she has joined – I will lead in and destroy the whole shooting-match. We have them finely in the bag! They can never get out except on the land-wind just before sunrise. How Cochrane will envy us!'

Stephen looked at him: did Clonfert, in his euphoria or his leaping excitement, really believe that he had done well, that his position was tenable? 'You do not intend sailing away yourself in the *Néréide* to bring down the reinforcements, I collect?' he said.

'Certainly not. Pym ordered me to hold this fort, and I shall hold it to the last. To the last,' he repeated, throwing up his head with a look of pride. At the next word his expression changed. 'And did you see that dog?' he cried. 'The *Victor* struck her colours to me and then hoisted them again and made off like a scrub, a contemptible sneaking little God-damned scrub. I shall send a flag of truce to demand her. See where she lays!'

She lay between the two heavy frigates, and from the fort her crew could be seen busily repairing the damage the *Néréide* had inflicted: the French colours flew at her peak.

'They are too close by far,' said Clonfert. He turned to the artillery officer, haggard and quite wretched at having been separated from his men, at having lost the finest opportunity of his professional career, and said, 'Captain Newnham, will the brass mortar fetch them, do you think?'

'I shall try it, my lord,' said Newnham. He loaded the piece himself with a thirteen-inch bomb-shell, laid it – a long and delicate operation – set the fuse just so, and fired. The shell soared high in the clear air, a rapidly-diminishing black ball, and burst right over the *Bellone*. A delighted cheer went up: the French ships slipped their cables and stood farther in, to anchor out of range. The last shell, fired at extreme elevation, fell short: and it was the last shot of the day.

The remaining hours of light saw all the precautions taken that should have been taken the day before: by the next morning the Ile de la Passe was capable of sinking any ship that attempted the passage. The *Néréide* had crossed new topgallantyards, had repaired her boom and fished her wounded foremast; and she sent in a boat to demand the surrender of the corvette.

'I hope to God Webber has found the *Sirius*,' said Clonfert, gazing eagerly out to sea. But the day passed, and no sail showed beyond the cape. The night passed too, with boats rowing guard: before sunrise the perilous land-breeze began to blow – perilous

because it might bring the powerful ships and a swarm of boats across the lagoon in the darkness, but the French never stirred, and at dawn the reviving south-easter kept them where they lay. So two days went by, with no incident apart from the French commodore's refusal to give up the *Victor*. The soldiers drilled and polished their equipment; the artillerymen exercised their pieces; the master-gunner filled cartridge and checked his stores. Clonfert remained as cheerful and active as ever, and his spirits reached a new height on the third day, when the French ships were seen to move down to the far end of the harbour, right down among the shoals and under the batteries of Port South-East, mooring in a curved line that stretched from one end of the sunken reef that guarded the port's entrance to the other; for this, said he, must mean that Webber had found the *Sirius*. At least some of the blockading force must have disappeared from off Port-Louis, and Governor Decaen, fearing an attack upon the *Minerve* and *Bellone*, had surely sent the news overland to Port South-East. Clonfert was right. Some hours later the *Sirius* herself rounded the cape under a great press of sail.

'Look sharp with the signal,' said Clonfert, when they had exchanged numbers. The prepared hoist broke out, and he laughed aloud.

'What does it signify?' asked Stephen.

'*Ready for action* and *Enemy of inferior force*,' replied Clonfert with a slightly conscious look; and immediately afterwards, 'Look alive with the book, Briggs. What is she saying?'

The signal-yeoman muttered the answer, and the midshipman spoke up: '*Send Néréide's master aboard*, my lord.'

'Gig's crew,' cried Clonfert. 'Mr Satterly, bring her in as quick as ever you can.'

In she came, and her last signal before she entered the channel told the *Néréide* to get under way. The *Sirius* passed the fort almost as fast as the *Bellone*, and still under her topsails and courses swept by the *Néréide*, Pym leaning over the rail and hailing Clonfert to follow him. Down the long winding channel they went, more cautiously now, but the *Sirius* still with her topsails set, for there was not much daylight left. In the *Néréide* her black pilot was at the con; he had her under staysails, no more, and he was muttering to himself, for after the Horseshoe bank their course would lead them into a region of the inner harbour that they did not know well – a region that they had avoided, it being swept by the guns of Port South-East.

Past the Noddy shoal, with the lead going fast: past the Three Brothers, and a four-point turn to larboard. The leadsman's calls came sharp, quick and clear: 'By the mark ten; and a half ten; by the deep eleven; by the deep eleven; by the mark fifteen.' A good depth of water, a clear channel one would have sworn: yet at the last call the *Sirius*, only just ahead, struck hard on the tail of a bank and ran far up on to the submerged coral.

Yet if she had to go aground at least she had chosen a good place for doing so. The shore-batteries could not reach her, and the wind, blowing right on to the land, pinned the French frigates to their moorings. The *Sirius* and the *Néréide* carried out their warps undisturbed as the sun set over Mauritius, and they settled down to heaving her off in a seamanlike manner. But she would not come off at the first heave, nor in the first hour of heaving, during which the tide began to ebb: however, tomorrow's flood would be higher and there were great hopes of floating her at about eight in the morning; and in the meantime there was nothing to be done except to ensure that no French boat-attack could succeed.

'What have you to say to our patient's present state of exaltation?' said Stephen to McAdam. 'In these circumstances, does it pass the limits of reasonable conduct? Do you find it morbid?'

'I am at a loss,' said McAdam. 'I have never seen him like this, at all. He may know what he is about, but he may be bent on wiping your friend's eye, and damn the whole world, so he does it. Have you ever seen a man look so beautiful?'

Dawn, and still the French had not moved. For once no holystone was heard aboard the *Sirius* or the *Néréide*; no swabs beat the decks, littered as they were with cables, hawsers, heavy tackles, all the resources of the bosun's art. The tide rose, the capstans turned, slower and slower as the full strain came on and as all hands who could find a place at the bars heaved and grunted in the increasing heat: and at last they heaved her grinding off into deep water, where she anchored by the *Néréide* and all the carpenters crowded about her bows, cut deep by the sharp and jagged coral. The exhausted hands were piped to their late breakfast, and they were beginning to set the still-encumbered deck into some kind of fighting-trim when the *Iphigenia* and *Magicienne* were seen in the offing.

Clonfert sent his master to bring them in, for Mr Satterly, though harassed and ashamed, now certainly knew the channel

up to this point very well; but he had grown so cautious that it was not until after dinner that they dropped anchor and all captains gathered aboard the *Sirius* to hear Pym's plan of attack. It was clear: it made good plain sense. *Néréide*, with her black pilot, was to lead in and anchor between the *Victor* and the *Bellone* at the northern end of the French line; *Sirius* with her eighteen-pounders was to anchor abreast of the *Bellone*; *Magicienne* between the *Ceylon* and the powerful *Minerve*; and *Iphigenia*, who also carried eighteen-pounders, abreast of the *Minerve*, closing the line on the south.

The captains returned to their ships. Clonfert, who did in fact look extraordinarily gay, young, and lighthearted, as though possessed by some happy spirit, went below to put on a new coat and fresh white breeches; coming on deck again he said to Stephen, with a particularly sweet and affectionate smile, 'Dr Maturin, I believe we may show you something to be compared to what you have seen with Commodore Aubrey.'

The *Sirius* made her signal, and the *Néréide*, slipping her cable, led in under staysails, her pilot conning the ship from the fore-topmast yard. The *Sirius* followed her, then the *Magicienne*, then the *Iphigenia*, each falling into line at intervals of a cable's length. On through the winding channel with the steady breeze, the shore coming closer and closer: with successive turns in the channel the intervals grew wider, and the *Sirius*, hurrying to close the gap and misjudging her swing, struck hard and grounded on the rocky edge. At the same moment the French frigates and the shore-batteries opened fire.

Pym hailed his ships to carry on. In five minutes the *Néréide* was out of the narrow pass. The *Magicienne* and the *Iphigenia*, judging the channel by the stranded *Sirius*, pressed on after her but now at a somewhat greater distance; and in the last wind, four hundred yards from the French line, the *Magicienne* took the ground. By now the French broadsides were sweeping high over the *Néréide*'s deck from stem to stern to disable her as she ran down, making for the *Victor*'s bow. 'Warm work, Dr Maturin,' said Clonfert, and then, glancing over the taffrail, '*Sirius* has not backed off; she is hard and fast,' he said. 'We must tackle the *Bellone* for her. Mr Satterly, lay me alongside the *Bellone*. Lay me alongside the *Bellone*,' he said louder, to be heard above the din; for now the bow guns were answering the French. 'Aye, aye, sir,' said the master. For another cable's length she held on, straight through the French fire: another fifty

yards, and the master, waving his hand to the watchful bosun, ordered the helm put up.

The *Néréide* swung round, dropped her anchor, and lay there broadside to broadside, abeam of the big Frenchman, and her twelve-pounders roared out at point-blank range. She was firing fast: the Marines and soldiers packed tight on the quarterdeck and forecastle were blazing away over the hammocks with steady pertinacity: stray ropes and blocks fell on to the splinter-netting overhead: smoke hung thick between the ships, continually renewed as it blew away, and through the smoke the *Bellone*'s guns flashed orange – flashes from the *Victor* too, on the *Néréide*'s starboard quarter.

Stephen walked across to the other side: the *Magicienne*, hard aground on her sharp piercing reef with her figurehead pointing at the French line, could nevertheless bring her forward guns to bear and she was hitting the enemy as hard as she could, while her boats worked furiously to get her off: the *Iphigenia* was close alongside the *Minerve*; they were separated by a long narrow shoal but they were not a stone's throw apart and they were hammering one another with appalling ferocity. The volume of noise was greater than anything Stephen had ever experienced: yet through it all there was a sound familiar to him – the cry of the wounded. The *Bellone*'s heavy guns were mauling the *Néréide* most terribly, tearing gaps in her hammocks, dismounting guns: presently she would use grape. He was a little uncertain of his position. In all previous engagements his place as a surgeon had been below, in the orlop; here it was perhaps his duty to stand and be shot at, to stand with nothing to do, like the army officers: it did not move him unduly, he found, though by now grape was screeching overhead. Yet at the same time men were carrying below in increasing numbers, and there at least he could be of some use. 'I shall stay for the present, however,' he reflected. 'It is something, after all, to view an action from such a vantage-point.' The glass turned, the bell rang: again and again. 'Six bells,' he said, counting. 'Is it possible we have been at it so long?' And it seemed to him that the *Bellone* was now firing with far less conviction, far less accuracy – that her ragged broadsides had far longer intervals between them.

A confused cheering forward, and from the *Iphigenia* too: a gap in the cloud of smoke showed him the weakly manned and weakly armed *Ceylon*, battered by the grounded *Magicienne* and by the *Iphigenia*'s quarter-guns, in the act of striking her colours;

and in one of those strange momentary pauses without a gun he heard the captain of the *Iphigenia* hail the *Magicienne* in a voice of thunder, desiring her to take possession of the Indiaman. But as the *Magicienne*'s boat neared her, pulling fast through water whipped white with small shot and great, the *Ceylon* dropped her topsails and ran for the shore behind the *Bellone*. The boat was still pursuing her and roaring out when the *Minerve*, either cutting her cable or having it cut for her by the *Iphigenia*'s murderous and continual fire, swung round, got under way, and ran straight before the wind, following the *Ceylon*. She steered better than the *Ceylon* however, for the Indiaman blundered right into the *Bellone*, forcing her too to cut. They all three drifted on shore – a heap of ships ashore, with the *Minerve* lying directly behind the *Bellone* and so near that she could not fire. But the *Bellone*'s broadside still lay square to the *Néréide*, and now men were pouring into her from the land and from the *Minerve* and the *Ceylon*: her fire, which had slackened, now redoubled and grew more furious still, the broadsides now coming fast and true. The *Iphigenia*, directly to the windward of her shoal and only a pistol-shot from it, could not stir, and it was clear that in these last few minutes the face of the battle had totally changed. There was no more cheering aboard the *Néréide*. The gun-crews, for all their spirit, were growing very tired, and the rate of fire fell off. By now the sun had almost gone: and the shore-batteries, which had hitherto played on the *Iphigenia* and the *Magicienne*, now concentrated their fire on the *Néréide*.

'Why do we swing so?' wondered Stephen, and then he realized that a shot had cut the spring on the *Néréide*'s cable, the spring that held her broadside-on to the *Bellone*. Round she came, and farther yet, until her stern took the ground, thumping gently with the swell and pointing towards the enemy, who poured in a steady raking fire. She still fired her quarter-guns and her stern-chaser, but now men were falling fast. The first lieutenant and three of the army officers were dead: blood ran over her quarterdeck not in streams but in a sheet. Clonfert was giving the bosun orders about a warp when a messenger from below, a little terrified boy, ran up to him, pointing at Dr Maturin as he spoke: Clonfert crossed the deck and said, 'Dr Maturin, may I beg you to give a hand in the orlop? McAdam has had an accident. I should be most infinitely obliged.'

McAdam's accident was an alcoholic coma, and his assistant, who had never been in action before, was completely over-

whelmed. Stephen threw off his coat, and in the darkness, weakly lit by a lantern, he set to work: tourniquet, saw, knife, sutures, forceps, probe, retractor, dressings, case after case, with the sometimes perilously delicate operations continually interrupted by the huge, all-pervading, sonorous jar of heavy shot smashing into the frigate's hull. And still the wounded came, until it seemed that half and even more than half of the *Néréide*'s company had passed through his bloody hands as she lay there, quite unsupported, her fire reduced to half a dozen guns.

'Make a lane there, make a lane for the Captain,' he heard, and here was Clonfert on the chest before him, under the lantern. One eye was torn out and dangling: maxilla shattered: neck ripped open and the carotid artery laid bare, pulsing in the dim light, its wall shaved almost to the bursting-point. A typical splinter-wound. And the frightful gash across his face was grape. He was conscious, perfectly clear in his mind, and at present he felt no pain, a far from uncommon phenomenon in wounds of this kind and at such a time. He was not even aware of the scalpel, probe and needle, except to say that they were oddly cold; and as Stephen worked over him he spoke, sensibly though in a voice altered by his shattered teeth, he told Stephen that he had sent to ask Pym whether he judged the ship could be towed out or whether the wounded should be put into the squadron's boats and the *Néréide* set on fire. 'She might wreck the *Bellone*, when she blows up,' he added.

His wounds were still being dressed when Webber came back from the *Sirius* with one of her officers and a message from Pym, a message that had to be shouted above the crash of the *Bellone*'s guns. Pym suggested that Clonfert should come aboard the *Sirius*. The *Iphigenia* could not possibly warp off from behind her shoal until daylight and in the meantime the *Néréide* lay between her and the French ships; she could not fire upon them; Lord Clonfert might certainly come aboard the *Sirius*.

'Abandon my men?' cried Clonfert in that strange new voice. 'I'll see him damned first. Tell him I have struck.' And when the officer had gone and the dressing was finished he said to Stephen, 'Is it done, Doctor? I am most truly grateful to you,' and made as though to rise.

'You will never get up?' asked Stephen.

'Yes,' he said. 'My legs are sound enough. I am going on deck. I must do this properly, not like a scrub.'

He stood up and Stephen said, 'Take care of the bandage on

your neck. Do not pluck at it, or you may die within the minute.

Shortly afterwards most of the remaining men came below, sent by the Captain: the routine of the ship was gone – there had been no bells this hour and more – and her life was going. Some clustered in the orlop, and from their low, muted talk and from those who came and went their shipmates learnt what was going on: a boat had come from the *Iphigenia* to ask why the *Néréide* was no longer firing, and would the Captain come aboard of her – told, had struck, and the Captain would not stir – Captain had sent to *Bellone* to tell her to stop firing, because why? Because he had struck; but the boat could not reach her nor make her hear. Then there was the cry of fire on deck and several men ran up to put it out: and shortly after the mainmast went by the board.

Lord Clonfert came below again, and sat for a while in the orlop. Although Stephen was still working hard he took a look at him between patients and formed the impression that he was in a state of walking unconsciousness; but after some time Clonfert got up and began moving about among the wounded, calling them by name.

It was long past midnight. The French fire was slackening; the British fire had stopped long since; and now after a few random shots the night fell silent. Men slept where they had chanced to sit or throw themselves down. Stephen took Clonfert by the arm, guided him to the dead purser's cot, well under the water-line, directed him how to rest his head so that he should not endanger his wound, and returned to his patients. There were more than a hundred and fifty of them: twenty-seven had already died below, but he had hopes for about a hundred of the rest: the dear knew how many had been killed outright on deck and thrown overboard. Seventy or so, he thought. He roused Mr Fenton, who was sleeping with his head on his arms, leaning on the chests that formed their operating-table, and together they looked to their dressings.

They were still busy when the sun rose and the *Bellone* began to fire at the *Néréide* again: on and on, in spite of repeated hails. The gunner came below with a gushing splinter-wound in his forearm, and while Stephen applied the tourniquet and tied the artery the gunner told him that the *Néréide*'s colours had not in fact been struck: they were flying still, and they could not be hauled down. There was a rumour that they had been nailed to the mast, but the gunner knew nothing of it, and the bosun, who

would have had the true word, he was dead. 'And not a scrap of rigging to come at them,' he said. 'So his lordship's told the carpenter to cut the mizen away. Thank you kindly, sir: that's a right tidy job. I'm much obliged. And, Doctor,' he said in a low rumble behind his hand, 'if you don't much care for a French prison, there's some of us topping our boom in the cutter, going aboard of *Sirius*.'

Stephen nodded, looked over his worst cases, and made his way through the wreckage to the cabin. Clonfert was not there. He found him on the quarterdeck, sitting on an upturned match-tub and watching the carpenters ply their axes. The mizenmast fell, carrying the colours with it, and the *Bellone*'s fire ceased. 'There, I have done it properly,' said Clonfert in a barely intelligible murmur, out of the side of his ruined, bandaged face. Stephen looked at his most dangerous wound, found him sensible, though by now at a far remove, and said, 'I wish to go to the *Sirius*, my lord: the remaining boat is fit to leave, and I beg you will give an order to that effect.'

'Make it so, Doctor Maturin,' said Clonfert. 'I wish you may get away. Thank you again.' They shook hands. Stephen took some papers from his cabin, destroyed others, and made his way to the boat. It was no great climb down, for the *Néréide* had settled on the sea-bed.

Although Pym received him kindly aboard the stranded *Sirius*, his conduct did not raise Stephen's opinion of him as a commander or as a man of sense. The *Iphigenia*, having at last warped herself free of the long shoal that had stood between her and the *Minerve*, sent to ask permission to stand in, to attack the immobilized French ships, boarding them with extra hands from *Sirius* and *Magicienne*, and not only taking them but rescuing the *Néréide* too. No, said Pym, who needed her help to heave his own ship off, she must go on warping towards the *Sirius*. Twice he sent back this categorical reply, each time as a direct order. With the *Iphigenia* warping out, the French fire concentrated on the *Magicienne*, hard and fast on her reef, badly holed, with nine foot of water in her hold and only a few guns that could be brought to bear. The French shot poured in upon her, and sometimes upon the other ships, and upon the frantically busy, exhausted hands in the remaining boats all that long, appalling, bloody day. It was impossible to get her off; it was impossible that she should swim if she were got off. Her men were ordered

203

into the *Iphigenia*, and after sunset she was set on fire, blowing up in doleful splendour about midnight.

The next day the French had a new battery ready on shore, closer to, and the battery and the ships began to fire on the *Iphigenia* and the *Sirius* as they strove to heave Pym's frigate off her reef. At last, after incessant labour all in vain, and after some ugly scenes with the captain of the *Iphigenia*, who was utterly convinced (and Stephen, together with many better-qualified observers, agreed with him) that his plan would have meant a total victory and who could barely bring himself to speak civilly to the man who had forbidden it, Pym realized that the *Sirius* could not be saved. Her ship's company were taken into the *Iphigenia* and the *Sirius* too was set on fire, Pym thereby relinquishing his command, twenty-four hours too late; and the now solitary *Iphigenia* returned to her warping.

She was obliged to warp – to carry out an anchor on the end of a cable, drop it, and wind herself up to it by the capstan – because never in the daylight did the wind cease blowing dead on shore. She could make no progress whatsoever in any other way, for when the land-breeze got up before dawn she dared not attempt the dark and unseen channel, and it always died with the rising of the sun. So hour after hour her boats, carrying the ponderous great anchors, dragged out the sodden nine-inch hawsers; and if the anchors held, if the ground was not foul, she then crept a very little way, rarely more than fifty yards, because of the turns. But often the ground was foul, and sometimes the anchors came home or were broken or were lost altogether; and all this exhausting labour had to be carried out in the blazing sun by a dispirited crew. Meanwhile the French ships in Port South-East had been heaved off, and a French brig was sighted beyond the Ile de la Passe, probably the forerunner of Hamelin's squadron from Port-Louis.

However, there was nothing for it, and the *Iphigenia* warped on and on towards the fort, fifty yards by fifty yards with long pauses for the recovery of fouled anchors, the whole length of that vast lagoon. It was two full days before she reached a point about three quarters of a mile from the island, and here she anchored for the night. The next day, when the *Bellone* and *Minerve* had profited by the land-breeze to advance far into the lagoon whose channels they knew so well, and had there anchored, she set to again; and by eight o'clock, when she was within a thousand feet of the fort, of the open sea and the infinite delight

of sailing free, she saw three ships join the French brig outside the reef: the *Vénus*, *Manche* and *Astrée*. They were exchanging signals with the *Bellone* and *Minerve*; and the wind, still right in the *Iphigenia*'s teeth, was bearing them fast towards the Ile de la Passe, where they would lie to, just out of range.

The *Iphigenia* at once sent the soldiers and many of the seamen to the fort and cleared for action. She had little ammunition, however: even before the end of the Port South-East battle she had had to send to the *Sirius* for more, and since then she had fired away so much that half an hour's engagement would see her locker bare. The clearing was therefore largely symbolic, and it was carried out, as her captain told Stephen privately, to let the French see that he would not surrender unconditionally, that he still had teeth, and that if he could not get decent terms he would use them.

'That being so,' said Stephen, 'I must ask you for a sailing-boat before the *Vénus* and her consorts close the entrance to the channel.'

'For Réunion, you mean? Yes, certainly. You shall have the launch and my own coxswain, an old whaling hand, and young Craddock to navigate her: though I should not carry the news that you must take, no, not for a thousand pound.' He gave orders for the preparation of the launch – stores, instruments, charts, water – and returning he said, 'You would oblige me extremely, Dr Maturin, by carrying a letter for my wife: I doubt I shall see her again this war.'

The launch pulled along the wicked channel in the darkness, touching twice for all their care; pulled out well beyond the reef, set her lugsail and bore away south-west. She carried ten days' provisions, but although she had many of the *Iphigenia*'s hungry young gentlemen and ship's boys aboard – their captain could not see them spend those years in a prison – the stores were almost intact when, after a perfect voyage, Stephen made his laborious way up the *Boadicea*'s side as she lay at single anchor in the road of St Paul's, close by the *Windham* and the *Bombay* transport.

'Why, Stephen, there you are!' cried Jack, springing from behind a mass of papers as Stephen walked into the cabin. 'How happy I am to see you – another couple of hours and I should have been off to Flat Island with Keating and his men – Stephen, what's amiss?'

'I must tell you what's amiss, my dear,' said Stephen: but he sat down and paused a while before going on. 'The attack on

Port South-East has failed. The *Néréide* is taken; the *Sirius* and *Magicienne* are burnt; and by now the *Iphigenia* and the Ile de la Passe will almost certainly have surrendered.'

'Well,' said Jack, considering, '*Minerve, Bellone, Astrée, Vénus, Manche*; together with *Néréide* and *Iphigenia*: that makes seven to one. But we have seen longer odds, I believe.'

Chapter Eight

'All hands unmoor ship,' said Jack. The bosun's calls wailed and twittered; the Boadiceas ran to their stations; the fife began its thin piercing tune; 'Stamp and go, stamp and go,' cried the bosun's mates; and in the midst of the familiar din of proceeding to sea Stephen turned from the rail, where he had been staring under his shading hand at the ship lying within the frigate. 'I could almost swear I had seen that vessel before,' he said.

'Oh, not above a hundred times,' said Jack. 'She is the *Windham*. The *Windham* Indiaman again. This time she was outward-bound, and they took her in the Mozambique channel. *Sirius* very nearly retook her when she shied away from Port South-East. Did not Pym tell you?'

'Faith, we had little conversation, Captain Pym and I.'

'No: I suppose not. But, however, Pullings snapped her up in his little schooner just as she was running under the guns of Rivière Noire: a good, seamanlike officer, Tom Pullings . . .'

'Up and down, sir,' called the bosun.

'Thick and dry,' came Jack's answer, as automatic as a response in church; and he continued '. . . and he brought her in, cracking on regardless. That was the first I knew of the affair. Let fall, there,' he cried, directing his voice upwards.

The topsails flashed out, the frigate's head swung to the north-east and steadied: she heeled, steeper and steeper as the courses, topgallants and staysails were sheeted home in smooth succession and the way came on her, the water slipping fast and faster still along her side. She shaved the cruel reef off Saint-Denis, altered course two points to eastward, and setting a flying-jib she stretched for the Ile de la Passe, making her ten knots watch after watch, her wake a straight green line of phosphorescence in the dark.

Every minute counted. Stephen's voyage had taken so little time that there was a possibility the fort had not yet surrendered, and that the *Iphigenia* still lay under its protection, within the reef. Every minute counted, and although sailcloth and spars were so precious they drove her through the sea as though they had a Spanish galleon in chase: with an even greater zeal indeed; so great that they raised the island before the light of day.

When he had two peaks of the Bamboo Mountain in a line and the Pointe du Diable bearing N 17 W Jack reduced sail, carried a night-glass up to the foretop, and took the ship in, ghosting along under topsails on the edge of the land-breeze. His eyes were used to the night, helped as it was by the stars and the sickle-moon: he had made out a good deal of what lay inshore and out to sea, and when the first dawn came up before the sun he was not surprised to see the *Manche* and *Vénus* – but not the *Astrée* – lying two miles off the reef to leeward, the *Iphigenia* just inside it, the *Bellone*, *Minerve*, *Néréide* and *Ceylon* Indiaman far over by Port South-East, and the charred wrecks of the *Sirius* and *Magicienne* in the lagoon. But what did give him a shock was the sight of a fifth ship down there, just astern of the shattered *Néréide*. Leaning his telescope on the rim and focusing with care he discovered what she was: the *Ranger* from Bombay. She was only a transport, but she would have been a treasure-ship to the remnant of his squadron, for she carried spare yards and topmasts, besides three hundred tons of invaluable stores, and he had been looking for her arrival at St Paul's these many days – the *Otter*, quite unfit for sea, was heaved down in expectation of what she should bring; the *Staunch* lacked almost everything; and if the *Boadicea* carried away a spar, she would have to whistle for it. And here was the *Ranger* fitting out the enemy. The *Bellone*, which must have suffered terribly in the long action, already had her topgallantyards across. His face took on a harder look.

No colours were flying yet from either the fort or the *Iphigenia*: had they surrendered? If not, conceivably his boats might tow the *Iphigenia* through the channel, covered by the *Boadicea* and the fort, and with even a battered consort he could set about the *Vénus* and the *Manche*; for although he was short of stores, he was rich in men and ammunition. And this was no time for timid defensive measures. He came down on deck, gave orders for the ensign, the private signal, and a hoist stating his intention. The *Boadicea* stood in as the sun came up, signals flying, one eye on the French frigates, the other on the fort and the *Iphigenia*. Farther and farther in, and still no colours, though the sun was now a hand's-breadth over the horizon. Another few minutes and the *Boadicea* would be within random shot.

'A gun to windward, Mr Seymour,' said Jack. 'And shiver the foretopsail.'

In reply the British colours ran up the not so distant flagstaff:

yet still the *Boadicea* hung off. Then after a pause in which hoists jerked up and down without the flags breaking out but with a crafty pretence of the halliard's jamming, the private signal.

'Hands about ship,' said Jack, for the island's private signal was ten days out of date.

Not one of the Boadiceas was unprepared for this, and she came about on to the larboard tack as briskly as a smuggling schooner, staying in her own length. The fort's seaward guns sent plumes of white water leaping from the swell two hundred yards short of her; a derisive cheer floated after them, and a little later a line of boats, carrying prisoners, put off the island for the *Manche*.

The *Manche* took them aboard and stood after the *Vénus*, which was already beating up under easy sail as though to get to the windward of the *Boadicea*. As soon as the *Manche* was up, both French frigates set their topgallants. They could be seen clearing for action, and they came on as though they meant it. Jack gazed at them with the utmost intensity, his eye hard to his glass, examining their captains' handling of their ships, gauging their sailing qualities, watching for ruses designed to mask their speed; and all the while he kept the *Boadicea* a little ahead, just out of range. By the time the watch had changed he knew he had the legs of them: he also knew that the *Vénus* could outsail the *Manche* and that if he could induce them to separate . . . but while his mind was running on to the possible consequences of this separation – to a night-engagement – to a boat-landing on the reef behind the fort – the French gave over the chase.

The *Boadicea* wore and pursued them, setting her royals to bring them within the extreme range of her brass bow-chaser, perched on the forecastle, and firing at the *Vénus*, which wore Hamelin's broad pendant. The *Vénus* and the *Manche* replied with guns run out of their gunroom ports, so low as to be ineffectual at this distance; and so the three ships ran, neither side doing the other any damage, until a lucky shot from the *Boadicea*, skipping three times over on the smooth swell, came aboard the *Vénus*. The midshipman high on the foremast jack reported a commotion on the *Vénus*'s quarterdeck: immediately afterwards the French ships went about, and once more the *Boadicea* ran south and west.

All day she ran, trying every kind of ruse and lame-duck trick to lure the faster-sailing *Vénus* ahead of the *Manche*: but nothing would serve. Hamelin had no romantic notions of single combat,

and he was determined to fight at an advantage. The two Frenchmen kept within half a mile of one another, doggedly chasing the *Boadicea* over the whole stretch of sea between Mauritius and La Réunion.

'At least we are tolerably well acquainted with our enemies,' said Jack to Seymour and the quarterdeck in general, when the lights of Saint-Denis bore south-west two miles, and all hope was gone.

'Yes, sir,' said Seymour. 'We could have given them topgallants at any time. Dirty bottoms, no sort of doubt.'

'*Manche* was precious slow, shifting her sheets over the stays,' said Trollope. 'I remarked it twice.'

'Surely, sir, they are not what you would call enterprising?' said Johnson.

'Slowbellies,' said an unidentified voice in the darkness.

In the cabin, over a late supper, Jack said to Stephen, 'Here is Fellowes' list of our requirements. May I beg you to go to Farquhar, tell him how things lie, and ask him to rouse out all that can possibly be found and have 'em down by the waterside at St Paul's in the morning? Make my excuses – I have a thousand things to do – he will understand.'

Before Stephen could answer, Spotted Dick walked in and said, 'You sent for me, sir?'

'Yes. Mr Richardson, you will take the *Pearl* aviso with four good hands and run up to Port-Louis, find the *Staunch*, and bring her down. Mr Peter has her orders ready for you to take.'

'So much responsibility for that pimply lad,' observed Stephen, through his Welsh rabbit.

'Aye,' said Jack, who had brought a prize hermaphrodite into Plymouth from far off Finisterre before his voice had broken. 'We must depend on our small-fry now, men and ships. If we had had the *Otter* or even the *Staunch* with us today, we could have made a dash at that unhandy *Manche*, you know.'

'Could we, indeed?'

'Lord, yes,' said Jack. 'And I trust we shall tomorrow. I have sent Seymour galloping over to St Paul's to bid Tomkinson leave the *Otter* where she lies, shift all his people into the *Windham*, and join me in the roadstead. With this wind getting up, Hamelin will stand off and on tonight, I am very sure.'

Hamelin was more off than on in the light of dawn when the *Boadicea* ran down to St Paul's, and the *Vénus* and the *Manche* were a mere flash of topsails against the western sky. But they

were there, and once he had settled that fact beyond any hint of a doubt, Jack Aubrey turned his glass to the distant shipping in the road.

'What in Hell's name is the *Windham* thinking of?' he cried. 'She has not even crossed her yards. Mr Collins: *Windham proceed to sea immediately*, with a gun; and give her another gun every minute until she weighs. God rot the . . .' He clapped his mouth shut, and clenching his hands behind his back he paced up and down. 'His face is darker than I have ever seen it,' observed Stephen, looking at him from the taffrail. 'Up until now, he has borne these reverses with a singular magnanimity, greater by far than I had looked for. Not a word about Clonfert's disastrous folly; nothing but sympathy for his wounds, and a hope that the French hospital may set him up. No reflection upon Pym's dogged stupidity. Yet there is no greatness of mind without its limits: is this his breaking-point?'

'Shot the next gun,' said Jack, stopping short in his stride, with a furious glare at the far-off Hamelin.

'Sir,' said Trollope timidly, 'a transport is rounding the point. The *Emma*, I believe. Yes, sir, the *Emma*.'

The *Emma* she was, and quite apart from her signal it was evident that she wished to speak the *Boadicea* as she hovered there, backing and filling in a black fury of impatience; for the slab-sided transport had already spread a great press of sail.

'*Captain come aboard pendant*, Mr Collins,' said Jack.

The *Emma*'s stern-boat splashed down, pulled across, hooked on, and Pullings came up the side. 'Mr Pullings,' said Jack, 'what is this caper?'

'I beg pardon, sir,' said Pullings, pale with emotion. 'I have *Windham*'s guns aboard: Captain Tomkinson declined the command.'

'Come below and explain yourself,' said Jack. 'Mr Seymour, carry on: course nor'-nor'-west.'

In the cabin it appeared, from Pullings' nervous, involved, embarrassed statement that Tomkinson, having looked into the Indiaman's condition, had refused to take her to sea until she should be made seaworthy, and had returned to the immobilized *Otter*. Pullings, a witness of this, had come to an agreement with the *Emma*'s captain, sick ashore; had moved his men and a score of volunteers into her, she being in a better state than the Indiaman, and by inhuman labour all through the night had shifted the *Windham*'s guns and his own carronades across, helped by

211

Colonel Keating, who had also given him gunners and small-arms men.

'This Tomkinson,' cried Stephen, who could speak openly before Pullings, 'must he not be hanged, or flogged, or at least dismissed the service, the infamous whore?'

'No,' said Jack. 'He is a poor creature, God help him, but he is within his rights. A captain can refuse a command, on those grounds. Tom,' he said, shaking Pullings' hand, 'you are a right sea-officer; I am obliged to you. If you can get eight knots out of your *Emma*, we shall have a touch of those Frenchmen out there, before long.'

The two ships bore away in company, steering a course that would give them the weather-gage in a couple of hours, well north of the island, where the wind came more easterly. But in far less time than that it became apparent to all hands that the *Emma* could not keep up. Six or at the most seven knots was her utmost limit, even with the wind abaft the beam – studdingsails aloft and alow, and even kites, strange sails without a name, all set and drawing – and once they had hauled their wind three points, even six was beyond her power, driven though she was with all the resources of seamanship and an able, willing crew. The *Boadicea* had to take in her topgallants to keep the *Emma* in sight at all; while on the other hand, Hamelin, the necessary complement of a quarrel, kept steadily ahead, with never a sign of reducing sail, still less of heaving-to to wait for them.

Yet for all that, Hamelin had now run so far to the westward that he would have to go up to Port-Louis rather than Port South-East, which was something gained, since it would allow Jack to look into the Ile de la Passe again: and the *Emma* was there to perform a most important task that should have fallen to the *Otter*.

'Back the foretopsail, Mr Johnson, if you please,' said Jack, just before the hands were piped to dinner; and when the *Emma* had come labouring up he hailed Pullings, directing him to make for Rodriguez, acquaint the military with the situation, and then to cruise between that island and 57° East to warn any King's or Company's ships he saw, at the same time taking all appropriate measures. 'And Mr Pullings,' he added, in his strong voice, 'I shall not object to your taking one of their frigates, or even two: that will still leave plenty for me.'

The joke was limp enough, in all conscience; but the tone in which it was said, or rather roared, caused Pullings' distressed,

tired face to spread in an answering grin.

The *Boadicea* looked at the Ile de la Passe, which greeted her with a roar of heavy guns: she looked beyond it, over the billowing smoke, into Port South-East, and there she saw the *Bellone*, new-rigged and ready for sea. The *Minerve* now had jury topmasts and the *Néréide* something in the way of a main and a mizen, while caulkers and carpenters were busy about them both: the *Iphigenia* had already sailed. There was nothing to be done, and the *Boadicea* turned about for La Réunion.

'Mr Seymour,' said Jack, in that curiously detached, impersonal tone that had come on him since the news of the defeat, 'when did we last exercise the guns?'

'Several days ago, sir. Much longer than usual,' said Seymour, searching wildly in his mind for the exact date; for this new and somewhat inhuman commodore, though neither fault-finding nor severe, put the fear of God into the quarterdeck. 'It was last Saturday, I believe.'

'Then we will advance quarters by half an hour, and rattle them in and out. We can afford two – no, three – rounds a gun; and I believe we may fire upon targets.'

If Hamelin was the man Jack thought him to be, he would surely have *Astrée* and one or two of his corvettes cruising between Mauritius and Réunion by now, and the sound of gunfire might bring them down: so late that afternoon the sky echoed to *Boadicea*'s thunder. The gun-crews, stripped to the waist and gleaming with sweat, plied the massive cannon with even more than their usual diligence, for they too had long since caught their commander's mood: he watched them with a grave satisfaction, a remarkably healthy crew, well fed on fresh meat and garden-stuff, in fine fettle and high training. Good men; a rapid, accurate fire, surpassing anything the *Boadicea* had yet achieved by a clear eight seconds. Although the *Boadicea* was not and never could be an outstanding sailer, he need not fear any single French ship afloat in these waters; nor any two, if only he had the support of a well-handled sloop and if only he could bring them to that perilous thing, an engagement in the darkness, when high discipline and true aim counted for so much. Yet when the guns were housed and cool again the sea remained as empty as it had been before, a vast disk of unbroken blue, now fast darkening to deep sapphire: there was to be no action that night.

Nor the next day either, in the twenty miles of sea before the

frigate dropped anchor at St Paul's again. No action at sea, but enormous activity on shore. Jack flung himself into the task of getting the *Otter* and the *Windham* into fighting-trim. He took little notice of Captain Tomkinson, now perhaps the unhappiest man on La Réunion, but directed the work himself: with the Governor's total, intelligent support, he had a sovereign hand in the yards of St Paul's and Saint-Denis, and there, labouring through the night by flares, every artificer in the island did all that could conceivably be done to turn a sixteen-gun sloop and a decayed, cruelly battered Indiaman with no guns but what the soldiers could afford her into honorary frigates, or at least into something that might have some remote chance of standing the enemy's fire, of holding him long enough for the *Boadicea* to run alongside and board.

On the Sunday morning, with the *Otter* in her final stage of refitting but with the *Windham* still heaved down, he was taking a very late breakfast after four hours of the deepest sleep he had known, taking it in the company of Stephen Maturin, whom he saw but rarely these days: he had resolutely dismissed the problems of the dockyard from his mind for twenty minutes, when Stephen involuntarily brought them back by asking the significance of the devil, among those that followed the sea, as in the devil to pay, a phrase he had often heard, particularly of late – was it a form of propitiation, a Manichaean remnant, so understandable (though erroneous) upon the unbridled elements?

'Why, the devil, do you see,' said Jack, 'is the seam between the deck-planking and the timbers, and we call it the devil, because it is the *devil* for the caulkers to come at: in full we say, the devil to pay and no pitch hot; and what we mean is, that there is something hell-fire difficult to be done – must be done – and nothing to do it with. It is a figure.'

'A very elegant figure, too.'

'Was you a weak, superficial cove, and feeling low, you might say it described our situation at the moment,' said Jack. 'But you would be wrong. With *Staunch*, and *Otter* and *Windham* in a day or two ...' he cocked his ear, and called out, 'Killick, who is that coming aboard?'

'Only an army officer, sir.'

The clash of Marines presenting arms on the quarterdeck: a midshipman to ask whether the Commodore would receive Colonel Fraser, and then the Colonel himself, his face as scarlet

214

as his coat from galloping under the torrid sun.

'Good morning, Colonel,' said Jack. 'Sit down and take a cup.'

'Good morning, sir. Doctor, how d'ye do?'

'Colonel Fraser should instantly drink something cool, and throw off his stock,' said Stephen. 'Your servant, sir.'

'Happy to do so, sir, in one minute; but first I must deliver my despatch – verbal, sir: no time to call for pen and ink. Colonel Keating's compliments to Commodore Aubrey, and HMS *Africaine* is in Saint-Denis. Captain Corbett –'

'Corbett? Robert Corbett?'

'I believe so, sir: a little man, looks rather black and cross when put out – the same that was here before – splendid disciplinarian. Captain Corbett, sir, proceeding to Madras, learnt of the state of affairs here from one of your ships when he was putting in to water at Rodriguez, so he turned off to La Réunion. He had some kind of a small engagement with a schooner on the coast of the Mauritius on the way and he is now landing his wounded: Colonel Keating has given him twenty-five men and an officer to take their place, because, sir, two French frigates and a brig are coming in after him. And Captain Corbett charges me to say, with his duty, that he has taken the liberty of hoisting your broad pendant, to amuse 'em, that he is clearing for action, and will put to sea the moment all his wounded are ashore.'

'Colonel,' said Jack, 'I am infinitely obliged to you. Killick, light along a jug of something cool for Colonel Fraser – sandwiches – mangoes.' These words he called backwards as he ran on to the quarterdeck. 'Mr Trollope, all hands from the yard immediately, and prepare to slip the moment they are aboard. Mr Collins, to *Otter* and *Staunch*: *proceed to sea immediately* and *enemy cruising east-north-east*. Pass the word for the gunner.' The gunner came running, for the news was spreading fast. 'Mr Webber,' said Jack, 'how much have you filled?'

'Thirty rounds a gun, sir,' said the gunner, 'and twenty-three for the carronades: we been at it all this forenoon.' And then, encouraged by old acquaintance and by the glowing change in the Commodore, 'May I hope to fill some more, sir, for the right true end?'

'Yes, Mr Webber,' said Jack. 'And none of your white letter stuff. Let it all be our very best red large grain.'

Rounding the Pointe des Galets at noon, the *Boadicea*, followed by the *Otter* and the *Staunch*, made out the French ships in the

offing: two frigates. The French brig was already topsails down to the northwards, no doubt hurrying off to tell Hamelin what was afoot. There was a general hum of satisfaction, tempered by the fact that the Frenchmen were no longer standing in, but had gone about on the starboard tack, and by the sight of long white lines far out, which meant that the wind, south or south-east to the leeward of La Réunion, was blowing from the east to the north of it, so that the enemy would have the weather-gage. They also saw the *Africaine*, and the actual sight of her raised Jack's heart still higher: she was a thirty-six-gun eighteen-pounder frigate, French-built of course, and one of the finest sailers in the Royal Navy, particularly on a wind. She must have been the plum with which Corbett was rewarded when he brought home the St Paul's despatches. 'He will certainly handle her well,' reflected Jack. 'A capital seaman. Let us hope he has taught his men how to point their guns this time, and that he has made himself more amiable aboard her.' A plum sometimes had that effect upon a disappointed man; and Corbett had often been disappointed.

When he caught sight of her, the *Africaine* was also on the starboard tack, under a press of sail, about eight miles south of the enemy. The two ships exchanged numbers, no more. Jack had no intention of worrying the *Africaine* with signals: Corbett was a fighting captain; he knew very well what to do; there was no doubt that he would do it; and in the meantime he must be left free to concentrate on making up at least seven of those eight miles. The same applied with even greater force to the *Boadicea*: although she could hit harder than the *Africaine*, she could not rival her in speed. Happily one of the Frenchmen was their old *Iphigenia*, now the *Iphigénie* once more, and she was no flyer: the other was probably the *Astrée*, whose qualities he did not know.

He would soon find them out, however, he said, smiling, as he took his glass into the foretop and the six ships settled down to the long chase. An hour later he knew that she had an able captain, that she was faster than the *Iphigenia*, but not faster than the *Boadicea*, while the *Africaine* could give her topgallantsails at least. If the wind held true, the *Africaine* should be up with them before sunset, and the *Boadicea* not long after dark. If the wind held true: that was his chief concern. For were it to back more easterly or even a little north of east as it sometimes did by night, then the *Boadicea* would be dead to leeward of the Frenchmen, and they might be able to run up to Port-Louis before that leeway

216

could be made up. For the *Boadicea* was not at her best on a bowline: and although he would not have it generally known, she could not come up so close to the wind as some other ships, not by half a point, in spite of all his care.

Yet taking thought would neither keep the wind south of east nor improve the *Boadicea*'s sailing: he came down, glanced at the now distant *Staunch* and *Otter*, he told Seymour that he was to be called in case the position changed, and went fast to sleep in a hammock slung in the desolate clean sweep fore and aft that had once been his array of cabins, knowing that his officers would sail the ship admirably well and that he must keep his wits as sharp as they could be for what might well be a difficult night-engagement, calling for instant decision.

When he came on deck again the *Otter* and the *Staunch* were barely in sight from the masthead: the *Africaine* was something better than two leagues ahead and she was gaining visibly on the Frenchmen. At his second hail the lookout replied, after a studying pause, that *Staunch* and *Otter* had vanished now: and while the lookout was answering, an unpleasant rattle accompanied his voice: the wind had come too far forward for the studdingsails to set, and they were shivering, in spite of fiddle-taut bowlines. The *Boadicea* took them in: she lost way at once, and presently the *Africaine* was a full eight miles away, pursuing the now invisible French towards the coming night.

A dirty night, though warm, with sudden squalls and a mounting cross-sea that kept forcing the *Boadicea*'s head northwards. The best helmsmen in the ship were at the wheel, with Jack behind them, standing by the master at the con. For some little while after full darkness he saw the rockets and the blue lights that showed the *Africaine*'s position. Then nothing. Hour after hour of low driving cloud, very heavy showers of rain, the seas breaking over her starboard bow, the wind in the rigging as she stood on and on; but never the sound that the silent, listening men were waiting for.

Nothing until seven bells in the middle watch, when the breeze turned gusty before dropping to something near a calm: at seven bells and again at the changing of the watch flashes were seen under the cloud to windward, and remote gunfire followed them. 'God send he has not engaged close without me,' murmured Jack, altering course for the flash. That fear had occurred to him in these hours of waiting, together with others, equally wild: but he had put it away – Corbett was no Clonfert; and in

217

any case Corbett knew the *Boadicea*'s rate of sailing perfectly.

The gunfire was louder every glass; but at every glass the breeze grew less; and at last the *Boadicea* had scarcely steerage-way. The short twilight before dawn was veiled by a last sheet of tepid rain. It faded slowly in the still air as the sun rose up; and all at once there was the whole stretch of sea, brilliantly lit, and upon it, four miles away, the *Africaine* with one French ship within pistol-shot on her bow, another on her quarter. She was firing an occasional gun: the enemy answered with full broadsides: then she fell silent.

Four miles away: clear in his telescope Jack saw her colours waver at the peak and come slowly down, down, right down on deck; and still the French kept firing. For a quarter of an hour they kept firing into her silent hull.

Never had he had to master himself with such force: the sight was so horrible that if the breeze had not got up while he was watching it seemed that his heart must break with grief and rage. The royals took it first. The *Boadicea* gave a gentle heave against the sea and the water began to whisper along her side. Jack gave his orders automatically; said, 'Mr Seymour, the slow-match needs renewing,' and took the *Boadicea* down towards the Frenchmen as they lay about their prize, the boats coming and going. 'Masthead, there,' he called. 'What do you see of *Staunch* and *Otter*?'

'Nothing, sir,' came the reply. 'Nothing to windward, nothing to leeward.'

Jack nodded. The breeze was freshening; he could feel it on his cheek, coming beautifully though soft from the south-east and even south of that – the breeze that would have brought him up. The *Boadicea* stood on; and as they watched the *Africaine*'s masts went by the board; first her foremast, then the mizen, then the main. The *Astrée* and the *Iphigenia* did not appear to have suffered at all.

Whatever it cost, he must resist the temptation to run down and engage them: it would be criminal folly. But the temptation to set the *Boadicea* right between the two, firing both sides, was terribly strong; and with the wind as it lay he might be able to yield just so far and still regard his duty – a quick hard strike and away was allowable: it was even called for.

'Mr Seymour,' said he, 'I am going to run down to within musket-shot of the windward ship. When I give the order, let the starboard guns fire, starting from forwards: deliberate

fire at her stern, the smoke to clear between each shot. When the last gun has fired, about ship, and then the larboard broadside as we go about to come up as near as she will lie. Mr Buchan, lay me for the *Iphigenia*.'

The *Boadicea* was bringing up the wind. The Frenchmen had steerage-way, but little more, while she was moving at three knots; and the *Astrée*, behind the *Africaine*, had not run clear before Jack said 'Fire.' The guns went off in steady, even succession, undisturbed by the ragged broadsides from the *Iphigenia*, the first two wild, the third deadly enough: the *Boadicea*'s was a deliberate fire, aimed with hatred, and hammocks and splinters of rail leapt from the *Iphigenia*'s stern; one fine shot from number twelve struck her between wind and water very near her rudder and a cheer went up. Then the cry 'Helm's a-lee,' and the *Boadicea* came up into the wind. She was in stays when the *Astrée*, clear of the *Iphigenia* and the *Africaine* at last, let fly. She hit the *Boadicea* very hard, shattering the stern-boat on its davits and giving her such a blow that for a moment Jack thought she was going to fall off – that he had risked her just that hair's-breadth too far. 'Flat in forward, there,' he cried, felt the fine balance change, and with infinite relief called, 'Mainsail haul.' Round she came and filled, the way still on her: round, round, till her larboard ports stared full at the *Iphigenia*. With one great rippling crash her broadside went off, and she sailed clear of her smoke. At the same moment a shot from the *Astrée* struck the master in the back, cutting him in two at Jack's side. Jack saw his astonished, indignant face jerk forward, knocking the starboard helmsman down. He took the man's place for a moment, bringing the frigate still farther round until her head-sails shivered and a quartermaster seized the spokes; then stepping over the body he walked to the taffrail. The *Iphigenia*'s stern had suffered, but her rudder had not gone, nor yet her mizenmast. She had dropped her foresail and was now before the wind, moving down towards the *Astrée*, masking her fire again: he heard the master's body splash into the sea as he considered her: a scratch crew, no doubt, with not much sense and still less appetite for a close engagement with the *Boadicea*. And as the *Boadicea* stretched away close-hauled and the distance widened, he saw the *Iphigenia* put up her helm and fall foul of the *Astrée*, just as the *Astrée* tried to slip through the gap between her and the *Africaine* to rake the *Boadicea* at extreme range.

He took the frigate some way to windward and there heaved

to. In the brilliant sunlight he could see the French ships perfectly, the people on their decks, even the state of their rigging. Sitting on the slide of the aftermost carronade he contemplated the scene; for this was a time for contemplation. No sudden decisions were called for at this point, nor would they be required for some considerable time. The *Astrée* was a formidable ship; she was undamaged; she had disentangled herself from the *Iphigenia* and had worn clear at last; the sea between her and the *Boadicea* was clear. Yet she did not come on. Her shivering foretopsail – her deliberately shivering foretopsail – told him a great deal about her commander, and a score of less obvious details told him more: a competent seaman, no doubt, but he did not mean to fight. He no more meant to fight than Hamelin, at an even greater advantage, had meant to fight; neither this man nor his commodore chose to risk the throw. The conviction, growing stronger as he watched, filled him with grave joy.

On the other hand, said his reason as it compelled his heart to be quiet, the *Astrée* carried a great broadside weight of metal, her gunnery was accurate, and although she was not faster than the *Boadicea* she could haul closer to the wind: then again, attack and defence were two different things; in a close action the *Astrée* would do tolerably well, and although the *Iphigenia* was handled by a nincompoop, tackling the two of them together by daylight would be unjustifiable in the present balance. Yet he must necessarily retake the *Africaine* ...

'On deck, there,' hailed the lookout. 'Two sail right to windward, sir. I think it's *Staunch* and *Otter*.' Some minutes later, 'Yes, sir: *Staunch* and *Otter*.' With this wind it would take them two or three hours to reach him: very well. He stood up smiling and looked across to the lee side, where his first lieutenant, the carpenter and the bosun were waiting to report.

'Three wounded, sir,' said Seymour, 'and of course poor Mr Buchan.' The carpenter had only four shot-holes and eight inches of water in the well: Fellowes gave an account of a fair amount of damage to the sails and rigging forward. 'I reckon an hour will see it to rights, sir,' he added.

'As smartly as ever you can, Mr Fellowes,' said Jack. 'Mr Seymour, let the hands go to breakfast; and the watch below must have some rest.'

He went down into the orlop, where he found Stephen reading in a small book, holding it up to the lantern.

'Are you hurt?' asked Stephen.

'No, not at all, I thank you: I am come down to look at the wounded. How are they coming along?'

'Colley, the depressed cranial fracture, I will not answer for: he is comatose, as you see. We must operate as soon as we have peace and quiet and light – the sooner the better. The two splinter-wounds will do very well. Your breeches are covered with blood.'

'It is the master's. He lost the number of his mess right by me, poor fellow.' Jack went over to the patients, asked them how they felt, told them that things looked very well on deck, that *Staunch* and *Otter* were coming up hand over fist, and that presently the Frenchmen might be served out for what they did to the *Africaine*. Returning to Stephen he said, 'Killick has a little spirit-stove on the go, if you could fancy breakfast.'

And standing by the stern-window while the coffee flowed into them by the pint, he explained the situation, pointing out just how the French lay now and how they had lain at different stages. 'I know you will think it illogical,' he said, his hand firmly gripping the wooden frame, 'and maybe even super-stitious, but I have a feeling that the tide has turned. I do not mean to tempt fate, God forbid, but I believe that when the *Staunch* and *Otter* join, we shall retake the *Africaine*. We might even snap up the *Iphigenia*: she is shy; I think we may have hit her hard – look at the people over her side; and the captain of the *Astrée* don't trust her. But I will not go so far as that: the *Africaine* will be enough.'

On deck once more, and a surprisingly respectable deck, with the knotting and splicing almost finished, the swabbers of the afterguard washing the last pale smears from by the wheel, the davits righted, a new foretopsail bent: over the water the French boats were still removing prisoners from the *Africaine*, the *Iphigenia*'s pumps were going hard, and from the look of the feverish activity among the parties inboard and outboard of her, she would be in no way to get under sail for some time. The *Astrée* had moved into a better position to cover her and the *Africaine*: her captain might be no fire-eater, but clearly he meant to cling to his prize if he possibly could. But now from the deck the *Staunch* and *Otter* could be seen hull up; and the breeze was blowing fresher.

An early dinner, cold, and the grog cut by half; yet there was no grumbling. The Commodore's look of contained pleasure, his certainty, the indefinable change that had come over him, had

spread a feeling of total confidence throughout the ship. The hands ate their good biscuit and their execrable cheese, wetted with more watered lime-juice than rum, and they looked at him, they looked at the Frenchmen in their uneasy heap to leeward, they looked at the two ships coming closer every minute, and they talked in low cheerful voices: there was a good deal of quiet laughter in the waist and on the forecastle.

With a piece of chalk the Commodore drew his plan of attack on the deck: the captains of the sloop and the brig watched attentively. The three were to run down in line abreast, the *Boadicea* in the middle, and they were to endeavour to separate the two French frigates; there were many possibilities, depending on the movements of the *Astrée*, and Jack explained them clearly. 'But at all events, gentlemen,' he said, 'in case of the unforeseen, you will not go far wrong by closing with the *Iphigenia*, ahead and astern, and leaving the *Astrée* to me.'

With the wind three points abaft the beam, and under topsails alone for freedom of manoeuvre, they bore down, the brig looking pitifully small on the *Boadicea*'s starboard beam and the sloop a mere wisp to port. Jack had given them plenty of time to feed and rest their hands; he knew that they were thoroughly prepared and well manned, and that their commanders understood his intentions beyond any sort of doubt.

He had foreseen a great many possibilities, and he stood on with a confidence that he had rarely felt so strongly before, a steady rising of his heart; but he had not foreseen what in fact took place. They were still a mile and a half away when the *Astrée* passed the *Iphigenia* a towline and both frigates made sail. Abandoning the *Africaine*, they gathered way, packed on more sail and still more, hauled their wind and stretched to the eastwards as fast as they could go, the fine-sailing *Astrée* keeping the *Iphigenia*'s head right up to the wind, closer than ever the *Boadicea* could lie.

By coming to instantly it was conceivable that since she was somewhat to windward the *Boadicea* might bring them to action at the end of a very long converging chase, in spite of the *Astrée*'s superiority on a bowline; but neither the *Otter* nor the *Staunch* could possibly keep up, and in the meanwhile it was probable that Hamelin's reinforcement, brought by the French brig, would be down for the *Africaine*. No: this, alas, was a time for discretion, and the *Boadicea* stood quietly on for the sad dismantled hulk.

which lay wallowing on the swell with no more than her ensign-staff to show the French colours.

The *Boadicea* came alongside: the *Africaine* fired two guns to leeward and the French colours came down, to the sound of immense cheering from the prisoners still aboard her. 'Mr Seymour,' said Jack, with a feeling of anticlimax, yet with a deep glowing satisfaction beneath it, 'be so good as to take possession. What the devil is this?'

This was the sight of a score of Africaines plunging into the sea, swimming across, and swarming up the side of the *Boadicea*. They were in a state of wild enthusiasm, joy and rage strangely mingled: nearly all sense of discipline was gone and they crowded dripping on to the quarterdeck, begging the Commodore to renew the action – they would fight his guns for him – they would be happy to serve under Captain Aubrey – not like under some brass-bound buggers – they knew him – and they knew he could serve those French farts out for what they done – take on two of them at any time like kiss your hand – 'I know you can do it, sir,' cried one with a bloody dressing round his upper arm, 'I was shipmates along of you in *Sophie*, when we fucked the big Spaniard. Don't say no, sir.'

'I am glad to see you, Herold,' said Jack, 'and I wish I could say yes, with all my heart. But you are a seaman – look how they lay. Three hours stern-chase, and five French frigates to northwards ready to come down for the *Africaine*. I understand your feelings, lads, but it's no go. Bear a hand with a towline, and we shall take your barky into St Paul's and refit her: then you shall serve the Frenchmen out yourselves.' They looked longingly at the *Astrée* and the *Iphigenia*, and they sighed; but as seamen they had nothing to say. 'How is Captain Corbett?' asked Jack. 'Did the French take him aboard?'

Silence. Then, 'Don't know, sir.' He looked at them in surprise. In front of him was a row of closed faces: the rare, immediate, man-to-man contact was entirely gone: he had run straight into the brick wall of lower-deck dumbness, the covering-up solidarity he knew so well, often stupid, generally transparent, but always unbreakable. 'Don't know, sir,' was the only answer he would ever get.

Chapter Nine

Slowly the *Boadicea* dragged the *Africaine* southwards through the rising swell: she behaved like a sodden tree-trunk of enormous size, now lagging sullenly so that the *Boadicea*'s masts complained and Seymour's hoarse whisper – all that was left of his voice – desired the hands 'to start that — sheet before everything carried away', now darting unpredictably at the *Boadicea*'s stern and then slewing so that the towline jerked from the sea, a rigid bar of rope on the verge of rupture, squirting water from every strand; and above all she rolled, a dead lurching drunken gunwale-roll that made the surgeons' work even more hazardous and delicate than usual.

Stephen was there, helping poor Mr Cotton, an elderly cripple who had scarcely recovered from a bout of dysentery and who had been overcome with work from the first few minutes of the action. Even now, after a shocking number of deaths below, sixty or seventy cases remained, lying all along the berth-deck: there was plenty of room, at least, since the French had killed forty-nine men outright and had taken fifty prisoners away. The Africaines who remained, helped by a party from the *Boadicea*, were busily lashing what spars they possessed to the stumps of the masts, and towards nightfall they were able to set three staysails, which at once gave the frigate back her life, so that she moved like a sentient being once more, with no more of a roll than a reasonable ship.

'What a relief,' said Mr Cotton, plying his saw. 'At one time I feared I was about to be seasick again – seasick after all these years afloat! A ligature, if you please. Are you subject to the seasickness, Dr Maturin?'

'I have known it in the Bay.'

'Ah, the Bay,' said Cotton, tossing the detached foot into a bucket held by his loblolly boy, 'that dismal tract. You may let him go,' he said to the patient's messmates, who had been holding him; and into the grey, sweating face he said, 'John Bates, it is all over now. You will do very well, and that foot will earn you a Greenwich pension or a cook's warrant.'

The grey, sweating face murmured in a tiny voice, thanking

Mr Cotton, and might he keep the foot, for luck?

'That finishes our urgent cases,' said Mr Cotton, looking round. 'I am infinitely obliged to you, sir. Infinitely obliged; and I wish I had something better to offer you than a dish of tea. But the French stripped us, stripped us like a pack of savages, sir. Fortunately they do not care for tea.'

'A dish of tea would be most welcome,' said Stephen, and they walked aft to the deserted gunroom. 'A bloody action,' he observed.

'I have rarely seen a bloodier,' said Mr Cotton. 'Nor, I suspect, a more unnecessary waste of life. Still, the captain has paid for it, for what comfort that may be.'

'Killed he was?'

'Killed, or call it what you choose. At all events he is dead,' said Cotton. 'He was brought below at the very beginning – metacarpals of the left foot all abroad. I did what I could, and he insisted on being carried up again – he was a brave man, you know, with all his faults. Then he was hit a second time, but who fired the piece I will not say; nor will I absolutely assert that in the confusion of the night-engagement his own people tossed him over the side; but in any case he disappeared. I dare say you have known similar cases.'

'I have heard of them, of course; and in this particular instance I had some hint of it long ago. Captain Corbett's reputation as a flogging captain had spread pretty wide, I believe.'

'So wide that the hands mutinied when he was appointed to the ship: refused to take her to sea. I was on leave at the time, and when I came back I was surprised to find that the officers sent down from London had persuaded them that he was not as black as he was painted – had persuaded them to return to their duty.'

'Why were you surprised, sir?'

'Because those reputations are never wrong. He *was* as black as he was painted. He flogged those men down to the line, he flogged them across it, and he flogged them all the way up from the Cape.'

'A parenthesis – did you carry any mail for the Cape, any mail for us?'

'Yes; and we were to carry yours on to Rodriguez. But as you know, we never touched there – turned right about the moment we had spoken the *Emma* – and I am sorry to say the Frenchman got it all.'

'Well, well. And yet the men fought with great spirit, I collect?'

'With very great spirit; and that was because they had a decent set of officers. Captain Corbett was scarcely on speaking-terms with any of them: never dined in the gunroom but once, never invited. And the men would have fought her even better if they had been taught how to use the guns: never exercised with them once, all because of that holy deck. It must be in a pretty state at this moment. No: the hands had nothing against the officers, who were a decent set of men, as I say, and game to the last – Tullidge fought the ship after the captain was gone, and he was wounded four times; Forder, the second, had a bullet through the lungs, and Parker's head was shot off. Good officers. Once, when we were off Cape St Roque and Corbett was handing out fifty lashes right and left, they asked me whether they might confine him, and I said no. I was sorry for it afterwards, because although the fellow was sane enough ashore, he was mad at sea: mad with authority.'

'Sure, it is a dangerous draught,' said Stephen. 'Yet some resist it. What is the source of their immunity?'

'What indeed?' replied Mr Cotton. His weariness was too great for speculation, though not for civility, and when Stephen took his leave he said, 'You were a God-send, Dr Maturin: may I in my turn be of any use to you?'

'Since you are so good,' said Stephen, 'it does so happen that I have a singularly delicate depressed fracture waiting for me tomorrow, and if by then you feel sufficiently recovered, I should be most grateful for your support. My young man has no experience of the trephine, and my hands are not so steady as they were – they do not possess your admirable firmness of grip.'

'I shall be with you, sir, at any hour you choose to name,' said Mr Cotton; and Mr Cotton, long accustomed to the ways of the Navy, was true to his word and exact to his time. At the first stroke of six bells in the forenoon watch he came swarming up the *Boadicea*'s side, using his powerful arms alone and trailing his withered leg. Once aboard he shipped his half-crutch, saluted the quarterdeck, brushed an officious bosun's mate aside, and stumped aft. Everything was ready: under an awning that spread the brilliant light stood an upright chair, made fast to cleats, and in it sat Colley the patient, lead-coloured, snoring still, and so tightly lashed by his friends that he was as incapable of independent movement as the ship's figurehead. The deck and the

tops were strangely crowded with men, many of them feigning busyness, for the old Sophies had told their present shipmates of that memorable day in the year two, when, in much the same light, Dr Maturin had sawed off the top of the gunner's head, had roused out his brains, had set them to rights, and had clapped a silver dome over all, so that the gunner, on coming back to life, was better than new: this they had been told, and they were not going to miss a moment of the instructive and even edifying spectacle. From under the forecastle came the sound of the armourer at his forge, beating a three-shilling piece into a flat and gleaming pancake.

'I have desired him to await our instructions for the final shape,' said Stephen, 'but he has already sharpened and retempered my largest trephine.' He held up the circular saw, still gleaming from its bath, and suggested that Mr Cotton might like to make the first incision. The medical civilities that followed, the polite insistence and refusal, made the audience impatient; but presently their most morbid hopes were gratified. The patient's shaved scalp, neatly divided from ear to ear and flensed away, hung over his unshaved livid snorting face, and now the doctors, poised above the flayed, shattered skull, were talking in Latin.

'Whenever they start talking foreign,' observed John Harris, forecastleman, starboard watch, 'you know they are at a stand, and that all is, as you might say, in a manner of speaking, up.'

'You ain't seen nothing, John Harris,' said Davis, the old Sophie. 'Our doctor is only tipping the civil to the one-legged cove: just you wait until he starts dashing away with his boring-iron.'

'Such a remarkable thickness of bone, and yet the metopic suture has not united,' said Mr Cotton. 'I have never seen the like, and am deeply gratified. 'But, as you say, it confronts us with a perplexing situation: a dilemma, as one might say.'

'The answer, as I conceive it, lies in a double perforation,' said Stephen. 'And here the strength and steadiness of your left forearm will prove invaluable. If you would have the goodness to support the parietal here, while I begin my first cut at this point, and if then we change hands, why, there is a real likelihood that we may lift out the whole in one triumphant piece.'

Had it not been for the need to preserve the appearance of professional infallibility and god-like calm, Mr Cotton would have pursed his lips and shaken his head: as it was he muttered, 'The Lord be with us,' and slid in his flattened probe. Stephen turned

back his cuffs, spat on his hands, waited for the roll, placed his point and began his determined cut, the white bone skipping from the eager teeth and Carol swabbing the sawdust away. In the silence the ship's company grew still more intent: the midshipmen's berth, ghouls to a man, craned forward, unchid by their officers. But as the steel bit down and down into the living head, more than one grew pale, more than one looked away into the rigging; and even Jack, who had seen this grisly performance before, turned his eyes to the horizon, where the distant *Astrée* and *Iphigenia* flashed white in the sun.

He heard Stephen call out the measurements to the armourer as the second cut began; he heard a renewed hammering on the anvil forward; but as he listened a movement far over there to windward seized upon the whole of his attention. Both the Frenchmen were filling: did they mean to edge down at last? He clapped his glass to his eye, saw them come right before the wind, and shut his telescope with a smile: from the busy way they were passing their sheets it was obvious that they were merely wearing once again, as they had done five times since dawn. Yes, they had hauled their wind. Although they had the weather-gage they did not choose to bring him and the crippled *Africaine* to action; and if he was not very much mistaken, this last manoeuvre had put it out of their power, now that the mountains of La Réunion were looming on the larboard bow and the breeze was likely to veer two points inshore. To be sure, the *Africaine* still had all her teeth intact, and the *Staunch* and the *Otter* could give a shrewd nip in a mêlée; but even so . . . He laughed aloud, and at the same moment he heard Mr Cotton cry, 'Oh, pretty. Oh, very prettily done, sir.'

Stephen raised the piece of skull entire and held it up to peer at its underside with a look of sober triumph – a moment during which the audience might gaze with fascinated horror into the awful gulf, where Mr Cotton was now fishing for splinters with a pair of whalebone tongs. As he fished, and as a long transverse splinter stirred the depths, an awful voice, deep, slow, thick-tongued and as it were drunk, but recognizable as Colley's, spoke from behind the hanging skin and said, 'Jo. Pass that fucking gasket, Jo.' By this time the audience had dwindled, and many of the remaining ghouls were as wan as Colley himself; they revived, however, when the surgeons placed the silver cover on the hole, fastened it down, restored the patient's scalp to its usual place, sewed it up, washed their hands in the scuttle-butt,

and dismissed him below. A pleased murmur ran round the ship, and Jack, stepping forward, said, 'I believe I may congratulate you, gentlemen, upon a very delicate manoeuvre?'

They bridled and said it was nothing so extraordinary – any competent surgeon could have done as much – and in any case, they added, with a sincerity that would have caused Mrs Colley a dreadful pang, there was no call for congratulation until the inevitable crisis had declared itself: after all, it could not be said that any operation was wholly successful unless the patient at least outlived the crisis. After that the cause of death might reasonably be assigned to a host of other factors.

'Oh, how I hope he lives,' said Jack, his eye still on the distant enemy. 'Colley is a prime seaman, a capital, steady hand, and can point his gun as well as any man in the ship. Has a large number of children, too, as I recall.'

All this was very true: Tom Colley, when sober, was a valuable though pugnacious member of his division; he had been bred to the sea and he could hand, reef and steer without having to take thought, and it was a joy to see him dance a hornpipe: the ship would not be the same without him. But beneath this valid reasoning lay a region that the kind observer might have called a sort of mysticism and that others, perhaps more enlightened, would have described as brutish superstition. Jack would not have had it known for the world, but he equated the seaman's recovery with the success of his campaign: and from the behaviour of the *Astrée* and *Iphigenia* over there, Colley was in a fair way to resurrection. If Hamelin had been present, flying his broad pendant aboard the *Astrée* rather than the *Vénus*, would the French attitude have been more determined? Would those two ships have risked the battle, to destroy all his hopes, whatever the cost to themselves? From what he knew of the French commodore, he doubted it.

'An impressive document,' said Governor Farquhar, handing back the copy of Pius VII's excommunication of Buonaparte, the hitherto unpromulgated but effective personal, *greater* excommunication, authenticated by the bishop's seal, 'and although some of the expressions are perhaps not quite Ciceronian, the whole amounts to the most tremendous damnation that I have ever seen. Were I a Catholic, it would make me extremely uneasy in my mind, if I were obliged to have anything to do with the wretch. The Bishop made no difficulty, I presume?' Stephen

smiled, and Farquhar went on, 'How I regret your scruples. This would be of the greatest value to the ministry. Surely we should make another copy?'

'Never concern yourself about the ministry, my dear sir,' said Stephen. 'They know of its existence. They know very well: it is a tolerably open secret, I assure you. But in any event, I must not imperil my source of information: and I have given an undertaking that only three men on the Mauritius shall see it, and that I shall then commit it to the flames.' He lapped the document, heavy with curses, in his handkerchief, and thrust it into his bosom: Farquhar looked wistfully at the bulge, but he only said, 'Ah, if you have given an undertaking . . .' and they both glanced at the slips of paper upon which they had noted the subjects they were to discuss.

Stephen's were all crossed off: one remained on Farquhar's list, but he seemed to find it difficult to broach. He paused, and laughed, and said, 'The form in which I have written this will never do. You would find it offensive. I reminded myself – very unnecessarily, I may add – to beg you to give me an explanation – oh, not in any way an *official* explanation, you understand – for the Commodore's abounding sanguine activity. He really seems to assume that our plans for invading the Mauritius can go forward in spite of this appalling disaster at the Ile de la Passe: he has thoroughly infected or perhaps I should say *convinced* Keating, and the two of them dart from point to point, day and night, flying in the face of the clearest evidence. Naturally I second him with all my power – I scarcely dare do otherwise, now that he has taken on his present heroic Jovian stature. He runs into this room, says, "Farquhar, my good fellow, be so good as to cut all the tallest trees on the island and set all the carpenters at work directly. The *Africaine* must have masts by dawn on Thursday at the latest," and runs out again. I tremble and obey: but when I reflect that the French possess seven frigates to our one and a pitiful wreck, and when I reckon up the guns at their disposal as opposed to ours, why, I am seized with an amazement.' He stared out of the window, seized with retrospective stupor; and to fill the gap Stephen observed that the number of guns counted for less than the accuracy with which they were pointed and the zeal with which they were served, adding that although the *Africaine* was not yet fit for battle, her guns were available for the other vessels, such as they were.

'Very true,' said the Governor. 'But I will confess that a per-

haps unworthy explanation of the Commodore's eagerness thrust itself into my mind: it occurred to me that he might possibly have some encouraging intelligence that I did not share. Do not take my words amiss, Dr Maturin, I beg.'

'Never in life, my dear sir,' said Stephen. 'No: I have told him nothing that I have not told you. The answer lies on another plane entirely. As I understand it, Commodore Aubrey has arrived at an intimate conviction that we have a moral superiority over our opponents; that the initiative has changed sides; and that, as he puts it himself, although they want neither ships nor seamanship nor conduct, they do lack spirit. They lack an earnest desire to engage, to risk everything on one throw; and he is of the opinion that Hamelin also lacks the sense of the decisive moment in the ebb and flow of a campaign. Furthermore, it is his view that Commodore Hamelin is more interested in snapping up Indiamen than in gathering laurels at the one moment when they lie ready to his hand. He quoted your remark about Fortune with great approval, declaring that Hamelin would find the wench's forelock hellfire hard to grapple, now that she had forged ahead.'

'I made that remark in a very different context,' said Farquhar; but Stephen, carrying on with his thought, continued, 'I am no strategist, but I know Jack Aubrey well: I respect his judgment in naval matters, and I find his conviction, his military intuition, wholly persuasive. There may also be some illogical factors,' he added, being perfectly aware of the reason for Jack's frequent hurried visits to the hospital and his immoderate delight in Colley's recovery, 'such as seamen's omens and the like, that need not detain a rational mind.'

'So you are persuaded,' said the Governor doubtfully. 'Well then, I too am persuaded; though at one remove. But at least there is no prospect of his stirring until the *Africaine* is ready for sea? No prospect, in this extremely dangerous situation, of his dashing out like a sea-borne Bayard to engage at seven to one?'

'I imagine not, but I would scarcely answer for it. Now, sir,' said Stephen, standing up, 'I must beg to take my leave: the boat is no doubt waiting, and I shall have harsh words if I do not hurry.'

'I shall see you again very shortly?' asked Farquhar.

'Yes, with the blessing. This journey takes me no farther than the south-west tip of the Mauritius, the Morne Brabant,

where I see two officers of the Irish troops and another gentleman; and I think I can promise that the Commodore and Colonel Keating will have little trouble with the more Catholic members of General Decaen's garrison, when they come face to face.' As they walked through the hall he said in an undertone, tapping his chest, 'This is so very much more portable than a hundredweight of gold, and so very, very much more effective.'

The great door opened, and in the entrance they were very nearly run down by Mr Trollope, who came bounding up the steps of the Residence four at a time. He recovered himself, cast a reproachful look at Stephen, plucked off his hat, and said, 'I beg your pardon, your Excellency, but I am charged with the Commodore's respectful compliments and might he have seven hundred and fifty blacks before the evening gun? I was also to remind Dr Maturin that he asked for the aviso at five and twenty minutes past four o'clock precisely.'

Stephen looked at his watch, uttered a low howl, and set off at a shambling run for the harbour, where the *Pearl of the Mascarenes*, the fastest aviso in the island, lay champing at her buoy.

At dawn on Sunday the two quartermasters at the signal-station high above Saint-Denis were weighing the probabilities of duff today: last Sunday they, like all the Boadiceas and all the Africaines, Staunches and Otters, had been deprived of their duff, on account of the furious pace of work in the dockyards; and it looked very much as though the same might happen today. As they leaned out to peer at the yard below the strong land-breeze whipped their pigtails forward, obscuring their view: automatically they grasped them with their teeth and peered on: judging by the feverish activity down there, the parties of blacks and seamen and artificers and soldiers already toiling like so many ants, Sunday duff seemed as remote as wedding-cake. Even beef was by no means certain.

'Some foreign mess again,' said William Jenkins, 'and ate cold, no doubt. How Goldilocks does crack on. Slave-driving ain't in it, when you consider two weeks of no duff; and it was much the same in Simon's Town. Hurry, hurry, hurry, and don't you dare sweat the glass.'

Goldilocks was Jack Aubrey's nickname in the service, and the other quartermaster, Henry Trecothick, had sailed with him when the locks were indeed golden, rather than their present

232

dull sun-bleached yellow. He felt that Jenkins was coming it a little high, and he said coldly, 'He's got a job of work to do, ain't he? And dogged does it. Though I must say a man likes a hot dinner, as being more natural and – Bill, what do you make of that craft out there?'

'Where away?'

'Nor-nor-east: just coming round the point. Behind the islands. She's dowsed her mainsail.'

'I can't see nothing.'

'What a wall-eyed slab-sided Dutch-built bugger you are, to be sure, Bill Jenkins. Behind the islands.'

'Behind the islands? Why didn't you say so? She's a fisherman, that's what she is. Can't you see they're a-pulling? Ain't you got no eyes?'

'Light along the glass, Bill,' said Trecothick. And having stared fixedly he said, 'She ain't no fisherman. They're pulling like Dogget's coat and badge; pulling right into the wind's eye like it was a race for a thousand pound. No fisherman ever pulled like that.' A pause. 'I tell you what, Bill Jenkins, she's that little old aviso, *Pearl* by name.'

'You and your fancies, Henry. *Pearl* ain't due back this tide, no, nor the next. Was that thunder? A drop of rain would –'

'Christ, she's broke out a signal. Get your fat arse out of the way. *Enemy in sight* – what's red white chequer? – *due north*. Bill, jump down and rouse out Mr Ballocks. I'll fix the hoist. Bear a hand, mate, bear a hand.'

Up flew the signal, out banged the gun: the station above St Paul's repeated within a matter of seconds, and into the dining-cabin of the *Boadicea* darted the midshipman of the watch, who found the Commodore pink and cheerful, surrounded by papers and already dictating to his blear-eyed, unshaved secretary as he devoured his first, or sunrise, breakfast. 'Mr Johnson's duty, sir,' he cried, 'St Paul's repeating from Saint-Denis *enemy in sight, bearing due north.*'

'Thank you, Mr Bates,' said Jack. 'I shall be on deck directly.'

There he found the whole quarterdeck motionless, all faces turned towards the distant flagstaff: he said, 'Prepare to slip, Mr Johnson,' and then he too fixed his eyes on the hill. Two full minutes passed with no further hoist, and he said to the signal-midshipman, 'Repeat to Saint-Denis, *Staunch and Otter proceed to sea immediately: attend to pendant's motions.*' Then stepping to the taffrail he hailed the *Africaine*. 'Mr Tullidge, I have room

233

for fifty volunteers, no more.'

The Africaines were less remarkable for their discipline than for their ferocious eagerness to serve the Frenchmen out, and now began a disorderly savage jostling race, whose fifty winners, headed by a powerful master's mate with a face like a baboon, came aboard the *Boadicea* by boat or strong swimming as her buoyed cable ran smoking from her hawse and she cast to the fine land-breeze.

The sails came crowding on; she gathered way, and the good breeze carried them up towards Cape Bernard, the high land that barred out all the ocean due north of Saint-Denis as well as the town itself. With studdingsails on either side, the *Boadicea* threw a bow-wave that came creaming down to the mainchains, but even so the cape moved tediously slow, and Jack found it something of a relief to have his impatience distracted by the ugly scene that developed when it was rumoured that the Africaines were to take over the forward starboard guns. Loud angry voices, rarely raised aboard the *Boadicea*, could be heard on the forecastle, disturbing the holy calm of a well-run man-of-war: the bosun came hurrying aft, spoke to the first lieutenant, and Seymour, crossing the quarterdeck to the rail where Jack was staring at the station in the hope of some more definite signal, coughed and said, 'I beg your pardon, sir, but the men of Mr Richardson's division believe that their guns are to be taken from them, and with the utmost respect they wish to represent that they would find this a little hard.'

'Let the hands come aft, Mr Seymour,' said Jack, with his telescope still trained on the flagstaff, now at the far limit of his view. When he clapped the glass to and turned there they were before him, the whole waist of the ship crowded with men, whose utmost respect (though genuine) was for the moment scarcely discernible beneath their rage at injustice.

'What a precious set of old women you are, upon my word,' he said testily. 'You clap on to a silly buzz with no truth in it and set about one another like a parcel of fish-fags. Look at Eames there, with a bloody nose and on a Sunday too, for shame. And all this before we know whether the enemy is anything more than some stray sloop, or whether he will be so polite as to stay until you have stopped clawing one another. Now I tell you what it is: if we have the good fortune to come into action, every team is going to fight the gun it's used to. That's justice. But if any Boadicea is hurt, then an Africaine takes his place: and if we

234

board, then the Africaines board first. That's flat and that's fair all round. Mr Seymour, be so good as to have cutlasses and boarding-axes served out to the Africaines.'

The general opinion was that this was fair enough: and although for the present the Boadiceas could not be brought to love the Africaines, they did at least treat their guests with a distant civility – no oaths, no blows, little more than a covert kick or nudge, accidental done a-purpose.

Cape Bernard at last, and the frigate rounded it, shaving the reef so close that a lobbed biscuit might have reached the wicked breakers. And as she rounded it, opening new skies, so her people heard the sound of gunfire, the growling of heavy guns a great way off in the north.

'Jump up to the masthead, Mr Richardson,' said Jack, 'and tell me what you see.'

As the midshipman vanished aloft Saint-Denis came into sight: the *Staunch* was still working out of the harbour, and the *Otter* was only a mile ahead of her. Jack frowned; he was about to call the signal-midshipman when he saw fresh canvas break out aboard both of them. It was true that neither had been ready for action, ready to slip at a moment's notice, as the *Boadicea* had been these last twenty-four hours; it was true that they must have had most of their hands ashore or in the yard; but even so he was not pleased, and he meditated a rebuke. 'Am I growing pompous?' he wondered, and the answer 'Probably' had taken disagreeable form in his mind when Spotted Dick, after a scrupulous examination of the distant northern sea, hailed him. 'On deck, there. Sir, I believe I can make out three ships hull-down two points on the larboard bow.' And as if to confirm his words, the distant thunder growled again. Every man aboard listened with all his might, strained ears trying to pierce through the song of the rigging and the slap of the sea to the underlying silence; and every man aboard heard the popping of a musket, weak, but nothing near so remote as the great guns.

Again the masthead hailed the deck, reporting, perhaps a little late, the presence of the aviso a couple of miles away, almost invisible against the reef. She was still pulling strongly against the wind, still announcing that the enemy was in sight, with a musket-shot to underline the signal.

'Close the aviso, Mr Seymour,' said Jack.

As the *Boadicea* swept down the *Pearl* set her jib and mainsail, spun about and ran quartering before the wind, clear of the reef

and its islands, so that when the two vessels converged they were both running fast on almost parallel courses – Dr Maturin could be restored to the frigate without the loss of a moment.

His standard of seamanship being tolerably well-known aboard the *Boadicea*, no orders were required for his reception: there was not time for a bosun's chair, but a whip appeared at the main-yardarm; and now, as they tore along together with no more than a few feet of foaming, heaving sea between them, Bonden, poised on the rail of the *Pearl*, seized the line, made Stephen fast, adjured him 'to take it easy', called out 'Heave away, there: cheerly now', sprang across the gulf and ran up the frigate's side like a cat to receive the Doctor as he came aboard. He had timed the roll exactly, and all would have gone well if Stephen, with some notion of steadying himself, had not grasped at the *Pearl*'s rigging. A slack slabline at once took a turn about his dangling legs and jerked him into a maze of cordage that he could neither name nor disentangle. A fairly heavy swell was running, and for a moment it seemed that Stephen must come aboard in two pieces. A nimble Pearl raced aloft and at great cost to the aviso's rigging cut him free; but this he did at the very moment when the Boadiceas, realizing that they were tearing their surgeon apart, let go; and Stephen therefore swung in a sickening downward curve to strike the frigate's side a little below the waterline. Now, urged by cries, they heaved again, but he stuck under the chains, and the ship's next roll plunged him deep. Unfortunately for Stephen he counted none but friends aboard, and a large pro-portion of these sprang to his rescue; powerful hands pulled him in different directions by the arms, legs and hair, and only the violent intervention of the Commodore preserved him. He reached the deck at last, more dead than alive, oozing blood from scratches inflicted by the barnacles; they emptied some of the water out of him, carried him below, and plucked off his clothes.

'There, there, take it easy,' said Jack, looking anxiously into his face and speaking in that compassionate protective voice which has vexed so many invalids into the tomb.

'There is not a moment to lose,' cried Stephen, starting up.

Jack pressed him back into the cot with irresistible force, and still in the same soothing voice he said, 'We are not losing any time at all, old Stephen. Not a moment. Do not grow agitated. All is well. You are all right now.'

'Oh, your soul to the devil, Jack Aubrey,' said Stephen, and in

an even stronger tone, 'Killick, Killick, you mumping villain, bring on the coffee, will you now, for the love of God. And a bowl of sweet oil. Listen, Jack' – writhing from beneath his hand and sitting up – 'you must press on, crack on, clap on, as fast as ever you can go. There are two frigates out there battering one of ours. And one of them, the *Vénus*, has lost masts, rigging – Bonden will tell you the details – and you may catch her, if only you will make haste, and not sit there leering like a mole with the palsy.'

'Pass the word for my coxswain,' called Jack, and to Stephen he said, 'We are already making haste, you know.' He named the sails that were now urging the *Boadicea* towards the distant battle, and he assured Stephen that the moment she cleared the land-breeze and entered the region of the south-easter offshore, he would let fall his maincourse and set his staysails, for then they would have the wind on the quarter, rather than right aft; and Stephen was to take notice that the presence of the captain on deck was not essential to the progress of the ship, once he was blessed with a seamanlike set of officers. The appearance of Bonden and of Killick bearing the sweet oil cut off Stephen's reply: he groped among the heap of wet clothes, brought out his watch and dipped it in the oil, observing, 'It has survived several grave immersions; let us hope it may survive this. Now, Barret Bonden, I shall give the Commodore a succinct account of the position, and you will supply the technical details.' He collected his mind, and went on, 'Yesterday evening, you must understand, I was standing on the most elevated point of the Morne Brabant, where it overlooks the sea, and conversing with some gentlemen who among other things told me, and this I must not omit, that the *Bellone*, *Minerve* and *Iphigenia* are undergoing heavy repairs, with their guns all out, and will not be fit for sea this fortnight and more: Bonden was at a certain distance –'

'A cable's length, sir,' said Bonden.

' – when I perceived a ship sailing down from Port-Louis in the direction of La Réunion. One of the gentlemen, who had followed the sea for many years, asserted that she was an Indiaman. He pointed out her general mercantile appearance, and the presence of a subsidiary posterior deck, or platform –'

'Poop,' muttered Bonden.

' – the infallible mark of your Indiaman; and he remarked that it would be strange indeed if Monsieur Hamelin, then in Port-

Louis, should let such a prize escape him. And in fact shortly afterwards we described the *Vénus* and a smaller frigate – '

'Pardon me, sir,' said Bonden,' *Wenus* and a *sloop*.'

'The little one had three masts,' said Stephen sharply. 'I counted them.'

'Yes, sir; but she was only a sloop.' And addressing Jack, Bonden went on, 'Sixteen-gun corvette *Victor*, sir.'

'Well, never mind. They pursued the alleged Indiaman, the *Vénus* outsailing her companion: and then to our surprise the Indiaman turned out to be no Indiaman, at all. She took down or folded a number of sails, allowed the *Vénus* to come close, and discharged a number of guns upon her, at the same time displaying a banner indicating she was a man-of-war.'

Jack looked at Bonden, who said, '*Bombay*, sir; a country-built Indiaman bought into the service in the year five. My cousin George, he sailed in her one commission, gunner's mate; said she was a good sea-boat, but mortial slow. Twenty-four eighteen-pounders, two long nines, and fourteen twenty-four-pounder carronades.'

'At this,' said Stephen, 'the *Vénus* drew back, waiting for her consort, and the *Bombay* pressed on. The sun had set: we descended the cliff, made our way to the aviso, and there I resigned the conduct of affairs into Bonden's hands.'

'Well, sir,' said Bonden, 'I knew you would be wishful to know as soon as ever could be, so we nipped through the Dutchman's Passage with barely a scrape, though the tide was out, fetched the *Victor*'s wake, crossed under her stern in the dark just before moonrise, and worked up to windward with all she could wear and well-nigh more. We was well ahead, running nine-ten knots by the time the moon was well up, and we see *Wenus* coming up on the *Bombay* hand over hand, seven knots to her six, maybe; and at the beginning of the middle watch, when we had sunk the land long since, she ranged up alongside and they set to hammer and tongs. I ought to of said, sir, that *Bombay* had a tidy packet of redcoats aboard, and there seemed to be plenty of soldiers in *Wenus* too, her decks were that crowded with men. Well now, *Wenus* didn't care for it overmuch, and presently she wore out of range, new-gammoning her bowsprit, as far as I could judge. Howsoever, in a couple of glasses she perked her spirits up again, and the wind having backed two points she set her stuns'ls and bore down. The action started again in the morning watch, a running fight, with both on 'em under royals

and larboard stuns'ls; but by now we was so far ahead I couldn't rightly see how it went. I did see *Wenus* lose her foretopmast and her gaff, and *Bombay*, she lost her main and mizen topmasts, and her courses were chawed up something cruel; but she was standing on for Saint-Denis and giving as good as she got when last we see her plain, and the sloop was still a league and more astern.'

While he was speaking the *Boadicea* began to heel to larboard; she had run beyond the land-breeze, which came from aft, and she was now in the south-easter, a gentle wind today, untimely gentle. In spite of his words about seamanlike officers Jack went on deck the moment Bonden's account was done. He automatically checked the spread of canvas against the force of the wind, and found something of a disproportion: like so many others, young Johnson still entertained the delusion that more sail meant more speed, and in his eagerness he was pressing her down by the head. Jack did not wish the change to have the appearance of a check, however, and first he hailed the masthead. 'Masthead, there. What do you see?'

'They are hull-up now, sir,' called the lookout. 'Heavy frigate, Indiaman, and a ship-rigged sloop or maybe a jackass frigate, all wearing French colours; pendant aboard the big frigate. No firing since four bells. Frigate's lost her topmasts, all three of them. Indiaman too. Sloop unwounded, I believe.'

Jack nodded, took a turn or so, told Johnson that he might find her labour less with the flying-jib hauled down, slung his glass, set his hands to the shrouds, and swung himself up: up and up, through the maintop, up again to the crosstrees, slower than he would have climbed twenty years before, but still at a respectable pace.

All that the lookout had told him was true; but what the lookout had not been able to tell him was the spirit of the scene far over there to the north, so far over that the shimmering air sometimes gave the distant ships their masts and sometimes took them away; and it was this that he had climbed his airy pinnacle to make out. After a backward glance at the *Staunch* and the *Otter*, both of them a couple of miles astern and losing steadily, he settled down to a prolonged study of the position. Between them the *Vénus* and the *Victor* had certainly taken the *Bombay*, having reduced her to her lower masts alone: the *Vénus* had paid heavily, however, losing not only her fore and main topmasts but the greater part of her mizen too. The sloop had not

suffered at all. There was great activity aboard the *Vénus*, and it appeared to him that they were preparing to send up a new fore-topmast: they had certainly fished a fine great spar of some kind to the stump of the mizen. Boats were passing between the ships. The distance was too great for any certainty, but it looked as though bodies of men were moving in both directions: as though it were not merely a shifting of prisoners. Did Hamelin intend to man his prize? It was by no means impossible: sailing from his home port he might very well have doubled his crew with seamen drafted from his other ships, to say nothing of all the soldiers in Port-Louis. If he could spare enough men to serve the *Bombay*'s forty guns, and if he had the hardihood to do so, that would change the situation.

Within himself Jack had not the slightest doubt of victory, but it would never do to let this conviction take the form of even unspoken words; it must remain in the state of that inward glow which had inhabited him ever since the retaking of the *Africaine* and which had now increased to fill the whole of his heart – a glow that he believed to be his most private secret, although in fact it was evident to everyone aboard from Stephen Maturin to the adenoidal third-class boy who closed the muster-book. So leaving that to one side he set himself to a cold, professional, objective examination of the factors that might delay or even prevent it.

The first was the wind. The south-easter was slackening; already there were glassy patches of sea on the starboard bow, forerunners of the usual midday lull, which might leave him without steerage-way or compel a very slow advance, head-on, into the combined broadside fire of the *Vénus* and *Bombay*, and which might allow Hamelin time to set up a jury-rig that would at least give him twice his present power of manoeuvring.

The second was the arrival of reinforcements. He had no very high opinion of the French commodore's enterprise, but Hamelin was no halfwit. On finding himself in such a position at dawn, with La Réunion looming large on the south horizon, he would certainly have sent his best cutter racing back to Mauritius for support. In Hamelin's place he would have done so the moment the *Bombay* struck.

While he turned these things over in his mind, the pattern to the northward grew clearer. The boats had been hoisted in; the *Victor*, all sails abroad, had taken the *Bombay* in tow; the *Vénus*, dropping her fore and main courses, had put before the wind.

And now a foresail appeared aboard the *Bombay*. They still had a fresh breeze out there, and presently they were moving at about three knots, while the *Boadicea*, with all her noble spread of canvas, was making little better than five and a half. 'However,' he reflected, 'there is nothing much I can do about that.'

What little he could do, he did. Having finished 'Plymouth Point', the surest of tunes for a wind, he was whistling at random when he became aware that Sophie was in his mind, present with an extraordinary clarity. 'Was I a superstitious cove,' he said, smiling with singular sweetness in the direction of England, 'I should swear she was thinking of me.'

The smile was still lingering on his face when he reached the deck, and this encouraged Seymour to ask whether he might start to clear the ship for action.

'As to that, Mr Seymour,' said Jack, looking at the log-board, 'it might be a little premature. We must not tempt fate, you know. Mr Bates, be so good as to heave the log.'

'Heave the log it is, sir,' said the midshipman, darting to the lee-rail with his attendant boy and quartermaster. The boy held the reel, the quartermaster the thirty-second sand-glass: Bates threw the log, watched the mark go clear, called 'Turn' and the quartermaster held the glass to his eye, while the boy held up the reel with a hieratic solemnity. The log went astern, the knots in the line passing smoothly through Bates's fingers. 'Nip', cried the quartermaster. The midshipman nipped, then jerked the line; the boy reeled in, and Bates crossed the deck to announce, 'Just on the five, sir, if you please.'

Jack nodded, glanced up at the frigate's towering array of canvas, at the fire-hose in the tops wetting all the jet could reach, at the buckets hoisting to the crosstrees to damp the topgallants so that they should catch every last ounce of thrust, and said, 'No, Mr Seymour. Without the gods are kind, we have more time on our hands than I could wish. It would be a pity to dowse the galley fires so soon; so let the men be piped to dinner at six bells, and since they went without their duff last Sunday, let there be a double ration of plums today. On the other hand, only half the grog will be served out this spell: and no plush allowed.' The faces of the men at the wheel, the quartermaster conning the ship, the yeoman of the signals and the nearer members of the afterguard took on a stony look. Jack paced fore and aft and continued, 'The rest will be kept for supper, wind, weather and the enemy permitting. And Mr Seymour, since we shall be

pinched for time, dinner being so early, church will not be rigged today; however, I believe we may proceed to divisions. Mr Kiernan,' he added, nodding towards the baboon-faced officer, 'will muster his Africaines on the forecastle.'

From this moment on time raced by aboard the frigate. Every man, with little notice and even less expectation of this solemn event (practised on every peaceful Sunday, but never, *never* when bearing down on the enemy), had to present himself, an hour earlier than usual, washed, shaved, and in a clean shirt for inspection by his particular midshipman and officer and then by the Commodore himself. Furthermore, there was a general determination to wipe the Africaines' collective eye by a brilliantly striking appearance. All along the gangway and on the forecastle the tie-for-tie pairs swiftly and silently combed and plaited one another's pigtails, while impatient groups clustered round the barber's tub, urging him to even greater speed, whatever it might cost; and anxious Marines pipeclayed and polished in the blazing sun.

The inspection itself was a creditable affair, with the officers, in full dress and wearing their swords, accompanying the Commodore in his slow progress along the lines of trim seamen in their best; and the hairy Africaines in their dirty shirts were brought suitably low. But the ceremony was marred by an extraordinary degree of distraction: remarkable things were happening in the north – the *Bombay*'s towline had parted, the *Victor* was having a devilish time passing another, the *Vénus* had first sheered off and had then come up into what wind there was to lend a hand, and above all the vast stretch of ocean between the *Boadicea* and the French had narrowed surprisingly. Even while the Commodore was on deck, few men apart from the rigid Marines could resist glancing northwards and passing remarks; and when he was exploring the galley and the berth-deck with the first lieutenant, Mr Trollope was obliged to call out 'Silence, fore and aft' several times, and to take the names of the more loquacious, for future punishment.

The moment divisions was over, the bosun and his mates piped loud and shrill to dinner. Every man aboard knew that the order *clear for action* would follow in a very short time indeed, for the wind had freshened markedly this last half hour, and that he must make up his mind at once between fighting the ship in his best clothes and missing if not his beef then his double-shotted duff. Most plumped for the duff, which they ate on deck, by their

242

guns, holding it carefully away from their snowy shirts, their silk neckerchiefs, and trousers beribboned at the seams. Scarcely was the last crumb down when the expected order came. Mess-kids vanished and the men, some still chewing, set about the familiar task of making a clean sweep fore and aft: they had done so, and they were standing at their action-stations staring now at the enemy, not far from extreme range, and now astern at the distant *Staunch* and *Otter*, when Stephen appeared on the quarterdeck, bearing a plate of sandwiches.

Doctor Maturin was a God-send to the Boadiceas: not only would he accost the Commodore with a freedom impossible to any other man aboard, but he would ask questions that none but he might propound, and receive civil answers rather than a severe set-down. Any gentlemanly reluctance to overhear private conversation had long since died away, and casual chat on the quarterdeck fell silent, in case any word between the Commodore and the Doctor should be lost.

He did not disappoint them now. 'Why, sir,' said he, looking about him, 'what splendour I see: gold lace, breeches, cocked hats. Allow me to recommend a sandwich. And would you be contemplating an attack, at all?'

'It had crossed my mind, I must admit,' said Jack. 'Indeed, I may go so far as to say, that I am afraid a conflict is now virtually inevitable. Did you notice we have cleared for action?'

'Certainly I did. I have not ploughed the ocean all these weary years without learning the significance of this wild disorder, the cabins vanishing, my papers, my specimens, flung upside-down into the nearest recess. That is why I am come out here, for a little peace. Dear me, how close they are! It would be indiscreet, per-haps, to ask what happens next?'

'To tell you the truth, Doctor,' said Jack, 'for the moment I am in two minds. The corvette, do you see, has cast off her tow for good and all, and she is bearing away for the Mauritius under all sail, no doubt on her commodore's orders, while he is coming down towards the *Bombay*. Now if he has manned his prize, if he has sent enough men aboard the *Bombay* to serve her guns, then his plan will be to fight us with both ships in close support; and in that case we must run between 'em, firing both sides. But if he has not manned her, and if he is only covering the *Victor*'s retreat by this manoeuvre, why, then he means to meet us alone. And in that case we must run down on his bow, or his quarter if he wears, and carry him by boarding, so as not to damage his

hull nor those precious spars I see on his deck. Another ten minutes will tell us what he means to do. If he don't back his foresail just before reaching the *Bombay*, so as to heave to beside her, you understand, that will mean she is not manned and that he must fight us by himself. Masthead,' he cried, 'what do you see in the north?'

'Nothing, sir, bar the sloop,' replied the masthead. 'A clear horizon all round. Sloop's carried away a kite on the main: is setting another.'

After this there was a prolonged silence aboard the *Boadicea*: the men stationed at the guns stared over the barricade of hammocks or out through the open ports at the *Vénus*; the splinter-netting over their heads sent a strange shifting rectangular pattern down on the deck; the wind hummed and sighed through the rigging.

The minutes passed; ten minutes passed; and then a general murmur ran through the ship. The *Vénus* had not backed her foresail and now she was well beyond the *Bombay*. She was ugly, with her stumpy masts, but she was dangerous, determined, and her gunports were all open; she carried heavy metal, and her decks were crowded with men.

'Mr Seymour,' said Jack, 'topsails and forecourse alone, and draw the guns. Reload with grape. Not a shot is to touch her hull. Sweep her decks, but do not touch her hull. D'ye hear me, there?' he cried, raising his voice. 'Any gun-crew that wounds her hull will be flogged. Mr Hall, lay me for her bow.'

Closer and closer. Jack's opinion of Hamelin rose: the Frenchman was staking everything on coming so close before he yawed that his broadside must do the *Boadicea* irreparable damage – staking everything, because after that one turn the *Vénus*, with no more sail than she could spread, would never come up into the wind again, but must lie there to be battered to death.

Closer still in the silence: they were within pistol-shot. The *Vénus*' bow guns cracked out; the turn began, and the moment before her side came into full view Jack said, 'Hard a-port.' The *Boadicea* moved fast, heeling abruptly, and the thundering broadside from the *Vénus* cut no mast away. The foretopsail yard was wounded, two studdingsail booms had gone, some rigging hung loose; the starboard cathead was shattered and the best bower swung free; but Hamelin had lost his bet.

'Duck up forward,' said Jack, and at once the foresail puckered,

checking the frigate's speed as she swept through the enemy's smoke. The *Vénus* turned, turned until she was almost before the wind and stern-on to the *Boadicea*. 'Bear a hand with the clew-line,' said Jack. 'Mr Hall, clear her starboard quarter, and bump me her bows.' The *Boadicea* shot forward, and it was clear that she would range up on the *Vénus* before the Frenchmen had had time to reload. 'Africaines stand by to board over her bow,' he cried. 'Boadiceas, come aft: we go for her quarterdeck. And we give the Africaines one minute's law, mark what I say. Steady there by the guns,' he said, loosening his sword. 'Bonden, where are my pistols?'

There was Killick at his side, holding an old pair of shoes and a coat over his arm. 'You can't go in your best silver-buckled shoes, your honour, nor in your number one coat,' he kept saying in an angry whine. 'It won't take you a minute to change.'

'Nonsense,' said Jack. 'Everyone else is going in his best, so why should I be left out?'

The *Vénus's* soldiers were firing from her stern, but it was too late. The *Boadicea* ranged alongside, Jack said 'Fire,' and the *Boadicea*'s grape swept the *Vénus's* deck at head-height and in the smoke grapnels flew over the side; topmen ran out and lashed the Frenchman's yardarms tight; their bows ground together, and Jack roared 'Africaines away.' A moment later their sterns swung in, and the two ships lay side by side.

For a full minute he stood at the head of his boarders, while the Marines behind him plied their muskets as though they were on parade and the small-arms men in the tops kept up a fire on the guns. A full minute of vast din and shouting forward, the crackle of pistols and the bellow of a carronade that the Africaines had turned into the waist of the *Vénus*. Then he cried, 'Boadiceas, come along with me,' vaulted on to the torn hammocks, leapt sword in hand across to the shrouds of the mainmast, slashed the boarding-netting, slashed at a head below him, and so down to the *Vénus's* quarterdeck, followed by a cheering mass of seamen.

Before him stood a line of soldiers – the seamen were in the waist, facing the Africaines' furious attack – and in the second before the wave of Boadiceas broke over them a little terrified corporal lunged at Jack with his bayonet. Bonden caught the muzzle, wrenched the musket free, flogged three men flat with the butt and broke the line. On the deck behind the soldiers lay several bodies – officers – and in the momentary pause Jack thought he saw a French captain's uniform. Then the aftermost

group on the larboard gangway, led by a young officer, turned and came for the Boadiceas with such a rush that they were swept back to the wheel, and the next few minutes were a furious confusion of violence, cut and parry, duck the pistol, kick and thrust and hack.

But the Vénuses were no match for the boarders; they were oppressed and hemmed in by their own numbers; they were worn out by their long night's battle and the toil that had followed it; their spirits were crushed by the sight of the *Otter* and the *Staunch* coming up fast, and by the certainty of eventual defeat. A body of Croatian soldiers, who had no real concern with the quarrel, leapt down the now unguarded main hatchway; others followed them, seeking safety below. The remaining Frenchmen on the gangway made a last desperate charge, and a short, broadshouldered seaman with a knife grappled Jack round the waist. Jack dashed his hilt into the seaman's face, trampled him down, broke free; and there in the clear space by the fife-rail stood an officer, offering his sword and pointing aft, where a boy was hauling down the colours.

Through the enormous cheering that spread from the *Vénus's* quarterdeck to the *Boadicea*, Jack roared out, "Vast fighting, there. Forward there, Africaines, 'vast fighting. She's struck.'

Men fell apart, stared impersonally at one another, and moved slowly away. The extreme tension died with extraordinary speed and within moments a new relationship had established itself, a kind of primitive social contract – men could no longer hit one another.

Jack accepted the officer's sword with a civil bend of his head and passed it to Bonden. The man he had trampled upon got to his feet without looking at him and stumbled away to his shipmates, who were standing where the battle had left them or who had gathered in little groups by the lee-rail, silent, as though the act of surrender had drained their spirit away, leaving them quite numb.

Still the *Boadicea* was cheering, and the exultant din was echoed by the *Bombay*, a quarter of a mile away: she had rehoisted her ensign, and her crew was skipping and waving and roaring all along her side and in her tops.

'Commodore Hamelin?' said Jack to the officer, and the officer pointed to one of the bodies close by the wheel.

'I was sorry about Hamelin, however,' said Jack, as he and

Stephen sat over a late dinner. 'Though when you come to think of it, a man could hardly ask better.'

'For my part,' said Stephen, 'I could ask for very much better. A grapeshot in the heart is not my idea of bliss, and I should do my utmost to avoid it. Yet your grief does not affect your appetite, I find: that is the eighth chop you have eaten. Nor, which strikes me with peculiar force, do I find that this battle has produced the melancholy reaction I have so often noticed in you.'

'That is true,' said Jack. 'An action clears your mind amazingly, for the moment; but afterwards the black dog comes down. The butcher's bill, the funerals, the men's widows to write to, the mess to be cleared up, the knotting and splicing, the pumping – you feel done up, hipped, as flat as ditch-water; though there is more to it than that. But this time it is different. To be sure, we have come off scot-free or very near, but that is not the point. The point is that this dust-up is only the beginning of the real action. *Africaine* will be ready for sea on Tuesday: with the spars preparing at St Paul's and what we have captured today, *Vénus* and *Bombay* will not take much longer, working double tides – their hulls would already pass a survey, you know. That is four capital frigates, plus the *Windham*, three good sloops, and all our armed transports: while on their side they have only *Astrée* and *Manche* ready for sea. *Bellone* and *Minerve* must certainly be heaved down; and *Iphigenia* and *Néréide* are little use to man or beast even when they are repaired. They have lost their commodore; and the captain of the *Astrée* at least is a booby. And where is their spirit? No: I tell you what, Stephen, by the end of the week Keating and I will carry out our plan – that will be the real action, what I call the real action; and I don't care how glum I grow after it.'

'Well, my dear,' said Stephen, 'politically Mauritius was ready to fall like a ripe plum, or mango, even before the Ile de la Passe; and now that you have repaired the disaster and more, I believe you may install Governor Farquhar at Port-Louis within a week of landing your troops.'

Chapter Ten

'You have been very much in my mind these days, sweetheart, even more than usual,' wrote Jack, continuing his serial letter to Sophie, a letter that had been building up to its present bulk ever since the *Leopard* had sailed from St Paul's for the Cape, his last contact with the flag, 'and I should certainly have wrote, had we not been so uncommon busy. Since Monday morning we have been on the run, with all hands turning to, to make the squadron ready for sea; and such a sawing of carpenters, a thumping of caulkers, and a busyness of bosuns you never heard in your life. Poor Trollope, an active officer but of a bilious turn, was overcome with a sunstroke, while a black blacksmith, that had wrought eighteen hours on a stretch, was carried off in a dead swoon, quite grey. But now it is done. Now we are at sea, sinking the land as the sun comes up' – he looked, smiling, out of the *Boadicea*'s stern-window, and there in her wake, two cable-lengths away, he saw the *Vénus*, her sails pearly in the growing light; beyond her he could make out the *Africaine*, and far to leeward the last three transports. As the pendant-ship, the *Boadicea* was sailing in the middle of the squadron with the *Bombay* and the *Windham* ahead of her, the *Staunch*, the *Otter* and the *Grappler* far up to windward, and under her lee the transports, comfortably full of soldiers – 'and a very respectable body we are. It is true some of our masts would make the dock-yard mateys stare, but they will serve: they may not be very pretty, but they will serve. We took many of the spars out of *Bombay* and *Vénus*, and the Devil's own job we had to bring them home: I had promised the men the other half of their grog should be served out with their ration for supper, which might have been well enough if they had not found their way into the enemy's spirit-room, too. Lord, Sophie, we rolled back that night like a whole herd of Davey's sows, with seven Boadiceas and seven Africaines in irons, and most of the rest not fit to go aloft. Fortunately the *Otter* had *Bombay* in tow, or I doubt we should ever have brought them both in. As it was, any French brig in her right wits could have snapped us up.

'By the morning most of the hands were sober, and I harangued them on the beastly vice of inebriation; but I am afraid the effect

of my words (and thundering good words they were) were quite lost because of the welcome they gave us ashore. Rockets, Bengal lights you could hardly see because of the sun though kindly intended, salvoes from all the fortifications, and three times three all round the port: the Governor, a capital determined fellow, with a good head on his shoulders, and thoroughly understands cooperation, was so pleased at the sight of two frigates bringing in that he would, though a tea-drinker himself, have made the men drunk again directly, if I had not represented to him, that *we must make hay while the sun shone*. Colonel Keating was positively overjoyed, and expressed himself in the most obliging manner; and he too thoroughly agreed that *we must strike while the iron was hot*.

'Nothing could exceed his zeal in harrying his staff-officers and other slow-bellies and in getting his men aboard with all their proper accoutrements and in the right order: for I will tell you, my dear (since no eye but yours will see this letter, and that only after the event), that we mean to invade the Mauritius the day after tomorrow; and we have a very fair hope of a happy outcome.' He cast a furtive glance at Stephen Maturin as he wrote these words, so offensive to all his friend's principles and so contrary to all his repeated injunctions, and Stephen, catching his eye, said, 'Should you like some encouragement, joy?'

'If you please,' said Jack.

'Then you must know that the captain of the ship the *Jefferson B. Lowell* –'

'The barque, Stephen. The American was a barque; and an amazing fine sailer, too.'

'Bah. Was so good as to tell me of the various rates he and his colleagues trading to St Louis have placed on Mauritius paper money. Before our arrival it was very nearly at par with cash; then it dropped to twenty-two per centum below, and so rose and fell according to the fortunes of the campaign, rising to ninety-three after the Ile de la Passe. But now it is not admitted upon any discount at all, and gold is absolutely insisted upon. There is cool, objective testimony for you.'

'I am delighted to hear it, Stephen: thank you very much,' said Jack. He returned to his letter, and Stephen to his 'cello.

'Keating would, I am sure, have been as busy as a bee in any event, out of zeal for our joint campaign (and never did army and navy work so well together, I believe, since ships were first found out); but in this case he was as busy as two or even more,

249

from an uneasiness in his mind at what he had heard from the army officers we released from the *Vénus*. They spoke of a General Abercrombie, who was to command them and a very considerable force gathered from all parts of India: it is difficult to make much sense of what they said, for their colonel was killed in the action, and the junior officers had only fag-ends of gossip; but the general notion is that they were to rendezvous at Rodriguez with several regiments from Fort William and some troops from the Cape and that they were then to make a descent on La Réunion; which, when you come to think of it, is absurd. Even so, Keating was much concerned: "If any gouty old fool of a general comes along to snatch the bread out of my mouth again the very moment it is buttered," cries he in a great passion, "I shall sell my commission to the highest bidder, and be d—d to the service: to be choused out of the glory when we have done all the work, would be more than flesh and blood can bear." And he told me again of the siege of some Indian city whose name I forget, where he had carried the approaches right up to the walls, had repelled sorties by the score, had made a practicable breach, and was on the eve of storming the place when a general appeared in a palanquin, took over, gave the order to attack, wrote a despatch giving himself all the credit for the victory, was promoted and given the Bath, with an augmentation to his coat of arms. Keating added some pretty severe reflections on the Bath and old men who would do anything for a trumpery piece of ribbon, which I will not repeat, they being somewhat too warm.' Jack paused, meditating a witticism in which *hot water* should combine with *Bath* to produce a brilliant effect, but his genius did not lie that way, and having chewed his pen for some time, he carried on: 'For my own part, I could not make much more sense out of poor Graham of the *Bombay*, either. He had had a cruise after pirates in the Persian Gulf, and when he put in, precious short-handed, he was at once ordered to take a whole heap of soldiers aboard and to rendezvous with the *Illustrious*, 74, just south of the Eight Degree Channel – had nothing but ill-luck all the way – sprang a leak low down under his fore-peak ten days out, had to put back, beating up with the wind in his teeth, pumping hard and his men falling sick – endless delays in the yard – missed his first rendezvous, missed the next, so bore away, sick himself with a low fever, for Port-Louis, where he expected to find us blockading – and was taken, after a long and tolerably bloody running fight. I am afraid the

heat and the wear and the anxiety and the action may have sent his wits astray, for the unfortunate wight absolutely struck to a sloop, which he took for a second frigate in the darkness. (It is true she was ship-rigged: our old sixteen-gun *Victor*, but a very mere cockle in fact.) Stephen was of my opinion about his intellects, filled him to the hatches with opium-draughts, shaving and blistering his head just before we left. But in any case, I cannot find that he ever had orders for Rodriguez; so it is a hundred to one that Keating was nourishing a chimaera, as they say. But since it made him so desperate eager to present any lurking general, hungry for honours, with a fait accompli, viz. a conquered island with HM Governor already installed, and since his eagerness chimed in with my eagerness to get to sea before the French had the *Minerve* and *Bellone* afloat (there is a rumour that someone, a Royalist or Papist or both, damaged their bottoms with an infernal machine: but I find it hard to believe that even a foreigner could be so wicked) – why, I fairly caressed the chimaera of his. Stephen,' he called, over the growling 'cello, 'how do you spell chimaera?'

'Many people start with ch, I believe. Have you told her about my stink-pot petrel?'

'Is not stink-pot a hellish low expression for a letter, Stephen?'

'Bless you, my dear, a mother that tends her own babies will not boggle at stink-pot. But you may put thalassodrome, if you find it more genteel.'

The pen scratched on; the 'cello sang deep; a midshipman tapped on the door. He reported a sail on the starboard quarter, adding that from a curious patch in her foretopsail she was thought to be the *Emma*.

'Aye, no doubt,' said Jack. 'She has made amazing good time. Thank you, Mr Penn.' The *Emma* had been called in by aviso from her station off Rodriguez, but he had not looked for her sooner than Thursday. 'Tom Pullings will be aboard presently,' he said to Stephen. 'We must keep him for dinner. After all this to and fro-ing off Rodriguez he will be glad of a bite of fresh mutton.' He called out to Killick: the saddle of yesterday's sheep was to be ready at five bells precisely, together with half a dozen of the red Constantia and a drowned baby. They discussed Thomas Pullings, his indifferent prospects, his real deserts, his probable appetite; and the midshipman reappeared, breathless and staring: *Staunch* had just signalled four sail, bearing northeast.

'What says *Emma*?' asked Jack.

'I don't know, sir,' said the midshipman.

'Then be so good as to find out,' said the Commodore, with some asperity.

The *Emma*, it appeared, had nothing to say. No *enemy in sight* flew from her fore; no gun called for the pendant's attention; yet the *Emma*, with a seamanlike captain aboard, was nearer those four sail than the *Staunch*. The conclusion was obvious: the four sail were Indiamen . . . unless, he reflected, with a cold grip in his heart, they were English men-of-war.

Stepping thoughtfully out of the cabin, he took over the deck, hailed the *Africaine* that he was leaving the line, and hauled up to close the *Emma*. Hitherto the *Boadicea* had been proceeding under easy sail, at a pace suited to that of the transports, but now topgallants broke out, and with the fine breeze two points free she began to move like a thoroughbred. Her wake stretched white and long; her bow-wave rose to the bridle-ports and the spray came sweeping aft from her forecastle, making rainbows in the sun. Spirits rose high, and the boys and the younger topmen laughed aloud as they raced aloft to loose the royals: but a few sharp, unusually vehement orders from the quarterdeck did away with their more obvious mirth. The afterguard and the waisters moved as mute as mice, ludicrously tiptoeing when they could not be seen; those forward exchanged covert winks and nudges; and those high above murmured, 'Watch out for squalls, mate' with a knowing grin. Little passes unnoticed in a man-of-war, and although only the Marine sentry and one or two members of the anchor-watch had seen Jack and Colonel Keating come aboard after Governor Farquhar's farewell dinner, the whole ship's company knew that the skipper 'had taken a glass', that he had been 'as pissed as old Noah', that he had been 'brought down in a barrow, roaring for a woman – for a black girl in his cot', and they smiled indulgently, whispering quotations from his homily on the beastly vice of inebriation, as he called out to know whether that tack was to be brought to the chess-trees this watch or not.

Now the *Boadicea* was really lying down to her work, shouldering the long swell aside with a fine living motion and making her ten knots with no effort, so that for all those untormented by vile premonitions it was a pleasure to feel her sail.

'This is what I had imagined life at sea to be like,' said Mr Peter, a rare visitor to the quarterdeck – he spent most of his

days in an airless paper-lined hole beneath the waterline, dividing his time between seasickness and work. 'Do you not find it exhilarating, sir?'

'Sure, it is like a glass of champagne,' replied Stephen; and Mr Peter smiled, looking significantly at Colonel Keating, greyish-yellow and blinking in the sun. It was in fact the Colonel who had been brought down in a wheelbarrow; it was he who had so often cried 'Let copulation thrive.'

The *Boadicea* and the *Emma* were approaching at a combined rate of sixteen knots, and every few minutes pushed the eastward horizon back another mile. Soon the lookout told the deck of the four sail reported by the *Staunch*: then came another hail – two ships bearing east-north-east, and a hint of topgallantsails beyond them.

Six ships at least: it was almost impossible that so many should be Indiamen. Jack took a few turns, and his face grew more forbidding: he tossed off his coat, borrowed Seymour's telescope, and made his way up to the foretopgallant masthead. He was nearly there, with the shrouds creaking under his weight and the wind sweeping his long hair away to the north-west, when he heard the lookout mutter 'Sixteen, seventeen . . . 'tis a bleeding armada. An invincible bleeding armada. On deck, there . . .'

'Never mind, Lee,' said Jack, 'I can see 'em myself. Shift over.' He settled himself into the crosstrees and trained his glass east and north-east. There they lay, the greatest concentration of men-of-war he had ever seen in the Indian Ocean. And presently, to knock any lingering ghost of hope on the head, he made out the *Illustrious*, a two-decker wearing a vice-admiral's flag at the fore.

By this time the *Emma* was well within range. They had long since exchanged signals, and now the *Emma* was coming under the *Boadicea*'s lee in her heavy wallowing fashion, while the frigate backed her foretopsail and lay to.

Jack took a last long look at the fleet, men-of-war and transports, and then lowered himself heavily down through the rigging, much as another man might have walked heavily down the stairs in his house, thinking not of the steps but of his own problems. He reached the deck and put on his coat as Pullings came up the side; and the contrast between the lieutenant's beaming face, white teeth flashing in the deep ruddy tan, and the Commodore's sombre look would have struck an eye far less observant than Stephen's. However, the mere force of Pullings's

253

grin, his evident pleasure, brought an answering smile; and the smile grew a little more lively at the sight of a large bag hoisting up from the *Emma*'s boat, the much-loved familiar mail-sack.

'There is no one so welcome as the postman, Mr Pullings,' said Jack, inviting him into the cabin. 'Whence come ye, Tom?' he asked, once they were there.

'Straight from the Admiral, sir,' said Pullings, as though this were the best news that could ever be brought.

'From Mr Bertie?' asked Jack, whose protesting mind had faintly offered a hypothetical force bound for Java, perhaps, under a different vice-admiral, one with no responsibility for the Cape – an admiral who was merely passing by.

'That's right, sir,' said Pullings cheerfully. 'And he gave me this for you.' He took a dog-eared Naval Chronicle from his pocket and plucked an official letter from among its pages, marking the place with his thumb; but holding the letter aloft, not quite delivering it, he said, 'So no post, sir, since I last saw you?'

'Not a word, Tom,' said Jack. 'Not a word since the Cape; and that was out of order. Not a word for the best part of a year.'

'Then I am the first,' cried Pullings with infinite satisfaction. 'Let me wish you and Mrs Aubrey all the joy in the world.' He grasped Jack's limp, wondering hand, wrung it numb, and showed the printed page, reading aloud, 'At Ashgrove Cottage, Chilton Admiral, in Hants, the lady of Captain Aubrey, of the *Boadicea*, of a son and heir,' following the words with his finger.

'Give it here,' said Jack. He grasped the magazine, sloped the page to the light and pored over it intently. ' "At Ashgrove Cottage, Chilton Admiral, in Hants, the lady of Captain Aubrey, of the *Boadicea*, of a son . . ." Well, I'll be damned. God bless me. Lord, Lord . . . upon my word and honour . . . I'll be damned to Hell and back again . . . strike me down. Killick, Killick, rouse out a bottle of champagne – pass the word for the Doctor – here, Killick, there's for you – God love us all – ha, ha, ha.'

Killick took the handful of money, put it slowly into his pocket with a look of extreme suspicion and walked out of the cabin, his lips pursed in disapproval. Jack leapt from his seat, took several turns fore and aft, chuckling from time to time, his mind filled with mingled love, happiness, fulfilment, and a most piercing nostalgia. 'I thank you, Pullings, I thank you with all my heart for your news,' he said.

'I thought you would be pleased, sir,' said Pullings. 'We always knew, Mrs P. and I, how you wanted a boy. Girls are very well, in course, but they are not quite the same; you could not wish them about all the time. And then you never know what they will be at. But a boy! – Our nipper, sir, if ever I get a settled command of my own, shall come to sea the minute he is out of coats, and properly breeched.'

'I trust Mrs Pullings and young John are quite well?' said Jack; but before he could learn much of them, Stephen walked in, followed by the sack of mail. 'Stephen,' said Jack, 'Sophie is brought to bed of a boy.'

'Aye? I dare say,' said Stephen. 'Poor thing. But it must be a great relief to your mind.'

'Why,' said Jack, with a blush, 'I never had wind of it, you know.' Calculation had already established the fact that the distant nameless wonder was conceived the night of his leaving, and this made him bashful, even confused.

'Well, I give you joy of your son,' said Stephen. 'And I hope with all my heart that dear Sophie does well? At least,' he observed, as he watched Jack busy with the mail-sack, 'this will make a baronetcy more welcome: will give it more point.'

'Lord, what am I at?' cried Jack. 'Orders come first.' He dropped the sack, broke the seal of the Admiral's letter, found the expected words directing and requiring him to proceed with all possible dispatch to the flag at or off Rodriguez immediately upon receipt of these orders. He laughed, and said, 'If there is any baronetcy in the wind, it don't come this way. I am superseded.'

He went on deck, gave one order for the signal that should set the squadron on its new course, away from Mauritius, and another to splice the mainbrace. To Seymour's astonished expression he replied, in a voice as offhand as he could make it, that he had just learnt of the birth of a son. He received the congratulations of the quarterdeck and many a kind look from the seamen nearby, invited Colonel Keating to take a glass in the cabin, and so returned. The bottle was soon out, the letters distributed; and Jack, giving Keating his packet, said, 'I hope, Colonel, that your news may be as pleasant as mine, to offset the rest; because you were too good a prophet by half, and I fear there may be a general waiting for you at Rodriguez, just as there is an admiral waiting for me.' With these words he retired with his letters to the quarter-gallery, his own private place of ease,

leaving the soldier transfixed, pale and even trembling, with indignation.

A little before dinner he came out and found Stephen alone in the great cabin. Pullings had now, for the first time, learnt of the squadron's destination; and realizing that a little tactful delay on his part would have allowed the Commodore to carry out his plan and to reap honour and glory, had withdrawn to the taffrail, where he stood by the ensign-staff, cursing his untimely zeal. 'I wish you too may have had very good news, Stephen?' said Jack, nodding at the pile of open letters at Stephen's side.

'Tolerably so in parts, I thank you; but nothing that causes me a joy comparable with yours. You are still in a glow, brother, a roseate glow. Pray tell me of Sophie's condition.'

'She says she has never felt better in her life – swears it passed off as easy as a letter in the post – finds the little chap a great comfort, and excellent company. Now I know you are about as partial to children as old Herod, Stephen, but –'

'No, no. I am not doggedly, mechanically set against them, though I freely admit I find most babies superfluous, and unnecessary.'

'Without there were babies, we should have no next generation.'

'So much the better, when you consider the state to which we have reduced the world they must live in, the bloody-minded wolfish stock from which they spring, and the wicked, inhuman society that will form them. Yet I do admit of exceptions: the replication of such a creature as Sophie, and even I may say of yourself, can be seen as a good. But I am afraid I interrupt you.'

'I was only going to say, that you might like to hear Sophie's description of him. It appears that he is a most unusual, exceptional child.'

Stephen listened with a decent show of complaisance: the smell of roasting meat drifted aft, and that of fried onions; he heard the drum beat 'Heart of Oak' for the gunroom's dinner; his stomach called out for his own; and still the tale ran on.

'You cannot conceive, Stephen, how it extends a man's future, having a son,' said Jack. 'Now it is worth while planting a walnut-tree! Why, I may even lay down a whole plantation of oaks.'

'The girls would have gathered your walnuts. The girls would have sported under the oaks; and their grandchildren would have felled them.'

'No, no. It is not the same thing at all. Now, thank God, they have portions; and so eventually they will marry some greasy

fellow called Snooks – you must admit, Stephen, that it is not the same thing at all.'

Just before five bells Jack was cut short by the arrival of Pullings, still sadly reduced, and of the Colonel, still trembling with rage; and at five bells itself Killick announced, 'Wittles is up,' with a courtly jerk of his thumb, and they moved into the dining-cabin.

Pullings ate his mutton silently, with little appetite; Colonel Keating, though allowed by convention to speak freely at the Commodore's table, remained almost equally mute, not wishing to spoil a happy occasion by giving vent to the words he longed to utter; Stephen was lost in reflection, though from time to time he did respond to pauses in Jack's cheerful flow. When the long meal was over, when the King, Mrs Aubrey and young Stupor Mundi had been drunk in bumpers of luke-warm port, and when the guests had moved into the open air to dissipate the fumes of their wine, he said to Jack, 'I scarcely know which I most admire, the strength of your philoprogenitive instinct, or your magnanimity in the face of this disappointment. Not many years ago you would have clapped your telescope to your blind eye; you would have evaded these orders; and you would have taken the Mauritius before Mr Bertie knew what you were at.'

'Well, I *am* disappointed,' said Jack, 'I must confess; and when first I smoked the Admiral's intentions I had a month's mind to steer due west for a while. But it would not do, you know. Orders is orders, bar one case in a million; and this is not one of those cases. The Mauritius must fall in the next week or so, whoever is in command, or whoever takes the glory.'

'Keating does not take it so philosophically.'

'Keating has not just heard he has a son. Ha, ha, ha: there's for you, Stephen.'

'Keating already has five, and a sad expense they are to him, as well as a grave disappointment. The news of a sixth boy would not have mollified his indignation, unless indeed it had been a daughter, the one thing he longs for. Strange, strange: it is a passion to which I cannot find the least echo, when I peer into my bosom.'

Colonel Keating's indignation was shared throughout the *Boadicea* and her companions. It was universally held that the Commodore had been done out of his rights, cheated of his due, and wiped in the eye if not stabbed in the back: and there was not a man in the squadron who did not know that two captured

Indiamen lay in Port-Louis, together with a large number of only slightly less magnificent prizes, and that the appearance – the totally unnecessary appearance – of a seventy-four, eight frigates, four sloops, and maybe a dozen regiments of lobsters, would reduce the share of all who had done the real work to half a pint of small beer, if that.

The indignation increased with brooding, and as the two bodies slowly converged, meeting at Rodriguez, it grew to such a pitch that when the *Boadicea*'s salute to the flag roared out, the gunner said, 'And I wish they was loaded with grape, you old –' without a word of reproach from the officers near at hand. When the last gun had been fired, and before the flagship began her reply, Jack said, 'Strike the pendant. Hoist out my barge.' Then, a mere post-captain again, he stepped into the cabin and called for his breeches, cocked hat and number one coat to go aboard the Admiral. It had been a hard moment, the striking of his pendant – for a pendant could not fly in the presence of a flag without the unusual compliment of a direct invitation – but little comfort did he meet with below. Killick's sense of injustice had been inflamed by the extra ration of grog served out to all hands. It now overflowed on to the principal victim, and in his old shrewish voice he said, 'You ain't got no number one coat, sir. All bloody and mucked up, with figuring away aboard the *Vénus*, when two minutes would of changed it. The scraper will pass with a shove' – spitting on the lace of the cocked hat and rubbing it with his sleeve – 'but you'll have to wear it athwartships, on account of the rats. As for coats and breeches, this is the best I can do – I've shipped the old epaulettes – and if any jumped-up new-come son of a Gosport fart don't like it, he may –'

'Bear a hand, bear a hand,' cried Jack. 'Give me my stockings and that packet, and don't stand muttering there all day.'

The same sullen resentment was obvious in the bargemen who pulled Captain Aubrey across to the *Illustrious*; it was evident in his coxswain's rigour, in the vicious stab of the boathook that clamped on to the two-decker's chains, removing a good hand's-breadth of paint, and in the expressionless reserve that met the friendly advances of the seamen peering out of her lowerdeck ports.

Admiral Bertie expected it; he knew very well what he was doing, and he was fully armoured against all reactions except cheerfulness. From the outset he adopted an attitude of jovial bonhomie, with a good deal of laughter: he spoke as though it

were the most natural thing in the world to find a ready and willing compliance, no trace of ill-feeling or resentment; and to his astonishment he did find it. The Naval Instructions clearly laid down that he must find it, and·that anything less than total abnegation, total perfection of conduct, would render a subordinate liable to punishment; but his whole service life had proved that there was a world of difference between the Navy in print and the Navy in practice, and that although in theory a senior post-captain must be as submissive to an admiral as a newly-joined midshipman, in fact an oppressed commodore, growing froward under ill-usage, might make things extremely awkward for his oppressor and still keep the right side of the law: he had himself used obstruction in all its refinements often enough to know what it could accomplish. He had been prepared to meet the cunningest ploys or the most violent expressions of dissent (his secretary was there to note down any choleric word): none appeared: he was taken aback, rendered uneasy. He probed a little deeper, asking whether Aubrey was not surprised to see so many ships coming to queer his pitch? And when Jack, with equal joviality, replied that he was not, that the greater the number the less the bloodshed (so repugnant to him, as to all right-feeling men), and that the more the merrier was his motto, the Admiral glanced at his secretary, to see whether Mr Shepherd shared his suspicion that Captain Aubrey was somewhat disguised, cheerfully disguised, in wine.

The suspicion could not be maintained. As soon as the captains of the fleet were assembled aboard the flagship, at the Admiral's request Jack Aubrey delivered to them a singularly lucid, cogent account of the situation, with all the facts, all the figures at instant command. To the anxious words about the notorious difficulty of the reefs surrounding Mauritius, the wicked surf that beat upon them, and the paucity of harbours, he replied with a chart, a little masterpiece of hydrography, showing Flat Island and the Grande Baie, exactly surveyed by himself, with triple-sextant-bearings and double-checked soundings showing plenty of room and clean anchorage for seventy ships, as well as sheltered beaches for a very great number of men. He ended his exposition by observing that in view of the lateness of the season he would respectfully suggest an immediate descent.

The Admiral was by no means so sure of that: long before Captain Aubrey was born the Admiral's old nurse had told him 'The more hurry, the less speed.' He would take the matter under

consideration – urgent consideration – and advise with General Abercrombie and the gentlemen of his staff.

When the meeting broke up he kept Jack for a while, by way of plumbing his mind: for Aubrey was either a nonpareil of docility (and that was not his reputation at all), or he had something up his sleeve. It made the Admiral uneasy. It seemed to him that beneath all his proper deference Jack regarded him with a certain detachment and something not far from a secret amused contempt; and since the Admiral was not altogether a scrub he found this extremely disagreeable. Then again, Mr Bertie had invariably met with hostility from those he had over-reached, a hostility that gave him a retrospective justification; and here there was none – continuing cheerfulness, even benignity. It made him feel nervous, and on parting with Jack he said, 'By the way, Aubrey, it was quite right to strike your pendant, of course; but you must hoist it again the moment you set foot aboard the *Boadicea*.'

Admiral Bertie was more uneasy still by the time he reached his cot. In the interval, as the fleet lay at anchor in the road of Rodriguez and the visiting boats passed to and fro, Mr Peter had called upon his near relation Mr Shepherd. Mr Peter had seen a good deal of Dr Maturin, a simpler, more penetrable man than he had been led to suppose, particularly since this last flood of letters and information from home: and from Maturin's casual remarks, some of them really far from discreet, Peter had formed the conviction that General Aubrey, the Commodore's father and a member of parliament, was probably playing a very deep game, that he might be about to change sides, that he was secretly very well with the ministry, and that it was by no means impossible that he might shortly appear in an office connected with honours and patronage, if not on the Board of Admiralty itself. Stephen had poisoned too many sources of intelligence to derive much satisfaction from this elementary exercise; but in fact the sneaking underhand little tale was admirably suited to the ears that received it a few minutes after Peter's departure. It explained Aubrey's disconcerting nonchalance: a man with such allies must be handled with care.

In the morning a council, attended by the captains and the senior army officers, considered the plan of attack worked out by Jack and Colonel Keating. General Abercrombie's plea for delay, strongly supported by his staff, was brushed aside with even greater strength by the Admiral himself. The General looked

surprised and even injured: he was a stout old gentleman, and he stared across the table at nothing in particular, with a look of hostile stupidity in his protuberant eyes, as though he did not quite understand what had happened. But having repeated himself for the space of about three quarters of an hour he yielded to the Admiral's insistence; and the plan, scarcely mangled in any important respect, was agreed to, though with very little grace. Half an hour later the flagship directed the fleet to get under way, and the leading frigate stood out to sea, with a fine topgallant breeze to send her north about Mauritius for Flat Island and the beaches up the coast from Port-Louis.

The conquest of Mauritius ran its leisurely course, with the regiments marching and countermarching in a scientific manner that pleased the generals on either side. The infantrymen sweated, but few of them bled. They had been landed smoothly, without opposition, and they presented General Decaen with an insuperable problem. His numerous militia was no use to him at all: most of its members had read Stephen's broadsheets, many of them had already seen copies of Governor Farquhar's proposed proclamation, all of them were more concerned with the revival of their strangled trade than with the welfare of Buonaparte's empire. His Irish troops were clearly disaffected; his French regulars were outnumbered by well over five to one; and his navy was blockaded by an overwhelming force of ships. His only concern was to delay General Abercrombie's advance until his surrender should meet certain arcane military requirements, so that he should be able to justify his conduct at home and obtain honourable terms at Port-Louis for himself and his men.

He succeeded to admiration, and Abercrombie particularly praised his orderly retreat on the night of Thursday, when his flanking battalions fell back from Terre Rouge and the Long Mountain, changing face at the double in the most professional way. 'That is real soldiering,' said the General.

While these ritual gestures were being made the emissaries passed to and fro, and although Port-Louis was still nominally French Stephen Maturin walked up to the military hospital without his usual detour; and there he found McAdam on the verandah. 'How is our patient this morning?' he asked.

'Och, the night was good enough, with your draught,' said McAdam, though with no great satisfaction. 'And the eye

shows some wee improvement. It is the neck that keeps me so anxious – slough, slough, and slough again, and this morning it looked as ugly as ever. He will pluck at the dressing in his sleep. Dr Martin suggests sewing flaps of healthy skin across the whole morbid area.'

'Martin is a fool,' said Stephen. 'What we are concerned with is the artery-wall itself, not the gross exfoliation. Rest is the answer, clean dressings, lenitives and peace of mind: there is physical strength in galore. How is the agitation?'

'Fair enough this morning; and he has been sleeping since my early rounds.'

'Very good, very good. Then we must certainly not disturb him; there is nothing like sleep for repair. I shall come back about noon, bringing the Commodore. He has a letter from Lady Clonfert at the Cape; he wishes to deliver it himself, and to tell Clonfert how the fleet praises his noble defence of the *Néréide*.' McAdam whistled and screwed up his face. 'Do you think it imprudent?' asked Stephen.

McAdam scratched himself: he could not say – Clonfert had been very strange these days – did not talk to him – no longer opened his mind – remained silent, listening for gunfire hour after hour. 'Maybe it would be best if you was to come a few minutes ahead. We can sound him out, and if we judge the excitement would not be too much, the Commodore can see him. It might do him a world of good. He liked seeing you,' said McAdam with a burst of generosity that he instantly balanced by asking in a sneering voice, 'I suppose your Big Buck Aubrey is prancing about on shore, the lord of creation? How are things going along down there, will you tell me?'

'Much as we had expected. Mr Farquhar has landed from the *Otter*, and I dare say the capitulation will be signed before dinner.'

They talked about other wounded Néréides: some were doing well, some were at death's door. Young Hobson, a master's mate emasculated late in the battle, had passed through it that night, thankful to go. Stephen nodded, and for a while he watched two geckoes on the wall, paying some attention to McAdam's account of the French surgeon's words about the impossibility of saving patients when the vital spring was gone. After a long pause he said, 'McAdam, you know more about this aspect of medicine than I do: what do you say to a patient with no physical injury, no tangible lesion, who loses all real concern with his life? Who

262

takes a disgust to the world? A scholar, say, who has edited Livy, Livy his sole study and his delight: he stumbles on the lost books, carries them home, and finds he has not the courage, the spirit, to open even the first. He does not care about Livy's lost books, nor about his books that are known, nor about any books or authors at all. They do not interest him. He will not lift the cover; and he sees that very soon his own animal functions will not interest him either. Do you understand me? Have you seen cases of this sort in your practice?'

'Certainly I have. And they are not so rare, neither, even in men that are kept busy.'

'What is the prognosis? How do you see the nature of the malady?'

'I take it that here we are to leave grace to one side?'

'Just so.'

'As to the nature, why, I believe he perceives the void that has always surrounded him, and in doing so he falls straight into a pit. Sometimes his perception of the void is intermittent; but where it is not, then in my experience spiritual death ensues, preceding physical death sometimes by ten years and more. Occasionally he may be pulled out by his prick.'

'You mean he may remain capable of love?'

'As between men and women I use the term lust: but call it what you like: desire, a burning desire for some slut may answer, if only he burns hard enough. In the early stages, however,' said McAdam, leering at the geckoes, 'he may tide himself over with opium, for a while.'

'Good day to you, now, Dr McAdam.'

On his way down through the growing heat Stephen overtook two crippled boys, the one with his leg taken off at the knee, the other with an empty sleeve pinned over his breast, midshipmen of the *Néréide*. 'Mr Lomax,' he cried, 'sit down at once. This is madness: your stitches will burst. Sit down at once on that stone: elevate the limb.'

Pale young wraithlike Lomax, propped by his crutch and his companion, hopped to the stone, the mounting-stone outside a rich-looking house, and sat upon it. 'It is only another hundred yards, sir,' he said. 'All the Néréides are there. You can see the ship from the corner; and we are to go aboard the minute her colours go up.'

'Nonsense,' said Stephen. But having considered for a while he knocked at the door: a little later he came out with a chair, a

cushion, and two stout anxious care-worn black men. He put Lomax into the chair, properly padded, and the black men carried it down to the turn in the road where the little group of mobile survivors looked down on their frigate, tight-packed among the Indiamen, the merchant ships and the men-of-war in Port-Louis harbour. Some of their eager life seeped into him. 'Mr Yeo,' he said to a lieutenant with a great bandage covering most of his face, 'you may do me an essential service, if you will be so kind. I was obliged to leave a valuable bolster in your ship, and I should be most grateful if you would order the strictest search when you go aboard. I have already mentioned it to the Admiral and the Commodore, but – ' His words were cut off by cheering away to the right, a cheering that spread as the French colours came down on the citadel, and that redoubled when the union flag replaced them. The Néréides cheered too, thin and piping, a poor volume of sound that was lost in the salvoes of artillery and then in the deep rolling thunder from the guns of the fleet.

'I shall not forget, sir,' said Yeo, shaking Stephen by the hand. 'Pass it on, there: the Doctor's bolster to be preserved.'

Stephen walked on, now quite through the town, where the closed shutters gave an impression of death, and where the few white people in the streets looked oppressed, as though the plague were abroad; only the blacks, whose lot could scarcely change for the worse, showed any liveliness or curiosity. He attended to various points of business, and met Jack at their appointed place. 'The capitulation is signed, I collect?' he said.

'Yes,' said Jack. 'Uncommon handsome terms, too: they march out with colours flying, match burning, drum beating – all the honours of war – and they are not to be prisoners. Tell me, how did you find Clonfert? I have his wife's letter here in my pocket.'

'I did not see him this morning: he was asleep. McAdam seems to think his general state to be much the same. He should come through, I believe, barring accidents: but of course he will be horribly disfigured. That will have a bearing on his state of mind, and in these cases the patient's mind is of great importance. I propose leaving you under the trees near the gate, while I attend to his dressings with McAdam. He may be in no state to receive you.'

They made their way up the hill, talking of the ceremony. 'Farquhar was astonished you had not been invited,' said Jack.

'He checked the Admiral so hard we all looked away – said your work had saved innumerable lives and that the slight must be repaired: you should be given the place of honour at his official dinner. The Admiral looked concerned, and salaamed, and said he would instantly do everything in his power – would mention you with the greatest respect in his despatch; and then he ran off like a boy to start writing it – had been itching to do so since dawn. And a precious document it will be, I am sure, ha, ha, ha. Much the same as most of 'em, only more so; but it will certainly have a whole Gazette to itself.'

'Who is to carry it?'

'Oh, his nephew, I dare say, or one of his favourite captains: it is the greatest plum to carry these last five years and more – attendance at court, kind words and a tip from the King, dinner at Guildhall, freedom of this and that: promotion of course or a damned good billet. I shall give the lucky man my letters to Sophie – he will go like the wind, cracking on regardless, homeward bound with such welcome news, the dog.'

Jack's mind flew off to Hampshire, and it was still there when Stephen said in louder tone, 'I repeat, what do you think is our next destination?'

'Eh? Oh, Java, no doubt, to have a crack at the Dutchmen.'

'Java: oh, indeed. Listen, now: here are your trees. There is a bench. I shall be with you directly.'

The hospital courtyard was in a strange state of disorder: not only the confusion of a defeat, with people making the most of a vacation of power to carry off everything portable, but something quite out of the common. Stephen walked faster when he heard McAdam's raucous northern voice calling out, and he pushed through a knot of attendants staring up at the verandah. McAdam was drunk, but not so drunk that he could not stand, not so drunk that he did not recognize Stephen. 'Make a lane, there,' he cried. 'Make a lane for the great Dublin physician. Come and see your patient, Dr Maturin, you whore.'

In the low-ceilinged room the shutters drawn against the noonday sun made Clonfert's blood show almost black: no great pool, but all there was in his small, wasted body. He lay on his back, arms spread out and dangling, the unshattered side of his face looking beautiful and perfectly grave, even severe. The bandage had been torn from his neck.

Stephen bent to listen for any trace of a heart-beat, straightened, closed Clonfert's eyes, and pulled up the sheet. McAdam sat on

265

the side of the bed, weeping now, his fury gone with his shouting; and between his sobs he said, 'It was the cheering that woke him. What are they cheering for? says he, and I said the French have surrendered. Aubrey will be here and you shall have your *Néréide* back. Never, by God, says he, not from Jack Aubrey: run out McAdam and see are they coming. And when I stepped out of the door so he did it, and so bloody Christ he did it.' A long silence, and he said, 'Your Jack Aubrey destroyed him. Jack Aubrey destroyed him.'

Stephen crossed the blazing courtyard again, and under the trees Jack stood up, expectant. His smile vanished when Stephen said, 'He is dead,' and they paced down in silence through the town. A town busier now, with the shops opening, men posting up the proclamation, large numbers of people walking about, companies of soldiers marching, parties of bluejackets, queues forming outside the brothels, several French officers who saluted punctiliously, putting the best face they could on defeat. Stephen stopped to kneel as the Sacrament passed by to a deathbed, a single priest and a boy with a bell.

'I trust he went easy?' said Jack in a low voice, at last.

Stephen nodded, and he looked at Jack with his pale, expressionless eyes, looking objectively at his friend, tall, sanguine, almost beefy, full of health, rich, and under his kindly though moderate concern happy and even triumphant. He thought, 'You cannot blame the bull because the frog burst: the bull has no comprehension of the affair,' but even so he said, 'Listen, Jack: I do not much care for the taste of this victory. Nor any victory, if it comes to that. I shall see you at dinner.'

The dinner was nothing in comparison with those usually eaten at Government House under the rule of General Decaen: many of his cooks and all of his plate had vanished in the brief inter-regnum, and a stray mortar-bomb had destroyed part of the wall. But even so the creole dishes made a pleasant contrast with the hard fare of recent days, and above all the ceremony provided an ideal occasion for speeches.

Something, reflected Jack, something came over officers who reached flag-rank or the equivalent, something that made them love to get up on their hind legs and produce long measured periods with even longer pauses between them. Several gentlemen had already risen to utter slow compliments to themselves, their fellows, and their nation, and now General Abercrombie was

struggling to his feet, with a sheaf of notes in his hand. 'Your Excellency, my lords, Admiral Bertie, and gentlemen. We are met here together,' two bars of silence, 'on this happy, eh, *occasion*,' two more bars, 'to celebrate what I may perhaps be permitted to call, an unparalleled feat, of *combined* operations, of *combination*, valour, organization, and I may say, of indomitable will.' Pause. 'I take no credit to myself.' Cries of No, no; and cheers. 'No. It is all due,' pause, 'to a young lady in Madras.'

'Sir, sir,' hissed his aide-de-camp, 'you have turned over two pages. You have come to the joke.'

It took some time to get the General back to his eulogy of Abercrombie and all present, and in the interval Jack looked anxiously at his friend, one of the few black coats present, sitting on the Governor's right. Stephen loathed speeches, but though paler than usual he seemed to be bearing up, and Jack noticed with pleasure that as well as his own he was secretly drinking the wine poured into the abstinent Governor's glass.

The General boomed on, came to a close, a false close, rallied and began again, and at last sank into his chair, glared round in surly triumph and drank like a camel with a broad desert before it.

A broad desert threatened, to be sure, for here was Admiral Bertie, fresh and spry, game for a good half hour: and his first words about his inability to match the gallant General's eloquence struck a chill to Jack's heart. His mind wandered during the Admiral's compliments to the various corps that made up the force, and he was in the act of building an observatory-dome of superior design on the top of Ashgrove hill – he had of course purchased the hill and felled the trees on the summit – when he heard Mr Bertie's voice take on a new and unctuous tone.

'In the course of my long career,' said the Admiral, 'I have been compelled to give many orders, which, though always for the good of the service, have sometimes been repugnant to my finer feelings. For even an Admiral retains finer feelings, gentlemen.' Dutiful laughter, pretty thin. 'But now, with His Excellency's permission, I shall indulge myself by giving one that is more congenial to the spirit of a plain British sailor.' He paused and coughed in a suddenly hushed atmosphere of genuine suspense, and then in an even louder voice he went on, 'I hereby request and require Captain Aubrey to repair aboard the *Boadicea* as soon as he has finished his dinner, there to receive my despatches for the Lords Commissioners of the Admiralty,

and to convey them to Whitehall with all the diligence in his power. And to this, gentlemen' – raising his glass – 'I will append a toast: let us all fill up to the brim, gunwales under, and drink to England, home and beauty, and may Lucky Jack Aubrey reach 'em all with fair winds and flowing sheets every mile of the way.'